THE WAR WITHIN

THE WAR WITHIN

BOOK TWO OF THE GREAT GOD'S WAR

Stephen Donaldson

GOLLANCZ

LONDON

First published in Great Britain in 2019 by Gollancz
an imprint of The Orion Publishing Group Ltd
Carmelite House, 50 Victoria Embankment
London EC4Y 0DZ

An Hachette UK Company

1 3 5 7 9 10 8 6 4 2

A CIP catalogue record for this book is
available from the British Library.

ISBN Hardback 978 1 473 22170 3
ISBN Export Trade Paperback 978 1 473 22171 0
ISBN eBook 978 1 473 22172 7

Printed and bound by CPI Group (UK) Ltd, Croydon, CR0 4YY

www.orionbooks.co.uk

To Rocky Kearney and Evelin Yourstone Wheeler
Four Decades Of Enduring Friendship

And To Jennifer Dunstan
For Her Generous Love

CONTENTS

PLANS IN MOTION

From the high windows of his workroom, the tall librarian, white-haired and bearded, studied the battlements that defended the gates, and below them the wide plateau lying like a porch at the foot of the Last Repository. He had wasps of anxiety buzzing in his brain. During the night, he had dreamed of his own death—and not for the first time. In itself, the idea of dying did not trouble him. A new librarian would take his place. His special relationship with the Repository's store of knowledge would pass to someone else: the sorcery preserving the continuance of that bond had been in effect for many centuries. And any new librarian would protect the books, scrolls, and papers as stringently as he did. But he did fear that his replacement might not share his vision of the library's defense. If that happened, all of his efforts would accomplish nothing. He could not bring himself to leave his post at the windows.

He was blind, of course. He had lost his sight when he had become the librarian. The gift or curse of knowing every text stored on the levels above him always exacted the same price. But he was more than a librarian. He was Magister Sirjane Marrow, and powerful. He saw with senses other than human vision. The midafternoon sun warmed his face but did not require him to lower his head or turn away.

In any case, he did not need sight to tell him that Set Ungabwey's caravan was arriving. He heard the grinding of its wheels on the distant stone of the plateau. Subtle vibrations reached him through the soles of his sandals. He could smell the importance of what was coming.

The caravan master's ornate conveyance, his traveling home, was already at rest in front of the gates, waiting for Magister Marrow himself. The wagon's teamsters were tending their horses, while several of Master Ungabwey's servants worked to clean the stains and grime of a hard journey from the vehicle's carved, gilded sides. In addition, the librarian detected a number of smaller carriages settling on their wheels. They housed the caravan's serving-folk, and some of them showed signs of damage: shattered spokes in their wheels, cracks and even holes in their roofs, deep scrapes along their sides. But the other wagons that had left the Repository almost three fortnights ago were not in range of the Magister's senses.

Those wagons were the most essential conveyances in the caravan. If they did not come—

They were Sirjane Marrow's latest gambit: only the most recent of his moves in the game he played against ruin, but by no means the least crucial. He had started to put his plans in motion more than a hundred years ago. Twenty years ago, he had beaten down Prince Bifalt's pride and hostility so that Belleger and Amika might be able to negotiate for peace. But since then, he had done little more than watch and wait. Oh, he had approved when the devotees of Flesh had proposed to give the two small realms their singular aid. And he had actively encouraged the devotees of Spirit to travel the continent with Allman Dancer's Wide World Carnival, looking for hints of the library's enemy, seeking out potential allies. In the intervening years, however, he had concentrated his own efforts on training the Repository's sorcerers, on preserving communications with Magister Facile in Belleger, and on keeping watch. He had not urged Set Ungabwey to attempt the mountains until he knew the enemy was coming.

Now the enemy was close. If Master Ungabwey had failed, the librarian's entire defensive strategy would fall apart.

Set Ungabwey and his ever-changing train had come to the Repository several times in recent years, but not on an occasion as fraught as this one; not since he had indirectly delivered Prince Bifalt.

Twenty years ago, however, Magister Marrow had had other stratagems ready if his plans for the Prince failed. Now he had no idea what he would do if the caravan did not accomplish its purpose.

An irascible man at the best of times, Sirjane Marrow scowled at the plateau as if the shapes he discerned made him furious.

Still the bedraggled line of conveyances continued to come. Tired oxen tugged more carriages onto the high porch of the library, bringing teams of guards and scouts as well as mechanicians and trained laborers. The condition of the vehicles gave further proof—as if the librarian needed it—that they had emerged from hostile terrain.

But not from human hostility. The state of the wagons did not suggest battle-damage. Before the caravan set out, Master Ungabwey's interpreter, Tchwee, had reached an understanding with the Quolt, the strange mountain folk who could have barred the wagons' road. In exchange for a trivial portion of the Last Repository's abundance, the Quolt had promised safe passage, guidance, and aid. They must have kept their word.

No, the hostility was that of the Wall Mountains themselves. They were so tall that even in summer they remained clogged with ice and flailed by snow, scourged by winds only granite could endure. Granite and, apparently, the Quolt. Centuries ago, when the guardians of the library had chosen to build their Last Repository here, they had believed the peaks and elevation and weather would protect them from any assault at their backs. Now, of course, they knew better. The Quolt had testified to that.

But Magister Marrow refused to consider the hardships and dangers the caravan had endured. The library's survival was his driving obsession. He already had too many piercing anxieties, and each of them felt like a fresh sting.

Then he made out the first of the immense conveyances for which he had been waiting. Gusting steam from their nostrils in the mild air of the heights, six illirim hauled their burden onto the plateau. They were huge, tusked beasts, massive as bullocks, shaggy as sheep: the only animals muscular enough to pull the weight of their long wagon with its enormous load, and tough enough to keep going day after day.

That load was tightly sheeted in canvas to protect it from rain or hail or snow or lesser rock-falls; but the librarian knew what it was.

Set Ungabwey had taken three such wagons into the mountains. One had returned.

But while it settled into its place on the plateau, more illirim impinged on Sirjane Marrow's senses. More beasts dragged their wagon into view. Like the first, their burden was sealed in canvas; stoutly tied. And undamaged.

Rubbing his sightless eyes, he allowed himself to imagine that where there were two, there might be a third. And when the third appeared, he allowed himself a moment of relief.

Unfortunately, the return of the caravan did not indicate success. It demonstrated only that Set Ungabwey's people had made the attempt, and had survived with their massive catapults intact. To know the truth, the blind librarian would have to hear it.

He could have sent a messenger to get the caravan master's report; but for several reasons, Sirjane Marrow wanted to hear Master Ungabwey's tidings in person. He and Set Ungabwey had dealt with each other for a long time. He owed the house-bound master the respect of a personal visit. In addition, he trusted his own hearing more than anyone else's; his own ability to detect what lay behind what was said. And if the caravan had succeeded, he had another challenge for it. He would have to negotiate.

Set Ungabwey was a faithful ally, but he was also a merchant. He would have to be paid. Determining and then accepting—or refusing—his price was the responsibility of the Last Repository's librarian. And if Magister Marrow could not meet that price, he would have to offer some other payment, something Master Ungabwey valued even more highly.

Sounding more irate than he intended, the librarian summoned a servant to inform the caravan master that Magister Marrow would come to him shortly.

The man who answered was not a monk devoted to the Cult of the Many. He gave his diligence and effort for pay: a detail that made no difference to the librarian. No doubt Magister Rummage, the hunchback—and therefore deaf Magister Avail—knew the man's name, where he had come from, how long he had served the Last Repository. They could vouch for him. Sirjane Marrow did not hesitate to trust him.

If the librarian had focused his remaining senses, he would have perceived a young man with a diffident manner wearing a blue tunic and pantaloons instead of a monk's grey robe, black hair tousled on his forehead, sturdy boots on his feet. But the Magister did not trouble himself. He had other issues on his mind. To the servant, he said irritably, "Please tell the caravan master I will attend him. And send someone else to Magister Rummage. He should know I am about to leave the library."

The young man did not speak: he had not been asked a direct question. Instead, he bowed and left.

Studying the wounded and comparatively small caravan below him, Magister Marrow wondered, Will they be enough? There were no Quolt in Belleger's mountains. Without guides, Master Ungabwey would need to consult with the rulers of Belleger and Amika.

That idea vexed the librarian. Some of his preparations would be exposed. But he had to face the consequences. He did not have many choices left. And he could not ask Set Ungabwey to brave another range of mountains without leaving the Master free to determine his own course.

Muttering curses under his breath, the old man turned from his windows and began to make his unerring way down through the keep toward the mustering hall and the gates.

Before he reached the hall, the servant he had sent to Master Ungabwey stepped in front of him. "With your permission, Magister," the man said to explain himself. "I have delivered your message. Now the most holy Amandis asks you to await her."

"*Await* her?" snapped the sorcerer. "Why? Master Ungabwey awaits *me*. What can she want that prompts her to delay me?"

The servant took the liberty of replying, "She did not say. You know her, Magister. She does not account for her wishes. She merely states them and expects compliance."

That was true, but the librarian had not expected a servant to tell him so. He regarded the young man more closely. "Will Flamora accompany her?"

The servant held his head so that his hair hid his eyes. "She did not say," he repeated. His tone did not suggest discomfort. "However, I imagine the most holy Amandis waits for the most holy Flamora."

Magister Marrow snorted his impatience. But he could not justify venting his irritation on any servant, certainly not on a young man who felt so little awe in his presence. An attitude that Magister Rummage would have called impudence—if the bitter hunchback had been able to speak—Sirjane Marrow found refreshing. More mildly, he said, "Inform them, please, that I will await them in the hall. But I will not wait long. If the devotee of Spirit cannot bear to be parted from her antagonist, and the devotee of Flesh cannot tear herself away from her self-regard, I will speak with them when I have consulted with Master Ungabwey."

He thought he heard a muffled chuckle from the servant, but he was not sure. He had already gone past the young man, walking briskly.

Amandis and Flamora were in the keep, of course, as they had been at irregular intervals for decades. In their separate ways, or by their separate means, they knew as well as he did that events were approaching a crisis. It might be the *last* crisis: the last in the library's besieged millennia of existence. They gave the Repository their support because they knew its worth. But they also had their own singular priorities—or their own peculiar styles of support. Magister Marrow did not care how fond of Elgart Flamora had become, but he still rued the impulse that had led Amandis to say too much to Bifalt twenty years ago. In his bones, the librarian believed that the more his designs became known, the more opposition they would attract.

Bifalt and the Amikan, Commander Forguile, who had somehow become the Prince's ally, already knew more than they should. No doubt Elgart did as well.

But those misjudgments were long past. They could not be corrected. What mattered now were the conclusions that Belleger and

Amika drew from their premature insights. So far, the librarian had no cause for regret. Those two realms were doing what he required of them.

Knowing every intricacy of the Last Repository, he reached the mustering hall that fronted the gates in a short time.

Those gates were the only entrance to the keep, and they were barred and strutted with heavy iron to protect the books, the scrolls and tomes, the loose papers. Nevertheless they were the most easily breached of the Repository's defenses.

Warned, no doubt, by the caravan's arrival, servants who were also students of sorcery had already lit the many cressets, filling the huge space with light Magister Marrow did not need. Urged by the buzzing in his head, he would have gone straight to the massive gates, confident that they would open as he approached. Instead, he went to the staircase customarily used by the devotees. There he paused to compose himself. Much as he wanted to rail at Amandis, he had no intention of doing so. His allies were too few: he could not afford to indulge a petty frustration at any of them. In any case, his ire would be wasted. The assassin had often demonstrated that she was impervious to insult.

In his place, another man might have peered upward, reflexively trying to see despite his blindness. But after more than a century of service, Sirjane Marrow had almost forgotten he still had eyes. Watching the staircase with his other senses, he concentrated on preparing himself to meet Set Ungabwey.

If he had bothered to count his heartbeats, he would not have reached fifteen before Amandis began to descend the stair.

As always, she glided downward like a woman floating on water rather than treading on stone. As always, she was demurely cloaked from neck to floor, and carried her arms with each hand resting on the opposite forearm inside her wide sleeves. As always, she did not return Magister Marrow's bow of respect.

She did, however, acknowledge his presence by saying, "We will await the devotee of Flesh."

For lack of any other useful gesture, the librarian raised his eyebrows. "We will? Why, Devotee? Master Ungabwey has returned.

His task was hazardous and necessary. His tidings are urgent. I must hear them."

Amandis replied with a slight shrug. "We will wait here, librarian, or we will wait in Master Ungabwey's domicile. He will not speak until the devotee of Flesh is present." After a moment's consideration, she conceded, "If Magister Avail's voice in his mind commands him, he may comply. Otherwise not."

With both hands, Sirjane Marrow rubbed the surprise off his features. He had known, of course, that Master Ungabwey's acquaintance with devotees of Flesh and Spirit was older than his own. Now he was forced to admit that he had no idea what their relationships entailed when they were not encamped in front of the Last Repository. His attention—his obsessions—had always been elsewhere. He had no curiosity to spare for anything that did not pertain to texts—or to the library's survival.

While the librarian wondered why Set Ungabwey required the presence of a trained killer and a gifted courtesan, a servant came toward him from the back of the hall. She was one of the monks, and she was in a hurry. The slap of her sandals sounded like scurrying in the cavernous space. When he and Amandis turned to face her, she slowed and halted; assumed the deferential posture habitual to all the monks, head bowed, hands clasped in front of her. Under her grey robe, she was breathing heavily.

Magister Marrow assumed that she carried some message, perhaps from Magister Rummage or one of the Repository's other defenders. But when he opened his mouth to question her, the devotee of Spirit forestalled him.

"She will accompany us," said Amandis crisply. "Like ours, her presence is required."

Before the old man could stop himself, he demanded, "Master Ungabwey requires *a servant*?"

"Not *a* servant," explained Flamora's antagonist or opposite. "*This* servant. The monk known as Third Father is absent. She is known as Fifth Daughter. She stands in his stead."

Sirjane Marrow gave up on restraint. "A servant, an assassin, and a courtesan. Are there *other* requirements that have been kept from me?

Does the caravan master need a team of acrobats, or perhaps a dancing *sow*? He did not rely on such an audience when we last met."

Then, abruptly, he swallowed his irritation. The gravity of the small devotee's attention hinted at peril: a warning, not a threat. He knew her too well to imagine that she might harm him. But her manner reminded him that there were things he did *not* know, matters that belonged exclusively to Set Ungabwey.

Then Flamora called out from the top of the staircase, "Librarian!"

Her voice tugged at him. It was a strange instrument. It gave the impression that viols and lutes were speaking simultaneously, each playing a distinct tune, yet each in harmony. The effect was delicious. No doubt, it was intended to be seductive.

Magister Marrow was in no mood for it; but he could not pretend that it did not affect him.

She came down the stairs in a waft of loose muslin thin as gauze. It floated around her as if to suggest that she was much more than she seemed and yet had nothing to hide. Tiny bells on her anklets chimed silver at every step. Her face and figure invited close scrutiny—or so the librarian had been told—but his lack of sight enabled him to ignore that distraction.

Unfortunately, he could not ignore her voice as well, or her scent, or the floating of her raiment.

She spoke as she descended the staircase. "Thank you for waiting, librarian. You are kind to the vanity of women." Her tone resembled an arched eyebrow. "I mean to the vanity of *some* women. The most holy Amandis has her own pride, but it takes other forms. For example, she takes pride in being obscure. No doubt she has not mentioned that Master Ungabwey has chosen us to be his counselors. He relies on us.

"In a perfect world, others would join us. Alas, they are too distant to be summoned."

The old man contained himself until the most holy devotee of Flesh reached the foot of the stairs. Then he asked, "Master Ungabwey requires counsel? You know this?"

He might have added, How? More than that, he wanted to ask, *Why?* Why does Set Ungabwey need advice *now*? What has happened?

But Flamora answered, "We know *him*, Magister." Before Sirjane Marrow could pose his other questions, she gestured toward the gates. "Shall we? I have kept him waiting too long."

By repute, her smile could ravish oxen. It did not touch Magister Marrow. Nevertheless he headed for the gates as if he were obeying her; as if he had not also been kept waiting too long. When Flamora slipped her arm through his, he did not shrug her off.

"Do you ever wonder, librarian," she offered as they walked, "how it happens that Master Ungabwey is able to travel this continent in peace and profit? There are many people, many languages, many customs. Some treasure their isolation. Some are warlike. Most are suspicious of strangers. Certainly, Tchwee is able to speak for Master Ungabwey, but how does he win trust? And not only the trust of other merchants. The trust of entire caravans? Many refuse to set out until they can join their wagons to Master Ungabwey's."

The devotee of Flesh held Magister Marrow's attention in spite of his anxieties. Knowledge had that power over him. In the abstract, he was acquainted with the homelands and natures of the peoples she mentioned. He had learned enough about them to recognize that few of them were likely allies, although they hungered for what the Repository offered. But he had never asked himself how Set Ungabwey had become so successful.

For a man who never left his rich conveyance—

"I will tell you," continued Flamora. "He relies on his counselors to win trust for him. If people are threatened, his guards aid them. If people are hostile, the most holy devotee of Spirit knows how to answer them. If they are merely suspicious, the Wide World Carnival entertains them. If they are rigid in their isolation"—she laughed like an ensemble of instruments—"well, I make friends easily. And the Cult of the Many is everywhere, teaching by example even when people do not realize they are being taught.

"Also Master Ungabwey is wise," she concluded. "He knows that trade and knowledge benefit all who consent to share them. If we saw no worth in him, or in what he does, we would not be his counselors. In our separate fashions, we benefit also."

Magister Marrow nodded to himself. Flamora had told him enough: he could imagine most of the details she left out. And ahead of him, the reinforced gates were opening. Casting his senses through the gap, he discerned Set Ungabwey's elaborate residence only a few dozen steps away.

In front of the carriage door stood Tchwee, waiting.

Sirjane Marrow was tall, but Master Ungabwey's black interpreter was taller. He was naked to the waist, clad only in a dhoti cinched below his navel; and his strong torso and muscled arms gleamed in the afternoon shadows as if his skin had been burnished with oils or sweat. In the mountain breeze, his chest and hairless scalp steamed like the labored breathing of the illirim. By that sign, the librarian understood that Tchwee had just emerged from the uncomfortable heat of Set Ungabwey's home.

Eager now, desperate to *know*, Magister Marrow passed between the gates onto the plateau with Flamora still holding his arm, Amandis and Fifth Daughter close behind him.

"Librarian," greeted Tchwee in a good-natured subterranean rumble that made his grin audible. "Make us welcome with wine and song. I do not hope for women." His tone implied a teasing glance at the most holy devotee of Flesh. "But our need for other pleasures is severe. We are much scathed, and more than a little humbled. Nevertheless we have returned."

Sirjane Marrow disentangled himself from Flamora and bowed to the interpreter. "Honored Tchwee." He tried to match the black man's manner. "Some women may be willing, but if you are wise, you will not wish for song. You have not heard me sing."

Tchwee chuckled. But when the librarian heard his own attempt at banter, he gave it up. His mood was too dark. More brusquely, he added, "Will Master Ungabwey speak with me?" When Flamora nudged him, he amended, "With us? Will he speak with us? I need his tidings."

Tchwee barked a laugh that sounded too cheerful to be insulting. "Certainly," he answered. "Master Ungabwey awaits you. He emulates the patience of stone, but his eagerness does not diminish."

With a flourish of his arm, he invited Magister Marrow's small company forward. Then he ascended the steps to the door, opened it, and went in.

"Master Ungabwey." His voice seemed to echo out of the carriage. "Your guests have come."

Sure of his footing despite his blindness, Magister Marrow entered Set Ungabwey's domicile.

The circumstances felt strange to him, portentous in both obvious and obscure ways. He had been here on other occasions, but none of them had stung him with so many different concerns. The future of the Last Repository was at risk, as it had been when he had asked Master Ungabwey to dare the mountains. Of *course* the situation felt portentous: he did not know whether the caravan had succeeded or failed. But when he had explained what he wanted a few fortnights ago, he had been alone with Set Ungabwey; alone apart from Tchwee and the caravan master's four ochre-robed daughters. Yet now the Master wanted his counselors around him? Positively required them?

What had changed? Clearly, the stakes were higher now, for Set Ungabwey as well as for the Repository—but *why*?

To the extent that Magister Marrow bothered to perceive its details, the Master's council chamber matched his memory of it: excessive warmth, a floor covered with rugs and strewn with satin pillows, doors ornamented with gems and silver, a starscape painted on the ceiling. As usual, brass trays crowded with goblets and ewers were set among the pillows. A dozen lanterns gave light for those who needed it—and added heat without regard for those who preferred cooler air.

Set Ungabwey's daughters sat in their customary places against the walls. They were older than they had been when he had last focused his attention on them: over the years, they had become mature women. But as far as he could tell, they had not moved a muscle since he had left their domicile half a season ago.

Nor had their father. While Amandis and Flamora entered behind Sirjane Marrow and chose pillows, then urged the monk to do the same, the tall old man studied Set Ungabwey.

The caravan master was immensely fat: so obese he could hardly stand without help; so laden with excess flesh he could barely open his eyes. Indeed, he would have looked absurd if he had not wielded such power and respect. As he sat cross-legged, his thighs supported his belly, while his shoulders provided resting places for his jowls and ear-lobes. Like Tchwee's, his skull was bald; but unlike his interpreter, he lacked both eyebrows and lashes. For clothing, he wore sheets of ochre muslin.

His only acknowledgment of the librarian's arrival was a slight nod that made his cheeks wobble. If he spared a glance for his counselors, Magister Marrow could not detect it. Apparently, he took their attendance for granted.

As usual here, Tchwee knelt beside the caravan master. On this occasion, however, he was not alone.

In a far corner near one of the doors to the carriage's private rooms stood a hulking figure that made the librarian think instinctively of a bear. Not as tall as Tchwee, but much broader. Covered from his hooded head to his bare feet in furs that he wore as if they were his natural skin. A flat face deeply tanned, a look of absence in his glacial blue eyes. Despite his size, he had an air of uneasiness, a discomfort that seemed to have nothing to do with wearing winter garments in a chamber heated like the western desert.

Sirjane Marrow had read about such people. As with other distant races, he knew where they came from and how they lived. And he had heard Tchwee's description of them. But this was his first encounter with one of the Quolt in person.

The way the man stood gave the impression that he would have preferred to crouch on all fours. If he looked like a bear, perhaps he walked like one as well.

Still standing, the Magister bowed to his host. Prompted by uncertainty or intuition, he bowed to the Quolt as well.

To his surprise, the man responded by uncovering one hand from his furs, touching his fingertips to his forehead, then resting his palm briefly over his heart.

The skin of his hand was a startling white, the hue of clean snow.

"Please, librarian," said Tchwee comfortably. "Be seated. Take wine. I will explain."

Staring blindly, Sirjane Marrow sat down as if he had been dropped. He was too shaken to touch the wine. What was going on here? Did Set Ungabwey need his counselors because the Quolt was present? Had something fatal happened?

There were Magisters in the Repository who could see events and individuals at any distance; but Sirjane Marrow, the oldest sorcerer, had not asked them to turn their sight eastward. Because their gift was rare, he had too few of them—and too many other places that required watching. His own thoughts were fixed on Belleger and Amika. He had trusted Set Ungabwey to send or deliver timely reports. After all, there was nothing the librarian or his fellow sorcerers could have done to aid the caravan master's efforts.

Smiling as if he were unaware of Magister Marrow's confusion, his growing alarm, the interpreter asked, "Devotee of Flesh?"

"Gladly," replied Flamora. Filling a goblet from one of the ewers, she held it up, first to Set Ungabwey, then to Tchwee, then to the Quolt. Both the caravan master and his strange guest ignored her; but Tchwee nodded his approval. With a sigh of appreciation, she drank.

Amandis and Fifth Daughter did not follow her example. For their own disparate reasons, neither the devotees of Spirit nor the monks of the Cult of the Many indulged in wine or ale.

When the devotee of Flesh lowered her goblet, Tchwee began.

Sonorous as the groan of rock shifting deep in a distant mountain, he said, "Librarian, this man is Sirl Hokarth. He has been chosen to speak for the Quolt. In their name, he has given you a gesture of respect. In his tongue, however, 'respect' has an added meaning. It entails a bond of kinship. His gesture calls you his brother."

While the Magister tried to imagine why *any* Quolt would call him brother, the interpreter turned to Sirl Hokarth. In a language full of harsh consonants, exaggerated fricatives, and piercing sibilants, Tchwee presumably repeated what he had just said to Sirjane Marrow. The sounds hurt the librarian's ears, but he thought he understood: not the words themselves, of course, but the style of speech. A people who spoke the tongue of the Quolt would be able to make themselves plain across great distances, or in high winds: a useful ability among the ragged peaks, sheer valleys, and masked crevasses of the Wall Mountains.

But his tension was rising. He had no patience to spare for a language he had never heard before. As soon as Tchwee stopped, the Magister demanded, "Why?"

He meant, Why does he call me brother? He does not know me.

But he also meant, Why have I been kept waiting? Did I not explain that the library is threatened? My need is urgent. I need to know. Did you succeed? *What has happened?*

Before Tchwee could respond, Set Ungabwey raised his head. In a high, thin voice, a falsetto croon, he said, "Because I believe."

There he stopped. Apparently, he considered that he had said enough.

No one moved or spoke. The lanterns seemed to give off more heat. Magister Marrow felt moisture on his forehead. Sweat dripped down his spine under his robe.

As if to ease an awkward moment, Tchwee offered in tones the old man felt in his chest, "You will understand, librarian, that we had no cause to credit your fears. You speak of a terrible foe, but no one confirms your concern. Throughout our travels, no one. And who would threaten such a storehouse of knowledge? *How* could they threaten it?"

"If you had consulted me," interjected Amandis, "I would have confirmed it. The Wide World Carnival travels more widely than your train, and some of my sisters in Spirit go with it. From rumors and hints, they have determined that the threat has substance."

Magister Marrow gave the devotee of Spirit a quick glance of approval; but both Set Ungabwey and Tchwee appeared to ignore her. While they remained silent, one of the Master's daughters rose. Filling a goblet with wine, she carried it to her father and helped him drink, then returned to her seat. As she settled herself, the interpreter resumed addressing the librarian.

"Master Ungabwey accepted your request because it was *yours*. And he delayed naming his price because he did not know what difficulties awaited him, or whether your request was possible, or how high its cost in lives might be. But he also delayed because he was not certain his task was necessary. From the first, he was prepared to turn back—and to suffer your disappointment."

The Magister struggled to contain himself. "But *now* he believes?"

Instead of responding directly, Tchwee faced Sirl Hokarth with another translation. This time, his spate of sounds had a querying cast. When the fur-clad man nodded, Tchwee returned his attention to Sirjane Marrow.

"He does," stated the interpreter. "We have become better acquainted with the Quolt. We have heard their tales. They have explained their straits—and their desires. We know now why they offered their protection and guidance. We begin to understand the threat you seek to guard against."

Abruptly, Sirl Hokarth stepped out of his corner. Almost roaring, as if he wanted to be heard atop the Last Repository, he delivered a speech: perhaps an announcement or proclamation he had prepared in advance, perhaps a spontaneous outpouring, Magister Marrow could not tell which.

After an instant's hesitation, Tchwee matched Hokarth's oration with a simultaneous translation or paraphrase. He spoke in a low voice to avoid distracting the Quolt, but he managed to make his words clear.

"For many and many generations," the interpreter explained on Sirl Hokarth's behalf, "this block of stone"—he indicated the library—"has been a peaceful neighbor. It does not intrude. Its people do not intrude. When men come into our mountains from the block of stone, we remain hidden. We see they do no harm. When they depart, they do no harm. And they do not send other men to follow in their footprints. There is peace between us.

"The men who came from the east were not peaceful."

Involuntarily, the librarian flinched. He was right about the danger. But he schooled himself to remain motionless, silent, so that Sirl Hokarth and Tchwee would not stop.

"They were warriors, many warriors. Our speakers met them to warn them away. The mountains are our homeland. They are enough for

us. We will not share them. But the men from the east slew our speakers. They found our nearest camps and destroyed them. They stole food.
They savaged women and children who failed to flee. And we could not
stand against them. We are strong, but we could not. They threw forces
at us, forces of fire and disease and killing thirst. In battle, they made
infants of Quolt with clubs and spears.

"When they found the ways through our mountains—the ways to
the block of stone—they marked them for all to see. Then they returned
to the east, laughing at the jest of our resistance."

By now, Magister Marrow was able to recognize the anger in Sirl
Hokarth's manner, the restrained fury. But the Quolt did not pause,
and Tchwee did not.

"We were humbled. And we were threatened. We knew those men
would return. Many and many more would return. Why otherwise had
they marked the ways? When the black man who speaks our tongue
came, some among us wanted his death. A small death to show our
courage. But he came from the block of stone, the place of peace. And
we understood his words. We understood what he asked. We liked his
purpose. It was retribution of a kind we relish. A reward we could not
obtain alone. When we were agreed, we offered our help. To restore
what the men from the east took, we asked only tokens of friendship."

When Sirl Hokarth and Tchwee were done, the silence resembled a
distant thunderclap. While the Quolt returned to his corner, Magister
Marrow sat momentarily stunned. The posture of the devotee of Spirit
retained its usual relaxed poise, but Fifth Daughter was rigid on her
pillows. None of the Master's young women gave any sign that they
were aware of the charged atmosphere in the chamber. Their attention
was fixed on their father as if their only desire was to read his mind, or
to guess his needs.

Then Flamora allowed herself a strained sigh. Flourishing her gauzy
raiment, she refilled her goblet, drank again. She sounded uncharacteristically subdued as she said, "So the matter is settled, is it not? The
threat has substance."

With the grace of the innocent or the oblivious, thought Sirjane
Marrow, the daughter who had served Set Ungabwey earlier stood to

give her father more wine. When the obese man was satisfied, she wiped his chin with the sleeve of her robe. For a moment, she stroked the crown of his head: a gesture of affection that the librarian had not witnessed from any of the caravan master's daughters before. Yet she looked as unconcerned or unaware as her sisters as she returned to her seat.

Deliberately or not, she had given the Magister time to gather himself. He was able to say almost calmly, "So, Master Ungabwey. Is the matter settled, as the devotee of Flesh claims? Will you *now* speak of your task in the mountains? Will you tell me what you have done, or not done?"

If Set Ungabwey's wagons and men had failed, everything the librarian had just heard was chaff. It confirmed his fears, yes—but he already knew the threat had substance. Its stings were everywhere in his mind. If the Master had not succeeded, all of Magister Marrow's machinations for the past century were blown away like leaves on the wind. And he did not have time to devise a different strategy for the Last Repository's defense.

Instead of answering, Tchwee translated the librarian's question for Sirl Hokarth. After a moment, the Quolt replied with a sound like laughter.

Tchwee's grin showed his amusement. "Forgive me, librarian," he said as if he were chortling. "Have we not already answered? Why else is Sirl Hokarth here? His presence answers you."

Before the Magister could swear at him, the interpreter continued, "But yes, and again, yes. Master Ungabwey has done as you asked. Sirl Hokarth will vouch for what I say. The passes are closed, all of them. The Quolt know their mountains with the intimacy of lovers. Their guidance and counsel enabled Master Ungabwey's engines to seal every eastern approach to the library.

"Mishaps we had, and some were grievous. Rock and ice are capricious. Every avalanche does not fall where it is intended. Wagons and men were lost. But your foes cannot traverse our barricades. Give them hordes of men wielding destructive sorceries of every kind, and still they cannot."

As he heard this, relief flooded through Sirjane Marrow. For a moment, everything else was washed out of his head. Success! Set Ungabwey had *succeeded*. The library was safe from the east.

When Flamora reached for an empty goblet and murmured, "I recommend the wine, Magister. It is excellent," he gaped at it as if he did not know what it was.

Fortunately, he was spared the necessity of a prompt reply. To Sirl Hokarth, Tchwee translated the answer he had given the white-haired old man. Nodding, he listened to the Quolt's response.

While they spoke to each other, Magister Marrow had time to think. With each thud of his heart, he regained control of himself. He was beginning to understand why the caravan master treated him this way; why Master Ungabwey had arranged a meeting with Hokarth and an audience of counselors while he kept the librarian in suspense.

He was already bargaining.

Turning from the Quolt, Tchwee said, "Here are Sirl Hokarth's words. When men come from the east again, scouts or armies, they will not be opposed. The Quolt will not make that mistake again. Instead they will hide, hide and watch. If they find the chance, they will drop rocks on the heads of your enemies. But they will not risk themselves. Let the killers learn for themselves that there is no road. The Quolt will laugh when the forces of fire and disease and thirst fail."

Magister Marrow glowered in his mind, if not with his useless eyes, until the interpreter was done. Then he made a show of appreciation to mask his relentless anxiety; his need for more than he had just received. "Give Sirl Hokarth my thanks," he replied. "Give him and all the Quolt the thanks of the Last Repository. Thank them on behalf of every man or woman everywhere who needs or loves knowledge.

"When you have expressed my gratitude"—he turned to Set Ungabwey—"we can begin."

Tchwee shook his head, smiling. "There is no need, librarian. Sirl Hokarth knows your gratitude. His own is as great. But Master Ungabwey is not ready to 'begin,' as you call it. He has more to say."

Once again, the caravan master nodded: a slight shift of his head, a gentle wobble in his flesh.

Mentally, Sirjane Marrow gritted his teeth. But now he was prepared for what would follow. "Then say it," he answered. "I will hear you."

As if in response, the interpreter spoke briefly to Sirl Hokarth. At once, the Quolt nodded, then left his corner again. Without another word, he strode across the chamber to the door, opened it, and was gone. Magister Marrow imagined him running on all fours toward the nearest approach to his mountains.

In his wake, a delicate waft of coolness entered the carriage. But it lasted for only a moment before it faded in the overheated air.

For the first time, Tchwee's expression was serious, almost somber, as he addressed the librarian.

"Master Ungabwey has not named his price. It will be high. He has counted his losses, and they are grave. He will want recompense, if not for himself, then for the families of the men whose lives are gone. Also he will need wains and wagons to replace those taken by rock- and ice-falls. He will need men to manage them and serve him. That cost, also, will not be small."

In other words, Magister Marrow muttered to himself, the wealthiest man on the continent wants more wealth.

"But there is more," said Tchwee, "a larger matter to consider." His voice seemed to grow deeper, more profound, as if he spoke for the stone that fronted the library. "From the Quolt, Master Ungabwey has learned to understand the peril that drives you. Now he dreads what you will ask of him next.

"Speak of that, librarian. When Master Ungabwey has accepted your task, or refused it, he will name his price."

Sirjane Marrow did not hesitate. He was done with patience and delay. He did not care what Set Ungabwey's price might be. He would pay it, whether he could afford it or not. His sole concern was that the caravan and its master, its engines and its men, would continue to serve the Repository's survival.

"If I must," he said as if he did not share the caravan master's dread. "Master Ungabwey, I need"—he paused for emphasis—"the *library* needs more of what you have already done."

He heard a small hiss of surprise or disapproval from the devotee of Flesh. Fifth Daughter echoed it in her own way. But the librarian ignored them. Concentrating his senses exclusively on Set Ungabwey, he explained.

"To the southwest of Belleger, there are other mountains. They are not as high as the Wall"—he gestured toward the Quolt homeland—"but they are no less jagged and treacherous. Their western cliffs confront the sea, permitting no approach or harborage. Along their northeastern face, where they are known as the Realm's Edge, they form the border of Belleger, extending to the edges of the desert. But on the south, they relax into inhabited lands, where there are harbors aplenty, and warlike people."

Simply saying the words stung Magister Marrow's mind. He wanted to shout to convey their urgency. He kept his voice level by clenching his fists.

"Already those people send raiders through the mountains, seeking passage for a great army—and doing what harm they can to Belleger. However, that army in its throng of ships has not been sighted. It is coming, but it has not come yet.

"My request is this. Travel to the Realm's Edge with your engines and mechanicians. Barricade the passes, as you have done here. I will give you what maps I have, but they are unreliable. Belleger's war with Amika has discouraged exploration. And you will find no people like the Quolt to guide or instruct you. However, I am confident that you will be able to follow the tracks of the raiders. And you will not *stop*"—there his control slipped—"until every passage from the south into Belleger is closed."

Just for an instant, the Repository's primary guardian thought he saw a stricken look in the slits of the caravan master's eyes. But he did not falter. The stakes were too high.

"Agree to undertake my task, Master Ungabwey, and I will meet any price you name. If it is within my power, I will pay it. If it is not, I will seek it out for you."

For a long moment, Set Ungabwey gazed at his guest like a man who had lost interest in what he was hearing. Perhaps he had lost interest some time ago. But then, with an effort that made his flesh tremble, he turned his head to Tchwee. At once, the interpreter leaned close to the caravan master; so close that their foreheads almost touched. In that pose, they appeared to confer, although the librarian heard nothing, sensed nothing.

When the Master was satisfied, he resumed his former posture. For a while, Tchwee regarded the rugs as if he were unsure of his response. Then he lifted his eyes. In a subdued rumble, he said, "Master Ungabwey will hear the thoughts of his counselors."

The interpreter was looking at Fifth Daughter.

Goaded by tension or heat, Fifth Daughter yawned: an unseemly display of common humanity that Sirjane Marrow found comforting. He was not alone in his anxiety.

"Mountains?" she ventured. "Mountains again? If the enemy comes that way, the passes must be closed. But surely he has scouts? They will tell him the mountains are impossible. He will come another way."

"Another way?" prompted the librarian. For her sake, he made his voice gentle.

With an air of desperation, she asked, "Can he not come through Amika? Are there not safe coasts and harbors in the north? Alleman Dancer's carnival folk speak of them."

Still gently, the Magister replied, "You have not seen the maps, monk. Yes, there are safe coasts and harbors. The enemy can use them. But they are not in Amika. They are far to the north. And between them and Amika lie the ungiving steppes of the Nuuri. If he chooses that approach, he will be forced to march his entire army and all of his sorcerers and slaves *and* all of their stores of food and water for themselves and their animals across three hundred leagues before they reach kinder terrain. In addition, the Nuuri are not tolerant of intruders who harm their graze-lands. If their herds of zhecki cannot range widely, unimpeded, the beasts will starve. The enemy will be forced to do battle for *three hundred* leagues before he encounters the opposition of Amika. And the Nuuri are adept at such warfare."

Flatly, Amandis stated, "He will not come that way. He did not become what he is by being a fool."

Magister Marrow expected the assassin to continue. But instead Tchwee thanked Fifth Daughter and turned his attention to Flamora. "Most holy devotee of Flesh?"

"Oh, my." Flamora flapped her hand in a vain effort to fan her face. "All that marching. And mountains. And killing. All that brave blood spilled in the dirt—and for a bad cause. My heart grows weak when I imagine so much slaughter. Master Ungabwey, my thoughts will be of no use to you."

The interpreter nodded like a bow, but he did not relent. "Still he wishes to hear them."

The devotee of Flesh raised her chin, straightened her shoulders. Her kohl-rimmed eyes flashed. "Then my thought is this." Between one word and the next, her manner changed. The Magister had never heard her sound so firm—or so grim. "If Belleger and Amika do not stand together, they will both perish. And the Last Repository will not outlive them."

To himself, Magister Marrow breathed, Yes. Unless their deaths save it.

Tchwee nodded or bowed again. Then his gaze turned to Amandis. "Most holy devotee of Spirit?"

As her eyes met the black man's, the librarian sensed a subtle shift in her posture. It seemed to become both more tense and more relaxed, more dangerous, as if she readied herself to face an opponent who might prove fatal. Her tone made him think of a blade carving a block of wood.

"You do not need my counsel, Master Ungabwey," she replied. "Whether or not you choose to serve the library, the enemy will face Belleger's strength, and Amika's. But if you allow him to pass through the Realm's Edge, he may not meet opposition until he is a hundred leagues closer to the Last Repository. And he will have allies from the south, allies and resupply. In contrast, if you seal those mountains against him, he will be forced to fight his way across the whole of Belleger."

All of the Magister's hopes depended on that.

Tchwee made a low musing sound. With questions in his eyes, he observed, "Master Ungabwey has heard that ships cannot land on

Belleger's coast. In the west, the lands of both Belleger and Amika rise against the sea. There are no sheltered coves or bays. The cliffs are both sheer and rugged. And the waters are defended by fangs of rock and tearing reefs. How can the enemy land an army there?"

Removing one hand from her sleeve, Amandis made a dismissive gesture. "The land rises, yes. Its slope forces every watershed in both Belleger and Amika to join the Line River on its way to the sea. For that reason, the outlet of the Line, the Cut, is a deep gorge, a fiord easily defended. Even if the Cut were not defended, ships could not sail against the current far enough to pose a threat.

"But you do not know the enemy. He will *make* his harbor. With sorcery and siege weapons—with powers we do not know how to anticipate—he will batter the reefs and rocks and cliffs until they welcome him, both him and his great army."

As if he were arguing against himself, Magister Marrow countered, "I do not know what Master Ungabwey has heard. Or from whom. *I* have heard that the King of Belleger now fortifies his coast. And the Queen of Amika aids him."

But Amandis scorned his efforts. "*Fortifies* it?" she retorted. "With *what*? Cannon? Rifles? Emplacements? The enemy will sweep them aside. And sorcery will not impede him. The sorcerers of Belleger and Amika are *limited*. Their numbers are too few, and they cannot fling their Decimates across any considerable distance. The King of Belleger may hope to rely on them when the enemy comes near, but they will not suffice. Then they will be dead."

Now she sounded more like an axe chopping timber. "Master Ungabwey, if you do *not* seal those mountains, the enemy will enter Belleger unhindered. Worse, he will be reinforced and supplied by the people in the south, just as my sister foresees. His might will be that much greater. But the choice is not as simple as the librarian suggests. Consider it with care. If you *do* seal the Realm's Edge, Belleger will be invaded directly. From coast to desert, the whole land will become a killing-field. The enemy will make carrion of every life he encounters."

While the assassin's assertion hung in the stifling air, Flamora tapped Magister Marrow's arm. "And *that*, librarian," she murmured privately, "is what you have desired from the first. It is why you forged peace between Belleger and Amika."

Sirjane Marrow ignored her. Prince Bifalt had guessed the truth twenty years ago. Even that small piece of premature understanding might be the Last Repository's undoing.

"Choose, Master Ungabwey," growled the Magister. "Choose now. And name your price." The caravan master would need his own resupply. More men. More wagons. More incentive. "Our time grows short."

Silence held the chamber. The lanterns blazed as if they had been lit to scorch the air. No slight breeze made breathing easier. If the sorcerer had bothered to concentrate, he would have heard every lung in the room straining. But he had no attention to spare for anyone or anything around him, except the caravan master.

Then Set Ungabwey braced his hands on his knees. He leaned forward. Fighting his weight with every muscle, he struggled to stand.

The effort made his whole body quiver. Sweat beaded and ran on his forehead. A pallor like a failure of heart swept the color from his face. He would have failed; but Tchwee rose to help him. With his arms wrapped around the great mass of flesh, Tchwee heaved the Master to his feet.

Magister Marrow stood as well. Whatever Set Ungabwey might intend, the librarian meant to face it upright.

Panting heavily, Master Ungabwey spoke.

"Sanctuary." His high voice had a chilling edge. It was a gasp of ice in the heated chamber. "For my daughters. Absolute sanctuary."

On the faces of his four women were identical expressions of shock.

Shocked himself, the Magister babbled. "For them? Yes. Of course. Certainly. Why not?"

But then he caught himself. Surely he was a better man than *this*? Surely he could afford to be more honest with his host? More generous? Instead of accepting the obese man's terms, he countered unsteadily, "Master Ungabwey, that is not a price. It is a gesture of friendship." He was pleading. "And it is yours. While the library stands, your daughters are welcome among us.

"But you must understand me. There is no *absolute* sanctuary on this continent. The enemy wields indescribable might, and his hunger for the Last Repository's destruction cannot be sated. If the worst comes to us, I will contrive to deliver your daughters to the Quolt. That is the best I can do. Sirl Hokarth's people threaten no one. They have no sorcery. No one covets their homeland. Your daughters will be safe among them. As safe as this life permits.

"My word stands. Name another price. I will pay it."

Set Ungabwey could not answer: he was collapsing. Without the support of Tchwee's prodigious strength, he would have toppled. Only his interpreter's help enabled him to sink back down onto his pillows and resume his former posture. He struggled for breath until, one gasp at a time, his pallor receded.

At once, his daughters rushed to him. Tchwee moved aside, then knelt again while one woman brought a filled goblet and held it ready at her father's lips. Another stroked the sweat from his brow. The third arranged the pillows to brace him in place, while the fourth dashed through a doorway into a back room, returning with a damp cloth and a flask of water. These she used to cool his face and pendulous cheeks, his neck, his flaccid hands.

When the Master finally felt able to drink, the skin of his face regained its normal hue.

His daughters did not return to their places. Kneeling like Tchwee, they clustered around Set Ungabwey. Until now, none of them had made a sound. Now one of them asked softly, "Why, Father? How can we leave you?"

In a low murmur, the interpreter answered, "Because he loves you. His life is forfeit in this war. He and his train cannot hide among the Quolt. You can. Therefore you must remain here. Then he will have good cause to risk himself and his men and all his wealth for the library's sake."

Still standing, Magister Marrow asked with as much care as he could muster, "Will he do it? Will he seal the Realm's Edge?"

Tchwee gave the sorcerer a glance that would have withered a less stubborn defender. Brusquely, he answered, "Yes."

"And the price?"

The black man sighed. "The gift is the price. There is no other."

"Then you have my word." The old man could hardly contain his relief—or his disgust at the use he was making of the caravan master. "I speak for the Last Repository. His daughters will be made welcome. Send them to us when they are ready. While it can be done, they will be kept safe."

Goaded by an unwelcome shame, Magister Marrow turned to the door, opened it, and stepped out of the carriage into the blessed cool of early evening, leaving Amandis, Flamora, and Fifth Daughter to depart and join him when they saw fit. As he strode toward the gap between the keep's heavy gates, he cursed his fate, and the library's, and his own desperation.

He had won an important victory; but that was just one more reason to swear at himself. Set Ungabwey deserved better. His life was indeed forfeit, as Tchwee had said. That was his, Magister Marrow's, doing. If he had made no more demands, the caravan master could have protected himself and his daughters for decades at the farthest edges of the continent. In effect, the librarian had urged the Master to sacrifice himself.

Sirjane Marrow regretted that. It was necessary, but he regretted it. In a less personal way, he even regretted the way he had manipulated Prince Bifalt twenty years ago. He regretted sacrificing Belleger—and, if his hopes and ploys did not fail him, Amika as well. Regrets he had in abundance.

But not scruples. The needs of the library were too strict to tolerate scruples.

PART ONE

ONE

AMONG OLD FRIENDS

In the mellow sunshine and cooling breezes of a gentle after-noon, Klamath rode without haste among the billowed hills of southwestern Belleger. He had always liked these rides. They pleased him. At heart, he was a man of fields and farms. He loved seeing Belleger at peace.

The purpose of his journey was another matter.

He had left the camps of the army outside the Open Hand two fortnights ago, wending first to the south, then gradually turning east-ward, visiting villages, hamlets, and farmsteads as he went. In the early hours, the sun reached his eyes uncomfortably, but when it did, the broad brim of his slouch hat protected them. Now his shadow led him on his way; and he rode with his hat pushed back, enjoying the warmth and air on his face, the hints of cooling weather in the winds, the vistas around him.

This was sheep-grazing country, fertile enough for crops, and well fed with streams wandering through the shallow valleys, but too hilly for wheat or barley, millet or hay or sugar beets. The only signs of cul-tivation were occasional olive groves and vineyards. As a result, thickets of scrub oak and rhododendron grew wild, and flowers sprang up where they willed. But the soft slopes dipping here and there into wooded hollows or marshy swales were ideal for sheep. Animals almost ready for shearing wandered wherever their shepherds and dogs allowed them, cropping the sweet grasses in contentment.

From time to time, a distant shepherd hailed Klamath. More than once, he saw a sheepdog lose its head and chase a rabbit into a thicket. But he did not pause to speak with the shepherds or watch the dogs frighten their quarry. He was in no hurry, but he did not dally. He still had a long way to go. His manner and his gait may have been casual, but he took his duty seriously.

He had come far enough from the Open Hand and Belleger's Fist to see the Realm's Edge Mountains high on the horizon to the south. Even now, the tallest peaks remained wrapped in their cloaks of snow and ice, vestments white with dazzles when they struck reflections from the sun; and even the lower slopes were clotted with winter among their granite bluffs. The sight of them used to lift his heart whenever he rode this way. Now they made him uneasy. They held secrets he could not have imagined in earlier times.

Ever since Belleger's new army had begun to take shape, he had required these rides of himself every three years or so. Despite his new instructions from his King, and his more recent awareness of the dangers of the Realm's Edge, he still relished the ride itself. The beauty of the countryside, like the increasing health and prosperity of its people, and the open air in every kind of weather, refreshed his spirit. The effects of peace wherever he went—the growing families, the better farms, the new abundance of staples, fabrics, and tools supplied by the merchantries—touched him where he lived inside himself. And this was especially true since sorcery had been restored to the realm. The benefits of theurgy were everywhere. The weather could be wet or dry, according to the needs of the region. Diseases were rare: fires, rarer. Before his eyes, Belleger was recovering from its long war with Amika. The new vitality of his homeland made him glad.

Apart from his two mules and their diminishing burdens, he had no one with him. He wore the homespun shirt and trousers of a farmer. At need, he could wrap himself in a canvas rain-cape. Hats like his were worn by half the men in south Belleger, and by a good number of women. Even his saber was packed away. Only the rifle slung over his shoulder, and the satchel of ammunition at his saddle-horn, marked him as a soldier: only those things, and the high moccasins rising to midcalf that he had learned to wear during his time in the eastern desert with Prince Bifalt and Elgart, searching for the Last Repository. To any cursory glance, Klamath looked like a farmer riding to market, or returning home.

But he was not truly alone. He had an escort. Years ago, two men were enough. Now, at his King's command, he was guarded by a squad of ten. Oh, they stayed out of sight among the hills; even out of earshot. They camped without him, rode on without him. But his path and his stopping-places were well known to them, and they followed a parallel track. He could summon them with a shot. They would reach him in minutes.

The King of Belleger considered Klamath too valuable to lose.

His purpose was an awkward one. Often unpleasant. Sometimes cruel. Being too valuable to lose was not a status that Klamath had ever wanted. He considered himself a common man, despite his uncommon experiences. He belonged among other common men. Yet it was only his elevated status that allowed him to insist on rides like this when his King argued against them.

The halloo of a shepherd reached him from a far-off hillside. Dogs barked, seconding their master. Klamath waved to them and their flock, and rode on. He was nearing his next destination. Under other circumstances, he would have been eager to reach it. Now he could imagine the distress it would cause. But it was his duty, and he did not delay facing it.

After another league, he rounded a hill near its crest and came in sight of the place where he expected to spend the night. Below him lay a dell that cupped a flourishing copse of birch and sycamore beside a languid stream; and across the water stood the cottage he sought. Sunlight still held the tops of the trees. It gilded the tall chimneys of the house. The rest of the farmstead—the barn and sheep-pens, the cottage itself—lay in the spreading shadow of the hill.

It was a welcome sight. The cottage was unharmed. Under its meticulously thatched roof and the high peak of its rooftree, its walls were snug and sturdy. The windows on all sides had only sheets of canvas for shutters, but they were open to catch the softer evening air. The smoke curling from the kitchen chimney became spun gold in the light of the setting sun; and when the breeze brought the smoke to Klamath, he smelled clean wood and mutton.

In the south, the flock he had noticed a short time ago was coming closer, herded homeward by its sheepdogs. Now he recognized the shepherd. And as he started down into the dell, a child who may have been playing or hiding or doing chores among a cluster of bushes beside the stream stood up and looked in his direction. Then the child gave a squeal and ran for the cottage.

A young girl, Klamath saw. Knowing the family, he did not have to search his memory for her name. It was Mattilda. And she did not sound frightened. She sounded excited, announcing a visitor. A visitor her parents had learned to expect in this season every third year.

Trotting down the slope, Klamath smiled as an anxiety left him. The family here was one of his favorites. He did not think that they were close enough to the Realm's Edge to be in danger. Being who he was, however, he had feared they were. That fear did not leave him entirely now. He knew too little about the secrets hiding in the mountains. But for one night, at least, he could let himself relax.

His visits here were always awkward. This one would be more than unpleasant. But despite his gentle disposition, he was a veteran of Belleger's battles with Amika. He knew killing and savage sorcery. He did not shy away from unpleasantness and hurt.

As he made his descent, a woman came out onto the porch. Stout and strong. Flaxen hair raddled with grey, just like her husband's. Hands and forearms red from washing dishes or cooking. She did not smile when she recognized Klamath; but he did not expect that. Her wave was welcome enough.

"Matta!" he called in answer. "My blessing on this house, and the King's as well! You are a sight to make a weary man glad."

Her reply was a scowl, but she did not turn her back.

In a moment, her husband, Matt, joined her on the porch. He was a tall man, upright and solid, with a frame made for heavy lifting and sturdy construction. The sun had baked his face bronze. His hair and beard were the same mixed hues as his wife's, showing his years. But his eyes were an unclouded blue, while hers were a stormy grey.

His daughter, seven-year-old Mattilda, the youngest child, accompanied him. She stood close beside him, staring at their visitor with wide eyes. He rested one broad hand on her head as if she needed his protection, although of course she did not.

"Matt," said Klamath with pleasure. "You look well. And your home"—he glanced around the front of the cottage—"looks strong enough to withstand the Decimate of earthquake. The King will be relieved to hear it."

"Klamath." Matt did not smile. His smiles were rare. But when they came, they lifted his face like a new day. "Be welcome in our house. While you stay, it is yours."

Sternly, Matta corrected him. "*General* Klamath. He commands an army now." Her gaze held Klamath's like a challenge. "He may have a hundred men nearby at this moment."

Klamath did not look away. If he did, she would distrust him. "Now, Matta," he said kindly, "you know better. I am Klamath, nothing more. A title is only as good as its power to command. No one here has ever obeyed a command of mine. And you know as well as I do, your husband has never obeyed *any* command since he was released from the King's guard. Nineteen years ago now, that was. When Belleger and Amika finally found peace."

"When King Bifalt married Queen Estie," piped up Mattilda, eager to show what she understood.

At the same time, Matta objected, "But you took—"

Matt silenced her by putting his other arm around her shoulders. "Now, Matta." He almost smiled. "Mattwil left by his own choice. No one *took* him. And Klamath is more than our guest. He is an old friend. We know why he visits us. He does it because he must. But if we treat him well, he may give us the news of the realm. He may even give us news of our eldest."

Still scowling, Matta forced an unconvincing smile. "Then be welcome, Klamath, general or not. Our home is yours. Mattin is out with the sheep. He will return at sunset. But Mattson does chores in the barn. He will settle your animals. When you come into the house"—she wrinkled her nose—"and wash, you and Matt can tell old war stories while I do what I can to ready a meal."

Klamath was slow to answer. He was remembering the last time he had tried to convince King Bifalt that he was the wrong man to command the combined armies of Belleger and Amika. With his usual curtness, his air of suppressed impatience, the King had replied, *No one who wants command should be allowed to have it.* Then he had added, *I will not command them. I am not trusted.*

He may have meant, Not trusted by the Amikans. Or by the Magisters of the Last Repository. Or even by Queen Estie. But Klamath suspected he meant that he did not trust himself.

To cover his lapse of attention, Klamath swung down from his mount. Smiling as well as he could with King Bifalt on his mind, he replied, "I remember your cooking, Matta. You will give us a feast."

Then he turned away, leading his horse and his trailing mules to the barn.

Most of his memories of his King troubled him. Something deep inside King Bifalt had been changed by his time in the great library. Klamath had heard the tales, but he did not understand them. *Prince* Bifalt would not have hesitated to command any army.

Klamath spent a few minutes chatting with Mattson, Matt and Matta's third child, now around twelve years old. Klamath understood the similarity of the names. After the long depredations of the war, Matt and his wife had sought to renew or reinvent their sense of *family* by giving their children names that belonged together, names like their own. For a boy his age, Mattson asked piercing questions; but Klamath gave them inconsequential answers. The time would come when he would have to confess the truth about his visit, although Matt and Matta understood it already. But Klamath was in no hurry to arrive at that moment. As soon as he could without being rude, he left his animals with Mattson and went to the cottage.

When he crossed the porch and opened the door, he saw—as he had seen before—that the front room was more spacious than it appeared from outside. It reached from wall to wall, with the kitchen at one end to his left, a cluster of chairs and stools near the hearth on his right, and a large table for dining in the middle. Doorways in the back led to the bedrooms.

Matta was in the kitchen, working. With Mattilda beside him, Matt sat in a chair at the dining table instead of near the low flames wavering in the hearth. With summer lingering in the air, no one needed the hearth for warmth. But Klamath did not greet them, or walk into the room. He knew better.

Inside the door stood a washstand, soap, small towels, and a jug of water. Matta was imperious about cleanliness. Smiling for her sake as much as for his own pleasure, he leaned his rifle and ammunition against the wall, stripped off his shirt, and made himself presentable with liberal amounts of soap and water.

From her place by the stove, Matta scowled at his gun and bullets. While she watched him wash, however, her expression softened into a frown. He would have liked to think that she felt compassion at the sight of his various scars. But they were old now, faded, practically invisible. No doubt she was simply gratified by his respect for her wishes.

He did not need her to tell him that she would never forgive him for the departure of her eldest son.

As soon as Klamath finished washing, while he was buttoning his shirt, Matt waved him to a seat at the table. "Sit, old friend. You have had a long day in the saddle. Be comfortable."

Klamath murmured his thanks. So that Matta could watch his face while he talked with Matt, he sank into a chair at the end of the table.

Glancing at his wife, the sheep-master said casually, "Matta expects war stories. But in truth, old friend, I am not in a warlike mood. Nor,

I suspect, are you. What shall we discuss? Shall I tell you how the sheep are faring? Are you interested in the weather?"

Klamath would have listened to talk like that happily for an hour. But Mattilda announced, "*I* want to hear about Mattwil." Apparently, she felt daring in Klamath's presence. "I miss him. Ever since he left, Mattin and Mattson are too busy to play."

Matt squeezed her shoulder. "Hush, child," he said softly. "Our guest is tired. He will speak when he is ready."

"I *am* tired," admitted Klamath. He feigned a groan. Then he winked at the girl. "But not too tired to talk about Mattwil."

The sparkle in her eyes and the flush on her cheeks was more reward than he deserved.

Matt's expression froze for a moment, then resumed its usual grave calm. Abruptly, Matta turned her back on the table, busied herself over one of the pots on the stove. But Klamath was not misled. He knew she could hear every word, and every word made her tremble. She turned away so her face would not betray her.

"He is well," said Klamath to ease her. "I spoke with him the last time he was given leave to visit the Open Hand." That had been a year ago, but Klamath did not say so. "He sends his love, and made me promise to tell you he is well."

Mattilda clapped her hands, and Matt nodded. Matta's shoulders slumped an inch—but only an inch. She was waiting to hear more.

"He is not a soldier," continued Klamath, the unwilling general. "As soon as he arrived, he was commandeered for work as a stonemason." Mattwil had his father's frame, his father's strength. "And he does not work with the crews that fortify the coast. For reasons of his own, King Bifalt fears an attack by sea. But if there *is* an attack, Mattwil does not stand in its path."

Matta's shoulders slumped farther. Grabbing a dish towel, she wiped her face.

Wincing in anticipation, Klamath finished, "Instead he works in Amika."

At once, Matta flung her towel aside, whirled away from the stove. "In *Amika*?" she demanded. "*In Amika?*"

"Now, Matta," her husband murmured, trying to soothe her. "Now, Matta." But she ignored him. Hot with fury, her glare was fixed on Klamath.

The General spread his hands as if he were helpless. With a tinge of sadness in his voice, he said, "We are allies, Matta." Her reaction was all too common. Common and dangerous. "Belleger and Amika stand together because they must. We are bound to each other by treaty, and by the King's marriage, and by fears he and Amika's Queen share."

"But *Amika!*" retorted Mattwil's mother. "Killers! Butchers! They made war on us for *generations*. We have peace now—you *say* we have peace—but twenty years without bloodshed do not restore the men we lost. It does not comfort the families left fatherless, sonless. It does not heal the people made homeless, driven into poverty, because they were not *enough* to tend the crops, raise the cattle, herd the sheep. It does not make us *forget*.

"Amikans *made* the war. They have no *right* to my son!"

"Matta!" said Matt more sharply. "None of this is Klamath's doing. Mattwil left because he chose to go."

"Because," snapped his wife, "*General* Klamath chose to visit us. Because he chose to speak of his need for men."

"Still," insisted the sheep-master, "the choice was Mattwil's. He was not commanded. Klamath does not command here."

Then he addressed his guest. There was iron in his voice. "What use does Amika make of Mattwil?"

Klamath sighed. "Queen Estie desires a road to connect the Open Hand and Maloresse with the Last Repository of the sorcerers. King Bifalt does not approve. His distrust"—Klamath could have said, His loathing—"of those Magisters endures. He wants no contact with them. But Queen Estie supports his fortification of the coast. He cannot refuse to support her road.

"Mattwil works with the teams on that road. Already it extends from the Open Hand to Maloresse and more than seventy leagues eastward. He is skilled with stone. He shapes blocks of granite and places them to bear the weight of horses and oxen, heavy wagons and marching men."

While Klamath spoke, Matta slowly recovered her composure. Matt watched her until she turned back to the stove. Then his own manner eased. When Mattilda squirmed away from him, he released her. He may not have realized how tightly he had gripped her.

"But why?" protested the child. "They say Queen Estie is the most beautiful woman in both realms. Why does she want a *road*?"

Trying to ease the tension of his hosts, Klamath asked Mattilda, "What will *you* want? When you are the most beautiful woman in both realms?"

The girl blushed; but she did not hesitate. "A crown," she said promptly. "And a fancy gown for special. And men who kiss my hand. And—"

"And," put in Matta sternly, "a good husband who loves you and can be trusted and does not think of war."

Klamath nodded. "All of that, yes." Then he said to Matt, "But Queen Estie wants a road to speed contact with the Last Repository. She wants to be able to send aid, or receive it. She wants caravans to include us in their trade routes. And she wants our Magisters, Belleger's and Amika's, to visit the great library, where they can grow in knowledge and usefulness.

"Also she hopes the Magisters of the library will visit *us*, so that we can learn to understand their purposes."

Klamath had not been there when those Magisters had forced Prince Bifalt to approach Amika and try for peace. He had heard the tales, however, both King Bifalt's terse version and Elgart's more elaborate account. He knew that the Prince had won Elgart's heart there. But he also knew that no one in Belleger or Amika truly understood why the sorcerers of the library did what they did. The King had his own explanation, and feared it. Only his closest advisers shared his certainty.

Breathing against his own tension, Klamath waited for Matt's next question. He knew what it would be. Why does King Bifalt fortify the coast? It is impassable. Men who want to sail there have tried too often. Too many of them have died. They cannot survive the reefs and rocks, the turmoil of cross-currents.

But before the sheep-master found the words he wanted, he was interrupted by the clatter of boots on the porch. Mattson came in from the barn, hurrying. "Are they telling war stories?" He did not try to mask his eagerness. "I want to hear."

Peremptory with her rules, Matta reminded him, "Wash!" Then she muttered darkly, "If they are not war stories now, they will be soon."

Ducking his head, Mattson turned to the washstand. While his mother watched, he brushed the straw from his hair and shirt, splashed water on his face, scrubbed the dirt and droppings from his hands.

Klamath used the distraction to glance over his shoulder at the hearth, where Matt's rifle hung from iron pegs set into the chimney near the ceiling. As he expected, dust coated the weapon. Despite her attention to cleanliness, Matta refused to touch the rifle. And clearly, Matt had not handled it, although he must have heard that the Realm's Edge had become dangerous.

The soldier returned his gaze to the family as Mattson passed Matta's inspection. At once, the boy scooted to the table and took a chair. Sharp with anticipation, his eyes flicked back and forth between Klamath and his father.

At the same time, Klamath heard the bawling of sheep and the yips of their dogs, the mild commands of their shepherd, the low rumble of hooves. The herd was being driven into its pens. Mattin, the second of Matt and Matta's three sons, would come to the cottage as soon as he watered the sheep and gave them grain to supplement their grazing.

Privately, Klamath sighed. He was running out of time. Soon— after the family had eaten at the latest—he would have to talk more seriously. Of course, Matt and Matta knew the reason for his visit. Mattin probably did as well. But they knew it from the perspective of their own lives, lives far from the more populous regions of Belleger and the threats King Bifalt feared. Klamath was here, at least in part, to make them look at a larger picture.

"Mattilda," said Matta from the stove. "Set the table." She managed a more comfortable smile for her daughter. "Mattin is home. He will be hungry." Then her frown returned. "And our guest has come a long way. He will be hungry as well."

Perhaps for Klamath's sake, the girl seemed to be on her best behavior. At once, she jumped up from her chair, went to a cupboard near the stove, and began taking down plates, bowls, and mugs with a child's care.

Speaking to be overheard, Klamath said, "She is a fine girl, Matt. And Mattson gave me good help in the barn." He was entirely sincere. He hoped it showed. "I trust you and Matta to be proud of them."

Matt almost smiled, but he spoke gravely. "We are. They are a great comfort to us. Mattin is also." After a pause, he added, "But we will not be whole, old friend, until Mattwil returns."

That, thought Klamath, would not be for a long time. Queen Estie's road still had to cross the eastern gorges of the Line River, and her need for men increased constantly. So far from Maloresse and the Open Hand, desertion by workers who resented the primitive conditions and long absences was a growing problem. Queen Estie had been forced to keep her laborers under guard. But Klamath only nodded to Matt, and did not answer.

Without question, his visit was going to be difficult.

To cover his reluctance, he called, "Hells, Matta! Your stew smells wonderful. I am hungrier than I knew. And is that the scent of baking bread?"

Matta nodded, but did not shift her attention from the stove.

Her husband frowned at her manner, then gave a small shrug and left her alone.

Soon heavier boots thumped the boards of the porch. With more circumspection than his younger brother, Mattin opened the door. He confirmed Klamath's presence with a quick glance and nodded once to his father before moving to the washstand. He was a young man now—only seventeen, by Klamath's reckoning—but he moved with his father's calm dignity: a way of carrying himself that made him look older than his years. Only the openness of his face and the thinness of his beard betrayed his youth.

When he had made himself as clean as he could without a full bath, he went to the stove and kissed his mother's cheek. Looking at her work, he asked, "Almost ready, Ma? The whole herd is not hungrier than I am."

"Soon," she replied. Klamath heard affection in her tone. "When you have greeted our guest. And asked your brother and sister if their chores are done. Our guest's arrival may have distracted them."

Mattin patted her shoulder, then came to the table. Before he seated himself, he gave Klamath a nod as formal as a bow. "General Klamath, sir. Ma and Da have welcomed you. So do I. We have too little excitement." With one hand, he tousled Mattson's hair. "And Mattilda tires of teasing mere brothers. Your visits stir us up."

Klamath answered with a more casual nod. "It is good to see you, Mattin. You have become a man in my absence. You wear it well."

Matt pointed at a chair. "Sit, Son. You have not missed much. My old friend has only had time to tell us Mattwil is well. He works with teams building a road for Queen Estie."

There was relief in Mattin's eyes as he seated himself. But he did not question Klamath further. Instead he looked around the table. "And your chores are done?" he asked his siblings. "Mattson? Mattilda? *All* done?"

Clearly, the girl adored her older brother, "Yes," she said, deliberately cheerful, as she put plates, bowls, and mugs for six in their proper places on the table. Then she returned to the cupboard for utensils: spoons and forks of tin, a sign of the family's renewed prosperity.

Mattson was more self-conscious. "Of course," he muttered past the hair hanging in his eyes.

"Very good." Mattin smiled more readily than his father. "And you, sir?" he added to Klamath. "How can we make you more comfortable until Ma feeds us?"

Klamath scratched his whiskers. "You can start," he offered, "by not calling me *sir*. Your father and I have been friends since the war. And my title is a reluctant one." He grimaced wryly. "I would abdicate, if soldiers had the freedom of Kings." King Smegin of Amika had done so after his daughter Estie had married Bifalt—and after old King Abbator of Belleger had passed away. "I am Klamath."

While Klamath was speaking, Matt whispered to Mattilda, "Not the ale. Our guest prefers water." But the reluctant general chose to ignore this. After all, it was true.

Almost tottering under the weight of her pitcher, Mattilda brought fresh water from the kitchen cistern. With exaggerated care, she filled the mugs on the table. When she came to Klamath, he drained his mug as soon as she filled it, then held it out to ask for more. Smiling, she complied. He thanked her with another wink.

"Klamath, then," conceded Mattin. "What is the news of the world? We are remote here. We hear too much of our own doings, and too little of anything else."

"When we have eaten," commanded Matta. In her reddened hands, she brought a stewpot to the table. "Whatever else he may be, he is our guest. We will talk later, no doubt for hours. Your questions can wait."

Obedient to his family's rituals, Matt moved to sit at the head of the table. Now Klamath remembered that he was in Matta's chair. While Mattilda set another pot beside the stew, this one steaming with stewed greens, he shifted to sit across from Mattin and Mattson. When the girl finished her duties by delivering a tray of warm bread redolent from the oven, accompanied by a plate of butter—another sign that the family prospered—she seated herself between Klamath and Matt as if she were claiming a place of honor.

Matta remained on her feet until she had ladled stew into the bowls, and had passed around the pot of greens. Then she took her seat opposite her husband.

"A feast," remarked Klamath. He felt almost reverent. He had eaten field rations too often on his trek. "As I predicted."

Matt watched Matta until she was ready to meet his gaze: another of their family rituals. While they regarded each other, he gave her a nod as formal as the one with which Mattin had greeted Klamath.

At once, Mattilda and Mattson began to eat like children who had not seen food for weeks. Mattin made a show of approaching his meal with his father's dignity, his mother's care; but soon he abandoned the charade as hopeless. Attacking his stew, greens, and bread, he had devoured his first helping and was reaching for seconds before Klamath had finished spreading butter on a slice of bread with the back of his spoon.

Klamath was slow because he had to suppress laughter. His pleasure demanded an outlet; but he swallowed it so he would not seem rude—or worse, scornful.

No one spoke until Klamath's plate and bowl were empty, and he had accepted more stew. Then, with an obliqueness Klamath recognized, as if the question were inconsequential, Matt asked him, "Did you take your usual path on this ride? Did you pass through the village?"

He named a place Klamath had visited two days ago.

The soldier groaned to himself. He was not ready. Without looking up from his stew, he answered, "I did."

"Then you have heard what happened."

"Happened?" This was the news Klamath had come for. He knew the outlines, but he wanted more details.

"To sheep-master Lessen," said Matt.

"And to his wife," added Matta sharply.

Matt nodded agreement. "And to his seven children. Six of them girls. And to his farmstead. Even to many of his sheep."

Klamath put down his spoon, wiped his mouth, and faced his host squarely. With a hint of command in his voice, but softly, he said, "Tell me."

"Matt," his wife warned him. "Mattilda is too young."

Mattin sat straight in his chair, his gaze fixed hard on Klamath. Mattson had his elbows propped on the table and his fists knotted in his hair. He looked nauseated.

The sheep-master frowned. "She will hear gossip, if she has not already. The tale will do less harm if she hears it from us."

Matta scowled back at him; but she did not argue.

Matt held Klamath's gaze steadily as he answered the soldier. Behind his mildness, he had as much courage as any man Klamath knew. He was the underlying reason for Klamath's visit.

"It was seven"—Matt consulted the ceiling with a glance, then met Klamath's eyes again—"no, ten days ago. Evening was near. The sheep were wandering home. The boy was their shepherd, but he did not hurry. He was not late. The rest of the family, Lessen himself, Abiga, his wife, their six daughters—all were in or near the house, busy with their chores. Only the boy survived.

"Men came out from behind the shelter of a hill. They were mounted. The boy counted eighteen or twenty. He had never seen garb like theirs. Garments like nightgowns head to foot, loose and flowing, open only for their faces. White cloth marked with black streaks like shadows. Short spears—he called them short spears, but I think they were jave-lins. And silent. If any of them spoke—*ever*—they did so in whispers. Only the sound of their hooves warned the boy to hide and watch."

Without pausing, Matt picked Mattilda up from her chair, pulled her onto his lap, wrapped his arms around her. Wide-eyed with fright and incomprehension, she stared at Klamath.

"Riding hard," said her father, "they surrounded the farmstead. Lessen was brave or foolish. Or maybe he could not believe he was in danger. He went to meet them. They gutted him. Abiga and her girls ran into the house. No doubt they barred the door. But a man threw a flaming brand onto the roof. Another followed, and another. Other men dismounted. The boy heard Abiga and her girls screaming. When fire and smoke drove them outside, they were taken."

Abruptly, Mattilda squirmed in Matt's arms, twisted to hide her face against his shoulder. For a moment, he gave her his attention. Stroking her hair, he murmured, "Lessen was never a soldier. He was helpless. I am not. I will protect you better."

When he felt some of her tension ease, he faced Klamath again.

"Men entered the house. They took as much food and drink as they could before the roof collapsed. They made Abiga witness while they had their way with the girls, all of them. One by one, they slaughtered the children. Last they used and killed Abiga. Then they feasted.

"After the house burned down, and their feast was done, they fired the barn, the outbuildings. Then they mounted their horses and rode a sweep around the farmstead, killing any sheep they found. Soon they were gone.

"The boy watched all this. He was helpless. He did his best by hid-ing. But the shock was too great for him. When the signs of fire brought help from a neighboring farm, he could not utter a word. Days passed before he was able to say what he had seen."

While Matt spoke, Mattin breathed deeply to contain himself. He studied Klamath with thoughts of fire in his eyes. Pulling at his hair, Mattson bent slowly forward until his nose almost touched the table. Matta sat like a woman carved in stone until her husband was done. Then she spat one word.

"*Raiders.*"

Her vehemence seemed to break a spell over the family. Matt lowered his gaze. Mattilda turned to look at her mother. Mattson slowly raised his head, blinking as if he had been asleep.

With care, Mattin placed his hands flat on the table. "Raiders?" he asked in a strained voice. "I do not understand. They took nothing. They came from the Realm's Edge, destroyed a farmstead, and rode away. Taking *nothing*? Why would raiders do such a thing?"

He kept watching Klamath.

Klamath spread his hands. He was not sure of his answer. "To provoke us? To probe our defenses?"

"Defenses?" snapped Matta. "We have no defenses. Our King ignores us. *General* Klamath does nothing.

"We are *Bellegerins*. Are we to be sacrificed because we live in the south? Are we too far from the Open Hand to deserve protection?"

"Now, Matta," said Matt without lifting his gaze. "These raids are too recent. They did not begin until the first of summer. Klamath is here to learn the extent of the danger. He has not had time to respond."

"*Will* you send the army?" asked Mattin at once. "Will you defend us?"

Klamath squared his shoulders. "No." He had feared that this would be unpleasant. He did not shirk it. "Our border along the Realm's Edge is too long. And we do not know where these raiders emerge from the mountains. Our whole army is too small to guard every farm."

"Then," insisted the young man, "will you give us rifles? Will you arm the farms? The villages? The towns? Will you make us able to defend ourselves?"

Again, Klamath said, "No." For the first time, he told this family a lie. He hoped devoutly that it would be the last time. "We do not have enough."

In truth, Belleger had more rifles than the army could use. Making them had been the realm's primary industry for at least a decade. But they had been forged and assembled behind screens of other activities. And they were stockpiled in hidden vaults among the foundations of Belleger's Fist, the King's high keep. As for the bullets, crates of them were concealed in rooms and cellars around the Open Hand. Guns and ammunition were King Bifalt's most severely guarded secret. He refused to release them.

Preserving that secret was another of Klamath's duties.

To forestall a further question, he added quickly, "But I *will* send companies of scouts and trackers." That King Bifalt would approve. "They will search until they learn where the raiders come from, or where they go. Then I will know how many men I must commit to prevent more raids."

Matta snorted her scorn. "And while your men scout and track, *we* have to die. Our only recourse is to abandon our home. Our *home*."

"Matta," said Matt more sharply. "Enough. General or not, Klamath cannot do more than he has promised. *He* does not send raiders to kill us. He cannot oppose them in an instant."

His wife made a sound like a snarl; but she did not say more. Stamping to her feet, she began to clear the table.

Matt gave her a moment. Then he said gently, "Mattson, Mattilda, help your mother."

Mattson jumped up immediately, snatched his plate, bowl, and mug from the table. Klamath suspected that the boy had already heard too much. He might not come back when the task was done.

Mattilda responded more slowly, but she, too, obeyed. While she moved back and forth between the table and the kitchen, she did not look at Klamath; did not so much as glance in his direction. So far, he had said almost nothing—and yet he felt that he had already betrayed her. Her and her mother both. He was here for more reasons than news-gathering, but he had not spoken of them.

When all the dishes and utensils were in the sink to be washed, and the remaining food had been put away, Matta hugged Mattson and Mattilda. With a kindness she reserved for her family, she suggested,

"Mattson, perhaps there is some game you and Mattilda can play in your rooms? What you have heard is not for children, and there may be worse to come. I will not refuse if you want to hear what your father's friend will say. But I encourage you to avoid it."

In a small voice, Mattilda asked, "Can Da really keep us safe, Ma?"

Keeping her back to Matt and Klamath, Matta said stoutly, "If a living man can do it, your father can. There is no one better."

During his time in the wars, in the aftermath of his rides into hell, and on other occasions as well, Klamath had wept easily: a reaction to the shock of swords and killing, the horror of terrible sorcery. But he had not shed tears for many years. Now he had to fight them back.

Like Matta, he believed there was no one better than Matt.

For a moment, Mattilda gave her father a pleading look. Then she left the common room, no doubt heading for her bedroom at the back of the house.

Mattson hesitated beside his mother. Like Mattilda's, his face had a pleading cast. But his gaze was fixed, not on Matt, but on Mattin.

At a nudge from his father, Mattin turned in his chair. Over his shoulder, he told his younger brother, "Go with Mattilda, Mattson. You are old enough to reassure her. Later, I will tell you as much as you ask to hear."

Klamath said nothing. He did not trust his voice.

The way Mattson bowed his head as he followed his sister made his relief plain.

When the boy was gone, Matt patted Mattin's shoulder. "Well done, Mattin," he whispered. "Thank you."

Matta was wiping her face with a dish towel again. Her voice muffled, she said, "They are good children. They deserve better."

Klamath knew that she meant, Better than what he could do for them. Better than the reasons for his visit.

While his mother began to wash the dishes, Mattin faced Klamath again. Pressing his hands on the table, he said in a tight voice, "Now, sir. You have our news. Perhaps you will tell us the news of the realm."

Klamath pushed back his chair so that he could stretch the tension out of his legs. He made an effort to appear relaxed. Loudly enough to be heard over the noise of running water and washing, he said, "A feast, Matta. You have my gratitude."

When she ignored him, he allowed himself another inward sigh. Then he looked, not at Mattin, but at Matt.

"Some of what I say," he began, "you have heard before. It has not changed. But I must start somewhere.

"Twenty years ago, Prince Bifalt returned from the Last Repository with Commander Forguile of Amika and faced the challenge of forming an alliance with King Smegin. Now nineteen years have passed since the marriage of Prince Bifalt and Princess Estie sealed peace between Belleger and Amika." He did not need to assemble his thoughts. He had made this speech many times. "A season or two later, old King Abbator passed, and Bifalt became King in Belleger's Fist. At once, King Smegin of Amika abdicated his throne, making Estie Queen in Maloresse so that her rank and authority would match her husband's.

"After the Prince and Princess had married, Prince Bifalt and Commander Forguile went back to the Last Repository. There Prince Bifalt demanded the knowledge that would restore sorcery to Belleger, and to Amika also. When they came home, the Prince and his companion brought with them a sorcerer, Magister Facile. Her aid reawakened in the Magisters of both realms their inborn gift for theurgy. Belleger and Amika had been equally deprived. By her efforts, and Prince Bifalt's, they were equally restored."

Klamath grimaced. "And still, after so many years, there is discord between the realms. It seldom flares into serious conflict. King Bifalt and Queen Estie are open in their disagreements—and open in how those disagreements are resolved. They do what they can to set an example for their people. There are no pitched battles. Discontented brigands do not prey across the border. But the peace remains uneasy. Disputes are common. Insults often lead to brawls. Belleger and Amika were at war too long, and the land heals faster than the people. Families do not forget their losses, and what they do not forget, they do not forgive.

"You know all this."

Ruefully, Matt commented, "You have told us often enough."

With a hint of tartness, Klamath replied, "It is necessary. I cannot explain more recent events without it."

Matt's expression did not change. "No doubt."

Mattin had been containing himself while he waited for an opening. Now he asked, "What are their disagreements? King Bifalt's and Queen Estie's?"

Klamath turned his attention to the young man. "I have told your parents of one. You know there is much rebuilding to be done in both realms. Belleger provides Amika with wool and fabrics and meat, which Amika repays with timber and carpenters. But in addition, King Bifalt works to fortify Belleger's coast. He has won Queen Estie's support. She has promised to supply cannon made with knowledge given to Amika by the King. For her part, she desires a road to join the Open Hand and Maloresse with the Last Repository. The King wants no dealings with the library and its Magisters. Nevertheless he has relented. He allows her to claim Bellegerin stonemasons, and also other workmen who are either unwilling or unfit to be soldiers. Mattwil is among them.

"On other subjects," he added after a pause, feeling his way, "our rulers stand together. They are united in their desire to foster peace. Also they seek to increase the size and skill of their combined army."

From the kitchen, Matta remarked sharply, "An army you now command."

Grateful for the interruption, Klamath nodded. "And I am not a commander by nature. I need counsel. Amikans are willing soldiers, but they resist serving with Bellegerins. And our people do not trust Amikans." Matt was a former rifleman: he knew the harm that fighters hostile to each other could do. "I struggle to combine them, but I fail to make them effective."

Matt considered the matter. In a musing tone, he suggested, "Then keep them apart. Make them compete against each other. Contests of archery. Marksmanship. Riding for parade and for hell. Sword-work. Combat without weapons. A company of Amikans against a company of Bellegerins. Allow the winner to keep the captain responsible for its training. The losing captain must accept a place in the other army. The losing company must accept a captain from the other army.

"Or if the competition is only one against one, the loser's teacher must become a student of the winner's teacher. The loser is given a new teacher, again from the other army."

Motivation, thought Klamath with a grin of relief. Familiarity. *Respect*. All acquired in small increments. Even with a Bellegerin captain, an Amikan company would not lose deliberately. Those soldiers were proud of their own skills. And if they lost, their next captain might be worse. Only a winning captain would be able to keep his own people.

From the heart, Klamath said, "*Thank* you, Matt." Already the sheep-master had justified his visit. "That is good counsel. I will try it."

But Mattin was not deflected. As soon as he could, he asked, "Are there other disagreements?"

Hoping to soften the young man's stare, Klamath tried a smile. "There is this. They have no children. After nineteen years together, none. That surely causes some unpleasantness."

He knew his King. And he had seen how the Queen watched her husband. He believed that their childlessness was Bifalt's choice, not hers.

According to Elgart, who in his weak moments sometimes disclosed secrets, the marriage was still unconsummated. The King refused to bed his wife, the loveliest woman in both realms—and perhaps the cleverest as well.

Elgart and Klamath had shared the ordeal of Prince Bifalt's search for the Last Repository. They were friends. Elgart knew he could trust Klamath's discretion. However, Klamath did not always appreciate Elgart's revelations.

Clearly, the subject of King Bifalt's childless marriage interested Matt. But thinking about the King's burdens and decisions was uncomfortable for Klamath. When his attempt at a more lighthearted reply failed to ease Mattin, he resumed his duty.

"Also we are troubled by priests," he said with a shrug in his tone. "They have come to Belleger from Amika, but they are not Amikan. Rather they passed through Amika from some unknown land. They preach peace, but their preaching spreads confusion. They speak of god or gods, one god or several or many, to people who have never imagined such beings. People who also cannot understand why gods need priests."

This appeared to surprise Matt. His eyebrows came up. His attention intensified. But he did not interrupt.

"King Bifalt and Queen Estie disagree on this," said Klamath, still addressing Mattin. "She has no interest in priests and their religion, but she sees no harm in them. *He* does not trust men from strange lands. He has met many foreigners, and few of them did not mean harm to both Belleger and Amika."

"A moment, old friend," put in Matt. "I do not understand. What are 'gods'? For that matter, what are 'priests'? You did not speak of them on your earlier visits."

Klamath confessed his uncertainty. "They are recent in Belleger. I do not understand them myself. The whole matter baffles me.

"I have been told that gods can be considered living sorcery." That was Elgart's explanation. "Or personifications of sorcery. Or perhaps *sources* of sorcery. They may or may not be *alive* as we know life. But they are mighty beyond comprehension. Their influence and wishes cover the world.

"Priests, I am assured," he went with more confidence, "are *not* gods. They are mere men, the ambassadors of gods, or the interpreters. The spokesmen. They travel from place to place, building places of worship they call 'churches,' and they teach"—honesty prompted Klamath to modify his assertion—"they *say* they teach how to live in harmony with their god or gods, so that people everywhere will have peace.

"That is as much as I know. It all confuses me. To my mind, sorcery is a natural force, as natural as wind and lightning." He had his examples ready. He had made this speech before. "Wind is destructive in one place and gentle in another. Lightning strikes where it wills—or where it can—without discrimination. The talent for sorcery is the same. *Every* talent is the same. One man is naturally gifted to train horses. His neighbor struggles to control them. One man adores his wife. Another fears his.

"I do not understand the need to talk of gods, or to become priests.

"But"—Klamath returned to Mattin's question—"the disagreement between King Bifalt and Queen Estie is more specific. Some of our folk want one of the priests, their archpriest, given a place among the King's advisers. The Queen agrees. If this archpriest, she reasons, speaks for a portion of Belleger's people, and of Amika's, his voice should be heard. But the King refuses."

And he seldom gave his reasons. Privately, however, Klamath had heard his King say that in troubled times, people were like sheep. They scattered and became easy prey. Or they bunched together and ran into peril. Then he had said, *I will not trust my flock to strangers. Especially to strangers who do not think for themselves. Their god or gods are too much like the library's Magisters.*

For a while, both Matt and Mattin were silent. Matt's troubled gaze roamed the room from the hearth to the kitchen stove, from Matta's back hunched over her washing to the doors leading to the rear of the house. Whenever his glance touched the neglected rifle above the fireplace, the small muscles around his eyes winced.

While Klamath spoke, Mattin had lowered his stare. Now he seemed to study his hands on the table. His shoulders bunched as he pressed his palms hard against the wood. He watched them as if he wanted to see them turn pale under their sun-brown hue.

Klamath used his opportunity to finish answering the young man's question.

"In addition, the presence of priests gives our King and Amika's Queen another source of disagreement." His tone hardened as he prepared for the most hurtful of his duties. "By their coming, they remind us that Belleger and Amika are small in the world. We are a little people sharing a large continent with many other races speaking many other tongues. And this continent itself is only one among several. The world beyond us now seems as vast as the heavens, and we are made smaller because we did not know our own smallness.

"King Bifalt and Queen Estie argue about what we who are small must *do* in a world that is large. She believes that we must ally ourselves with the Last Repository. Only there can we find the knowledge we lack. *He* insists that our allegiance must be to our own people alone, our own survival."

Over her shoulder, Matta snorted, *"Survival."*

Like an echo, Matt asked, "Survival?" With a deepening frown, he faced his guest again.

Klamath braced himself.

"How are our people threatened?" continued the sheep-master. "How are Amika's? We have told you what we know of raiders. We are in danger, certainly. But a raid on a farmstead—or a dozen—or even a few villages—does not threaten the realm. Raids do not threaten *both* realms."

The big man leaned forward. "*Tell* us, old friend. I think I can grasp Queen Estie's reasons for wanting a road to the Last Repository. And I can imagine the uses of a combined army, if Belleger and Amika are not at peace. An army may serve to make the more warlike men into comrades. But *why*—?"

He put his palms like Mattin's on the table. "*Tell* us. Why is King Bifalt determined to fortify an impassable coast? Make us understand *that*. Make us understand before Matta loses patience entirely, and I begin to question our long friendship."

Klamath did not hesitate. "Because," he replied in a tone like falling gravel, "our King expects a war that will make our rides into hell against Amika look like skirmishes. Why else did the Magisters of the Last Repository abuse him until he agreed to attempt an alliance with our old foe? With King Smegin, who proclaimed his desire for our destruction?"

Matta whirled away from her dishes, gaped at Klamath openly. Mattin jerked up his head. In the hearth, an ember cracked, spilling a small spray of sparks. Matt sat like a stone, expressionless and waiting.

Klamath wanted to hide his head, but he refused the impulse. He had chosen this task. He and Matt had been friends for a long time.

"King Bifalt," he stated, "expects war because those Magisters fear it. They have an enemy, and they want Belleger and Amika to defend them. But they do not fear the deep south past the Realm's Edge, or the far north beyond Amika. If they did, they would not need us. And they are defended in the east by their own mountains."

While Matt, Matta, and Mattin watched him as if he were a poisonous snake, Klamath explained, "Those Magisters chose us to be their barrier, their buffer, because they believe their enemy will come from the west. But in the west, there is no conceivable approach except by ship against Belleger's coast.

"Yes, we call that approach impassable. The cliffs are high. All are sheer. And even the most accessible of the rare bays are barricaded by reefs and rocks like jaws. In addition, only one offers a break in the cliffs, and even there the turmoil of currents alone is enough to swamp any vessel our people have tried. Hells, Matt! Even dry planks are torn apart and scattered beneath the waves.

"But King Bifalt believes an enemy mighty enough to threaten the high fortress of the Last Repository will have power enough, and knowledge enough, to impose a harbor on our coast. Therefore he fortifies—"

"But the raiders!" protested Mattin, aghast. "They come from the Realm's Edge. You said they probe our defenses. They must know the passes. An army can find a road. Why does the King believe the enemy will not come through us"—he slapped the table—"*here?*"

Klamath met the young man's distress without flinching. This was an argument, not a battle. It caused fear and pain: it did not shed blood.

"King Bifalt does not discount that threat. But he asks himself what *he* would do, if he were a sorcerer of unimaginable might, with an army of inconceivable size and a vast relish for slaughter. There may well be passes through the Realm's Edge. But if the enemy comes that way, his movements will be restricted. His army cannot march in a mass. He may find himself made vulnerable. If we can discover his road, we can prepare for him.

"In his heart, the King expects a more direct assault. He expects the same careless arrogance he met in the Last Repository.

"*That* is why he fortifies the coast. And it is why the soldiers of Belleger and Amika must become a unified force, ready to plunge into a hell that exceeds their worst nightmares. Without that force—without rifles and cannon—without every man we can find and train—we may all be lost."

The family's silence made Klamath's face feel burned, but he did not look away. Mattin's eyes were full of terror and pleading. Matt sat with his arms locked, appraising his old friend. No one moved except Matta.

Leaving the kitchen, she came to stand behind her son's chair. With both hands, she took hold of the knots in his shoulders and began to massage them. She did not glance at Klamath; but the way she avoided his gaze made her defiance plain.

Abruptly, Mattin groaned, "Why did you tell us? It would be better if we did not know. We could live as we are until we were killed. We would not spend the rest of our days afraid."

"Mattin," said his mother: a gentle reproach. "You know what this is. He has made his purpose plain. He needs *men*. He is here to gather them."

The young man twisted against Matta's hands to face her. "Does he think I will ride away with him? To become a soldier? A sacrifice in a war that has nothing to do with us?"

"Foolish boy!" Without much force, Matta slapped the back of her son's head. But her scorn—her suppressed fury—seemed to light up the room. "*General* Klamath is not here for you. Oh, he will not turn you away. He will not turn *any* able body away. But he aims higher, or worse.

"He is here for your father."

Klamath only nodded. What else could he do? She was right.

General was an Amikan title. Klamath had left his First Captain, his lead commander, in charge of the army. The man was a brilliant fighter and a capable teacher; but his heart was not in it. He was no leader. He dreamed of solitary contests, one champion against one antagonist, with all the world at stake. He would abandon his command as soon as King Bifalt gave permission.

Klamath wanted Matt.

Still suppressing herself, Matta finally looked at her guest. Her voice shook.

"Do you expect to command us, General?"

Leaning back in his chair, Klamath allowed himself to sigh aloud. "Of course not, Matta. Who would obey me? I am only here to *tell* you. Tomorrow I will ride to tell someone else. In a fortnight or two, I will return to the Open Hand and resume the task my King has given me.

"I can only do what I can. But what I *can* do, I will."

His quiet promise silenced the family. Matta bent to kiss her son's head, a soft apology for her slap, then continued rubbing his shoulders.

She did not look up. Mattin turned away from her to study his hands again, as if their emptiness or their littleness dismayed him. Matt appeared to contemplate the air above the table. With one hand, he reached out to add his clasp to his wife's on Mattin's shoulder. His expression was oddly blank. It revealed nothing.

Whatever their answer was, or might become, Klamath accepted it. It could have been worse. He had been spared Matta's blistering outrage. Matt had not spurned his appeal—or his friendship. Given time, they would be able to reassure Mattin. They might even be able to explain Klamath's visit to Mattson and Mattilda in terms that did not frighten the children.

Without speaking, Klamath rose to his feet and went to the door. There he paused to offer the family a bow. But none of them seemed to notice it. Not even Matt—

When he had reclaimed his rifle and ammunition, Klamath went alone into the night.

In the barn, he unpacked his bedroll from one of the bundles his mules carried for him. With straw for a mattress, he made a comfortable place where he would be able to rest. Everything he had said and heard gnawed at him. He wished that he had handled this visit better. He wished that he were a better man—a better spokesman for Belleger's plight—a better servant of his King. But whatever else he was, or was not, he was a soldier; a veteran. He did not waste any chance to sleep.

He thought that he had roused himself in time to be gone before the family in the house began to stir. But when he sat up in the first gloom of dawn, he found that he was not alone. Matt was working quietly nearby.

With some chagrin, Klamath saw that the sheep-master had already fed and watered his horse and his mules.

Refusing to embarrass himself further by hurrying, Klamath climbed out of his blankets, adjusted his clothes, and repacked his bedding. He did not speak to his host until he had settled his bedroll among the burdens his mules would bear. Then, awkwardly, he said, "I did not expect to see you again, Matt. I am grateful for your care. Please assure Matta that I am grateful for hers as well. And tell your sons and daughter that I understand why you are proud of them."

Matt came closer until he was near enough to clasp Klamath's shoulders. Even in the dimness of the barn and the new day, Klamath could make out the big man's smile.

"It is always good to see you, old friend," said Matt. "Matta considers you a wolf among chickens." His smile became a grin. "I think you are more like a hound trying to chase too many wolves away.

"We are as small as you say. But we share one occupation with King Bifalt and Queen Estie. We agree—and disagree. Together, we will think what to do."

Klamath answered the sheep-master with a quick hug. Then he went to one of his bundles and took out two new rifles, two full satchels of loaded ammunition clips. With both hands, he offered them to his old friend.

"Teach Matta to shoot," he said hoarsely. He could not control his voice. He sounded like a man who had spent the night weeping. "You are a fierce defender. She will be fiercer.

"And teach Mattin, if you think it wise."

Matt nodded. Gravely, he accepted the guns and bullets. He did not speak again.

When Klamath rode away, he was alone once more. Matt had already gone back into the house; back to his family.

TWO

MAKING PEACE

Princess Estie of Amika was a young woman of fifteen when she met her first Bellegerin.

Her father, King Smegin, had filled her with his ambition for dominance, his ready fury at Belleger's resistance. She had spent her life thinking what he wanted her to think, feeling as he instructed her, desiring what he told her to desire. But he had also protected her. He had kept her swaddled in the many luxuries of his hard fortress, which his ancestors had named Amika's Desire. The war did not touch her, except as he and his generals talked about it, or as he explained it to her. He and her tutors had taught her to understand his attempts and dreams. But in her whole life, she had never set foot outside the precincts of Amika's Desire. Certainly, she had never wandered the streets of Maloresse, Amika's only city, or seen how its people lived. She was her father's favored, pampered daughter, and she was proud of who and what she had become. Her life was blessed.

Being young, she did not understand Belleger's fatal refusal to be conquered. Her father had a natural right to those lands. He had told her so. They should have been his. Belleger had started the war by killing Malorie, King Fastule's bride-to-be. And King Smegin foresaw a time—or said that he foresaw it—when he or his descendants would need everything Belleger offered. Once a year, representatives of the Nuuri in the north met with Amikan merchants to discuss trade and boundaries. From gossip at those meetings, King Smegin knew that there were more people in the world than Amikans, Bellegerins, and Nuuri: other realms, other rulers, other ambitions. If the greed of those rulers turned southward, they would eventually cross the inhospitable steppes of the Nuuri to reach the fertile fields and hills and forests of Amika. King Smegin *needed* to conquer Belleger so that Amika would become a larger, stronger people, better able to turn back any potential invasion.

But instead of submitting to their necessary defeat, the Bellegerins had devised *rifles*. When the news of what had happened in the last battle had been brought to King Smegin, Princess Estie had shared his consternation as well as his fury. Belleger was a foul land inhabited by foul desires. Only foulness could have hit upon the way of making weapons as evil as *rifles*, weapons that could kill faster and more accurately at greater distances than any archer.

That development was a calamity. Neither King Smegin nor his generals knew how to counter it. But there was worse to come. Between one evening and the next dawn, every Amikan Magister lost the ability to wield the Decimates. The whole realm was deprived of sorcery. Despite his pride in his gift, and his eagerness to use it, even King Smegin was made powerless.

During that time, Princess Estie—like her father—was an overheated stew of rage and fretting. Her distress boiled over incessantly; and it did not begin to ease until the King's spies reported that Belleger also had no sorcery. Apparently, the same force which had struck Amika had left Belleger impotent as well.

Still, Belleger remained poised for victory. Amika's enemy had rifles. Estie feared that her father's people stood on the brink of slaughter. Shaken by unimaginable disasters, she did not begin to hope until after King Smegin had dispatched Commander Forguile to the Last Repository.

Of course, previous kings had sent emissaries to the library for their own reasons; but they had obtained little satisfaction. The sorcerers of the Repository had been polite rather than helpful. They kept their secrets for themselves. However, Commander Forguile's mission was of another kind. After all, he could not ask those Magisters to restore

Amikan sorcery. How could he? Belleger would be restored at the same time—and Amika could not withstand both theurgy and rifles.

But King Smegin had reasoned that theurgists who withheld their understanding of the Decimates might feel less protective of other kinds of knowledge. He sent the Commander to learn what he could about new weapons. And eventually a messenger, Forguile's only companion, came home to report that the Commander had read about the existence and uses of cannon. Somewhere in the library, there was a book that taught the making of guns bigger and more destructive than rifles.

Then King Smegin and Princess Estie were able to hope again. Even an *army* of riflemen could be scattered by the heavier shots of cannon. The Open Hand and Belleger's Fist could be reduced to rubble, given enough big guns, enough powder, enough iron.

While Commander Forguile was away, Princess Estie slowly taught herself to believe that she would feel secure, finally at peace, when he returned to Maloresse with the knowledge to cause Belleger's destruction. King Smegin gnawed his knuckles and fumed while he waited.

But when the Commander came back to face his King, he brought a Bellegerin with him.

At that moment, Princess Estie's future changed. It became a place she had not been taught to recognize.

Commander Forguile brought Prince Bifalt.

He was not simply the first Bellegerin she had ever seen. He was the first Bellegerin to enter the ceremonial hall of her fathers since the terrible day when Fastule, the first King of Amika, had stood there, helpless, while Malorie, the love of his life, had been murdered during their wedding.

The hall had seldom been used in recent generations. Like his fathers, King Smegin had no foreign dignitaries to honor, no definitive victories to celebrate, and few significant marriages to commemorate, apart from his own. But word of Commander Forguile's return had run ahead of him. All Maloresse and Amika's Desire knew that he was coming—and that he was not coming alone, although the identity of his companion was kept hidden. Who could it be? A representative of the Last Repository? A Magister with some unguessed Decimate? A smith who knew how to fashion cannon? For that reason, King Smegin had ordered the hall opened and aired, swept and polished. The tapestries gleamed in the high stained-glass windows, and the mighty statues of the King's forebears shone like promised victories. Displays of weapons glittered as if their edges and points were still keen. His daughters—all three of them—had never seen the place look so majestic.

But only Princess Estie was instructed to join her father; to sit at King Smegin's side when he welcomed Commander Forguile.

As for the Queen, Estie's mother, she had of course seen the hall clean and bright for her own wedding. But she was too empty-headed to wish that her husband made a place for her on important occasions. Or perhaps the Queen simply did not much like her husband. Her only apparent interest was in what her daughters wore. For that reason, and only to please her mother, Princess Estie was dressed to dazzle, with jewels in her hair, subtle tints on her face to emphasize the perfection of her features, and a rich gown designed to be both demure and womanly. She was a delight to everyone who saw her when her mother, blessedly ignorant of what was at stake, sent her to meet Commander Forguile and his unknown companion.

Entering the hall, Estie did not care how she looked. She had no desire to impress, much less attract, any man she knew. She was blessedly ignorant herself when she took her place at King Smegin's side. It was sitting with her father that mattered to her, not her jewels and tints and gown. She only knew who her first Bellegerin was because the seneschal of Amika's Desire announced him after speaking Commander Forguile's name.

Prince Bifalt, the eldest son and heir of Belleger's King Abbator.

Her immediate reaction was revulsion, indignation: a reaction shared by the few courtiers, functionaries, and honor guardsmen whom King Smegin had gathered for the occasion. She felt outrage that *any* Bellegerin dared, or had been permitted, to enter this hall. And *outrage* was too small a word to convey her horror and disgust that the Bellegerin proved to be a descendant of despised King Brigin, who had planned and carried out the murder of Malorie, Amika's intended Queen.

King Smegin rose as Commander Forguile and the Prince approached him. Amika's monarch was not a large man, but he dominated every room he entered, even one as high and deep as the ceremonial hall. He was a master of hauteur and waspish sarcasm, quick to anger, and not slow to punish those who angered him. He was also cunning. Princess Estie had learned in her private hours with him that he was capable of profound insights, thoughts so swift and deep that she had to exercise her whole mind in order to ride their currents. In manner, if not in body, he towered over the commander of his honor guard and the son of his bitter enemy.

Commander Forguile's face was strictly controlled, as blank as an unused slate. But in his eyes, Princess Estie saw a seethe of emotions: fear, anger, shame, even guilt—and, perhaps, a desperate hope. He had taken the time to make himself presentable for his King, washing away the grime and stains of hard traveling, changing into clean garments. His freshly waxed goatee and moustache, like his orange headband, accentuated the sallow hue of his skin, the heritage of his blood. In its leather scabbard dyed the precise hue of his headband, his sword hung ready at his hip. Over one shoulder, he carried a satchel that had seen rough use.

Entering the hall, Prince Bifalt had discarded the disguise of his hooded cloak. At Commander Forguile's side, he came forward, comporting himself as if he were the Commander's equal in King Smegin's presence. As he drew near, Estie saw that he, too, had made himself presentable. In particular, she noticed the cut lines of his visage, the tight trim of his beard. She knew from her studies that he was not more than eight years older than she was; but where she had been pampered, his life had been one of hardship, familiar with privation, defined by scars. He looked a decade older than his years.

In addition, Princess Estie recognized the image of the beleaguered eagle on his breastplate, the emblem of a Bellegerin soldier. Seeing it quickened her breathing, her pulse. Her revulsion. That symbol and his face assured her that he had fought and killed in battle. *Amikans* had died at his hands.

Yet his breastplate was his only accoutrement of war. He had come weaponless into the hall, without his sword and dagger, without his bow and arrows. Without even his rifle.

His rifle—

Seeing the Prince unarmed, Estie did not need Commander Forguile's reputation for courage, loyalty, and intelligence to convince her that Prince Bifalt had not come to attack King Smegin. No, not even to threaten him. Belleger had no more sorcery than Amika. The son of King Abbator was as helpless as a man could be in the hall of his foes.

He was not here for blood. He had other intentions.

King Smegin's daughter could not imagine what they might be.

So far, the Prince had not deigned to glance at her. Standing beside Commander Forguile twenty paces from her father, he held his gaze fixed on his enemy; on King Smegin, who more than any other Amikan craved Belleger's eradication.

The King ignored the Prince. With his fists clenched in front of him, he regarded Commander Forguile as if the man had approached him alone. Until the Commander gave him an Amikan bow, touching the heels of both palms to his forehead, then spreading his arms wide, King Smegin did not speak; and the men he had gathered to witness this meeting did not breathe. Then he said, "Commander Ennis Forguile." His voice buzzed dangerously. "Why have you not butchered this Bellegerin brat?"

Prince Bifalt did not bow. He kept whatever he felt to himself.

"Majesty," replied the Commander with admirable steadiness, "I gave him my word."

"Your *word*?" snapped King Smegin at once. "*Your* word? It is not yours to give. It is *mine*."

Without any visible tremor, Commander Forguile repeated his bow. "Then, Majesty," he said, "I have given *your* word. And I did not give it to Prince Bifalt privately. I gave it in the full presence of the Magisters of the Last Repository. I gave it in the hearing of a hundred or more onlookers. Also I gave it to King Abbator in front of his counselors and lead commanders. He welcomed me for it, thanked me for it, and urged me to keep it.

"If you command me to kill the Prince now, I will do it. If you command it, I will kill myself. But the Magisters of the Last Repository will know you have broken your word. All of our world will know."

While he spoke, Commander Forguile's audacity held Estie's attention, and her pulse beat in her throat. She knew her father's mounting fury—and his willingness to accept any dare. In some sense, she shared it. King Smegin's *word* was not a coin that any soldier could spend on a whim. But Prince Bifalt interrupted her, and the King.

"You will be forsworn, King of Amika." His voice was raw, strangely hoarse. He sounded like a man who was done with shouting: a man who had already shouted enough to last him until he died. "And you will never hear what occurred in the Last Repository. You will never understand *why* Commander Forguile gave his word, or what the Magisters of the library want from you, or what gift we have brought to show that I have come in good faith. You will never know what promises the Magisters and Belleger are prepared to offer."

Princess Estie felt his assertions as if he had insulted *her* rather than her father. "You *dare?*" barked King Smegin. "In *my hall?*" A moment ago, she had been amazed at Commander Forguile's audacity. Prince Bifalt's insolence was worse. The Bellegerin had only heartbeats left to live.

But then she realized that his attention had shifted. He was looking now, not at King Smegin, but at her.

Formally, as if she rather than her father ruled here, Prince Bifalt bowed. "My lady," he said in the same raw, hoarse voice, "you are enough. You will be worth what you cost."

His expression had not changed. His features might have been stone, too rigid to alter their own lines. But when she faced him, the dark smolder of his gaze seemed to scorch her. A flush rose in her cheeks. The skin of her whole body felt the same heat. In an instant, her revulsion and disgust became a passion like hate. She hated him—oh, she *hated* him—because he was Bellegerin.

And because he was not hers.

As soon as he turned his attention back to her father, she understood how it happened that men and women fainted. All the blood seemed to rush out of her. She had to grip the arms of her chair to hold herself upright.

Somehow, King Abbator's son had given her a reason to be afraid.

King Smegin must have been as amazed as his daughter. He did not give the command that would have ended Prince Bifalt's life.

"Then *tell* me, braggart," he snarled. "Whelp. Insignificant son of a petty dotard. Butcher. Tell me all these things that I will not understand or know if you do not live to speak."

The corner of Prince Bifalt's mouth clenched at the word *butcher*. He betrayed no other reaction. For the first time, however, he addressed the King in a tone of careful courtesy.

"Majesty," he said, "my coming shocks you. It must. What I have said offends you. It must. I understand your ire. I share it. But I hope you will believe me when I say that you will prefer to hear my tidings alone. You will not want witnesses until you have had time to consider my explanations. My gifts. My promises."

"Please, Majesty," put in Commander Forguile. "Grant us a private audience. I will be there"—abruptly, he drew his sword—"to ensure that Prince Bifalt speaks only the truth."

The Prince opened his arms. "And I have no weapon, as you see. I cannot harm you. More than that, I do not *wish* to harm you. Our history of battle and bloodshed has become—" He hesitated for an instant. "I will not say it has become meaningless to me. *That* you will not believe. My own losses are too severe—and too recent. But our history has lost its poison in my heart. I have tasted too many other venoms. I have come to you because I have new concerns."

Almost whispering, the Commander repeated, "Please, Majesty."

New concerns. Other intentions. As Princess Estie had guessed. But still she could not imagine them.

She was not conscious of caring what answer her father would give. She only hoped that Prince Bifalt would not look at her again.

Or that he would.

If she had glanced at the King, she would have seen that he was torn. He was quick to anger, yes, and quick to punish insults. And his repeated failures to defeat Belleger had abraded his nerves until they cried out at any provocation. But he was not a fool. Any reference to the Magisters of the Last Repository was not a subject he could ignore. His dismay at what had been taken from him was too great.

Temporizing, he demanded, "Tell me, Commander. Are you persuaded by this Bellegerin brat's absurd protestations of 'good faith'?"

Commander Forguile had resumed his blank mask. Without pause or qualm, he answered, "I am, Majesty."

He did not return his blade to its scabbard.

"And when you gave him *my* word," continued the King, "were you confident that you were doing what I would have asked of you?"

Again, the captain showed no reluctance. "At first, Majesty, I was not. Now I am."

"A long journey," sneered King Smegin, "the Last Repository to Maloresse. Especially considering that you went first to Belleger's Fist. We will speak of *that* disloyalty later. But you have had time enough for Abbator's whelp to fill your ears with every kind of nonsense. No doubt *that* is why you are now confident."

In response, Commander Forguile surprised Princess Estie by letting a hint of iron into his tone. "No, Majesty. I am not so foolish—and Prince Bifalt is not so dishonorable. I have reason for my confidence. Your word gives him reason to trust *me*."

As if he were losing patience, the Prince said, "You know the power of secrets, Majesty. No doubt you believe I will use mine to do you or Amika some hurt. In your place, I would think as you do. But when you know my secrets—and Commander Forguile has vouched for them— the power will be yours. In your place, any ruler must study my secrets before he shares them."

"Brigin!" rasped King Smegin: a common Amikan expletive. "Brigin and *pestilence*, boy! Do you suppose I *need* your counsel? Will you advise *me* how to rule? My father died young. I was King in Amika before you were born. Your life is already forfeit. I will do what I please with your secrets."

Before Prince Bifalt could attempt a reply, the King whirled away. Over his shoulder, he snapped to Commander Forguile, "*Bring* him." Then he strode from the hall, leaving his daughter still seated in her chair.

The Commander allowed his mouth to twist ruefully. Saying nothing, he gestured for Prince Bifalt to precede him. His bared blade hung loose in his hand with its tip pointing aimlessly at the stone of the floor.

Instead of obeying, King Abbator's son took a moment to look at Princess Estie again.

His gaze was brief, but its heat touched her nonetheless. She might have been sitting too close to a bonfire. Sensations like flames spread down her body from her face. She could feel them in her feet. Her lips parted, unbidden, as if she were on the verge of some involuntary utterance: an expression of disgust, perhaps, or a demand to know his intentions. *My lady, you are enough.* But she could not find the words she wanted, or they caught in her throat. Or she was afraid to hear what he might say.

Prince Bifalt answered her silence with a nod like a shrug. He, too, did not speak. Instead, he turned back to Commander Forguile and murmured his acquiescence. Like a man who had come to the end of fear when he was done shouting, he followed after King Smegin with his companion, the Commander, at his back.

Although her father's courtiers, functionaries, and guards remained around her, shocked motionless, Princess Estie was alone.

Despite the anxious hovering of her maids and attendants, the half-interested queries of her mother, and the curiosity of her flighty sisters, Princess Estie stayed alone in her apartments, or in herself, throughout that long day and its interminable evening. Her father did not send for her until after midnight.

No doubt she could have distracted herself with her studies, or with one of the activities that was supposed to interest young, highborn women: dances, music, designs for elaborate or seductive gowns. But her thoughts were full of other things, subjects that compelled her emotions, and therefore her attention—although she could hardly explain them to herself. She despised Bellegerins. Why did she care how Prince Bifalt looked at her, or what he said, or how he said it? Why did she fear his gaze? Why was she so interested in the precise cut of his mouth, or the scarred shapes of his hands? Why did the memory of his raw voice affect her like a fever?

You will be worth what you cost.

No! she told herself. *No.* I will not think about him. I will not wonder why he is here, or why he has put himself in such peril, or what he wants from me. I *will* not.

But she was her father's daughter. He had taught her much; but he had not taught her to rule her mind and heart. He was Amika's King: he did not trouble to practice *self*-rule. His daughter did not know how to find an inward quiet.

Brigin! she swore to herself as if the curse were an explanation. Brigin and pestilence! Brigin and *treachery.* The man was *Bellegerin.* Her enemy. Reviled. A nightmare for children. How was it possible that he had so much power over her?

In desperation, she tried to think about Commander Forguile instead. The Bellegerin's *unwitting* companion, surely? Ennis Forguile was more than the commander of King Smegin's honor guard. He was the most *proven* man in Amika. At times, Estie had suspected that her father intended her to marry the man when he returned from his mission to the Last Repository. That was unfortunate, as far as it went—she was not drawn to him—but it was less distasteful than a sour marriage with any son of Amika's older families. She supposed that she could accept it, if her father insisted.

However, she had known from the first that Commander Forguile's mission would be a long and challenging one. A trek across the eastern desert was not a task to be undertaken lightly, even by a man who knew the way. He would need courage, fortitude, and an abundance of supplies. He would need *time.* And then he would have to face the many pitfalls of the library itself. Its Magisters were known to be prickly men, sure of their stature, indirect in their intentions. They had stubbornly refused to share their knowledge of theurgy. And their stored knowledge on every other conceivable subject was *vast.* If they declined to help Commander Forguile themselves, he would have to search through a *mountain* of books to find what King Smegin wanted.

But whether he succeeded or failed, the Princess had known that he would be gone for a long time. Perhaps a very long time.

Much might change before the Commander returned. Especially if he brought with him the secrets of making cannon. *Then* King Smegin's mind would be consumed by preparations for Belleger's absolute defeat. His daughter might by spared the prospect of an unsatisfied marriage almost indefinitely.

Meanwhile, spies brought news from Belleger. A season or more after Commander Forguile's departure, Prince Bifalt and a squad of riflemen left the Open Hand to search for the Last Repository.

For generations, Belleger's ignorance of the library's existence had been a source of comfort and pride in Amika. King Abbator's realm was primitive indeed if it did not know the Last Repository. But then Amika's superiority was threatened by more than rifles. Inspired by desperation, perhaps, or by a spy who had somehow slipped through King Smegin's nets, Prince Bifalt set out on a mission of his own. Princess Estie understood perfectly when her father declared that it was imperative to stop the Prince. The Magisters who had refused Amika might choose to help Belleger instead.

In haste, an ambush was prepared, a combination of soldiers to strike and destitute, starving villagers to serve as bait. Their orders were to get well ahead of Prince Bifalt, then to find their way into Belleger through the gorge. Once there, the villagers would locate abandoned huts or hamlets and live there as Bellegerins until Bifalt's company passed that way. When the Prince had been seen often enough to confirm his position and heading, the soldiers would attack. By King Smegin's command, they would leave neither Bifalt nor his escort alive.

Estie considered it a good plan, likely to succeed. Yet it failed. The villagers were scattered, and only three of the soldiers returned to Maloresse. Surprise had not enabled them to defeat Bellegerin rifles.

This news made Commander Forguile's mission more than merely arduous and complicated: it was now endangered. Suddenly, King Smegin and Princess Estie and Amika had to hope that Prince Bifalt would fail to find the library. Or that Commander Forguile would kill the Bellegerin on sight.

But now— Ah, now. Commander Forguile had certainly been away longer than anyone had expected. But finally he had come back. Bringing with him Amika's most dangerous enemy: a man who had clearly found the Last Repository, and had gained what he wanted from the

Magisters. And *now*, of all times, the outcome of Commander Forguile's purpose, and of King Smegin's hopes, was kept from Princess Estie.

Worse, the Bellegerin's intentions were kept from her. She had spent half of the morning, all of the afternoon, and a long evening waiting; and *still* she did not know what Prince Bifalt had said to her father, or shared with him, or given him. She did not know if or when her father had ordered the Prince's death. She did not know what had been, or would be, done with his body. Burned among the crippled and impoverished on the charnel-field outside Maloresse? Sent back to King Abbator to show Amika's contempt? Left for the crows along some roadside?

She felt unspeakably galled that King Smegin had chosen *now* to exclude her from his thoughts and decisions. At unexpected moments, the image of Prince Bifalt with his eyes dulled, his mouth stopped, his body ruined by Commander Forguile's blade, almost brought her to tears.

She did not shed them. Unlike her mother, she was not a woman who wept. She took pride in that.

But when the summons to attend her father finally knocked on her door, long after the hour when she would normally have been in bed, she came close to fainting for the second time in her life.

Instantly, what she feared changed. Now it was not that Prince Bifalt had been killed. It was that he was still alive. That she would be forced to meet with him, and endure his gaze again, and hear the worn-out sound of his voice. That she would be expected to speak with him—

Nevertheless she hurried to answer the summons. She was more afraid of being left in ignorance than she was of any life or death she might be asked to face.

King Smegin's apartments were not as luxurious as hers. He saw no reason to impress anyone who attended him there. And he was proud of the years he had spent as a soldier when his father was still alive. His rooms looked like a soldier's. But his first room was far larger than hers. Where hers served as a sitting room, a place where she could entertain guests or herself, his was his council chamber. It held an abundance of sturdy chairs and a long table strewn with maps, letters, and tomes. But there was no desk. When he wrote something himself, he did so in a more private room.

One thick tallow candle with a tall flame gave the only light in the chamber. It stood on the table. There were shadows and darkness everywhere outside its reach, lurking like bad omens.

By candlelight, Princess Estie found the King sitting in an armchair beside the table. He was alone—and obviously very drunk. There were four empty wine jugs lying on their sides on the table, he had his fist wrapped around the neck of another, and two more waited nearby. His greying hair stood up from his head as if he had spent hours trying to pull it out. A few droplets of wine hung in the disarray of his beard. When he turned his head to regard his daughter, his eyes seemed unwilling to focus.

Seeing him like this, his wife would have turned and left, shutting the door softly behind her. His younger daughters might have fled, letting the door slam to mask their squeals of laughter. Princess Estie closed the door, bolted it to ensure that no one intruded on the King in his condition, then crossed the room to stand in front of her father.

She had been alone with him on similar occasions in the past; but he had not been *this* drunk. Perhaps those earlier occasions were not similar at all. Perhaps his excess now was unprecedented.

Feeling simultaneously relieved and appalled, she scanned the floor for signs of blood. But there were none.

So. The Bellegerin was not here. She would not be expected to face him. And he had not been killed here. He might still be alive.

Unless King Smegin had ordered him killed elsewhere. Or Commander Forguile had slain the Prince hours ago, giving the servants time to clean the floor. Or the stains were hidden in shadows.

Almost at once, Estie dismissed those possibilities. The Commander was obviously Prince Bifalt's ally. They had a shared purpose. Ennis Forguile had promised to kill the Bellegerin on command, but Estie did not believe that he would obey without protest. She could imagine him protesting at length, especially when he and Prince Bifalt were alone with the King; when no one else would hear him present arguments that sounded disloyal.

Standing in front of her father with her hands on her hips, Princess Estie spoke in a voice that no other person still living dared to use with King Smegin.

"Did you kill him?"

The King rolled his eyes. His head lolled on his neck. "Kill him?" he asked. In a drunken attempt to sound crafty, he countered, "Who?"

Estie stamped her foot. Her father would tolerate a display of impatience from her, if from no one else. "You know who. You are the King of Amika. Answer me like the King. Did you kill King Abbator's son? The inheriting Prince of Belleger?"

Her tone and manner had the effect she wanted. They made her father marginally more sober. Peering up at her, his gaze came into focus briefly. Then it wandered away.

"Him?" he muttered. "That arrogant puppy? He was *rude* to me. His people are butchers. His father is a dying goat. Why do you care?"

She did not relent. "I do not care about him." She tried to believe that was the truth. "I want an answer."

King Smegin belched indecorously. Then he sighed. "Did I kill him? No. He and Forguile went off together. By now, they are probably as drunk as I am." Sighing again, he shuddered. "Celebrating."

Celebrating? Princess Estie raised a slim eyebrow. His reply told her much and nothing. It told her that her father had been swayed, but it did not reveal what he had accepted, or why he had accepted it. What had he given away? And how had Commander Forguile been persuaded to support Prince Bifalt?

Moving slowly, she pulled a chair closer so that she could sit facing him. Her knees almost touched his as she gently took hold of his wine jug, urged his fingers to let it go, then put it down on the table. Wrapping his hands in hers, she stroked them tenderly.

"What do they have to celebrate, Father?"

Without looking at her, he snorted sourly. "Success. What else?"

"Success?" She made her voice as sweet as she could, as musical. "What did they gain?"

"Gain?" For a moment, he tried to meet her gaze; but his sight was blurred with tears, and he had to turn away. "Gain?"

Abruptly, he jerked his hands free, lurched to his feet. Snatching up his wine jug, he took a sloppy drink, then walked out into the center of the room, catching himself on the backs of chairs when he staggered; putting distance between himself and his favorite daughter. Beyond the light of the candle, he appeared to move furtively from one place of concealment to another.

"That arrogant. Arrogant." He made a visible effort to shout, but he did not have the strength for it. "Arrogant. Son of a diseased bitch." His voice sank to a whisper. "Has humbled me. I am his pawn. He does what he wants with me."

Princess Estie did not move. She watched her father with concern and love and something like terror in her eyes. Restraining herself, she waited until he drank again. Then she said as firmly as she could, "I do not believe you. You are the King of Amika. No one does what they want with you."

Clearly, King Smegin had been shaken to his foundations. Prince Bifalt had that much power over him. Where had a prince of Belleger acquired so much force? *How* had he acquired it?

"That Bellegerin does," answered the King more strongly. "I should have seen it. Ennis Forguile is not a man who gives his loyalty to the first foe he meets. But I was too angry to think—"

While her father drained his wine jug and tossed it aside, the Princess composed herself. "Then tell me," she said when he was done. "What did the Bellegerin reveal? What did he give you? What did he promise?"

She did not ask, What did you give him in return? That question she held in reserve.

Bracing both arms on the back of a chair, King Smegin faced her across the room. Shadows masked his features. She could not read his expression. But despite his inebriation, his tone was terrible in its clarity and venom.

Behind it, she heard an ache of fear—and a strangely abased hope.

"There is a war coming," he said. "It will not come soon, but it is certain." Each word was distinct. "And when it comes, it will trample both Belleger and Amika, if we do not stand together.

"Prince Bifalt believes that. He learned it from the Magisters of the Last Repository. It is not *our* war. It is aimed at *them*. At the library. A great army with unimaginable numbers and unimaginable sorceries will come to attack the Last Repository. It will not be content until every book is burned and the whole stronghold is rubble. But it will come through *us*. We will be destroyed because we are *in the way*.

"The Prince believes this so strongly that he does not fear me. He does not even fear to sacrifice his people. And he does not choose to crush *us*, although he was offered the means. Instead, he hopes we will not crush Belleger. He wants to unite our realms. But if I refuse, he will give me the power to defeat him. He *has* given it. To show his 'good faith.' When the real war comes, the enemy must face two realms that fight as one.

"And he believes all this so *strongly* that his father believes it as well. Abbator is a failing dotard, worn down by a war he cannot win even with rifles, but he *believes* his son. And he has the courage to risk what I will do with his son's gift."

Sitting motionless in her chair, Princess Estie trembled deep within herself. Her own foundations were no longer sure. She did not know how to understand what she heard.

With an effort of will, she made herself sound calm. Softly, she asked, "How did you answer him, Father?"

He wants to *unite*—?

In response, King Smegin's voice slipped into exasperated slurring. "I laughed at him. What did you expect? I am the King of Amika. I laughed in his face."

She knew her father too well. She could hardly see his features, but she could interpret every flick and snarl of his tone. His sudden slurring was a mask. She heard venom, yes—but she heard other emotions as well, hints of ideas and desires that he did not want to acknowledge, even to her.

She surprised herself by refusing to believe that he had laughed at the Prince.

Still calmly, she asked, "And what has King Abbator's son given you, Father?"

Braced on a chair-back, he seemed to crouch at the farthest edge of the candlelight. She watched him release the chair while he turned his back on her. She thought she saw him cover his face with his hands.

Muffled and distant, he said like a plea, "Can you not guess? It must be obvious. Why else does Ennis Forguile stand with him? Why else is that arrogant puppy so fearless?" With one arm, he made an obscure gesture. "It is on the table."

Princess Estie did not glance aside. She kept her gaze fixed on her father. Despite his drunkenness, she was not inclined to spare him the burden of telling her the truth.

"What is it?" she insisted. "There is too little light. How will I know it when I see it?"

A wrenching movement of King Smegin's shape made him look like he was clawing at his hair. "It is a *book*," he snapped, absurdly furious. "A *heavy* book. The writer is Sylan Estervault." Then he appeared to sag. "It is *A Treatise on the Fabrication of Cannon Using Primitive Means*."

Commander Forguile's mission.

"The Magisters surrendered it"—for a moment, Estie's father sounded almost broken—"but not to Forguile. They gave it to that cursed Prince. *He* gave it to Forguile. And he gave his word that he would not take it back. Forguile *vouches* for him."

Princess Estie was stunned. At first, she could not think at all. Then she could only think, Cannon. Victory. Cannon could defeat rifles. Not easily, perhaps. Not quickly. But with enough of them—

The Magisters had put the book in Belleger's hands. Belleger would have rifles *and* cannon. That meant victory. The enemy could cut through Amika like a scythe through wheat.

But Prince Bifalt had made a different choice. And he had convinced his father to support him. He had *given*—

What manner of man *was* he, this Bellegerin Prince? How could he—?

Estie sounded small to herself as she asked, "Do you credit his tale, Father? A great army. A war against the library. Amika and Belleger destroyed. Do *you* believe him?"

"I *must*!" cried the man whom she had trusted for all of her short life. "He learned of it from the Magisters of the Last Repository. The *Magisters*! Commander Forguile did not. He learned nothing. He was given nothing. It was all that rude whelp. *He* learned. *He* was given. And then he *gave*. With the book and his new knowledge, he persuaded my best soldier. Brigin, Daughter! He persuaded his *father*! Of all men living, Abbator has more cause to hate me, yet he put his life and his people and his realm in his son's hands. How could I doubt that Prince?

"Could *you*?" demanded the King as if she had challenged his authority. "I saw how he looked at you." As if she had turned against him. "Could *you* doubt him?"

She had no answer. She did not think about Prince Bifalt at all now. Her father's fear had come out of hiding, emerged from its concealment of distance and wine. It scattered her thoughts in unbidden directions. For the first time in her life, she wondered whether he had truly foreseen an invasion from the north. Had that been nothing more than an excuse? A way to justify his desire for Belleger's destruction? If he had prepared himself for a larger war, why was he frightened to hear that it was aimed, not at Amika, but at the Last Repository?

And why did she hear a note of abject hope mingled with his fear and fury?

His distress, like his explanations, raised as many questions as they answered. Instead of answering his demand, as a dutiful daughter should, she pursued her earlier queries. Summoning her composure, she spoke like a woman who knew her own mind.

"You told me what he knows, Father. You told me what he gives." She nodded at the table. "The book is here. We can make cannon. Now tell me what he promised."

When she knew that, she would know what the King of Amika had given away.

He replied with a strangled curse. It rose into an inarticulate yell of frustration. Then he cut it off. At the edge of the chamber's darkness, he seemed to shake himself as if he were casting off his drunkenness. A moment later, he came back into the candle's wan light.

He moved stiffly, like a man who had been beaten with clubs, but he did not lurch or stagger between the chairs. His mouth was clenched with anger, yet his eyes were full of plain dread. When he reached the place beside the table where his daughter sat, he did not meet her gaze. Instead he sat down in front of her, where he had been sitting earlier. Tentatively, as if he expected a rebuff, he took both of her hands, folded them in his.

"He wants peace," said the King in a low growl. "He has already come far to win it. He has promised to do more.

"If I will make peace with him—if I will agree to his terms—he will restore sorcery." Her father's clasp tightened momentarily. "I mean he will provide for its restoration. And not only in Belleger. It was the Magisters of the library who made us impotent." Just for an instant, his tone was hot enough to raise blisters. "They made *me* impotent." Then he subsided. "But if that Prince can arrange peace between us, they will reawaken sorcery in both realms. They will do so themselves, or they will teach their pet Prince how it is done.

"Commander Forguile confirms this. He was present when the Prince and the Magisters struck their bargain. He was *included* in it by the Prince."

None of this shocked the Princess. It was too much for her to comprehend in an instant: it had too many ramifications. But it fit with what she had heard in her father's voice, the fear and the hope. It fit the man he was becoming in her eyes. And it told her what he would say next.

Suppressing a small shudder, she asked the top of his head, "What answer did you give him?"

Without looking up, he replied like a man who had knots in his throat, "We will have peace. I gave my word. I will not take it back. My fathers in their graves will curse me, but I will not take it back. How can I refuse a Bellegerin who would rather see his homeland destroyed than face his future without Amika? A man who knows so much more than I do, and is not afraid? A man who has promised to restore me?

"I must have my gift." He was barely whispering, yet his voice held his oldest passions. "I am not whole without it."

She understood him now. He had made himself clear. He was not afraid for Amika. He was afraid for himself. He did not grasp at hope for his people. Prince Bifalt had given him hope for his own needs.

His gift was the Decimate of lightning. She had seen him use it more than once, when he was furious at one or another of his subjects. The sight had made her wonder about herself. She still wondered. What had she inherited from him? Did she, too, have a gift? If so, what was it? How could she wield it?

But she understood other things as well. She should have realized long ago that he was not primarily concerned for Amika. He did not resemble Prince Bifalt, who was not afraid to face death or risk his own people. King Smegin's first thoughts were for himself.

She wished that he would look at her, but he did not. Instead, he seemed interested only in her hands. He held them, stroked them, as if they had the power to give him what he wanted. What he needed.

Unable to see his face, Princess Estie studied the tangled mess of his hair. It resembled her confusion. She did not know how to name what she felt. Was it dismay? Could she feel disgust for the man who had made her his favorite while he scorned his wife and ridiculed his younger daughters? Was she able to imagine that he had sent his men to fight and die against Belleger—sent them over and over again—for no better reason than personal pride? What had their deaths cost him, apart from frustration and a sense of diminishment?

In fact, he had not suffered a personal blow until Amika had been deprived of sorcery. And now he was prepared to forget all of those battles and all of that bloodshed, all of that history, so that he could be *whole* again?

Had he always been so petty?

How *much* had she inherited from him?

"Is there more?" She sounded eerily detached. Her thoughts were elsewhere. "Tell me."

"There are conditions," he answered more bitterly. "I am required to meet his terms. It is not enough that we put an end to our fighting. We must work together. We must prepare ourselves to face the library's enemy. We must help each other prepare. And we must combine our armies."

King Smegin paused to curse. "Under *his* command, naturally. Amikans must serve with Bellegerins. Bellegerins must serve with Amikans. They will not do it, but they must." He sighed heavily. "He does not demand the rule of Amika. He does not offer the rule of Belleger. To that extent, he is not deranged. But we must support each other as if we are one people, as we were before."

Estie knew what he meant. Before Brigin and Fastule divided their father's realm. Before Brigin murdered Malorie on King Fastule's wedding day.

Now the Princess herself was frightened. She had heard too much in too short a time. With every word, her King changed her world. He changed its very substance. All of its solid facts had become liquid. She could not hold them: they leaked between her fingers. Her father's hands seemed to squeeze them away.

The light of the one candle shrank around them until it illuminated only the King bowed forward in his chair and the Princess sitting upright. She still wore the gown her mother had chosen for her meeting with Commander Forguile and the disguised Bellegerin Prince. Her voice trembled as she asked, "Is that all, Father?"

It was already too much. But she knew by King Smegin's manner that he was not done.

He was not done with *her.*

His shoulders hunched as if he meant to crush her hands, break the bones so that they could not resist the shape of his desires. But he only held her tightly. He did not hurt her. His voice was soft. It was also harsh. It was tender and cruel.

"Abbator has one further condition. That Prince is content, but if we do not satisfy his father, we will not have peace.

"The King of Belleger insists that you must wed the Prince, his son and heir. He knows nothing about you, except that you are my daughter. And he does not care what his son's inclinations may be. He cares only that you two are wed.

"Also the ceremony must be held in Belleger's Fist. According to the fables Bellegerins tell themselves—lies to appease their guilt—that is where King Fastule killed Malorie to prevent her from marrying Brigin. Abbator believes that your wedding there will heal the oldest of our wounds.

"They have rewritten the past." Estie's father did not mask his scorn. "We know the truth. We do not need lies to shore up our honor. But truth is not the issue. The issue is Abbator's condition. His demand.

"If you do not comply, there will be no sorcery. Amika and Belleger will pursue their war with rifles and cannon until the library's enemy comes to destroy us all."

Abruptly, King Smegin reached the end of his restraint. He let his anger take flame.

"And that Prince said all this to me—to *me*—with no flicker on his face. No disdain. No triumph. No desire. No *fear*. As if he were certain of my answer and could not imagine doubt.

"Do you understand *now* why I call him an arrogant puppy? Why I say his father is a failing dotard? Why I deride Belleger and its rulers and its people? He dares to *demand* you from me. He knows I cannot refuse. He knows *you* will not refuse, if I ask it."

Raging quietly, he commanded, "Give me your answer, Daughter. State your willingness. Then I can send that Prince away. Let him go back to his father and be proud of his success. We can leave the negotiations to my chancellor and whoever serves Abbator. You will not need to sully your eyes with the sight of any Bellegerin again until the time comes for your wedding."

Estie quaked in her father's grasp. She had realized a moment ago that he wanted *something* from her. Why else had he performed his explanations like an elaborate masque? He could have had her understanding—even her sympathy—without so much effort.

But *this*? To give herself to a Bellegerin? The inheriting Prince of a people whom he had taught her to despise? A man whose features might have been carved with a knife? A man with scarred hands and such heat in his gaze? A man whose raw, hoarse voice betrayed the cost of his self-control? She would rather she died, or he did. Or her father—

Trembling, she asked, "Will I be killed, Father? In Belleger's Fist? Where I will be helpless in the hands of my enemies? Is that how they will heal their oldest wound?"

"What?" The King jerked up his head, met her pleading gaze. She accomplished that much, if no more than that. "No. Of *course* not. Spare me such nonsense. You are not a child. The arrogance of that Prince is beyond endurance, but he *believes* what he says. He *believes* that Belleger and Amika must have peace. He will do nothing to endanger it."

Finally, her father was looking at her; but she found that she could not bear it. She turned her head away as if she were ashamed. She was supposed to be a young woman, old enough to marry, old enough to want marriage. But she felt like a girl threatened with a punishment she did not understand or deserve. She wanted to beg—

The *Prince* had done this to her, Bifalt of *Belleger*. Even the memory of his drained voice made her heart quake.

Avoiding her father's eyes, she stared at the candle flame. There was no air in the chamber, hardly enough to breathe, but the flame danced and hesitated, as uncertain as her future.

"Then will you not kill him?" she asked. "For my sake? To spare me—?"

King Smegin's answer was a twisted, unconvincing smile. "How can I? He will be your husband." Then he said more roughly, "And without him, we will not have sorcery. I *must* have my gift."

Instead of sighing aloud, or attempting a brave, false response, Princess Estie blew out the candle so that her father would not see the tears running down her cheeks.

THREE

THE QUEEN IN COUNCIL

Queen Estie of Amika, the Queen-Consort of Belleger, was already late for the King's council meeting, but she continued studying herself in her glass for a little longer.

She did not much like what she saw.

At fifteen, when she had met her first Bellegerin in King Smegin's ceremonial hall, she had been a beauty. At twenty-five, nine years after her wedding, and eight after her father had abdicated his throne, making her Queen in Amika, she had been ravishing. But now she was thirty-five. Time and suppressed grief had engraved their fine lines around her eyes. Anger and hard choices had left their marks at the corners of her mouth. The loss of the luxuries she had known as a princess had rubbed a subtle roughening into her skin. And her eyes themselves seemed to have lost their luster. She was a disappointed wife, apparently unloved, certainly childless. In addition, she was the ruler of an endangered realm, vexed in its uneasy alliance with Belleger, uncertain of its future. And she was always afraid.

On some days, her fears seemed so vaporous that they hardly deserved to be named. On others, she knew precisely what she feared, and why. And on others, her only real fear—the only one she cared about—was that she had proven herself unworthy.

She was deliberately late to King Bifalt's council meeting.

But she had not chosen to delay her arrival out of pique. She had too much pride for that, and the issues were too important. She only faced herself in the glass to pass the time.

She could just as easily have occupied herself by making a mental tally of the austerities imposed on her by her apartments high in one of Belleger's Fist's turrets. Until her wedding day, she had been accustomed to sumptuous living in Amika's Desire. When she was here, she occasionally pined for a few of the indulgences that awaited her in Maloresse.

However, she was not petty enough to complain. After all, King Bifalt's quarters were no more comfortable than hers. *Nothing* in the Fist was comfortable. Every scrap of wealth that her husband acquired, he used to relieve the privations of his people; or to feed and house the workmen who labored on his various fortifications, here and on the coast; or to provide for his army. Privately, she admired his lack of interest in fine furniture and pampering. In fact, she had modeled her rule of Amika on his conduct as Belleger's King—much to the consternation of the few functionaries and fewer courtiers she had retained after her father's abdication.

And whenever she exceeded her tolerance for discomfort and strict living, she could return to Amika's Desire. Her husband did not hold her here. Oh, he needed her. She understood what drove him well enough to know that she was needed. But he did not pretend to rule her. And he honored her commitment to Amika. When she absented herself from Belleger, he did not even ask when she might return. Instead, he visited her in Maloresse faithfully, taking his place as the King-Consort of Amika for a few days or a fortnight, until his own responsibilities called him away, or until she expressed a wish to return.

She could not complain about how she was housed and served in Belleger's Fist without seeming as silly as her sisters.

A casual observer might have thought that she was late to important meetings because she was vain. She wanted to make an entrance when everyone else was already at work so that she could command their attention. No doubt some of King Bifalt's adherents saw her in that light. But any closer study would have discovered that she was early almost as often as she was late; even very early. At times, she tested the King's patience. At times, she encouraged him to think that he was testing hers.

In fact, his council meetings were as significant to her as they were to him, whether they were public or private. They dealt with matters she could not ignore. She was the Queen of Amika. She had the needs of her own people to consider; her own fears to take into account; her own heritage to understand. Every issue, every disagreement, every decision had a direct bearing on the eventual survival of both realms. She did not want to miss *any* council meeting. She found no pleasure in being late.

Nevertheless she was routinely late—or early—in an effort to shore up her battered self-esteem; her sense of her own existence. Like many of her comments and arguments during those meetings, her unpredictable arrivals were an attempt to nudge King Bifalt off balance. He was too rigidly controlled, too patient with her. None of her vagaries—like her unannounced departures for Maloresse, her unexplained returns—unlocked the iron door of his tolerance. He had told her his terms on their wedding night. Now he lived by them. Her complete freedom was the price he exacted from himself for the life he had refused to give her.

Apparently, he did not grasp—or perhaps simply declined to acknowledge—that she also paid a price. He made her feel insubstantial. At times, she doubted her own reality.

Well, freedom had its advantages. Certainly, she appreciated the fact that she could spend as much time as she wished or needed in Amika. And she did him the justice of valuing his willingness to play the role of the dutiful husband on those occasions when she sat her throne in Amika's Desire. As the years passed, however, she felt less inclined to fill the same role in Belleger's Fist. Her freedom had disadvantages as well.

One was that she was completely and solely responsible for what she did, or wanted, or feared. If she had a problem—if she felt unhappy and needed comfort—if she did not know how to manage her doubts—she could not turn to her husband. *He* did not turn to *her*. In effect, they never spoke to each other unless there were other people present. As a result, being married to him was far lonelier than living alone.

But there was a worse price to be paid for the conditions of their marriage. Before she had been his wife for five years, she knew with absolute assurance that she could have taken half a dozen lovers and flaunted them without ruffling the surface of his self-command. He would not offer her any sign of disapproval, or betray so much as an air of disappointment. And certainly, he would not treat her as she treated him. *He* did not take lovers. His cold bed was part of what she received in exchange for what he had refused to give.

So of course Queen Estie of Amika had never taken a lover. She did not want one.

She wanted *him*. She wanted the heat of his gaze, the touch of his battle-cut hands, the hoarse sound of his voice in her ear. She had wanted him, and only him, since the first moments of their wedding.

That truth—or its hopelessness—shamed her. And over the years, it had made her strive to provoke some kind of *personal* reaction from her husband. She ached for something more ordinary than an argument about policy or a disagreement over the distribution of resources. She teased him, even taunted him; contradicted him in public; tried his patience. She wanted to make him feel *something*. Anything. If he had rewarded her goading with a flicker of chagrin or irritation, she would have been pleased. If he had slapped her face, she might have called that a victory. It would have confirmed her to herself.

But he did not do those things. And she could not console herself with the protest that she did not deserve to be treated so distantly. With her rational mind, she understood that his rigidity was not directed at her. Its effect on her was an unfortunate consequence of his rigidity in all things, his inflexible resolve to save what he could from a war he had not chosen and did not want. In addition, she *believed* what he had told her about that war. More than that, she believed in *him*. It was no wonder that she hungered for him. She was convinced that his restraint—his stern focus on his one true burden, to the exclusion of every distraction—was all that stood between their two realms and destruction. If he failed to be less than who and what he was, the Last Repository's enemy would treat both Belleger and Amika as fodder, and move on. If she, Estie of Amika, diminished Bifalt of Belleger in any way, her people and his would suffer for it.

So she, too, restrained herself. Her small efforts to vex him encouraged the view that she was petty or vain; but they were all *small*. She did not permit herself lovers, or tantrums, or deeper forms of betrayal. As much as she could, she defused conspiracies in Amika. Whenever her desire to provoke her husband threatened to exceed the bounds she had set for herself, she retreated to Maloresse and Amika's Desire, and stayed there until she regained her self-control.

Still she did not understand why he did not want *her*. Twice he had tried to explain himself, once on their wedding night, once years later, and still she did not understand. She had done what she could to make herself the wife he needed, the partner he needed, the ally he needed. As far as she was concerned, Amika was a friend Belleger could trust. Nevertheless he remained distant. And so her wish to provoke him persisted, and her secret grief; and her face in the glass hinted at the depth of her disappointment.

What was *wrong* with her? How had she failed to win her wedded husband? What did she lack that he might crave?

Sighing, she turned away. She intended her deliberate provocations to be small. And she did not want to miss anything of substance that might be said in the meeting. This was one of King Bifalt's public councils: it was open to anyone in the realm who wanted him to judge a grievance. But larger issues would be discussed as well—and discussed as freely as if the meeting were private. The King did not fear disagreements. He was not reluctant to answer criticisms. And he could compromise, despite his unbending manner, when he was presented with solid arguments. More than once, he had sacrificed his own plans and preferences because his Queen-Consort had stood her ground. Her road toward the Last Repository was a good example. Despite his loathing for the library's Magisters, he had given her as much support as Belleger could afford.

Queen Estie of Amika did not intend to avoid her chance to hear what he heard, and to have her say. Putting on the calm demeanor of a woman who was never late, she left her rooms.

When she walked into the hall where King Bifalt held his public councils, Chancellor Postern of Amika and Land-Captain Erepos of Belleger were arguing. However, their disagreement was a familiar one, and she ignored them for a moment while she surveyed the chamber.

The space was perhaps half the size of the ceremonial hall in Amika's Desire, and almost entirely unfurnished, apart from the rows of backed benches arranged on the floor four shallow stairs below the dais that held the King's heavy, uncushioned armchair and her own, the Queen-Consort's. The benches could have seated at least a hundred people, but on this occasion, she counted no more than thirty. She allowed herself a brief satisfaction when she saw that some of them were Amikan.

None of the lamps were lit. Even this late in the afternoon, the many windows admitted enough daylight. In the streaks of sunbeams, motes of dust danced like snow-flurries. The King did not waste the efforts of the keep's servants on sweeping the hall.

King Bifalt was in his place, listening to the Chancellor and the Land-Captain with apparent attention—and gripping the arms of his chair like a man who wished that both functionaries would drop dead. As soon as he saw Queen Estie enter, he rose from his seat and bowed. Without asking the Chancellor and the Land-Captain to pause, he said as he always did, "My lady Queen, you are very welcome. Thank you for coming." Then he came closer to hand her into her chair.

She replied with her customary curtsy. Ignoring his depleted tone, she said, "Thank *you*, my lord King. I am intimately interested in these discussions, as you know."

His frown had nothing to do with her. "The subject is an old one."

Because he was frowning, she smiled. "So I surmise, my lord."

Too late for courtesy, Chancellor Postern and Land-Captain Erepos noticed her presence. Abruptly, both men fell silent.

Still smiling, Queen Estie let her husband settle her in her chair. While he reseated himself, she continued to scan the people in the hall.

As usual, there were a few guards standing against the walls. As usual, they had nothing to do. Looking for the individuals she wanted to see, she noticed a Bellegerin merchant grinning with evident satisfaction. And a few rows from him, an Amikan trader sat slumped in dejection. Clearly, King Bifalt had already judged their grievance.

In contrast, an Amikan housewife on one of the last benches nodded to herself happily while a Bellegerin tinker nearby chewed his beard in frustration.

Whatever King Bifalt's emotions might be, Queen Estie could trust her husband to dispense his judgment with an even hand.

Continuing her search, she was surprised to find both of King Bifalt's brothers present. No doubt, Jaspid, the older, was here because he was General Klamath's second-in-command, the First Captain, and the General had not yet returned from his search for veterans willing to rejoin the army. Jaspid sat with a soldier's carriage, a soldier's high head and jutting chin—and a soldier's profound boredom. Estie knew him well enough to know that he would not have spent a moment in this hall if his King had ever given him permission to abandon his duties. Jaspid did not want command. He was a gifted fighter, and he yearned to prove himself on his own terms. Preferably against overwhelming odds.

Characteristically, Lome, the youngest of King Abbator's sons, stayed as far away from his martial brother as he could. A smaller man, in finer clothes that were less well kempt, he sprawled on his bench like a sot who had already made a good start on a day of heavy drinking. His presence at this—or any—council baffled the Queen-Consort. He had refused any role in Belleger's affairs. Apparently, he preferred ale and wine to any useful task. Estie considered him the Disappointed Son, too young to have any hope of gaining the throne, too inept to compete with his older brother. Over the years, she had spent time comfortably with Jaspid often, on a few occasions at length. She had no patience for Lome.

Unfortunately, the two people she most hoped to see were absent: Magister Facile, the Last Repository's representative to King Bifalt's court; and Elgart, who appeared to have no function in Belleger's life, and yet had contrived to make himself a treasure-house of secrets, some of which he shared. Queen Estie had expected to find both of them here. Elgart seldom skipped a council meeting; Magister Facile, never.

Oh, well. She would have to look for them later. The sorceress came closer than anyone else to being Estie's confidant. She seemed to understand the Queen-Consort's dilemmas. And Elgart might be able to answer a question or two that had been nagging at the Queen recently.

Land-Captain Erepos had already resumed his argument. In council, he was a bitter badger of a man. In private, he was pleasant company: warm and genial, almost self-effacing. Estie missed his elderly predecessor, but she liked Erepos well enough. To King Bifalt, he was saying, "I have said it before, Majesty. I will say it again. That road is an extravagance. No doubt, it will prove its value, given time. But we do not *have* time. The coastal fortifications must take precedence. The necessity of that work is absolute."

Now that his Queen was present, the Chancellor addressed himself to her. "The same tired argument, Majesty," he sighed without quite looking at her. He was a tall man with a straggle of white hair, a full grey beard, and a furtive glance: an air of misdirection which he had learned during his years serving Estie's father. "The Land-Captain wants more men. Belleger's King wants more men. Levies for the army I try to understand. But fortifying the coast? It is an impossible task. Worse, it is wasteful. Everyone knows that the sea is of no use to Belleger. It will be equally useless to invading ships—if we are compelled to assume that such ships will ever come. We have already given too many men and years to a foolish task."

"It is *not* foolish," snapped Erepos. "Your ignorance of Belleger betrays you, Chancellor. There is only one bay that does not confront the sheer walls of the Realm's Edge in the south, or the high cliffs that form the Line's Cut in the north. It lies due west of the Open Hand. And in that one place, the cliffs subside. They are like staged battlements. It is as if nature intended them to hold cannon. We have already carved a road down to the edge of the sea. Now we make fortified positions to catch encroaching ships with our fire. If you doubt *my* word, ask Commander Forguile. He commands there, with Captain Flisk of Belleger. Ask *him* if he needs more men.

"Those ships *will* come, Chancellor. King Bifalt has told us. If we are not ready for them, they will have their way with us."

In response, Chancellor Postern made a show of sighing. "Do you hear him, Majesty?" he asked his Queen. "It is always the same. More men for a misguided task." Lowering his voice in the hope—or the pretense—that only Estie could hear him, he added, "King Bifalt has been to the Last Repository. I do not know what he heard there, but it frightened him. Belleger has a frightened King, and his decisions are made in fear. He—"

Queen Estie held up her hand. "You will stop there, Chancellor. You have said too much already." She had never liked the man; but recently she had begun to doubt him. "When I was sold to Belleger to be King Bifalt's wife, the price was agreed." She had the satisfaction of seeing the muscles around her husband's eyes tighten slightly at the implied insult: the suggestion that he considered her nothing more than an item of barter. But he betrayed no other reaction. "He abides by it. *I* abide by it. We are allies. If a war is coming, we must prepare for it together."

Chancellor Postern tried again. "But, Majesty—"

"No," she said sternly. "Do not obscure your disagreement with the Land-Captain. The subject is men, not the use to which they are put. That use is not yours to determine. My lord King and I have agreed on it. The matter is closed.

"What is your objection to supplying the Land-Captain with more men?"

While the Chancellor almost looked at her, his mouth unbecomingly ajar, King Bifalt cleared his throat. "Chancellor Postern says, my lady, that Amika has no more men. They are all at work on your road."

Land-Captain Erepos nodded. Then, bowing to no one in particular, he went to the nearest bench and seated himself. Clearly, he was content to let his King and Queen-Consort make his arguments for him.

Estie did not doubt that her husband quoted the Chancellor accurately. But she had returned from Maloresse at the end of summer. She knew that Postern's statement was false.

Of course, he knew that she knew. He was not fool enough to imagine that she kept her eyes shut when she visited her home. He had been trying to mislead Land-Captain Erepos and King Bifalt. She intended to discover how far he would go, and why.

"What, *all*?" she asked the Chancellor, smiling brightly. "Are you quite sure? I can hardly credit what I hear."

"Majesty." Chancellor Postern did not let himself move a muscle. He made a vague study of her right ear. Sunlight from the nearest window outlined him with a penumbra of drifting dust. It gave him an innocent look. "Not *all*, naturally. But all that can be spared. Your honor guard is much reduced. There are scarcely enough men now to defend Maloresse. And—"

"From *what*?" demanded Jaspid loudly. He was paying more attention than Estie had realized.

"From unrest, Majesty," answered Postern uneasily. "From unruly Bellegerin traders. From hostile Amikan merchants." Then he added, "And your father requires his retinue. Surely, King Smegin deserves a measure of protection in his declining years?"

Requires? mused Queen Estie. Protection? The Chancellor was trying to pacify her; but he did not have that effect. Instead, her doubts began to take shape.

"Protection!" snorted General Klamath's second-in-command. "I will ask again. From *what*?"

Still smiling, Estie urged, "Answer the First Captain, Chancellor."

Postern appeared to flinch. But he did not falter. Without a quaver, he replied, "From the Nuuri, Majesty."

"The *Nuuri*?" exclaimed Jaspid.

Before he could go on, King Bifalt silenced him with a short gesture.

The Nuuri, indeed? thought Estie. Interesting. Now she was actively suspicious. Everyone knew that the Nuuri were fierce fighters; but they were not warlike. They had no interest in the affairs of Amika and Belleger. They only fought to defend their lands from intrusion.

But she did not challenge Chancellor Postern directly. She could sense his discomfort. She meant to undermine him further.

With no hint of ire in her tone, she changed her ground.

"I understand, Chancellor. Now tell me. What progress is being made on my road? How does the work progress?"

He shifted his gaze to her left ear. The tension in his shoulders betrayed an increasing unease. "Well enough, Majesty." He made a visible effort to sound confident; to tell her what she wanted to hear. "You will not be displeased."

Sweet as honey, Estie asked, "And this is done without calling on my honor guard? Without the aid of my father's retinue?"

Postern was taken by surprise. He was not accustomed to being questioned like this; and he made the mistake of letting his irritation show. "We have our slaves, Majesty."

Abruptly, peril filled the air. The audience was slow to react. Prince Jaspid and the Land-Captain were not. They sprang to their feet. "Majesty!" began Erepos. "We did not condone—!"

But King Bifalt dominated the hall. *"Slaves?"* He did not shout, but his voice was hot with fury. Before the onlookers had time to understand his demand or grasp what was happening, he was on his feet, moving like a thunderhead toward the Chancellor. "Do you mean *Bellegerin* slaves?"

At once, Estie leapt from her chair. In that instant, nothing mattered to her except her husband. With three quick steps, she managed to put herself in front of him.

"My lord," she whispered urgently, "think a moment. You know me better than that. If your people have been made slaves, Amikan heads will pay for it."

His rage was fixed on Postern. Black murder filled his eyes. He raised one hand to thrust the Queen-Consort out of his way.

But then he caught himself. His gaze shifted to her. Slowly, he seemed to remember who she was.

"I do," he rasped. "Know you better." Slowly, the darkness in his eyes faded. The hard lines of his face relaxed. "He is *your* Chancellor. Deal with him."

Turning abruptly, he went back to his chair and sat down.

Queen Estie took a deep breath. Without looking at Postern, she asked softly, dangerously, "Chancellor?"

"A mistake of the tongue, Majesty," he replied quickly. He knew his danger. He was Amikan: he must have believed that King Bifalt would kill him. "I meant to say *laborers*. They are not slaves. We do not enslave our allies. They are slaves only to the extent that we do not allow them to leave." As if he were scoring a point, he explained, "We lose too many men to desertion. Most are Bellegerin."

There she had him. She could get the truth from him now, while he was afraid of her husband. She nodded to King Bifalt, then went to the edge of the dais and down the first step so that Chancellor Postern could at least try to look at her straight.

Giving him no chance to prepare himself, she changed her ground again.

"What threat do the Nuuri pose to my father?"

Floundering, he focused on her mouth as if her words were as deadly as King Bifalt's hands. "Who knows, Majesty? They are strangers. Primitive." Then he seemed to tighten his grip on himself. "But they are massing along the border. You know your father's retreat, Majesty. They can reach it in two days."

Smiling like a woman who wanted blood, Queen Estie released the jaws of her trap. "How do you know this, Chancellor? How often do you communicate with my father?"

His reaction betrayed him. The blood left his face. His head jerked as if she had slapped him. "Majesty!" he protested. "I do not! How can you think—?"

"No!" Estie's voice cut like a whip. King Smegin had taught her how to be savage when she needed to be. "I will not *have* it, Postern! I may call it *treason*. I have my own sources. Their reports are sure. I will know a lie when you speak it.

"How *often* do you communicate with *my father*?"

In fact, she had received no reports. But Elgart had hinted at secret messengers. She had been increasingly troubled by Chancellor Postern's efforts to obstruct King Bifalt's preparations. She knew how many armed soldiers remained in the vicinity of Maloresse. She could guess at the size of King Smegin's retinue. And she knew her father.

Almost stammering, the Chancellor admitted, "Every fortnight." He stared at Estie's mouth as if it horrified him. "Once or twice." Desperately, he tried to assure her of his loyalty. To fend off her next question. "He supports your road, Majesty. He wants it completed for you. He is proud of what you do. Only the Last Repository can help us."

But she was Queen Estie now, not a mere princess who could be flattered into compliance. And she was married to King Bifalt of Belleger: she knew the stakes. She did not relent.

Postern was her Chancellor, but until now she had not realized that he still served Amika's former monarch.

"I am *familiar* with my father's pride, Chancellor. I know its worth. He keeps it for himself.

"*How* does he support my road?"

The man continued to hold himself still—and yet he looked like he was tottering. "He supplies laborers."

If Estie could have made her voice raise welts, she would have done it. *"Laborers?"*

"Workers," croaked the Chancellor. Then something in him seemed to collapse. "He supplies slaves." As if he wanted to condone his own actions, or King Smegin's—as if they *could* be condoned—he added, "They work well enough under the whip."

For a moment, the Queen simply stared at him. She let the shock of his revelation pass through her; pass through the hall. She did not need to ask who the slaves were, or where her father had acquired them. Why else were the Nuuri massing on the border? Nor did she waste time on *how* he had captured any of them. King Smegin was a Magister.

Then the urgency of the situation came over her. She could deal with Postern later. He had already disgraced himself enough. He was harmless now. King Bifalt would not let him leave. Turning her back, she returned to the dais; walked straight to her husband sitting rigid in his chair.

The deep smolder of his gaze made her feel weak with shame. Facing him, she wanted to drop to her knees. A terrible crime—a *dangerous* crime—was being committed, and the fault was hers. When her father had abdicated his throne, she had allowed Postern to remain as her Chancellor. At the time, she had believed rightly enough that he knew more about the practical business of managing Amika than she did. And she had believed that she knew how to manage *him*. She had accepted him without examining his loyalties. Now she felt that she had spent too much time obsessed with her own circumstances, her own emotions. She had paid too little attention to the underlying conflicts and motives of her people.

And while her back was turned, King Smegin had contrived to enslave some of the Nuuri.

His actions must be comparatively recent. Otherwise she would have heard about them from someone she could trust.

Still the fault was hers.

But she had no time to castigate herself. Her father had to be stopped before the Nuuri crossed the border in force. Before they started a war that neither Amika nor Belleger could afford.

In that instant, she ceased to be a woman who wasted herself on trivial provocations. Trembling, she said, "Forgive me, my lord King. I must go to Amika. Lives have been taken. There are more at risk. I will depart as swiftly as I can.

"Imprison Postern. Do what you wish with him. He is no longer my chancellor."

As she spoke, King Bifalt surged to his feet, caught her by the elbows as if he feared that she might be in danger of falling. "My lady—"

She shook her head fiercely. "I know your questions, my lord. When I return, I will answer them."

Nodding, the Land-Captain sat down. He seemed relieved.

At the same time, Jaspid strode forward. Before Postern could move, the First Captain reached him. Gripping the appalled Amikan by one arm, Jaspid gestured for guards.

King Bifalt studied Estie for a moment that felt long to her. His gaze seemed to lay her bare. Then he released her.

"I have no doubt," he said drily. "You will track this crime to its cause. But perhaps you do not know *all* of my questions. There is another matter to be discussed here. You will wish to hear it."

"Majesty!" Postern tried to protest; but the rough hands of the guards silenced him as they dragged him away.

Queen Estie did not glance at him. She wanted to go. Oh, she wanted to *go*, before the atrocity of Nuuri slaves ignited an explosion. But her husband's eyes held her. His tone reached deep into her. It forced her to *think*—

Abruptly, she realized that she needed to talk to Elgart before she left. And to Magister Facile. Earlier, she had wanted advice. Now she wanted more.

Feigning steadiness, the Queen-Consort dropped a small curtsy. "As you suggest, my lord."

Without waiting for his reaction, she returned to her chair and sat down. In an effort to reclaim some portion of her image of herself, she added, "When you are ready, my lord King."

Belleger's King did not waste her time. Looking out over the hall, he said in a voice like dry cornstalks rustling against each other, "Forget King Smegin's lackey. He will answer for what he has done. Slavery is a great evil. The Queen-Consort will deal with it. We have another question to consider.

"Prince Lome, you wish to speak. I mean no disrespect when I ask you to be brief. My lady Queen has urgent tasks elsewhere."

"*Lome?*" Prince Jaspid paused on his way back to his seat. "*Lome* wishes to speak?" Across the benches, he asked, "What ails you, Brother? Have wine and ale eaten your mind? Are you too drunk to understand Postern's confession?"

Other people shared Jaspid's surprise. Murmurs ran like a breeze from place to place. Even the few Amikans knew Lome's reputation.

King Bifalt cut through the ripple of voices. "First Captain." His tone was mild, but it did not soften his reprimand. "Lome is a Prince of Belleger. He is my brother as much as yours. And he is familiar with regions of the Open Hand you seldom visit. He does not need to swing a sword to offer his service. We will hear him."

Away from the training-field and trials at arms, Jaspid was impulsive; but he was not slow-witted. He accepted his King's reproach. As mild as his brother, he replied, "As you say, Majesty."

Before he took his seat, he bowed an apology to Queen Estie.

While she smiled for the First Captain, and for her husband's defense of his second brother, Prince Lome lurched upright. "I have a request," he said too loudly. "Majesty. You have heard it before. You must reconsider." Drink or his uncharacteristic temerity made him sound belligerent. "It concerns the Church of the Great God Rile."

Blocked by turrets and ramparts outside the windows, the sunlight was fading. Prince Lome was an indistinct figure, slurred by shadows and gloom.

"Will you be more specific, Brother?" If King Bifalt felt any displeasure, he kept it to himself. "You know my position. I have allowed the building of churches because my lady Queen sees no harm in them. I have not resisted the worship of this 'great god,' whatever he may be. But I do not trust these strangers. Their purposes are unclear to me.

"What must I reconsider?"

"A place on your council." Prince Lome's effort to speak assertively scattered saliva. "Your private council. Where Belleger's future is decided. A place for Archpriest Makh, who leads the Church of the Great God.

"You have rejected any priest." The Prince spoke strongly, yet he did not sound strong. He sounded frightened. "You are wrong. The Archpriest is *more* than his disciples. He is *wiser*. And he preaches peace. We do not have it now. We are allied with Amika, but you cannot pretend we are at *peace*. Even *you*, Brother. You cannot pretend we have peace.

"Only hear him *once*. Only let him speak in your council *once*. Then his purposes will be clear." To keep his balance, Lome braced his arms on the back of the bench in front of him. "You will know how wrong you are."

There was silence in the hall until Land-Captain Erepos suggested to Lome laconically, "Majesty."

At once, Prince Lome's confidence seemed to abandon him. "Majesty," he echoed in a smaller voice.

With what Queen Estie considered admirable restraint, King Bifalt repeated, "You know my position, Brother. I will not restate it." Then he turned to her. "But if my Queen-Consort has any new thoughts? We have spoken of this before. What do you say to Prince Lome's request now?"

Estie had forgotten her impulse to provoke her husband. This was not an occasion for an unloved wife's frustration. It was a time for the Queen of Amika.

In her most soothing tone, she asked Lome, "Will you answer one question, Highness? What do you say to one of the Nuuri on the King's private council? Will you hear him?"

Vague in the dimness, Prince Lome gaped at her, but no words came.

She gave him a moment to gather himself. When he did not respond, she said, "Then I will tell you how I view your request.

"I see no threat in the priests, or in strangers. The world holds many people, and they each have their own wisdom. We can learn much from strangers.

"But I place great value on privacy. King Bifalt's private councils are private, as mine are, because they consider private matters, matters that do not concern strangers. In those meetings, every voice and opinion can be heard and answered without fear. Beliefs and desires can be debated there, thoughts that cannot be addressed publicly because they might give rise to rumors and confusion.

"In private, any stranger can only be a distraction. I do not call it *wise* to admit any priest, even the Archpriest, to the King's private council. I would not admit him to mine."

For the briefest of moments, King Bifalt's severity eased. Then he stood. Crisply now, he told Prince Lome, "You are answered, Brother. And my Queen-Consort's need to depart is grave. If you remain dissatisfied, speak to me alone. *This* council is ended."

To his wife, he gave a formal bow; but he did not look into her eyes. As soon as she replied with a curtsy, he turned away and left the dais, heading toward the passages that led to his personal rooms in Belleger's Fist.

Doing her best to emulate her husband's manner, Queen Estie also turned away. But before she departed, she could not resist one more look around the hall.

Prince Lome had collapsed into his seat. Almost immediately, however, he lurched to his feet and rushed toward the public exit. His brother Jaspid stood back, letting other people pass around him; watching Lome with a smile that might have been sardonic or rueful. Grinning, Land-Captain Erepos bowed elaborately to the Queen-Consort before making his own departure.

But Elgart and Magister Facile were still absent.

Queen Estie of Amika needed them.

FOUR

"IN THE BEGINNING . . ."

Elgart was in a hurry, so he took his time, sauntering indi-rectly instead of striding toward his destination. Men in a rush were noticed, especially in the late afternoon on the less reputable streets of the Open Hand, before the few lamps were lit, when laborers with unclean habits and filthy clothes were leaving work, heading home to their families, or jostling together on their way to the taverns. Elgart did not so much walk as insinuate himself down the roadways and alleys. He avoided notice whenever he could.

For the same reason, he wore a nondescript brown shirt with ragged sleeves, stained breeches a size too short for him, and battered boots with holes in the creases. Since the long scar that divided his face was his most recognizable feature, he had on a crumpled hat with a wide, floppy brim, and he ambled with his head lowered. In that way, he gave the impression that he could hardly see where he was going: a sensible precaution in this part of the Hand, where there might be trouble for any man who looked askance at another at the end of a hard day. No one who glanced at him would have guessed that he wore a wire garrote wrapped around his waist as if it were part of his belt. The long poniard strapped to his left forearm under the sleeve was well hidden.

Attracting as little notice as possible, Elgart noticed everything as he passed. Among his other gifts, he could see past the brim of his hat better than anyone would have supposed, and his hearing was acute despite his years as a rifleman. He marked every face that came near him, and would remember many of them. He heard snatches of conversation or complaint among people who imagined they were alone in the crowds: men and women exchanging gossip; merchants bragging or whining about their day's profits; thugs whispering descriptions of past or future victims; tirades, solicitations, admonitions, advice, warnings. Some were entirely innocent, others were conceivably treasonous: most were harmless. In addition, he smelled the fetor of open sewers, the rank reek of garbage, the breath of too much ale or the assault of too much perfume. He knew when to step aside from a drunk's stagger; when to shoulder past an ostentatious tradesman or clothier. In particular, he knew when to touch his hat to a personage elevated by birth or violent habits who expected acknowledgment. Occasionally, he passed someone who knew him. At those times, the touch of his hat was a sign that he could not stop to talk.

Since almost everyone who served Belleger's ruler was a "captain" of one sort or another, Elgart considered himself King Bifalt's Captain of Spies. Amika delighted in titles: Belleger did not. "Queen-Consort" was a rank that King Bifalt imposed on his wife only because he was called King-Consort in Amika. Thinking of poor Klamath saddled with a title like "General" made Elgart chuckle to himself. As a Captain of Spies, Elgart ferreted out secrets, listened to disputes or diatribes, interpreted rumors, collected tidings from his various aides—two of whom were watching over him now at a discreet distance—and reported what he had learned to his King. At times, he intercepted messages. When he felt needed, he went so far as to step into the middle of some useless protest over the price of grain, perhaps, or the wealth of certain merchants, or the conscription of men for one or another of King Bifalt's demanding projects. Whatever the cause, he quieted the clamor by knocking a few heads together. For the most part, however, he made himself effective by remaining unnoticed.

That he performed essentially the same services for the Queen did not trouble him. He stood by King Bifalt. They had crossed the desert together, argued about their purposes, survived the Last Repository, and faced each other in what could easily have been mortal combat. They knew each other's minds. But sometimes, when she needed it,

Elgart shared what he knew with Queen Estie, for his King's sake. At other times, he kept his mouth shut for the same reason.

At all times, however, he encouraged her to believe that *her* secrets were safe with him. Most of them were. He had no reason to expose her. In her own way, she was as loyal to her husband as her long sorrow allowed. And he valued her too highly to betray her heart. With a dagger at his throat, he would not have told King Bifalt that Estie was slowly dying of unrequited love.

Apparently aimless in his movements, Elgart made his way where he meant to go.

When he was within a few hundred paces of his destination, however, he heard the noise of an imminent brawl in a nearby tavern. He was already late, so he opened the tavern's often-mended door and went in to see what was happening. What could be more natural for a nondescript laborer wandering through the Hand without a thought in his head?

He found two groups of men snarling obscenities at each other across a narrow span of open floor. The men nearest him were Amikan soldiers. Accidentally or deliberately, they had entered an alehouse frequented almost exclusively by Bellegerin farmers and stable-hands. No doubt, one of the Amikans had remarked on the pervasive odor of sweat, dirt, and manure. Or one of the farmers may have sneered at soldiers who did not know when they were not welcome. In truth, it made no difference who had delivered the first insult. They were Amikans and Bellegerins in a confined space that served copious amounts of ale: a brawl was inevitable. They had not come to blows yet, but they would soon.

While Elgart paused to consider his alternatives, however, the situation changed. A woman with an avid smile stepped into the clear space between the groups. She was comely enough to insist on notice, shapely enough. But what most drew the attention of every man was her raiment. She was dressed like an exotic courtesan, a woman who bedded princes and entranced rulers in some far-off land. Diaphanous silks hinted and revealed at every movement. Small bells tinkled on her anklets with every step. Her bangles chimed. The ribbons binding her rich hair begged to be undone. The ordinary folk of Belleger and Amika had never seen a woman like her before.

Elgart knew her. Grinning, he allowed himself to wait and watch.

For a moment—only a moment—she surveyed the two groups. More quickly than Elgart could have done, she identified the leader on each side: not the man who shouted the loudest, but the one who would strike the first blow. Then she went to the Amikan she had selected, wrapped her arms around his neck, and kissed him like a woman who had spent her whole life dreaming about him.

If a cannonball had crashed through the wall, it would not have startled the tavern more completely, or silenced it more quickly. When she finished with the Amikan, he looked dazed, disoriented, as if he had been struck by a shard of debris.

At once, she turned to the Bellegerin leader. Him she kissed as well, and as thoroughly, until he forgot how to breathe. Then she hooked her arm through his, drew him into the gap between the antagonists, and clasped the Amikan on her other side. Holding both men close to her, she said musically, "Come, now. I have a room nearby. Two such strong men will surely be able to satisfy me."

With gentle insistence, she moved them toward the tavern door. They accompanied her as if they had no choice and could hardly remember their own names. The Amikans parted to make way for her like men in the presence of royalty.

Down the aisle of soldiers, the woman winked at Elgart.

He would have laughed aloud if he had wanted to call attention to himself. Instead, he opened the door for her and her new lovers, then followed them out into the early evening.

No one shouted after him, or made threats, or cursed. He heard the scraping of chairs and tables, but no voices. He imagined them all, Amikan and Bellegerin, sitting lost in themselves; vaguely stupefied by dreams of exotic women. Eventually, someone would rouse himself to call for more ale. Others would do the same. But there would be no brawl.

Still grinning, Elgart continued on his way. He was late for an appointment, but that did not worry him. He knew exactly how the crowd behind him felt. The woman was a devotee of Flesh, a sister in holiness if not in blood to Flamora, the devotee who had been one of his teachers in the Last Repository. She had initiated him into the more private pleasures of lovemaking, as well as—indirectly—into the trade of spying. Together, she and Amandis, the most holy devotee of Spirit, had taught him how to be whole despite his divided nature. They had made him into the Captain of Spies King Bifalt needed.

Over the years, a number of Flamora's sisters and a few of Amandis' had come to the Open Hand. Elgart knew most of the devotees of Flesh by sight, had spoken with some of them. They were here to do what they could to ease the distrust that lingered between Belleger and Amika. From his perspective, their successes were remarkable. But the devotees of Spirit had kept their intentions to themselves. He could find one or another of them if he needed them. But he had no idea why they explored the Hand. Or whom they might want to eliminate. After all, they were assassins, gifted fighters and killers. When he remembered how often—and how easily—Amandis could have killed *him*, he shuddered.

However, his appointment tonight had nothing to do with devotees of Spirit or Flesh. He did not expect it to require his full attention; but it might. It might be more than it seemed. His suspicions had been growing for some time. Although they were vague, he trusted them. Tonight he trusted them enough to miss one of King Bifalt's public council meetings, despite the illumination those occasions offered.

Soon his destination loomed in front of him, stark against the darkening sky. It was a crude block of a building, as tall as it was wide, and reported to be considerably longer. A single lamp shed its pale light over its one door, a flimsy construct that a lesser man than Elgart could have broken down. In fact, its very flimsiness suggested its real purpose. It was not intended to keep people out. Instead, it promised that the building contained nothing worth stealing; that the men who worked inside had nothing to hide; that anyone who considered the door worth breaking was welcome to enter. The only sign of the building's purpose was a hastily painted cross on the wall between the lamp and the lintel.

For some reason, the shape of the cross was irregular. On the left, it included a quarter circle between the head and the arm. The uneven lines of the quarter circle gave the cross an oddly deformed look.

It represented the Church of the Great God Rile.

The presence of the Church—of any church—was comparatively new in Belleger. Like Amika before the priests came, Belleger knew nothing of religion. Indeed, the vast majority of King Bifalt's people did not understand the concept. Their long experience of sorcery had spared them from imagining supernatural magicks and deities. Did they want to see theurgy? There it was. Did they want to understand why some individuals could exert it while others could not? Look at the weather. Like sorcery, it came and went according to the natural forces of the world. No other explanation was necessary. Certainly, no one needed to rely on beings like "gods" and invocations like "prayer."

And yet Bellegerins attended the Church of the Great God Rile. Over time, they attended in increasing numbers.

Hence Elgart's suspicions. What did ordinary, practical, hardworking people find here that they could not get anywhere else? What did they lack that only religion could supply?

In his personal opinion, Belleger's acceptance of the Church was a reflex. Perhaps it was an instinctive response to the pervasive uncertainties of King Bifalt's overlong and overarduous preparations for an overdue war. Or it may have been a reaction to the years when the realms had been bereft of sorcery. But those were only opinions. Elgart was a practical man himself: he wanted facts.

Because he was late, he did not encounter other arrivals in the street outside the Church. The other worshippers were already inside. Only one person waited beside the door: his appointment. At a distance, he could not read her expression by the thin shining of the lamp, but her stance told him that she was losing patience. Perhaps she had already lost it.

Smiling shamelessly, Elgart went to greet Magister Facile.

She had come to Belleger in middle age, accompanying the newly married Prince of Belleger and Commander Forguile of Amika when they had returned from their journey to obtain Hexin Marrow's *Seventh Decimate* from the Last Repository. Now she was an elderly woman who moved stiffly and walked with a cane: a condition she blamed, not on her years, but on her protracted absence from the library. *There*, she insisted when she was in the mood to complain, an assortment of sorcerous physicians would have delayed her aging, as they had done for the librarian himself, extending his life well into his second century. *Here*, there was no relief for her inevitable ailments and weaknesses. Yet she remained, although no one would have tried to stop her. No one would have dared. She was not just a sorceress. She was a Magister of the Last Repository: the woman who had restored theurgy to Belleger and Amika, using only Hexin Marrow's book and her own gift.

"You are late," she snapped as Elgart approached. "The ceremony is about to begin."

Over her grey Magister's robe, she was wearing a cloak of the same color for warmth. Its hood did little to hide her features. Her face resembled a poorly kneaded pastry, with currants for eyes, a baked fig for a nose, and a mouth like a line of slivered almonds. Although she was a woman alone, and far from Belleger's Fist, she was in no danger. Sorcerers were too powerful to be threatened. Under the circumstances, however, Elgart wished that she had been more circumspect. Especially here, he wanted to avoid attracting attention.

Still smiling, he bowed. Behind his careless manner, he respected her. "But not too late, Magister," he replied like a man who found her amusing. "I believe they call it a 'service,' not a 'ceremony.' And I am told they always delay to accommodate stragglers like myself."

She sniffed her impatience. "I hope your sources have not misled you, spy. I have come a long way, and"—she stamped her cane—"not easily. Also, I have missed a public meeting of the council. *My* sources hinted that this one would be of particular interest. Yet I am here. Your summons was peremptory."

Elgart made an effort to sound serious. "A matter of timing, Magister. I have ignored my suspicions too long. Now I hear that events are quickening. Our time has come. We must know where we stand before the ground is taken from under us."

"Quickening how?" she demanded.

Briefly, he considered what he could afford to say. Then he risked telling her, "There is a rumor that Queen Estie now has slaves working on her road."

Magister Facile gave a hiss of surprise. "Slaves?" Then she demanded, "Does the Queen know? Does she permit it?"

Elgart shook his head. "It is a rumor. She knows, or she does not, or it is false. I have no better answer." He was not prepared to admit that he trusted the man who had whispered the news. Klamath certainly did, but Elgart's acquaintance with him was less direct. In any case, the man was a deserter. Like Elgart, he could not afford to attract notice. If he kept his promise to attend the service tonight, Elgart would contrive to hear a full report afterward.

Taking his companion's arm, he urged her toward the door of the Church. "Come, Magister," he said softly. "We have other answers to hear."

Magister Facile snorted her disapproval, but she did not resist the pressure of his hand.

As he held the door open for her, Elgart waved a gesture for the spies following him, a signal that told them to wait and watch. Then he followed the Magister inside.

He knew what to expect: he had heard descriptions from various people. The hall he and Magister Facile entered—the "sanctuary"—was as crudely made as the Church's exterior. But it was only half as long as the building itself. The rear half served some other purpose. However, the front was clearly meant for a respectful gathering, rather like the place where King Bifalt held his public council meeting. Respectful and quiet: Elgart had been told that the people who came to the Church were not intended to speak. Rows of benches with backs—"pews," in this case—gave seating for forty or fifty worshippers. The pews faced a dais at the front of the sanctuary, a wooden platform extending from wall to wall, and standing well above the floor.

On the dais to the left was an obscure shape that some folk called a "pulpit." To the right was a less definite shape that may have been the figure of a man. But Elgart could not make out details. The lighting in the sanctuary was strange.

Oil lamps set into the walls toward the rear gave enough illumination for people attending the service to find seats. Scanning the space, he had no difficulty locating the flaxen hair and strong frame of the man he had hoped to find: Mattwil, son of Klamath's old friend Matt. But there was no light on the dais. Crowded with shadows and unseen possibilities, it loomed like the mouth of a cave that stretched indefinitely toward the back of the building, a dark cavity where predators or hermits contemplated their singular appetites.

In silence, Elgart steered Magister Facile to a seat on the nearest empty pew, close to the door. Nothing that he had heard gave him cause to suspect trouble; but because he was suspicious, he wanted to be able to leave the sanctuary without hindrance.

The congregation was quiet. Altogether, it represented a trivial portion of the Hand's residents. In its own way, however, it was as peculiar as the lighting. People gathered like this usually murmured to each other, or rustled their feet restlessly, or squirmed in their seats. Here, they were so still that he could hear them breathe. They seemed unaccountably reverent.

Then even the sound of their breathing stopped as a darker figure materialized behind the pulpit. Although he was watching, Elgart caught no hint of arrival. The vague shape of a man was simply there, as if he had been condensed from the obscurity of the dais.

Without acknowledging the congregation or explaining itself, a sonorous voice said, "Hear the reading of the scripture of the Great God Rile."

Magister Facile astonished Elgart by gripping his hand.

The congregation sat motionless, as if every man and woman had been carved in place.

Elgart had no idea what a "scripture" was. The voice of the indefinable speaker made it sound like a ritual of some kind, or an incantation. An implacable judgment.

"In the beginning," proclaimed the voice, "was the Name, and the Name was god, and the Name was Folly.

"And in the beginning was the Name, and the Name was god, and the Name was Pride.

"And in the beginning were two Names, and the Names were god, the two who were also one, and the Names were Truth and Faith.

"Then on the many people of the earth, Folly begat Lust, the lusts of the flesh, greed and gluttony and drunkenness, adultery and sloth.

"And on the many people of the earth, Pride begat Lust, the lusts of the mind, lies and knowledge, contempt and arrogance, and above all, power.

"And together, on the many people of the earth, Lust and also Lust begot anger. They begot hate. Together, they begot fear, the greatest and gravest of all their get.

"But Truth and Faith, the two who were one, stood apart. They did not impose god on the many people of the earth. From the essence of themselves alone, they brought forth honesty and courage, love and peace.

"So they remained, Truth and Faith, standing apart, until their hearts were moved by pity for the many people of the earth, who lived and died in wretchedness under the yokes of Folly, and of Pride, the chains of the two Lusts. Because they were moved, they came among the many people, Truth and Faith, to stand against the earth's misery. By the essence of themselves alone, by honesty and courage, by love and peace, they drew people to them, all who could hear and understand their call.

"Alas, the coming of Truth and Faith filled Folly and Pride and their Lusts with wrath. They opposed the two who were one whenever and wherever they could, citing as their justification the nature of the earth's people, for were not all men and women born of Folly and Pride and Lusts? Yet Truth and Faith were not swayed, and they did not relent. Unafraid, they held fast to what they were. And now their name was Rile. They are the great god who does not know Folly, or Pride, or any Lust.

"Thus the wretchedness of the earth was made less."

Then there was a pause. A long moment filled only with silence and indrawn breath passed before the voice said like a commandment, "This is the scripture of the Great God Rile. Hear and understand."

At that instant, an intense blaze of light struck the right side of the dais, leaving the speaker on the left masked in gloom.

Half of the congregation gasped, although surely some of them had seen this before. Magister Facile herself gasped. Through his teeth, Elgart hissed, "Hells!"

Revealed by the explosion of light, a statue dominated that side of the dais. It was only a little taller than a man, but it seemed much taller. While his eyes were dazzled, Elgart thought that it was nothing more than a cross: a bronze, polished, and perfect version of the rough emblem over the door of the Church. Then his sight adjusted, and he saw more clearly.

Behind the cross stood a man. Naked. As tall as the cross. He faced the congregation with his arms draped over the arms of the cross. The way he cocked his head to the side so that he could regard his worshippers resembled the quarter circle outside.

And he was flawless, a man of glory. Every muscle of his powerful arms, and of what could be seen of his strong legs, was meticulously delineated. His hair formed ideal waves. There was strength in the lines of his face, in the shape of his mouth, in the blinking of his piercing gaze.

Yet he was a statue, not a living man. Cast or molded or sculpted in gleaming bronze, not born. No breath stirred his chest behind the cross. The blinking of his eyes was an illusion caused by the way they caught and reflected the light.

His eyes were rubies, as red as blood in the blaze of focused lamps. His teeth were ivory. All the rest of him was metal. His expression seemed both rueful and sardonic. At one instant, the eyes seemed to weep compassion. At the next, they held the mad glare of scorn.

Elgart had trained himself to see conspiracies and harm in the simplest glance. Even here— But he knew himself. He knew that his first impression was often mistaken. When he studied that face more carefully, he did not see malice. Or pity.

He saw authority.

Magister Facile clenched his hand more tightly.

Then the man who had delivered the scripture stepped out of shadows into the edge of the light; and she flinched.

He was all in black. He wore a black cassock cinched with black rope, black sandals on his feet. His hair and his full beard were ebony. His eyebrows formed thick streaks of obsidian on his forehead. His eyes were so dark that they resembled pits leading into the heart of midnight.

His deep, full voice rolled out over the congregation, but now it did not sound commanding or implacable. It sounded like solace after a severe storm.

"You have heard the scripture," he said. "I will help you to understand it."

Tugging Elgart's arm, Magister Facile pulled him close. Her mouth at his ear, she whispered urgently, "I must leave. There is theurgy here. I do not know what it is, but it may detect me. If it does, it may end me."

Before he could protest, she slipped away. A moment later, the door closed behind her.

He had no gift for sorcery. He could not imagine what she had seen or felt. The spectacle of the sculpture draped over the cross was already losing its effect on him.

The priest on the dais gave no sign that he was aware of her departure. Resonant and mild, he began.

"The world is war. In every land, there is war. Here there is war between Belleger and Amika. At one time, it was open bloodshed. Now it is called an alliance. But it remains war, resentment between one neighbor and the next, one merchant and the next, one farmer and the next, one soldier and the next. Within every family, there is war. Wherever there is disobedience and disrespect, anger and punishment, hunger and futility, there is war. You know this. In your hearts, you know it.

"But there is more. In the man or woman sitting at your side, or in front of you, or behind, there is war. In *you*, there is war. In *each* of you, there is war. It does not end. It cannot find peace. If you stood on a mountaintop alone, with no one to trouble you, there would still be war within you.

"You know this. In your hearts, you know it."

Elgart blinked. The radiance of the cross and the man behind it seemed to be growing brighter. Hidden servants of the Church were lighting more lamps, or the bronze brilliance of the reflection was making his eyes tired.

"What is this war?" asked the priest. "In some, it is a venal craving that cannot be satisfied. It cannot *accept* satisfaction. In some, it is a more admirable aspiration to be a better man or a better woman, a better father or a better mother, a better neighbor or a better subject. But for that yearning also there is no end. One aspiration leads always to another, for further betterment, or for recognition of what has been gained, or for relief from striving. In some of you, it is a raw hunger for love and friendship, but that hunger is never fed.

"From such struggles, there is no escape. They are made inevitable by the war around you, and the war beside you, and the war within you.

"But for all of you, the war has one name, and it is *lack*.

"Here I do not speak of unsatisfied cravings, or unattainable aspirations, or unrelieved loneliness. I speak of a *lack* that lies behind those lacks, a deeper absence, a more profound need. It is the sense that you have been *kept out*. That you are the only stranger, the only one who does not belong. In your hearts, you suspect that everyone around you shares a secret which is withheld from you alone. That you and you alone are cursed with an ache that can never be assuaged.

"Lie to me if you wish. Lie to each other if you must. But do not lie to yourselves. If you have no other courage, have the courage to tell the truth to yourselves. You have come to hear the wisdom of the Great God Rile because you *lack*."

The congregation listened with an attention as acute as the keenness of a blade or the thirst of a dying man. But Elgart was no longer conscious of them. He felt unaccountably drowsy. The priest's voice poured over him like syrup. He wanted to lie back in it and float.

"But what do you *lack*?" said the speaker. "I will tell you. In its simplest terms, you lack sorcery. Some men have it. Some women have it. You do not. Seeking always to sow wrath and fear, Pride and Folly grant the Decimates to a few, but they do not sow widely. Thus some men are great, and greatly feared, and greatly needed, able to deal out death or life wherever they go. Some women are. You are not. They are blessed. You are blighted.

"Yet you must not let simple terms mislead you. Sorcery is not *in itself* what you lack. If I could wave my hand and gift all of you with the talent for theurgy, you would not be at peace. First, you would require the knowledge to make use of your gift. Then you would require the knowledge to perfect the use of your gift. Then you would require the knowledge to protect yourself from others whose needs and desires oppose yours. And from this pursuit of knowledge, you would learn two things.

"The first of these is an awareness of your superiority. The greater your knowledge, the greater your power—and the greater your standing above those around you. Thus knowledge becomes arrogance. In truth, knowledge breeds arrogance the way a corpse breeds maggots. And arrogance breeds manipulation. It justifies the making use of those with less knowledge or power as if they were your tools or playthings. As if they were your slaves.

"At its foundation, knowledge exists to feed the greed of some at the expense of others. It wears many masks, but it has no other purpose.

"You have seen the outcome. You know it in your hearts. The Magisters of the Last Repository exercised their knowledge to make use of King Bifalt, so that he would waste his years and yours in preparation for a battle that will never come, but they did not tell him *why*. They did not tell him how his efforts profit *them*. Nevertheless he complies, diligently, honestly, because he believes them, because he is ignorant where they are not, and because he fears to fail his people.

"Belleger remains at war with Amika, and Belleger remains at war with itself, and you remain at war within your own hearts, because the Magisters of the Last Repository are arrogant."

Elgart had been warned. *There is theurgy here. I do not know what it is.* And he had his own suspicions. But the priest's voice, or the brightness of the statue, slowed his thoughts. The effect was cloying and inescapable. He heard the words. He even remembered them. But all he wanted was sleep.

Still the priest did not release him.

"The second thing that the pursuit of knowledge teaches is fear. Does the Magister who now sits beside you, or in front of you, or behind you have more knowledge? Then he or she has the power to destroy you. If you seek the perfection of what you *lack*, and you desire to enjoy it, you must first ward yourselves from your neighbor. You must ward yourselves from every neighbor. From every kinsman. Every Bellegerin. And from Amikans, and Nuuri, and all the people of the world. To pursue knowledge is to live in fear.

"The blessing of arrogance is that it conceals your fear from you. The curse of arrogance is that your fear rules you secretly.

"Do you understand? Knowledge cannot amend your *lack*. It is forever insufficient. Or it breeds arrogance and fear. Or it is controlled by men whose purpose is to keep you out. If you crave peace instead of war within yourself, or between the realms, or in the world, you must amend your *own* lack. You must find peace within who and what you are."

Fine, thought Elgart. Certainly. I hear you. But he did not say the words aloud. He did not have the strength to say them. Only the priest spoke to be heard.

"And how is this done? I will tell you. The Great God Rile sends his priests throughout the world so that they can say what I will say.

"When you have told yourselves the truth about your *lack*, you must have faith. Only faith. Said as I have said it, simply, it sounds both too simple and too difficult. But I tell you that its power is within the grasp of every man and woman. And with that power—without arrogance, without fear—faith brings true peace.

"Faith in *what*, you ask. Faith, I answer, in the nourishment that feeds your hunger. The Great God teaches that faith is a form of theurgy. It is theurgy by another name, the theurgy that *transforms*. It will give you the honest power of who and what you are. And when you have that power, you will have neither fear nor *lack*. Indeed, your power will become like a stone cast into a lake. Its ripples will spread. *Peace* will spread. One man or woman of faith can soothe a family, or a neighborhood. A handful can put a town at ease. With the Great God's wisdom, and enough men and women of faith, the Open Hand can become a place of peace. Then Belleger will follow, and after it, Amika. If King Bifalt can be swayed to set aside his trust in knowledge, there will be no war, and this realm will blossom like wildflowers after a spring rain.

"That is the Great God Rile's will, and his hope. All of his efforts are bent toward it. When it is accomplished, Belleger and Amika and all the world will know peace because they will know Truth and Faith. They will know god.

"Perhaps you understand me. Perhaps you do not. But hear me when I say that every great crime is enabled by knowledge, and is condoned by it. Every act of simple goodness is done by those who know the truth of who and what they are, and have faith in their hearts."

After that, the priest may have said more; but Elgart had stopped listening. As soon as he closed his eyes against the glare from the dais, he fell asleep.

When a hand on his shoulder disturbed him, the priest and the congregation were gone. The brightness on the dais had been extinguished. Only a few lamps near the rear of the sanctuary had been left burning. Out of consideration, no doubt, some servant of the Church had kept those lamps lit so that he would not flounder in darkness while he made his way to the door.

Startled, Elgart wrenched himself awake.

The hand, he saw, belonged to one of the aides he had set to watch the Church until he returned after the service, a woman named Flax. She stood in front of him wearing a clenched frown of concern. As soon as Elgart opened his eyes, she asked, "Have you been harmed, Captain? Were you drugged? We saw Magister Facile depart. Howel followed to watch over her. But you—"

Elgart flapped a hand to silence Flax. He liked being called Captain. It gave him stature. And it was not King Bifalt's doing. He had chosen it for himself. But he was not ready to talk about a form of theurgy that he had never encountered before. And he had a more immediate concern.

There was a man sitting in the pew beside him.

Shaking his head to clear it, Elgart recognized Mattwil, the oldest son of Klamath's friend Matt. It was Mattwil who had whispered a few quiet words recently about *slaves*—and had promised to say more after the service.

"I did not know what to do," explained the young man. His manner suggested that even now he was afraid of being overheard. "The service ended, the priest and the congregation left, but you slept. I feared for you. But then this woman entered." He indicated Flax with a glance. "She appeared to stand guard. And I must speak to *someone*. Yours is the only name I can trust. My father knows you. I decided to wait with you."

Elgart clapped the young man's shoulder. "That was well done, Mattwil. Thank you. I have the King's ear. I can do everything that needs to be done with what you say." Then he rose to his feet, pulling Matt's son with him. "But we will not speak here. At this hour, we will be more alone outside."

On the way to the door, he asked, "How did the service affect you, Mattwil? Did you sleep as well?"

The young man shook his head. Elgart knew his own strength, but he suspected that Matt's son could break him in half. Mattwil had hands that shaped granite, and the chest and thighs of a man who could lift an ox. His voice was husky with caution.

"I know your name. I know General Klamath thinks highly of you. But I do not know *you*. I will tell you what I must. My father and mother would be ashamed if I did not. Then I will surrender myself as a deserter to the First Captain."

Elgart could not suppress a grin. Out in the empty street, beyond the reach of the lamp over the Church door, he replied, "You have nothing to fear, Mattwil. It will not be obvious to you, but you are under my protection now. First Captain Jaspid is a good man. King Bifalt is a better one. They will do more than treat you well. They will understand."

At Elgart's side, Mattwil chewed his thoughts in silence until their taste satisfied him. Then he began to talk about slaves. Not Bellegerin or Amikan: Nuuri slaves.

Because Elgart was in a hurry, and what he heard was urgent, he took his time. He listened until Mattwil was done. He asked a number of questions, some of which the young man could answer, some he could not. In the King's name—and the Queen-Consort's as well—he thanked Matt's son again. Then he instructed Flax to guide Mattwil to the First Captain's command-post. Jaspid might or might not be there; but Flax could use Elgart's name to ensure that Mattwil was handled with respect while the young man waited to surrender himself.

When they were gone, and Elgart saw that the streets around him were empty, he broke into a run, heading for Belleger's Fist.

FIVE

THE QUEEN IN CONSULTATION

Queen Estie paced her rooms in King Bifalt's keep, fretting. Her preparations to depart had been completed hours ago. The distance between the Open Hand and Maloresse was little more than two hard days on horseback, and she traveled without carriages, carts, or extra mounts. For her journey, she only had to take riding garments, a heavy cloak to protect her from the vagaries of the weather, enough food and water for two or three meals, and a few personal items, such as oils for her face, a brush for her hair. Anything else she could obtain at one of the inns that had sprouted along the road since the alliance had been established. And Anina, her maid, had already done the packing. Her groom, Blurn, had been waiting since sunset with their horses. The small company of riflemen that her husband insisted on sending with her whenever she went to or came from Amika was ready.

She had to *go*. There were Nuuri massing on Amika's northern border. An unfamiliar threat: they were not warlike. But she had baited now-former Chancellor Postern into revealing that some of them had been made slaves, forced to work on her road.

That was her father's doing. She was sure of it.

Her road's need for more men was unquestionable. So far, good progress had been made. But her teams of surveyors, stonemasons, diggers, carpenters, rope-makers, and levelers, followed by their trains of food, water, tents, bedding, field physicians, and other supplies, were nearing their worst obstacle. They had to construct a bridge to cross the deep gorge of the Line River—and they had to build it before they reached the dunes of the eastern desert, where they might be unable to find foundations solid enough to support the weight of the bridge.

When they came to the desert, of course, the sorcerers of the library would be able to clear a way for the road, as they had done for Set Ungabwey's caravans long ago. But tonight, that was irrelevant to the Queen of Amika. The bridge itself was irrelevant. The need for more men was a mere detail. She knew where to find them.

To her mind, no justification sufficed for enslaving Nuuri. That was an unprecedented crime. No previous monarch of Amika would have tolerated it. The thought of it made her sick. The careless cruelty of it appalled her. And it would provoke a war. For all she knew, the Nuuri had already started raiding.

She *needed* to go.

Instead, she waited. Before she left, she absolutely *had* to consult with both Magister Facile and Elgart, if for different reasons; but neither of them had come. She had summoned them hours ago, as soon as she left the council meeting, and still they had not come.

Because she was frustrated and angry, she wanted to imagine that they would have appeared instantly if King Bifalt had called for them. But she knew better. The Open Hand was a sprawling, confused mess, and both of them might be anywhere. Her summons might take a long time to reach them. Elgart in particular could be difficult to locate.

In any case, the King never demanded prompt attendance from his counselors and functionaries. He trusted them to use their own judgment and come when they could.

Of course, he was more patient with Elgart than with the sorceress. He did not truly trust any Magister. It was no accident that so few of them came to his public councils—and none except Magister Facile were admitted to his private meetings. Nevertheless he trusted her reasons for being here. He believed that he understood why the Last Repository needed both realms.

But Queen Estie was not her husband. Her thoughts grew increasingly grim as she paced. Perhaps Postern's collusion with her father reached farther than she knew. Perhaps Magister Facile had been caught in some web of conspiracy that she, Estie, had failed to divine. Perhaps Elgart, King Bifalt's right hand, lay knifed in a ditch somewhere, betrayed by his own daring as he pursued the Open Hand's secrets. What then? Should the Queen depart without knowing what had happened to her only real advisers? *Could* she?

In growing agitation, she paced around and around her parlor. A low fire in the hearth warmed the air. Nevertheless she felt a chill in her heart until Anina finally entered from the antechamber of the suite and announced brusquely, "One has come."

At *last*.

By Anina's manner, Estie knew that the arrival was Magister Facile. A blunt, outspoken woman who disliked all things Bellegerin, the maid ordinarily introduced visitors—especially Elgart—with some harsh epithet. But she was curiously reserved around the sorceress. As for King Bifalt, well, he had only come twice, and both times Estie had expected him.

As the old woman came into the parlor, and Anina returned to her post in the antechamber, Queen Estie forgot her fears and remembered her anger. With her head high and her eyes flashing, she snapped, "I summoned you some hours ago, Magister."

Leaning on her cane, Magister Facile met Estie's gaze without any obvious dismay. She was breathing deeply, and a dew of sweat glistened on her pastry face. There were many stairs between the main levels of Belleger's Fist and the Queen-Consort's turret. But her self-command was equal to the challenge. She did not apologize. Instead she allowed herself a sniff of impatience.

"I had a long way to come, Majesty. Your messenger did not find me until I was halfway here. And even then I was delayed. I had a necessary appointment."

Before Estie could demand a fuller explanation, the sorceress warned, "My tidings are grave, Majesty. I cannot linger with you. When we have spoken, I must go to King Bifalt. Events are quickening. He must be told."

Quickening? Startled out of her exasperation, Estie asked, "You *know* of the Nuuri?"

Did *everyone* know? She was the Queen of Amika. Was she the last to hear common knowledge?

But Magister Facile replied with a snort of surprise. "The Nuuri? What of them? I have heard only a rumor. I doubted it. I know nothing more."

Her gaze asked questions that she did not pose aloud.

It was Estie who looked away. She needed a moment to gather herself. She wanted to hear that rumor. She wanted to know where the old woman had heard it. But Magister Facile's demeanor insisted that her own reports were imperative.

In a smaller voice, the Queen said, "Then tell me, Magister. What are your tidings?"

The sorceress grimaced. "The enemy is coming, Majesty. Already his allies scout Belleger and Amika, seeking a road for his armies. *He knows where the library is.*

"Now I must go."

Stamping with her cane, she turned away.

Instantly incensed, Queen Estie called, "Anina, bolt the door! The Magister will not leave until I am satisfied!"

She believed that Magister Facile could shatter the door with a bolt of lightning, or break it by making the floor shudder, or burn it down. But she also believed that the sorceress would not do any of those things. Until now, the Magister had behaved as if she were Estie's friend.

The old woman turned back; opened her mouth for an angry retort, then stopped herself abruptly. For a moment, she seemed to rearrange her face, knead it into a new shape. Conflicting priorities raced to catch up with her thoughts. Finally, they settled on sternness. Resigning herself, she sighed.

"Majesty." Her tone was bleak. "That is unnecessary. I see that you are distraught. No doubt, you have some good cause. And King Bifalt's need of you does not diminish with time. I will answer. When I explain, he will not complain of the delay."

Queen Estie took a deep breath to control the rush of her own emotions. "You say that events are quickening." Her ire did not pass in an instant; and King Smegin had taught her how to sound peremptory. "The enemy is coming. How do you know this?"

Magister Facile sighed again. "Surely, Majesty, it has occurred to you that I speak with the Last Repository."

That admission shocked the Queen of Amika into silence. There were aspects of Prince Bifalt's quest to find the library that she did not understand. How many uses did theurgy have? How did men like Magister Marrow know what happened in Belleger, or elsewhere? How had they known when to intervene to preserve the Prince's life? And how had they heard him when he had finally surrendered to their summons?

Magister Facile was telling her.

"You know King Bifalt's tale." The effort to restrain her impatience was plain in her voice. "You know that Magister Avail has the gift of speaking to any mind he chooses. He could as easily have sent his summons to King Smegin, or to one of the Nuuri. Near or far, there are no obstacles.

"But he cannot *hear* that mind. No Magister can. Sorcery does not extend to the reading of thoughts and secrets. They must be spoken aloud—and spoken within reach of the Magister's ears. Hearing speech at any distance is an altogether different gift.

"It is easily learned by an apt student, but it is terrible to know. Many who learn it are driven mad, or choose death. For that reason, no Magister practices it. It is taught only to apprentices who understand its perils, and who dedicate themselves to surviving it, to the exclusion of all other theurgy."

Magister Facile regarded Estie with a glare; but her tone softened as if she meant to speak of a personal pain.

"Consider it, Majesty. The ability to hear any voice at any distance is the ability to hear *every* voice at *every* distance. It is an incomprehensible clamor, a deafening chaos. That it causes madness is no surprise. That men and women die of it, or kill themselves, is no surprise.

"Over the course of generations, those who study the possibilities of theurgy have learned that few or none can endure the gift of hearing unless they have first been trained to close the ears of their minds. They must learn to hear only when they *choose* to hear. In addition—a harder discipline—they must learn to hear only *whom* they choose to hear.

"For that reason, each apprentice who claims the cruel gift of hearing is taught to hear only *one* voice among the world's multitudes. The training is long and rigorous, and it suffers no distractions. But those apprentices who master their disciplines of choice and concentration are treasured. They are necessary.

"One apprentice hears only King Bifalt. Another hears only a most holy devotee of Spirit who travels with the Wide World Carnival." Just for a moment, the Magister's voice ached with sorrow. "And one, Apprentice Travail, hears only me."

She tried to sound brisk: tried and failed. "That was my appointment. Between us, Magister Avail, Apprentice Travail, and I select times when I am confident of being alone. Magister Avail speaks in my mind. I reply aloud, saying what I need to say. Apprentice Travail hears me. With signs, he tells Magister Avail what I have said.

"When we are done, Apprentice Travail rests in complete isolation for days at a time. He must. He is a good man, and strong, loved by many, precious—" For an instant, the old woman's voice faltered. "Precious to me. But," she finished, "even *his* heart will break if he is asked to hear too much."

Briefly, Queen Estie felt torn. She heard sympathies in Magister Facile's voice that had never revealed themselves before. Clearly, the sorceress had a relationship with Travail that was more than Magister and apprentice. After all these years— Estie wanted to know more.

But Elgart had come in unannounced. If Anina had bolted the door, she had opened it quietly. And Elgart had done or whispered something to keep the maid silent. He stationed himself against a wall without making a sound that might distract Magister Facile. His divided face grinned on one side, scowled on the other.

Because he did not speak, Estie did not let her surprise show. She hardly glanced at him. Instead she studied the sorceress.

Magister Facile recovered her more characteristic manner. "Tonight," she continued, "Magister Avail told me that the enemy is coming.

He told me that we are being scouted by the enemy's allies. In turn, I told him what I have learned."

"And that is?" prompted the Queen.

The old woman grimaced again, rearranging her thoughts. "Majesty, there is theurgy in the Church of the Great God Rile, a sorcery unknown to me. I cannot guess its uses, or its reach. But it is a strange coincidence that the Church enters Belleger from the north while raiders from the Realm's Edge attack farmsteads in the south."

"I believe," said Elgart unexpectedly, "that the priests of the Church call their theurgy 'faith.' They say it has the power to make peace in any conflict. And they say it is *mighty*."

Magister Facile was visibly startled by his presence, but she suppressed her reaction in a moment. Perhaps she had expected his coming. Still facing Estie, she concluded, "You will understand, Majesty, why I must go to King Bifalt. Elgart knows more of the Church than I do. If you have questions, ask him."

Privately, Queen Estie was shocked. She had heard talk about raiders in her husband's private councils, of course. Those people and their lands were unknown in Belleger. They might well have an accessible coast. By ship, they might have negotiated agreements with distant powers. But the idea that the Church of the Great God Rile might be allied with the library's enemy hit her hard. Were the priests and their followers scouting Belleger? Then they had already learned whatever they wanted to know about Amika. And she had condoned their presence in her realm. Worse, she had encouraged King Bifalt to do the same.

The Church's coming might be nothing more than coincidence. That was possible. The priests seemed harmless enough. She had been told that their preaching resembled pleading more than exhortation. They made no apparent effort to foment unrest. On the contrary, they encouraged a quiet calm, a private passivity.

But the timing—

She was Amika's Queen, Belleger's Queen-Consort. She could not discount the implications of Magister Facile's observation.

And she had not forgotten her own need to speak with the sorceress and Elgart.

"A moment, both of you." Her voice trembled slightly, but she made no effort to steady it. "I will not keep you long. King Bifalt must hear your reports. But you have not heard mine."

Elgart's eyebrows twitched on both sides of his scar. He looked suddenly eager, whetted, as he left his place against the wall to stand with Magister Facile.

Glancing at him, the old woman scowled furiously. "I told you, did I not," she rasped, "that I should not have missed the King's public council?"

He treated her to an amiable smile. "You did. Now it is the Queen-Consort's turn to speak."

Their exchange gave Estie a moment to master herself. Deliberately, she set aside as many of her emotions as she could. "There are slaves," she said harshly, "working on my road. *Nuuri* slaves. That may be the rumor you heard, Magister. If so, I thank you for discounting it."

"But it is true, Majesty," said Elgart. Then he bowed an apology for interrupting her.

"I know it," she retorted. "Chancellor Postern confessed it. However, there is more. The Nuuri are massing along our border. Postern fears that they gather to threaten King Smegin."

Elgart's expression betrayed his surprise. Magister Facile's features seemed to crumple in consternation.

Queen Estie had wanted advice from both of them. Facile might be able to tell her how to face King Smegin's sorcery. Elgart could suggest ways to approach her father's retreat. But a new urgency had taken hold of her. King Bifalt needed to hear what she had heard.

Forcing herself to set aside her own concerns, the Queen-Consort declared, "You understand the dangers. I will not recite them. I mean to confront them. I will depart for Amika tonight. King Bifalt knows this. I will answer to him for the enslaving of Nuuri. And for any other atrocities my father has chosen to enjoy."

As if to herself, the sorceress muttered, "Nuuri enslaved. Nuuri massing. King Smegin threatened. A war we are unprepared to wage." Then she faced Estie squarely. "Majesty, all this *cannot* be coincidence."

Elgart had a different reaction. His mouth made a serious line under his nose, but his eyes sparkled with something like glee. "Majesty," he asked, "who goes with you?"

The Queen shrugged. "My maid. My groom. A small company of the King's guards. I mean to make haste."

Magister Facile gripped the head of her cane with both hands. She seemed to wrestle with it as if it were twisting away from her; as if some internal force tried to tug it from her grasp. Then, like a repudiation of herself, she hissed through her teeth, "And I." Abruptly, she stamped her cane on the floor. "*I* will accompany you."

Hearing her, Estie felt a different kind of shock. She could guess why the sorceress had struggled with her decision. Surely Magister Facile's place was with King Bifalt, where she could speak for the Last Repository. Nevertheless she, the Queen of Amika, was shaken by relief. She had not thought of asking for the old woman's company, but now she wanted it. When she was honest, she could admit that she feared her father. If she had inherited any part of his talent for sorcery, she did not know it. She could not impose her will on him. With a hundred riflemen at her back, she could not.

Magister Facile might be stronger.

Elgart seemed to think so. Bowing to the sorceress, he said, "Well said, Magister. Well done."

Magister Facile ignored him. To Estie, she insisted, "But *first* I must speak with King Bifalt. I require you to wait until he is done with me."

Before the Queen could respond, Elgart said, "And I also must ask you to wait, Majesty. Magister Facile's support is much, but it is not enough. I will find another companion for you. Grant me an hour, no more. You will understand when you meet her."

Without waiting to be dismissed, he took the old woman's arm and drew her toward the antechamber, urging her along as if she were reluctant—or as if he feared that she might change her mind. At the threshold of the outer room, however, he paused. Grinning, he said over his shoulder, "At some other time, Majesty, I would like to hear how you wrung a confession from the Chancellor."

Then the Queen's counselors were gone. She heard the outer door open and close. This time, she heard Anina throw the bolt.

In spite of her own desires, her taut yearning to prove herself to her husband, Queen Estie of Amika was still forced to delay her departure.

The stables of Belleger's Fist were not extensive. Opening on the bailey between the bulk of the castle and its gated outer wall, they were large enough to house and feed twenty horses, no more. King Bifalt kept only that number for his own use, for officials like the Land-Captain, for messengers, and for his Queen-Consort. Every other mount that Belleger could muster was bedded near the training-fields outside the walls of the city, where they were needed for the army and its exercises.

At this hour of the night, the bailey usually had only a few torches and guards; and the stables were dark apart from a lantern or two so that the ostlers could see where they were going. Queen Estie expected to find only her usual escort of five Bellegerin riflemen in addition to her groom, Blurn, and the two companions she had been promised. But when she and Anina finally reached the bailey, more than an hour after Magister Facile and Elgart had left her, it was bright with torches and crowded with horses.

First Captain Jaspid was there. At his back waited at least fifty mounted riflemen. In the unexpected light, their bronze breastplates with the beleaguered eagle of Belleger on their chests seemed to blaze, filling the bailey with gold.

All Bellegerin. No Amikans among them.

The Queen stopped; stared. "First Captain," she demanded. "Why are you here? Has there been an attack? Is the Fist threatened? Or the Open Hand?"

The King's brother bowed. "Majesty." He was tall and strong, but not heavily muscled. To the men he trained, he preached that speed was more important than strength. Speed delivered power, he said: strength inhibited speed. And unlike most of the men Estie knew, he was beard-less. She had heard him declare that a man with too much hair gave a weapon to his enemy. He kept his own hair cropped close to his skull, and encouraged his soldiers to do the same.

His saber hung from his belt on one side, his dagger on the other. But he did not have his rifle and ammunition. That was enough to tell Estie that he was not going with her.

Standing as straight as a spear, he explained, "There is no threat *here*, Majesty. But I have confirmation of Chancellor Postern's revelation." His mouth twisted sardonically. "Your purpose is dangerous. King Bifalt offers more men to escort you. He does not wish *you* threatened."

Waiting and fear had exhausted Estie's patience as well as her courtesy. For a moment, she forgot where she was. "Brigin and pestilence!" she snapped as if she still belonged in King Smegin's court. "I am the *Queen* of Amika. Do you imagine I cannot find enough loyal men to protect me in my own realm?"

The First Captain looked momentarily stricken. Then he stood even straighter. "Your pardon, Majesty," he said stiffly. "I meant no offense."

Estie had not intended to reproach Jaspid, but she was in no mood for regret. "Your King did," she retorted. "Does he doubt me because I am Amikan, or because I am a woman?"

Or because, she thought, he does not love me?

Jaspid did not move a muscle, yet he gave the impression that he had taken a step backward. His reply was rigid. "You misjudge King Bifalt, Majesty. By his instructions, we are *offered* to you. We have not been *commanded* to accompany you. The choice is yours." Without softening his tone, he added, "The choice is always yours. Surely, you know that?"

Queen Estie could not think of a graceful way to recant her outburst. She managed to say, "Now I ask *your* pardon, Jaspid." Then other emotions carried her forward. "You and your men are dismissed, with my regret that you were roused at this time of night. I am content with my customary escort."

The First Captain bowed again. However, he did not withdraw. The intensity of his gaze undermined his attempt to sound casual.

"You have two other companions, Majesty. They are in the stables readying their mounts. One of them the King does not know. But Elgart—" Jaspid paused, searched his memory. "The phrase is 'stand surety.' Elgart stands surety for her. King Bifalt is satisfied."

Before Estie could ask if Jaspid knew anything more, the First Captain continued. "The other is Magister Facile. I am to tell you that she may not be what you expect. King Bifalt wants to know if you trust her."

Trust her? The *sorceress*?

There had been too many surprises. The Queen of Amika had a crisis ahead of her—a conspiracy, a possible war, her father—and had already been intolerably delayed. She should have been ten leagues away from the Open Hand by now.

King Bifalt did not trust *any* Magister.

Taking Anina by the hand, Estie left Jaspid where he stood. As she passed him, heading around the crowd of horses and men toward the stables, she breathed fiercely, "Let him ask me himself."

Soldiers watched her go, but they did nothing to stop her. The King's brother did nothing.

Along the way, Anina hissed one word, the worst curse she knew: "Bellegerins."

The Queen missed a step, struck by a sudden fear that they were all going to die. Every rifleman in the bailey. Every Bellegerin she knew.

She could not imagine that her husband loved her; but she could imagine his horror as his realm was put to the sword, slaughtered in front of him.

She was not going to fail him. She was *not*.

SIX

UNPREPAREDNESS

Against a flailing wind, Captain Heren Flisk climbed the crude road that ascended from the jagged strand. At his back, the seas crashed toward the rim of the cliffs that opened here onto the westernmost plains of Belleger.

He hated working in the relentless winds. Chaotic and cruel, they thrashed the bay behind him. They were always bitter, rebounding from the sheer precipices on both sides, edged like knives by the spume and vexation of the rock-bitten waves. Often they carried spray that hit like hail from the wild boiling of the breakers. And they were always cold. They made his shoulder ache, giving new life to the damage done by an Amikan arrow.

Twenty years had passed since Prince Bifalt had sent him back to the Open Hand and King Abbator because he was too badly injured to continue the quest for the Last Repository, and still his shoulder ached. His journey to the Hand had taken too many days. The wound had festered. There had been talk of amputation. Even now, that arm was weaker than the other. When he had been chosen to accompany Prince Bifalt's search, he had been the youngest of the veterans. Hampered by his shoulder, he still felt like the youngest man in any company, despite his years in the army and his rank. Asked to share command of the laborers who would fortify this bay, his first impulse had been to refuse. "Find someone better," he had wanted to reply. "Someone you can trust." But the man who had asked him was King Bifalt, and Heren Flisk did not have it in him to say no.

Nevertheless his King's confidence only exacerbated his uncertainties. At all times, he doubted himself. Any challenge might prove too great for him. He blamed his shoulder; but the truth was that he had suffered a wound deeper than an arrow when Prince Bifalt had been forced to send him home. Except for Elgart and Klamath, every other rifleman on the Prince's quest had died defending King Abbator's son and heir. All of them had given their lives for the Prince, and for King Abbator, and for Belleger. And in other ways, even Elgart and Klamath had done so, although they still lived. They had become the hands of King Bifalt's will. Only Flisk had been forced to abandon the Prince's quest and ride away.

After so many years, the Captain's deepest wound was still shame. Shame that he lived on after his comrades died. Shame that he had done nothing to equal them; nothing to justify their sacrifice. Instead, when better men were gone, King Bifalt was compelled to rely on a soldier who had once failed him.

That was one of Flisk's many reasons for hating this climb. It reminded him that he was weak. There was no shelter from any accusation the sky might throw at him, or the sea, or the intolerable exhaustion of his men. Under other circumstances, he would have sent someone else up the road in his place. But a lookout stationed atop the cliff had signaled that a rider was approaching from the direction of the Open Hand. A second signal had informed him that the rider was a Magister. That was not a summons Captain Flisk could ignore.

Nor could the other man who shared Flisk's responsibility for Belleger's defenses in the bay. Commander Ennis Forguile of Amika strode upward at his side. Behind the blank mask of the Amikan's resolve, Commander Forguile made it look easy.

For a year or more after Queen-Consort Estie had insisted that Forguile should have an equal role in preparing the fortifications, Flisk had resented the man's presence and authority. Of course, he had understood the Queen-Consort's reasoning. A task as prodigious as the one King Bifalt contemplated would require men from both Belleger and Amika, hundreds of them in relays; and her people would work better for a respected Amikan than they would for any Bellegerin. By the same argument, men from Belleger would do their best for Captain Flisk, but would resist Commander Forguile's orders.

King Bifalt had agreed with her. And Heren Flisk knew they were right. Belleger and Amika were allies now; but the certainty that Amika desired Belleger's destruction had been ground into his bones. He could not simply shrug it off. His own hostility demonstrated the accuracy of the Queen-Consort's judgment.

Nevertheless his resentment had been more personal than that of the men he commanded. He was a soldier. He had ridden into the hell of battle. He had seen dozens of his comrades killed. But he had also seen uncounted Amikans fall. He was able to welcome the end of the war. His former enemies could do the same. Given time, men who had once tried to kill each other would learn that they had more in common than their wounds and fears. They would begin to work effectively together. But Commander Ennis Forguile had been a special case.

With his air of earned assurance, his physical prowess, and his greater experience, Forguile cast a shadow on the Captain's questionable competence. And he had known Flisk's King since they were in the Last Repository together. They had returned together, persuaded King Abbator to offer peace together. Together, they had convinced King Smegin to accept. With his own hands, Commander Forguile had put Sylan Estervault's book on cannon in King Smegin's hands.

Forguile did not vaunt himself or boast; but the simple fact of his accomplishments made Heren Flisk's whole life seem trivial. They made King Bifalt's trust look foolish.

Doubting himself, the younger man had compensated with bellig-erence. The two officers had argued constantly, opposing each other on almost every topic, Commander Forguile with rigid calm, Captain Flisk often shouting. In particular, they had fought over the treatment of their laborers. When the Commander wanted another hour of work before calling a halt, the Captain insisted on rest. When the Amikan urged risks, the Bellegerin demanded safety. When Forguile pushed the men to work in storms and heavy rain, Flisk sent them to their shelters and kitchens.

Flisk had foreseen a day when he and Forguile would come to blows. He had dreaded the beating he would receive: the humiliation more than the pain.

Fortunately, he no longer felt such antipathy. For him, the turning point had come late one night after a particularly angry dispute had reached an impasse. During a pause in the wind's keening, Ennis Forguile asked suddenly, "Do you know Prince Bifalt once swung his saber at my neck? It was in the refectory of the library, before—" He shrugged. "Before many things. I think now he meant to check his cut, but he was not given the chance. Magister Rummage broke his wrists."

"You provoked him," snapped Flisk instantly.

The Commander shook his head. "I am Amikan. There was no other provocation. Not on that occasion. Later, yes. But not then."

Flisk stared. "But you aided him. You stood before King Abbator with him. You took him safely into Amika. Without you, he would have been killed. You supported him in front of King Smegin." Helpless with confusion, the Captain protested, "You should have hated him."

Forguile nodded. "Yes. I did. But my loathing passed. That is what I want you to understand. I learned to know him better. I suspect he *became* better. He humbled me in front of the Magisters. Then he made me his comrade. He answered each of my doubts, of which I had many. He shared his reasons and his secrets. And he shared his travels, both returning from the library and going there again after he was wed, to obtain the restoration of sorcery. I know what he knows about the plotting of those Magisters.

"I believe in him, Captain. Estie of Amika is my Queen. I serve her. But I *believe* in King Bifalt."

Before Flisk could find a reply, the Commander added, "He did well when he chose you. You care for the men. Amikan monarchs like King Smegin show no concern for those who do their bidding."

After that confession, Flisk's self-doubts and defenses lost their virulence. He and Forguile still argued incessantly. They were of Belleger and Amika: it was their nature that they would disagree. But now they argued peaceably, like friends. Over time, Flisk learned to be glad that he was not alone with his burdens, and that his companion was Forguile.

Working his way up the road now to meet with a Magister from the Open Hand, Heren Flisk had one more reason to be glad. A single rider from the Open Hand was a messenger. The message might be from the Land-Captain: good news, perhaps, or bad, about the latest delivery of food and supplies, the latest relay of men to relieve exhausted laborers. But a single Magister was a messenger from King Bifalt. Therefore the message was urgent.

Captain Flisk was grateful that he would not have to face the Magister and his message alone.

When the two men passed the crest of the road, and Flisk saw who the Magister was, he felt even more gratitude for his companion.

Commander Forguile's sight was not as keen as his. To warn his companion, Heren Flisk said through the wind, "It is Magister Lambent." The sorcerer was riding hard. "And in a hurry."

Frowning, Ennis Forguile replied with a grunt of distaste. He knew Lambent better than Flisk did, and had his own reasons to dislike the man.

From the shelter of a stone hut built for the purpose, the lookout waved a salute. Then he resumed his duties.

Shoulder to shoulder, the Bellegerin and the Amikan waited for King Bifalt's messenger.

In a clatter of hooves muffled by the moaning of the wind past the ridge, the Magister arrived. He flung himself from his mount as if he could not abide even an instant's delay. But when he stood on his own feet, he took a moment to adjust his robe and settle himself. From one of his saddlebags, he took out a heavy cloak. Carrying it over one arm, he approached the officers as if *he* had been the one waiting for *them*.

He was tall, with the thin chest and protruding belly of a man who exercised little and ate too much. The slope of his granite-grey robe from his neck to his elbows gave the impression that he had no shoulders. Above a mouth like a purse, he had a nose like a raptor's beak. But his eyes were weak, already watering in the sting of the wind. The effort of fast riding had left him short of breath.

As he came near, he managed to say without panting, "Commander Forguile." Captain Flisk he ignored, as he always did. The sorcerer was Amikan.

Like his companion, Flisk bowed without any obvious disrespect. Then the Commander observed drily, "You rode hard, Magister. Your message must be alarming. What drives you? What do our King and Queen command?"

Magister Lambent huffed. "I am instructed to survey your progress. Then I will have more to say." He glanced briefly at Captain Flisk; but he did not deign to address servants directly. Instead, he told Commander Forguile, "I have indeed ridden hard. It would be courteous to offer me ale."

Clearly, he expected Flisk to run off in search of some refreshment. But the Captain stood where he was. For Forguile's sake, he did not answer the sorcerer with an insult.

"Then, Magister," replied Commander Forguile without enthusiasm, "you must descend to our camp. There is nothing for you here. We do not allow ale to our lookouts. Their duty is tedious, and we do what we can to discourage slackness."

Wiping his eyes, the Magister muttered, "Brigin! What a place." However, he did not insist. His reasons for coming may have been as urgent as his riding had made them seem. When he had pulled on his cloak and covered his head with its hood, he gestured for Commander Forguile to lead the way.

While they turned back toward the bay, the Commander winked at Flisk. But the Captain kept his face as blank as he could. His long struggle with himself had taught him to resent being treated like a menial. Whenever his shoulder ached, his resentment intensified.

From the top of the road, the three men faced the bay.

It formed a rough U with a notch in its deepest point, a cut that reached from the height where the men stood down to the water. Walled on both sides by unassailable cliffs, as they were everywhere else along the coast of Belleger, the seas boiled and thundered, battering each other to spray in a mad clamor of cross-currents. The crooked reef that blocked the top of the U ripped every surge of the ocean into breakers.

Then the waves heaving over the claws of the reef met other obstacles. Everywhere within the bay, raw rocks bit the air like fangs, tearing the surges into new breakers, forcing them aside, driving them into collision with each other. When the sky was clear, and the sun shone on the waters, the white-cap-raddled turmoil of blue looked like it was about to erupt. During a cloudy midday, as now, the seas took on an evil hue, the restive bitter grey of hunger and malice.

But at night under an open sky, the bay became a place of beauty, as wondrous as sorcery. In its turmoil and savagery, the water was bright with dazzles, the eerie shining of torn and crashing seas: a sight that entranced even the exhausted teams of Bellegerins and Amikans. They knew why the place was named the Bay of Lights.

Yet always, day or night, winter or summer, the water roared against the rocks. At times, its insatiable tumult was louder than the winds. At others, the squalling of lashed air among the stones and along the cliffs covered even the agony of wracked waves. On some occasions, it was louder than thought. Captain Flisk and Commander Forguile gave their instructions by signs and signals because they could not be heard.

The whole bay would have been inaccessible without the notch in the bottom of the U.

The formation of the bay itself was strange. Here, some ancient force had caused the rim of the cliff to collapse, leaving a steep slope of boulders and rubble down to the strand: the slope which teams of Bellegerins and Amikans had eventually made into a road. From this distance, the fan of rocks where the collapse met the sea looked like nothing more than debris. But the making of the notch had dropped astonishing sections of the cliff into the bay. In fact, the fan was composed of ragged boulders taller than a man.

And the force which had formed the original notch had other effects as well. For perhaps three hundred paces in both directions, left and right, the cliffs were no longer sheer. Instead they fell away in a series of ragged shelves or terraces. There were five of these terraces, the highest thirty or so man-heights below the rim of the precipice, the lowest no more than ten above the fury of the seas at high tide.

With years of effort, endless amounts of supplies and fresh men, and some deaths, the teams of laborers had leveled those shelves until they were suitable for the construction of emplacements for cannon; of heavy housings to store and protect gunpowder; of enclosures waiting to be filled with cannonballs and chain. All of those structures were made of stone.

In contrast, the bunkhouses, dining halls, and kitchens for the men were built of wood. Wooden shelters provided scant relief from the wind, and little from the rain and hail, but they could be taken apart and moved wherever they were needed, so that the men were able to sleep and eat near where they were working.

Nine years ago, when King Bifalt was satisfied by his progress rebuilding Belleger and the army, he and his Queen-Consort had ridden here with Heren Flisk and Ennis Forguile. From the top of the slope that was now a road, they had discussed every aspect of the King's fears and desires.

By that time, Amika had become proficient in "the fabrication of cannon using primitive means." Early in her reign, Queen Estie had recognized the advantages of making her guns in standard sizes according to their desired ranges and the weights of their balls. That way, the same castings and molds could be used repeatedly instead of being refashioned for each new cannon. During the years that followed, Amika had produced a number of cannon in three calibers: the long guns intended to fire twenty-pound balls across great distances; the medium guns with their shorter ranges and heavier loads, able to throw sixty-pound balls or an equal weight of chain; and the massive siege guns, the barrels of which were too thick to be made long, but which could fling hundred-pound balls at least that many paces.

Together, King Bifalt, Queen-Consort Estie, and their chosen officers had decided to assume that the bay's reef would not prove insurmountable to invading ships. The enemy would find a way to break through it. On that basis, they agreed that the two highest terraces would be armed with long guns, cannon that might be able to do damage as soon as their targets passed the reef. The next two shelves would hold medium guns to defend against ships deep in the bay. Siege guns would fire from the lowest terrace, wreaking their terrible havoc at close range.

Once those decisions had been made, the small company—standing where Flisk, Forguile, and Magister Lambent stood now—had talked for a long time about the practical problems of the task. It would require immense numbers of men over several years; mountains of tools and heavy rope; stonemasons, carpenters, cooks, physicians. And it would depend on an endless train of supplies ranging from gunpowder for blasting to fresh recruits to ordinary blankets, clothing, food, and water. In short, the task would depend on all of the same resources that Queen-Consort Estie needed for her road to the Last Repository. King Bifalt and his lady would have to negotiate with each other almost daily.

And when the labor of building and shaping was done to the satisfaction of King Bifalt and his officers, the fortification would need forty Amikan cannon: sixteen long guns for the two highest levels, sixteen medium for the next two, eight siege guns on the lowest terrace.

Unfortunately, the work that Captain Flisk and Commander Forguile had been given was far from complete. On the Bellegerin side, the three highest terraces were done: four widely spaced cannon emplacements with their shield-walls, their gun-ports, and their smooth stone floors on each shelf, each emplacement with its storage for shot and chain, and its strong housing for gunpowder. But on the Amikan side, only the first two levels and half of the third were finished.

Every man who could still stand was working there before moving down to the next level. To Flisk's eye, they seemed to move as slowly as insects in syrup. Nevertheless he was proud of them. Far below him, Bellegerins and Amikans shared their burdens, helped each other with their tasks—and hardly noticed that they were doing so. By the time their duty ended—if it ever ended—they might not remember that they had once been enemies.

He and Ennis Forguile had accomplished that much, at least. Their own comradeship and the near prostration of the men had taught this small portion of the two realms to work as one.

Magister Lambent was not impressed. He started down the road, heading for the bunkhouses and kitchens now on the third terrace. As the officers joined him, he remarked sourly through the wind, "I expected more progress, Commander. I expected more from Amikans.

Their officer should have expected more. These workmen are needed elsewhere."

He had visited the Bay of Lights often enough, and more frequently in recent seasons. He knew what Flisk and Forguile were up against. But he was Amikan, more loyal to Queen Estie's road than to King Bifalt's fortifications, which he considered useless. If the Queen-Consort had not spoken to him severely on the matter, he would have refused to serve as King Bifalt's messenger.

Captain Flisk's shoulder ached acutely. But Commander Forguile did not offer the obvious explanation: he and Captain Flisk had too few men; and the men they had were not relieved often enough. Instead, the Commander said, "Captain Flisk and I argue incessantly. That delays us." When he thought that men who outranked him were stupid, he had a private way of mocking them. "And more often than not, events prove him right. That delays us further."

Like any number of other sorcerers Flisk could have named, Magister Lambent believed himself a superior being, too high above ordinary men to care how he affected them. Clearly, however, he knew when he was not being taken seriously. And the angle of the descent made his legs tremble. With heavy asperity, he demanded of Forguile, "Have you accomplished *anything*? Anything at all since my last inspection?"

Heren Flisk swallowed a curse.

The Commander showed Flisk another wink. In a tone of exaggerated innocence, he asked, "Do you see the reef at the mouth of the bay, Magister?"

"Of course I see it," snapped the theurgist. In all likelihood, he did not. The way the wind made his eyes water would have blurred the vision of a man with stronger sight.

Forguile took the Magister's arm, tugged him to a stop. "Then watch." To Lambent's stare, he insisted, "The reef, Magister. Watch the reef. We will demonstrate."

Flisk knew what his comrade wanted. He took out one of his signal-flags, waved it at the nearest emplacement.

Unfortunately, the fortifications of the bay in their present state included only three cannon, all long guns, all on the highest terrace.

Fortunately, Captain Flisk and Commander Forguile had agreed long ago that every man who worked in the bay needed to learn how to load, aim, and fire a cannon—and to do it safely. All day every day, there were relays of laborers in teams of four at each of the guns. Under the supervision of a lash-tongued Amikan cannoneer, the teams practiced as long as they were allowed. It was their only respite from more strenuous tasks. And it gave them the sense that their efforts served a purpose.

Under other circumstances, one of the long guns would have fired at any moment. Flisk's signal simply gave the cannoneer an excuse to fire *now*.

Snatched away by the wind, the report was barely audible; little more than a clap, a muffled thud. Flisk knew the interval: he counted his heartbeats until he saw the small splash of the shot among the brawling seas.

"There!" Commander Forguile pointed. "Did you see it, Magister? No more than thirty paces within the line of the reef. The perfect distance." With a chuckle in his voice, he added, "Amika makes fine guns."

Magister Lambent scowled, blinking furiously. "Do you call *that* an accomplishment, Commander? One iron ball at the bottom of the bay?"

Captain Flisk was confident that the King's messenger had seen nothing.

"*We* do," retorted Forguile. "*You* must imagine it. Imagine that a vessel has just breached the reef. In itself, a significant feat. But now it has a hole in its hull. If it is a small vessel, one hole is enough. The waves have already swallowed it. And no man survives those rocks and breakers." He shrugged. "If it is a large vessel, of course, one hit may not sink it. It may need three holes, or five, to send it down."

Then Forguile rounded on the sorcerer. "The point of our demonstration is this, Magister. Our work here is not complete to your satisfaction, or to ours, yet already we are able to defend the bay."

Magister Lambent tried to pull himself up to his full height so that he could glare imperiously at Commander Forguile, but the trembling of his legs worked against him. Instead of attempting a retort, he started down the road again. Dragged along by his belly, he was barely able to refrain from running.

The two officers followed more slowly. Commander Forguile looked like he was laughing privately. Captain Flisk rubbed his shoulder and hoped to see the sorcerer fall on his face.

Half an hour later, both men ran out of patience. They had followed the slope-shouldered Magister to the nearest kitchen, where he had demanded ale and food. Being a sorcerer, he was obeyed with only one quick glance at the officers for confirmation. They watched him eat and drink. While they waited, the Commander asked Flisk in a whisper if he thought Lambent would need help to climb back up the road. But now the Magister stood with his back to them near one of the stoves, holding his cloak open to gather warmth; and he still had not delivered his message from King Bifalt.

Around the kitchen, winds groaned between the boards of the walls. But they were muted here, comparatively quiet. Men did not have to shout to be heard.

Abandoning deference, Commander Forguile said abruptly, "It is time to speak, Magister. Tell us what the King wants us to hear. We have work to do."

Lambent did not turn from the stove. "Nevertheless you will wait until I am ready, Commander. These are weighty matters. I must decide what you are fit to hear."

At once, Forguile snapped, "You have nothing to decide. We command here. You do not. We serve the King's purposes. You do not. Your delay is an insult. King Bifalt will hear of it.

"Queen Estie will hear of it."

To a loyal Amikan, that was a more personal threat.

The sorcerer whipped around with the heat of the stove shining on his cheeks. "Do you dare to speak of insults? Ignorant lackey! I am *Magister* Lambent. I can take your life, and the lives of every man here, without lifting my arms."

Well, he was Amikan—and obviously bitter about the alliance. But Captain Heren Flisk was Bellegerin. He had his own resentments. Without raising his voice, he replied, "And you will answer for it. Have you forgotten King Bifalt's nature? Have you forgotten that the Queen-Consort stands with him?

"Come, now, Magister. You are weary. You have ridden hard, and have far to go. Tell us what the King wants us to know. Then you can turn your back on us and go. You will be able to say honestly that you have done your duty."

Magister Lambent huffed for a moment. Then he seemed to deflate. "Commander," he sighed without looking at Flisk. "I was hasty. I *am* weary. It makes me short of temper. I will be brief."

Flisk understood then that the sorcerer had delayed because he was afraid.

"Through Magister Facile," reported Lambent stiffly, "King Bifalt and Queen Estie have received word from the Last Repository. Events are quickening. The enemy is coming. He knows where to look for the library. You have labored for years. The time remaining to you is measured in fortnights.

"The King asks for a list of your requirements. Make it complete. This may be your last chance to summon supplies and aid from Amika, if not from the Open Hand."

Short as it was, the message shocked Flisk. Glancing at his comrade, he saw that the Commander had been hit hard as well. There was a flush that Flisk recognized on Ennis Forguile's cheeks. It was not cold. It was not even fury. It was chagrin. The officers had labored here together for the better part of nine years, they were both exhausted to the core by the work and the winds, the cold and loneliness, the slow creep of their progress—and yet, suddenly, they were not ready to be done. With King Bifalt and the Queen-Consort, they had talked about so much more—

But Commander Forguile recovered first. He had experienced much that his comrade had not, and had risen higher under a crueler King. He held the Magister's gaze until the man looked away. Then he said in a voice that was almost a drawl, "A list, is it? Do you have yours, Captain Flisk? I have forgotten mine."

Even now, he defied the Amikan sorcerer's prejudice by refusing to take precedence over his Bellegerin comrade.

The Commander's question—and his attitude—freed Heren Flisk from his dismay. He always had the fortification's needs in mind. He recited them to himself daily.

"Men," he said at once. "At least three hundred. A hundred to relieve those here. They are prostrate on their feet. Two hundred to speed the work. Also food and cooks and serving-men. And bedding for two hundred. What we have is rotting in the damp and salt. Wood for more bunkhouses, wood and stoves for new kitchens."

Magister Lambent listened, nodding as if he knew all this, and had already lost interest. His gaze wandered.

But Captain Flisk did not pause. With more force, he added, "Also we need cannon, at least forty, more if they can be spared. Long, medium, and siege guns. King Bifalt knows the numbers. Ask the Queen-Consort to send experienced cannoneers, men who can work the guns with accuracy and speed. And tell the King that we must have carpenters."

That surprised the theurgist. Without a sound, his mouth shaped the word: Carpenters?

"*Skilled* carpenters," insisted Flisk. He did not bother explaining that Amika delivered new cannon on wheeled carts which could not take the strain of repeated firing: the violent recoil, the hard jolt of impact with the restraining ropes, the force of being hauled back into the gun-ports. In addition, the carts did nothing to hold the guns' aim. The defense of the Bay of Lights required cannon mounted on battle trucks: trucks wheeled, roped, and balanced according to his and Commander Forguile's specific instructions. As soon as the guns started to arrive, carpenters who could do more than saw and hammer boards would be essential.

"And Magisters," finished Captain Flisk firmly. "All who can stomach the risk when the attack comes."

"*Magisters?*" sputtered the sorcerer. For the first time, he looked directly at Flisk. "Have you lost your wits? The distance is too great." He jerked a gesture toward the bay and the reef. "No Magister can aid you. No Decimate can be extended so far."

"Do you think so?" The Bellegerin feigned confidence. "Consult King Bifalt. Consult the Queen-Consort. If she will speak to you, consult Magister Facile. There is much you do not know."

That was the pain in Flisk's shoulder talking. In truth, he had always believed what Lambent did: the range of every theurgist's Decimate was limited. Why else had Belleger and Amika fought all their battles in a valley with ramparts from which their respective sorcerers could not reach each other? But King Bifalt and Commander Forguile had different ideas. Even Elgart did. The Magisters of the Last Repository had challenged all their preconceptions. And Magister Facile had come from the library.

How could she receive *any* word from that stronghold of knowledge, when hundreds of leagues and a lifeless desert intervened?

For reassurance, Flisk looked at his comrade. Commander Forguile's barely suppressed grin showed his approval.

"Do you affirm all this, Commander?" demanded the sorcerer. He looked shaken; but he was too angry to admit it directly. "Do you stand behind this Bellegerin's madness? Does Queen Estie stand behind *you*?"

With veiled impudence, Forguile answered, "Ask her yourself, Magister. You know she supports King Bifalt. You know she affirms his commands in all matters pertaining to the defense of the realms. How do you imagine she will respond?"

That reminder of the Queen-Consort's commitment to the alliance—and to her husband—made Magister Lambent wince. For a moment, he turned away to hide his expression. Muttering bitterly to himself, he appeared to consult the stove. Then he wrapped his cloak around him. Without a word, he headed for the door.

As he passed, Flisk glimpsed the white glare of alarm in the sorcerer's eyes.

When the King's messenger was gone, the Captain asked his comrade, "Should we?"

"Accompany him?" Ennis Forguile grinned openly. "Not at once. Give him a little time, for the sake of his dignity. Then we can see how he fares. If his struggles are painful to watch, perhaps we will assist him."

Heren Flisk nodded; but his mind had already veered. He was thinking, Fortnights? *The time remaining to you*— Aloud, he said, "We cannot be ready in fortnights."

The Commander's grin faded. "We can only do what we can. If we are fortunate, the enemy will send scout ships ahead of his main force." Then he shrugged. "If we are *unusually* fortunate, the enemy will send his scouts *far* ahead. And if we are *extravagantly* fortunate—and if we are able to drive off his scouts with what we have—he may send his main force elsewhere."

"Or abandon his attack altogether?" asked Flisk.

Forguile shrugged again. "The library's Magisters do not think so. Their enemy has nurtured his malice too long. He will not allow any obstacle to prevent his assault on the Last Repository.

"But we have this advantage. He does not expect us to be prepared. Certainly, he does not expect us to be prepared *here*." He clapped Flisk's shoulder. "I foresee that you and I will have the honor"—he laughed sourly—"of striking the first blow against him. Perhaps the first and the second."

At that moment, Heren Flisk felt daunted by Ennis Forguile. And he did not know how to explain himself. He had not helped Prince Bifalt force an alliance between Belleger and Amika. He had not even made the arduous journey to the library and back, a feat which Commander Forguile and Prince Bifalt had accomplished twice. And he could not ask his comrade to understand him.

The Amikan had never been sent home wounded. Forguile did not know the shame of that; or the relief, which was another kind of shame. Flisk had lost friends in that ambush long ago: men he had known and trained with since he was old enough to sit a horse and aim a rifle. He was only alive now because he had been more fortunate than Captain Swalish and the others—and less fortunate than Elgart and Klamath, who had seen the Prince's quest through to its end. Like Commander Forguile, they had no cause for shame. Even the dead had no cause.

Were Belleger and Amika at peace with each other? Truly? It made no difference. Heren Flisk was still trying to come to terms with himself.

PART
TWO

SEVEN

PRINCE BIFALT'S COURTSHIP
OF PRINCESS ESTIE

To her surprise, Princess Estie fell in love with Prince Bifalt on their wedding day. She was sixteen years old.

It was not the fact of getting married that swayed her. He was Bellegerin, and she was too Amikan to be dazzled by a union with the ancient enemy of her people. In addition, she was too much her father's daughter to believe that marriage had anything to do with love.

And she was not impressed by the hall where the ceremony took place. It was considerably smaller than her father's royal hall in Amika's Desire, and had none of that chamber's glory. Nor was she overcome by the size of the gathering, which was not large, or by the finery of the guests and witnesses, most of which was shabby as befitted the people of a lesser realm impoverished by a long war. Also, there were no bright trumpets, no swooning choruses; no music at all.

At an earlier time, the comparative magnificence of her own apparel might have made her feel exalted in front of so many Bellegerins. Now it did not. In fact, she was hardly aware of the jewels in her hair, around her neck and wrists; the hues that enhanced her luminous eyes; the elaborate elegance of her gown.

Furthermore, the ceremony itself was brief, almost perfunctory: an uneasy combination of Bellegerin and Amikan traditions hammered out by King Smegin's Chancellor and King Abbator's Land-Captain. Estie was only acquainted with the Land-Captain because he had participated in the peace negotiations, and because he had presided over her welcome to Belleger's Fist. She knew him as an elderly man with kind eyes and a gift for perfect courtesy, nothing more. But she suspected that her father had instructed Chancellor Postern to belittle her wedding as much as possible. The word *love* was not used.

In short, there was nothing in the occasion itself to sweep a young woman of sixteen off her feet; to persuade her that she was in love with a man she should have despised.

And yet her first sight of Prince Bifalt as he came to stand near her at the head of the gathering undid her. Before leaving Maloresse, she had promised herself that she could tolerate this marriage for Amika's sake, and for her father's. Now, suddenly, she wanted it.

Like his hall and his subjects, Prince Bifalt's appearance was not splendid. Oh, his soldier's breastplate and helm shone brightly enough. They had been strenuously polished. And his brown shirt, trousers, and boots were clean, finely made, well fitting. His form was strong, his movements sure, his features chiseled in a way that suggested determination rather than handsomeness. Still, he did not resemble a maiden's vision of a bridegroom. Like Belleger's Fist itself—like the chambers assigned to the Princess, her family and retinue—he looked functional, made for use rather than display. He could have gone into battle dressed as he was.

Still *he* was splendid—or his effect on her was indistinguishable from splendor. This alliance between ancient enemies was entirely his doing. By force of will, generosity of spirit, and inflexible courage, he had altered the fundamental assumptions of life in both Amika and Belleger. And now his eyes held the same dark smolder that she had seen in them when he had risked entering Amika's Desire to demand peace; when he had said to her in his raw, exhausted voice, *My lady, you are enough. You will be worth what you cost.* The scars on his hands were as plain as language, and the severity of his mien promised more passion than she had dared to imagine. She hardly heard what he said to affirm their vows. She was not aware of her own responses. She could not look away from him. If he had offered to kiss her at the ceremony's end, she would have collapsed in his arms.

She called what she felt then "love" because that was the word a woman expected herself to use at her age. But when she looked back on the occasion with more knowledge of people, and more awareness of herself, she recognized that the change in her attitude toward her husband was not as sudden as it had seemed at the time. She also learned other names for the emotions which had mastered her during—and after—her wedding.

In retrospect, she realized that her view of the Prince began to shift when she became conscious of the difference between his firm resolve and King Smegin's debased hunger for victory and power. She was Amikan: she was supposed to loathe Bellegerins. But during the year between Prince Bifalt's first arrival in Amika's Desire and the date set for their marriage, Princess Estie had attended many of the sessions in which the terms of the alliance were debated; and—unlike her father—the Prince had been present at most of them. Despite her instinctive reactions, she had been impressed by the clarity of his demands and concessions.

For his father's sake, he had asserted that his union with Princess Estie was a necessary condition of any alliance. At the same time, however, he had demonstrated that he had no interest in assuming the rule of Amika, even indirectly. In particular, he left the fabrication of cannon to Amika exclusively. Likewise, he refused to concede any detail of Belleger's sovereignty. The making of rifles belonged to Belleger alone. But he had been adamant about his preparations for a terrible war, a distant but inevitable invasion. Where those preparations were concerned, he had insisted that Amika and Belleger had to work together. Their firepower would be combined and shared when the war came. In that struggle, Belleger and Amika had to fight as one—and fight under his command.

On all the other details of the alliance, he had been flexible, conciliatory, even magnanimous. Decisions about the security of borders, about the freedom of bridges over the Line River, about the rights of trade, even about the establishment of inns and way-houses to facilitate travel: all were more Amikan than Bellegerin. At times, Princess Estie's mental jaw dropped at Prince Bifalt's willingness to concede. As the seasons and sessions passed, she had become more and more conscious of the ways in which the Prince surpassed her. And when she had grown accustomed to being impressed, she had slipped by unremarked increments into admiration.

She had assured herself that she could endure this marriage. It might be unpleasant: it would not be unbearable. Now thoughts of her future husband occupied her for hours; and as her attitude toward Prince Bifalt became more favorable, her fascination with her father diminished. She felt less pride in being King Smegin's favorite daughter. She learned to dislike his sarcasm and disgust. She began to enjoy his absences from the sessions of negotiation. The possibility of seeing Prince Bifalt again did not repulse her. She almost looked forward to each opportunity.

Naturally, inevitably, she felt both wounded and relieved when King Smegin announced that he would not attend her wedding. She wanted her father's support: she did *not* want his manners to rule the occasion. But instead, he proclaimed, Amika would be represented by his wife and Estie's sisters. By the Chancellor, of course, and by a squad of honor guards. And by as many Amikan courtiers and functionaries as dared to enter Belleger. The King himself would remain in Amika's Desire. Drinking, he said. To mourn his losses. He said.

To no one's surprise, his announcement cheered his wife immensely. For the first time, Queen Rubia seemed to believe that her eldest daughter would actually marry—and would marry the man who had put an end to Amika's horrid war. She became excited and made plans, arranging for Estie's trousseau and her younger daughters' display. Before long, she began to count the days.

As for Estie's sisters—unkindly named by their father Demure and Immure to distinguish them from his favorite—they vacillated between eagerness and scorn. They were going to Belleger, to the Open Hand and Belleger's Fist. Every man they met would be Bellegerin, repugnant suitors for Amikan princesses. On the other hand, the Queen's party would only be in the Fist for a fortnight: time enough for flirtation and even dalliance without consequences. It might be fun to break the hearts of a few handsome enemies—if there *were* any handsome enemies—

before returning home. Together, Demure and Immure made no secret of the fact that *they* did not consider Prince Bifalt handsome.

Princess Estie disappointed her sisters by not expressing an opinion. In silence, she affected a profound disinterest in her future husband's face and form. For the most part, she was able to avoid the subject by avoiding Demure and Immure.

But then the day of departure came; and the Queen and her three daughters were dispatched together in King Smegin's second-best coach to travel to Belleger. With their maids, servants, and baggage in a much larger coach behind them, and a company of ten richly appointed cavalry soldiers around them, they left the heavy fortifications of Amika's Desire and went out into Maloresse for the first time in Estie's life.

For a while, she was as interested as her sisters in what she could see from the coach's windows. Their conveyance rolled along a well-paved boulevard through a region of mansions and manor-houses: a region in which elegance and wealth had the stature of virtues. Graceful trees shaded the roadway. Shaped hedges lined the approaches to the houses. Immaculate lawns and elaborate gardens were everywhere, and most of the homes boasted stables with lanes and paddocks carpeted in sawdust.

Twittering incessantly, Demure and Immure flitted from side to side, naming the family of each manor-house and mansion, tracing lineages to or from their father's line, gossiping excitedly about possible marriages, liaisons, and scandals. Estie, however, was silent. Listening to King Smegin for years, she already knew too much about the families her sisters dissected. Instead, she studied where and how those families lived, and drew conclusions.

She had not realized that the riches of Maloresse extended so far beyond the walls of Amika's Desire. And she wondered—not for the first time—how a people so prosperous had failed to conquer a realm as poor as Belleger.

But then Queen Rubia announced wearily, as if she were already tired of traveling, "It is not all like this, girls."

At once, Princess Estie settled herself to listen.

When Demure and Immure had squabbled themselves back to their seats, their mother explained.

"We are on the west road. Around us, every family of wealth or birth has staked its claim. We have already passed my own home. But long ago, the kings of Amika decreed that any invasion from Belleger, however inconceivable it might be, must not threaten the riches of Maloresse. For that reason, the habitations of the common people are now primarily in the south, and the poor are *only* permitted there. And beyond them, farther south, are the encampments and training-fields of the army.

"The south road is more direct. Our route will add a day to our journey. But your father commanded us to it. He does not wish you to witness the ugliness of those who are made victims by our old war. Those who do not gain from it." After a moment, she added, "Or do not benefit from trade with the Nuuri."

The girls were shocked. "Nonsense, Mother!" protested Immure. She and Demure shook their heads, disarranging their ringlets; enjoying the drama of their own emotions. "Maloresse is rich!" added Demure. "Everyone knows that."

The Queen sighed. "Everyone you know is rich. Amika is not. War impoverishes a hundred for every one who profits."

Patting Estie's hand, Queen Rubia sank back into her corner of the coach and closed her eyes.

Princess Estie was mildly shocked herself. But she was not surprised. King Smegin had never mentioned his policy of using Amika's poor as a buffer to protect the more privileged inhabitants of Maloresse. A year ago, she would have felt sure that he had good reasons. She would have teased or badgered him until he explained them. But the process of negotiating peace with Belleger had made her aware that she, too, had been buffered, if in a different fashion. At times during those sessions, her ignorance of her homeland had dismayed her. The debates taught her more about the costs of the war than her father had ever told her.

Hoping for a few moments of privacy, she waited until her sisters had resumed their chirping at the windows. While their commentary grew more caustic as the scale of wealth around them diminished, she leaned close to her mother. In a low voice, she asked, "Where are the hospitals, Mother? Are they with the army in the south?"

She meant, Do they also buffer Maloresse from attack?

The Queen opened her eyes, raised an eyebrow. Almost without a sound, she countered, "Hospitals?"

"The harm of our battles must be extreme," explained Estie quietly. "If it were not, we would surely have conquered Belleger. There must be many grievously wounded, many maimed. Where are they given care?"

Queen Rubia winced. For a moment, Estie feared that she would not answer. But then the Queen shook herself. Whispering as if she were taking a great risk and did not want to be overheard, she said, "There are none, Daughter."

What, *none*? Suddenly, there was not enough air in the coach. The unevenness of the roadway seemed to jostle Princess Estie off balance. None for the men who came back injured or dying from King Smegin's war?

"You are a woman now, not a child," continued her mother. "You must live in the world as it is, not as your father wishes you to believe. There are no hospitals because there are no wounded. At your father's command, our Magisters kill them all after every battle." Although her voice was barely audible, she sat forward, and her manner sharpened. "Your maids would have told you, if you had thought to ask. It has been the custom of Amika's kings for many years."

Estie felt the reprimand. In dismay, she breathed the words, "But why?"

Why would the King order his own men killed?

The Queen slumped again. "He says that he does not want Amikans captured and tortured. He says that Belleger's cruelty is terrible. But you will soon marry Prince Bifalt. You will be able to form your own opinion."

A year ago, Estie would have believed that explanation. She had been taught that Bellegerins were capable of any atrocity. But since then, she had spent time in Prince Bifalt's presence, if not in his company. As far as she knew, no Amikan except Commander Forguile had as many scruples as the Prince. And her mother's oblique comments warned her to think more clearly about her father.

More than once, she had seen him use the Decimate of lightning to savage men who displeased him.

After a long moment, she murmured, "If Father allowed his men to be tortured, what would they reveal? What secret does Amika have that must be kept from Belleger?"

Queen Rubia cast a sharp glance toward Demure and Immure. But they were still talking at each other, too engrossed in their own interests to eavesdrop. To Estie, the Queen whispered brusquely, "Did. Not does. The secret is known now."

Estie stifled an impulse to shout. Forcing herself to silence, she mouthed, What secret?

"The Last Repository," answered the Queen: a mere breath of sound. There was a glisten in her eyes that may have been anger or sympathy. "Your father learned of it from his father. Belleger was ignorant of it. Our Magisters killed our wounded to keep the secret. Prince Bifalt was the first Bellegerin to discover it."

For a while, Princess Estie had trouble breathing. The shock was too great. If King Smegin had not made his own motives plain to her when Prince Bifalt first came to Amika's Desire, she would have doubted her mother. But the King had explained in terms she could not fail to understand that he was willing to accept peace with Belleger for the same reason that he was prepared to force her to marry the Prince: not to save Amikan lives or Amika's future, but to regain his talent for sorcery. Now she had no reason to question anything the Queen told her.

Later, Princess Estie realized that she should have been able to name King Smegin's secret for herself. Why else had he arranged to ambush Prince Bifalt's quest for the library? An attack like that would have been futile if the Prince had already known that the Last Repository existed; if his search had been anything more than a desperate gamble.

In retrospect, Estie was horrified by what her father had done. But once again, she was not surprised. He was in fact the man he had revealed to her in his chambers after his one conference with Prince Bifalt. The only real surprise was the scale of his obsession.

The Queen, on the other hand—

There the surprise was not what she had revealed about her husband, but rather what she had revealed about herself. No doubt King Smegin would have been furious at his wife. In contrast, Estie was grateful for every sign that her mother was not as empty-headed as she commonly seemed. Now Estie imagined that behind Queen Rubia's apparently exclusive fixation on matters of appearance and ceremony was a woman who was not loved by her husband, and did not love him: a woman with the stature of a Queen who had no role in Amika's life because her husband's dealings were repugnant to her. Her vacuity was a mask. It protected her from a man who might have burned the flesh from her bones if she had stood in his way.

Or perhaps not. Princess Estie was overwrought: shaken by what she had learned about her father, alarmed by her coming marriage, uncertain of her ability to straddle the gulf between Amika and Belleger. She may have been exaggerating her mother's circumstances. But she could too easily see herself in a similar position, unloved and unloving, with no part to play except that of a pawn between two natural enemies with entirely different reasons for making peace.

For her, the ride to the Open Hand threatened to drag on forever, and yet could not drag on long enough.

On the far side of the Line River, the bride-to-be with her family, her retinue, and her guards were met by a company of mounted Bellegerin riflemen.

This escort had been discussed and agreed fortnights ago. Nevertheless the two groups of men bristled with hostility as they faced each other. The Amikan commander had his orders, but now he questioned them. He and his soldiers could not stand against rifles.

Involuntarily, Princess Estie remembered her fear when King Smegin had told her that she had to marry Prince Bifalt—and marry him in Belleger's Fist. She had imagined that the offer of peace was a trick to lure her into Belleger, where she could be killed.

But then the captain of the Bellegerins dismounted. He was a young man, surely no more than twenty, but he bore himself with an air of earned confidence and calm as he approached the commander. The Amikan commander remained in his saddle: an act of overt rudeness which failed to trouble the Bellegerin. They spoke with or at each other. Estie could not hear them clearly; but she thought that the commander used the word *treachery*. The captain's reply resembled a vow of some kind. After a few moments, the commander nodded. While he addressed his men, telling them what he had decided, the Bellegerin captain returned to his horse.

Before the Queen could summon him, their commander trotted his mount to the side of the coach. At once, Demure and Immure beleaguered him with questions, working themselves up into frenzies of fright. However, their mother silenced them with a severity that none of her daughters had heard from her before. As soon as Estie's sisters retreated, trembling, to the far side of the coach, Queen Rubia leaned out of her window to hear the commander's report.

By an act of will, Princess Estie forced herself to sit passively and await the commander's verdict.

"Majesty," said the man grimly, "this escort was agreed. Numbers, location, purpose, even weapons. Words on paper. Easily ignored. I do not trust them.

"But the Bellegerin captain is Prince Jaspid, King Abbator's second son, Prince Bifalt's brother."

Instantly, Demure and Immure forgot their fright. Another Prince! Flinging themselves to the windows, they gaped at the riflemen.

The commander rolled his eyes. To the Queen, he continued, "Our spies know his reputation. He is said to be honorable. Unbeaten in combat. Held in awe. And fiercely loyal. He has promised me his life if he fails to earn my trust.

"Majesty, his instructions from his father are explicit. *Our* men are responsible for your safety. His are responsible for *ours*. They will guide us, but they are mine to command."

Queen Rubia inclined her head. "I am content, Commander. No Bellegerin can think well of us, but they will not act against the wishes of their King."

"As you say, Majesty." Dismissed, the man rode away to organize his soldiers—and Prince Jaspid's.

Demure and Immure sighed as if they were smitten. As one, they declared that Prince Jaspid was much better looking than Prince Bifalt. More handsome in every way. *And* unbeaten in combat. "You should marry *him*, Estie," added Immure. "He is held in awe. *Your* prince is too common."

Their mother's response was an entirely different kind of sigh.

Estie said nothing; but she permitted herself a private smile. Watching Prince Bifalt while he negotiated his alliance with Amika, she had come to believe that his desire for peace was sincere. He would not jeopardize it by harming her—or by permitting her to be harmed. And any man who could make her tremble simply by meeting her gaze was far from common.

The Queen may have been impatient with her younger daughters. With surprise, Princess Estie found herself feeling impatient for the end of her journey.

But the passage from Maloresse to the Open Hand could not be hurried. The route commanded by King Smegin had added a day; and two nights of heavy rain turned the road to mud, slowing the coaches. Prince Bifalt's bride-to-be did not catch her first glimpse of her destination on the horizon until midmorning on the day before her wedding.

By then, Queen Rubia was letting Demure and Immure drink indecorous amounts of wine. Without it, their restless glooms and boredoms might have driven both their mother and their older sister wild with exasperation. Fortunately, they were asleep when Estie discerned the smudge of the Open Hand in the distance.

Surrounded by their double escort, the Amikan coaches approached the city at a slow trot: the best pace that the horses could manage. For a time, Princess Estie's destination seemed to recede, keeping its distance;

but then the towers and turrets of Belleger's Fist became visible against the dark background of retreating rainclouds. Soon the fortifications of the original city began to emerge: the walls and heavy gates, the ramparts, the guardhouses. And she could see that the Open Hand itself was substantially larger than the portion contained by its defenses.

From her studies with her father, whose spies kept him well informed, she knew that the city had begun spreading beyond its walls generations ago. Belleger was dying by migration as the army's demands drew men from farther and farther around the realm; and as the men came to the Open Hand, they were eventually followed by their families, their hamlets, their villages. Fewer and fewer people remained to work the land. This in turn had reduced the growing of crops, the tending of herds, the harvesting of timber, even the mining of metal. By increments, Belleger lost more and more of the labor it needed to support itself. In effect, the realm was already crippled by poverty.

And *still* Amika had failed to defeat its enemy: a fact that had infuriated King Smegin. Some cruel mischance had enabled Belleger to develop rifles just when the realm was ripe for the taking. And then, before Amika had been able to devise a response, all sorcery had been quashed. Suddenly, King Smegin and his people had found themselves comparatively defenseless, despite their prosperity. Now a land that should have crumbled under the weight of its own penury had been able to set the terms for an alliance with its natural conquerors.

As her coach drew near to the outskirts of the city, Princess Estie found that she had paid a high price for the sheltered wealth of her girlhood. Despite her place at her father's side—despite her status as King Smegin's favorite daughter—she had been raised in ignorance. Until she faced the ruined sprawl of the Open Hand for the first time, she had no real understanding of words like *poverty* and *penury*. She had not known what they *meant*.

That changed when she in her grand coach with its heavy escort entered the crooked alleys that served as streets, walkways, and sewers on the fringes of the city.

If there were any merchantries or other places of business in this region, she could not identify them. Every structure was a dwelling.

And all of them leaned against each other as if they had been struck by pestilence. A few of them—a very few—had actual timbers at the corners, or weathered and warped boards in the walls. But most of them—walls, roofs, doors—were made of wattle or some other springy wood that could be woven when it was green. Then the gaps were filled or covered, in some cases with tar, in some with waxed cloth, in most with dried dung. The leaks in their roofs probably filled buckets. The warmth inside may have been less than a handful of candles.

And the smell from the sewers was appalling. Although the coaches hardly seemed to move, their wheels flung clods of mud and excrement at the mounts of the soldiers. The rank odor of ordure filled the air. The assault on Estie's senses made her stomach clench until she was forced to swallow bile.

Startled, Demure and Immure awoke. At once, they gasped, covered their noses, huddled against each other. Fortunately, they were too horrified to say anything that could be heard outside the coach.

Grimacing, Queen Rubia leaned out of her window. In another voice that was new to her daughters, she demanded, "Is there no other road?"

"Highness!" the honor guard commander barked at Prince Jaspid.

Without obvious difficulty, the Prince guided his mount through the tight cordon of Amikans to ride beside the coach. "Majesty." Briefly, he bowed his close-cropped head to the Queen. "I regret your discomfort. The Open Hand is not all like this. The smell will ease as we near the walls of the city proper.

"There are other roads. Several are worse. None are better. This is the most direct."

Queen Rubia held his gaze for a moment. Finally, she said, "Then we will endure it. Thank you, my lord Prince."

"Mother!" wailed Demure. Immure made retching noises, but produced nothing.

Grinning, Prince Jaspid returned to his place at the head of the escort.

For a fleeting moment, Princess Estie wished that she might see Prince Bifalt smile. His brother's grin was promising. It was full of amusement, but there was no malice in it. If her husband-to-be smiled like that—

Apparently, the arrival of coaches and soldiers was an event in this part of the Open Hand. As they labored along the lanes, Estie noticed people hurrying from their homes to watch. The size of the vehicles and their escort forced most of the onlookers to stand with their backs against the dwelling walls, but they squeezed aside to make room for more and more of the slum's inhabitants. Women in tattered skirts and stained blouses, with grime on their faces and knots in their hair; emaciated men draped in whatever rags they could find to cover their stringy arms and distinct ribs; youths who looked like they supported their families by rummaging in middens, or by selling themselves in alleys: more and more of them. And children— Estie felt a different kind of nausea as she stared at little boys and girls, some wearing only loose shirts, others entirely naked, and all filthy. Their bellies were bloated with hunger, but their legs looked too thin to carry them. She had seen children with sparkling eyes in and around Amika's Desire. These here watched her pass with the glazed, gaping gaze of constant hunger. She could have drawn half a dozen of them together without finding one complete set of teeth.

For a moment, her attention was caught by a naked girl with the body of a three-year-old and the aged features of a browbeaten woman. Standing ankle-deep in sewage, the child sucked her thumb as if it gave her the only nourishment she had ever known. Her wide eyes followed the royal coach without blinking.

"Mother!" squealed Immure. "Make them go away! They are disgusting!"

"Hideous!" added Demure. "They are an insult. Take us home! We cannot stay!"

"*Girls!*" For the first time in Estie's life, she heard her mother sound like a trumpet. "Have some *sense*! They are Bellegerin. They can *hear* you!"

Queen Rubia's tone more than her words sent Demure and Immure trembling into a corner. From the front of the escort, Prince Jaspid called cheerfully, "Well said, Majesty!"

Princess Estie of Amika found herself looking back and forth between her mother and her sisters as if she had never seen any of them before. But she knew the truth: at that moment, she saw too much of herself in her sisters, too little in the Queen.

Years passed, however, before she knew herself well enough to realize that her first approach to Belleger's Fist through the Open Hand had been a form of courtship. The plight of Belleger's people had done what Prince Bifalt himself had not: it had wooed her away from her most basic assumptions about the war. It had shown her that *poverty* was not merely a word. It was another name for suffering.

As the coaches and their escort labored toward the city's original fortifications, the condition of the dwellings improved by small increments. First entire walls of planks appeared, then crude cornerstones, then entryways guarded by actual doors rather than covered by sheets of cloth or leather. Some of the structures did not lean. Here and there, a few faded signs over the doors suggested shops.

At the same time, the road gradually became wider. After a while, it began to resemble a street. Its surface had been improved with sand to control the mud. In places, the sewers were deep enough to contain their burden of wastes. The general reek diminished. The travelers were able to move a little faster.

But the widening of the street made room for more of the Open Hand's inhabitants. Soon there were crowds on both sides. They were better fed than the people Estie had seen earlier; somewhat better clothed. They had more energy. As a result, they were more engaged with the spectacle of the Amikan Queen's company. A clamor arose around the coaches: men and women talking to each other, or calling to their neighbors and acquaintances; voicing their reactions. Estie heard a growing swell of anger.

The sound mounted to a roar. An erratic chanting began, a repeated, staggering shout of "Amikans!" as if the word were an obscenity. Individuals yelled, "Pollution!" Others were more candid: "Whores!"

Demure and Immure had gone pale. They sat rigid in their places, too afraid to move.

Abruptly, Prince Jaspid halted the company. *"Enough!"* he roared at the throng. "Are you fools! Do you hope to resume the war? Have you not shed enough of your blood, or lost enough of those you love? Is this your respect for King Abbator and Prince Bifalt, who have given you a chance for peace? They will not be *amused* when they hear how you have treated women who have trusted their lives to us."

Apparently, King Smegin's spies were right. Prince Bifalt's younger brother was indeed regarded with awe. His rebuke quelled the shouting. For a moment, there was complete silence. The only sounds Princess Estie could hear were her own heartbeat and the whimpering of her sisters. Then the noise returned as King Abbator's subjects resumed talking. But now it was muted. There were no more shouts; no more chants or insults. The mood around the coaches and their soldiers remained sullen, but it was not primed with outrage.

"Do you see, girls?" said Queen Rubia gently. "We are safe. The Prince knows his people. He knows how to protect us."

Crying, Demure and Immure flung themselves into their mother's arms and let her comfort them. But Estie sat where she was, hardly daring to breathe. She was frightened in ways that she had not expected. She had told herself that she could tolerate this marriage. She had never considered that Prince Bifalt's people might not tolerate *her*.

She had decisions to make.

She had never dreamed that anyone would ever call her *whore*.

When they passed the gates in the outer wall of the old city, they left the crowds behind. Here King Abbator's guardsmen kept better order. The coaches rumbled upward along cobbled streets between houses that may have been the Hand's humble version of mansions, homes for the King's functionaries and adherents; for merchants who had once been wealthy; for Magisters and ironsmiths who were always needed. Estie saw inns and taverns on almost every corner, a few apparently thriving, most disreputable. At one time, clearly, there had been an abundance of merchantries. Now many of them were boarded shut, empty of goods and supplies—or of Bellegerins who could afford to buy. Those that remained open had a shabby, embarrassed air. Ostlers lounged in the doorways of stables, hoping for work and pay that seldom came.

Fortunately, the sewers here were well drained. As the cobbles made their gradual ascent toward the hillcrest where Belleger's Fist raised its turrets at the sky, the air cleared, leaving behind the noxious fug of the lower city. Even the persistent smells of horse dung and urine were gone, washed away by the recent rains.

Ahead of the travelers, the gates into the bailey of the Fist were open. On each side of the entrance, a rank of guardsmen stood at attention, their helms and breastplates clean, their rifles slung safely over their shoulders. And in the gateway itself waited a man Estie recognized: the elderly Land-Captain of Belleger.

Seeing him, she sighed to herself. She had hoped to find Prince Bifalt there. The taunts and indignation earlier had left her shaken, unsure. She wanted the reassurance of a greeting from her husband-to-be. She wanted to see his eyes smolder darkly when he looked at her, and to hear his worn voice—

Queen Rubia took her hand, squeezed it firmly. As the coach rattled to a halt near the guardsmen and the gates, the Queen said quietly, kindly, "Now it begins, dear. Until this moment, you have been little more than a girl, a game piece. A pawn in a far greater struggle. When you step from this coach, you will be a woman ready to marry. The struggle will be yours.

"Remember who you are. You were not chosen at random. You have power here. Remember to form your own opinions—and act on them. Remember that Amika's well-being is in your care." She kept her face turned away, avoided the pleading in Estie's gaze; the uncertainty. "And remember that your mother thinks of you with pride."

Demure and Immure had been subdued since their earlier fright.

Saying nothing, they stared at Estie. They were too young to understand why their sister had tears in her eyes.

But she did not weep. With an effort, she summoned a smile for the girls.

"Soon, now," she whispered to them as if she were sharing a secret. "Soon you will come face to face with Prince Jaspid, who is held in awe. You will be able to judge his handsomeness for yourselves. True, he is Bellegerin. But you will not let that flaw sway you."

As they grasped what Estie was saying, Demure and Immure began to look more hopeful.

When the coach had rocked to a halt outside the bailey, the Amikan commander dismounted. Formally, he opened the door, placed a stepstool in front of it, then stood aside, ready to offer his hand to anyone who needed support.

Queen Rubia did not. Holding her skirts, she stepped down from the coach with her head high and her lips smiling tightly. On the cobbles, she waited.

Taking each of her sisters by the hand, Princess Estie followed. Fortunately, she did not wobble on the stool. Still, she was glad that an Amikan was there to steady her.

In spite of her increasing anxiety, she could not help noticing how dirty the commander was. In the lower slums, the horses had kicked up quantities of mud and excrement; and the wheels of the coaches had added more. Like his men, he was stained and clotted almost to the shoulders.

As were Prince Jaspid and his riflemen. The Prince, too, had dismounted, although he did not approach. His legs and breastplate looked like he had been brawling in a pool of filth. Until that moment, Estie had never seen the emblem of King Abbator and Belleger, the beleaguered eagle, look pitiable.

At a word from the commander, the collection of maids and servants in the second coach stayed where they were, waiting to be welcomed.

With as much circumspection as she could manage, Princess Estie scanned the area in front of the walls; the gateway and as much as she could see of the bailey; the battlements above her; the companies of her

Amikan and Bellegerin escorts standing apart from each other; the rows of guards. But she did not see Prince Bifalt anywhere. As her heart sank, she felt a growing tightness in her chest. His presence might have eased her fear that her reasons for coming were based on a false belief: the idea that Belleger and Amika could ever achieve peace.

His people would never tolerate her. They had called her *whore*.

Then the Land-Captain came forward, extending his hands. His smile looked more genuine than the Queen's, and there was no reluctance in his kind eyes. When he was near enough, he bowed to Queen Rubia. "Majesty." To Estie. "Highness." To the girls. "Princesses."

In succession, the Queen, Princess Estie, and the girls replied with their best curtsies.

"My good ladies," continued the Land-Captain, "you are very welcome here. I hope you will feel welcome when some of the strangeness has worn off. We have apartments prepared for you, with food, warm fires, water for bathing, and soft beds." He nodded toward the second coach. "Also there are accommodations adjoining yours for your servants. We will make you as comfortable as we can."

Sounding rueful, he added, "This is an occasion without precedent. It deserves Belleger's utmost. King Abbator regrets that he is not here to greet you. Sadly, he is unwell. When we had sorcery, the Decimate of pestilence might have eased him. Its loss dooms him. If he obeyed his physicians, he would not leave his bed. However, his decline is slow. He hopes you will grant him an audience. In two hours' time, perhaps? If that is convenient? He would come to you if he could. Instead, I will escort you to him."

As the man spoke, Queen Rubia's smile softened a little. Acknowledging his speech with a nod, she replied, "Accept my thanks, Land-Captain. You are indeed gracious. It grieves me to hear that King Abbator is not well. He is a man of courage and compassion, I know. What other monarch would send his eldest son and heir to demand peace from his oldest enemy? We are here because we trust him, Land-Captain, and you."

Estie's mouth hung open. She had to remember to close it. Her mother had surprised her again. She had spent her childhood hearing

Queen Rubia talk about nothing except clothes and ornaments and comeliness. Since leaving Amika's desire, however, she had witnessed iron in her mother, and understanding, and clear judgment: qualities she had never observed before. And now she learned that her mother was capable of matching courtesies with a man like King Abbator's Land-Captain.

Suddenly, she felt that she had never truly met the Queen until the past few days, while they were isolated from anyone who might report what Queen Rubia said to her husband.

And she was not the only one listening. Without warning, Prince Jaspid began to applaud, striding closer as he clapped. When he stood, besmirched and foul-smelling, in front of the Queen, he bowed deeply, then snatched her hand to his lips and kissed it. "Well said, Majesty," he proclaimed as he straightened to his full height. "Once again, that was well said."

Grinning, he added, "Who knew that Amika produced such women?"

Another man might have added, Or that King Smegin would marry one? But the Prince did not. He had better manners.

An unforeseen blush tinged Queen Rubia's cheeks. Before she could respond, however, King Abbator's second son turned to Estie. "My brother," he said as if he were suppressing mirth, "is a better man than you know, Highness." His amusement did not imply scorn. His features did not look capable of disdain or malice. Instead, his gaze was bright with appreciation. He was obviously handsome—and just as obviously, he did not take his looks seriously. "If you are half the woman you appear to be, you will make him better still."

With another bow, he turned away; went back to his men.

It was fortunate that he had not kissed *her* hand as well. If he had, Demure and Immure might not have been able to contain their titters.

As if nothing had disturbed her composure, Queen Rubia addressed the Land-Captain again. "But speaking of Prince Bifalt," she said with a hint of sternness, "I confess disappointment. I had hoped that the groom would wish to greet his bride. Has some duty called him away?"

Her tone said, Is this how he tries to secure peace? What duty could be more important than his duty to my daughter?

Princess Estie found herself nodding.

"Ah, Prince Bifalt." The Land-Captain sighed, but without any discernible discomfort. "The man of the hour. He follows his own path for his own reasons. No doubt he considers them good. At times, I confess, they baffle me. But you can be sure that he will make his presence felt when he thinks the time is right. By his own standards, he does not fail any duty."

Then the man gestured toward the gateway through the heavy wall; the passage into King Abbator's strongest fortifications.

"Will you accompany me, Majesty?" he asked. "The bailey has been cleared so that you will not be troubled by well-wishers or other attentions after your journey. You will not be asked to take notice of anyone except myself until after you have spoken with King Abbator.

"And bring your retinue. Let us make them welcome as well. No doubt you will have need of them. Our servants will deliver your baggage to your apartments."

The Queen gave him another curtsy. Again, she said, "Thank you. You are gracious, Land-Captain. My daughters need food and rest. After the noises of the city, I will be glad for quiet."

With a nod, she conveyed her acceptance to the commander of her escort. One of his men opened the door of the second coach; and after a moment, maids and servants began to debark. They were hesitant at first, fearful of Bellegerin rifles; fearful of setting foot in the city, and of entering Belleger's Fist. But soon they realized that Queen Rubia and the princesses did not feel threatened. The Amikan soldiers were as relaxed as they could be in the precincts of their ancient enemy, and every rifleman in sight had his gun hanging by its shoulder strap at his back. Once the Land-Captain had given them his welcome, they came with more alacrity to accompany the Queen.

While he spoke to her people, Queen Rubia turned to Demure and Immure. Taking their hands, she encouraged them softly.

"It is time, girls. Soon we will do what no other Amikans have done for an age. We will meet the King of Belleger, who has caused your father so much consternation. It will be an experience to remember. When we return to Amika's Desire, everyone you know, and many you do not, will want to hear every detail of your adventure. Indeed, they will be amazed by the tale of your daring and comportment."

When she was satisfied by the easing of her daughters' tension, the hints of relish in their eyes as they began to consider the prospect she described, the Queen faced the Land-Captain again, still holding the girls' hands. "We are ready, kind sir," she told him.

Proclaiming himself pleased, the elderly adviser led his charges through the gate and into the bailey; into Belleger's Fist.

As Queen Rubia had said, they were the first Amikans to enter there since the start of the war.

That fact alone was another form of courtship. But when, much later, Estie recognized the truth, she forgave herself for not seeing it more clearly at the time. She had been too frightened to see it.

At the time, however, she was less alarmed than her maids and servants, or even her sisters, at being among the first of her kind to hazard the Fist after generations of warfare. She was more afraid of a realization that had been growing in her since she had entered the Open Hand. Her mother had expressed it for her. *The struggle will be yours.* The time was coming—perhaps in as little as two hours—when she would have to stop letting other people negotiate her future for her: the time when she would have to start speaking for herself.

The time when she would have to confront the dilemma of Prince Bifalt's false belief that he could achieve peace by marrying her.

The Queen had said that she would be glad for quiet; and Princess Estie, too, wanted it. She needed silence and solitude to help her think. But there was none to be had in their apartments. Demure and Immure rushed from room to room, exclaiming in horror at the severity of the furnishings. The maids and servants were busy settling themselves in their own chambers and dealing with the baggage as it was delivered. Queen Rubia herself did not rest: she was in her domain, sorting clothes and ornaments, choosing what she and her daughters would wear to meet King Abbator, and refreshing Demure's, Immure's, and Estie's faces—when she could get them to sit still. And the whole company was hungry. Even Estie found that she could eat.

Full of noise, decisions, and food, the time passed too quickly. Long before Princess Estie felt ready, a polite knock on the outer door announced the Land-Captain.

"Girls!" cried the Queen. "Your hair!"

In haste, a servant went to the door to forestall the King's adviser while maids scrambled to make sense of Demure's and Immure's ringlets.

When her daughters finally satisfied Queen Rubia's inspection, they followed her to admit the Land-Captain.

With a smile of approval, he led them away.

While he guided them along passages so empty and silent that Estie suspected the Fist's other inhabitants and guards were being kept out of sight, the old adviser entertained the Queen with descriptions of how life was managed in King Abbator's keep. Her own soldiers, he said, the Amikan commander and his company, were housed two levels below her apartments. If they were needed, they could be summoned by a rope in the chambers of one of her servants: the rope was attached to a bell in the commander's quarters. And arrangements had been made to give the commander quick access to Prince Jaspid, who had pledged his life to the safety of the King's guests. In fact, Prince Jaspid commanded the household guardsmen, twenty soldiers in all: King Abbator's version of King Smegin's honor guard. There were no riflemen in Belleger's Fist who had not chosen to share the Prince's pledge.

Because the King wished to speak with Queen Rubia and Princess Estie in comparative privacy, explained the Land-Captain, he himself would be the only counselor present. Naturally, King Abbator's physicians would attend him—as would Prince Jaspid and Prince Lome, his youngest son. But the Queen and her daughters would not be asked to meet other Bellegerins until they felt prepared to do so.

Without prompting, the elderly man admitted that he had no idea whether Prince Bifalt would appear. At present, the inheriting son was somewhere else doing something else: he had not told anyone where or what, or indeed why.

Queen Rubia compressed her lips to stifle a reproach. Demure and Immure looked at each other, avoided glancing at Estie, and laughed behind their hands. But the bride-to-be hardly noticed them. Her own thoughts held her. She imagined that she knew why Prince Bifalt had absented himself.

He was reconsidering his marriage.

He had good reason.

For her part, she meant to help him make up his mind.

Then the Land-Captain led them to a set of high doors that spoke of better times. They were of fine wood, and finely carved with the emblem of the beleaguered eagle spread majestically across both sides. Only the hinges and fittings betrayed the decline of generations. Belleger's kings no longer wasted the labor of their servants on tasks like polishing such things.

At the doors, the Land-Captain paused. "When you are ready, Majesty?" he inquired.

"I am ready now," replied the Queen at once. "It is unlikely that my life will grant me a second chance to meet Belleger's King and take his measure."

Smiling, the old man put his hands on the handles and pushed the doors open. Without waiting for an announcement, he walked into the chamber where King Abbator waited to meet his guests.

Queen Rubia and her daughters followed immediately. In Amika's Desire, that would have been an excoriating offense. But clearly the Queen believed that if the adviser did not need to be announced, neither did the wife and daughters of King Smegin.

The room they entered appeared to be King Abbator's private sitting room; but only its size distinguished it from the quarters prepared for his Amikan guests. It was large enough to hold six heavy armchairs and two couches in a comfortable semicircle in front of his own seat. But the furnishings were no better than those in the guest apartments; the armchairs and couches were worn by long use; the woolen rug that eased the chill of the stone floor was threadbare in patches. And the air was cooler here. There were fires in the hearths at opposite ends of the chamber, but they did not cast enough heat. Instinctively, Princess Estie shivered. She expected courtesy until she said what she had to say. Then she anticipated coldness.

On either side of one hearth stood two men. Since Estie recognized Prince Jaspid, she assumed that the other was Prince Lome, the King's youngest son. She had been told that he was two years older than Demure, but he looked younger. He had an unformed air, as if parts of him had been left out when he was made. He was dressed plainly in a shirt and trousers of fine-spun wool. Despite the gloss on his black boots, they had a handed-down look.

Prince Lome's older brother had bathed and changed his garb since the Queen's party had left him. In fact, his short hair was still damp. Apart from the scuff marks on his boots, his apparel matched Prince Lome's. But his demeanor was entirely different. The younger Prince was scowling like a boy who wanted to be taken more seriously than his years and features allowed. Prince Jaspid's grin suggested that he was enjoying himself.

At that moment, Princess Estie learned that her mother had more surprises in her. Ignoring—ignoring!—King Abbator in his seat, the Queen turned to Prince Jaspid. "Do we amuse you, my lord Prince?"

If Queen Rubia intended to claim stature equal to her host's, she did so in a way that would have pleased King Smegin.

At once, the rifleman bowed. "Not you, Majesty," he explained, still grinning. "The situation. It amuses me. You have brought Princess Estie all the way from Maloresse to marry my brother, and he is not here.

"There is no fool, Majesty, like a thoughtful fool. Sadly, Prince Bifalt's thoughts run deep enough to blind him. Any other man would be eager to meet with you and your daughters, but he will not let himself see you."

Estie's future husband had seen her before. She had felt the heat of his gaze. Perhaps she should have been grateful that he was not here. If he were looking at her now, her thoughts and sentences might fray into incoherence.

"For shame, Brother." Prince Lome tried to sound old enough to scold, but his voice cracked. "These Amikans are rude to Father, and you encourage them."

Instantly, Prince Jaspid banished his humor. "Forgive me, Father," he said with contrition—but without any real regret. He did not glance at his brother. "You know me. Take away my saber and armor, and I become a rattling half-wit. I will stop now."

Still King Abbator said nothing. His silence as much as the awkwardness she had caused drew Queen Rubia's attention toward him. It drew Estie as well. Somehow, Demure and Immure contrived to appear respectful without quite looking away from Prince Lome and his more dashing brother.

Backed by two attendants in loose, flowing robes—his physicians—the King of Belleger sat in a plain armchair, high-backed and uncushioned, which occupied a low platform facing his guests. In Amika, he was said to be a tall man, strong, and only a decade older than King Smegin. But he did not look tall or strong, and he could have been much older. Slumped in his seat and his heavy fur cloak, he appeared to be dwindling by the moment. His hands were thin, yet they trembled as if they were too heavy for his emaciated arms.

Like his frame, his face had lost too much flesh. Still, its lines had been cut deep. His full white beard could not hide the erosion of his features. Above the blade of his nose, fever gleamed in his eyes. In his own way, he looked as beaten down as the folk in the Open Hand's slums. His people had paid too high a price for Belleger's war with Amika. So had he.

Now the Land-Captain spoke. "King Abbator of Belleger," he said formally, "I present Queen Rubia of Amika, wife of King Smegin, and also her daughters, the princesses Estie, Demure, and Immure."

Perhaps to compensate for her discourtesy, the Queen curtsied to the floor. Immediately, Princess Estie followed her example. After an instant of uncertainty, Demure and Immure did the same.

Above them, King Abbator braced his hands on the arms of his chair and began trying to push himself to his feet.

At once, his physicians intervened. "No, Majesty," said one of them. "No. You must not exert—"

The King resisted them. "I will stand." His voice quavered, but it had not lost its habit of command. "Queen Rubia has honored us with her trust. She has put her life in our hands, and the lives of her daughters. They have come to seal the alliance. I will rise to greet them."

There was chagrin on the faces of both men; but now they helped their patient upright.

Standing, the King showed that he was indeed tall—or would have been tall, if he did not stoop so much. With one hand, he gripped a physician for support. The other he extended toward Queen Rubia.

Her surprise at his effort and his gesture was evident, but she did not hesitate. Rising from her curtsy, she approached King Abbator to take his hand.

For a moment, he looked like he wanted to bend over her fingers to kiss them; but he lacked the strength, or his physicians prevented him. Instead, he clasped her hand and did not let it go.

"My lady Queen." Estie could hear his breathing rattle in his throat. "You are very welcome. I hope you will be made to feel welcome. In a better world, you would be my sister in rule, if not in blood, and King Smegin would be my brother.

"Offering your eldest daughter to my eldest son in marriage, you grant my deepest wish."

"Majesty." To Estie, her mother seemed flustered. But the Queen quickly found a reply. "Your Land-Captain has been gracious. You are more so. My voice is not heard in Amika. If it were, our war would have ended years ago. We will do what we can—we will do anything we can—to end it now."

Estie knew that her mother's last sentence was an admonition. It was directed at her.

"Thank you, my lady Queen." The fever in King Abbator's eyes glittered. "Whatever transpires, you have blessed me with more than your trust. Your support is a gift I will treasure.

"Now." Finally, he released her. "I see that your daughters do not share your sentiments." In fact, both Immure and Demure looked shocked by their mother's assertions. "I hope the day will come when your younger princesses will think better of me. But first I must speak with Princess Estie." He attempted a smile. "While I am still able to stand."

Queen Rubia nodded. With another curtsy, she stepped aside, clearing the way for Estie to take King Abbator's hand.

Princess Estie's heart beat so hard that she could hardly draw breath. Her time had come to speak. It was now. She had tried to prepare herself for it. But she had not expected the effect of the King's frailty and politeness; of his plain sincerity. He wanted peace as much as Prince Bifalt did. He may have wanted it longer. She trembled as she took her first steps toward the King of Belleger.

Like her mother, she dropped a curtsy. Like her mother, she rose again to accept King Abbator's grasp. But she could not meet his gaze. She feared the heat of illness in his eyes.

"My lady Princess," he began, "you are very—" Abruptly, he stopped himself. "But what is this? Are you frightened?" The rattle of his breathing threatened to suffocate her. "Do you think that I will share my ailment? No, be at ease, Highness. My physicians assure me that my infirmity does not spread. I choose to believe it is an effect of age and woe, not of some pestilence. Your safety is precious to me.

"Come, child." His clasp on her hand urged her in spite of its gentleness. "Look at me. You will see nothing to fear."

Princess Estie wanted to turn away, but the impulse shamed her. Her time was *now*. Was she not the daughter of King Smegin and Queen Rubia? And had her father not taught her to speak? Had her mother not given her guidance for this moment?

Still trembling, but more privately now, she raised her head to King Abbator.

"It is not you I fear, my lord King. It is your people."

"My people?" He raised his eyebrows. His breathing strained. "Why do you fear them? Do they not want peace? Do they not *need* it?"

In a small voice, Estie answered, "When we were seen in the street, Majesty, I was called *pollution*."

She would not say the word *whore*. In Prince Bifalt's presence, she would not have dared to speak of *pollution*.

Those words still echoed in her ears. But they did not haunt her as much as the sight of a naked little girl standing up to her ankles in sewage.

The King's grip on Estie's hand tightened. In a harsh croak, he demanded, "Jaspid?"

"It is true, Father," answered the soldier. Every trace of amusement was gone from his tone. "There were insults. *Pollution* was not the worst."

Glowering, Prince Lome muttered, "It *is* not the worst."

"They will learn—" began King Abbator fiercely. But then a fit of coughing took him. It wracked his lungs until he collapsed into his seat, losing his hold on Estie's hand. With murmurs of reproach, one of his physicians steadied him while the other wiped his mouth.

When the fit passed, and he was able to breathe, he began again.

"They will learn to know you better. Peace with Amika will not pollute us. It will save us. You must not let gutter insults daunt you."

"They did not, Majesty," said Queen Rubia stoutly. "They will not."

Earlier, the Queen had shown a clear understanding of her daughter's situation. Now she missed the point of her daughter's fears.

Strangely, Queen Rubia's miscomprehension steadied Estie. And King Abbator's weakness reminded her of her own strength. *You were not chosen at random. You have power here.* When she raised her head once more, she was able to speak with more confidence.

"Forgive me, Majesty," she said as if she were calm. "I express myself badly. I will try to do better.

"My lord King, I fear that my place here rests on a false belief."

King Abbator's eyes widened. The fever in them made him look alarmed. Rasping for breath, he said, "You surprise me, Highness. How can it be false? Yours is a political match, not a union of lovers. You hardly know my son. And no one has asked for your consent. You are here by your father's choice, not your own. If you should chance to loathe Prince Bifalt, that will be unfortunate, but there can be no blame in it for you. The matter is simple enough. We must have peace. Therefore you must wed."

Princess Estie shook her head. "Let me explain, Majesty.

"Prince Bifalt has cited the oldest history of our enmity. We were told that I must marry your son here, in Belleger's Fist, because it was here that King Fastule of Amika killed Malorie during her wedding to

King Brigin of Belleger. We were told that you believe my union with your son here will help to heal an old and festering wound. In your view, the fault of the war is Amika's. Therefore the gesture of reconciliation must be made by Amika. It is not required of Belleger.

"By your reasoning, my fears are unfounded.

"But your understanding of King Fastule's conflict with King Brigin is mistaken. The truth is that Malorie chose Fastule of Amika, not Brigin of Belleger. King Fastule named his city Maloresse in her honor. The ceremony of their wedding took place in his fortress, Amika's Desire. And it was in Amika's Desire that Bellegerin Magisters murdered her. Our war was ignited by King Brigin's rage and jealousy."

Prince Lome opened his mouth to shout a protest. Instantly, Prince Jaspid swept to his side; silenced him with a hard grip on his arm.

Estie did not allow herself to be distracted. "Majesty," she continued, "my wedding *here* will not ease an old wound." Her voice shook, but she was determined to have her say. "It will feed our hostility. The gesture is not one of reconciliation. It is one of appeasement." His people had called her *whore*. "It will offend the pride of Amika, and the wounds that Belleger has suffered will not be so easily soothed.

"*That* is my fear."

"Majesty," put in Queen Rubia quickly, "forgive my daughter. She repeats what her father has taught her. But old debates over the start of the war are moot. King Smegin has given his consent to this marriage. His consent to the alliance of our realms is absolute. We have come to demonstrate his sincerity."

King Abbator did not so much as glance at the Queen. His gaze remained fixed on Estie. But now the intensity in his eyes did not resemble alarm. It looked more like relief. Her explanation gave him an opening that he appeared to welcome.

"Now, my lady," he replied with as much gentleness as his lungs allowed, "you astonish me. If it were not rude to do so, I might contest your account. We have believed what we have believed for a long time.

"But history is like memory. It changes for reasons of its own. Perhaps the tales told in Amika are mistaken. Perhaps our own are. Neither version falsifies your place here.

"It is true, my lady, that I desired your wedding in Belleger's Fist to relieve the stain of an ancient crime. But I had another purpose as well, one that carries more weight. My son and heir shares it. When I name it, you will grasp its necessity.

"You are here because we wish you to *witness*. To witness, and then to *testify*.

"We want you to see how we demonstrate our desire for peace. We want you to measure what we have lost, so you can be sure that our need for this alliance is desperate. We want you to understand that we recognize the generosity of your presence. We want you to know that we have asked for your father's best because we offer our best in return.

"In addition, we hope to persuade you that our rifles no longer threaten Amika. Your realm has been given the gift of cannon—a gift that we could have kept for ourselves, and did not. Remember that when you doubt me. Riflemen weakened by loss and hunger cannot stand against cannon. Also my son has promised to secure the return of sorcery for both realms when you are wed. Your own Commander Forguile will accompany him. Remember that as well."

King Abbator grew visibly weaker as he spoke, but he did not pause. "And then, my lady, we hope that you will report what you have seen and felt and observed. We hope that you will vouch for us in Amika. Whenever your people question the honesty of our alliance, we hope that you will speak for us.

"My son has taught me an unfamiliar term. It is 'stand surety,' and it implies an acceptance of responsibility. My lady Princess, the war is old. Its effects will endure for years or decades. And while they last, we hope that you will stand surety for us. We implore you—*I* implore you—to give us the credibility of your support, both as King Smegin's eldest daughter and as Prince Bifalt's Princess-Consort."

Queen Rubia had contained herself during the King's appeal. When he was done, she could not keep silent.

"Well said, Majesty," she proclaimed. "I applaud you. You spoke of your deepest wish. Mine has been to hear such sentiments expressed. King Smegin will not do so. He does not have them in him. For that reason, I am doubly grateful to you.

"I am not my daughter's confidant. I am not her teacher. Her father has claimed that place in her life. But if she will heed me now, she will heed you."

For a long moment, Princess Estie remained speechless. What could she say? She had been answered in ways that she did not expect. King Abbator had done more than acknowledge her importance and stature. He had confirmed that she had power. He made it plain that he and his inheriting son needed her more than she needed them.

This, too, was a form of courtship that she did not recognize until much later. While King Abbator watched her with pleading in his gaze, she was only aware that her fear was gone. It had been replaced by a sense of affirmation. She was King Smegin's daughter. If she had power in Belleger, she could use it.

And if the use she made of it did not please her father, he had no one to blame but himself.

During these exchanges, Demure and Immure had grown increasingly restless. What they heard meant nothing to them, and Prince Lome refused to meet their most flagrant glances. Squirming with impatience, Demure finally tugged on Queen Rubia's skirt. "Mother," she hissed. No doubt, she thought that she was whispering. "Is this all they do in Belleger? Make speeches? We're bored."

Before the Queen could slap her daughter's hand away, the Land-Captain cleared his throat. "Perhaps, Majesty," he suggested, "it would be well to excuse the girls. If we prevail upon Prince Lome, he might show them the view from the highest tower. Or if he declines"—the boy made his disgust obvious—"I could escort them myself."

His thoughtfulness ended Princess Estie's self-absorption. It confirmed her impression of him—and by extension, of King Abbator. Turning, she gave the elderly adviser her best smile.

"Thank you, Land-Captain. You are indeed gracious, as my mother often remarks. But there is no need. Enough has been said. We are almost done."

She liked the way she felt.

To Prince Bifalt's father, she said, "My lord King, I share my mother's gratitude. I will marry your son. When we are wed, I will do what I can to justify your hopes."

Ignoring Queen Rubia's surprised approval and the Land-Captain's more discreet approbation—ignoring Prince Jaspid's wild grin and Prince Lome's petulant snarl—Princess Estie waited for the King of Belleger's response.

Despite his weakness, his smile gave her exactly what she wanted.

She had no idea what her marriage to Prince Bifalt would be like. She could not imagine how his passion would affect her, or his severe sense of duty, or his preparations for a war that no one else seemed to fear. But she believed that she would be able to make good use of her role as his Princess-Consort.

She spent the rest of the day in a haze of anticipation. She hardly noticed the courtesies of the Land-Captain, or the squabbling of her sisters, or the warm appreciation of her mother. She counted the passing of time. Nothing else held her attention.

That evening, Belleger's Fist offered a feast to welcome the King's Amikan guests. It was a small gathering. In addition to Queen Rubia and her daughters, it included only Prince Jaspid and Prince Lome, King Abbator's advisers and lead commanders, and a few functionaries, most of whom were the sons and daughters of families that had been prosperous until they had sacrificed their wealth and comfort for Belleger. The Land-Captain presided: the King himself was too weak to attend. Prince Jaspid was merry in the manner of a man who would have preferred to be somewhere else, perhaps training with his riflemen. For some reason, Prince Lome had reconsidered his attitude. Swallowing much of his sullenness, he set himself to learn as much about Amika as he could, a challenge he undertook by seating himself between Demure and Immure, and flattering them until they were both chattering like magpies in his ears. Princess Estie suspected that they were filling his head with the scandals of King Smegin's court; but she did not trouble herself to listen. While the Land-Captain chatted amiably with Queen Rubia, the other guests studied Prince Bifalt's bride-to-be with varying degrees of caution, distrust, and plain hostility; but Estie took no notice of them.

Every thought in her head revolved around Prince Bifalt's absence. His apparent determination to avoid her filled her with so much tension, so much eagerness and trepidation, that everything else seemed vaguely unreal.

She had declared herself to his father. Was her future husband *that* certain of her? So certain that he felt no need to pay attention to her? No need to woo her in any way? Or was he so consumed by his own passions that the mere sight of her might render him incapable of controlling himself until their wedding night? Was he that *hungry* for her? Or—a thought that seemed more terrible now than it had earlier—was he reconsidering their marriage? Had he absented himself so that he could think? So that he could search himself for the courage or the resolve to do what his father wanted?

Trying for calm, she told herself that she could discount one of her suppositions. She had witnessed Prince Bifalt's self-command when he had first met her father. She had seen it often during the negotiations. She had good reason to believe that he could rule any of his passions. Nevertheless the idea that his hunger might be too great to be contained pleased her deeply. Even while she discounted it, it made her tremble with a kind of delicious fright that she had never felt before.

Unfortunately, other possibilities were more plausible. They were also more disturbing. If he was sure of her, he would take her for granted. And if he was unsure of *himself*—

Brigin and pestilence! If he was unsure *enough*, he might not appear even at the wedding.

No, she told herself. No! *That* is impossible. His first words to her had been, *My lady, you are enough.* The man who had said that would not turn away when the whole alliance and his realm's survival depended on their marriage.

Still, the notion that he *might* reconsider had a nightmare quality. When it took hold of her, she did not know how to break away.

By the time the feast ended, her nerves were drawn so tight that she feared they would break if she did not see Prince Bifalt soon.

When she and her family returned to their apartments, she closed herself in her bedroom; but she did not sleep. She spent the night staring at one blank wall of her chamber as if it had been left bare to conceal her future.

Although she did not know it at the time, her state of taut, troubled anticipation played its part in courting her. It forced every nerve in her body to concentrate on the moment when she would finally *see* him.

When the hour came for her wedding the next day, she allowed her mother to dress her in her most eye-catching gown, her brightest jewels. She sat still while her maid made a confection of her hair; applied subtle tints to her face. She murmured approval when Demure and Immure paraded their finery for her inspection, although she did not notice what they wore. Her mother's solicitude, advice, and instructions passed across the surface of her mind and left no ripples in their wake. Whenever someone mentioned Prince Bifalt's name, she trembled inwardly. But she kept her agitation to herself. Outwardly, she was a model of passive composure.

An interminable amount of time passed. Then she entered the hall of the ceremony, took her place on the dais, and seemed to awaken.

Someone had told her that every inhabitant of the city had been invited to witness the confirmation of the alliance; yet the hall was no more than two thirds full. Estie probably should have been able to recognize a few faces, but she could not. However, the Land-Captain was there to preside once again, smiling with placid kindness. Prince Jaspid was there, a soldier from head to foot. He gave her a smile more personal than the Land-Captain's, but did nothing to ask for her attention. At his side, Prince Lome glared at her as if he considered her a mortal insult; yet he, too, did nothing, said nothing.

King Abbator's seat on its low platform had been placed to one side of the dais. Like his sons, his attendants, and a number of his people, he had entered the hall before Princess Estie arrived. Now he sat wrapped in his heavy robe with his physicians at his shoulders. No doubt, he rather than the Land-Captain should have performed the ceremony. But clearly he was too weak.

Not too weak, however, to greet his inheriting son's bride with another of the unconflicted smiles that had touched her heart the previous day.

Then, when the Land-Captain had asked for and received silence, Prince Bifalt entered the hush. Like a man with stalking on his mind, he came toward Princess Estie until he reached the spot assigned to him by the requirements of the ceremony. There he stopped. But his eyes held her as if she were the only other person in the hall—or in the world.

The dark heat of his gaze seemed to answer all of her doubts.

From that moment on, Estie believed that she was in love. To an extent, she was. But there were other names for what she felt when she married Prince Bifalt. Eventually, she learned them.

The time between her wedding and her wedding night, she passed in a different kind of haze. Superficially, she was present with her mother and sisters. Later, during the wedding feast, she was able to exchange courtesies with some of the guests, observations with others. She noticed what happened around her, and tried to remember names. Occasionally, she attempted a small jest. But in the back of her mind, as in every nerve of her body, she was already in bed watching her husband come to her.

King Abbator could not attend. He had been returned to his bed by his physicians. Friendly and firm, Prince Jaspid was everywhere, reassuring his fellow Bellegerins more by his manner than by anything he said. For the most part, Prince Lome spent his time avoiding Demure and Immure. Believing that they had made a conquest, they pursued him, flirting outrageously. But his attitude had changed again. He dodged the girls whenever he could. And when he felt safe, he drank wine and ale like a boy who only felt alive when he could no longer think.

For this feast, as for the wedding, everyone in the city had been invited. Of course, many thousands of the Open Hand's residents lacked the desire, the will, or the resources to come. Only a few hundred people entered Belleger's Fist for the occasion. But even that number was too many for the Fist to accommodate. Within an hour, the food was gone. Soon after that, the wine casks were empty.

When the hogsheads of ale began to run dry, Prince Lome crept away. But surprisingly few of the other guests followed his example. They had made the effort to come; and, fed or not, they stayed to hear the speeches.

To Princess-Consort Estie, even those people who had feasted adequately appeared distrustful. However, the mood in the hall did not appear hostile. Instead, the crowd seemed willing to be persuaded. After all, King Abbator was a good ruler, easily loved. And Prince Bifalt had risked everything he had in an effort to win peace. He had promised to do more.

From the dais, Prince Bifalt spoke briefly. When he had welcomed his father's guests, and explained King Abbator's absence, he thanked Princess Estie for marrying him. He gave her credit for ending the war. "By her acceptance," he asserted, "she has made us allies." Despite his hoarseness, he had no difficulty making himself heard. "Together, she and I will ensure that peace endures." Overriding lukewarm applause, he added, "And together, Commander Ennis Forguile of Amika and I will ensure that sorcery is restored to our realms."

A grimace suggested that this last promise pained him.

Nevertheless the shouts and clapping that greeted it thundered around the hall. To his audience, the return of sorcery was more desirable, more necessary, than promises of peace.

After Prince Bifalt, the Land-Captain spoke at greater length, detailing the terms of the alliance. Subtly, he emphasized the benefits Belleger would receive and the concessions expected of Amika; but he did not slight what Amika would get, or what Belleger would be expected to give.

His recitation was greeted with silence. He might have been speaking to a hall of stones.

The Land-Captain raised his eyebrows. In a conversational way, he asked, "How many loved ones have you lost?"

At that, a low growl arose from the Bellegerins. Men snarled through their teeth; muttered to each other. Women groaned deep in their throats, or swore softly.

"Then rejoice that the war is ended," suggested the old man as if he were speaking to a small group of friends. "You will return to your towns and villages and farmsteads. The Open Hand will be rebuilt. Fields will be planted, herds and flocks replenished. Your lives will be renewed. To all this, King Abbator has pledged his word, and his honor, and his own life. In Amika, King Smegin has done the same.

"Old enmities are not easily set aside. Concessions must be made. Gifts must be given and received. Peace cannot be gained by other means. But when it *has* been gained, it can be made to endure.

"*That* is what Prince Bifalt has achieved for you. It is what his Princess-Consort achieves for you, and for Amika. If you cannot rejoice, remember your grief. Remember that your bereavements will have time to heal. Remember that with every year of peace your hunger and poverty will diminish. While you do your part, and King Smegin is true to his word, you will lose no more of those you love and what you need to our war with Amika."

Princess Estie watched in suspense until she saw the stones begin to stir. People shifted in their seats. They murmured to each other, and nodded or shook their heads. Some of the faces in the hall lifted in relief. Others were clenched around their distrust. She did her best to remember them all so that she would know who might side with her and whom she would need to persuade. But the crowd was too large, and the faces blurred.

Also every detail of her husband's presence distracted her. She thought that he might express some reaction to the Land-Captain's support, or to the doubts of his people. And she knew what he could have said. "King Smegin will keep his word. I can grant or deny his most urgent wish. He will not defy me." But the Prince did not speak again. With his arms folded on his chest, he sat motionless, keeping whatever he felt to himself.

Throughout the occasion, he had offered her nothing more than bland courtesies. In fact, he had hardly spoken to her; had paid no specific attention to her. But his distant demeanor only whetted her eagerness. She imagined that he was saving everything he felt and wanted for her bed.

At the end of the evening, when the guests had been sent home, she was escorted to new quarters: the Princess-Consort's rooms in their turret, where she would live as Prince Bifalt's wife. They were no more comfortable than the accommodations set aside for Queen Rubia, her daughters, and her servants. But they had been prepared for Estie during the feast and the speeches, with fires crackling in the hearths, and an abundance of lamps and candles. All of her clothes and other belongings had been set out for her. And her maid had an adjoining suite.

She had expected this, of course. Her own living space was one of the terms of the alliance. When she had dismissed her maid for the night, she was more truly alone than she had been at any time since she had left Amika's Desire. Under other circumstances, she might have felt lost.

But her husband would come. That was what mattered.

In her bedroom, she removed her gown and ornaments, her underthings. With care, she washed away the signs and scents of a day spent on formal occasions. Then she slipped her finest night-dress over her head, a thin garment as soft as gossamer, as filmy as gauze. After a moment's thought, she arranged and lit candles by the head of the bed so that Prince Bifalt would see her in a flattering light. Next she blew out the lamps and piled pillows against the headboard.

When she was satisfied with her preparations, she took her place on the bed, sitting propped on the pillows and facing the door. She felt as ready as she could possibly be for whatever her husband craved. After all, she hardly knew him. As a young woman in bed, she did not know him at all.

She anticipated a wait, perhaps a lengthy one. No doubt he had more duties than she could imagine. But the knock on her door came so promptly that her heart stuttered.

Opening the door a crack, Estie's maid announced softly, "Prince Bifalt, Highness."

At once, the Prince entered. For an instant before he closed the door behind him, the Princess saw him clearly by the light from the outer chamber. Apart from his helm, he was still clad as he had been for the wedding and the feast. Then the door closed, and he became a figure of shadows and darkness. Her candles revealed nothing more than his general shape. Fitful gleams from the dying fire in the hearth touched the line of his jaw, the angle of his arms, the bronze of his breastplate. His eyes caught only brief sparks. In glimpses, she saw that his hands were fists.

Instead of approaching, he stood with his back against the door. He may have been studying her. Her heart beat against her ribs while she waited for him to address her. To come closer.

"My la—" Some congestion seemed to block his throat. With an audible effort, he cleared it. "My lady wife. Princess of Amika. Princess-Consort of Belleger. I must speak."

His discomfort startled Estie. With less gentleness than she intended, she said, "Then speak." After a moment, she remembered to add, "My lord husband."

"Highness." He made a growling sound like a snarl of disgust. "I do not speak well. I prefer to remain silent. Many things"—by a glint from the fire, she saw his hands open, then clench again—"would have happened differently if I had remained silent in the Last Repository. But my father commands me to speak. He is my conscience when I have lost my way."

Like a man who intended brutality, he said, "I will leave the Fist in an hour. Commander Forguile has agreed to meet me at the Line. We will ride to the library. If those Magisters have any truth in them—if they are not laughing at us even now—the Commander and I will return with the means to restore sorcery."

Princess Estie sat up straight. With one part of her mind, she understood what she heard. Another part was too shocked to comprehend him.

"In an *hour*?"

Firelight found a flash of ferocity in his eyes. "Hells, girl! Do not make this harder than it is." Then he stopped himself. His whole body receded into shadows. Flicks of light along his breastplate hinted at the weight of his breathing; his restraint. "Forgive me, my lady." His hoarseness made the words sound like curses; but he was cursing himself. "My father is right. I must speak. There is too much of me that you do not know. Too much that you do not know has been done to me."

For his sake, she swallowed her dismay; found a moment of composure. "Then speak," she repeated more gently. "I am your wife." She meant, I am *yours*. "I am also your ally. If you cannot speak to me, how can I be your wife? How can I be your ally?"

Shrouded by shadows, he appeared to bow his head. "Then hear me," he said more softly. "I will try to say what I must."

Still he hesitated. Shifting firelight left his features in darkness. Her candles did not soften him. Before she could prompt him, however, he began.

As raw as the milling of a grindstone, he said, "Understand this, my lady. You are my wife in name. I hope that you are my ally in fact. But I cannot pretend that you have chosen to be where you are. I cannot pretend that you have chosen me.

"I have used you without honor or scruple. I manipulated your father to bring about our alliance. For that, I feel no shame. We *must* be allies. But to manipulate him, I have treated you like an object of barter. This for that. Cannon in exchange for peace. Your hand in marriage for the restoration of sorcery. For *that*, I am deeply ashamed."

Ashamed? Exposed by candles and her thin night-dress, Estie might as well have been naked. *Ashamed?* But she did not draw back or cover herself. Instead she protested.

"But I *have* consented. To your father." In front of her mother and sisters. In front of the Land-Captain and Prince Bifalt's brothers. "I gave my consent."

"Yes," answered her husband out of his private shadows. "You consented. Freely, my father says. Sincerely. It shows the goodness of your heart. And it deepens my shame. But it was—" He faltered for a moment. "Forgive me, my lady. It was an empty gesture. What else could you have done? You were not asked for your consent in a way that you could have refused.

"Do you imagine that King Smegin would tolerate it if you spurned me?" Now Prince Bifalt's voice held a rasp of anger. "No. You have come too far, and the stakes are too high. Especially for him, the stakes are too high. He does not know me. He can suppose too easily that I will ride to the Last Repository alone. That I will obtain the restoration of sorcery for Belleger alone. He has his own hunger for theurgy. I saw it in him when we spoke. And he does not fear the war that haunts me. If you had tried to refuse me, he would have had you married in chains.

"If you doubt me, ask your mother. Ask the commander of your escort. They have King Smegin's orders."

Now Estie wanted to cover herself. Deliberately, she forced herself to remain as she was, visible, vulnerable. The girl she had once been, King Smegin's favorite, would have responded with insults and venom: the woman she had become could not. She knew her father too well. What Prince Bifalt said was true. The only surprise was that he, too, knew Amika's King so well.

She would never forget her father's confession during his last honest hour with her. *I must have my gift.* His oldest passion. *I am not whole without it.* No price was too high for his ability to wield the Decimate of lightning.

He required her consent. He did not need it to be sincere. If she had forced him to coerce it, he would have done so.

Recognizing the truth when the Prince named it, she looked for a way to tell him that he had said enough. She needed time to reconsider her marriage: hours or days; perhaps fortnights. But he was not done— and his anger did not lessen. It made her tremble. His voice had been worn raw. It was familiar with agony. The sound of him as he spoke still had the power to shake her, even when his gaze and his passions were hidden.

"I see that you understand, my lady. Understand this also. I, too, have been manipulated without honor or scruple. I, too, have been used like an *object*. It was done by the Magisters of the Repository. They summoned me, but did not ask for my consent. They allowed the deaths of my men, but did not ask for my consent. They lied to me and misled me, but did not ask for my consent. They said nothing of their desires until they had blocked every possible refusal.

"My own conduct in the library was not above reproach. I lack your goodness. But whether I acted well or ill had no effect. The outcome was assured. I was allowed no choice except consent.

"And the cost to them?" His tone was the scrape of a whetstone along the edge of his anger. "The price they paid for using me? It was nothing." A bursting ember found an instant of flame in his eyes. "The cost to me is my whole life."

Despite her determination to face him bravely, Princess Estie shrank back as if he had threatened to strike her. In her heart, he had mastered her. His voice and even his bitterness had that power. At that moment, he could have taken anything he wanted from her. Her every nerve ached for whatever he might do.

Nevertheless a whimper of fear filled her mind. She strained for breath as if he had used up all the air in the room. She had fallen in love with him—and he did not want her. He would never want her. The things he said could not be a preamble to love.

"Now I say *this*," he continued. "Princess of Amika. Princess-Consort of Belleger. My lady wife." With every word, his tone softened. He was not threatening her: he was trying to persuade her. But she had already been persuaded. His efforts were worse than threats. "I have made promises. Most I have kept. Some I *will* keep, if I live. This is my promise to you.

"I will not use you as I have been used. While I live, never. I will make no claim on your choices, or"—she saw his fists tighten—"on your body. I will not touch you. I *will* not. I will not risk a consent that you may learn to regret. You will go where you wish, live where you wish, do what you wish. Until now, you have been bartered. Now your life is your own.

"I ask only that you honor the terms of our alliance. When war comes to us—and it *will* come—it will threaten both Belleger and Amika. We must stand together." He may have been pleading with her. If so, she could not hear it. She heard only the iron severity of his restraint. His refusal. "As my wife, my lady, my Consort, you are bound to that duty. You have no other."

His words wrung a response from her. She gave it no thought and did not count the cost. "You do not want me."

"Hells, woman!" he cried as if she had cut him deeply. "I *do*. Of *course* I do." He took a step toward her, into the light of the candles; let her see the anguish on his face.

Without thinking, she reached out to him.

At once, he snatched himself back, retreated to the darkness of the door. When he spoke again, his voice was metal.

"I *do*," he repeated. "But not more than I want life for my people. That life depends on you. It depends on your stature in Amika. And to have stature, you must be present there. You must witness and testify, as my father has said. But you must also be loyal to your own realm. You must convince Amika of your loyalty.

"If I claim a husband's privilege with you, how can Belleger believe I have not been seduced by Amika? And if your consent comes from the heart, how can Amika trust your allegiance?

"Eventually, you will become Queen. King Smegin has no other heir. And when you are Queen, I pray that we will still stand together." For an instant, his self-control broke. In that brief moment, she heard his misery. "If you can bear to stand beside a man who has used you as if you were coin.

"In your place, I could not do it."

The darkness around him was absolute. If she had not heard the door open and close, or seen the momentary flash of light from the outer chamber, Estie would not have known that Prince Bifalt had left.

She stared at his absence for a time. Then she collapsed against her pillows like a woman whose limbs and will had failed.

She did not weep. Oh, she did *not*. She was not a woman who wept when she was wronged. But her whole body seemed to burn. She called that fire *fury* because she refused to give it its true name. She would not admit that she was bereft, or that her heart was broken, by her husband's rejection. She *would* not. She was not a child, to complain of it when her husband clung to his honor while she offered herself.

She would insist that she was infuriated, and she would repeat it to herself until she found a measure of calm. After that, she would keep her secret to herself. She would say nothing to anyone. Ever.

Seasons or years had to pass before she understood that what she had felt for Prince Bifalt then, during her wedding and afterward, was not love. It was desire, the enflamed craving of her body and senses for his. Love was something else entirely.

It came later.

EIGHT

THE GENERAL'S RETURN

General Klamath rode hard, trailed by his escort and his recalcitrant mules. Ten days after his visit with Matt and Matta, he had cut short his circuit of southwestern Belleger. Crossing rumpled hills of gorse and bracken far from the sweet grasses of sheep-herding country, he had headed as straight as he could for the Open Hand. And he had pushed the laboring horses hard. Now at last he was in sight of his army's training-fields beyond the outskirts of the city.

First Captain Jaspid's summons had been peremptory. It had also been cryptic. "Come," it had said. "Events are quickening."

It was typical of Prince Jaspid that he had not bothered to offer an explanation. And his messenger had no answers. He had told the man nothing. Despite Jaspid's devotion to his brother the King, he detested his duties. In subtle ways, he often tried to disqualify himself as Klamath's second-in-command.

Still, the General drew conclusions. Something urgent must have happened, but events were not desperate. Even at his most insubordinate, Prince Jaspid would not have withheld details that Klamath needed immediately.

Under a baking sun in the middle of the afternoon, the General reached the crest of a low hill and halted his company.

From that vantage, he had a good view of some of the training-fields. Spread out below him were the circular arenas of packed sand where his soldiers trained in sword-work and unarmed combat; the field of bare dirt that served as a parade ground; and, in the distance, the long ranks of archery butts. The rifle ranges were out of sight beyond another hill where stray bullets would do no harm.

At the moment, the butts were not in use. On the parade ground, a hundred men worked their horses in a series of complex drills, harried by an Amikan commander who clearly knew what he was doing. However, soldiers should have been practicing in all of the combat arenas, and they were not. Instead, Bellegerin and Amikan, they had gathered around one of the circles. Almost two hundred men stood watching the First Captain teach.

General Klamath stepped down from his lathered horse. Giving his reins to his escort, he told the riflemen to report to his command-post. When they had cared for the beasts, they could consider themselves relieved of duty for the rest of the day.

They were reluctant to go. Prince Jaspid's lessons were always entertaining for the spectators, if not for the participants. But Klamath was obeyed.

Stretching the kinks out of his muscles, the General studied King Bifalt's brother.

Jaspid was demonstrating tactics of defense against multiple opponents. He stood surrounded by a wide circle of six men, three Amikan, three Bellegerin. Shining on Klamath's back from its place in the southern sky, the sun clung to the bronze breastplates of his own people. It made the orange headbands and insignia of the Amikans look like blood.

All seven combatants held training swords fashioned of thin strips of wood bound together. The weapons had no edges or points, and delivered wounds no worse than bruises; but they made a satisfying *thwack* when they hit. In this style of drill, a man was considered killed when a sword struck his head. No other blow was an excuse to stop fighting.

Prince Jaspid spoke for a moment, no doubt instructing his opponents. Then he raised his sword and nodded.

At once, the Amikans attacked in a mad rush.

The Bellegerins knew Jaspid better. They approached more cautiously.

In a blur of speed, the First Captain dove between two Amikans; rolled; snapped to his feet. He was fast enough to take out one of them with a rap to the head—but not fast enough to prevent a nearby Bellegerin from hacking hard at his ribs.

"Good!" shouted Jaspid. Undisturbed by the hit, he danced away.

A low growl of disgust rose from the Amikans. There were a few cheers from the Bellegerins—but only a few. The odds were still heavily against their champion. And the First Captain judged the conduct of his own people harshly. The Amikans were far from their homes. Worse, they were often forced to obey Bellegerin officers. In Jaspid's view, the Queen-Consort's soldiers deserved sympathy from Belleger.

Now the Prince moved at a trot, circling so that his opponents could not surround him again. And while he dodged and parried, he talked easily, advising the men he fought, pointing out mistakes to his audience. Soon the Bellegerins and Amikans forgot their reluctance to work together. Forming a loose arc, they tried to trap their tormenter against the edge of the arena.

Jaspid knocked a Bellegerin sword down, grabbed the man's wrist, heaved him against the next attacker. A flick of Jaspid's weapon on the man's ankle completed the parry: the Bellegerin fell, tangled with an Amikan. While his opponents scrambled to react, the Prince whirled through the opening, countering as he moved, and escaped again.

Surging up from the sand, the Bellegerin charged Jaspid, tried to tackle him. A smack on the head removed the man from the exercise.

With only four opponents, the First Captain changed his tactics. Instead of circling, he challenged one man, drove that man back with a flurry of cuts. At once, other combatants moved to take him from behind. But he seemed to feel them coming. He spun in time to catch the nearest of them by surprise. Swinging his sword with astonishing speed, he forced that man to stagger away. Then he leaped aside to engage another attacker. Darting from side to side, he assailed each of his opponents. With cuts and thrusts, he maneuvered them so that they had the sun in their eyes.

But now, instead of talking, he shouted. "Good!" heard Klamath again. And, "Follow up! Follow up!" And, "No! Avoid the sun!"

An instant later, another Amikan was removed from the contest. This time, the Queen's side of the audience watched without a sound. One young Bellegerin cheered. The men near him silenced him with their elbows in his ribs.

Klamath nodded his approval. He had known what the outcome of the contest would be before it began. But he was never sure how his people and Amika's would react when they worked together.

The last three men wiped the perspiration from their eyes, gasped for breath. The sand shifted under their feet, draining their strength. In contrast, Jaspid breathed steadily, moved lightly. He seemed to know how to use the sand instead of resisting it. Despite the heat, he did not appear to be sweating.

As the Prince started toward his next victim, however, the last Amikan dropped his sword and pointed.

General Klamath sighed. The soldier was pointing at him.

The First Captain glanced up at the crest of the hill, then dropped his own sword. He took the time to give each of his opponents a few words of praise or advice. Then he sent all of the men back to their training arenas. While they dispersed, he started toward Klamath.

Trotting like a man who fed on exertion, Prince Jaspid ascended the rise.

With a shake of his head, Klamath walked down to meet him.

As they neared each other, the General felt an entirely private relief when he saw that in fact his second-in-command *was* sweating. The Prince was human after all.

Jaspid did not salute. That suited Klamath. He did not like salutes. Of course, he understood that they were intended to show respect for his authority. But on his side, they had the effect of making him feel excluded from ordinary men. In his mind, he was nothing if not an ordinary man.

Instead of greeting the Prince or asking any of his questions, Klamath feigned severity. "You were lax. I saw four openings you did not use."

The First Captain grinned. He had a look of hilarity in his eyes. "There were five," he retorted. "But a contest that ends too quickly teaches little. I extended the encounter so my students could see at least some of what I hoped to convey."

Klamath masked his approval with a noncommittal grunt. Touching Jaspid's arm, he said, "Walk with me. We must talk."

The Prince nodded like his grin. Together, the two men angled across the hill in the direction of the General's command-post.

The training-fields were off to one side. Ahead of them was the complex of tents that formed the command-post; the sturdier structure of the hospital where cuts, bruises, concussions, broken limbs, and a few accidents with bullets and arrows were treated; and the long, well-built halls of the stables. But where Klamath and Jaspid walked, they were effectively alone. No one was near enough to hear them.

"Your message was incomplete." Klamath ignored the fact that he was addressing a prince of the realm. "Why was I summoned?"

The First Captain considered the question, then said reluctantly, "You should ask the King. He is eager to see you. And he can explain better than I can."

"Hells, Jaspid," muttered Klamath. More strongly, he asked, "Must I order you? 'Events are quickening.' That was your message. What 'events'? How are they 'quickening'?"

Prince Jaspid grinned, this time without humor; but he did not argue. "If you insist, General.

"Magister Facile has heard from the Last Repository. Apparently, she has spoken with one or more of those sorcerers, how I cannot imagine. She claims the library's enemy now knows its location. And he is coming. Signs have been sighted. Belleger and Amika are being scouted. But who scouts us, or how, she does not know.

"King Bifalt told me that much. I have not spoken with Magister Facile. If she had more to report, I have not heard it."

Scowling, Klamath demanded, "Why not? It must have occurred to you to question her."

The Prince made a placating gesture. "Naturally. But I could not. She is gone. She has left Belleger's Fist. In fact, she has left Belleger. She is in Amika with the Queen-Consort."

Stopped by surprise, General Klamath stared at his second-in-command. "Gone? To *Amika*? Why?"

Queen Estie went to her own realm whenever she wished, but the sorceress had never accompanied her before.

Prince Jaspid faced him and shrugged. "I cannot explain it. You must ask King Bifalt.

"This much I know. Five days ago, in one of the King's public meetings, Chancellor Postern confessed that there are *slaves* working on the Queen-Consort's road." To Klamath's sudden consternation, Jaspid explained, "*Nuuri* slaves.

"He also revealed that Nuuri are massing on the border. He believes they are a threat to King Smegin." Klamath did not need to be reminded that Amika's former monarch had withdrawn to a private manor some distance from Maloresse after his abdication. "It is not difficult to imagine," continued the Prince, "that Smegin has infuriated the Nuuri by forcing some into slavery.

"Why he would do such a thing is unclear. The Queen-Consort has gone to Amika to obtain answers. And she has Magister Facile with her, as well as a woman I do not know. Elgart sent her."

Klamath's surprise became dismay as he tried to absorb what he heard. It became outrage. "But not you?" he demanded. "Not the best warrior we have? The Queen-Consort has gone to face King Smegin and the Nuuri. She may face a war. Yet you did not consider it your duty to accompany her?"

At once, Prince Jaspid's eyes kindled. His whole face seemed to become sharper. Every lingering trace of humor vanished.

"Of *course* I considered it. You know me better than that. But the King denied me. The *King* denied me." Gradually, he forced himself to relax. "I did an amount of shouting. He insisted I am needed here.

"What else do you think I should have done?"

General Klamath dismissed Jaspid's indignation. "So of *course*," he retorted, "you sent an escort with her. A hundred riflemen? Two hundred would be better. If the Nuuri are *massing*, two hundred good men with guns might not be enough."

King Smegin was reputed to be a sorcerer. At close quarters, two hundred good men might not be enough to protect the Queen-Consort from her own father, with or without guns.

"Enough, General," said Jaspid. He seemed to sigh. "Save your ire for the King. You consider me lax. Certainly, I am not suited for command. But I am not a fool. I offered the Queen-Consort a substantial escort. She called it an insult. An insult to her, an affront to the loyalty of her people. And by the King's order, I was required to respect her wishes.

"If you believe a fatal mistake has been made, say so to *him*. Otherwise"—in an instant, the Prince recovered his good humor—"you risk insulting *me*."

For a long moment, General Klamath glared at his second-in-command. Then he dropped his gaze. Jaspid was right. Of all the men in Belleger, King Bifalt's younger brother would have been the first to volunteer to protect Queen Estie. Clearly, the King had overruled him. And everyone knew that the Queen-Consort was headstrong, despite her complaisant demeanor. So she had gone to her own realm with only her maid, her groom, and her usual small escort—five men—to watch over her. None of this should have surprised Klamath. The only real surprise was that the Queen of Amika had taken companions, Magister Facile and an unnamed comrade of Elgart's.

Still, Jaspid's report was alarming. An unforeseen conflict with the Nuuri might cripple the King's preparations. If Queen Estie failed—if she died—the alliance might collapse. And Klamath knew of dangers that King Bifalt and Prince Jaspid did not.

The General gathered himself. "As you say, Highness," he conceded. "I will take my concerns to the King. But first"—he attempted a smile—"I must discover what you have done to the army in my absence."

He resumed walking. "Are there other events that your summons neglected to mention?"

At Klamath's side, Jaspid recovered his grin. "Wait and see, General." His tone hinted at amusement. "Other developments must speak for themselves. I cannot do them justice."

Having just vented his dismay and anger at a man who did not deserve them, Klamath swallowed his next questions.

His command-post was an elaborate complex of tents, all interconnected. It included his duty-room, where he could address his captains, or his captains could speak to their men; a smaller conference chamber for more private discussions; and an office with desks for the various clerks and scribes who kept his records and wrote his orders. In addition, it supplied his own living quarters and the First Captain's, personal chambers for his aides, and a modest kitchen for those occasions when he or his staff needed food at unexpected hours.

Beyond the stables, a far larger kitchen and hall fed the soldiers and their officers. It kept the men close to the field where they pitched their tents, as well as to their horses.

As Klamath and Jaspid approached the command tents, one of the General's aides rushed out to meet them. His name was Ulla, and he was little more than a boy, the son of an Amikan commander. But he was fast on his feet, rode like a veteran, and delivered Klamath's orders accurately. When he had first been accepted on the General's staff, he had carried out his orders in a constant state of consternation, and his cheeks were often streaked with tears. But Klamath, remembering his own youth, had divined the cause. In his most reassuring manner, he had told Ulla that the boy's only duty was to communicate orders: he was not expected to explain them, no matter who questioned him. After that, Ulla's relief was obvious, and his confidence improved. Now he was eager to do everything that Klamath asked.

"That boy," murmured Prince Jaspid before Ulla came close enough to hear, "believes the sun rises and sets at your command."

Briefly, Klamath wondered how the boy's father felt about Ulla's devotion. But he did not pursue the question. He was *General* Klamath. Attending to the concerns of the captains and commanders was the First Captain's duty. Similarly, those captains and commanders were expected to manage their men, deal with the residual hostility between

Bellegerins and Amikans. However, Jaspid ignored such matters whenever he could. As he said—often—he was not suited to command.

Then Ulla snapped to a halt in front of Klamath. "General, sir," panted the boy. Klamath had weaned him off saluting, but the *sir* persisted. "You have guests. They occupy the First Captain's quarters, sir. You will find them in the duty-room."

As he had been instructed, he did not explain.

The Prince nodded an acknowledgment. "And have been for some days." He had little use for his bed in the command tents. After a long day of training, he often spent much of the night wandering the streets and alleys of the Open Hand, looking for conflicts that he could defuse with his singular skills. Guests were always welcome to his rooms. "They await your return, General."

Well, thought Klamath. *Developments* that would speak for themselves. Guests fit that description. Perhaps his visits along the Realm's Edge front had been answered.

On the other hand, why would old veterans or new volunteers be kept waiting? Why had Jaspid not placed them in the army?

"Some days?" mused Klamath for the Prince's benefit. "Then I must not ask them to wait longer."

He would talk to King Bifalt when he was ready.

The First Captain nodded. "By your leave, General," he said, assuming an air of long-suffering patience. "Some of our more pitiable swordsmen need sterner lessons."

Without waiting for permission, he trotted away back toward the training-fields.

"Ah," sighed Klamath for Ulla's amusement, "the burdens of being both a prince and the First Captain. They are endless."

The boy's smile made him look five years younger.

Unslinging his rifle, Klamath gave it to Ulla for cleaning, along with his satchel of ammunition. While his aide hurried off, he entered the command-post.

The change from hot sunlight to the comparative gloom and cool of the duty-room blunted his vision for a moment. He saw two tall shapes rise from their benches, but he did not recognize them until one said,

"My old friend. At last," and the other added more crisply, "General Klamath, sir." Then his eyes caught up with his hearing.

Beside one of the tables stood Matt, taller than Klamath, and as strong as an oak, with grey in his flaxen hair and beard, and the purity of a clean sky in his blue eyes. The sight of him lifted Klamath's heart.

At first glance, the man standing opposite Matt might have been his twin: the same workman's build, the same hair and beard, the same eyes. But in fact he was twenty-five years younger. His hair had been bleached to the hue of linen by the sun, and his gaze did not meet Klamath's. He was Mattwil, Matt and Matta's eldest.

When Klamath had last heard of him, he was working with the teams of laborers on Queen Estie's road to the Last Repository. Now he was here?

Smiling broadly, the General shared a quick hug with his old friend. He wanted to greet Mattwil in the same way, but the young man's downcast eyes rebuffed him.

When he stepped back, he noticed that there were no plates or flagons on the tables. At once, he called for the command-post steward; asked Matt and Mattwil what they needed or wanted. But they had eaten well at midday, and were not thirsty. From the steward, Klamath requested water for himself. Then he urged Matt and his son to sit. They chose a bench together. Klamath seated himself across the table from them.

As soon as the steward brought a flagon of water and left, Klamath drank enough to wash the dust of traveling out of his throat. "So," he began. "We are here. 'At last,' as you say, Matt. The sight of you, both of you, is a happy one.

"But the three of us all have tales to tell, and they are all different," if for no other reason than because Matt and Mattwil had arrived from opposite directions. "You know mine well enough, at least in outline. I left my usual southern wandering when I was summoned. But I do not know yours.

"Tell me now. That is why you are here." If it were not, even Prince Jaspid at his most lax would have given them duties. "You have things to say that I must hear."

Matt sat upright. He faced Klamath with the confidence of long friendship. "As you say, General." He made the title into a form of teasing. "You do not need to hear how long Matta and I discussed your visit, or what we said to each other—or to our children. In the end, we agreed that if Belleger is threatened, I must serve.

"You know our family. You will want some assurance that they are safe. Both Matta and Mattin have rifles now, and can use them. Matta fires faster than I can. Mattin shoots with more accuracy than I do.

"But you should know that I bring a message from Matta." Matt's expression hinted at one of his rare smiles. "She wants you to understand that if any harm comes to me, you will answer to her. And you cannot expect pity."

Klamath made no attempt to hide his own grin. "Then I will find the safest possible duty for you. Matta *armed* is more than I can face."

Mattwil sat bent over with his elbows braced on the table and his head lowered, hiding his face.

The young man's posture troubled Klamath. The Mattwil he had known years ago did not sit like that. That man had faced whatever was in front of him squarely.

Klamath set his pleasure aside. "Have you spoken to the King?" he asked Matt. "Have you told him your tale of raiders from the Realm's Edge?"

The veteran's face hardened. He shook his head.

"But you have told the First Captain? *He* has told the King?"

Again, Matt shook his head. "I have said nothing to anyone except Mattwil. I told him only so that he would understand why his mother and brother now have rifles."

Klamath tried to contain his surprise, but his eyebrows betrayed him. "Hells, Matt," he growled. "The King needs to know."

Matt's shoulders lifted in a shrug. "You are his General. It is not my place to speak to him. I speak to you.

"And if I did speak to him, what would he do? What, except wait for you? If he commands the men in your absence, he undermines you. You would return to find your authority divided.

"The First Captain informed me that you were summoned. I chose to remain silent until your return."

For a moment, Klamath, the ordinary man, could not find his voice. The straightforward simplicity of Matt's attitude made his thoughts spin, not with surprise or disapproval, but with ideas. Matt was a veteran: he *understood*. Men spoke to their captains. Their captains spoke to the First Captain. The First Captain spoke to the General. The General spoke to the King. In this fashion, the lines of authority—of *responsibility*—were made clear.

Prince Jaspid took both too much responsibility on himself, and too little. Matt had every quality the First Captain lacked.

And raiders from the Realm's Edge were attacking villages and farmsteads in the south of Belleger.

And the Queen-Consort had gone, virtually unprotected, to Amika. She meant to confront the dangers of enslaved Nuuri and King Smegin and a possible invasion.

When Klamath recovered his balance, he said from his heart, "You did well, old friend. Thank you."

Mattwil raised his head to stare at the General. Clearly, he had not expected Klamath's reaction. Almost at once, however, he bowed his head again, resumed his blank consideration of the planking that served as the table.

Matt only nodded.

"Can I assume," continued Klamath, "that you have not spent all of your time in my absence sitting here? The First Captain gave you the freedom of the camp? You have observed the training, and the men?"

A glint in the veteran's eyes showed that he knew what Klamath was asking. "As you say, General," he replied. "Mattwil was here when I arrived. He and I have had more than enough time to wander the training-fields and watch the exercises."

"Good." Klamath narrowed his concentration on his old friend. "And what have you seen?"

Again, Matt almost smiled. "We spoke of this, you and I. I have seen men improving. Their skills progress, and their precision is"—he gave a second shrug—"almost adequate. Most of their officers are capable.

"But they are not united. Even in mingled groups, they remain apart. You have two armies, General, not one. And they are not well suited to each other."

Now it was Klamath's turn to nod. "So it seems to me."

But he did not say more on the subject. He had too much to chew over with King Bifalt before he took any action. Lines of authority and responsibility. The decisions he wanted to announce on the goad of the moment were all premature.

When he had thanked Matt again, he shifted his attention to Matt's son. "Now you, Mattwil," he said gently. "You are not under my command. I have neither the right nor the desire to order you. But I need to hear your tale."

Mattwil did not move. Watching the side of the young man's face, Klamath saw the muscles at the corner of his jaw knot in refusal.

Leaning back on his bench, Matt looked up at the taut canvas of the ceiling. As if he were addressing the empty air instead of his old friend, he said, "He does not speak of it. I know a sketch of his tale, but I heard it from the First Captain. I did not arrive in time to stand with him.

"He is a man. I do not doubt that he can bear his trials. But I am his father. A father should be allowed to stand with his son."

Thinking, Hells. Oh, *hells*, Klamath murmured, "Tell me."

Matt lowered his gaze until it met the General's. Like a man delivering a recitation, he answered.

"My son is a deserter." He let that assertion hang for a moment before he explained it. "King Bifalt and the Queen-Consort prepare for war. You told us this. Mattwil knew it when he volunteered. And he knew that at such time, men cannot be allowed to walk away from their tasks whenever they wish. Preparations for war require discipline from every man, not just soldiers. Mattwil knew this. And discipline on the road was enforced by Amikan guardsmen.

"But"—Matt sighed—"when my son saw Nuuri slaves put to work on the road—when he saw what Amika had done—he could not bear it. King Bifalt must be told. Taking his chance, he escaped. Alone, he crossed the Line River and Belleger to the Open Hand.

"But then he did not know how to proceed. Who would believe a deserter? Who would hesitate to make him prisoner? He knew only one name he might trust, your friend Elgart, but he did not know how to find him. I fear to imagine how he survived. Mattwil does not speak of it.

"But it seems that Elgart is widely known. Mattwil was able to meet with him in the Church of the Great God Rile.

"When he heard Mattwil, Elgart ran to the Fist. Mattwil was escorted here, where he was given sanctuary in Elgart's name. Soon the First Captain was summoned to the Fist. Then Mattwil was summoned. In the First Captain's presence, my son confessed his desertion. As justification, he said only that he had seen Nuuri slaves made to work by Amikans. He had left his duty on the road to warn Belleger.

"He must have been surprised that he was believed. But Elgart had already informed the King. And earlier in the day, the Chancellor of Amika had confessed the crime. The King thanked Mattwil and pardoned him. Then he freed him from any further service. He was given leave to return to his home."

Matt glanced at his son; faced Klamath again. "He did not go. You see that. With one hand, the King freed him. With the other, he asked Mattwil to stay. 'The times are perilous,' he said. 'Belleger needs every man who knows evil when he sees it, and does what he can. There are other forms of service, if you will accept them.'

"Mattwil replied that he would not serve with Amikans. He would not fight. But he also would not return to his home. He could not tell his parents—" Matt's throat closed. He struggled to speak. "He could not tell his parents that he had turned his back when Belleger was in need."

Abruptly, the veteran snatched the flagon from Klamath's hand, emptied it in three quick swallows. With elaborate care, he replaced it on the table.

More sourly, he told Klamath, "The King was pleased. If a man like King Bifalt is ever pleased. He assigned Mattwil to you. You will not make him a soldier, or give an Amikan command over him. You will offer him a more suitable place, if you have one. If you do not, you will pass him to Land-Captain Erepos. The Land-Captain's need for willing men in the Open Hand is endless.

"All this I have from the First Captain," concluded Matt with an ache in his voice. "Mattwil and I have been together for three days, but he does not speak of his trials. There is a wall between us. My son will not let me stand beside him."

Klamath wanted to reach out and clasp his old friend. Instead, he forced himself to sit where he was, motionless. He knew the wall between Matt and Mattwil. Its name was *pain*, but it had other names as well. Any move that Klamath made toward the father might push the son further away.

Throughout his father's recital, Mattwil sat still, head bowed, elbows propped, eyes gazing at the table or nothing. He hardly seemed to breathe. But when Matt was done, and there was a long silence, the lost young man breathed, "Da." His voice was almost inaudible. "I cannot."

Klamath was a man of ready sympathies and kindness, easily moved, easily grieved. But he was also a soldier trained to hard choices, a veteran who fought and killed when he was needed. In his own way, he was as divided as Elgart.

Deliberately, he folded his hands on the tabletop so that Mattwil could see that they were empty of threats. In that posture of expectation, he assumed what he hoped was a convincing tone of authority.

"Nonsense," he told Mattwil. "You can. You have already lived through it. Talking will only refresh the memory. It will not increase what you have suffered.

"Tell me what you did not tell the King. Tell me what you want to conceal from your father. Let him stand beside you, as a father should. I need to know."

He knew that he was twisting a knife in the guts of Mattwil's emotions. He was not proud of himself. But he was *General* Klamath, and King Bifalt had assigned this young man to his care. He could not obey until he understood what Mattwil needed.

For perhaps a dozen heartbeats, Matt's son sat like a statue carved to sit on that bench. He seemed lifeless. Only the slight lift and fall of his chest showed that he still breathed. Only the throbbing vein in his temple hinted that he still heard.

But then he joined his hands, tangled his fingers together, and tried to answer.

"I heard the priest." His voice was a husky whisper raw with hurt. "He spoke to my heart. He has such understanding— He knows there is war everywhere. He *knows*. It is between us. It is *in* us. It is in *me*. But I cannot find the way to peace. The priest described it. I heard him. But I cannot find it."

Without raising his head, he asked Klamath, "Do you need to know? Knowing will not ease you. It is a hunger. The more you know, the more you will need to know. It will prolong your own war. What you know can never be enough. The priest understands that as well.

"There is only one way to peace. It is the way of Truth and Faith. Knowledge is Pride. Desire is Folly. Only Truth and Faith bring peace. The truth of who and what we are. The faith that we will be sustained by the truth."

Mystified, Klamath said nothing. He had told Mattwil's family days ago that the notion of *gods* made no sense to him.

Matt, yearning to help, only watched his son.

"I will not *fight*"—Klamath was startled to hear Mattwil's voice crack—"because I am done with war. I *want* to be done with it. And I will not serve with Amikans because I have seen what they do. They make me want to kill them.

"I know the truth of who and what I am. But I have no faith. I cannot find it."

After a moment, Matt said, "There are other ways to faith." He spoke as if he were sure, but softly, treating his son with care. "Your family can help you. The love of your mother. The love of your brothers and sister. My love. We can sustain you, if you will let us."

Klamath shook his head. He had chosen his role and did not diverge from it. As if Mattwil had not moved him, he said, "There are other ways to *truth*. I do not believe you know who and what you are. You will not know until you speak of it. It is not enough that you do not want to fight, or to serve Amika. It is not enough that you want peace. You will not know the truth until you tell your tale. You must hear what your tale says about you."

"The priest—" began Mattwil in protest.

Klamath cut him off. "The priest does not know you. Tell your tale. Your own truth may lead you to a better faith."

At last, Mattwil raised his head. Klamath saw fury in his eyes, and scorn, and anguish.

"And *you* know me? We have not met more than half a dozen times. You are my father's friend, not mine. *How* do you know me?"

Unmoved, Klamath answered, "I know that you have not told your tale."

Abruptly, Mattwil surged to his feet. He strode to the far side of the tent, put as much distance as he could between himself and the older men. Facing away from them, he looked like he wanted to beat his head against the wall. If it had been made of wood or stone, he might have done so. But it was old canvas, too soft to cause pain.

"I cannot," he said; pleaded. "It is too much. The Nuuri—"

He made a visible effort to stop, and found that he had already begun.

"You do not know the Nuuri. They are small men, but strong, strong, and their courage does not fail. Hairy men with faces like wolverines. Wearing hides and furs and grime. But their garments were rags, shredded by their overseer's whip. He delighted in whipping them. Often he laughed while he struck."

"There are such men in Belleger." Klamath spoke in a voice of iron. "Such men and worse." But he knew that Mattwil did not hear him. The young man had spent days at the mercy of his memories. Now he was lost in them.

"He pretended to whip them because they refused to obey. I knew the truth. We all did. He whipped them because hurting them pleased him. They did not obey because they did not understand.

"They speak our tongue. We heard their protests. Their confusion and curses. They were too brave to plead, but they told the overseer again and again that they did not understand. They do not work with stone or dig in the earth. Everything we did to make the road, every tool we used— They did not understand.

"So they were whipped. When my crew came to where they worked, they had been whipped for a long time. Fresh blood ran down their backs and shoulders. Older cuts oozed pus, more and more pus. Some of them had cruel burns. They all reeked of infection.

"Yet they were made to do the hardest tasks. Lifting the heaviest stones. Carrying them. Digging holes when the work needed more stone, or when the men lacked latrines, or when their overseer wanted to use his whip.

"And the Nuuri could not escape. We were all guarded. There were soldiers everywhere. Amikan soldiers. Whenever a Nuuri sickened, when he was too weak to stand, the soldiers tossed him into a latrine and left him."

Without moving, Matt strained toward his son. But Klamath ignored his old friend. Rigid with authority, he told Mattwil, "Finish it. Say it all. You need to say it."

Mattwil's whisper was like a wail. "I should have killed that overseer. I *should* have. He *deserved* it. Every Bellegerin there should have risen up. But there were so *many* soldiers. When the overseer laughed, so did they. We were all cowards. *I* was a coward. I should have *killed* him."

There the son of Matt and Matta broke. Covering his face, he began to sob. Great, wrenching gasps were torn out of him by what he had witnessed and failed to stop.

At once, his father went to him. Grim-faced, Matt wrapped his son in his arms. With tears in his voice, he said over and over again, "My son. My son." Then he went further. "If you rose up—if you defended the Nuuri—those soldiers would have killed you. How would that be better? Oh, my son. They might have killed every Bellegerin who rose up. How would that be better? What would be gained?"

General Klamath knew the answer. It was: Nothing. Mattwil could not have stopped what was happening. And the bloodshed, Bellegerins and Amikans killing each other, would have consequences. It would undermine the alliance.

Deserting, Mattwil had made the best possible choice.

Heart-stricken, Klamath left the duty-room, left the complex of tents. He had provoked Mattwil's crisis. He could not comfort it. That role belonged to Matt.

What could the Queen of Amika do against men like that overseer, those soldiers? What could she do against her father, who was a sorcerer?

Klamath was in no mood to talk to King Bifalt. He wanted someone to yell at, and his King was the wrong choice. But he had ridden through hell as often as Belleger's sovereign. Fierce battles and horrible slaughter had taught him to set his emotions aside. They would find the outlet they needed later.

Of course, he could have vented his outrage in his King's presence without fear. A harsh reproach was the worst punishment King Bifalt might inflict on a man who had been his loyal comrade and supporter for twenty years. Still, the disciplines Klamath had learned during the old war served him. There were things he had to say. If he remained calm, he might be able to understand his King's answers.

When he entered King Bifalt's private council room, he found the King alone. Because Klamath had spent so long with Matt and Mattwil, he arrived at an inconvenient time. The King was due for his usual supper with his personal counselors: the Land-Captain; the Purse-Holder; the Royal Surveyor, who planned the restorations of the Open Hand and mapped roads to serve the towns, villages, and hamlets of Belleger; Elgart and Klamath himself when they were available; and the Captain of the Count, perhaps the most vital, certainly the least understood, of the King's officials, the man responsible for numbering every Bellegerin and identifying where they all lived. But Klamath knew his King. King Bifalt would not hurry him. And the King's supper council would not complain when he was late. He was not the Queen-Consort, late on a whim.

There were no lamps lit in the chamber, no fires in the hearths. Instead, all of the windows were open, letting in the day's last sunlight and the evening's fresher air. The result was a comfortable dimness. It revealed faces and expressions, but softened their edges. Night would come soon enough.

King Bifalt was at his desk, a wooden expanse cluttered with a few maps and any number of reports. He commonly worked on many different projects, and now events were quickening. He had received a great many reports. But he looked up as soon as Klamath arrived.

Standing in front of the desk, Klamath took a moment to study his sovereign's visage.

Usually, he took that familiar face with its cut lines, its piercing eyes, and its iron mouth for granted. Now he noticed, as he had once or twice before, that King Bifalt looked younger than his years; perhaps much younger. As Prince Bifalt, he had aged at least a decade during his quest for Hexin Marrow's *Seventh Decimate*. But since then, time had touched him lightly. Another man's features might have crumpled under the strain of so many burdens. King Bifalt's other sacrifices seemed to shield him from the cost of his days.

To Klamath's eye, the King only looked his age when he was watching his Queen-Consort walk away from him.

Dropping a densely written sheet of parchment, King Bifalt rose to his feet. Across the debris on his desk, he met Klamath's gaze. "I am glad of your return, General." A sardonic lift of one eyebrow mocked Klamath's title. But he was not mocking his old friend. He knew how Klamath felt about being in command of the combined army—and about having to carry that weight while bearing an Amikan title. "Your trek troubles you."

Klamath wondered what his King saw in him. "Does it, Majesty?"

King Bifalt shrugged. "How could it not? The library's war is coming. You must have seen signs of it."

Of course, rumors of raids had reached Belleger's Fist before Klamath left on his round of visits. Otherwise, the King would not have required him to take more than his usual escort.

With a private sigh, Klamath nodded. "And the library's Magisters believe we are being scouted. The First Captain told me. What I learned on my road troubles me. What I have heard since my return makes matters worse."

More sharply, King Bifalt said, "Tell me."

Trying to sound composed, Klamath related Matt's description of one specific raid; but he could not keep his bitterness out of his voice. Then he added, "I heard other, similar tales, a dozen or more, but they were less detailed. Those attacks left no survivors."

The boy watched all this, the slaughter of Lessen and Abiga and his sisters. *Days passed before he was able to say what he had seen.*

With an effort, Klamath unclenched his jaws. "Majesty, if we are being scouted, those raiders are the scouts. They come through passes in the Realm's Edge to probe our defenses. If they had any other purpose, they would forage for their people. Food, ale, sheep, cattle. Horses. And if they come only to feed an evil hunger for harm, they would not be content with ravaging isolated farmsteads and hamlets.

"They are scouts. They serve the library's enemy."

Considering Klamath's assertion, King Bifalt frowned. Darkness gathered in the hollows of his eyes, refusing the glow from the windows. Like a man thinking aloud, he replied, "We must believe they serve the library's enemy. We cannot afford to believe otherwise. But they may have another purpose.

"They may be a diversion. Their purpose may be to distract us from a greater peril."

"*What* peril?" demanded Klamath. His King did not require courtesy when they were alone. "There is no sign of the enemy anywhere, except in the south."

Still musing, King Bifalt replied, "The enemy can come against us from the sea. If he has enough power to threaten the Last Repository, he can force a landing in the Bay of Lights."

Klamath understood. This aspect of Belleger's defense had been argued endlessly. Men who were badly needed in the army were hard at work fortifying that bay. "Majesty," he said with as much circumspection as he could muster, "I cannot fear the Bay of Lights. I try, but I cannot. It is an impossible approach. The enemy must use some other route."

Then he felt a flush, as he sometimes did when the King's concentration shifted from his own thoughts to his General. That was often the strongest impression people had of him: his attention had force. Everything else was locked away. Of course, there were small signs. The lift of an eyebrow. The slight clench of his mouth. But the sting of King Bifalt's focus was almost tangible.

"We have rifles, Klamath," he answered obliquely. "If we use them well, they can defend us against raiders. But why were we given cannon? Why did the Magisters of the library go to such lengths to give us cannon? If the enemy comes at us from the Realm's Edge, or from the lands of the Nuuri, those guns will be useless. They are too heavy to be moved quickly. They will never be where they are needed most.

"I believe we have cannon because those Magisters want us to guard the Bay of Lights. They fear it if you do not."

Despite Klamath's efforts, patience eluded him. "Hells, Majesty!" he objected. "That is speculation. The raiders are fact. We must protect the south. Too many of our people are helpless. Too many fields and crops, too many flocks, too many herds. We must respond."

The tightening of King Bifalt's brow implied a frown. "Yes, my friend. We must. That is the essence of a diversion. We must respond. We cannot take the chance that it is *only* a diversion.

"Yet I am reluctant to weaken our forces here. And if these raids are more than a diversion, we may face a war on several fronts. We do not know how many passes there are through the Realm's Edge from the south."

Then his manner announced that he had reached his decision. "Our best trackers, Klamath. Send them in three squads of twenty riflemen. You will know best where they can look for trails.

"But hear me well, General. Their task is to track, follow, and observe. I do not want them to engage. Hells, I do not want them *seen*. We need to know the routes of these killers, and their numbers if we can, far more than we need to bloody them.

"A prisoner or three might be useful, if they can be taken secretly. But no word of our response must be allowed to reach the enemy's servants. If these raids are only a diversion, we will punish them when we are ready. And if they are not, we must conceal our knowledge of the danger."

Klamath loosened the tension in his neck, settled his shoulders. He approved. "As you say, Majesty." Left to himself, he would have taken the same actions.

"Then hear this also," continued King Bifalt. "Understand me." Now he sounded grim. "I want an Amikan in command of each squad."

Now Klamath stared. He could not see the King's face clearly. The dusk in the room obscured it. Dimness seemed to hide his meaning. Did he doubt his own people?

The King answered before Klamath could question him.

"Our riflemen will obey and fight for Belleger. Amikan commanders will obey and be wise to prove themselves. They will be more cautious than our people. If you send only Bellegerins, the Amikans will feel slighted. And if you put our people in command of mixed squads, the Amikans may wish to show that they are better fighters. They may exceed their orders to compete.

"Also, there is this," he added, sighing. "During the years of the war, Amikan spies knew what we did. You have not forgotten how their spy Slack betrayed us. I have heard it said that Amikans are a more subtle people. How else were they able to continue their attack on us when we knew they would come? If Spliner and Winnow had not saved us, every hope for Belleger would have failed."

Memories of that night were written on Klamath's mind. The Amikans had tried to hamstring the oxen. That tactic would not have occurred to him. If it had, he would not have acted on it. It was too cruel.

And yet King Bifalt wanted Amikans to command Belleger's response to the raids?

"Certainly," continued the King, "my lady Queen is more subtle than I am. She used only words to surprise Postern's secrets out of him. I would have relied on my fists and rage."

Like the voice of the gloom, he concluded, "We must learn from our past, Klamath. Amikan commanders will be better able to detect spies and snares than our blunt Bellegerins. Our squads may be ambushed. I want them led by suspicious, subtle men."

That was one reason why Klamath followed Bifalt of Belleger; why he accepted command of the army when he did not want or deserve it;

why he followed orders and trained his men as well as he could. His King thought further ahead than he did. Bifalt's quest for Marrow's *Seventh Decimate* had changed him. He had become formidable.

Like most of Belleger, Klamath would not have said that he loved his sovereign. King Bifalt was too severe, too self-contained. He seemed impossible to touch. But he inspired something more dangerous than love. He made men *believe*.

Men *and* women. Klamath had not forgotten the Queen-Consort. Or that she was in peril.

To the King's waiting silence, he said hoarsely, "As you say, Majesty." He had to swallow several times before he could repeat, "As you say."

Then he took hold of himself. "But there is another matter."

In the dimness, King Bifalt seemed surprised. "My friend, do you hesitate? After all our years together?"

"I do." As it did in battle, a sudden fury beat in Klamath's temples. As he did in battle, he used it: it did not use him. "I told you I have spoken with the First Captain. I know Amika is threatened by the Nuuri. I know Nuuri have been enslaved to serve the Queen-Consort's road."

If he let himself, he would remember Mattwil's sobs.

"This must be King Smegin's doing. Because her people are involved, she has gone to confront the danger. For that, she will need men. But you did not give her an adequate escort.

"Hells, Majesty! Smegin is a sorcerer. He must be, if he can enslave Nuuri. And many Amikans remain loyal to him. But you *let her go* with only Magister Facile, five riflemen, and some friend of Elgart's.

"You say her life is her own. I have heard it often enough. But this is madness, Majesty. You could at least have asked Prince Jaspid to watch over her. But you did not.

"You did not."

King Bifalt's concentration was intense. It seemed to increase. His voice held an undertone that could have been wrath or dismay.

"Her escort is small," he said, "yes. And its captain is young. But she is safe in Belleger. Have you forgotten? Our riflemen accompany her only to the border. An *Amikan* company waits for her in the Fivebridge garrison. Twenty men with a commander she trusts. *Her* men in *her* realm.

"She was right to refuse a larger escort here. I was wrong to offer it. I let my loathing for her father sway me." He may have meant, My fear for her. "Sending fifty riflemen, or a hundred, or two hundred would have been worse than an insult. It would have undermined her authority in Amika, her *autonomy*. Some of her people would have seen it as the first step in an invasion. King Smegin would certainly have seen it that way.

"She is safe enough in Belleger. I cannot protect her in Amika. She must protect herself."

General Klamath understood. But he did not relent. Stiffly, he retorted, "The First Captain tells me she has been gone for five days."

The King lifted an eyebrow. His attention did not waver. "I would call it six."

Goaded by the pulse in his temples, Klamath asked, "Has her escort returned?"

Gathering dusk muffled King Bifalt's features. He seemed to glare at the General. He did not reply.

"Majesty," rasped Klamath, "it does not take six days for men on horseback to reach the Fivebridge garrison and return. It does not take four."

Like Prince Jaspid, the King knew the trick of appearing to stand straighter without moving a muscle. He chose his words with care. "Magister Facile is old. Even a slow pace is likely to exhaust her. My lady desires haste. She may not get it. She *needs* Magister Facile."

General Klamath dismissed that argument. "Six days, Majesty!" he protested. "What will you say if six becomes seven? If it becomes eight?

"The Queen-Consort's life is too precious to risk."

King Bifalt had once said the same thing about Klamath himself, and he was only an ordinary man.

For a moment, the King maintained a turbulent silence. He did not move. He hardly seemed to breathe. Nevertheless his concentration was a thunderhead charged with lightning. When it released its force, it would burn—

Somehow, he contrived to sound calm. "What do you advise?"

General Klamath did not hesitate. "Send Prince Jaspid now."

"Now?" The King did not mask his surprise. "What can he do? She is six days ahead of him."

As if he were inspired, Klamath explained, "He can travel at speed. As you say, her companions will slow her. And she will be delayed in Maloresse. She cannot avoid that. She must make preparations. He may be able to catch her in time."

King Bifalt's focus was like a hand at Klamath's throat. "You do not need your First Captain?"

Klamath forced himself to breathe more slowly. "You know your brother, Majesty. He does not want the post. And I can replace him. I have found a better man. I mean a better First Captain. A veteran of the wars. You may remember him. His name is Matt. He understands what the army needs. He understands what I need from my second-in-command."

In the same tone, the King asked, "Have you promoted him?"

Standing his ground, the General replied, "No, Majesty. I did not know what you would say."

"Then do so," answered the King at once. "My brother will be on the road before you reach your command-post."

For an instant, Klamath felt stunned, not by shock, but by recognition. Here was another reason why he followed King Bifalt; why he served. The King listened to his counselors, even when their arguments had the effect of accusations. If he saw merit in what he heard, he acted on it without hesitation.

An impulse to salute almost overcame Klamath. He needed an effort of will to stifle it. "At once, Majesty."

Turning away from the desk, he headed for the door.

Before he reached it, his King stopped him. "Do you trust me, my friend?"

Startled by the question, Klamath gripped the door's handle to steady himself. Cautiously, he countered, "Have I given you reason to doubt it?"

"No." Outside, a residue of sunshine still held the battlements. Within the chamber, the light was almost gone. King Bifalt spoke like a shadow. "But at times, I confuse you. You may have reason to be unsure of me." His voice held an unfamiliar note of loneliness. "I feel a need to be understood.

"Long ago, the Magisters of the library tried to teach me that I am a lesser being, incapable of understanding their motives or honoring their desires. Before I left them, I promised myself I would teach them to respect ordinary men, men who were not born to sorcery. But I cannot keep my word if I do not prove worthy."

Klamath had no answer. Baffled and hurrying, he left as soon as his King let him go. But as he half ran down the many stairs of Belleger's Fist, he wondered about loneliness.

King Bifalt should have asked the Queen-Consort his question. It was her understanding he needed, not Klamath's. If he could not find it with his wife, he would not find it anywhere.

Klamath did not need to understand. He *believed* in his King. That was enough for him, despite the way his heart was torn.

NINE

QUEEN ESTIE'S COMPANIONS

From the gates of Belleger's Fist, Queen Estie of Amika rode at a quick canter through the streets of the Open Hand in the middle of the night. Led by Rowt, its captain, the small squad of her escort surrounded her and her companions: her maid, Anina; her groom, Blurn; the sorceress Magister Facile; and a woman the Queen did not know, an acquaintance of Elgart's. Their journey had just begun, and already Estie was gritting her teeth in frustration.

She wanted to reach Maloresse in two days. Men like Prince Jaspid traveled that swiftly. So did urgent messengers between the Fist and Amika's Desire. She ached to match them. Her city was not the end of her journey. Her father's retreat—the sanctuary King Smegin had established for himself when he had given her his throne—lay another two days east of Maloresse. If she did not reach him in time to forestall an incursion by the Nuuri, Amika would find itself embroiled in a war it could not afford. Queen Estie's promises to her husband and her people and Belleger—her promises to herself—would fail.

But already her pace was too slow. At least two of her companions could not keep up with her.

Oh, Blurn was hardy enough. She had never seen him tire. And she had no concern for her guards. They only had to watch over her until she reached the Line River. In the garrison that straddled the bridge, a larger company of fresher Amikan cavalry would be waiting for her, kept in a constant state of readiness. She could release King Bifalt's soldiers there. As for Elgart's acquaintance—a tall figure who should have been ungainly—she rode with the fluid grace of a woman in harmony with her horse. The hood of her long cloak kept her features hidden, but the easy flow of her movements suggested that she could go on indefinitely. Like Blurn, she could probably leave Amika's Queen in her dust.

But Anina was another matter. She was only ten years older than Estie, and active enough in her own sphere; but the nature of her duties—and her stubborn distrust of all Bellegerins—confined her to her Queen's rooms. As a result, her joints had stiffened. And Magister Facile had left middle age behind long ago. She walked with a cane, and looked too brittle to go without it. Anina could be left in an inn when she was exhausted, but Queen Estie had to keep Magister Facile with her. King Smegin was a sorcerer. His daughter would need a sorceress to ward her.

So a hard two days to Maloresse would stretch to three or even four. And there the Queen had responsibilities. She hoped to dispatch them quickly. But then the ride to her father's retreat would stretch as well.

Brigin and pestilence! How long would the Nuuri mass and wait before they decided to answer King Smegin's predations? How long would they wait before they swept past his retreat and attacked the crews abusing their enslaved kinfolk?

Queen Estie wished that she had Magister Avail's voice; his ability to address distant minds. She had never met the deaf theurgist. As far as she knew, his inability to hear was a consequence of his power to *speak*. But while she rode away from Belleger's Fist, she considered his deafness inconsequential. She did not need to hear: she needed to make herself *heeded*. If nothing else, she could use sorcery like Magister Avail's to startle and confuse her father; to disturb his concentration when he tried to call down lightning. By the same means, she could reassure the Nuuri. She could give them promises and offer restitution in terms that would convince them.

Sadly, she had no theurgy in her. She had not inherited any version of her father's gift. Her only hope was to reach him—and the Nuuri—in time.

And her journey had just begun. Bitter with frustration, and furious at her father's betrayal, she needed all of her self-command to canter instead of galloping.

Her route through the Hand was the same one that had brought her to Belleger's Fist for the first time; to King Abbator and her wedding. It had changed over the years—and some of the alterations were dramatic. Crushed gravel packed the roadbed. Slate-lined gutters carried sewage away from the streets. Most of the homes had been rebuilt with sturdy timbers and tarred roofs. Some had walls entirely of stone. The people in the city's lower reaches lived in better comfort and suffered fewer diseases. More of them had work. More of them had enough food.

But Queen Estie did not notice the improvements now. She had passed this way many times; witnessed the increments of its transformation. They did not surprise her. King Bifalt's labors on behalf of his people were equaled only by his efforts to prepare for the library's war. Talking to people like Prince Jaspid, Land-Captain Erepos, and Elgart, Estie had learned that Belleger did not love its King. His character discouraged that kind of devotion. Instead, his dedication inspired a loyalty that resembled awe.

When she was not gritting her teeth or restraining her desire for speed, Queen Estie prayed that she had earned a comparable fidelity from her own people. She was going to need it.

She had certainly tried to follow King Bifalt's example, not in her demeanor, but in her deeds. By her commands, dozens of her father's most grasping supporters had been reduced in both prestige and wealth. Of course, they hated her. Fortunately, they also feared her. She ruled Amika's soldiers. When she had ascended to the throne, her first priority had been to convince the army that her reign would not resemble King Smegin's. The war with Belleger was ended. She meant to keep the peace. And if by some catastrophic misfortune the conflict resumed, no more Amikans would be killed simply because they had been wounded. Never again would Amikan Magisters murder Amikan soldiers. To demonstrate her sincerity, she had begun the work of building army hospitals and gathering physicians.

Later, when she was sure of her forces, she had set about using the wealth she stripped from her father's adherents to ease Amika's long-unacknowledged burden of poverty. During her first journey to the Open Hand and Belleger's Fist, her mother had surprised her by saying, *War impoverishes a hundred for every one who profits.* Over the years, thousands of lives that King Smegin scorned had been bettered by Queen Estie's reign. If her father had kept his throne, he might have had a more insidious use for peace. Estie had done what she could to match her husband.

. After nineteen years as King Bifalt's wife, and more than eighteen as Amika's Queen, Estie was satisfied with her efforts. Most of her people were content. Of course, there were exceptions. Clearly, King Smegin and Chancellor Postern had betrayed her. Perhaps some of her father's old supporters connived against her. Her soldiers still resisted their union with King Bifalt's. But most Amikans had learned to trust her. Her duty as their monarch required her to care for them.

What she needed now, however, was going to demand more of them, and of her, than any previous challenge. Beneath her anger and frustration squirmed a fear that she had not done enough to prove herself worthy of her people, or of the alliance, or of her husband.

But eventually her company left the outskirts of the city behind. Now the horses could run safely, without risking themselves on loose gravel, or endangering unexpected people in the streets. They were on the road that Queen Estie intended as a lifeline between the Open Hand, Maloresse, and the Last Repository; and its surface was fitted stone that struck sparks from iron horseshoes. Galloping, she began to relax into the rhythm of her mount's strides.

Time and distance seemed to pass more quickly when she was lulled by the swift clatter of metal on rock.

She and her companions rode hard for the rest of the night. Hours before dawn, they paused at the first of the relay-posts that she and King Bifalt had established to supply fresh mounts for travelers in a hurry, primarily messengers between Belleger's Fist and Amika's Desire. Vaulting from her saddle, the Queen waited, pacing, while her escort and Blurn readied new horses, shifted the company's packs and bundles. Then Estie and her people mounted again and galloped on, running north.

Under a cloudless sky in the early grey before dawn, they came to an inn called, in true Bellegerin fashion, "Beds, Food, Ale." It stood in an isolated spot, a stretch of lower ground in a region of gentle hills with no villages, hamlets, or even farmhouses visible in any direction. On all sides, the inn's vistas were obscured by small copses where newer trees crowded around older oaks and sycamores. Like the grasses cloaking the hills, the trees still held their summer greens, dark and rich mingling with pale and young. Autumn was late this year for both Belleger and Amika: a sign that winter was likely to be harsh.

But Beds, Food, Ale did not need to rely on local custom. Instead, it served travelers who were not in a hurry to leave or reach the Open Hand. As a result, it was prosperous. Merchants, messengers, soldiers, supply trains, tradesmen, families, and functionaries going back and forth between Belleger and Amika filled the purses of its owners. The main building was well made and expansive, with a roofed porch to welcome guests and a second story of bedchambers above the public rooms, kitchens, and servants' quarters. A large barn extended on one side. On the other were a large corral and paddock, both unused at this hour. Behind these structures, a wood spread up the slope of a hill. Perhaps because the inn harvested firewood and timbers there, the trees had a kempt look unlike the tangled growth of the copses.

Queen Estie knew the place well. She had spent the night here on many occasions, when her duties called her to Maloresse, or when her husband's refusal to love her—his refusal to even *touch* her—drove her away. In fact, she had an agreement of long standing with the innkeeper and his wife. Every year, she made a generous donation to their profits. In return, they kept rooms available for her and her escort; they did not trouble her for payment; and they protected her privacy, primarily by keeping her presence and identity to themselves.

In Amika, she did not insult her people by taking such precautions. But in Belleger, she was only the Queen-Consort; and she had not forgotten being called *pollution*. Or *whore*.

Still, Beds, Food, Ale was a welcome sight. She felt safe there. And now savory smoke drifting from the chimneys reminded her that she was hungry.

More than food, however, she wanted a little rest. Perhaps she would choose to lie down for a while before she ate.

As her company approached the inn, a clutch of stable-boys ran out to secure the horses, and the innkeeper appeared on the porch. He was a tall whippet of a man with one walleye that gave him a look of permanent confusion. Recognizing the Queen, he bowed deeply.

"To arrive so early, Majesty," he said with a nice blend of unction and confidence, "you must have ridden through the night." He may or may not have glanced at the Magister and Elgart's emissary. "Some of my best rooms are ready. But even my lesser chambers are comfortable, as you know. Shall I send up food for you? Do you prefer to sleep undisturbed?"

Estie held up her hand to promise an answer. Masking a wince of soreness, she lowered herself from her mount; handed her reins to a stable-boy. Before she committed herself, she wanted to gauge the condition of her companions.

The stranger stepped to the ground with the ease of long practice and toughened muscles. Upright, she stood more than a head taller than the Queen. In the glow of dawn over the eastern hills, Estie noticed for the first time that the woman's hooded cloak was white, the purest white she had ever seen. But the hem of her hood masked the woman's face. The Queen still had not seen her features.

Anina's weariness showed in the compression of her lips, the tight squint of her eyes, the trembling of her hands. Fortunately, she was as familiar with the inn as her Queen. She did not need an invitation to begin her tasks. In a hoarse voice, she demanded Estie's packs and bundles from the riflemen. Her manner suggested that her stamina would last a while longer.

Magister Facile's state was worse than the maid's. She dismounted as if all of her bones had been shaken loose. When she gained the ground, she looked unable to stand without her cane. Hanging her head and muttering to herself, she resembled an aged crone more than an effective sorceress.

Too late, Queen Estie remembered that the theurgist had had a difficult night before this journey began. But there was nothing she, Estie, could have done to spare the Magister. She had to reach her father before he forced a war on her.

She felt a need for a stronger epithet. *Brigin and pestilence* was worse than inappropriate: it had outlived its effectiveness. Experimentally, she breathed, "Gods!" It seemed to fit. If she let Magister Facile sleep at the inn, the old woman might not awaken until evening.

But what choice did Estie have? Could she trust her fate to one of Amika's sorcerers? They knew King Smegin too well. Which one of them would be willing to challenge her father's lightning?

Swallowing her urgency, Queen Estie went to the old woman's side. "We can rest here for the day, Magister," she offered softly. "I will need you. You will be useless if you prostrate yourself."

For a moment, Magister Facile went on mumbling. But then she raised her head. She seemed to glare as she answered, "A quiet hour or two, Majesty." Her voice quavered, but she lifted her shoulders and leaned less on her cane. "At my age, I cannot sleep longer. Then a hot meal, and I will be ready.

"As ready as I *can* be."

Estie studied her, wondering, until she recognized the determination in the old woman's gaze. When she had given herself an inward shake, the Queen turned to address the proprietor of Beds, Food, Ale.

"Thank you, innkeeper." She felt stretched too thin to be gracious, but she tried to sound pleasant. "I value your welcome. My escort will accept it when they have assured themselves that all is well. My companions and I will sleep for two hours. Then we will break our fast in the common-room."

The thin man looked away with one eye, faced Estie with the other. "As you say, Majesty." Bowing again, he held the door open, invited his guests to enter. At once, Anina hurried ahead to prepare the Queen's chamber. Supporting Magister Facile with one hand, Estie followed with the stranger at her back. Of course, Blurn would be given a room as well; but at the moment, he was busy helping the stable-boys.

Before she crossed the threshold, Queen Estie shared a glance with her escort's captain, Rowt. Beds, Food, Ale was a safe place. It had to be, catering as it did to Bellegerins and Amikans of all persuasions, in addition to some locals and a few priests. A reputation for trouble would have done the inn irreparable harm. But hers was not a safe journey. The circumstances of her departure from the Fist had made that obvious. She saw in the Captain's nod that he intended to take extra precautions.

Giving the innkeeper the best smile she could manage, Estie led her companions into the common-room of Beds, Food, Ale.

The large space, cool and companionable, was as familiar to her as many of the halls and chambers in Belleger's Fist. A servant had already lit lamps to brighten the room until the sun climbed high enough to make them unnecessary. Between the wall of windows on one side and the long bar on the other stood more than a dozen wide, round tables with plenty of chairs. At this hour, however, they were unoccupied. The inn's other guests had not emerged from their bedrooms yet. They were probably still asleep.

Nevertheless the innkeeper's wife stood behind the bar, ready to serve ale from the array of barrels at her back, or wine from the inn's discouraging selection. That she was an industrious partner to her husband was demonstrated by the sheen on the bar itself. The wood was as smooth as skin, and it wore so many coats of varnish that it seemed to glow with its own light. Servants presumably kept the floor clean; but the bar was the innkeeper's wife's domain, and she tended it with care.

Acknowledging the woman with a nod, Queen Estie headed for the staircase. As she followed Anina upward, she kept her hand on Magister Facile's arm. Behind her, the woman Elgart had sent along leaned over the bar, exchanged a few soft words with the innkeeper's wife, then disappeared into the back rooms.

With a mental shrug, Estie let the woman go. No doubt she would get a chance to question Elgart's choice later. For the moment, she concentrated on helping the sorceress avoid a fall.

Soon she and Anina were alone in a room across the hall from Magister Facile. The chamber was one of the inn's best in the sense that it held two beds without crowding. It was not luxurious in other ways. But it was well aired and clean, its mattresses did not smell, and there was a leather shade on the window. Anina wanted the Queen to change into her bed-clothes; but Estie removed only her boots in the gentle gloom, then stretched out on her bed and closed her eyes. She had no intention of sleeping. She simply wanted to rest for a while.

Yet only a moment seemed to pass before Anina shook her shoulder. "Majesty," whispered the maid brusquely, "you said two hours. Those Bellegerins will think Amika's Queen is indolent."

Prodded by an unexpected alarm, as if she had been dreaming of ruin, Estie sat up. At once, she pulled on her boots and stood. Again, she disappointed her maid by refusing to put on fresh garments. There was a mirror on the wall, but she did not glance at it. She had no interest in how she happened to look. Other concerns were more urgent.

In the common-room, she found Magister Facile there ahead of her. With Elgart's acquaintance, the sorceress sat at the table farthest from the entrance. In the middle of the room, Blurn was eating a substantial breakfast. Captain Rowt and two of his men had a table near the door. Presumably, the other two were on guard outside.

While Anina went to join Blurn, Queen Estie scanned the other guests in the room: a dozen men and half that many women. None of them seemed unusual. They all had Bellegerin faces and wore Bellegerin dress, apart from a solitary individual who was clearly an Amikan merchant. She assumed that the people breaking their fast had spent the night in the rooms upstairs. Other men stood at the bar, but they had the look of local folk: farmhands who had already brought in their crops, perhaps, or woodsmen with no compelling reason to pass the morning without a flagon of ale.

Harmless, thought the Queen. All of them. Of course, they recognized Magister Facile as a sorceress. But they showed no particular interest. Over the years of the alliance, the slate-grey robes of theurgists had become more common on the road. Estie saw no reason for alarm.

Nevertheless her attention sharpened with every beat of her heart. Postern's betrayal had undermined her assurance. Involuntarily, she remembered Bellegerins shouting insults.

No one who knew the state of her marriage would call her a *whore* now.

A few people glanced at her as she crossed the room toward the Magister and the cloaked woman, but their eyes did not linger. Most of Belleger had never seen the Queen-Consort. It was likely that her stained riding garments and sweat-clumped hair served as a disguise. The Amikan merchant had his back to her and kept his attention on his meal.

Still, she was glad that Magister Facile and Elgart's emissary had chosen a table where they were in no danger of being overheard above the general murmur of voices.

When she was seated, the innkeeper came over to ask her what she wanted. Checking on her companions, Estie saw that the strange woman had only water. She must have eaten earlier. But Magister Facile had a flagon of thin ale and a bowl of porridge. Queen Estie requested the same for herself, then made a pretense of relaxing in her chair as the innkeeper moved away.

She forced herself to wait for a few moments before she said to Elgart's representative, "You are unknown to me. I do not know how to address you."

The woman's features were comely enough—smooth and regular, even rounded—and she smiled easily. Her eyes were the hazed blue of a summer sky when there was too much dust and moisture in the air for perfect clarity. Yet somehow her face seemed to resemble the blade of a hatchet. Instead of answering, she looked at Magister Facile.

The sorceress held her companion's gaze briefly, then snorted, "Foolishness." Her blunt visage twisted into a grimace. "You carry circumspection to extremes."

To Estie, the Magister said irritably, "Majesty, I present Lylin, a most holy devotee of Spirit. You have heard King Bifalt speak of the devotee Amandis. Or if not him, then Elgart. Lylin is her sister in devotion." Returning to her companion, she asked, "Do you prefer 'sister' or 'daughter'?"

Lylin's smile broadened. "Either," she replied in a husky, unfamiliar accent. "Neither. We do not rely on the distinction."

Tapping the floor with her cane for emphasis, Magister Facile added, "Elgart asked her to join us for your protection, Majesty. The devotees of Spirit know you are valued in the Last Repository. They know your alliance with the King is precious. They do what they can for the sake of the library."

For reasons of her own, the old woman snorted again. "I am glad of her company. She can do much that would surprise you. No doubt she will. When Elgart asked you to wait for an escort of his choosing, I feared he would summon a devotee of Flesh. If he had done so, every man here would crowd around us. You would have an unyielding escort, but you could not leave your seat."

Clearly, Lylin found the idea amusing. Her smile took on a teasing cast. When she flicked aside the fine silk sleeves of her cloak, Estie glimpsed daggers.

"The devotees of Spirit and Flesh," said Lylin, "serve the same purpose by different means. Ask Elgart, Majesty. He will explain—if he is bold enough."

Queen Estie did not know how to react. She *had* heard her husband speak of Amandis. He credited the most holy assassin with giving him the clues he needed to decipher the machinations of the library's Magisters. And he was impressed by her skills. But what were such women doing in Belleger? How many trained killers had infiltrated the Open Hand? And were any of them pursuing their secret intentions in Amika?

There were other questions as well. Clearly, the Magister and the devotee knew each other. How? Lylin looked thirty years younger than the sorceress, yet Magister Facile had left the Last Repository almost twenty years ago. Was the devotee older than she looked? Had she been spared the toll of years by sorcery?

On occasion, Magister Facile had remarked that theurgy could work such miracles, in the right hands—

But that strange effect of sorcery held no interest for Queen Estie. She did not suffer under the illusion that King Bifalt would love her if she were younger. She had been young enough when they married, and still he had not touched her.

Finally, she managed to say, "If Magister Facile is glad of your company, Lylin, I am glad as well. But I trust we will not need your protection. The Fivebridge garrison will provide a larger escort. When I reach Maloresse, I can command as many guardsmen as I need."

The devotee lowered her head to shield her grin. "But first, Majesty, you must reach the garrison."

Estie was inclined to take offense. "King Bifalt rules Belleger," she snapped. "I am in no danger here."

He had demonstrated his loyalty—and earned hers—a thousand times. He grieved her. At times, he infuriated her. But she had no patience for people who doubted him.

With a lift of her shoulders, Lylin shrugged the Queen's irritation aside. "Then, Majesty, I will have a pleasant ride, and acquire new knowledge of the terrain. My time with you will not be wasted."

Estie tried to match the devotee's manner. Still, the thought of threats lingered in her. She had been suspicious of Chancellor Postern for years, but she had ignored her concerns. Now an irrational alarm muttered warnings in the background of her mind. She feared that she had not challenged Postern hard enough. Perhaps he had not confessed the full extent of his treachery. Perhaps he had allies. Perhaps—

But her companions could not answer those questions. Deliberately, she pushed them aside. Postern was in the King's custody. If the man had more secrets, her husband would learn them. And he would act on them. She had no cause for concern.

Facing Magister Facile, she turned her attention to a different topic.

"In any case, Magister, I am glad of *your* company. When you announced that you would join me, I was unprepared. I had not thought ahead. Now I understand. I must challenge my father, yet I cannot outface him alone. He, too, is a Magister, as you know. He wields the Decimate of lightning. I have some hope that he loves me. But he loves his gift more. I will need your support, if you choose to hazard yourself against him."

Surely that was why Magister Facile had come?

"Yet in all these years, Magister, I have not learned to name your power. No one speaks of it. I have not seen it unveiled." Perhaps that was why Prince Jaspid had asked her in King Bifalt's name if she trusted Magister Facile. "Now I must know. What is your Decimate? Can it counter lightning in the hands of a man who has made himself adept?" So skilled that he could coerce Nuuri without killing them? "Are you enough to equal my father?"

While the Queen framed her question, the old woman raised her hands to her face, kneading her features as if she could change their shape. When she was done, she had made her mien bland, almost featureless; devoid of expression. Only her eyes, as black as currants in dough, hinted at what she felt.

Keeping her voice low, she replied, "King Smegin's gift is known to me, Majesty. I would rather speak of yours."

With those words, she struck Queen Estie dumb.

How often had Estie asked herself why she had not received her father's talent for sorcery? For most of her life, in the darkest recesses of her heart, she had felt bereft, fundamentally disinherited, because King Smegin's most personal legacy had not been left to her.

Of course, her sisters had been denied as well. That was no loss. Estie shuddered to think of the use Demure or Immure would have made of any Decimate. But she, Estie herself, had been their father's favorite—

She had to force herself to hear what Magister Facile was saying.

"I understand your confusion, Majesty. Your gift is apparent to me, but you are not aware of it. That is the experience of every latent sorcerer. The talent is not recognized by any sign or impulse until it is awakened. The intervention of another sorcerer is required.

"And how it passes from parent to child, from one parent to this child but not to that, or to neither, but to a grandchild instead, is a question without an answer. It passes in the blood. That much is known. But how the blood chooses who will receive the gift, or in which generation— The librarian insists that no book in the Last Repository holds such wisdom. We can only say that the passing of the gift is always unpredictable, and always singular.

"Nevertheless the presence of a gift that *can* be awakened is apparent to anyone whose gift is already alert." For a moment, Magister Facile's tone dripped acid. "King Smegin has known since your birth that you are capable of sorcery. That he kept his knowledge secret tells us much about him."

The old woman might have said more, but Lylin touched her wrist to stop her. "Allow her a moment, Magister," urged the assassin softly. "You are turning her world on its head. She cannot comprehend so much in so little time."

A moment? cried Estie to herself. A moment was not enough. *Days* might not be enough. She would need to reexamine every interaction she had ever had with her father, every vague notion that had crossed her mind while he spoke, every nameless ache he had inspired, looking for hints of the truth about herself: the truth he had concealed. He had betrayed Amika as well as Belleger when he had used sorcery to enslave Nuuri. He had betrayed King Bifalt, for whom the coming attack on the library was as plain as if it had been etched onto his forehead. But to his own daughter—his *favorite*—King Smegin had done something worse. He had kept the essence of who she was from her.

Now she understood his scorn for his younger daughters. He had seen with every glance that they had no talent for theurgy. But she, Estie herself, would have preferred scorn. His unexplained preference for her presence, her closeness, was like a grenade with a fuse decades long. When it exploded, it left rubble in its wake.

Nevertheless her reaction was quicker than thought, despite the breakage inside her. So suddenly that she startled the sorceress, Queen Estie surged forward against the edge of the table as if she meant to fling herself at the old woman. In a strangled gasp, she demanded:

"Awaken me!"

She did not see the consternation on Magister Facile's face. In that instant, only her own fury and desire existed.

"Majesty." A hand like iron gripped Estie's shoulder: the devotee of Spirit. "You will be overheard." The pressure of Lylin's fingers was too strong to resist. It forced Estie back in her chair. "Speak softly."

The warning was a different kind of concussion. With her own outcry still in her ears, Estie remembered where she was. Men and women at other tables turned their curiosity toward her. At the far end of the common-room, Captain Rowt shifted in his seat; braced his hands on the table in case he needed to leap to his feet. Too many people had heard her. Some of them might draw conclusions—

Queen Estie leaned back as if she had been slapped. Dismayed at her indiscretion, part of her snapped, Fool. *Fool*. Another part wailed, Father! You bastard!

Her awareness of the inn's other guests and customers was like fire in her nerves. She did not move another muscle until the people who had looked at her returned to their food and drink, their companions; until the Captain allowed himself to relax.

As Estie composed herself, the assassin said, whispering, "The shock is great. You feel betrayed. You do not understand yet." Her tone became more soothing. "But now you have one of King Smegin's secrets. It may be the greatest of them—and it is yours. Its *power* is yours. Not the power of its use. The power of its secrecy. At times, the secret itself is more potent than the strength it conceals."

Studying Estie's face, Lylin concluded, "It was not Magister Facile's intention to cause you pain. She has more to say. If you can hear her, she will say it."

While the devotee intervened, the old woman rubbed at her features again. When she was done, they wore an expression of concern—and perhaps of regret.

Hardly moving her lips, Queen Estie commanded, "Speak."

"Majesty," began the Magister hesitantly, "I cannot awaken you. I must not attempt it. But the devotee speaks truly. Knowing that you *have* a gift is powerful in itself, especially when your awareness is kept hidden. You intend to confront King Smegin. He can see your ability in you while it slumbers. But he will not fear it unless it comes to life. And he will not fear it *at all* if he believes you are unaware of it. Your secret protects you even when your power does not."

Slowly, Estie nodded. She could follow Magister Facile's reasoning. Still, she *wanted* sorcery. Under other circumstances, she might have wondered why her father had kept her ignorant of herself. He could have raised her to be his ally. But she was too shocked and angry to dwell on that question. She thought she knew the answer. King Smegin had concealed what he knew about her so that he could control her if she ever dared to oppose him.

Now she ached to match him strength for strength; to make him pay for his dishonesty, his selfish cunning. But she did not know which Decimate she would be able to wield. Hers might be useless against his, or simply weaker. Unlike him, she had not spent decades perfecting her mastery of theurgy.

Without moving her head, she scanned the room; reassured herself that no one was studying her, trying to eavesdrop. Then she breathed harshly, "I understand. You must not. Now tell me why you *cannot.*"

She still needed to know the nature of Magister Facile's gift.

King Bifalt wants to know if you trust her. —she may not be what you expect.

The old woman squirmed; rearranged her features into lines of pleading. "Because I cannot name it, Majesty. It is too dangerous. I do not know what I would awaken.

"This is imperative, Majesty. I must beg you to understand it. A gift *must not* be awakened if it is not recognized.

"In Belleger and Amika, only six Decimates are known. They are all you know of sorcery. They can be roused, and roused safely, because they are known. But there is a further restriction. It is that like speaks to like. Like speaks *only* to like. A Magister of earthquake can recognize the same gift in another, but he can only recognize *that* gift. For any sorcerer you know, only his own gift can be identified in others. He can awaken that gift safely because he *knows* it. More, he can teach its uses—and its limits.

"But there are many different forms of sorcery. Surely King Bifalt has spoken of this. Some are Decimates. Some are like Decimates. Some are not. Some only heal. Some are fatal. Some are worse than fatal." With an ache in her voice, she reminded Estie, "I have told you of Apprentice Travail, who can hear enough to destroy him." Then she resumed.

"For that reason—*hear* me, Majesty—even the most foolish theurgist would not awaken a gift he cannot name. He *cannot guess the outcome.* What he rouses may be a holocaust that destroys him and all those with him, a power like the final Decimate. Or it may be a small talent with few uses, such as the ability to grow or prevent beards.

"For the same reason, no sane sorcerer speaks of a sleeping gift he sees but cannot recognize. None of your Magisters have told you that you have a gift. None of King Bifalt's Magisters have told you. They do not dare."

Magister Facile rubbed her face again. Now she made her expression severe. "It is far better for you, Majesty," she concluded, "that your gift and your awareness of it are kept secret until you know what it *is*. You would not thank me if I sent you to face King Smegin armed only with the sorcery to make him bald."

Queen Estie stared. She felt shaken to the core. She could not think—or she had too many thoughts at once. Her conceptions of herself seemed to crumble. Whom could she trust? Every Magister she had ever met knew that she had a gift? And had said nothing? Because she was too dangerous?

Some are fatal. Some are worse—

Before she knew what she was going to say, she asked, "Does King Bifalt know? Did you tell him?"

Was that why he could not love her?

"No!" retorted Magister Facile at once. "*No.* I did not. Others would not. His distrust is too well known. Only a sorcerer who hopes to end the alliance would whisper your secret. That is why I have remained with you when my heart aches for the Last Repository. To protect you— and him."

That small reassurance steadied the Queen. Her husband did not know. She was safe from his clenched loathing, the revulsion he kept to himself because he could not afford to act on it. She took a shuddering breath and began to calm herself. As soon as she mastered her turmoil, she intended to ask more questions.

If my secret is so dangerous, why did you speak of it?

But before she could be clear, she was distracted by the sight of two men descending the stairs from the inn's bedchambers.

Judging by their garb, they were Bellegerin. And laborers by the same measure: boots cracked by hard use, stained canvas trousers torn in places, stiff leather jerkins made stiffer by mud or ordure. One was beardless, young. The face of the other, the older, was covered from the eyes down by an unkempt tangle of greying whiskers. If Estie had not been alarmed by her own outburst earlier, she might not have noticed them at all. She certainly would not have noticed that their hands and necks were clean, or that their skin was too smooth to belong to laborers.

As indirectly as she could, she studied them. If they were not laborers, they must be travelers. But if they could afford to travel, why did they wear those clothes?

Both men seemed to feel her gaze. At once, the bearded one turned his face away. But the younger one looked straight at her. She saw boldness in his smile, and daring. She saw cunning.

For an instant, Magister Facile followed Estie's glance. Then she went rigid. She sat with her back to the stairs; made no effort to watch the men behind her.

Prompted by an instinct of her own, Lylin looked aside, hiding her face with the edge of her hood.

A moment later, the men reached the foot of the stair. Without pausing, they crossed the room toward the door.

"Majesty?" whispered the devotee, a question so soft that Estie barely heard it.

The Queen waited until the two men reached the door; until she was sure that they were leaving. Over the pounding of her heart, she breathed, "I know those men. They are not Bellegerin."

Magister Facile muttered a curse. Quiet as a breeze, Lylin observed, "They wear Bellegerin raiment."

"I *recognize* them," said Estie more firmly as the door closed. "The younger one is—" Her memory refused to release his name. Grimacing, she said, "He is a lesser son of one of my father's courtiers. I dismissed the father when I took my throne. I did not like him. He looked only at my form, never my face. But I have forgotten the names of his sons.

"The other is a Magister."

Magister Facile nodded once, viciously. She had seen—

"His name is Flense," explained Estie. "A crawling sycophant with a craven air. I find him unpleasant. But I cannot dismiss him. Amika needs its sorcerers. Instead, I give him tasks that remove him from Maloresse. He has no cause to be here.

"His Decimate is fire."

Lylin let her smile show. "A tidy plot, Majesty," she remarked. "Those men were here to confirm your presence. There will be an attempt on your life."

An instant flush heated Estie's face. "What do you mean?" Her voice was a croak. "That is impossible." Unthinkable. "We are in Belleger. Some of my father's adherents hate me. I know that. But if they want my death, they will wait until I reach Amika, where King Bifalt cannot hunt for them."

"No, Majesty." The assassin was sure. "I will explain. But you must not alert your captain. Knowing that you are in peril is an advantage. We must seem oblivious until we are ready to act."

Before Estie could challenge Lylin, Magister Facile urged, "Heed her, Majesty. She has skills that we do not."

Staring, Queen Estie took a deep breath; held it to contain the tumult of her heart.

"Consider it, Majesty," began the cloaked woman. "If the Queen of Amika is killed in Belleger by seeming Bellegerins, the alliance will break. Even King Bifalt's resolve will not hold it together. And with your death, Amika will have no choice but to plead for King Smegin's return.

"Consider *that* outcome, Majesty. With sorcery and cannon, he will renew his war against the land that murdered his daughter. He will call it his duty to claim the rule of both realms. If you die in Amika, he will lack any excuse for war. No one will believe you were killed by Belleger."

"But how—?" Estie tried to ask. She meant, How can they threaten me? They are only two. I have riflemen. Magisters can be shot as easily as other men. But her throat closed on the question.

"First," said Lylin, "your Magister Flense will set fire to the inn."

Those words seemed to stop the blood in Estie's veins. She felt a rush of weakness. Set fire— Of course. Brigin and pestilence! Gods! Of *course*.

Traitors who wanted her dead would not care that the inn was full of people.

Abruptly, Magister Facile rapped the floor with her cane. "He will *not*," she asserted.

Her certainty started Estie's heart pounding. It startled her out of her weakness. Helpless to close her mouth, she gaped at the old woman.

More awkwardly, the sorceress justified herself. "You called him craven. No doubt he intended to fire the inn. No doubt he was sincere. But his courage will fail."

That did not sound like the truth. The devotee appeared to accept it, however. At once, Lylin continued what she had been saying.

"And firing the inn will be only the first threat. It is an uncertain tactic. You might escape the flames. To ensure your death, there will be a force of arms waiting." She shrugged delicately. "But not openly. They cannot risk capture. Any one of them might be known as Amikan.

"They will strike from ambush."

Finally, Queen Estie managed to protest, "Captain Rowt. He needs to know."

Lylin's smile suggested relish. "He will. I will speak to him.

"If Magister Facile says there will be no fire, Majesty, there will be no fire. I will instruct your captain. And he will instruct me. I do not know the terrain along our road.

"When I leave the inn, I will use a door at the back. Begin your own departure then. But do not hurry it. Mask your alarm. Exchange a word or two with the innkeeper. Acknowledge a few guests. Smile. Nod."

Estie started to protest again, but the devotee stopped her. "For their protection, Majesty. If the folk here do not know of your peril, they cannot then be accused by Amikan traitors of warning you—or by the King's soldiers of failing to warn you."

Too stunned to think, Queen Estie simply stared at the tall woman. Lylin sounded sure of herself. But there were flaws or gaps somewhere. They pressed on Estie like panic.

How could the assassin know so much about a danger that had never threatened her before, not once in scores of journeys between the Open Hand and Maloresse? Still, the danger must be real. Why else were Magister Flense and that lesser son dressed like Bellegerin laborers? Why were they here *now*?

With quiet intensity, as if she had usurped Estie's command, Magister Facile said, "Go, devotee. We understand."

Her tone said, Time is against us. Delay serves our enemies.

Lylin responded with a quick grin that vanished as quickly. Shielding her face with her hood, she rose to her feet. Her back to the common-room, the other guests and customers, she said distinctly enough to be heard nearby, "We part here, friends. I have duties elsewhere. Travel safely."

With the easy grace of a panther, she disappeared into the back of the inn; into the chambers and passages she had explored earlier.

Speechless with confusion, Estie blinked several times; swallowed at the pressure of questions and fears rising in her throat. Somehow, when she had come down the stairs a short time ago, she had entered a world with only a superficial resemblance to the one she knew. She was the Queen of Amika, the Queen-Consort of Belleger: she had been here many times: she was accustomed to attention and respect: she had servants that she sometimes took for granted. King Bifalt himself treated her as an equal, argued with her as an equal. And he honored her rule of her own realm. Yet now she felt like a child being led by the hand; a child in a thicket who would have torn herself to shreds without an experienced guide who knew the path. She almost flinched when Magister Facile spoke.

"Come, friend," said the old woman. "We must depart as well. We have far to go. We should collect our horses."

Bracing herself on her cane, the sorceress pushed herself upright. Her expression had reshaped itself again. Now she wore the face of a tired woman who had resigned herself to more riding.

That signal, at least, both the Queen and her escort understood. While Estie pushed back her chair unsteadily and stood, the Captain and his men left the inn by the front door, pretending that they had nothing to do with the Magister and her companion at the far table.

Moving at Magister Facile's pace, Estie accompanied her among the tables to collect Anina and Blurn. Then they went to the bar, where the Queen thanked the innkeeper and his wife, taking her time. To maintain the charade that she was someone they did not know, she pretended to offer them coins, which they pretended to accept. To every guest and customer who glanced at her, she gave a crisp nod. Studiously, the sorceress ignored everyone: behavior that was common among Magisters.

When Queen Estie and her companions reached the porch, she received another jolt. Their escort was gone. There was no sign of the riflemen anywhere.

And Magister Flense and his young partner had vanished. They had hidden themselves or ridden away.

An attack could come from the woods behind Beds, Food, Ale.

No. The distance was too great for archers among the trees. It looked too great for a Magister wielding fire. If traitors disguised as Bellegerins wanted a chance to kill the Queen, they would have to come out into the open. They would have to take the risk of being seen; of being recognized as Amikans.

"The stables," commanded Magister Facile brusquely.

Numbly, Estie accompanied her toward the horse barn.

With its many stalls, its hay-loft, its collection of saddles and tack, its abundance of straw and droppings, it would burn more readily than the inn. If the sorceress had judged Magister Flense wrongly—

At the Queen's back, Anina hissed, "Bellegerins. They have abandoned us."

Blurn snorted. "Nonsense, woman." For a homespun man who never tired, his voice was unexpectedly light. "The King would flay them alive. Or the First Captain would."

Estie had to fight an impulse to hunch her shoulders, cover her head with her arms. Instinctively, she held her breath. She was exposed between the inn and the stables. The men who wanted her dead might be desperate enough for recklessness. Fire might fall out of the sky at any moment.

But as the Queen and Magister Facile approached the barn, its wide doors appeared to open by themselves. Inside them waited her escort. All of the horses were saddled and ready.

In a moment, Estie entered the gloom of the stables. With an effort, she forced herself to breathe again.

"Majesty," began Captain Rowt when she was near enough to hear his whisper. "That woman." He was obviously flustered. "The stranger. She asked questions. She gave us orders. I would have refused. I do not know her. We have seen no sign of an attack. But she said—" He choked on his uncertainty. "She said her orders were yours."

"They were," snapped Magister Facile.

The Captain ignored the theurgist. His eyes searched Queen Estie's face. "Majesty, I told her what she asked. We have obeyed her this far. We will continue to obey her, if that is your wish. But if we did wrong, the fault is mine. I accept your displeasure."

He did not need to add, And King Bifalt's.

While Estie tried to calm herself, she looked around the stalls for Lylin. When she was able to speak, she asked, "Where did she go, Captain?"

"Out the back, Majesty." Rowt squared his shoulders, visibly braced himself to face his Queen-Consort's ire. "With her horse."

"Did she warn you about the woods? Behind the inn?"

"She said they were safe. Although how she knew—" The Captain's voice faded.

She knew because she looked, thought Estie. The assassin could have scouted those trees several times while she, Estie, was sleeping.

Finally, the Queen answered her escort's anxiety.

"If you did wrong, Captain, so do I. She knew our peril before I saw any threat. She has skills I cannot imagine. Obey her as long as you can. We have reason to expect an ambush. The men are Amikan, but they are disguised as Bellegerin. They want King Bifalt to believe *his* people killed me.

"We must go. Before they finish preparing their attack."

Rowt started to ask, "What reas—?" then stopped himself; signaled to his men. At once, they rushed to mount.

"She said the same, Majesty," added the Captain, scowling. "Her orders were explicit. I would prefer to leave you and the Magister here until we have dealt with this ambush."

"*Obey* her," repeated Estie. "I need haste. I cannot wait for safety."

One more glance at her expression, and Captain Rowt sprang for his horse. Around him, his men readied their rifles.

While Anina blustered, "An ambush? By *Amikans*? *That* is nonsense," Blurn helped Magister Facile into her saddle. Despite her indignation, the maid watched over Queen Estie until the Queen was settled on her own horse. Then Anina let Blurn help her.

As the groom mounted, the Captain warned his men, "Remember the orders. Slow canter until the inn is no longer in sight. Then ride hard."

Estie understood his uncertainty. What reason did *her* people have to want her dead? For trying to kill her in a way that would end the alliance? She was not sure, but she believed Lylin. Men like Postern hoped to help King Smegin reclaim his throne. Men like Magister Flense and his companion—

Fervently, she prayed that her husband had secured Postern in the dankest cellar he had.

With five soldiers in formation around them, the Queen-Consort of Belleger and her companions rode out of the stables and onto the road between the Open Hand and Maloresse.

The morning was brilliant with sunlight. By noon, the air would be too warm for the season. As Queen Estie and her company left the vicinity of Beds, Food, Ale, she felt exposed again; vulnerable to fire. The sun on her face seemed to promise flames.

But then the road passed around a hill; the horses began to run; and Estie's impulse to flinch at every glimpse of the open sky diminished. Her mount's swift gait and the cool breeze on her face had the effect of steadying her. They seemed to shield her from her enemies. By increments, she began to think.

She had time. She knew every section of her road between the Open Hand and Maloresse. She had personally chosen every stretch where its workings diverged from the old wagon track among these hills: the track along which Prince Jaspid had escorted her through Belleger for the first time. Despite her inexperience with battles, with attempts on her life, she felt sure that she could judge where the ambush would strike. The best place was still a third of a league away. She had time to gather herself.

Lylin's explanation of the plot against her had flaws. It left gaps. The rhythm of Estie's horse and the wind that fluttered her hair helped her name them.

Somehow, Magister Facile seemed to know as much as the devotee of Spirit. Queen Estie wanted to ask the old woman, Why *now*? Why *this* time, when she had stopped at Beds, Food, Ale so often? But she could guess at an answer: because Postern had been tricked or pressured into confessing his complicity with her father. King Smegin's treachery must reach deeper and spread wider than she had allowed herself to imagine. The shock of hearing that he had enslaved some of the Nuuri had been enough to galvanize her. She had not asked herself *why* he would commit that bizarre crime.

The assassin had suggested one possibility. King Smegin wanted to bring about the end of the alliance. He wanted her people to plead for his return to the throne. A ruinous war with the Nuuri might be enough to give him what he desired. Or it might not. He had taken then-Prince Bifalt's measure: he knew what he was up against. King Bifalt might keep the peace between Amika and Belleger by sheer force of will.

His wife's death in Belleger, apparently killed by Bellegerins, would ensure King Smegin's success.

Was it possible? Was enslaving Nuuri only the beginning of King Smegin's machinations? Had Estie's father always planned to have her murdered so that he could reclaim the rule of Amika when he had per-fected his mastery of his Decimate?

The idea horrified her.

Like so many other things about King Smegin, however, it did not surprise her. He had that kind of cunning. Before the alliance, he had relied on the crude approach of trying to bludgeon Belleger into sub-mission. But when he chose to do so, he could be subtle. In the old days, he had kept his grip on Amika as much by manipulation as by flagrant cruelty.

But if Queen Estie accepted her own reasoning—if she believed that her father wanted her killed in a way that would restore his throne—she had only one question for Magister Facile.

Over the loud clatter of iron-shod hooves on stone, she shouted at the sorceress, *"How?"*

By some process of divination known only to herself, the old woman grasped what Estie was asking. Barely audible through the clamor of galloping, Magister Facile called back, "The Chancellor must have had an ally in the hall when he confessed!"

Of *course*, thought Estie. An ally. In the hall. Her mind rode the rhythm of her mount's strides. He had time. She had waited too long for the sorceress. For Elgart. She had given her enemies the rest of the afternoon and half the night. Postern's ally had time. More than enough to send a message. Or go himself. To trigger the ambush.

The attempt on her life must have been planned long ago. It must have been ready and waiting for seasons. Or years. Waiting for the Chancellor to crack—

No.

Gods! thought Estie suddenly. Oh, Brigin and pestilence! Postern's confession may have been deliberate. He may have chosen his moment after some signal from King Smegin. In fact, he *must* have. Otherwise her father's plotting involved too much uncertainty, too much waiting. Any traitor savage or foolish enough to attack Amika's Queen would eventually lose patience. Postern must have chosen his moment of weakness to suit her father's preparations.

Between one instant and the next, Queen Estie's fears vanished. Her confusion and helplessness burst like soap bubbles. She was too full of fury to feel anything else: fury at herself. Why had she failed to wonder why her father had turned his malice on the Nuuri? Why had she not considered the possibility that Postern's confession might be a ploy? And why, why, *why* had she refused Prince Jaspid's escort? Before her departure, she had been too shocked to think clearly. Too unsure of herself to act without consulting Magister Facile and Elgart. But that did not account for her refusal of the First Captain's men. *That* bit of pettiness she could only blame on wounded pride. On her private conviction that she was still no match for her husband. He did not love her for the plain reason that she did not deserve it. She had not proved herself.

Then she was out of time.

Her road had been winding among gentle hills, curving to accommodate their slopes. Now it faced a higher ridge clad in old forest and brush. Here the wagon-track that had carried travelers and soldiers in the early years of her marriage turned to the west, seeking its gnarled way through gaps where the land's gradual rise met the ridge. But Queen Estie had imagined a more direct line for her road. She intended her road to speed communication and armies between the Open Hand and Maloresse—and, when it was complete, between Maloresse and the Last Repository. At her command, her sappers and roadmen had gouged into a shallow valley until it became a deep cut: not as straight as she might have wished, but wide enough for her purposes, and at least five leagues shorter than the older track.

Thus, inadvertently, she had created the perfect place for an ambush. The cut's walls were not truly sheer, but they were too steep for most men; certainly too rugged for horses. And its rims were cloaked with broad oaks, spreading sycamores, brush, and brambles. Hidden archers could send swarms of arrows at riders on the road. A Magister like Flense could rain down fire without ever being seen.

Now Queen Estie believed in the danger. She believed the devotee of Spirit. And she remembered the attack that King Smegin had arranged for Prince Bifalt's quest to find the library. People at Beds, Food, Ale would recall that two Bellegerins had left the inn ahead of the Queen-Consort's party. The innkeeper and his wife would do so, if no one else did.

Urgently, she drew breath to call for Captain Rowt's attention. But he slowed the horses before she could shout. He brought the company to a halt. Then he wheeled to face Estie.

"Majesty," he demanded in a low voice, "I must know. That strange woman. Do you trust her? Do her orders stand? There is peril in them. The old track is safer. Her tactics are dangerous. You will be at risk."

"Captain!" muttered Magister Facile in vexation. "The Queen-Consort has already answered you. 'That strange woman,' as you call

her, is adept in these matters. Her orders will serve better than yours."
Then the sorceress seemed to relent. "Or mine."

"Perhaps not," snapped Estie. "Captain, will her orders save us if
those traitors use grenades?"

Rowt flinched at the idea. But almost at once, he shook his head.
"No, Majesty. They will not. I mean the traitors." Until that moment,
she had not realized how young he was. King Bifalt's army had few
veterans. "Grenades are an Amikan weapon. The King has forbidden
them in Belleger. If your traitors wish him to believe you were killed by
Bellegerins, they must strike as Bellegerins."

"Then," said the Queen distinctly, "her orders stand."

To his credit, the Captain did not object or hesitate. With a gesture,
he sent two of his riflemen racing away, one to the east, one westward.
"They will climb the ridge as soon as they can," he explained. "If we are
fortunate, Majesty, they will take your traitors from behind.

"Now we ride at an easy trot. We must give our men time to find
their way. And we have one advantage. In this cut, hidden attackers will
not see us until we near them. If we have come this far swiftly enough,
they will still be scrambling to conceal themselves. Then they will have
to wait while we approach at our own pace. They will not know that your
escort is diminished until it is too late for them to adjust their positions.

"Be prepared to run at the first arrow—or the first shot."

Queen Estie nodded her approval. "As you say, Captain." Then she
asked, "Can you spare a weapon? I am unarmed."

He gave her an appraising look that became a scowl of disgust or
regret as he took the long dagger from his belt and handed it to her.
"Useless against archers, Majesty," he muttered. "But if it comforts
you—"

Hefting the blade to test its balance, Estie ignored his manner. In
fact, the knife did comfort her. When she was a girl, her father had
made sure that his favorite received some rudimentary training. And
later, in the early years of her marriage, Prince Jaspid had made time to
work with her. No doubt, he, too, remembered the hostility that had
greeted her first arrival in the Open Hand. In her present mood, the
Queen was more than willing to defend herself, if she had the chance.

As the Captain turned to lead his company into the cut, Estie told Magister Facile curtly, "Use your Decimate as you see fit. We must live to reach King Smegin."

If she had lingered with the sorceress, she would have seen the dismay on Magister Facile's face, the brief despair in her eyes. But Queen Estie was already giving her own orders to Blurn.

"Watch over Anina. Do what you can. Do not hazard yourself for me. I have enough protection."

Another maid might have thanked her mistress, or said something kind. Anina took her mount to Blurn's side and gripped his arm. "Save me," she demanded in a harsh whisper. "I will curse you if you do not. I cannot bear to die in Belleger. Not at the hands of *Bellegerins*."

Blurn barked a short laugh, but he did not rebuff her.

With a rueful grimace, Estie urged her horse to catch up with Captain Rowt. Side by side, they rode into the cooler air and shadows of the cut.

Here there were occasional echoes. Bare rock reflected the iron clang of hooves: slopes of dirt and scree did not. Estie could have imagined a host gathering somewhere ahead of her; but she shook those fancies out of her mind. Even a host of traitors would not challenge riflemen head-on. When Rowt had examined his gun, confirmed that it was cocked and loaded, and settled it in his hands, she asked quietly, "What are your thoughts, Captain?"

"Majesty." She heard tension in his voice: the clenched anxiety of a young officer who had never faced combat. "If I planned an ambush here, I would set a barricade in the narrows." She knew the place he meant: a short stretch where her road squeezed between unyielding walls of granite. "Then I would prepare a rock-fall, or a few half-hewn trees, perhaps there." He pointed up at an overhanging rim of the cut. "When my targets passed, I would seal their retreat. Once they were trapped, I would pick them off at my convenience.

"Afterward"—his tone became a snarl—"I might use their rifles to kill some of my own men. To support the pretense that my victims fought hard before they—before *you*—were killed."

The Queen-Consort nodded. King Bifalt would not be fooled: she was sure of that. But King Smegin did not need to convince his enemy. He only needed an excuse.

Aloud, Estie observed, "Or they could simply target the horses." Unconsciously, she matched her tone to the Captain's. "Then they would not need barricades."

"Hells, Majesty!" He seemed startled; unaware of what he was saying. "I think like a Bellegerin. Real cruelty is an Amikan gift."

She winced at the insult, but she let it pass. Under the circumstances, she could not reproach him. She knew her father.

Her road was wide enough for six or even eight men to ride comfortably abreast. And the walls of the cut were not the cliffs of a natural formation like Belleger's coast, and Amika's. But from the rims, the thick boughs of oaks and sycamores covered the passage in shadows. At this time of day, quick bursts of sunlight spattered through the leaves. They struck Estie's eyes when she did not expect them; vanished before she could shade her gaze. The effect was dizzying: it distorted her sight like a heavy blow. Her tension became a throbbing headache.

She was nearing the narrows that worried Captain Rowt. Two more curves around blunt stone on one side, fallen debris on the other, and she would be able to see the barricade—if there *was* a barricade. If King Smegin's adherents made the effort to think like Bellegerins who did not have guns—

Close behind the Queen, Blurn and Anina followed her. Farther back, the two remaining soldiers scanned the rims of the cut through the sights of their rifles.

One more curve. Estie felt her pulse beating in her throat. The iron clack of hooves sounded louder; echoed more.

Then a rifle banged in the distance. Trees and undergrowth made the shot seem impossibly far away.

Squalling, birds sprang into the air, hundreds of them, thousands. Their lift swirled the leaves, the branches. The thunder of their wings filled the cut as if the sky had broken open.

Estie's mount did not flinch. It had been trained to ignore rifle-fire. But it knew what to do when she snapped her reins, dug in her heels. In three strides, it was galloping.

An arrow streaked across her vision like Anina's shrill cry. It struck the stone road and skittered away. Another passed overhead, embedded itself in a slope of scree.

The traitors were bad marksmen.

No. They had been startled by that gunshot. They were rushing their aim. The next shaft—or the next—

Rifles boomed behind her. A man screamed from the rim. He must have betrayed his position when he loosed his arrow.

More arrows. Estie heard a crash at her back, a heavy body falling; heard Anina wail, *"Blurn!"*

Before the Queen could react, she rounded the last curve and saw the narrows.

They were not barricaded: not with piled rocks or felled trees. Instead, six, seven, no, eight men stood there waiting for her. They wore Bellegerin clothes. They had long Bellegerin sabers. Most of them had the features and skin-tone of Bellegerins.

When they saw her, they started to howl.

She ran straight at them, daring them to strike at the Queen of Amika. *Their* Queen.

Another distant rifle spoke. The guardsmen in the rear fired again. Arrows hammered down on all sides.

Gods! How many traitors had Postern or his allies found to attack her?

An instant later, the Captain caught up with her. Leaping from his saddle, he grabbed at her, one arm around her waist, one hand on her reins. As he pulled her out of her seat, he wrenched her horse's head to the side.

Hauled off balance, the horse missed its footing and skidded into a fall. Estie landed hard on top of Rowt, hard enough to knock the air out of her lungs, hard enough to make the sun's dazzles spin like nausea across her sight—but not hard enough to mask the cruel sound of her mount's legs breaking, or the raw agony of the beast's screams.

Then those cries were cut off by arrows thudding into the horse's barrel. Another shaft made a clicking sound as it skimmed the Captain's helm. His mount danced away, ran back the way it had come.

Anina had stopped wailing.

With a grunt of effort, Captain Rowt heaved Estie aside. Snarling, "Stay *down*!" he squirmed over the stones until her horse lay between him and the narrows. With the still-quivering beast for cover, he opened fire on the blockade of traitors.

Eight of them. Six bullets in his clip. But those men did not stand waiting to die. After his first shot, they scattered, crouching for the partial shelter of the walls, or diving to lie flat.

Down? thought Estie. *Down?* Where she would be an even easier target for the bowmen above her?

With Rowt's dagger in her hand, she surged to her feet.

"You *dare*?" she yelled for no better reason than the desire to challenge her assailants. "You *dare* attack the Queen of Amika?"

More shots in the distance, their noise muffled by trees. They came from the soldiers who had been sent to take the ambush from behind. The riflemen in the cut were firing as fast as they could, although they could only guess at the coverts of the archers. But now fewer arrows flashed down from the rims. Most of them were aimed at the riflemen; at the only obvious threat to the men above the road. Past the blaring of guns, near and far, Estie heard a curse from one of her escort, a shout of pain and anger.

If Magister Facile was using her Decimate, the Queen saw no sign of it. No roar of fire reached her; no sizzle-and-burn of lightning; no blast of wind. What was the sorceress *waiting* for?

The Captain had emptied his clip. Slapping it out of the breech with one hand, he scrambled to snatch a fresh clip from his satchel.

In that pause, the swordsmen holding the narrows started their rush. Only two of them were down. One had a small red stain on his shoulder, a superficial wound. With the rest, he came running. The fury of their howls stunned Estie's heart. It made her own rage feel trivial, as if it were mere petulance.

If her attackers had feared sorcery, they would not have charged so recklessly.

Holding her dagger ready, she moved to meet them.

They were still twenty paces away when a body fell onto the road in front of them. It hit as if it had plunged out of the sky, or had been knocked off one of the heavy boughs overhead. As it landed, it flopped once, then lay still; lifeless.

The man had fallen without a sound. He had died before he fell. Someone must have thrown him from the rim of the cut.

The swordsmen froze in shock. The dead man had landed on his back. They could see his face as well as Estie could.

Magister Flense.

Glancing upward, Estie thought she caught a glimpse of white. But she could not be sure of it. While she paused to look, her foes recovered from their dismay; started toward her again.

Captain Rowt must have been surprised as well, but he did not let the fallen corpse slow him. The attackers were moving sluggishly, still shaking off their reactions. He shot one of them, and another, before the rest scattered.

Now they were harder to hit. And there was no supporting fire from the men with Magister Facile, Anina, and Blurn. Desperate to stop more arrows, the riflemen shredded the rims of the cut with bullets. Queen Estie and the Captain were alone.

Ducking and dodging, the four remaining swordsmen continued to close.

Doing what he could, Rowt crippled one with a bullet in the belly. Another he stopped by hitting the center of the man's thigh. His other shots missed.

Deliberately, Estie moved again, walking to meet her attackers.

The last two were almost near enough to strike. They no longer howled. Their blades concentrated their fury.

Estie readied herself to step aside. One of her tutors had taught her this. Prince Jaspid had practiced it with her. If she did not step too soon, or too late, she could make one of the sabers miss her. Then she would—

Abruptly, a dagger appeared in one of her foe's eyes. With a look of absolute astonishment, he toppled backward.

Estie's anger was clarity. It was focus. As she had been taught, she stepped away from the last swordsman's swing. She let his momentum carry him closer. Then she drove her dagger to the hilt into the side of his throat.

The traitor was already dying when the Captain shot him.

Queen Estie knew that she was going to start trembling soon. Her legs might fail her. She might be forced to empty her stomach. But not yet. Not yet.

With no surprise at all, she watched the devotee of Spirit stride easily down the steep slope of the wall. With every step, Lylin started dirt and rocks sliding; but she let each slide carry her to her next step until she reached the road.

"Majesty," she said in greeting. "You are unharmed. That is good."

While Estie stared, the assassin indicated the body of Magister Flense. "No devotee kills such a man willingly. He was defenseless, as craven as you described him. When I found him, I knew that he would not join the ambush." A brief flick of sunlight caught her eyes. For an instant, they looked like hot stones. "But some cowards discover bravado when their weakness is witnessed. Your purpose is urgent, and I feared leaving a traitor at your back if he recovered his self-regard.

"As for the rest—" She shrugged. "Those who were not slain by your escort are dead. They will not carry the tale of this encounter to their masters."

Estie tried to think of something to say. Nothing came to her.

Then Captain Rowt staggered toward them. He had a wild look in his eyes, and his face was deathly pale, as if he were bleeding from a wound he had failed to notice. "*You,*" he rasped, practically spitting in the devotee's face. "You are a *madwoman.* You took an insane risk. In what world is riding into an ambush called sanity? A *known* ambush? The old track would have cost us three hours, four at most, and *all these men*"—he brandished his fists feverishly—"would have nothing to report except failure. If they dared to report at all.

"The Queen-Consort would have been *safe*."

His outrage seemed to restart Estie's mind. She held up one hand, asking the man to hear her. "I understand, Captain. But a report of failure might be as fatal as success. King Smegin would learn that his intentions against me are known. He would prepare something worse for his next attempt."

Lylin nodded. "Also there is this. Eighteen traitors will attempt no further harm to the alliance."

Gaping, the Captain breathed, "Eighteen? There were *eighteen* of them?"

"You saw eight," answered the devotee. "Your men and I accounted for ten hiding above us."

The young officer's eyes rolled. He clamped his arms across his stomach. A moment later, he lurched away to vomit.

A reaction in the aftermath of unfamiliar extremity. Prince Jaspid had described the signs. Estie's turn was coming.

But while she could, she muttered, "Anina. Blurn. My escort." Suddenly, she thought, Magister Facile! Who had apparently done nothing.

Wheeling away, she trotted back down the road to the curve where she had lost sight of her companions.

Lylin retrieved the dagger she had thrown to save Estie; took the time to wipe it clean. Nevertheless her longer legs carried her swiftly. She was only two steps back when the Queen found the rest of her company.

Estie's trembling started then. It was going to get worse.

Splashed with patches of sunshine that moved like reflections on water, the riflemen stood in the middle of the road. One of them scanned the trees and rock above him through his sights, watching for more bowmen. Concentrating wildly, he did not appear to notice the

Queen-Consort's approach. The other struggled with an arrow in the meat of his shoulder. Gasping through his teeth, he tried to wrench out the shaft; but he could not work it free.

At the side of the road, Magister Facile sat on a fallen boulder. It must have broken off the wall sometime after the road was finished. She held her cane upright in front of her with her hands clasped on the handle and her chin resting on her hands. She looked exhausted, not hurt. Yet she had done nothing.

Trying to locate Anina and Blurn, Estie finally noticed that the horses were gone. They had run off during the fight. Perhaps their riders had sent them back down the cut to keep them safe.

Were Anina and Blurn still mounted when the horses ran? If so, they, too, were safe. And they could bring the other horses back with them.

Lylin touched Estie's arm, breathed softly, "Majesty." She was pointing at a swath of deeper shadows where the sun's angle did not reach.

When Estie peered in that direction, she made out a mounded shape that did not resemble rocks. It looked like bodies. Two of them, one on top of the other.

Anina.

Unsteadily, the Queen ran.

Blurn.

In four strides, she was sure. That was Blurn facedown at the edge of the road. He seemed lifeless. But then she saw his fingers clenching and opening, clawing at the stone, trying to find his strength.

Anina lay on top of him as if she had stretched herself there to protect him. She was facedown as well. Her hands covered his head.

Arrows jutted from her back, four of them driven deep. As the reek of gunpowder drifted away, the smell of blood pooling around the groom almost dropped Estie to her knees.

The maid was the most rigidly loyal Amikan Estie knew. Anina had never forgiven Belleger for the war. She had never forgiven King Bifalt for the alliance. Despite their years together, it was possible that she had never trusted her Queen. And she had begged Blurn to save her. Then she had done what she could to keep him alive.

After a moment that seemed to go on too long, the devotee of Spirit knelt beside the bodies. Gently, she lifted Anina aside, confirmed that the maid was dead.

At once, Blurn drew a gasp of air. Hunching his shoulders, he raised his head. None of the shafts in Anina had reached him. But his forehead was bleeding. He must have fallen hard, hit his head—

Wavering on her feet, Queen Estie turned away to confront the sorceress.

Captain Rowt had come back from the narrows. After exchanging a few words about Anina and Blurn with Lylin, he helped his injured rifleman. Once he had broken off the head of the arrow, the shaft slid out with comparative ease. Gritting his teeth, the soldier bore the pain in silence. He did not let himself groan or curse until the Captain bound his shoulder.

Magister Facile looked up as Queen Estie approached, but she did not move or speak. Her expression revealed nothing.

King Bifalt wants to know if you trust her.

Standing with her knees locked and her stomach sick, Estie demanded, "Where *were* you? What are you good for? How could you fail to defend them?"

Although the Magister raised her head, her eyes avoided Estie's. "Defend them how, Majesty? Should I have summoned an earthquake to topple our attackers? I would have broken your road. Should I have sent a blast of wind? I would have knocked you and everyone else to the ground. In the aftermath, trees or rocks might have fallen on us. Did you think the Decimate of pestilence is more precise? It can be—but only when its victims are visible. The bowmen were concealed. You were beyond the curve. Fire and drought are not so discriminating, and I have no gift for lightning. What do you imagine I could have done?"

Estie's mind twisted like her guts. Magister Facile's reply seemed to imply that she—unlike any theurgist Amika or Belleger had ever known—could wield more than one Decimate. That she could wield them all, if she chose.

The Queen started to ask, "Do you mean—?" but she could not finish the question. Her balance was gone. She was going to fall.

She heard the Captain say, "We have lost our horses."

She heard Lylin laugh. "If they do not return, I know where our attackers tethered their mounts."

Then the Queen of Amika was on her hands and knees, bringing up the contents of her stomach hard enough to tear muscles in her chest.

TEN

BEFORE THE FIRST ENCOUNTERS

In the middle of the afternoon on the fourth day after the ambush, Queen Estie of Amika approached the outskirts of Maloresse with an escort of twenty cavalrymen and her remaining companions, Magister Facile and the devotee Lylin.

Blurn and the wounded rifleman she had left to recover with the physician of the Fivebridge garrison, along with her strict orders for the garrison commander. From that moment on, she insisted, no one was allowed to leave or enter Belleger until she lifted the restriction in person. Representatives of King Bifalt were the only exception: riflemen, known messengers, or some other emissary. To explain herself, she told the commander that she needed a few days to identify and root out a threat to peace between the realms.

She did not tell him that she hoped to prevent any report of the ambush from reaching King Smegin, directly or indirectly. She did not mention the ambush at all.

Of course, there were other bridges over the Line River. They had been negotiated before her wedding. Belleger built and guarded some: Amika was responsible for others. But her road, the fastest and most direct route between Maloresse and the Open Hand, crossed the Line at Fivebridge. In one of his many unexpected concessions, then-Prince Bifalt had allowed Amika to claim authority there. The garrison now straddled the bridge on the Amikan side. No one could cross to or from Amika without passing through the defended heart of the garrison.

If some unsuspected traitor knew what had happened to the attack on her and wanted to warn King Smegin, the messenger would be stopped at Fivebridge. The man would be forced to make a detour that would cost days.

That was the only precaution Queen Estie knew to take against her father.

For different reasons, she no longer had any riflemen with her. Acutely reluctant, she had instructed the garrison commander to arrest her Bellegerin escort: a form of house-arrest that included every amenity except departure—and communication with Belleger's Fist. To Captain Rowt, who had saved her life, she had confessed privately that she dreaded her husband's reaction to the ambush. She did not want the King to know about it until she had ended the plot. Traitors in Amika were *her* problem. If King Bifalt made them *his*—if he feared for her life, or for her ability to rule—he might take some action that resembled an invasion. The uneasy balance of the alliance might not recover.

When she had given her reasons, she swallowed Rowt's blistering retorts and arguments. She understood well enough that she was forcing him to appear disloyal. But instead of debating with him, she assured him that the garrison commander would release him as soon as King Bifalt sent someone after her. Then she left the Captain to his indignation.

Now she was protected by her own men. Her escort in Amika—twenty men dedicated to that duty and no other—was led by Commander Crayn, whom she had known for years. And several of his soldiers were known to her as well. They sufficed. Under the circumstances, she was safe enough in her own land. As long as her father did not know the outcome of his ambush, he was unlikely to prepare more dangers for her.

Naturally, Estie wanted to push for speed. But Magister Facile's comparative frailty held her back. If the devotee of Spirit had not ridden beside the old woman to keep her in her saddle, the Queen's company would have taken even longer to reach her city.

On other, more leisurely returns, riding into Maloresse had often lifted Queen Estie's heart. Her improvements in the condition of her people and their homes had given her pleasure. Unlike the Open Hand, Maloresse had always maintained wide streets and boulevards. Her forebears on the throne had refused to let any of Amika's poor encroach there: the sick and the destitute had been forcibly banished. Now only the width of the main roadways remained. With her own wealth augmented by coin extracted from the realm's more grasping nobles and landlords, she had built solid homes all around the city. She had encouraged the establishment of shops, merchantries, ironworks, stables, smithies, taverns, inns. And she paid well for men and women who could construct homes, or repair streets and sewers and walls, or labor on her road, or join King Bifalt's army, or sweat in the foundries that forged her cannon, or help with the fortification of the Bay of Lights. Every year, her people became more prosperous. In turn, they paid better prices for food, ale, wine, timber, metals; and anyone she did not employ directly could afford to work the fields, or the forests, or the mines for Amika's benefit.

In her own way, Queen Estie had served her realm as diligently as King Bifalt served his.

But now she paid no attention to the results of her efforts. A gnawing tension drove her. Every hour that passed was like acid dripping in her stomach.

Long ago, Elgart had offered her one of his rare attempts to explain King Bifalt. He was not always who he is, Elgart had told her. The Magisters of the Last Repository shaped him into the man he became, but they did not rely on persuasion—or seduction. The only tool they used to refashion him was frustration. After a moment's reflection, the spy had added, Frustration and loss.

Estie was beginning to understand how her husband felt during his quest for the library.

Word of her coming to Maloresse ran ahead of her, as it always did. She knew how news traveled in the city. Many of her people were natural spies. Informers at the outskirts signaled to other informers, or to members of her honor guard patrolling the vicinity, and they passed the signal inward. She was not surprised to find Commander Soulcess waiting for her when she reached the main gate through the wall of the city's outer fortifications. She had made him the first officer of her honor guard as soon as she had found a better use for Ennis Forguile.

As usual, Soulcess had mustered a mounted squad to relieve Commander Crayn's company. The guardsmen sat their horses in the small plaza beyond the gate, holding fresh mounts for Queen Estie and the two women who were obviously her guests. Commander Soulcess himself stood in the throat of the gateway, looking as polished and correct as if four servants had spent the past hour burnishing his appearance. Estie could imagine that he had given at least an hour to his beard and moustache alone.

Personally, the Queen preferred the less ostentatious air of use worn by King Bifalt's guards. She had not promoted Soulcess for his immaculate garb and grooming—or for his questionable wits. In fact, she considered him obtuse; hampered by self-importance. But she respected his attention to detail. It extended beyond his own person to his command of her honor guard. He knew every man he led by name.

Before she dismounted to accept Commander Soulcess' welcome, she told Crayn to send a few of his men ahead with Magister Facile and the devotee. She named an inn, the Flower of Amika, where her guests could be sure of comfort, good food, and quiet. To Lylin, Estie added, "Make her rest. I will come for you at dawn."

Stunned with weariness, the sorceress did not react; but the assassin nodded her approval inside her hood.

As the two women and their smaller escort walked their horses past the confused first officer, Queen Estie asked Commander Crayn to join her. Then she swung herself out of her saddle and dropped to the cobbles of the roadway. With Crayn a step behind her, she entered the high arch and thick walls of the gate.

Because Commander Soulcess looked flustered, the Queen allowed him time to give her his most elaborate bow. But when he began on his customary fulsome speech of welcome, she cut him off.

"I ask your pardon, Commander," she said without a trace of contrition. "I am in haste. You heard me say I will depart at dawn. I will give your formality the acknowledgment it deserves on another occasion."

While Soulcess huffed through his moustache, apparently trying to find his way through what she had just said, Estie added in the same tone, "For the present, I want you to assemble my honor guard."

His eyes jumped wide as if she had just ordered him to strike her. "Assemble—?" The word was a croak. Swallowing, he began again. "Assemble, Majesty? The honor guard?"

Estie held his stare. "Am I not speaking plainly, sir?"

"But *assemble*, Majesty?" he protested. "They are here." He gestured at the horsemen in the plaza behind him. "What more—?"

"*All* of them, Commander." She knew better than to raise her voice. A display of anger would only make him rigid with bewilderment. Then she would have to repeat herself, perhaps more than once. "Assemble all of my honor guard."

Soulcess stared at her so hard that his eyes bulged. "All *fifty* of them, Majesty? Who will patrol the city, or watch the walls, or—?"

In silence, Queen Estie returned his gaze until his voice trailed away.

After a moment, Commander Crayn cleared his throat. "With respect, Majesty. I believe Commander Soulcess speaks of the fifty men who are now on duty. Will they suffice?"

She shook her head. She knew perfectly well that her honor guard numbered more than fifty. She had reduced King Smegin's force from three hundred to one hundred fifty, but she would not accept less. With an effort, she kept a grip on her temper. "Thank you, Commander Crayn. Now I understand Commander Soulcess' uncertainty.

"Commander," she asked the first officer, "how many men *altogether* are in my honor guard?"

The specificity of her question seemed to put Soulcess on surer ground. He had his answer ready. "One hundred thirteen."

Estie frowned in surprise. "You disappoint me, sir. Were my commands unclear? When I asked you to lead my honor guard, there were one hundred fifty. You were instructed to maintain that number. I trusted you to respect my wishes." Gods! She was *saving* those men for the day when the library's enemy attacked. No matter how many she gave her husband now, he was going to need more later. "How do you justify the discrepancy?"

An appalled purple stained the first officer's cheeks. "There *is* no discrepancy, Majesty. They are one hundred fifty." Then a thought worse than Queen Estie's displeasure struck him, and he sagged. "That is to say, one hundred thirty-one remain. But only one hundred thirteen serve."

"Explain," snapped Estie.

She meant to contain her frustration. She knew that the more confounded Soulcess felt, the more difficult he would become. But she was tired herself; dismayed by the attempt on her life; thwarted in her marriage; burdened by a gift she could not name or use. And now her father—

However, Commander Soulcess raised his head, stuck out his chin. Did his Queen want a list? He was the kind of man who had his lists ready.

"Seven," he said distinctly, "suffer from the flux, Majesty. Four were relieved for family reasons. One ailing wife, one child trampled by a horse, one mother dying, one grandfather dead this morning. Five are in the stockade for accepting bribes. Two have been dismissed for extreme drunkenness.

"The other nineteen are absent without leave."

"Nine*teen*?" demanded the Queen. The dripping of acid in her stomach was getting worse. "Do you know where they are?"

Discomfited again, Soulcess pulled on his moustache. "Know, Majesty? How can I know? They are not here. I cannot ask them where they are."

Again, Commander Crayn spoke. "With respect, Majesty, there are rumors. I would not expect Commander Soulcess to hear them. Folk do not confide in him. He is too lofty. But more common soldiers tell them to each other."

Queen Estie studied the leader of her escort. He must have been at least as old as she was, but his age was difficult to determine. If lines marked his face, they were obscured by his short, blond beard. His eyes were the timeless color of sandstone, and the hair curling around his headband was full enough to belong to a young man, although it had been bleached almost white by the sun. When he called Soulcess "lofty," he was not being obsequious. She knew him as a straightforward man, respectful but unafraid. His comments were his way of guarding the first officer's vulnerable pride; of giving Soulcess an excuse for being ignorant of whispers everyone else heard.

Facing the Queen squarely, Crayn explained, "Majesty, some among your honor guard consider their service in Maloresse an idle task. We are soldiers. We are trained to fight. But here there is no one to fight, apart from the occasional drunkard. Unless our thieves are luckless or stupid, there is no one to chase or snare. And more serious matters, such as killings and frauds, are not trusted to ordinary soldiers. Many of your honor guard are bored. Some are restless. They want excitement."

Estie clenched her teeth so that she would not spit vitriol. She thought she knew where Crayn was going. The man was still making excuses. But now he was making them for *her*. For her failure to keep the loyalty of her guardsmen.

The escort Commander appeared to consider what he should say next. Then he shrugged. "The rumors say there is an abundance of excitement at King Smegin's sanctuary."

"Rumors are only rumors, Majesty. I cannot vouch for them. But I believe the men who are absent without leave have gone to join King Smegin."

Gods! thought Estie. Oh, gods and folly! Why had she allowed her balked passion for her husband to distract her from her doubts about Chancellor Postern? All of this could have been prevented, if only she had paid more attention to her duties—and trusted her instincts.

After nineteen years of marriage, King Bifalt's rejection of her desire for him, her love and admiration, still weakened her.

But as soon as he understood Crayn, Commander Soulcess yelped, "What? Do you mean to say—?" He looked positively apoplectic. His whole face was a flush of purple. "Do you mean to tell me *my men* are not loyal to the Queen of Amika?

"Brigin and *pestilence*, Crayn! If I did not know you, I would strike you down. It is an insult—!"

"It is nothing of the kind." Queen Estie's tone, piercing as an awl, punctured the first officer's outrage. "It is time for you to calm yourself, Commander. Commander Crayn serves me well. As *you* will, sir. I told you I am in haste. Now you can imagine why."

Soulcess, she knew, could do nothing of the kind.

But she did not need him to guess her reasons. She needed him to obey explicit orders. And now she recalled why she had chosen him to be her honor guard's first officer. He had his weaknesses, but he also had this strength: if she made her orders explicit enough, he would obey them exactly.

Commander Soulcess took a deep breath, tugged on his beard, puffed his fury through his moustache. After a moment, the livid hue faded from his cheeks and forehead.

With towering dignity, he said, "Command me, Majesty."

"I will," Queen Estie assured him. But first she addressed Commander Crayn.

"Your men are tired, sir. They will be more so. Rest them now. Prepare them for travel and combat. I will require your escort in the morning."

Instead of a soldier's cursory salute, Crayn replied with a formal Amikan bow, touching his forehead with the heels of both palms, then spreading his arms. "We do not fear tiredness, Majesty," he replied with a scowl that may also have been a grin. "We will be ready at your word."

To thank him, Estie matched his bow. Then she turned her attention back to Commander Soulcess.

Stiff with umbrage and confusion, the first officer faced her like a man who meant to shout her down. But she knew him better than that. A slow-witted soldier who had never been in a battle, he had avoided the horrors of the war by the simple expedient of being dependable. King Smegin had grown accustomed to relying on him in mundane matters of detail and organization, and so had not sent him to fight. A lesser man than Soulcess might now have considered his position a sinecure. After all, Crayn was right: the Queen's honor guard had little to do. As long as the Commander fielded his men appropriately and looked his best, he could occupy his post in his sleep. But Soulcess took his duties to heart. He wanted to be trusted.

"Now, sir," began Estie. "The immediate burdens fall to you. I require three things.

"First, assemble my men. *All* of them." To ease his look of protest, she added, "All one hundred *thirteen* of them. Naturally, I will not disturb those you have excused." Some of the rest would be sleeping, either in the guard barracks or with their families. Some would be scattered among the many taverns. No doubt, some would be whoring. Rounding them up would give Soulcess a chance to exercise one of his gifts. "Assemble them in front of the gates of Amika's Desire before sunset. I will speak to them there."

Soulcess regained his composure as she spoke. He seemed to grow taller. "As you command, Majesty."

Queen Estie did not pause. "Second, I need a list. Give me the names of thirty—no, thirty-three guardsmen. You know them, sir. Choose them wisely. I want men who are brave, experienced, and hardy. But above all, I want men who are *faithful*. If worst comes to worst, they will be sorely tested."

Now the Commander frowned. She was probably alarming him. No doubt, he could have given her his list on the spot. But he did not understand. She had not told him what her idea of *worst* might be.

She had not explained herself to Commander Crayn either, but he was better able to draw conclusions from hints.

"Third," she continued with a severity that she no longer tried to mute, "when you have discounted those thirty-three, divide your men into two equal companies. As much as you can, divide them according to their endurance. I must have fidelity from all of my guardsmen. But one company will be asked to display greater stamina and withstand more hardship.

"Do you understand me, sir?"

Commander Soulcess no longer faced her. His gaze wandered as if he expected more reasons for confusion to spring on him from the walls of the gate. Chewing on his moustache, he muttered to himself for a moment. Then he mustered the will to say, "I understand your commands, Majesty. I do not understand their purpose. I cannot explain them to my men."

For his sake, Estie made an effort to smile. "Do not concern yourself, sir. I will explain when I speak to them. But now that you question me, I realize that I have a fourth requirement.

"I will leave Maloresse at dawn tomorrow. You will accompany me. Commander Crayn will direct my usual escort. You will take charge of the thirty-three men you select for me."

She needed Soulcess with her. He knew all nineteen of the honor guard's deserters.

At first, she feared that she had pushed her first officer too far. He seemed on the verge of a seizure. Clutching at his chest, he started to cough. His face and even the backs of his hands turned purple. Almost retching, he gasped, "In the field—?" But then he drew a great whoop of air, and his lungs relaxed. Gradually, the hue of his skin faded.

"As you command, Majesty," he croaked. "I understand." Forcing himself to breathe, he regained some of his usual manner. "That is to say, I do *not* understand. But you are Queen Estie of Amika. I will understand when you choose to explain."

Estie was satisfied. "Then, Commander, take me to Amika's Desire." She beckoned for her horse. "I must speak with the Vice-Chancellor. And also Queen Rubia."

In turn, Soulcess gestured to the guardsmen waiting in the plaza. "At once, Majesty." As he and Estie mounted, and her new escort surrounded her, he became himself again. "The Vice-Chancellor will be eager for news and messages from Chancellor Postern. And the Queen your mother often complains that she sees too little of you."

He may have hoped that she would tell him more, but Estie said nothing. She had given him enough to keep him occupied. Now her thoughts ran ahead of him, hurrying to her next tasks. Her visits with her mother were always awkward. This one might be more so. However, that was a secondary concern. She was more anxious to meet with her Vice-Chancellor—and anxious about seeing him. If she had misjudged him when she approved his appointment, he would be able to warn King Smegin before she could leave Maloresse.

Vice-Chancellor Sikthorn's workroom was small by the standards of Amika's Desire. In the servants' barracks of Belleger's Fist, it could have housed four. It did not have as many windows as Chancellor Postern's chamber high in one of the corners of the fortress; but at this time of day, the Vice-Chancellor had enough to let in an abundance of natural sunshine. However, he kept them shuttered. He preferred the light of his candles and lamps. As a result, the gloom that filled his corners and veiled his shelves seemed to crowd against the zone of illumination surrounding his heavy desk, his piles of books and reports, his sturdy stool. There were secrets all around him, while he and his work were brightly lit.

Queen Estie was familiar with the space, as she was with the man himself and his habits. Still, she always felt upon entering the workroom that she had to swim through shadows and confusion until she reached the desk, where she could see the Vice-Chancellor clearly.

She did not knock to announce herself. She was Amika's Queen: it was her policy to believe that her functionaries had nothing to hide from her. And on this occasion, her abrupt appearance did not startle Sikthorn. Like the rest of Maloresse, he had probably known she was coming by the time she met with Commander Soulcess. As she crossed his threshold into gloom, he rose from his stool and bowed. Without a word, he shifted a stack of papers off another stool and moved it so that she would have a seat at his desk across from him. Then he went back to his place. While she remained standing, he did not sit.

Frowning, Estie studied the Vice-Chancellor. He was a ferret-faced man, long of chin and nose, narrow of face, with powerful shoulders and thin legs—the consequence, no doubt, of spending most of his time hunched over his labor. Despite his habits, however, and his preference for wrapping himself in shadows, his eyes were almost preternaturally keen.

The Queen had often pretended to like her Vice-Chancellor. At times, she did like him. But *liking* and *trust* were not interchangeable.

She had approved Sikthorn's appointment, but she had not chosen him: he only worked for her through Chancellor Postern. She did not believe that he sided with her father. But if he did—if she was wrong—

Sikthorn faced her calmly; held her gaze with no particular expression on his face. When her silence made it plain that she was not going to speak first, he inclined his head in a small bow. "Majesty." For some reason, his voice always sounded like a rusty hinge. "No doubt, you are aware that the Chancellor has not returned from Belleger. How may I be of service in his absence?"

Estie said one word: "Deserters." Then she sat down.

The Vice-Chancellor followed her example. His eyes did not leave hers. "Yes?"

"Deserters," she repeated. "From my honor guard. Nineteen of them, by the first officer's count."

"Indeed." Sikthorn nodded. "And they are not alone. Others have left as well. However, their numbers are more difficult to tally."

Involuntarily, the Queen grimaced. "Others?"

"Thugs, Majesty," he replied. "Estate guards."

When she continued to stare at him, he explained, "Usurers must have protection. They hire thugs. And some of our nobles insist that your reduced guard is not adequate." He shrugged. "Or perhaps they owe coin to the usurers and do not choose to pay. They also hire protection.

"But now both thugs and guards are scarce in Maloresse."

Estie held herself still, but inwardly she squirmed. She understood the Vice-Chancellor too well. Early in her reign, she had forbidden the practice of usury: an edict that changed nothing. Her guardsmen were too widely scattered around the city to enforce it. And usury, like arrogance and other forms of greed, was too deeply embedded in the culture of her realm. From time to time, she thought that Brigin of Belleger had given rise to a land of ascetics. In contrast, Fastule of Amika had fostered the notion that wealth and ostentation were virtues. Estie herself had changed her views. She had sold or bartered most of Amika's Desire's wealth to improve the lives of her poor, to pay for her road, and to support King Bifalt. Nevertheless her people were slow to follow her example.

When she was sure of her composure, Queen Estie asked, "Do you know where they go?"

She did not fear where they went as much as she feared that Sikthorn would not tell her.

He did not. Hunching, he braced his elbows on his desk, steepled his fingers. The light of a dozen candles and lamps glittered in his eyes.

"Majesty," he said carefully, sounding more rusty than ever, "I have no answer. I am in a delicate position. My dilemma is one of loyalty. In general, of course, everything I do is for you. You are my Queen, Amika's Queen. In practice, however, I serve Chancellor Postern. I answer to him. If I disregard his instructions, is that not treason?"

With her best expression of innocence, Estie countered, "What an extraordinary question. Did Chancellor Postern instruct you to refuse to answer me?"

"Of course not, Majesty," replied Sikthorn at once. "That, too, would be treason. Still, I am at an impasse."

As sweetly as she could, she suggested, "Will it ease your dilemma if you consider that the Chancellor could not have foreseen my interest when he instructed you?"

The Vice-Chancellor spread his hands, then brought his fingertips together again. "Sadly, it does not."

There Estie saw her opening. At the same time, she saw that he had given it to her. And he was an intelligent man, as keen as his gaze: he knew what he did. He had already said enough to outrage Postern. He was probing her, looking for some hint—

She took her chance. Smiling like a woman whose smile commonly dropped men to their knees, she asked, "Will it ease your dilemma if I inform you that Chancellor Postern is King Bifalt's prisoner? The charge against him is already treason."

In surprise, Sikthorn flung himself off the support of his elbows. His mouth hung open. Light seemed to burst in his eyes. Then he sprang to his feet. Without a word, he strode to the far wall and began opening the shutters. In moments, his workroom was awash in late-afternoon sunshine.

When he returned to his stool and sat down, he looked entirely un-changed. The light of day exposed the patina of dust on his shoulders, emphasized the stains of ink on his fingers. In every other way, he looked like a man who had just been informed that his life was unchanged.

"Forgive me, Majesty." His voice betrayed a tremor so slight that Estie barely heard it. "I must ask. Is the Chancellor imprisoned in Bel-leger's Fist? Truly? Is he accused of some great crime?"

"He is." Clenching her fists out of sight below the edge of the desk, she prodded the Vice-Chancellor to explain his reaction. "He betrayed himself in my presence. And in King Bifalt's."

"Then, Majesty—" Sikthorn took a deep breath, held it. For a mo-ment, he allowed his eyes to scan the records and secrets that crowded his shelves. When he faced Estie again, his expression was subtly al-tered. Did he look relieved? Less wary? Or only more sure of himself? She did not know him well enough to interpret the change.

Emptying his lungs in a long sigh, he said finally, "My dilemma is resolved. I am entirely at your service.

"Shall we begin again? How may I serve you?"

Her hands were cramping. One at a time, she uncurled her fingers. She wanted to trust the Vice-Chancellor. Oh, she *wanted* that. But she had to be certain. When she was with her husband, she sometimes felt that she had touched the bottom of human loneliness; that no one could sink further. But when she was away from him, she was reminded that she also leaned on him: on his clarity of purpose, on his ability to act while she faltered.

Abandoning sweetness, she demanded, "Tell me where they are go-ing. My deserters. The thugs. The estate guards."

Once again, Sikthorn propped his elbows on the desk, made a stee-ple of his fingers. When he spoke, the tremor was gone from his voice.

"I am not intended to know this, Majesty. Nevertheless I do. If Chancellor Postern acted according to your wishes, I doom myself by speaking of it. But his imprisonment gives me hope.

"They go east, Majesty. Singly, or in small groups, they travel to King Smegin's retreat."

Gods! thought Estie. Crayn was right. Her father had always had a substantial retinue of servants and soldiers with him. Now he was gathering more men. Perhaps to help him capture Nuuri? Perhaps to protect his sanctuary? And he had taken wagonloads of riches with him when he had left Amika's Desire. He could afford to pay well.

She had to face him anyway. By right of birth as well as by formal grant, she was the Queen of Amika. King Smegin was her responsibility.

While she considered other questions, other details of Postern's conniving, she asked Sikthorn, "Do you know what they do there?"

"I do not," he admitted, "although I have certainly tried to discover the secret. My efforts have been hindered—"

Abruptly, he paused to reconsider his answer. When he was ready, he began again.

"Majesty, you must understand. I was only able to pursue my curiosity when the Chancellor was absent. He had made my duties plain. 'King Smegin,' he told me, 'served Amika long and diligently, and brought us peace. He should be left in peace for his declining years. Apart from his need for supplies, he is not our concern. You will not trouble him, or intrude on him, or speak of him. You will ignore him, as I do.' Those were his instructions to me, Majesty. It was my place to obey him.

"Nevertheless my curiosity was aroused. That he considered it necessary to warn me away from King Smegin disturbed me. And I—" Again, he said, "Forgive me, Majesty. On occasion, I heard him speak slightingly of you. That also disturbed me. Whenever he absented himself from Maloresse, I disobeyed him."

Slightingly, sighed Estie to herself. Her own Chancellor. The man should have known better. Still, she believed Sikthorn. More than once, when Postern did not know she was near, she had heard him mention her in conversation with one or another of King Bifalt's counselors. She means well, he had said. But she is a woman. She lacks a man's attention to detail. She does not have a man's understanding of the forces arrayed against her.

Of *course* she had been suspicious of him. He had given her cause. And she should *absolutely* have acted on her doubts sooner.

"But," the Vice-Chancellor was saying, "I had to rely on men who would not report to the Chancellor. That limited me. And King Smegin himself has frustrated me. If Amikans are adept at spying, King Smegin is supremely skilled at thwarting spies. My men traced your deserters and others to his retreat, but they could not cross the boundary he has claimed for his sanctuary without exposing themselves. I do not know what he does within that boundary, or why he does it."

Estie could have relieved part of Sikthorn's ignorance. But she said nothing. She did not know *why* her father did what he did. If all he wanted was to regain his throne, he could have chosen a more direct way to challenge her. He did not need to ignite a fatal war with the Nuuri. And he surely did not need to make enslaved Nuuri work on her road. As a means to reclaim the rule of Amika, his plotting was too complex, too vulnerable to discovery—and too cruel.

No, he had some other goal.

That was why she had told no one in Amika about the ambush, not even men she had reason to trust: men like the Fivebridge garrison commander and Commander Crayn and—now—the Vice-Chancellor. Of course, she did not want to risk being overheard by the wrong ears. If nothing else, the rumor of a conflict between Amika's former and present monarchs would make her people even more uneasy than they already were. In addition, one of King Smegin's spies would naturally rush to him with the news that she had survived an attack. But she had a deeper reason as well: she could not answer the questions that would follow. She would be asked, Why? And, Why? And again, *Why?*

To her cost, she did not know.

But Sikthorn was not done with his report.

"Still," he said as if despite his keen sight he could not see the worries squirming in her gaze, "I can tell you this, Majesty. No matter how cleverly he disguises his secrets, he cannot conceal the Decimate of lightning when he wields it at night. Night after night, he exercises his talent. When the skies are clear, his bolts strive to touch the stars. When the heavens are overcast, the clouds seem swollen with silver from horizon to horizon."

Then the Vice-Chancellor shrugged. "As I said, Majesty, I am not supposed to know this. Nevertheless I do. I am glad to learn that I have not committed treason."

His manner concealed whatever he felt; but he may have wanted more reassurance than he could draw from the fact that Postern was King Bifalt's prisoner.

However, Queen Estie had too many other concerns. Sikthorn had told her enough to confirm her worst fears. She could only learn other details and better explanations when she confronted her father. For now, she needed movement and a chance to think. And the glow from the windows told her that sunset was only an hour away. She had to prepare herself to command her honor guard.

If Sikthorn was clever enough to defy Postern, he would understand.

With a jerk, as if all of her muscles had stiffened, she rose from her stool. "Then, sir," she said, masking her fears with severity, "you may be glad to learn that you are now my chancellor. All of Postern's duties are yours. You will report to me, and you will conceal nothing. If you have cause to doubt me—if you become suspicious of me for any reason—you will tell me to my face. I will not fault you if I cannot justify myself.

"But your first task is to arrange for private communication between us, so that when I am in Belleger our messages for each other will not be delayed or intercepted." If King Smegin was *supremely skilled*, he had spies and agents everywhere. And she expected to return to King Bifalt. Once her father's plotting became known, he would change his approach. Whatever he did next, Sikthorn would learn of it long before the news reached Belleger's Fist by ordinary means.

Queen Estie hoped to prevent King Smegin from doing *any*thing next. But if she failed, she would need the ability to receive tidings and send orders swiftly.

Sikthorn stood when she did. Now he nodded an acknowledgment and waited to hear more.

"I will address my honor guard soon," she informed him. "When I am done with them, there will be no guardsmen left to watch over Maloresse. Commander Soulcess will tell you more. Together, you will need to ready the city for their absence.

"Later, I will spend time with Queen Rubia. Tomorrow at dawn, I will depart for King Smegin's retreat."

When Sikthorn nodded again, she went to the door.

As she opened it, however, she paused, struck by a belated thought. "At your convenience," she told the man, "you should take your place in the Chancellor's chamber."

As she left his workroom, she thought she saw him smile.

The place where Princess Estie had spent her whole life until her marriage was a luxurious dwelling, made to house its hundreds of inhabitants—servants, functionaries, courtiers, guardsmen, as well as its monarch's extended family—in rich comfort; and also to display its opulence and pride. In its design and fortifications, however, Amika's Desire was more a fortress than a castle. It did not rise up: it hunkered down. Its walls were as thick as King Fastule's stonemasons had been able to make them so that they would withstand any known form of siege. Its gates were an arm-span thick, oaken boles banded with heavy iron. And in front of the gates was a large open space three hundred paces on each side. It was originally intended as a killing-field in the event of an attack. But Amika's Desire—in fact, Maloresse itself—had never been attacked. Instead, the space was used as a parade ground. Here horsemen competed with each other in games of skill and agility to entertain the Amikan monarchs and their nobles. Soldiers marched from edge to edge in complex formations, demonstrating their precision. Or butts were set up for displays of archery. On rare occasions, Magisters took turns showing off their Decimates. And there were public executions.

Here, as the coming sunset cast long shadows like portents over the ground, Commander Soulcess had assembled Queen Estie's honor guard: one hundred thirteen men with their weapons and their armor, standing at attention.

Knowing that the Queen intended to speak, the first officer had instructed servants to set up a raised platform just outside the gates. From its elevation, Estie would be able to look out over her guardsmen and be sure that they heard her.

As she crossed the bailey from the fortress itself, Queen Estie found Soulcess waiting for her inside the gates, as ready as the men he commanded—and as bewildered. She had only addressed her assembled guardsmen once before, when King Smegin had abdicated and she had claimed the throne. That had been a long time ago. None of them knew why she wanted to speak to them now. Only the quick-witted among them knew that their former lives were finished, perhaps permanently.

"Majesty." The first officer bowed stiffly. "As you commanded." Without waiting to be asked, he handed her a sheet of parchment. "Here are the names you requested. Thirty-three trusted men."

While she glanced at the list, he continued, "In addition, you wanted forty men of proven endurance, Majesty. I have assigned them to sub-Commander Hellick. He has their names. He will muster them when he knows your wishes. The remainder will be led by sub-Commander Waysel."

"Thank you, sir." Estie rolled up the parchment to carry it in one hand. "I will be glad of your company in the morning.

"Now," she said more sternly, bracing herself for his reaction, "there is another matter that will require your attention. Chancellor Postern has been removed from his position."

Soulcess gawped. "Removed, Majesty? The *Chancellor*?"

She ignored his consternation. "I have appointed Vice-Chancellor Sikthorn in his place. Sikthorn will assume all of the Chancellor's duties immediately.

"When we are done here, I want you to speak with him. Answer any questions he may have. No doubt, he will be interested in my use of the honor guard. Also, advise him concerning the safety of the city's people in our absence."

Commander Soulcess flapped his hands as if he had lost control of them. "Majesty, please." His voice was a croak. "I can hardly understand you. The safety of the city's people? In the Chancellor's absence—*and* your honor guard's? It is impossible. There will be chaos. Crimes. Unrest. You cannot—"

"*Calm* yourself, Commander," snapped Estie. Her nerves were worn ragged. Patience eluded her. "The Chancellor is *not* absent. He is Sikthorn. The responsibility is his.

"But he lacks your detailed knowledge of Maloresse. He will have suggestions. Knowing the city, you will see the wisdom of them, or the folly. Then you may find that you, too, have suggestions. Together, you will devise a strategy. After that, your duty is at my side. The Chancellor will care for the city, or he will not, according to his abilities."

Soulcess wrestled with himself; but gradually, Estie's authority mastered him. Sounding oddly shamed, as if she had caught him in an abuse of his position, he choked out, "As you say, Majesty. It will be as you command."

"Then let us proceed, sir." Now she tried to soften the sting of her impatience. "Queen Rubia is waiting for me. She will not dine until I join her. And as you know, she has grown querulous since her husband left her. If I aggravate her, I will suffer for it."

Deliberately, she gave the Commander a chance to exercise his instinct for protective gallantry: an instinct that had failed him so far. But he recovered it when she gave him the opportunity. "At once, Majesty," he replied stoutly.

Straightening his shoulders and sticking out his jaw, he gestured her toward the open gates, the platform, the assembled guardsmen. "I will announce you. Then you will say what you must. Whatever you require will be done."

Making a show of courtliness, he offered her his arm.

She felt a little foolish accepting it. She was wearing the same travel-stained garments that she had worn for days and could not remember her last bath: a condition that would have shocked her nobles and adherents. Under the circumstances, she did not look like the kind of woman who clung to a man for support. Certainly not a man like the first officer. But she had provoked this reaction in him, hoping that it would overrule his confusion. Taking his arm was her only charitable choice.

As they walked, he leaned closer. "If you wish it, Majesty," he said softly, "I will send a servant to inform Queen Rubia that you have been delayed."

Queen Estie shook her head. "She knows, Commander." Again, her thoughts had run ahead of him. "She has already drawn her conclusions. It will not surprise me if she understands more than either of us."

The first officer nodded, doing his best to pretend that he knew what she meant.

When they had passed between the gates, he preceded her to mount the platform. While she waited for his announcement, Estie counted backward, trying to remember—

Then she had it. The Fivebridge garrison. Magister Facile had needed rest, and the garrison commander had required time to corral her Bellegerin escort. For their sakes, she had delayed in her quarters there. To soothe her frustration, she had bathed. Recalling Anina with a pang, she had put on clean clothes in the maid's honor.

The ride from the garrison to Maloresse had tarnished the effect; but perhaps she did not look as disreputable as she felt.

On the platform, Commander Soulcess was saying in his parade-ground voice, "Stand at rest, guardsmen." More loudly, he called, "You others, hold your tongues. This gathering is not for you. I have assembled the honor guard to receive the Queen's commands." Then he returned his attention to his men. "You will know more when you have heard her. She will address you now.

"I present Estie daughter of King Smegin, by right of birth and formal grant the Queen of Amika. She will test your allegiance. If you fail her, you will answer to me."

Estie sighed. No doubt she needed the Commander to vouch for her. It was likely that some of her honor guard did not know her by sight. Others might not recognize her without her robes and gowns of queenship.

But she did not hesitate. She had come too far to falter now—and still had too far to go. Ascending the stairs, she joined Commander Soulcess on the platform. There he gave her the respect of a full Amikan bow. When she had replied in kind, he withdrew, leaving her alone in front of one hundred thirteen armed and armored men.

Their numbers might have intimidated her at any time. Now they were not alone. As she scanned the assembly, she saw that Commander Crayn and his company had come to hear her as well. And behind the guardsmen, a throng had gathered. The rumor that something important was happening had probably reached every quarter of the city. For reasons of their own, hundreds of her people wanted to see and hear her. She had spent too much time away from her realm. Unlike her husband in Belleger, she had made herself forgettable.

Facing her audience, she tried to imagine what King Bifalt might say in her place. She wanted to visualize his example so that she could take a different path. He was too curt, too self-contained. As he could afford to be: he already had the loyalty of his people. She was not sure of hers. She had to reach out to them in her own way.

She waited a moment for silence. More than her honor guard needed to hear her. The crowd of Amikans behind them deserved to be forewarned as well. Nevertheless she had to be careful. She was certain that at least a handful of the people in front of her were loyal to King Smegin. Some of them were likely to be active spies. One or more of them might leave immediately to repeat what she said to her father. Then he would know that she had survived his ambush—if he did not already. But if she did not explain what she was doing *now*, he would have to guess how to defend himself.

She had to keep her intentions to herself.

"Men of the Queen's honor guard," she began when she felt ready to make herself heard. "Men and women of Amika. I am glad of your presence. Many years have passed since I have addressed you all. I have not felt the need to speak. And you know of my efforts to heal the harm of war and share the benefits of peace. I did not imagine that you needed to hear me.

"But now events have overtaken us. If we do not act, we may not live to regret our delay."

Shadows lengthened across hundreds of faces, darkening them like doubts; but Queen Estie did not let the sun's setting sway her.

"For decades," she continued more loudly, "King Bifalt of Belleger has warned us that war is coming, a great war that will dwarf all our conceptions of slaughter and devastation. It is not *our* war. Amika has no enemies. Belleger has none. Rather, it is the Last Repository's war.

The library has an enemy, a foe of such implacable savagery that he has gathered an unimaginable host and crossed oceans so that he can strike at the object of his hatred. And that enemy is *near*. He knows the Last Repository's hiding place. While I speak to you, he is *coming*.

"The library's war is not *ours*." She intended to speak calmly. "The library's enemy is not *ours*." She did not wish to frighten her people. "He cares nothing for Amika or Belleger. He does not come to strike at *us*." Nevertheless passion rose in her as she named the danger. She was sick with frustration and on fire with outrage. What she felt cried out in her voice. "But we are *in his way*. Before he can assail the Last Repository, he must pass through us.

"That is a danger we cannot flee. No doubt, it would ease our hearts if we could simply stand aside and let him pass by. But we do not have that choice. He is not *our* enemy—but he is also not a fool. He will not leave a living force behind him. He will not expose his back to any foe. Rather, he will roll over us until Belleger and Amika have been reduced to smoldering ash and rubble.

"We are fortunate that he is not here *now*. He is only *coming*. And King Bifalt has spent many years preparing for this day. For many years, I have stood with King Bifalt. For many years, Amika and Belleger have supported each other. We will not be taken by surprise. But the first threats are near. We will act against them now, while we can."

Deliberately, Queen Estie aimed her voice at the throng behind her guardsmen. "The first threats are in the north." That was as close as she let herself come to prevarication. Let a spy report to King Smegin. Let her father think that she meant to answer the massing of the Nuuri. "I have three tasks for my honor guard, three prongs for our response. If our good fortune holds, they will forestall the enemy. Otherwise, they will counter him."

Then she focused her attention on her soldiers. "Commander Soul-cess and I have made our choices. Sub-Commander Waysel will lead one company, sub-Commander Hellick, another. You will be mustered by your officers when I have given them my instructions.

"Commander Soulcess and I will undertake the third task. We will need men to ride with us. Because we will face the gravest threat, my life will be in the hands of my company, and I want my guardsmen to know our peril. I will call out the names of those who will accompany me so that they can ready themselves."

Unrolling the sheet of parchment, she held it in front of her and began to read the first officer's list.

Blissin.

Undit.

Rousel.

She thought that she would recite the thirty-three names and be done. But before she reached the fourth, a guardsman cheered. After the fifth, several men began to mark each name with a stamp of one foot. By the time she had named ten of them, half of her soldiers were stamping as if to confirm every added man. Then her whole honor guard was stamping, matching the rhythm of her list. She was allowed to say each name clearly. In the gaps between the names, the parade ground thundered.

Swaleman.

Hankerish.

Adour.

The platform seemed to tremble under her, shaken by the pounding of boots. Where the last sunshine reached between the shadows, she saw small bursts of dust rising to form clouds that held the light.

Kindrel: thirty-two.

Gurdin: thirty-three.

Deliberately, Estie rolled the parchment again and tucked it under her belt.

When the men realized that she was done, they raised their fists and shouted: the one hundred thirteen of the honor guard and the twenty of Commander Crayn's company, all of them eager to serve their Queen, or to serve Amika, or simply to have an enemy. And all of them seemed to know the men she had called out. Estie could almost believe that they approved of her choices.

Commander Soulcess had done well.

If her father had any sense, he would fear her.

The first officer knew his moment. After all, Queen Estie was not the first Amikan monarch he had obeyed. Returning to the platform, he quieted the men. In his stentorian voice, he told them to be fully supplied and ready for more explicit orders by dawn. Then he dismissed them.

Some of the guardsmen ran: those with families, perhaps, or those who had left too many duties or women unattended. Others moved away in small groups, talking among themselves; trying, no doubt, to guess what would be asked of them.

While the throng of Amikans thinned away to nothing, sub-Commander Waysel and sub-Commander Hellick came forward to join Soulcess and Queen Estie behind the platform. Estie looked for Crayn, but he and his men had left the parade ground with the others. They already had their orders.

She was in a hurry now; on the edge of a kind of nervous exhaustion. She did not wait for questions or offer to repeat herself.

"Sub-Commander Waysel," she began, "yours is an escort duty. The Chancellor will give the necessary orders when Commander Soulcess has told him what we do. You will take our first delivery of cannon, shot, and gunpowder into Belleger."

Before Waysel could open his mouth, the Queen explained, "You may think that forty men are too many for your task. But you will not take the wagons and their cargo to Belleger's Fist. You will deliver them to the Bay of Lights, where Commander Forguile and Captain Flisk require them. And when you arrive, you will help with their emplacement. Forty men will seem too few, but I cannot spare more."

If she did not entirely share King Bifalt's obsession with fortifying the coast, she supported it nonetheless.

While sub-Commander Waysel chewed on her instructions, considering their implications, Estie turned to Hellick.

"At dawn, sub-Commander, you will take your men eastward along my road. And you will ride hard." She clenched her fists to steady herself. "I have heard rumors of slavery among the teams of laborers. *Slavery*, sir. *Nuuri* slaves." She did not believe that any of her honor guard would desert in order to warn King Smegin. Not now. But on this point, she did not care if anyone reported to her father. She felt sure that sending slaves to work on her road was a small detail in King Smegin's larger designs. "It is a great crime, sub-Commander, and you will end it. You will deal with the slavers and care for the slaves.

"You also may think that forty men are too many. But I do not know how many slavers there are, or how well they fight, or how much support they can summon. I rely on you to carry out my orders."

Before either officer could ask the obvious questions, she dismissed them. They knew enough. She did not want them to know more. Nineteen guardsmen had already deserted. Despite her confidence, others might be tempted. For her own protection, as well as for the safety of the soldiers who remained loyal, she hid her secrets behind a mask of imperiousness until Waysel and Hellick left her.

The first officer was harder to dislodge from her side. If his subordinates were confused, he was entirely out of his depth. But she reminded him of his duties, of which he had many, and soon he hurried away.

Only then did Queen Estie let herself tremble.

Alone, she went back into Amika's Desire and made her way to the apartments that served as her home. She needed a bath and clean clothes—a chance to compose herself—before she faced her mother.

Queen Rubia's apartments were sumptuous by any standard. Estie could have slept better on any of the carpets than in her bed in Belleger's Fist. The tapestries on the walls—in which Estie had no interest—were said to be magnificent. All of the furniture had been fashioned by people who loved their craft. Some of it was almost comfortable. Even in this season, Queen Rubia's sitting room held a profusion of bouquets in vases of cobalt stoneware. The candlesticks and lamps were wrought in gold, and several were exquisite. Fortunately, the portraits—of Rubia herself, of each of her three daughters, even of King Smegin—were less admirable, and ill-lit in addition. Estie did not like looking at them.

As she was admitted, she felt a moment of profound relief to find that Demure and Immure had not been invited. She had no wish to see either of her sisters. And Demure would have brought her fat, foppish husband, a minor noble who had contrived to keep half his wealth by donating the other half freely to Queen Estie's various endeavors. For her part, Immure would have dragged along her latest suitor, whoever he was: a man too young for her whose only real interest was the hope that she had influence with one of Amika's queens. At any time, Estie would have found conversation with the four of them distasteful. At *this* time, it would have been agony.

But Queen Rubia, as always, knew what she was doing. The suddenness of Estie's arrival, and the extraordinary actions she had taken in the course of one afternoon, had told Queen Rubia everything she needed to know about the urgency of her eldest daughter's visit. She was too sympathetic toward Estie, and too concerned, to inflict Demure, Immure, and their men on her.

King Smegin's abandoned wife rose from her chair of state as Estie entered. Some other displaced queen might have greeted the ruling monarch with a deep curtsy, either as a purely ceremonial show of regard, or as a sarcastic display of resentment. But Queen Rubia did not offer homage. Instead, she came to meet Estie and wrap her in a long hug.

While they embraced, Queen Rubia murmured through her daughter's still-damp hair, "My dear. My dear." Then she stepped back; held Estie at arm's length to study her.

Smiling crookedly, Estie faced her mother. Queen Rubia had put on weight over the years. She had jowls now, plump cheeks, a thick waist. But she declared her attitude toward herself by wearing the most regal of her informal attire. Her hair was elaborately piled on her head, but it was held in place with ribbons, not with jewels. Altogether, she presented herself as one queen to another in the privacy of her home.

Since her husband had left her for his retreat, his studies, and his plots, her gaze had grown more and more shrouded, as if she were willing herself to go blind. Still, her sight was sharp enough to see what she wanted to see. When she was done looking at Estie, she dropped her daughter's arms and made a low sound like a snarl in the back of her throat.

"When you assumed the throne," she said harshly, "I was proud of you. You know that. You became the Queen of Amika. The *first* queen with no king to overshadow her. No king to wield the real power. Now I am ashamed of myself. I should have wept. I had no idea what would be expected of you, or what you would have to endure. It is too much to ask. Yet now I see—"

Estie felt a dangerous pricking in the backs of her eyes. "Is it so obvious, Mother?"

"Obvious?" The older woman took the question seriously. "You eat little," she began judiciously, "and care for yourself less. You should indulge yourself more. A little pampering would do you no harm. And that husband of yours—"

Then she stopped herself. "And yet—" Looking Estie full in the face, she let her daughter see that she was sincere. "Estie, I swear you have not aged a day in ten years. You carry your burdens well.

"You will tell me what they are." Queen Rubia took Estie by the hand. "I will not allow you to leave until you do. But I will not hear a word until you have eaten. Whenever I see you, you look famished. Now you seem ravenous."

Estie knew her mother well enough to understand that she was not talking about food—or not just about food.

Queen Rubia drew her daughter into her dining room, where a fresh-faced maid with a reticent demeanor served a hearty soup, slabs of bread with rich butter, and more other dishes than the cooks of Belleger's Fist could have provided. Estie sat opposite her mother on the long sides of the table so that they were not far apart. Faced with so much food, she felt a strange impulse to nibble at her meal instead of enjoying it. On some deep level, she needed to be hungry. She needed what her hunger implied about her; about her marriage; about her fears for her people, and for Belleger. As one of her tutors had told her long ago, Hunger teaches many things. None of her guardsmen would have a chance to eat this well before they risked their lives.

But she was hungry in more ways than she could confess to her mother. Her craving for a good meal was only one of them, at once the least important and the most necessary. When she realized that Queen Rubia had not touched her own food—that she was waiting for her daughter to begin—Estie gave up her reluctance. With a shiver that was both pleasure and revulsion, she allowed herself to repay the simplest costs of hard traveling and poor rations.

For a while as they ate, working their way from dish to dish, Queen Rubia smiled a mother's smile and did not speak. Gradually, however, her smile became a frown. It folded itself into a scowl: a sign that she was losing patience. Without waiting for her daughter to finish, she asked abruptly, "Still no child, Estie?"

Sighing, Estie put down her knife and fork. The topic was too familiar: it came up whenever she visited her mother. And it caused too much pain. "No, Mother," she admitted. "No child. No children. No heir."

She meant, No future. Not for me. Not for Amika. Not that I can see.

Queen Rubia made her snarling sound again. "I do not understand." With unnecessary vehemence, she threw her napkin onto the tabletop. "What manner of man *is* your husband? You are a desirable woman. When you married, you were in your best years for children. They would not be too much for you even now. How can he bear to fail you? How can he face himself, or his people? I thought better of him."

More deliberately, Estie put her own napkin aside. Whenever anyone insulted King Bifalt, she wanted to shout. For Queen Rubia's sake, she restrained herself.

"Mother, we have spoken of this before. I am done with it. I will say what I must. Then I will not speak of it again.

"No, I have no child. No man has bedded me. Certainly, King Bifalt has not. He does not love me. I believe that he cannot." He was ruled by promises that he had made before they ever met. "I am precisely as forlorn, as lonely, as grief-ridden as you expect me to be.

"But I have something that no woman of my acquaintance can match. I have a husband who deserves my admiration. A man whose given word is absolute. A man who has been abused by the Magisters of the library, and who refuses to abuse anyone else in the same fashion. A man whose concern for his people in every way, from bare survival to true well-being, is everything a king's should be. A man who is *not my father*."

In her mother's eyes, Estie saw what the woman wanted to ask. Do you call it *abuse* to be bedded by your husband? But Estie's last words stopped her. Queen Rubia sat back in her chair. The shroud came back over her eyes. In an abstract tone, a tone she might have used to discuss a minor relative's wife's gown with one of her maids, she said, "There it is. The truth that you have kept to yourself. You hoped to spare me."

Estie winced. She knew that tone. It was how Queen Rubia spoke when she was keeping her distance. Protecting herself.

Without heat, the older woman declared, "I have more than one cause to feel shame. You endure an unendurable marriage because I gave you an unendurable father."

Taken aback by the stab of the distress her mother withheld, Estie reached across the table to clasp her hand. But Queen Rubia's sudden harshness forestalled her.

"I know what I have done. I do not deny it, any of it. But as long as you are my daughter, I do not regret it. If you and I and all Amika now pay the price for your father's place in my bed, I call the bargain fair."

Queen Estie of Amika, who never wept, covered her eyes and bowed her head over the flawless white of the tablecloth.

She heard rather than saw her mother rise. "Come, my dear." Once again, Queen Rubia spoke in her abstract way, guarding her heart. "We will sit more comfortably. There will be a breeze from the windows. If it cools the room, it may help you to ask whatever you wish. I will try to answer."

Estie needed a moment to control her emotions. Then she left the table and followed her mother into the sitting room.

The night air stirred through the chamber, dissipating some of the season's persistent heat. The flames of the candles did their small dances, but if they flickered at all, the effect was banished by the steady glow of the lamps. In a negligent manner, as if she did not care where she sat, Queen Rubia claimed a chair that Estie recognized as the least comfortable in the room. Smiling wanly at her mother's self-abnegation, she seated herself where the light favored her view of the other woman.

"So, Estie," began Queen Rubia. "Ask."

Estie had her first question ready. She had been waiting to ask it for days. "Mother," she said with care, "what do you know of my gift?"

"Your gift?" Queen Rubia did not try to hide her surprise. "What do you mean? You cannot refer to a talent for sorcery? Surely, you know that you have none?"

With an effort, Estie forced herself to sound calm. "No, Mother. I do not know that.

"I am traveling with a Magister from the Last Repository. You know of her. She is Magister Facile, who came with Prince Bifalt and Commander Forguile to restore sorcery after the alliance was forged. She has told me that I *do* have a gift. She cannot tell me what it is. She cannot awaken it for me. But she assures me that I have it.

"Do you know anything of this? Did my father speak of it? Did you overhear him speak of it?"

"No," declared King Smegin's wife at once. "When he first saw you in my arms, he swore that you were flawed by a complete absence of talent. He made a great show of his disgust. He was outraged that his reign came to this, that his inheriting child was worse than female, she was a female who would never wield theurgy. I always believed"—she caught herself—"that is, I chose to believe that he made you his favorite to compensate for his initial scorn.

"Of course," went on Queen Rubia while Estie cursed to herself, "he only smiled when Demure and then Immure were born. They, too, he said, had no gift. But the harm, he said, was already done. One girl without sorcery or three made no difference."

More sourly, the older woman finished, "You know how he has treated them since they entered the world. That alone should have caused me to question his judgment of you. If none of you were gifted, why were you his favorite while your sisters were dismissed as hindrances? But in those days, I chose what I saw and what I did not. And I dreaded *his* use of theurgy. I was comforted to think no daughter of mine shared his gift."

Estie was fuming. But she had had days to absorb Magister Facile's revelation. *King Smegin has known since your birth that you are capable of sorcery*. Instinctively, she believed the sorceress, despite her reasons for distrusting the woman. Magister Facile's claim fit the way Estie had learned to view her father since then-Prince Bifalt had entered her life. *That he kept his knowledge secret tells us much about him.*

"Do not fault yourself, Mother," said Estie, trying to soften an old hurt. "If I have a gift, it has not been awakened. And if it is not awake, it is of no use to anyone." Much like her body's craving for her husband, and her love for the man himself. "Certainly, it is of no use to me."

Then she returned to her more immediate concerns. "Do you want to know what King Smegin is doing?"

Queen Rubia considered the question. Her pain was written in the folds and creases of her face. Finally, she decided, "No. I know too much. When my life as your father's wife ended, I decided that I had seen enough. I chose blindness. I did not wish to see him again, or know any of his doings. But now you have opened my eyes. I do not need to hear more."

Ruling herself sternly, Estie did not relent. "Nevertheless I will tell you this much. After all these years, he thinks the time is ripe to overthrow my rule in Amika.

"Mother, I cannot put it off longer. I must confront him."

The older woman threw back her head. Her mouth hung open. For a moment, she looked as stricken—as motionless—as a woman who had passed out of life between one heartbeat and the next. When she drew her next breath, it shuddered in her chest.

"Now I understand," she murmured. "Your haste. The sorceress with you. The elevation of Sikthorn. The disposition of your honor guard." Her maids told her everything that happened in Amika's Desire; in all Maloresse. "You must confront your father. You are making ready.

"You need my counsel."

Abruptly, Queen Rubia heaved herself out of her chair. But when she reached her feet, her strength seemed to desert her. Tottering as she moved, she made her way around the room, snuffing one unsteady candle flame at a time.

"Do you know he sent for me?" she said as if she were talking to the slow death of the chamber's light. "A year after he left Amika's Desire, he sent for me." One candle after another. "And again a year later. I stayed with him for almost a fortnight. Then he was done with me."

While Estie watched, transfixed by the force of her mother's desire to hide what she saw, Queen Rubia finished extinguishing the candles. In the same way, she began to blow out the lamps.

"I went because I am his wife. I could not forget the feel of his body, or the sharpness of his mind, or the quicksilver of his temper. But after my second visit, he was done. I could no longer conceal what I saw in him, and he did not like the view through my eyes. From that day to this, I have preferred blindness."

Then all the lights were gone. Yet Estie could still discern her mother. The illumination that came through open doorways from other rooms showed Queen Rubia as a knot of shadows. She could not hide from her daughter as she shuffled back to her chair, lowered herself into it, and closed her eyes.

Like a woman who had aged while she put out the lights, she said, "If you mean to confront him, there are two things you must know." Her voice quavered, and she was breathing heavily. "The first is this.

"He believes that his gift for sorcery serves him. It does not. He serves it. He has been enslaved by his own power."

Although her mother could not see her, Estie nodded. King Bifalt had made similar statements. He believed that eventually every Magister would be enslaved by what theurgy could do. The arrogance of men like the sorcerers of the Last Repository was only one step down the slope to that fate.

"Also," continued Queen Rubia as if her thoughts matched her daughter's, "you must understand that he will never forgive the Magisters of the library. At any time, they could have given him the power to destroy Belleger. He asked often enough, as his father did before him, and his father's father. But the Magisters refused them all. Whether they did so courteously or disdainfully changed nothing. Your father received their refusals as scorn.

"There are a number of crimes he does not forgive. The worst is scorn."

Estie was trembling again, but now she did not try to suppress it. If her mother had wanted to say more, she might not have been able to hear it. The clamor of her confusion threatened to deafen her. King Smegin would never forgive the Magisters of the library—and yet he enslaved Nuuri to speed the progress of her road? He wanted her and King Bifalt and every soldier that the realms could muster to be able to reach the Last Repository more quickly? She must have missed some crucial aspect of his machinations. Lylin and Magister Facile must have missed it. They had all assumed that putting Nuuri to work on her road was intended to do nothing more than provoke her; that King Smegin's underlying purpose was to incite a war that Amika and Belleger could not afford. They had assumed that all of his efforts were bent on breaking the alliance so that he could reclaim his throne.

And they had trusted their reasoning. She had. But if they were wrong—? If the massing of the Nuuri against Amika were merely a side effect? If King Smegin's true purpose required her road? For access to the library? So that he could achieve some unimaginable revenge?

Estie shook her head, trying to knock her thoughts into some semblance of order. A desire to reclaim his throne was cruel and destructive, ultimately ruinous; but she could understand it. An obsession with revenge against the immense fortress and vast powers of the Last Repository was insane.

Fortunately, Queen Rubia had fallen silent. With her head resting against the back of her chair, and her eyes closed, she seemed to be drifting toward sleep, exhausted by what she had compelled herself to look at and confess.

For what felt like a long time, Estie sat quietly, waiting for the worst of her trembling to pass. Then she left her seat and went to her mother. With all of her gentleness, she kissed her mother's forehead.

When she was sure that she had not roused King Smegin's bereft wife, she returned to her own apartments to get as much sleep as she could. As much as her fear and confusion allowed.

ELEVEN

POKING A NEST

Long ago, Elgart had been tutored by Flamora and Amandis in the Last Repository. As if they had known his future, the devotees of Flesh and Spirit had prepared him for his later life. Now he called himself King Bifalt's Captain of Spies. He was always busy plying his skills—and always suspicious.

Ordinarily, his duties revolved around keeping track of Amikans in the Open Hand: a task that he performed without bias for both his King and the Queen-Consort, if for different reasons. King Bifalt wanted to know how his wife's people behaved. His wife wanted to know how her people were treated. In lesser disturbances and difficulties—for example, in instances of dishonest dealings between Bellegerin and Amikan merchants and tradesmen—he intervened, usually by sending one of his personal enforcers to address the problem. Situations like that were normal everywhere: they were not worth troubling the King and Queen-Consort. But when he identified thugs or killers, agitators of any kind, gangs of bullies preying on the weak, or people whose stealth suggested conspiracies, he tracked them secretly, and reported what he learned.

To watch over a city as extensive as the Hand, he maintained a considerable network of subordinate spies, informers, bodyguards, enforcers, and casual gossips ranging from serving-wenches and off-duty riflemen to plain charlatans and lesser nobles. Their observations and his own kept him occupied at all hours of the day and night. Still, they were not enough.

Fortunately, he was aided by the devotees of Flesh. They were all courtesans in the best sense of the word: their gifts for distracting angry men were wondrous. Sometimes they used their bodies. More often, they offered music that had an almost-sorcerous power to encourage dancing; or they sang songs that made even thugs blink back tears; or they told tales that entranced everyone around them. And they heard secrets, some of which they shared with Elgart.

Directly and indirectly, they did more than relieve unrest and prevent fights. They also assisted him with the most covert and perhaps the most vital of his duties: the protection of the unremarkable houses, barns, cellars, and warehouses where Belleger's kegs of gunpowder and crates of bullets were hidden.

Although he had no proof, Elgart believed that the real purpose of the people who plotted against the alliance was to locate those stores. Rifles were useless without them. Belleger could not defend itself without them. And the rifles themselves, thousands of them, were locked away deep in Belleger's Fist, where only a full siege could reach them. General Klamath's soldiers and Prince Jaspid's guard had them: no one else did. The bullets were more vulnerable.

Elgart watched over them with particular care.

The Captain of Spies enjoyed all of his responsibilities. They suited his inquisitive and cynical nature. He liked uncovering connections and intentions. But his greatest pleasures involved identifying and tracking the Chancellor's—the former Chancellor's—agents and messengers.

Postern had employed a number of them, and they were good. If they provoked brawls or stirred distrust, they stayed in the background. If they passed secrets or wooed support, they kept to the shadows. None of them wore Amikan garb. Few of them looked Amikan. Elgart had to work hard to be sure of them, and he could never be sure that he had found them all. But when he *was* sure of them, he did not expose them, except by naming them to King Bifalt. Instead, he had fun with them. He assigned his least skilled underlings to follow them. He wanted them to know they were watched. That alone would inhibit them. And it would encourage overconfidence, reinforce the old Amikan belief that Bellegerins were too blunt-minded to be effective agents. As a result,

Postern's servants could be apprehended with comparative ease whenever King Bifalt wished.

Wisely, thought Elgart, the King chose to do nothing. He was reluctant to tilt the precarious balance of the alliance.

All in all, Elgart valued his duties in the Open Hand. They kept him honest. For him, frustrations were not obstacles: they were challenges to be overcome. Because of him, King Bifalt knew more about the state of his realm than anyone who opposed him would suppose. Because of Elgart, the King knew who could be trusted and who could not.

The obvious exception, of course, was the Church of the Great God Rile. Elgart still had not found a way to penetrate the secrets of those priests. But he had not forgotten them. Their turn was coming. They had reached Belleger through Amika, and their teachings were improbably persuasive. One way or another, Elgart intended to learn more about them.

But then the situation changed. Overnight, a lull came to the Open Hand, an unfamiliar quiet free of all but the least worrisome outbreaks. At the same time, Postern's agents and messengers went to ground like hunted animals. After his confession during the King's public council, and the Queen-Consort's departure for Amika: a lull. It was like removing a burr from under the saddle of a horse. The beast still fretted. It rolled its eyes and shied away. But it did not buck or fight its rider. Given time, it would become manageable.

Elgart was deeply suspicious. He drew the obvious conclusions—but he did not know how to answer them. It was not his place to question Postern. He did not think that the time was right to start arresting Amikan spies, a tactic the Queen-Consort's people could easily misinterpret in her absence. And he had done as much as he could for Estie herself when he had asked a devotee of Spirit to accompany her. In addition, she was protected by Captain Rowt's men while she traveled Belleger. In Amika, she would have her own guardsmen around her. Also, Magister Facile was with her. She should be safe enough.

In the meantime, Elgart chased his suspicions.

Because he was both curious and persistent, he knew by sunset of the same day that three men on horseback had left the Open Hand a few hours after Postern's confession, riding hard in the direction of Amika. An interesting detail, to Elgart's way of thinking, but not necessarily significant. Haste had many possible explanations. He did not learn until the next morning that the three men were Amikan, and then he was still only curious. During the afternoon, however, he heard that one of those three was a lesser son of a noble Amikan family that opposed Queen Estie's rule. His interest became more active. Asking the right people the right questions, he discovered that those Amikans had spent the previous afternoon drinking in an alehouse called the Beleaguered Eagle.

Coincidentally or not, the Beleaguered Eagle was Prince Lome's preferred tavern. The Prince spent some afternoons and most evenings there, drowning his resentments in sour ale and acid wine.

Well. A divided man himself, Elgart understood the Prince's bitterness. Before his brief study with Flamora and Amandis, Elgart's own contradictions had often made him bitter; caustic with his comrades; harsh in his judgments. He knew where the distress that haunted King Abbator's youngest son could lead.

And he knew that Prince Lome wanted the Archpriest of the Great God Rile, Makh, included in King Bifalt's private council. There was no obvious connection. Certainly, none of the three Amikans numbered among the spies and messengers Elgart had identified. But he never hesitated to jump to conclusions.

He informed King Bifalt that *someone* in Amika had an urgent interest in Chancellor Postern's downfall—and possibly in the Queen-Consort's reaction to it. But after that, unfortunately, there was nothing he could do to pursue the matter. In the back of his mind, he dithered, waiting for General Klamath's return, or for King Bifalt to take some kind of action. Meanwhile, he focused on other interests until one of his people happened to mention that the Beleaguered Eagle had more than one unusual patron. A priest of the Church also enjoyed disreputable drinking in the grotty tavern.

Wearing his twisted grin, half smile, half grimace, Elgart decided that the time had come to learn more about the Church and its Great God. He wanted to meet the Archpriest. He had a few questions.

But he did not go alone. Magister Facile had warned him. The bronze cross with the statue of a naked man standing behind it had warned him. And his personal guards, Flax and Howel—like Elgart himself—lacked even the slightest gift for sorcery. Since he could not ask for Magister Facile's company, he elected to invite Magister Pillion.

Pillion's gift was the Decimate of earthquake. At the King's command, he and his substantial family lived in a modest house just outside the walls of Belleger's Fist. In fact, King Bifalt had given all of Belleger's earth-shakers—all three of them—homes near the Fist's fortifications. He kept them close so that they could defend the walls if his keep was ever threatened by theurgy like theirs. But after twenty years of peace, the war he feared was an abstraction to most of his people. Few Bellegerins truly believed that the Fist—or the Open Hand— would ever be attacked.

Certainly, Magister Pillion did not. He was a small, unassuming man with little imagination and no apparent ambitions apart from an unfortunate love of gardening: unfortunate because most of his vegetables, herbs, and flowers died. But Elgart liked him, at least in part because—unlike many other Magisters—he allowed himself to be liked. Indeed, only his slate-grey robe marked him as a theurgist. As a man, he lacked the sense of power or superiority, the sense of being necessary, that characterized most sorcerers. In general, they were acutely aware of what they could do. In contrast, Pillion seemed oblivious to the fact that he could crack the ground and heave it aside with a thought. He loved his garden and his family, and did not understand why King Bifalt considered him important.

Elgart had known the man for years before he realized that Magister Pillion was more interested in his Decimate than he appeared to be. His passion for gardening exposed him. Elgart had seen the joy on Pillion's face when he made furrows and water-channels without having to dig them, or when he piled dirt without using his hands.

The Magister had more children than Elgart had bothered to count, and his wife was a woman twice his size who looked like she could have beaten off a gang of thugs or outshouted a blare of thunder. But she ruled her brood with even-handed affection, and treated her husband as if he were a fragile piece of crockery. Fragile and precious. Elgart only heard her raise her voice when she called Pillion in from the garden.

The Magister joined Elgart willingly enough, smiling his unpretentious smile. For years now, Elgart had called on him perhaps once a season, on those rare occasions when the scarred spy was in a mood to set aside his usual wary probing: often enough that Elgart's friendship became familiar, not often enough to disturb Pillion's preferred life. Their custom was to leave the house in the evening after the children were fed, walk to a secluded alehouse, drink two or three tankards, and talk about every inconsequential subject that came into their heads. For the most part, Magister Pillion rambled on about his gardening and his children. Elgart found their few hours together refreshing, a respite from suspicion and prying.

Clearly, Pillion assumed that this occasion would be like all the others. Distracted by his own concerns, he did not appear to notice the time of day until Elgart's path diverged from their usual walk. Then he raised his head, looked around with an air of surprise, and said, "This is midafternoon, Elgart. What are we doing?"

Elgart replied with his split smile. "*You*, Magister, are being a good friend. *I* am presuming on your generous nature."

The small man's brow wrinkled as if he wondered whether he ought to be anxious. "Whatever for?"

"The simple answer, my friend," said Elgart, "is that I want a witness." His tone made this subject sound as inconsequential as everything else he and Pillion had discussed. "I want you to accompany me, watch and listen, and say nothing. But I am reluctant to tell you why." He grinned broadly. "I fear your friendship. If you know my thoughts, you will be inclined to share them. When we are alone together afterward, I will want to hear *your* thoughts, not a reflection of mine. I will explain myself then."

Magister Pillion smiled easily; nodded like a man who did not suffer from curiosity and had nothing better to do. Then, abruptly, he gave Elgart a look of horror. "You are not taking me to see the King?"

"Certainly not!" vowed Elgart. "Even *my* presumption is not that extreme. If King Bifalt summoned you, you would have time to prepare yourself. And you would be expected to speak, not remain silent. What I am asking you to witness is an attempt to satisfy my curiosity, nothing more."

"Oh, well." The sorcerer relaxed. "If that is all. We are friends. I can trust a friend for a few hours."

Elgart patted his shoulder. "Of course, you can."

Just for a moment, the spy despised himself. He was behaving like Magister Marrow, the librarian of the Last Repository: he was making use of a more innocent man without explaining himself or obtaining an informed consent.

But he answered himself quickly. His desire for Pillion's uninfluenced observations was sincere. And he could not imagine that what he had in mind would harm his friend. In that respect, Elgart's actions were entirely unlike Magister Marrow's. To all appearances, the Church of the Great God Rile was benign. In fact, its presence in Belleger depended on that appearance. Its sanctuary was probably safer than the Hand's streets.

Had Magister Facile sensed theurgy in the Church? Had Elgart been overcome by an uncharacteristic drowsiness? Yes. But he did not think for a moment that his unexpected nap had been an effect of sorcery. That was impossible. Everyone else there had remained awake. No Magister in Belleger or Amika could exert power against just one man in a crowd.

While he and Pillion walked, Elgart recovered his peculiar equanimity; his point of balance between the opposing forces of his nature.

When they reached the Church of the Great God Rile, Elgart knocked on the door, but there was no answer. Although the lamp over the lintel was lit, his polite rapping returned the hollow sound of a door that opened on an empty room. The door itself, as hastily hammered together as the rest of the edifice, rattled in its frame: a sign, Elgart suspected, that it was not bolted. Perhaps it was never bolted. What could priests serving the Great God have to protect—or to hide?

Waggling his eyebrows—a show of amusement that he hoped would reassure Magister Pillion—Elgart opened the door and went from afternoon sunlight into the gloom of the sanctuary.

The hall was indeed empty, but it was not entirely dark. When the sorcerer closed the door, Elgart could still see the rows of pews for the worshippers, with the high dais beyond them. A few lamps set into the walls near the door had been left lit. In their dim illumination, he made out the blurred shape of the pulpit on the left side of the dais. With more difficulty, he discerned the outlines of the tall cross and its statue on the right.

Whispering for some reason, Pillion asked, "This is the Church? Why is it open and lit when it is not in use?"

Elgart put a finger to his lips: a reminder. Whispering himself, he answered, "I suspect the Church wants us to know that we may enter at any time. The priests have nothing to fear."

The Magister opened his mouth to ask another question, then grimaced ruefully, shrugged, and said nothing.

With a nod of approval, Elgart patted his friend's shoulder again. Together, they moved between the pews toward the dais.

He was willing to call out for some priest or servant. But as he and Pillion neared the dais, a robed figure came out of the darkness behind the pulpit.

A priest. In fact, he looked like the same man who had read the scripture and spoken to the worshippers when Elgart had attended a service. His black cassock was belted with black rope: he wore black sandals and a black beard: his eyebrows made ebony stripes on his forehead. As soon as he spoke, Elgart knew he was the same man.

"Be welcome in the Church of the Great God Rile." It was the same sonorous voice, deep and full. "All who are in need are welcome." It conveyed authority, sorrow, and kindness. "All who suffer, all who question themselves, all who are merely curious—all are welcome.

"You come strangely, a Magister and a laborer. Such men commonly avoid each other. But the Great God does not see outward distinctions. He sees within. How may his Church serve you?"

Elgart's unequal grin twisted his face. "Thank you," he replied, trying for meekness. "We have come for a purpose, as you already know. But your courtesy deserves courtesy in return. How may I address you?"

In the dim light from the back of the hall, the priest seemed to have no eyes; or they were hidden by the stark black of his eyebrows. If he smile or sneered, his beard concealed it.

"You may call me Father, my son."

"Thank you," said Elgart again, "Father. My companion does not choose to speak. I speak for him." Hoping to catch the priest by surprise, he asked at once, "Am I addressing the Archpriest Makh?"

The priest betrayed no visible reaction. "You are not, my son. I am Father Skurn."

In response, Elgart feigned embarrassment. "Forgive my presumption. We have heard your scripture and your explanation of it, and now we find that we have questions. We were told that the Archpriest could answer us. May we speak with him?"

"Not at present, my son," answered the priest. "He is absent from the Open Hand. There are many regions of Belleger that have not heard the tidings of the Great God Rile. He has gone to consecrate a new Church"—a small twitch of the priest's hand indicated the whole realm—"elsewhere. He will return in perhaps a fortnight.

"But if I may be of service—?"

Hoping piously that Pillion would remember to keep his mouth shut, Elgart made a modest show of enthusiasm. "Certainly, Father." He had no difficulty concealing his disappointment. After all, his interest in the Archpriest was mere suspicion. It was based on little more than Prince Lome's efforts to win King Bifalt's trust for Archpriest Makh. The spy's more concrete interest lay in learning what had frightened Magister Facile. "If you will not be offended by the ignorant questions of men who know nothing about gods, we will be glad for your spiritual guidance."

Father Skurn nodded with the dignity of a bow. "Then, my sons, await me a moment."

As if he had become mist, he evaporated into the darkness behind the pulpit. Almost at once, however, a portion of the wall below the dais shifted, revealing a door. Lamplight from an inner corridor silhouetted the priest, made him an incarnation of shadow.

"If you will accompany me, my sons?"

Holding his companion by the arm, Elgart drew Magister Pillion forward. With his free hand, he motioned again for silence.

When they had followed the priest a dozen paces along the corridor, they came to a small, doorless chamber that would have suited a scribe or secretary. Well lit by lamps, it held a table like a desk, although there were no papers, scrolls, books, or writing implements in the room. A single stool waited on the far side of the table. Several others stood closer to the entryway.

Father Skurn entered the chamber first; seated himself on the single stool. Then he gestured for Elgart and Magister Pillion to approach and take seats.

Now Elgart could see the priest's eyes. Deep in their nests of wrinkles, they looked like the eyes of a man who had seen a world of woe.

"Thank you, Father," said the spy again as he and his friend sat down. "You must have many duties. It is good of you to give us your time."

Resonant as an immense bell, but muted and gentle, the priest replied, "I am here to testify on behalf of the Great God Rile. You have questions, my sons? I will answer them if I can. What better use is there for my time?"

Elgart nodded. "As you say, Father. Still, it is good of you. I hope our ignorance will not strain your patience."

Out of Father Skurn's sight below the edge of the table, he put his hand on Magister Pillion's thigh and squeezed gently: another reminder.

"You know why we are ignorant," began Elgart. "We have no history of beliefs that resemble yours." Again hoping for surprise, he changed directions without pausing. "You come to us from Amika?"

"We did."

"And to Amika from the north?"

"Yes, my son."

"Through the lands of the Nuuri?" pursued Elgart. He wondered if the passing of the priests there had prepared the way for or inspired the hostility of the Nuuri somehow.

"We travel in peace wherever we go," replied Father Skurn. "But that is not your question, my son. You did not enter the Church to learn of our travels."

"Of course, Father." Elgart concentrated on seeming meek. "I was merely curious. Our need for guidance is more personal.

"We heard your scripture," he continued. "We heard you speak. We were moved. But I must confess, Father, that we found some of your insights confusing. For you, there is a clear distinction between 'knowledge' and 'truth,' but we do not understand it. How are they not the same?"

Father Skurn's posture did not change. No flicker of a muscle altered his expression. He sat upright on his stool, with his shoulders back and his hands folded on his chest. Nevertheless Elgart found it difficult to meet the priest's gaze. The light seemed to be growing brighter. It concentrated on the priest, making him somehow larger or more persuasive. Elgart had to stifle an impulse to yawn.

Beside him, Magister Pillion sat hunched over, propping his feet on a rung of his stool and bracing his elbows on his knees. He kept his head down like a man who was listening hard and did not want to be distracted by what he saw.

"Consider the distinction this way, my sons," said Father Skurn. "Knowledge is outward. It concerns the materials and use of *things*." He released one hand briefly to rap his knuckles on the table. "This is knowledge. The lamps are knowledge. The oil that burns, the making of the container to hold it, the setting of the flame. The use of such things is knowledge. Rifles are knowledge. Cannon are knowledge. Whatever their shape may be, they concern the materials and use of *things*.

"Truth is inward. Your confusion is a truth. Your inability to grasp the distinction is a truth. It comes from within you. It *describes* you, or a portion of you. Truth is concerned with who and what you *are*, in your hearts, in your thoughts, in your desires. It may guide the use you choose to make of things, but it is not the use of those things.

"The peace that the Great God Rile offers arises from truth, not from knowledge."

Elgart tried to nod. He wanted to maintain his composure, his air of calm interest and uncertainty. But now he realized that he *was* tired.

How many nights had he spent getting too little sleep? Too many. When he nodded, his head seemed to keep bobbing of its own accord.

With one hand, he pinched the soft skin inside his thigh. He needed the pain to steady him.

"I understand, Father." His voice sounded muffled to him, but he did not try to force it. "That is, I *think* I understand. Your explanation confuses me in another way.

"If the distinction is as plain as you say—if knowledge is merely outward—it can hardly threaten truth. Yet there is *some* threat in Belleger. That truth is obvious. Our alliance with Amika has endured for twenty years, but the uneasiness between us remains." He stopped himself from asking, Do you preach against the alliance? Instead, he inquired, "Do you consider knowledge a threat? When you spoke, you seemed to denounce it." During the service, he had heard Father Skurn proclaim, *At its foundation, knowledge exists to feed the greed of some at the expense of others.* "You were eloquent against it." *To pursue knowledge is to live in fear.* "I do not understand how knowledge can be an obstacle to truth. Or to peace between Belleger and Amika."

The priest sat motionless. "Again, my son, you misunderstand." His inflection did not change. "I did not denounce knowledge. The comprehension of *things* does not threaten either truth or Belleger. The discord here is King Bifalt's doing. With every passing year, it becomes more obvious that his preparations for war serve no purpose. There is no enemy. There will be no war. Naturally, resentment grows. I have never spoken against knowledge. Rather, I speak against the pursuit of knowledge *as if* it were truth.

"In itself, knowledge is a little thing. Like all little things, it can be of service when it is needed. And like all little things, it becomes a snare and a delusion when it is mistaken for a large thing. Then the lust for knowledge becomes mere *lust*. Like every other lust, it is a child of Pride and Folly. The craving for it is only more insidious than other desires. It is not wiser.

"The first step in every quest for peace and harmony and true power, the power that is made possible by ending the war within you—that first step is truth, and only truth."

Elgart had to swallow another yawn. Every thought in his head had become fuzzy, fogged with a need for sleep. With the sluggishness of a drunk or a drugged man, he realized that he was feeling an effect of sorcery. It had to be. It was too much unlike him to be caused by lamp-light or a sonorous voice.

Yet during the service, the congregation had not fallen asleep. Magister Pillion was not yawning now. Elgart did not understand.

But he understood that he had put his friend in danger.

He had put his *friend* in danger.

Goaded by chagrin, he fought to stay alert. His own arrogance appalled him. How could he have believed that Pillion would be safe where Magister Facile felt threatened? With an effort, he loosened the poniard hidden by his sleeve. But he did not draw it. He was not ready to declare his intentions. Instead, he tried to determine what was happening to his companion.

When he touched the Magister's thigh again, he found the muscles rigid from hip to knee. A small shift on his stool allowed his shoulder to brush Pillion's. The sorcerer's whole body was rigid, clamped around itself as if he were resisting a pressure Elgart could not detect.

Cursing himself, Elgart did not yawn, or close his eyes, or slump to the side. He meant to question the priest further, but he doubted his ability to form a consecutive sentence.

Deeply, gently, Father Skurn spoke for him.

"You asked for spiritual guidance. I can only describe what I see in you. My sons, you are as distinct inwardly as you are in appearance."

He looked toward Elgart's companion. "You, Magister, have truth in you. You know who and what you are, and you cling to it. There is no way forward for you except faith. When you have learned to rely on the Great God Rile, you will find every path made clear.

"But *you*, my son." The priest's woe-weary gaze turned to Elgart. "You feel a great need for sleep, do you not? Your eyes are heavy. The light now seems too bright for comfort. That is because you are at war with yourself. You know the truth, but you battle against it. My words resonate within you. They strike a chord of recognition that strives to become music. But you refuse to hear it. While your heart tries to leap up, your mind holds it down. You cling, not to the truth of who and what you are, but rather to an ill-fitting belief that you *ought* to be someone else. The struggle exhausts you.

"Tell the truth to yourself, my son, if you cannot confess it to me. You are not the man you try to be."

Between suppressed yawns, one side of Elgart's nature sneered sardonically. The other ached with sorrow.

But that contradiction was familiar to him, as familiar as breathing. It was a kind of strength. It enabled him to rally. Blinking rapidly, he forced himself to see through the intolerable brilliance of the lamps. With both hands, he gripped the edge of the table. By increments, he contrived to focus on the priest.

"Tell me one truth of your own, Father," he croaked. "Is your Great God coming?"

For the first time, Father Skurn betrayed a reaction. The small muscles around his eyes tightened until he was almost squinting. His hands tightened on his chest. "Coming?" he countered with a granite edge in his voice. "He does not come or go. He is here. He is everywhere and nowhere, in all lands and none.

"He is a god."

That was too much for Elgart. He would never forgive himself if his friend was harmed. With the last scraps of his defiance, he managed to say, "And if he is 'a' god, there must be others. Perhaps they, too, are worthy of faith."

Then he was done. An eerie haze closed over his mind. He could not refuse it. His concentration faded as if it had been dispelled by an enchantment. As far as he knew, he fell asleep.

Afterward, he could not remember how he and Magister Pillion left the Church. Had he excused himself, thanked the priest, promised to come again? Had Father Skurn dismissed him and his companion? He had no idea. He did not become himself again until he stood in afternoon sunlight outside and could draw clear, unambiguous air into his lungs.

While your heart tries to leap up, your mind holds it down. Could that be accurate? After all that he had learned from Amandis and Flamora long ago?—yes, and from King Bifalt since then? After everything that he had seen and done and served?

No. He did not believe it. Not when he could feel the sun on his face and breathe honest air. Father Skurn had sounded sincere. What he said had sounded true. But that was his form of theurgy: a form that Elgart had never faced before. Fortunately, Elgart was accustomed to his own divided nature. More than accustomed: *trained* to it. He could accept any assertion and question it simultaneously.

He had learned how to choose. And he loved his life.

In any case, he had more important concerns. He and the Magister were walking together. Pillion was heading home. Elgart was accompanying him. Almost undetectably, Howel and Flax escorted them, Flax some distance ahead, Howel lagging behind.

As the fog in Elgart's mind faded, he remembered that he and his friend needed to talk.

The Magister was walking rapidly, faster than his usual desultory amble. He strode ahead with his head down and his jaws clenched. Every line of his small form was tight with tension. Elgart could almost feel the knotted muscles inside his grey robe.

Hells! muttered the spy to himself. What had he done to his friend?

Carefully, matching Pillion's pace, he asked, "Magister?"

"How *could* you?" The man did not glance at Elgart. He snarled his indignation at the street in front of his feet. "I called you my friend. How could you inflict *that* on me? Without *one word* to forewarn me?"

"I *am* your friend," replied Elgart. He knew suddenly that he stood on the edge of the secret that had frightened Magister Facile. "I would take a knife for you.

"What did I inflict?"

"*That,*" snapped Pillion.

"Does it have a name?" asked Elgart. When his companion did not respond, he went further. "Were you offended by the priest's distinction between knowledge and truth?"

"That?" retorted the Magister. His tone was raw scorn. "It is absurd. The 'truth' of who and what I am is self-knowledge. The 'knowledge' of lamps and rifles is the truth of what they are and what can be made of them. Every word from that man's mouth was chaff."

"And you *know* it." Pillion still did not raise his head. "It put you to *sleep*." He tightened his fists, brandished them uselessly. "Why did you choose *me* to hear it?"

Groping for a response, Elgart insisted, "I am your *friend*. I would take a knife for you. And you are *mine*. There is no other Magister I can call my friend. No other Magister would call me his."

Without warning, the smaller man wheeled on Elgart; glared up at the spy with his fists between them. "*That* is why you chose me? Because I am a *Magister*?"

"Yes." Elgart had no better answer.

Abruptly, Pillion's anger began to crumble. The muscles of his face drooped as they relaxed. His shoulders sagged. Then his gaze fell to the ground. Opening his hands, he rested his palms on Elgart's chest.

"Forgive me, my friend," he murmured. "I have wronged you. You chose me because I am a Magister, and you are not. Without the robe"—his mouth twisted—"and the sneer, you cannot tell a sorcerer when you see one. You cannot see the difference between those who are gifted and those who are not. You needed a witness to advise you.

"That man offended me. I blamed you. I was threatened—" He glanced up at Elgart's face, then dropped his gaze again. "I should have trusted you, as I said I would."

Elgart gripped the man's shoulders so that he would be heard. "There is nothing to forgive. I did not prepare you." He had been too sure of himself. He had not taken the Church seriously enough. "Tell me what you saw."

"I know *this*," spat Pillion. For the first time, his voice held the reflexive disdain most theurgists felt for the ungifted. "That man is no sorcerer. He has no scrap of talent in him."

Again without warning, he turned away. Ahead of Elgart, he resumed his rapid steps. His shoulders clenched. His fists swung at his sides.

At once, Elgart hastened to join him. He needed to hear the secret that he had risked their friendship to learn.

Carefully, he asked, "How were you threatened?"

"There was sorcery in the room." Bitterness rasped in Magister Pillion's tone. "That man is no sorcerer, but he wields it. He borrows it or steals it from some other source. I did not know that was possible. I know it now."

Before Elgart could frame another question, he added, "It is not a Decimate. *That* I know. It cannot be used to inflict pestilence or rain down fire. But it is—" For a moment, he stumbled inwardly. When he continued, he was shuddering.

"Elgart, it is difficult to refuse. While you dozed, I fought for my life. That man showed me to myself. Not as I *am*. As I *could* be. As he wanted me to be. Respected. Revered. Able to bring down mountains. Known as the mightiest of my kind.

"He wanted me to believe I can be *that* Magister if I give myself to his Great God."

Elgart felt a pang that resembled horror. The priests used sorcery to win converts? Their theurgy was *persuasion*? The power to insinuate their will? Shaken, he asked, "How did you resist?"

"I have children," answered Pillion as if he were chewing curses. "I am their father. I have a wife. I am her husband. They will not be taken from me. I will not surrender them."

Then he declared, "No Magister can bring down mountains."

He did not speak again while he and Elgart crossed the Hand to his home. He did not speak while he entered the house and closed the door. And Elgart, too, said nothing. He had no words that he could bear to hear aloud.

Had Father Skurn tried to woo Magister Pillion with sorcery? By the same means, the priest had mastered Elgart. The spy did not have the single-mindedness that had defended Pillion. With his usual recklessness, he had assumed that he had more strength of will than his friend. Now he knew that he had less.

But he knew something else as well; something far more important than his rattled self-esteem. He knew that there were no circumstances under which King Bifalt could be allowed to meet with Archpriest Makh. The Archpriest's theurgy would destroy the King's world, and Elgart's. It would destroy Belleger.

TWELVE

KING'S SECRET

When Queen Estie rode to the Flower of Amika at dawn to collect her companions, the sight of Magister Facile relieved one of her many anxieties. The sorceress looked less frail. She must have slept longer than her usual few hours, or perhaps she had slept repeatedly. And the inn had fed her well, as Estie had known it would.

Seeing Amika's Queen, Magister Facile arranged her face in a dour scowl. Like Estie, she knew what was at stake. Unlike Estie, she knew why she had determined to travel with the Queen. When she assayed the Queen, her eyes were gimlet and probing. Then she shook her head as if she could name Estie's shortcomings and found them distasteful.

In contrast, the devotee of Spirit seemed unchanged. As she often did, she kept most of her face hidden by the hood of her white cloak; but the glimpses Queen Estie caught were of a wry smile and an air of eagerness. Lylin, too, knew her own intentions, if Estie did not. Unlike Magister Facile, the assassin had already demonstrated her worth.

Estie assumed that she herself looked worn-out, fretted with worry. She had spent a restless night after her talk with her mother. Queen Rubia's view of King Smegin dismayed her. It also confused her. Clearly, he hated the Magisters of the library. But how would a war with the Nuuri speed his approach to the Last Repository? How would his daughter's death help him get revenge?

Was it possible that he believed killing her would prevent King Bifalt from learning of his intentions?

No part of her father's plotting made sense to her.

But she did not let her concerns—or Magister Facile's expression—slow her. She needed to hurry. For all she knew, she was already too late. Dismissing even the most common pleasantries, she led her companions out of the inn.

Outside, Commander Crayn and Estie's familiar escort were waiting for her. Their presence gave the Queen a measure of reassurance. Over the years, they had spent long days together. Crayn and his men remained respectful and diligent; but they were able to relax in her company. And none of them were old enough to know what their lives would have been under King Smegin's rule. None of them had cause to fear her father.

Under the circumstances, Estie wanted soldiers who were loyal to her personally. In general, her honor guard served her because she was Amika's Queen. Confronted with a choice between her and King Smegin, those men might hesitate. Even the ones Commander Soulcess trusted most might hesitate. Her father could threaten them with the Decimate of lightning. But Commander Crayn and his company would not falter.

Smiling her gratitude, Estie vaulted from the porch of the inn into the saddle of her mount. She waited impatiently while the devotee of Spirit helped Magister Facile onto a horse. Then, trusting Lylin to join her, she wheeled away. With Commander Crayn at her side and five of his men ranging ahead, she went at a brisk canter toward the parade ground in front of Amika's Desire.

There she was reassured again. In the open field, she saw only Commander Soulcess and the men she had called out by name awaiting her, armed, armored, and mounted. Sub-Commander Hellick and his troop had already left to ride her road eastward, rushing to rescue enslaved Nuuri. And sub-Commander Waysel's company had no reason to be present. He could not depart until the cannon and shot were gathered from their several forges and storage sheds, loaded onto wagons, and secured for travel. His train might not depart for Belleger and the Bay of Lights until the next day.

But when Estie surveyed the gathered men and their horses more closely, she felt an unexpected pang of alarm. Apparently, Commander Soulcess had decided to exceed his orders. On his own initiative? She doubted that. It was more likely that Chancellor Sikthorn had made the suggestion. But the result was not what she wanted. It was too dangerous.

In a clutch off to one side, keeping their distance from common guardsmen, were three Magisters. Their fine horses demonstrated their intention to accompany her.

Estie swore under her breath. Those three were all that she had allowed to remain in Maloresse. Their Decimates were fire, drought, and pestilence: the city might need them. But she had sent every other Amikan Magister elsewhere, either to distant regions of the realm that required aid, or to Belleger.

"Majesty!" said Magister Facile tensely. "Your Magisters. They cannot come with us."

I *know*, snorted Estie to herself. Snapping her reins, she urged her mount toward Commander Soulcess.

Full of self-esteem and doubt, the first officer sat his horse at the head of his guardsmen. He may have been proud of himself for doing more than his Queen had asked; but he was also painfully aware that he had never commanded soldiers in battle, or fought for his life. When he saw the expression on Estie's face, he flinched, realizing suddenly that he had made a mistake, but unable to guess what it was.

Without greeting or preamble, the Queen snapped, "Deliver my thanks to those Magisters. Tell them to remain in Maloresse. By my command, they must not leave their duties."

Then she grabbed more self-control out of her vexation. "I value your forethought, sir," she added. "But I will not expose any Magister to our foe. I cannot refuse Magister Facile. I lack the authority to command her. *My* theurgists must obey me.

"See to it, Commander."

She did not explain that she also had another reason for leaving her Magisters behind. If the massing Nuuri had not already begun their march into Amika, they had surely sent scouts to watch her father's movements; and she did not want them to think that she intended an attack on them. From the perspective of the Nuuri, her soldiers were enough to pose a threat. A cadre of Magisters—even a cadre as small as three—would confirm the impression that she meant war.

The first officer gulped. "As you say, Majesty." His face showed a mixture of consternation and relief as he turned his mount and cantered away to dismiss the Magisters.

While Queen Estie watched Soulcess, Crayn brought his mount to her side. In a low voice, he asked, "A foe, Majesty? One that can threaten sorcerers? Where will we go to find such a foe?"

She did not glance at him. Commander Soulcess was approaching her Magisters. She wanted to watch their reactions. And she knew that she did not need to be cautious with Crayn.

"Where did you think we would go?" she murmured. "Before you heard me speak of a foe?"

"East, Majesty?" ventured her escort commander. "Pursuing deserters?"

Absently, Estie nodded. The first officer was speaking to the theurgists, but she could not hear him. At this distance, the faces of the Magisters were illegible. However, he had not dismounted: an act which he probably intended to emphasize her command, but which they would interpret as discourtesy.

Almost whispering, Crayn asked, "Will you punish them, Majesty? They belong to your honor guard. They took the oath. Do you mean to execute them?"

Like men crippled in battle, deserters had been summarily put to death during King Smegin's reign, often by the King himself.

Intent on the Magisters, Queen Estie answered, "Of course not." Now one of them was shouting at Soulcess. The other two turned away. In their postures astride their mounts, she saw disgust. But were they angry because she had refused their protection? Because she had denied them a chance to join King Smegin? Or merely because they resented the first officer's manner?

Her nerves were too raw. Fearing treachery, she looked for hints of it everywhere when in fact most Amikans had good reason to value their Queen. Certainly, none of her Magisters—with the obvious exception of Magister Flense—had resisted her reign.

Sighing, she turned her attention to Commander Crayn.

"Why would I execute them? I mean to bring them back." Later, she would make up her mind about the thugs and estate guards Sikthorn had mentioned; about King Smegin's retinue of soldiers. "They are Amikan. I want their lives, not their deaths. And the great war for the library is coming. We will need as many men as we can muster. Men *and* women."

Studying her escort commander, she saw approval in his sandstone gaze. "As you say, Majesty." He may have been smiling.

Queen Estie sighed again. She had encouraged Crayn to underestimate her intentions. Perhaps she had succeeded. Nevertheless she had told him the truth—or part of it. For that matter, she had told Commander Soulcess the same. If she could do it, she was not going to expose *any* Amikan lives to her father's sorcery. Magister Facile and the devotee of Spirit had chosen to accompany her. They knew what was at stake. The first officer's contingent of her honor guard did not. She wanted them with her, but not to fight. Instead, she hoped that Commander Soulcess and his men by their mere presence would daunt King Smegin's forces. Dishearten or shame them; sway them somehow. Convince them to stand aside. She meant to approach her father without bloodshed.

If her coming caused a battle, Amikan against Amikan, she might never get a chance to forestall the greater threat: the prospect of an invasion from the north.

With that bitter prospect souring her thoughts, she waited for Commander Soulcess to rejoin her. Then she led him and his company, her escort, and her companions off the parade ground to the nearest street heading eastward through Maloresse.

By the measure of Magister Facile's stamina, the Queen and her small army made better progress than she had expected. During the first day, they passed through a town large enough to refresh and resupply them. Pausing there gave the sorceress an hour of rest. And that night, they reached a village where Estie and everyone with her could unpack their bedding in various barns and stables. Apart from the men on watch, they were able to sleep in comparative comfort.

The next day was more difficult. They had gone beyond the fields and farms that clustered around Maloresse; the orchards and vineyards; the wide pastures of the horse-breeders; the many woods that had been reduced to copses by the city's appetite for timber and fuel. Their way took them into more rugged terrain, hills that discouraged grazing, stony flats that were not worth cultivating. Here there was no true road. Instead, the Queen's force rode along wagon-tracks with deep ruts, or on paths trampled flat by sheep, cattle, and horses. Occasional hamlets punctuated the landscape, habitations for folk who preferred isolation and could subsist on their gardens, their pigs, and their scavenging for veins of ores beneath the shallow topsoil; but Estie bypassed them. They had nothing to spare for a company as large as hers. Turning aside to visit them would have made her journey longer.

Pushing Magister Facile as hard as she dared until sunset, the Queen brought her force to the edge of the only substantial obstacle in her path: the place where King Smegin's spies would keep watch, and she might be attacked.

It was a vast forest of cedar, dense and deep, so crowded with trees that they blocked daylight, stunting most of the undergrowth. From the moment when she had first seen it, more than a year after she became Queen, Estie had loved it. Its trees were glorious in sunshine, its shadows thronged with hints of mystery, and the rich fragrance of its oils and needles was balm to her nerves. She had always meant to have it surveyed to determine its full extent, but more immediate concerns consistently demanded her attention. Early in her reign, she had worried that the wood would be harvested; that the forest would be gradually gnawed away. Now she knew better.

During the generations of the old wars, the forest had been called Solace Wood. In her studies of Amika's geography as a girl, Estie had learned that the Wood was known to hold a large glade near its center, a place of wild grasses where streams came together and ran south to join the Line River. But now the woodland had a new name: King's Secret. No one cut trees there because King Smegin had claimed the forest. He protected it.

His sanctuary was there, in the heart of the glade.

She had only visited him once, and only then at his invitation. A season after her coronation, he had sent a message asking her to come and see how he lived. At that time, she was still enough of her father's daughter to be pleased by the request. And she had wondered how long he would be content in his isolation. But the same message forbade her to bring her husband: a prohibition that cast her excursion in a more anxious light. Apparently, King Smegin still felt outplayed by his Bellegerin rival—and still resented his defeat.

Arriving in the glade, Queen Estie had found that his self-imposed exile was a polite fiction. He had a score of retainers with nothing to do except serve and entertain him, carry messages and spy for him. In addition, at least twice that many soldiers attended him as his personal guard. During the two days that she spent in his company, she had learned almost nothing about him; certainly nothing that explained his decision to isolate himself. He had obviously not lost interest in Amika. He asked questions by the dozens. And if she asked one herself, he used it as a pretext to hear more about how she ruled Amika; how she dealt with King Bifalt; how Amika and Belleger managed each other. When she finally forced herself to insist, he told her only what he had told her before, that he had withdrawn so she could rule over a clear field, one free of conflicting loyalties.

After that occasion, she had promised herself that she would not visit again. His interest in her doings had not flattered her. It had kept her at a distance. And she felt more than a little irate that he distrusted her husband, the man who had given Amika peace. During the years that followed, she found that promise easier and easier to keep.

But no longer. Now, while her company made camp at sunset on the edge of King's Secret, she wanted nothing more than to ride through the night until she reached the glade and the manor-house with its outbuildings that her father called his sanctuary. She wanted to *face* him and be done with it. To demand an explanation for his actions—and to compel his help in undoing them.

The track inward was plain enough. It had been kept clear by the passing of horses and wagons in both directions, many of them. All she needed was moonlight, and she could ride—

—until one of King Smegin's guardians objected to her presence. Or until she inadvertently surprised a band of Nuuri scouts. That could happen. The track wore a thick carpet of cedar needles. Even galloping, her mount's hooves would be almost silent.

Still, the trees called to her. Lit by the westering sun, they seemed to glow with invitations. They held answers. In their depths, she might discover what lay behind King Smegin's actions. She might even learn something about her purported gift for sorcery.

She did not notice Commander Crayn's approach. When he spoke, he startled her.

"Do not think it, Majesty," he warned. Her hunger to go on must have shown in her eyes, her manner. "There will surely be guards. If they cannot see who you are, you will end your journey with a clutch of arrows in your chest."

Because she trusted him, she said softly, grimly, "The risk is greater than you know. But the risk of delay is great as well." Then she shook her head. "Still, I hear you. I will avoid as many dangers as I can."

Crayn might have said more, but while he considered his response, Magister Facile came closer. Without Lylin's help, she might have fallen when she had dismounted. On her feet, she looked more than ever like a failing crone. Nevertheless she hurried toward Estie, leaning heavily on her cane.

"Majesty!" she called: a gasp intended to sound peremptory. "I must speak." Glancing at the Commander, she added, "Alone."

With a nod to Crayn, Queen Estie lowered herself from her horse; wavered a moment until she remembered the feeling of solid ground. Then she handed her reins to one of Crayn's soldiers and faced the sorceress.

With a bemused expression, Crayn rode away to settle his command. The soldier followed him with Estie's horse.

But when Magister Facile reached the Queen, she said nothing. Instead, she gripped Estie's arm with her free hand and drew Estie farther away from the slow seethe and confusion of more than fifty men dismounting, setting pickets, starting campfires, arranging their bedrolls. The older woman did not stop until there was no chance of being overheard.

Panting to catch her breath, she stood with her back to the rest of the company. By degrees, she eased her hold on Estie's arm.

Over the Magister's shoulder, Queen Estie saw the devotee of Spirit accost Commander Crayn. He dismounted to greet her.

"Majesty," began the sorceress, "understand this. It is vital. I must be nearby when you meet King Smegin. But I cannot enter his presence."

Almost at once, Lylin and Crayn began an earnest conversation. At first, they seemed to be arguing; trying to persuade each other. But soon their discussion changed. Clearly, the Commander was asking questions. With her usual ease, the devotee answered them.

"When we enter the forest," insisted the old woman, "I must not be known as a Magister. Until you reach your father, the solution is simple enough. I will put aside my robe. A servant's garb will disguise me. His men will not know me."

While Estie watched, the assassin and Commander Crayn reached an agreement. Together, they walked toward Commander Soulcess.

"But *he* will know me," said Magister Facile harshly. "He will see that I have power.

"Majesty, I *must* be nearby—and King Smegin *must not* catch sight of me."

The Queen could see that Soulcess did not like what Crayn and Lylin were saying. His first retorts were imperious. Then he began shouting. But the general clamor of the men and their animals masked his voice.

With an effort, Estie forced herself to give the sorceress her attention. In King Bifalt's name, Prince Jaspid had asked her if she trusted Magister Facile. Estie could not think of a reason why she should.

"Be plain with me, Magister." She held the old woman's blackcurrant gaze until Facile looked away. "I have heard that one sorcerer can sense another's power. Surely my father will feel your presence?"

The old woman replied with a hiss of scorn. "One sorcerer can sense another's power—*when* that power is used. When that power is with-held, no sorcerer can recognize another, except by sight. If he does not see me, he will not know what I am."

Estie had expected some such explanation. She accepted it with a nod. "Then tell me. Are you able to counter my father's Decimate?"

"If we are fortunate," snapped Magister Facile, "we will never know." But then she appeared to relent. "We have spoken of this, Majesty," she said like a sigh. "At times, a truth hidden has more power than a truth revealed."

Remembering the Magister's uselessness during the attempt on her life, Estie demanded, "Is that your answer? Do you expect it to content me? Magister, I have spent my life grieving because I have no gift. You tell me that I do. Then you give me nothing. Instead, you hide behind obscure utterances about the power of secrets. Do you imagine that I am able to trust you?"

In a flash of vehemence, the theurgist met Estie's gaze again. Her face twisted itself into lines that matched her ire. "Majesty," she said harshly, "you will trust me because I have chosen to accompany you for this sole purpose. You will trust me because King Bifalt does. You will accept my answers because he does. My secret will remain mine until I choose to reveal it. *Your* secret is beyond me. I will not touch it.

"I must be near when you meet with King Smegin. He must not see me."

Without Queen Estie's assent or comprehension, Magister Facile turned sharply and stamped away, jabbing at the ground with her cane as if she sought to pierce it to the heart.

Estie stared after her. It is my *life*! she wanted to shout. You are risking *my* life! I want my inheritance!

But that was unfair. She was risking her own life. She had come here because she was the Queen of Amika, not because of anything that Magister Facile had said or done. With or without the Magister's sup-port, she would have accepted the challenge of her father's treachery. The old woman's only role had been to slow her. Even the Magister's claims about an unawakened talent for sorcery were little more than taunts. They changed nothing. Certainly, they did not make King Smegin any more dangerous—or any less.

Still, Estie was furious. She was almost relieved to see Commander Soulcess storming toward her. Indirectly, he might give her an outlet for what she felt.

"Majesty!" he called as soon as he was near enough to address her without shouting. "Do I command your honor guard? Do I not?"

Old reflexes came to the Queen's aid. Instead of matching the first officer's tone, she replied evenly, "You do, sir. Who questions it?"

"That *woman*—!" He gestured uselessly behind him: Lylin was gone, although Estie had not seen her leave. "She dares to *instruct* me. She instructs *me*. As if I were a novice too ignorant to care for the Queen of Amika. She—!"

Fortunately, Commander Crayn had followed Soulcess. He stood at the first officer's shoulder. If he had not intervened, Estie might have snarled in the older man's face.

"With respect, Commander," offered Crayn diffidently. "Queen Estie has known the devotee of Spirit longer than we have. She knows better than we do that the devotee is easily misunderstood."

"Misunderstood?" huffed Soulcess. "What have I misunderstood? Did she not instruct me? Did she not assume command of my men?"

"Her manner is strange, Commander," replied Crayn. "That I grant." Estie saw amusement in Crayn's eyes, but his tone was soothing. "She is blunt and sure. The fault of misunderstanding is hers. She assumes that we are familiar with devotees of Spirit. If we knew her, we might hear what she says as counsel, not commands."

Soulcess turned on the escort commander. "Then explain her, sir. Tell me why I should hear any word or insult from her."

"Commander Soulcess." Estie kept what she felt out of her voice. Nothing good would come of it if she inflicted her ire at Magister Facile on him. "I owe my life to the devotee. She is a skilled scout. She is also a trained killer. It may be that she knows more of our peril than we do.

"But she does not command your men. Who would obey her? They do not know her. And she does not command *you*. *I* do.

"Sir, you will accept her instructions as counsel. If you are wise, you will be grateful for them. She is adept in matters that lie outside our experience. You and Commander Crayn will allow her counsel to guide you."

The first officer struggled visibly to regain his composure. In a congested tone, he answered, "As you say, Majesty. Of course." He tugged on his beard, trying to pull his expression into a more respectful shape. "But if I may ask. How do you know—?" He may have wanted to understand why Estie considered the devotee of Spirit trustworthy. If so, he changed his mind. "Do you know what she has told us to do?"

The Queen offered him a rueful smile. "I do not. Her manner is strange with me as well. She expects blind compliance. Perhaps all devotees of Spirit do the same.

"But she has proven herself to me, Commander."

Another man might have countered, But not to *me*, Majesty. Soulcess did not trust himself that far. He had dedicated his life to obeying his monarch's orders, and to making sure that his men obeyed as well. He did not challenge those orders. If he had, he might not have survived King Smegin's reign.

When Estie dismissed him, the first officer left at once, taking Crayn with him. But she did not follow them. She stayed where she was, studying the trail into King's Secret. At that moment, she did not care what Lylin had told Commander Soulcess to do. She was satisfied to know that the devotee had convinced Commander Crayn. Her thoughts were knotted around the dilemma of Magister Facile, and she wished to be alone with them.

King Bifalt wants to know if you trust her. How was she, Estie, supposed to do that? Magister Facile claimed that Belleger's King *did* trust her; but as far as Estie knew, her husband had never trusted any Magister.

A truth hidden has more power— The power to do *what*?

Estie had no answers. The trees told her nothing. When one of her escort came to say that her supper was ready, she went back to the camp because her efforts to understand led nowhere. Nothing would be made clear until she faced her father.

Deep in the night, she was roused by Commander Crayn's touch on her shoulder. "It is time, Majesty. We will enter the forest soon."

Time? As she rolled out of her bedding and stood, she found herself in the midst of turmoil. Time for what? By slivers of moonlight and the dull glow of embers, she saw men hurrying in all directions, packing their bedrolls, adjusting their headbands and weapons, seeing to their horses, snatching bites of food and gulps of water from the evening's meal. Her escort and half of the guardsmen were ready to mount. The rest would join them soon.

A short distance away, Magister Facile floundered out of her blankets, cursing to herself. In the confusion of the moon's faint silver, the ruddy emanation of dying fires, and the abrupt movements of the men, Queen Estie found no sign of Lylin. The hinted suggestions of the stars were not answers.

"Time for what?" repeated Estie, this time aloud. Her voice was a croak clogged with sleep.

"The devotee's instructions," answered Crayn. "She told us to rest until we could see the moon above the trees. Then we are to enter the forest at a canter. When she has made sure of the scouts and spies, she will rejoin us. She will tell us whether we can go on safely."

If he had been talking about anybody else, Queen Estie would have questioned him. But she knew what Lylin could do. Her only response was a curt nod of acquiescence.

While one of her escort brought her horse, she peered up at the night, the trees; the moon. The silvery crescent seemed to be cradled among the highest branches above her. The night was half gone. At a gallop, she could hope to reach her father's retreat by sunrise. She might be able to surprise him.

She allowed herself a moment to consider the idea of obeying her own desires. Then she discarded it. Her escort would be able to keep up with her: Magister Facile could not.

Like Lylin with Commander Soulcess, the sorceress had given Estie counsel in the form of instructions. Her father was a Magister. Only a fool would challenge him without the support of another Magister, even a Magister who had not proven her worth.

As soon as the Queen stepped up into her saddle, her escort arranged its formation around her.

In brief scraps of illumination, Estie watched Magister Facile. The theurgist was not ready. She had packed away the grey robe that announced her talent for sorcery. Now she was struggling into the garments of a camp-follower: clothes that she must have brought with her for this purpose. Her full skirts and open bodice looked ridiculous on her plump form; and the effect was not improved by her bangles and earrings, certainly not by her riding moccasins. But Estie doubted that anybody would notice, apart from the guardsmen immediately around her.

At last, the Magister climbed onto her horse, helped by one of Crayn's men.

From the head of his company, Commander Soulcess called his guardsmen to attention. To Estie's ears, his voice was too loud. Clearly, he was accustomed to addressing larger groups in larger spaces. "We will ride at a canter, men. We will ride in *silence*.

"Blissin. Swaleman." They were two of the guardsmen he had chosen on his Queen's behalf. "Take eight comrades. Ride ahead of the Queen and her escort. Halt at once if you catch sight of *that woman*"—resentment lingered in his tone—"the one in white who came with us. Speak only if you judge that Queen Estie is threatened.

"The rest of us, all of us, will say nothing. We will show the Queen that we can follow without a sound."

As if to prove that he could obey his own orders, he turned his mount away without telling his men to move out.

A few of them were still rushing around, putting out the last embers of the fires, cinching their horses. Ten took their places in front of Estie and her escort. The rest formed ranks behind the first officer.

Silent as a cortege, they approached Queen Estie and the trail into King's Secret. In rows of three and four, they entered among the trees and seemed to disappear, swallowed by shadows.

Estie could have ridden the trail alone, although it was only visible as a vague streak directly in front of her. Her horse would recognize a clear path even when the thick canopy of branches and leaves reduced her to blindness. And the way to King Smegin's retreat was wide enough for wagons. Several men could ride abreast. If her mount veered to avoid an obstacle, she would not lose her seat or strike a tree. Still, she was glad to have her escort around her. Dangers seemed to crouch among the cedars as she moved. King's Secret felt more threatening in darkness than it did when she had studied it at sunset.

In the lead, Blissin and Swaleman held the whole company to a steady pace, an easy canter that the horses could sustain for hours. Commander Crayn's men had positioned Magister Facile behind the Queen. Two of his soldiers rode at the Magister's sides, crowding close to catch her if her balance or her strength faltered. The rest ranged more widely around Estie, ready to intercept any unexpected attack before it reached her.

Estie tried to prepare herself to meet her father, but the trees drew her attention. They concealed everything they contained. What was the devotee of Spirit doing? Killing King Smegin's watchmen? Killing Nuuri scouts? Their deaths might be necessary, if they intended harm. But killing them might also prove ruinous. If the King's watchmen did not report at their assigned intervals, he would assume that his daughter meant to strike at him. And if Nuuri scouts did not return, their people would have proof that Amika's purpose was hostile.

Random instants of moonlight made the riders ahead of Estie real, then swept away, leaving them in darkness. So many cantering hooves on the dense carpet of cedar needles raised a soughing like the whisper of breezes in the high branches. She had no way to measure time or distance. They were quicksand. She sank into them and left no trace. She had become unreal herself, a figure in a dream. When the whole company slowed to a halt, she hardly noticed that she was no longer moving.

Then the tension of her escort swept over her like a breaking wave, and she understood. She was almost alert, almost herself, when Lylin reached her side.

The devotee of Spirit was on foot, but she was tall: her head came to the level of Estie's waist. Resting a hand on the Queen's knee, the assassin said mildly, "I hope, Majesty, that you thought to bring my horse."

In a gruff whisper, Commander Crayn answered, "We did." At once, one of his men approached with the devotee's mount.

"And you, Magister?" asked Lylin. "You are well enough?"

"Enough," croaked the sorceress at Estie's back. Clearing her throat, she added, "My lady Queen doubts me. I am too stiff-necked to fail her now."

Lylin chuckled softly. For a moment, she was gone. Then she returned astride her horse. At Estie's side, she called, "Walk on, guardsmen."

No one moved until Crayn referred the decision to Commander Soulcess. Fortunately, Lylin's instructions had prepared the first officer. "Walk on, men," he answered: a muted command that still sounded too loud. "We will go at the Queen's pace."

By increments, the small army shrugged itself back into motion.

Although she peered until her forehead throbbed, Queen Estie could not make out the assassin's features. Lylin resembled a shadow, an image cast by the cedars. She must have set aside her white cloak—or its fabric had the strange gift of blending with trees and darkness.

Keeping her voice low, Estie asked, "What have you done?"

"As you instructed, Majesty." The devotee chuckled again. "Or as you would have instructed, if you were more familiar with women of my kind."

Speaking so that only Estie would hear her, Lylin said, "I found a band of three Nuuri. There were several such bands. But they lack stealth in forests. They would be easy prey for King Smegin's watchmen if they ventured closer. I sent them back to their people with a message in your name. I told them, 'You do not need to advance. I will come to you, when I have ended the crimes committed against you.'"

Then the assassin shrugged. "The Nuuri I addressed were sick with rage. Their people will not wait for you. But your message will give their scouts a reason to escape these trees."

Estie listened with her mouth hanging open. If she could have thought of something to say, she might not have been able to say it. She had imagined the possibility of Nuuri scouts, but she never imagined that they might be in danger—or that she might benefit by their presence. She did not know how to think in those terms. Everything that she had done since hearing Chancellor Postern's confession was new to her.

Lylin's actions filled her with a kind of awe.

When Queen Estie did not respond, the devotee of Spirit continued.

"King Smegin's spies are more skillful. They are also more numerous. And they watch singly. It would have been an arduous task to gather them all. Fortunately, they can signal each other. They use a nicely judged code of whistles. When I had captured two of them, they agreed to warn the King of your coming. You ride with a force of arms to protect you, I told them, but your desire is peace. You wish to save Amikan lives, not lose them. Your only purpose is to speak with King Smegin.

"Also, I mentioned that I would kill any man who raises his hand against you." Lylin's tone implied a grin. "I believe that the ease with which I captured them was persuasive."

With an effort, Estie closed her mouth. The devotee amazed her. For a moment, she was faint with gratitude. She wanted to bless Elgart for the inspiration that had asked Lylin to travel with her. He had seen the dangers more clearly than she could.

But Elgart was not here. Queen Estie had to be content with thanking the assassin. Loud enough to be heard by everyone nearby, she proclaimed, "Most holy devotee of Spirit, I am in your debt. In more ways than I can count, I am in your debt. You have done more than save my life. Your forethought gives me hope."

Then she turned in her saddle and called for Commander Soulcess. When the first officer and Commander Crayn joined her, she gave them her orders. She explained her intentions, answered their objections.

When she was done, she instructed her escort and honor guard to resume their easy canter.

At that pace, they would not reach the glade of her father's retreat until midmorning or later. But now Queen Estie did not want speed. She wanted to arouse her father's curiosity. If she did not come at him like an enemy, he might be interested in hearing what she had to say.

The glade was larger than Estie's memory of it. A strong archer with a longbow might not have been able to land an arrow among the cedars on the far side. It formed a tilted basin deep enough to draw three distinct streams into its bottom and then spill them southward as a small river. The whole place was surrounded by the thick walls of the forest, but the expanse between them was open to the sky and sunshine.

At the time of Queen Estie's visit long ago, the slopes on all sides had been covered with a lush riot of wildflowers and grasses. Now most of the glade's bottom had been beaten down to bare dirt by the hard use of boots and hooves.

King Smegin's manor-house and its immediate outbuildings stood on the near side of the confluence of streams. The house itself was as splendid as Estie remembered it. In size, it was comparatively modest, only large enough for a monarch, his family, and his courtiers and functionaries. But in sunlight, its opulence seemed to glow with significance. Its porch and portico, its high doors, its bright windows: all spoke of ambition and anticipation, of ready eagerness.

During the intervening years, the adjacent servants' quarters had not been expanded. It was a plain structure, sturdy rather than luxurious. But the barracks for the King's men-at-arms was new to Estie—and it was substantial. It did not rise to three stories like the manor-house, or connect to the King's residence like the servants' quarters; but its length and depth occupied more ground.

If King Smegin needed that much space for his soldiers, he must have been gathering men for a long time.

The huge barn and long stables were on the far side of the river, laid out where they had plenty of space while remaining close to water: a precaution against fire. And beyond them were the fenced enclosure of the paddock and the wide stretch of the training-field where King Smegin's men could practice horsemanship, archery, and combat drills.

Altogether, the King's sanctuary looked like a place where an army larger than Estie's company could live and grow; prepare in secret. And perhaps ride out on raids. Other trails leading out of the glade to the north and south gave King Smegin's forces paths toward Nuuri lands on one side, the Line River and Estie's road on the other. The condition of those trails showed hard use over an extended time.

But when Queen Estie and her company emerged from the forest late in the morning, there was no one in sight anywhere. No one. Not on the polished porch of the manor-house. Not coming or going from the servants' quarters. Not watching from the barracks. Not near the barn or the stables, not in the paddock or on the field. Every window in every building was shuttered. Smoke curling from the chimneys of the main house and the servants' quarters insisted that those dwellings were occupied. But whoever was inside betrayed no awareness of the Queen of Amika's arrival.

The emptiness of the glade troubled Estie, but she was prepared for it. Obeying the orders she had given during the night, her escort and honor guard did not ride down into the glade. Instead, they fanned out along the edges of King's Secret until the last of them had left the trail. Then, like men who were just passing through and did not mean to intrude, they dismounted and began making camp. They strung picket-lines for their horses where the grasses were thickest; watered their mounts from their own waterskins; set out their bedrolls in no particular order. Some of them shared food from their packs. Others simply sprawled on the ground to stretch the kinks out of their muscles.

As much as they could, they all pretended that the manor-house and everything with it did not exist. At the same time, feigning indifference, they made excuses to draw their swords, unlimber their bows. They kept their quivers handy.

If King Smegin hoped the Queen's men would ride down into the basin so that his soldiers could surround them, he was going to be disappointed.

But Estie's precautions had another purpose as well: to avoid a show of hostility. If her father meant to risk killing the Queen of Amika on her own lands, he was going to need a better excuse than a visit that did not threaten him.

Dismounting herself, Estie studied the approach to the manor-house. She remembered a brief avenue of cherry trees, four on each side, apparently planted to welcome visitors. In springtime, they had worn their pink-and-white blossoms like promises of gladness and comfort: one of her few pleasant memories of her visit here.

Now they were dead. Their trunks looked burned, and their boughs formed a black and brittle tangle where there had once been twigs, leaves, flowers, fruit. Silhouetted against the richness of the house, they conveyed an impression of stark agony. Estie's first thought was that they had caught fire somehow. But no ordinary blaze would have killed them all equally. It would not have left so many of the thickest branches in place. And if they had been killed by fire, why had they not been cut down? King Smegin could have planted new trees to restore his wel-come.

Then she noticed the heavy shapes hanging from some of the limbs. As soon as she recognized those dark burdens, she spotted at least one in each tree. Three of the trees supported two.

"Majesty!" hissed Magister Facile: a warning. She did not need to explain it.

The shapes were human. Men? Women? Burned alive? *After* they were hung?

Unaware of what she was doing, Estie started down toward the trees. She began to run. She forgot to breathe.

Voices called after her, but she did not hear them. Lylin joined her. Commander Crayn caught up with her, his sword in his hand. Magister Facile followed more slowly. Crayn shouted something that kept the first officer and everyone else back.

Among the dead trees, Queen Estie saw the truth. The shapes *were* human. Men or women, she could not tell: their bodies had been burned until nothing remained except black crusts of flesh clinging to charred bones. But they had not been killed by hanging. Leather straps too stubborn to burn were knotted around their chests. They had been hauled up into the trees by those straps, suspended from the boughs, and then set on fire.

Oh, Father! moaned Estie to herself. What have you done?

Is *this* your legacy? Have I inherited *this*?

When she began to breathe again, every inhalation hurt, but she did not feel it. Burned by—? She could not finish the question. She feared that she knew the answer. It sickened her. Burned by—?

In a voice of gall, Magister Facile declared, "They are Nuuri, Majesty. King Smegin has used them to practice his Decimate. He desires precision. He craves the ability to inflict savagery without killing. These Nuuri have died to perfect his skill.

"He leaves them hanging so that other Nuuri will see them and fear him."

A moment later, one of the bodies appalled Estie by opening its eyes. The pain in them struck her like a blow.

Still alive? Gods! Still *alive*?

Snarling a curse, Crayn sprang forward. Before Estie could react— before she could think—he swung his sword, severed the living head from its body. When the head hit the ground, its eyes stayed open, staring its horror at the gnarled branches where its friends and kinfolk had died.

With her usual husky mildness, the devotee remarked, "I would have questioned him."

Crayn wheeled on her. He looked like he wanted to sob. "*Questioned* him?" he cried. "For what purpose? To prolong his *torment*?"

Lylin shrugged. "To determine if his mind still lived. If it did, I would have given him a gentler death. He would not have seen my blade. He would have known only that he was released.

"He has no use for mercy now."

Estie could not get past her questions. Burned by lightning? And still alive? So her father could learn—?

She had never expected to know of a crime worse than enslaving Nuuri and working them to death.

He believes that his gift for sorcery serves him.

What kind of monster—?

It does not.

But some response was expected of her. She was supposed to confront her father. Why else had she come? Her responsibility was not made less by the scale of this atrocity, or by her father's cruelty, or by her own nausea.

He has been enslaved by his own power.

Queen Estie did not weep. In spite of everything, she *did not*. But when she found her voice, it was congested with tears.

"You keep saying 'he.'"

The devotee nodded. "Yes, Majesty. If these are Nuuri, they are men. The women are bigger. And fiercer. If King Smegin had captured one of them, the Nuuri would have gone to war at once."

"Then we are fortunate to that extent." Queen Estie did not need to make decisions: she had already made them. *I know your questions*, she had promised her husband. *When I return, I will answer them.* A storm of fire arrows would be answer enough. Her men could burn the manorhouse and all its buildings to the ground.

But then there would be fighting. Amikan lives would be lost. Her father would end many of them before he fell himself. If he fell. And she would not get a chance to understand him.

"I have seen enough." She turned to face the house. "I will not wait to be noticed." With every word, she braided horror and outrage into a strand of strength. "Commander Crayn, go back. Hold the men where they are. Show no alarm. If you are needed"—she meant, *When* you are needed—"you will see it.

"Send the first officer to me."

Without glancing at the sorceress, she added, "Choose where you will make your stand." She did not believe that Magister Facile could do anything to counter the Decimate of lightning. "Go there when you think the time is right."

Then the Queen of Amika began walking down the slope toward King Smegin's sanctuary. Lylin accompanied her. By an act of will, Estie forced herself to move slowly so that Commander Soulcess could catch up with her. That was her only concession to her own power-lessness.

When the first officer reached bare dirt, she heard him hurrying after her. A moment later, he came to her side. He did not speak. He was breathing too hard, and he already had his orders. But he allowed himself to take her arm and stop her so that he could look into her eyes.

What he saw must have reassured him. Or perhaps it merely re-minded him that he had built his life on obedience. After a few breaths, he turned to the barracks and did what she had asked of him.

In a stentorian bellow, he shouted, "Pulltrop! Anderfall, come out!"

He knew every deserter by name. He knew their parents, their homes, their pleasures. If he could awaken their fidelity or their pride—if he could make them remember the men they had once been—King Smegin's authority might begin to crack. Even thugs and estate guards might start to question themselves.

But the Queen saw no sign that anyone had heard the Commander, not in the barracks or the servants' quarters or the house.

"You are deserters!" yelled Soulcess at the mute walls. "You and your comrades! I have come for you. Estie Queen of Amika is with me. She has come to *reclaim* you!

"Pulltrop, you have given six years to her service. Anderfall, you have given *nine*. Now she needs you! More than any Amikan monarch, she needs her honor guard. By her command, there is no punishment for desertion. She *needs* you. *Amika* needs you!"

Only silence answered him.

Briefly, he panted for air. A dangerous flush darkened his cheeks. His eyes bulged in their sockets.

"Brigin and *pestilence!*" he roared. "Come out! I am Commander Thren Soulcess, first officer of the Queen's honor guard! Estie of Amika stands with me! I *order* you to come out!"

She expected him to fail. She had always thought of him as ineffec-tual. But she had underestimated him. He was stringent with himself and demanded the same from his men. For some of his soldiers, if not for all of them, his right to command ran deep.

The nearest door of the barracks opened. A man stepped out into the sunlight. He still wore the livery of the honor guard.

"Anderfall!" called Soulcess, peremptory with rage. "Come! Explain yourself!"

After a few steps, the man stopped. "Commander Soulcess." He made himself heard without shouting. "You do not rule here. We serve King Smegin. Go back. Your presence will not be tolerated. You will all die."

Before the first officer could retort, Estie put herself in front of him. "But *I* rule, sir," she told Anderfall. "I am Amika's Queen. I rule wherever I go. Wherever I go, I am obeyed."

Anderfall flinched. As if reflexively, he bowed. "Majesty," he began, "I—"

She cut him off. "Say nothing, sir. I will not listen to your justifications until you answer one question. Do you *like* what you do in my father's name? Does his service *please* you? Does it protect your family, or your comrades, or those you love?"

The man tried again. "Majesty, I—" But what he would have said was too much for him. Abruptly, he turned; hurried back into the barracks and closed the door.

His manner said as plainly as words, I fear to defy the King.

Commander Soulcess drew breath to shout again; but the Queen stopped him. "Do not order them again, sir," she said softly. "And do not beg. They know their duty. They will do it, or they will not.

"Call them by name, all of them. Ask them if they remain Amikan. Ask them if they prefer to enslave and burn Nuuri while Amika is threatened. Use what you know of their lives in Maloresse. Remind them of what they sacrifice here.

"If your efforts seem fruitless, do not stop. You may accomplish more than you know."

The first officer gathered himself. The flush in his cheeks eased slightly, but the glare of ire in his gaze hardened. "As you say, Majesty. No man who has obeyed me once can refuse to hear me."

Stiff with indignation, he moved a few strides closer to the barracks. Then he began yelling names.

Through the shouts, Estie said to Lylin, "Now, Devotee, we will gain admittance to the house."

Leaving Soulcess behind, the Queen and the assassin walked toward the portico and the high doors of the manor-house.

Estie imagined pounding on the doors and hearing no response; but as soon as she and Lylin entered the shade of the portico, one door opened. In the gap stood an elderly man she recognized.

He was one of her father's oldest retainers. In fact, she had considered him old when she was a girl. Now she was inclined to call him ancient. His head wobbled on his neck, and his hands shook. Scraps of white hair fluttered from his scalp. He was clad in fustian dyed the purple hue King Smegin preferred, but he lacked the strength of frame to give it dignity. In a scabbard belted at his waist, he wore a heavy sword. On him, it looked more like a hindrance than a weapon.

In a tremulous voice, he demanded, "Tell that man to stop shouting. He disturbs the King."

"Sir." Estie supposed that her appearance had no more dignity than the retainer's; but she kept her voice steady nonetheless. "Perhaps you do not recognize me. I am Queen Estie of Amika. I wish to speak with my father. Admit us, if you please. Then inform the King that I am here."

Behind her, Thren Soulcess continued to blare names and demand answers. She did not hear any replies.

"Estie." The retainer's tone was querulous. "A slip of a girl. I remember. The King expects you." Then he addressed the devotee. "You are not welcome. Stay here. Silence that shouting fool while you wait."

"Sir," returned the Queen sternly, "she is more than my companion. She is a most holy devotee of Spirit, honored wherever she is known. My father would do well to make her acquaintance. She will enter with me."

"Will she?" snorted the old man. "Against the King's wishes? Ha!"

Trembling in every limb, he gripped his sword and tried to drag it from its scabbard.

Lylin stopped him by pinching his hand between her thumb and forefinger, then twisting his wrist. As far as Estie could tell, the assassin used no force at all. Nevertheless the surprise of the pain—if not the pain itself—dropped the retainer to his knees. His sword clattered on the floor.

"Majesty!" gasped the old man weakly. "Guards! Help!"

Estie stared at the devotee. Past the edge of her hood, Lylin met her gaze and grinned.

Softly, Estie suggested, "Let him stand. He will have the whole house in arms." Then she raised her voice. "Father! You know your daughter. You know I cannot harm you." That particular source of resentment made her stronger. "But I must speak with you. Do you truly mean to refuse me *one* companion?"

Behind the retainer, a dark hall led into the manor-house. From an open doorway a few strides beyond the entrance, the Queen heard a snarl that took the place of laughter when King Smegin wanted to hide his amusement. Like a swarm of wasps, he replied, "You are impetuous, Daughter. I have enemies. I could have killed you." As if he were making a great concession, he added, "The first chamber on the right. Bring your companion."

Staggering to his feet, the old man let Queen Estie and the assassin enter. He did not look at either of them again. As he began to close the door, Estie glimpsed a small squad trotting down the slope to support Commander Soulcess: ten of the men she had chosen. They would help him appeal to the deserters. If necessary, they would defend him.

Then the door was shut, and the first officer's shouting was reduced to a distant cry like the forlorn call of a tern.

For a moment, Estie hesitated. King Smegin had consented to Lylin's presence too easily. He knew nothing about her. How could he? Who could have told him? Yet he believed that she could not harm him. That she was not a Magister. Any flicker of doubt might have prompted him to forbid the devotee. Perhaps Estie should ask the assassin to wait outside after all? So that the King would not be able to exercise his Decimate against her?

Lylin's abilities were astonishing. She could throw a knife faster than her target could blink. But she was not a sorceress. She could not feel theurgy gathering in the instants before it was unleashed. If King

Smegin decided to kill the devotee, she would have no warning. Neither would Estie.

But before the Queen reached a decision, Lylin resolved the question by moving toward the doorway King Smegin had indicated. "Come, Majesty," said the devotee in her unfamiliar accent. Despite its huskiness, her tone had acquired a lilt like a hint of excitement. "This must be done. You are not alone."

As Queen Estie swallowed her doubts and approached the chamber, Lylin ushered her into her father's presence.

The room they entered was a large one, longer than it was wide. Down one side ran a number of west-facing windows. Under other circumstances, they would have admitted plenty of light; but they were shuttered now, leaving the room trapped in its own gloom. Opposite them stood a long row of shapes that almost resembled men in the dimness, although Estie suspected they were something else. An old odor of charred wood and burned fabric lingered in the air: a smell like garments tossed onto a bonfire. She supposed that her father sat or stood at the far end of the chamber, but she could not be sure without better light.

"Welcome, Daughter," said King Smegin. "It is good to see you." The harsh buzz of his voice contradicted his words. "But where are my manners? Visitors always want light." He was mocking her. "I have kept to myself so long, I forget the common courtesies.

"Here is a little trick I have mastered."

At the end of an alley walled by windows on one side and human-like shapes on the other, a small silver spark appeared. It lit King Smegin's fingertips as he touched it to the wick of a lamp. At once, the wick took flame. The lamp began to glow, spreading a buttery light around the King in his chair.

Now Estie could see the glee in his eyes, the secret ecstasy, as he repeated his little trick. Grinning, he produced a second silver spark at the ends of his fingers and used it to light another lamp on the opposite side of his chair. When the spark was no longer needed, it vanished.

In spite of herself, the Queen gaped. Her father was using the Decimate of lightning? To light lamps? She had never heard of a Magister who could exercise his talent with such precision. Such delicacy.

Magister Facile was right. He had used Nuuri for practice.

And not only Nuuri. His lamps left the space behind him shrouded in darkness, but they revealed that the shapes facing the windows were dummies, bundles of canvas stuffed with grasses and straw, and propped on wooden stands to resemble men. To one extent or another, they had all been burned. Some had lost their heads and torsos to King Smegin's sorcery. Others showed more focused wounds: a damaged shoulder here, a gutted stomach there. A few had been hit by bolts of theurgy so specific and controlled that the marks of fire and charring were no bigger than one of Estie's hands.

Her father had achieved a degree of mastery that seemed inconceivable.

"Do you wish refreshments, Daughter?" King Smegin did not raise his voice, but his tone implied a shout of delight. "Wine? Ale? Bread and fruit, perhaps? I seem to recall that guests expect to be made welcome with viands. You will get none here.

"No one will bring them. I have servants, enough for my needs. But they will not enter while you are here. They fear to stand in your presence."

Deep inside Queen Estie lived a little girl, a princess who held her father in awe. Even then, she had feared him; but her fear had hidden behind the pride and pleasure of being his favorite. Now she had many more reasons to be afraid—and no reason at all to feel pride. He had so *much* power—!

With an effort of will, she swallowed her dismay. "Is it me they fear, Father," she countered, "or their own shame?" She meant, Is it *you* they fear? Is it what you will do to me that frightens them? "Are they too timid to stand in front of their rightful Queen and confess that they do not serve her?"

The King gave a humorless laugh. "Or perhaps they fear to stand before you and confess that you no longer rule Amika. They are only servants, after all. Their duties do not require courage."

Estie wanted the devotee to say something; help her in some way. But Lylin stood silent and motionless, using her hood to hide her face.

As if he knew what Estie desired, King Smegin asked, "Shall I test your companion for you, Daughter? If you are Amika's Queen, she should be your servant. Shall we discover whether she serves any purpose at your side?"

"No," said Estie at once. Prompted by his threat, she put her weakness aside. "That will not be necessary. My rule of Amika is not in doubt. Nor is my companion's worth.

"Do you still imagine that you can resume your throne, Father? You cannot. There is no road to Maloresse that you can travel. Chancellor Postern has been discovered. He is King Bifalt's prisoner. Chancellor Sikthorn and Commander Soulcess serve only me. The honor guard serves me. When we are at war with the Nuuri—when it becomes known that you have caused them to attack us—there is no one in Amika who will stand with you."

"No," snorted King Smegin, "there is not. Not yet. But you have given your whole army to your fool of a husband. Apart from the honor guard, you are defenseless. If there is no one in Amika to stand with *me*, here *you* are alone."

Then a thought appeared to strike him. "Unless you have hidden a squad of Magisters in my forest." He grinned like a wolf. "If so, I tell you this. I know them all. They will not turn against me. And if they try, they will find themselves in their graves. My power has grown too great for them."

Forcing herself, Queen Estie made a dismissive gesture. "Calm yourself, Father. I have not risked any of Amika's sorcerers. My companion is not a Magister. You know that. But I do not need theurgy to demonstrate that I command here."

"Indeed?" Scowling, King Smegin raised his hand.

Outside the manor-house, the first officer's shouting had become a muffled clamor of voices. Some of his men had joined him, adding their calls to his. They, too, knew their former comrades. Now Commander Soulcess and his soldiers used every claim they had—friendship, kinship, love of home and homeland—to influence the guardsmen who had been lured away.

Other voices answered: frightened voices urging the first officer to retreat; angry voices threatening slaughter. But Estie did not hear fighting. Apparently, King Smegin's men were still in the barracks.

When her father raised his hand, an arrow shot out of the shadows behind his seat.

It was too sudden. Estie did not see it in time to react.

It was aimed at the assassin.

With a movement that seemed trivial, Lylin shifted aside. The shaft flashed past her. An instant later, it spent its force and skittered away along the floor.

King Smegin's eyebrows lifted. "Well." For a moment, he sounded impressed. "Now I see why you need her, Daughter. She does not deserve death. She is worthy of life. I will not destroy her."

Then he resumed his scowl. "But my patience wears thin. Do you believe that you command? Then say what you have come to say. You will not sway me, but I will be pleased to point out the flaws in your reasoning.

"The first is this. I do not require the rule of Amika. It will become mine when I deign to claim it. Do you propose to command *me*? Fine. Do so. Nothing will change. I will see my desires fulfilled, with or without your throne and your crown."

From outside, Estie heard a quick clash of iron, the thud of an arrow in flesh, a cry. Then silence. The brief struggle was over. Someone was wounded or dead.

There was worse to come. More men were going to fall.

In desperation, the Queen said sharply, "Enough! You have taunted me enough. Now *I* will speak.

"Father, you must stop."

The King squinted at her. He feigned incomprehension. "Stop what, Daughter?"

"Do not pretend senility with me," she snapped. She could not manage hauteur. That was one of her father's strengths, not hers. But she could draw on a deep well of outrage. "You know what you do. I have seen the corpses of your victims hanging. I know you have enslaved Nuuri and sent them to work on my road. I do not know how many. One would be too many. You must stop."

"Truly?" Now he mimicked sincerity. "Why?"

Cursing to herself, Queen Estie retorted, "Already, the Nuuri are massing. Soon they will come for you."

"Ha!" he snorted. "*Let* them." His bitter amusement cut like the blade of a saw. "They are no match for me. I have the might now, and the range, and the control. From this house, I can withstand the entire *race* of the Nuuri."

"You fool!" Estie's mother had warned her. Now she knew what Queen Rubia meant. "They will not attack you directly. They know what you can do. They will set fire to the house, the barracks, the stables. And if that fails, they will march against helpless hamlets, villages, towns. They will lay waste—"

King Smegin cut her off. "Is *that* your argument? You are the fool here, not I." His contempt lashed at her. "Those hamlets and villages and towns are helpless because you have made them so. You gave your army to Belleger. As for setting fires, well, the Nuuri do not use bows. Or arrows. The best they can manage is spears, which they will have to carry alight across open ground. I will pick them off at my leisure."

He held Estie's attention. She needed a moment to notice that she no longer heard voices. Commander Soulcess and his men had fallen silent.

In frustration, she cried, "But *why*, Father? What do you gain in all this? What purpose drives you? Why did you try to have me killed in Belleger? Why do you want war with the Nuuri? What *use* is there in Nuuri slaves?"

Abruptly, King Smegin tensed.

The cries and clangor of a melee became audible. Obscured by the walls of the house, they sounded impossibly distant. Estie did not know how many men were fighting, or why. Had Soulcess lost patience; tried to storm the barracks? Were some of the deserters resisting her father's guards?

King Smegin listened as if he knew what was happening. He raised his other hand.

Another signal.

Expecting a second arrow, Queen Estie flinched. She could not defend herself. She had little skill and no theurgy. She had to trust—

But the man or men hidden in shadows behind her father's seat did not fire again. Lylin remained still. The devotee seemed sure that she and the Queen were not threatened.

After a few heartbeats, Estie heard a boom like the detonation of a grenade. The explosion was too far away to be interpreted. An attack? A defense? A summons?

Outside, the melee ended as suddenly as it had begun.

The King relaxed as if he had been waiting for that sound.

As he regarded Estie now, his expression changed. She saw relish in his gaze, gratification in the twist of his mouth. When he replied, he sounded less like a swarm of wasps, more like a man who wanted to share his secret with his favorite child.

"Well, Daughter. Since you command it, I will answer."

Reliving a memory he enjoyed, he told her, "Some few years past, a troupe of men entered my sanctuary from the north. When they accepted my hospitality, they explained their presence in ways that pricked my curiosity. They described themselves as 'priests'—a strange word—and said they traveled from land to land, spreading the wisdom and peace and faith of their 'god'—another strange word. They called this being 'the Great God Rile,' but the name told me nothing. It was only a name, not an explanation. Their teaching, however—"

King Smegin leaned forward as if he were eager to convince Estie of something. "Daughter, they spoke at length of the war that rules every heart and home, every village and town, every people. They told me that every outer conflict is an expression, a reflection, of the inner struggle tormenting us all. We cannot be at peace in the world because we are not at peace in ourselves. And we are never at peace in ourselves because we are tortured by what we lack, whatever that lack may be. The lack of love, the lack of power, the lack of certainty. *Any* lack—but especially the lack of sorcery. Then the priests revealed how that lack can be amended.

"They assured me that if I acknowledge the truth of who and what I am, and if I have faith like theirs, I will know peace. And when I am at peace, I will understand that for me all things are permitted."

Surprised out of her silence, Queen Estie demanded, "The priests told you *that*? They gave you *permission*?"

The faint rumble of galloping hooves carried through the house, but she ignored it. She had come too far. Lylin could not save her. Her life was in Magister Facile's hands. As soon as she discovered the right words to provoke her father—

"Of course not!" he snarled. Throwing himself back in his chair, he crossed his arms over his chest to contain his vexation. "Those self-righteous idiots? Their insistence on their 'Great God' was ludicrous. But I drew the obvious conclusion.

"I have told myself the truth. I know who and what I am. I am at peace with myself and my desires. And if I *lack*, I know how to satisfy it. Whatever I do is right because *I* do it."

While Estie stared at him, he said, "If you can understand that I am at peace, Daughter, you may be able to understand that I have no specific interest in war with the Nuuri." Once again, he made an effort to sound sincere. "It is a means to an end. My only desire there, like my attempt to arrange your death, is to expose the madness of your alliance. Amika and Belleger should be one realm, and it should be ruled by Amika."

After a moment's consideration, he added, "But I do have a use for Nuuri slaves."

Like rising flames, Queen Estie demanded, "What *use*?"

"Why else?" he asked with false nonchalance. "To speed the completion of your road." But then his pretense failed him. He gathered himself; forgot his pose of sincerity; gripped the arms of his chair with hands like claws. "To open the way," he declared harshly.

"When it is ready, I will ride to the Last Repository in triumph"— his voice climbed—"and when I do, I will have a host at my back!"

The sudden nakedness of his malice shocked Estie. He was worse than treacherous: he was insane. But she could not afford to be daunted. "Gods, Father!" she cried. "You have allied yourself with the enemy of the library! You serve him!"

"*Serve* him?" He glared fury at her. "Paugh! I do not *know* him. I know only what all men know, that he is coming. If he allies himself with *me*, I will welcome him.

"But *first*, Daughter. *First* I will tear down that library and kill every man or woman or child who upholds it. I will teach those haughty Magisters that they do not know the true meaning of *power.*"

Later, no doubt, Estie would remember this and be appalled. But not now. Her mother had prepared her. Almost calmly, almost quietly, she replied, "No, Father. They will laugh at you. They scorn you now. When you face them, they will teach you the true meaning of contempt."

There. Those were the right words. They snatched King Smegin to his feet. His hands held silver lightning as if she had summoned it from the flesh of his palms, his fingers; as if she had ignited it.

"Do you believe that, Daughter? Have you learned nothing from me? *You do not know who and what I am!*"

Estie had no answer. She could not face her father any longer. Instead, she turned away.

In silence, she prayed, Magister Facile, please! If you were ever my friend, save me now. If you can fight him, do it now!

Aloud, she said to Lylin, "This is intolerable. It must end. Do me the favor of taking him prisoner."

The devotee raised her head, let Estie see the ferocity of her smile. She started forward.

But they had no time. Lightning crackled between King Smegin's hands. It spread up his arms. Bleeding tendrils of force, it reached his shoulders, his chest. Faster than Estie could think, he encased himself in lurid sorcery. Serpents of silver ruin writhed around him. From his head to his feet, he became a living bolt that strained for release.

Swift as lightning, Lylin flung a dagger at his throat.

Before the blade touched him, it evaporated in the blazing corona of his theurgy.

"*Now, Daughter!*" he roared. "*Scorn me and DIE!*"

From his whole body, sorcery erupted.

But it did not go anywhere. It did not strike and destroy. All of the hair on Estie's head seemed to stand upright. Ants crawled over her skin. The air vanished from her lungs. Yet she was not touched. Lylin was not.

As King Smegin's power erupted, it became mist. It dissipated and became nothing.

Just for an instant, he appeared to believe that he had succeeded. Then he saw the truth.

Wild horror filled his face. Waving his arms, he strove to summon his gift again. And again. And *again*.

Instead, the extremity of his desire made his muscles cramp. Spasms he could not control ran through his frame. Convulsing as if the after-effects of lightning lingered in his limbs, he collapsed in his chair. His eyes bled anguish. When he opened his mouth to wail, the only sound he could make was a thin whine.

Still convulsing, he struggled out of his chair. In a rush, he stumbled away to bash his head against the wall.

The first impact did not drop him. He tried again. He kept trying.

After that, Estie's mind went blank. She could not interpret the sequence of what occurred.

Without warning, the room was full of guards. Half a dozen of them. More. Waving their swords, they shouted confusion in all directions.

Estie found herself on the floor in Lylin's arms. They rolled from side to side, tripping one soldier, avoiding another. She saw the assassin cut a guard's hamstring. She may have heard him howl.

Then she was on her feet again, half carried by her companion; dragged along. Lylin batted blades aside as if they were meaningless. When the King's guards stopped shouting, the only sound in the long room was the steady thud of their monarch's forehead against the wall.

Estie nearly fell when Lylin shoved her through the doorway. There the devotee stopped; faced the room and the guards and the King. "Put up your swords." She did not need to shout. Her harsh accent gave her authority. "There is no one to fight. King Smegin has no more need of you. His reign is at an end."

When she was satisfied by what she saw, Lylin closed the door and came to support Queen Estie again.

The devotee did not speak. Estie did not. Her mind was gone, hidden away somewhere. She could not find it.

The beating of her father's forehead followed her like a knell as the devotee of Spirit helped her leave the house.

THIRTEEN

NOTHING WITHOUT HELP

An hour later, Queen Estie still sat with Magister Facile on the porch of the manor-house. They rested on stools against the outer wall of the room where Estie had faced her father. Inside that room, King Smegin could be heard beating his head on the far side of his chamber. The impacts came less regularly now. And they were less heavy: his strength was failing. Nevertheless he did not stop. Earlier, the devotee of Spirit had suggested a kinder location, one that would spare Estie the burden of listening to her father. But the Queen refused to leave him. He was broken now. She had nothing to fear. She stayed where she was to do what old King Abbator had once asked of her.

To witness.

When she tilted her stool and leaned on the wall, she could hear the remnants of her father whimpering between blows.

While Queen Estie sat back, Magister Facile hunched forward, bracing her elbows on her knees and gripping her cane with her aged hands. She was still wearing the absurd attire of a camp-follower; but she made no move to reclaim her grey robe. She had reached the porch in time to do what had to be done: that was all that mattered. Now she seemed content to rest with Amika's Queen until Estie was ready to hear her.

Before Estie had joined the Magister on the porch—while the Queen was still too stunned to react—Commander Soulcess had delivered his report. Under the circumstances, he had been admirably concise. Three of his deserters were dead. So were two of King Smegin's newer recruits, both former estate guards. Two of the King's soldiers were seriously wounded, one by Lylin's knife. There were no other casualties.

Apparently, King Smegin had expected Queen Estie's force to surround the manor-house. He had sent all but a handful of his guards to prepare a mounted counterattack from the concealment of the northward trail. A grenade had been their signal to charge. But when they pounded down into the glade, they found themselves flanked by the Queen's honor guard and her personal escort. There they discovered that their loyalty to the King had limits. Exposed in that fashion—too spread out to defend themselves effectively—they elected parley instead of battle.

Now that King Smegin no longer ruled his own house, his men—like Estie's honor guard and Crayn's command—were waiting for the Queen to make a few decisions.

At the time, Estie heard the first officer's report without attending to it. But she remembered it. When she had been sitting on the porch with Magister Facile for a time, she considered her choices briefly. Then she set them aside. They could wait until the first wave of her grief had passed.

The glade of King Smegin's sanctuary was hot in the midday sun. Waiting for Estie's recovery, his men were probably sweltering. But she was in no hurry to relieve them. The roof over the porch gave her shade. It helped soothe her overwrought nerves. If she kept her eyes half-closed, the world outside her sorrow and bitterness looked too dim to trouble her.

Eventually, Magister Facile moved. Groaning softly, she straightened her back, forced herself to sit upright. In a low voice that only Estie could hear, she said, "Now, Majesty, you comprehend why I cannot speak of my gift."

Do I? thought Estie.

As if the Queen had asked her question aloud, the Magister explained, "The secret protects me. If secrets are not more powerful than sorcery, they are often more useful. No Magister can harm me, but I have no defense against common violence. If that were known, I could not walk the streets of the Open Hand alone, and the ambush that tried to take your life would have been aimed at me as well. Only the belief that I can summon one of the six Decimates shields me.

"But my Decimate is the seventh. It is known as the Decimate of impotence, but I prefer to call it the Decimate of slumber.

"Majesty, it was I who deprived Amika and Belleger of sorcery. I did not destroy the talent for theurgy. I cannot. It is inborn. I merely made it sleep. Then I roused it again when your alliance was sealed."

As if to herself, she added, "Thankfully, I cannot affect a gift like yours, one that has not first been awakened. I can only restore a gift that I caused to sleep. Otherwise, I could never risk the use of my Decimate. The danger would be too great."

By degrees, Estie listened with more attention. In the intervals between the erratic thumping of her father's head, she found that she understood Magister Facile's vulnerability. Common violence— The old woman could have been killed by any chance bully or brawler; certainly by any traitor who feared her or Belleger or the alliance. She would have been an easy target. She had done nothing to defend Estie during the ambush because her power was meaningless there. Her secret kept her alive.

But once Queen Estie began to think, she had more questions.

"Do you mean to say, Magister, that Prince Bifalt and Commander Forguile did not use Hexin Marrow's book to restore Amika and Belleger? That they did not need it?"

"Majesty," replied Magister Facile bluntly, "they did not *have* it." Then she sighed. "King Bifalt will confirm what I say, now that you know my secret. He and Commander Forguile came to the Last Repository for the book, but the librarian did not release it. He sent me in its place."

Estie opened her eyes wide. With care, she set her stool squarely on the porch. "Why? He promised it to my husband. Prince Bifalt surrendered to the librarian's demands because of that promise."

Molding her features into a grimace of distaste, the sorceress stamped her cane on the floor. "Magister Marrow could not know how Prince Bifalt or Commander Forguile would use the book." She seemed to find the whole subject distasteful. "He trusted them to an extent, but he could not be certain." Despite her disapproval, she spoke too softly to be heard by anyone except the Queen of Amika. "Suppose King Smegin had ordered his loyal Commander to kill the Prince when they had the book in their possession. Suppose King Smegin had killed the Prince himself. You know your father. Can you imagine what he might have done if he could restore Amika and leave Belleger powerless?

"Or suppose the Prince betrayed his companion. You know how the librarian humiliated him. Perhaps you can grasp how deeply he was wounded. And you are familiar with his loathing for all sorcerers, especially for the sorcerers of the library. Can you be sure that he would have restored Amika as well as Belleger?"

Yes, thought Estie. I can be sure. He is a man of his word.

Still speaking quietly, Magister Facile glared out at the sunlight, the uneasy clusters of soldiers, the gloom-shrouded trees. "And if neither supposition troubles you—if your trust in both men is absolute—can you imagine that after the book was used it might not be used again? King Smegin would not have allowed it to remain in any hands but his. He would have defied the alliance to keep the book from Belleger. He did not have it in him to trust his former enemy.

"Magister Marrow explained all this to Prince Bifalt and Commander Forguile. In place of the book, he offered them me. And when he obtained their consent, he told them of my peril. My secret and my life would be in their hands."

The old woman sighed again. Her shoulders slumped under the weight of what she was saying. "Majesty, I am bitter that I cannot return to the library. My task here galls me, and I grieve for the loss of my life there. I grieve for the love I have left behind. But I am grateful daily that King Bifalt and Commander Forguile are honorable men. Today only they and you know what I can and cannot do." A moment later, she added, "And the devotee of Spirit, of course."

Estie could have asked then how the sorceress had met Lylin, how long they had known each other, how they had learned to trust each other. But those questions seemed trivial now. Suddenly, she was too angry to raise them. Magister Facile complained of her own bitterness and gall and grief, and yet she had—

Keeping her voice low, Queen Estie rasped, "You explain and explain, Magister, but you say nothing to excuse yourself."

At first, the old woman flinched. But then she made her expression blank. "What have I done, Majesty?"

"Why did you tell me I have a gift for sorcery when you can neither name nor awaken it?"

Magister Facile faced her without blinking. "You asked about *my* gift. I said what I did to distract you."

"Gods, woman!" snapped Estie. Then she remembered to speak softly. "Do not lie to me. You wanted me to fear my father. If I feared him enough, you would not need to expose your power. Or you wanted me too angry to shirk facing him."

As if involuntarily, the old woman's brows knotted in a scowl. "Majesty," she breathed: a reprimand. "I do not deserve your reproach. I am not Magister Marrow. I do not play on your heart to manipulate you."

"Then," retorted Estie, "give me a better answer."

Magister Facile took a moment to compose herself. Tapping her cane on the floor, she arranged her thoughts. Then she said with an air of sadness, "I wanted to distract you. That is one truth. Here is another. I did not know I would surprise you.

"I believed you were already aware of your talent. Surely some Magister has spoken to you? In all these years? Of course, none who are loyal to King Bifalt would do so. In itself, it is dangerous knowledge. Your husband's abhorrence makes it more so. His Magisters would say nothing to you—or to him. But surely one of your own theurgists—? They must see it. King Smegin did. I do. They *must*."

At once, Estie denied it. She knew her father. In fact, she knew him better now than she had a few hours ago. He *wanted* her kept ignorant. He would have forbidden every Amikan Magister to raise the subject with her. He had had the sixteen years of her girlhood in which to emphasize his orders, and he knew how to ensure obedience. In addition, every sorcerer knew what Magister Facile had said in the common-room of Beds, Food, Ale. Estie's secret was too dangerous to mention, even in passing. Any theurgist who did not recognize her gift could not take the risk of commenting on it.

Even the Queen's most trusted Magisters had said nothing.

Like Magister Facile, Estie slumped, borne down by a weight of sadness. "I cannot think of another reason why my father made me his favorite. He kept me close to ensure that I remained ignorant." Then she took hold of herself; shook off her regrets. "But you have told me two truths, and they are not enough. They are still excuses, Magister. You have a better answer. I want to hear it."

In exasperation, the older woman responded, "Because I want to fire your curiosity. I want you to have hope. I want you to *finish your road.*"

While her assertion echoed in Estie's mind, Magister Facile sagged to support her elbows on her knees again. In a lost, quavering voice, she murmured, "I want you to visit the library. I want to return there. We cannot without a road. The journey would be too cruel for you. It would end me."

Princess Estie might have retorted, So you *do* play on my heart to manipulate me. Queen Estie stifled the impulse. She had spent her girlhood being manipulated by her father. King Abbator had won her consent to marriage and the alliance by playing on her heart. Her husband's refusal to do as much as touch her felt like a kind of manipulation. She hated such things. But events were *quickening.* The enemy was coming. She could not afford to indulge her small hurts.

Instead, she said with as much steadiness as she could manage, "I understand your desire to return." Leaving Apprentice Travail—the only man who could truly *hear* her—must have hurt the Magister deeply. And of course Magister Facile had left behind more than the love of a good man, more than the companionship of people who shared her devotion to the Last Repository. She had also sacrificed her access to sorcerous health and vigor. "But why should *I* visit the library?"

"Why," sighed the older woman. "Why. Why. You know why. For answers. For help. For *knowledge.* No one in Amika or Belleger can guide you. Only *there* will you find teachers skilled enough and learned enough to name your gift.

"If you do not know what it *is,* how can you choose whether or not it should be awakened?"

From the room behind her, Estie heard a slumping sound, the limp stutter of thuds made by a falling body. King Smegin had finally collapsed, unconscious or asleep. She had borne witness long enough.

Weakness lingered in her muscles. It lingered in her heart. But she had one more question.

"Now tell me why you came *here* with me. You say you silenced all sorcery in Amika and Belleger. In one night, you made it sleep. Then later you reawakened it just as quickly. Why did you not end my father's power from the safety of the trees? Gods, Magister! Why did you not end it from the safety of *Belleger*?" King Smegin could have been stopped at any time. Certainly, he could have been stopped when his crimes against the Nuuri became known. "Why did you *allow* him to commit so much harm?"

To Estie's surprise, Magister Facile had an answer ready.

"Imagine a pond crowded with lily pads, Majesty. Throw a stone into the pond from any distance, and the ripples move every pad. To move a single pad, you must kneel at the pond's edge and touch the pad lightly with your finger. As I did with the Magister who meant to ambush you in Belleger."

Did that make sense? Estie was not sure. But she did not know enough to argue against it.

And she had other responsibilities. She had kept the men in the glade waiting long enough. She knew what had to be done. Forcing herself, she rose to her feet. For a moment, she tottered. Then she stood straight and looked around her like a Queen.

Like a Queen, she left the porch and went to tell her people what she expected of them.

It was not her place to give orders to her honor guard and her personal escort—or even to King Smegin's soldiers and his accumulated deserters, thugs, and estate guards. That chore belonged to Commander Soulcess. She talked to him and Commander Crayn at a little distance. But she kept the devotee of Spirit with her. That was her only concession to her own frailty.

In the manor-house, Lylin had saved her life for the second time. Queen Estie might need her to do more.

Her orders must have seemed obscure to the first officer. After all, she had told him nothing about Nuuri slaves working on her road or a Nuuri army massing on the border. But Soulcess and everyone he commanded had seen the blackened corpses hanging outside the house. They knew enough to guess that there were other crimes to consider.

By Queen Estie's command, King Smegin's household servants and Magister Facile would be escorted back to Maloresse. The servants had no lives to which they could return in the city, but they also had nowhere else to go. And the Magister was too old to endure a journey harder than the one she had already suffered. They would all be delivered to Chancellor Sikthorn. He would know how to care for them. Magister Facile could rest in the Flower of Amika until Estie returned.

The deserters would be given their former places in the honor guard. They would not be singled out or mistreated. Were they untrustworthy? They would be surrounded by staunch comrades. Did they want excitement? They would find excitement enough in her service. Were they merely brutal men who hungered for brutality? The coming war would feed them until they sickened of killing.

King Smegin's men—soldiers, estate guards, and thugs—were a problem with more thorns. Perhaps because they were afraid, or perhaps because they relished cruelty, they had enabled all of the King's crimes. They must have raided Nuuri lands to capture victims for his studies. And they had taken an unknown count of survivors to work as slaves on the road.

Unfortunately, they outnumbered the first officer's forces. Nevertheless Estie believed that Commander Soulcess would be able to control them. By submitting when they were flanked, they had demonstrated the limits of their fidelity. The Commander carried her authority as the rightful ruler of Amika: King Smegin was a broken vessel. And by now, everyone had heard that she had faced her father and shattered him. How the deed was done, they had no idea: none of them knew Magister Facile. They had to assume that Queen Estie was a more powerful sorcerer than King Smegin. They would not be inclined to defy her first officer.

On that footing, Commander Soulcess would disarm the King's forces and escort all of them to her road. There they would join sub-Commander Hellick's company. Then the King's men would be required to earn their release by sharing in the roadwork. Sub-Commander Hellick and a number of the honor guard would remain to oversee their labors. He would not be asked to deal kindly with any of the King's soldiers who deserted *that* duty.

As for the surviving Nuuri slaves: if there were any, they would be in the first officer's care. By this time, sub-Commander Hellick had presumably rescued the slaves and done what he could to treat their wounds and ease their fears. Surely, he had secured or driven off the King's men who had abused the Nuuri. Commander Soulcess and as many guardsmen as he needed would bring the remaining Nuuri north to the borders of their lands. If they were too weak or hurt to walk, he would have them carried in litters. If they needed crutches, or bindings for their feet, or decent garments, he would provide them. Whatever happened, he would see them safely to their homeland.

By Queen Estie's estimate, she had ordered nearly a hundred fifty people to abandon her father's refuge. And the distances she expected them to travel were considerable. Fortunately, they would not lack for provisions. King Smegin liked rich living. His larders and cold-rooms would be well stocked. She encouraged Commander Soulcess, Commander Crayn, and the servants to take as much as they could carry.

For herself, the Queen had a more urgent task. It was also more dangerous.

When she named it, she faced protests. The first officer had a list of them, but they came down to one: he was afraid for her. Would she take more men? No. Any force larger than her personal escort might be seen as a threat. Would she at least take Magister Facile? No. After all the harm King Smegin had inflicted on the Nuuri, *any* Magister would be seen as a threat. Then what could she hope to accomplish? To prevent a war.

But. But. But.

Queen Estie answered him with one more order. "Say nothing of me to your men. *Nothing*, Commander. For you and them, the road and the

surviving Nuuri are paramount. I will not have my honor guard distracted by new fears."

Then she walked away, leaving the first officer's outrage, anguish,
and doubt in Commander Crayn's capable hands. While Crayn did
what he could, she rejoined Magister Facile in the shade of the porch.

King Smegin had been right on one point. Amika was effectively
helpless against an enemy in the north because she had made it so. If
the Nuuri launched an assault with all their strength, Amikans would
be slaughtered because their Queen had put her faith in King Bifalt.
And because she had been too naïve to imagine that her father would
betray her.

She was not naïve now. King Smegin and Magister Facile had cured
her of that fault.

And she was learning to appreciate the power of secrets. Under the
circumstances, she needed to conceal the danger of an invasion. Commander Soulcess had vouched for the loyalty of her honor guard. She
had chosen men by name on the strength of his appraisal. But even loyal
Amikans might balk at the thought of Nuuri rampaging across the
realm: of villages torched, towns ransacked, homes and farmsteads
trampled. If they understood the peril, even the most faithful guardsmen might find it difficult or impossible to obey their Queen.

The matter of the Nuuri was urgent; but that burden was hers. Her
soldiers could not carry it for her.

She was in no hurry to face it. She was too tired. Nevertheless
she felt compelled to turn her back on her father's sanctuary. Perhaps
someday—if she lived—she would have his house burned to the ground.

More than an hour later, she left the glade with the devotee of
Spirit and her personal escort, riding north. Before long, she and
her small company left the sunlit glade and galloped into the deep
gloom of Solace Wood as if they had vanished from the world.

This trail was worn, but it had not been used as heavily as the track
that led toward Maloresse. It was rougher under the hooves of the
horses, narrower; more often obstructed by shrubs, fallen branches, and

low-hanging boughs. The riders could not gallop safely. Their passage through the cedar was going to take longer than Queen Estie had imagined. It might take much longer. She did not know how far the wood extended.

Still, the rich scents of the trees and their carpet of needles seemed cleaner than the air around the manor-house. Despite their dark cling, the shadows felt protective: they masked the reminders of King Smegin's madness and cruelty. There might still be Nuuri scouts lurking near the trail, but they did not carry the lingering reek of burned flesh. By increments, Estie began to relax. Eventually, her mount's easy gait made her pine for sleep.

She would have liked to reach the edge of Solace Wood before she halted for the night. Like her, however, Commander Crayn and his men had no idea how distant it might be. They had spent their years of service escorting her back and forth between Maloresse and the Line River, not exploring their homeland. And this was Lylin's first visit to Amika. When the Commander suggested a pause for rest and food, Estie accepted with involuntary relief.

Dismounting, she leaned her groaning muscles against the bole of a cedar, then slid down the trunk to ease the strain on her legs. From one of his saddlebags, Crayn produced a waterskin and packets of food for the Queen, the devotee, and himself. Estie drank gratefully, ate a little fruit and some bread that still smelled fresh. For a while, she concentrated on breathing like a woman who had never heard her father beat his head on a wall. Briefly, she closed her eyes.

When she opened them again, she was lying on a fragrant bed of cedar needles wrapped in the comfort of her bedroll. Through a fog of sleep, she felt cool air on her cheeks, saw darkness everywhere. Gradually, she realized that night had come. Overhead, a few stars glittered between the leaves, appearing and disappearing as the arch of boughs swayed in the breeze.

Time seemed to pass. She must have slept again. She was too close to dreams to rouse herself, but she managed to turn her head. Nearby, ruddy with gentle heart, the embers of a dying campfire blinked like the stars. On opposite sides of the coals, Commander Crayn and the devotee of Spirit faced each other. He sat cross-legged, erect like a soldier expecting orders. The embers made occasional reflections like flickers of interest in his pale gaze. She knelt with her weight on her heels. Her back was as straight as his, but she seemed more at ease, as if that posture were habitual. She had pushed back the hood of her cloak, but Estie could not see her face.

None of Crayn's men were visible within the small reach of the coals, but their absence did not trouble the Queen. She trusted her escort.

Still half asleep, she spent a while listening to the Commander and Lylin.

Apparently, he had surrendered to his curiosity. Sounding careful, he asked, "What can you tell me about your people?"

An interesting question, thought Estie. Yawning, she missed part of the assassin's reply. Then she heard Lylin chuckling softly. "We have more in common with the Nuuri than you might imagine. I have read about them in the library. The men are smaller than the women, more fleet, more enduring. They herd their zhecki across the whole of their steppes, which are vast. The women tend their hearths and tents. They birth their children. And when there is war, they fight.

"You will understand when you see them. The women stand head and shoulders taller than the men. They have twice the girth, and there is a killing strength in their limbs."

Crayn rubbed his face with both hands. "Your people are like that?"

The devotee laughed outright. "Yes and no. It is an example. In Amika and Belleger, men and women are divided in one way. In other lands, the divisions differ. Our men are goodly in size and strength. We desire them greatly. But they love hearth and home, children and fields, grazing and crops. The fire for dominance that burned in King Smegin, or for honor and responsibility that rules King Bifalt, does not trouble them. It flames in us, the women. The devotees of Spirit and Flesh."

Estie drifted. She missed another question or two, or perhaps an answer. Then she heard Lylin saying, "If I confuse you, forget Spirit and Flesh. Think of *fist* and *clasp*. My sister-devotees and I seek dominance and honor through the act of standing apart. No hand touches us. Instead, we impose our purposes and our sense of what is right on all who cannot match our skill and passion. We do not fight. We *are* the fight.

"The devotees of Flesh seek dominance and responsibility through the act of drawing close. Where we speak with the fist, they speak with the clasp. Their skills are as honed as ours, and as precise, but they do not strike or kill. Rather, they woo others to their purposes, their sense of what is right. In their own way, they also do not fight. They are the embrace that renders the fight meaningless."

Dozing, the Queen tried to understand. Then she gave up. After a while, she remembered to listen.

To some other question, the assassin explained, "Often together, but at times separately, we wander the lands, we women of Spirit and Flesh, seeking opportunities to prove ourselves. With Set Ungabwey and his caravans, we found many opportunities. He became our ally. But when we discovered the Last Repository, we understood its gifts. There we formed a new alliance. We do not serve. Nor do we impose our own purposes. Instead, Spirit and Flesh, we do what we can to preserve a threatened treasure."

This time, Estie heard Commander Crayn. She heard his confusion. His fascination. But it was not the library that transfixed him.

"You wander," he said gruffly. "Your men do not." If he had been less bewildered, or less entranced, he might have sounded scornful. "How do your people survive? How do you continue in the world? Your desires and their homes depend on children. They must. Surely your men do not bear your children for you?"

Another interesting question; but Estie did not hear Lylin's reply. Her husband refused to touch her. She would never know his embrace or bear his children. It was an old grief, but Crayn's probing made it fresh. Escaping, she went back to sleep.

In the morning, while the Queen and her company rode on between the cedars, they moved through dapples and splashes of sunshine, tree-filtered light that seemed to make them substantial and then dismiss them from one moment to the next. But when they emerged

from Solace Wood before noon, they found that the weather was changing. A stiff wind whipped the hair across Estie's face, and from the east
black clouds came boiling. They were still distant, but they piled over
the horizon like spume. Already, she could see bolts lashing among the
thunderheads. Brief silver flashes gave the depths of the storm a livid
look as if the clouds were bruised.

"Gods!" she panted. Urgently, she asked Commander Crayn if her
company could still travel when the storm hit.

"If we must, Majesty," he answered. Squinting, he studied the thunderheads. "But we have a few hours. The worst may not catch us until
midafternoon. Then—" He shrugged. "We have our rain-capes, and
enough canvas for two or three small shelters. If the downpour defeats
us, we can contrive to wait it out."

Then he added, "But it would be better, Majesty, to stay where we
are. The Wood will shelter us until the storm passes. While it lasts, it
may blind us. We may lose our way, or miss the Nuuri altogether."

Feeling stymied, Queen Estie chewed on her worries. The weather
foiled her assumptions. She did not know how far she was from Nuuri
lands—or how far the Nuuri might have come into Amika, if they refused her offer to meet them. They might be one league away, or thirty.
But that was a secondary fear. Crayn was right. The greatest danger was
that she and the Nuuri might not meet each other at all. If they could
not see—

Estie reached for Lylin's arm, drew the assassin closer. "Devotee,"
she asked, "can you guide us in that storm? Can you ensure that we do
not pass by the Nuuri?"

Lylin cocked an eyebrow. A twist at one corner of her mouth implied a grin. "I am one woman, Majesty," she answered. "I can guide
you. But I cannot both guide you and scout ahead. Heed the Commander. If we remain where we are, you will not be led astray. The
Nuuri will come to you."

Then she flicked a glance past Estie's shoulder. When she faced the
Queen again, she smiled openly. "Your concerns are groundless, Majesty. Look!"

With a gesture, the devotee directed Estie's attention northward.

Clearly, Solace Wood ended where it ran out of fertile soil. Beyond the trees, the ground sloped down to a basin as wide as the glade around the manor-house. Its bottom appeared to hold nothing except gravel: the slope itself was loose dirt. And on all sides except the south, the hollow was surrounded by low, rugged hills. They resembled stone heads, some upright, some lying on their sides, all indifferently covered with dirt and twisted shrubs as if some careless giant had lost interest before he finished burying them. Here and there, foreheads or cheekbones fronted the sky. Some of them implied scowls. In other places, knobs of granite jutted from the ground like fists. Boulders like broken fingers cluttered the rifts between the hills.

"Do you see? There," insisted Lylin, pointing, "and there. Do you see how folds in the hills funnel down to lower ground? If the *first* desire of the Nuuri is to punish King Smegin, they must use the trail we have used—and to reach it, they must approach through the hollow below us.

"Wait here, Majesty. Sooner or later, the Nuuri will come to you."

"But you said—" protested Estie. She was thinking too hard to form coherent sentences. "When you gave their scouts in the forest your message. You asked them to wait. You told them I would come—"

"Majesty." The devotee's tone was a reproach. "I did not expect them to comply. Would you? If villagers in Amika were tortured and killed, would you hold back, trusting a woman you do not know to answer the crime? Who would trust *you* afterward?

"I said what I did so the scouts would feel compelled to abandon their poor spying and deliver my message. But the Nuuri will come *here* for another reason as well. In your name, I said you would meet with them. Why would they go to vent their ire on helpless hamlets and villages when they can challenge Amika's Queen herself?"

Queen Estie looked away to hide her chagrin. Lylin was right. Of course she was. At every stage along the way, she had done and said what was needed when it was needed. Estie herself had not. She had been so horrified by her father and his crimes that she had let desperation rule her. How much time had she lost to frustration and treachery? She did not know: she could not count the days since she had heard Chancellor Postern's confession.

Without the devotee's help, Queen Estie's brave promises to her husband would have come to nothing.

Instead of meeting Lylin's gaze, she pretended to study the clefts among the hills where the Nuuri forces might appear. As if she expected the wind to hear her and answer, she asked her companion, "What are you doing here?"

Did women like the devotee of Spirit abandon their own purposes simply because Elgart appealed for help?

"Majesty?" inquired Lylin.

"I heard you last night." In retrospect, Estie understood why Elgart had insisted on the company of an assassin. "You said you impose your sense of what is right." But she could not imagine why the woman had honored his request. "You can't do that *here*." With a sweeping gesture, she encompassed King Smegin's retreat and the coming Nuuri. "Here *everything* is wrong."

"Ah, Majesty," replied Lylin: a sigh of comprehension. "No doubt, it seems so. But if you take a wider view, you will see that *here* is only a fragment of a larger landscape. *You* are not wrong. Elgart was not wrong to ask for my aid. Your alliance with Belleger is not wrong.

"Both Amika and Belleger have been wrongly used, but you do not respond wrongly. King Bifalt does not. You are like the Last Repository. I am here to preserve a threatened treasure."

That answer silenced the Queen. Estie did not consider herself a treasure, but she knew too well that she was in danger.

She had never met the Nuuri. They were as strange to her as any of the people her husband had encountered on his journey to the library. She did not know how to answer the righteousness of their fury.

While the wind grew stronger, and the thunderheads surged closer, mounting into the sky as they approached, Queen Estie and her company retreated into the cover of Solace Wood. They stayed near the fringes of the trees, where they could watch the rifts leading down toward the hollow; but they tethered their horses deeper among the trees, out of immediate danger. To the accompaniment of distant thunder and the lashing of branches and needles, Commander Crayn and his men shared out a meal, passed waterskins from hand to hand.

Estie was not hungry—she was scarcely thirsty—but she forced herself to eat and drink despite the knots like cramps in her stomach. The storm was still at least a league away, but she could feel the deep growl of thunder in her chest. At intervals, blasts of lightning glared through the canopy overhead: instants of silver-white so quick that they were only truly visible because they lingered in her vision. Moment by moment, the air lost its heat. Soon it would be cool. When the rain started, the whole forest would turn cold.

She was not surprised to find that she yearned for her husband. She had felt that wasted longing often enough to know that she carried it with her wherever she went. But she was surprised when she caught herself aching for the rudimentary comforts of Belleger's Fist. Even her unloved bed in King Bifalt's keep would be more kindly than hours or days drenched by cold rain.

Would the Nuuri march on through the storm? Would they pause to let it pass?

They herded their zhecki across their wide steppes in all of the world's weather. Why would they let a mere thunderstorm delay their vengeance?

"Majesty," breathed the Commander.

He spoke so quietly that Estie barely heard him. Perhaps he wanted a moment of private discussion. Something about shelter? Or setting a watch? Was it possible that some of King Smegin's spies in the forest had not joined his thwarted attempt to take her forces by surprise? Was it likely? Was she still in danger from her father's men?

No, she decided. Lylin could not be ambushed. The devotee was too canny. Any spy foolish enough to creep close would be captured or killed before he could threaten the company.

"Majesty," said Crayn again. The Queen heard more tension in his voice.

She raised her head; blinked at him. Her mind had wandered. She thought that she had already responded to him, but she must have imagined it.

When he had her attention, he said only, "The Nuuri."

She reached his side without making a conscious decision to move. He put his hand on her arm, guided her among the last trees. The devotee of Spirit joined them as if he had summoned her out of the air.

Crouching at the end of the trail, they looked down into the basin.

It held bright sunshine, nothing more. The highest clouds leading the storm would begin to mask the sun soon, but not yet. The light was so clear that Queen Estie could distinguish individual bits of gravel in the hollow-bottom. To the east, the storm front loomed over her as if dozens of Magisters had combined their Decimates to inundate her, drown everyone in the path of their theurgy. Like an undertone to the harsh wind, the cracking thunder, she heard a liquid sound like the first hint of a flash flood.

But there were no Nuuri.

Then she realized that Commander Crayn was pointing at one of the descending cuts off to her left. When she looked there, she saw a mass of people moving closer.

Dozens of them. More. They wore sewn leathers that flapped around their arms and legs. Their coming did not resemble a march: it looked more like a rabble in motion. But they stayed together.

They were all men. All of them carried weapons, heavy clubs of bone. Chest-plates and thigh-guards made of smaller bones bound with leather thongs protected them. In silence, they came quickly. But they did not run. Instead, they kept pace with the long strides of the taller figure in the center of their cluster.

If the devotee had not explained that Nuuri women were larger than their men, Estie would still have guessed that this figure was a woman. The men had short hair. Their limbs were lean and hardy. The woman wore long tresses that fluttered around her face. Her arms and legs were stout, bound with muscle. The bones of her chest-plate were thick, and they bulged to accommodate her massive breasts.

She carried a club heavy enough to crush rocks.

Crayn caught his breath. "Majesty," he murmured. "I estimate eighty."

"Their women are precious," remarked Lylin, "because they are few, but also because they are strong." She sounded unnaturally calm, almost nonchalant. "Each of them keeps a stable of men to hunt and forage for her, herd for her, father her children. In my reading, I learned that eighty is a large number. Most of the women command between forty and fifty men."

So, thought Estie, *that* woman is a kind of queen.

Then the Commander gasped softly. He pointed again.

Down another rift came a second mass of Nuuri similarly armed and armored. This company was smaller than the first, no more than half as many men. But the woman at its center was as big as the first, as strong. She looked fiercer.

A steady roar, soft and insistent, marred Queen Estie's hearing. For a moment, she thought that she was listening to the fear in her veins. Then she realized that it was the sound of a distant deluge.

Like the Nuuri, it was coming closer.

An instant later, Commander Crayn pointed again. Past a protruding forehead of rock in a third cut came another band of Nuuri.

After that, there were no more. Apparently, the Nuuri were only prepared to risk three women and perhaps a hundred fifty men in a direct assault on King Smegin—or on Queen Estie.

Estie did not doubt for a second that if she failed to stop this army, there would be war. Thousands of other Nuuri would strike into Amika elsewhere.

She expected them to stride straight across the basin and start up the slope without pausing. But she was wrong. The first mass halted in the center of the graveled bottom. When the second woman and her men arrived, the two women barked greetings or commands at each other. Their words sounded familiar, but they were too far away to be heard clearly. Then the third cluster or stable joined the army. The women spoke. The men did not make a sound.

In a moment, the whole force was facing up the slope toward the trail through Solace Wood.

Move, Estie ordered herself. Move! This was why she had come. It was time for her to forget the girl who had loved her father, the woman who still ached for her husband. They had to be set aside. Here she needed to be the Queen of Amika in fact, not just in aspiration.

As if to help her, the devotee of Spirit said, "Address the woman who steps out to meet you as Keeper. Women are the Hearth-Keepers. The one who speaks with you is *the* Keeper."

Trembling, Estie stood up from her crouch.

Her voice shook as she told the Commander, "Show ten of your men at the edge of the trees." Let the Nuuri see that she was not alone. "Hold back the rest. If I do not call for you, do not advance. Do *not*.

"Do you hear me, sir? This challenge is not for you. Your presence where you are is enough. I will not risk one more life in the name of King Smegin's crimes."

"As you say, Majesty," replied Crayn. She could not tell by his tone whether he was indignant or appalled.

Unsteadily, she took one step down the slope, and another; and another as if she were falling.

Just for a moment, the Nuuri men greeted her by beating their chest-plates with their clubs. The clash of bone on bone covered the wet rush of approaching rain, the slam of thunder. Then they stood still, waiting. Every flare of lightning emphasized their savagery.

A dozen steps. Two dozen. Halfway down the slope. More. Estie struggled to control her legs. Nevertheless she defied her fear. With every stiff-kneed stride, every jolt downward, she straightened her back more, squared her shoulders, set her jaw. She was the Queen of Amika by right of birth and formal grant, and she did not mean to dethrone herself.

But, gods! Those Nuuri—! The men looked ready to tear open her throat with their teeth. And the women towered over her. They glowered like thunderheads, with reflections of lightning in their deep-set eyes.

The Keeper who advanced a few steps as Estie approached, the one with the largest stable, was the tallest woman she had ever seen. Each of the Keeper's fists was big enough to grasp Estie's whole skull. Her club looked heavy enough to shatter iron.

Ten paces away, Estie stopped. Holding her head up with every ounce of sovereignty she could muster, she met the Nuuri's scowl.

"Keeper." Queen Estie fought down her impulse to shout. The storm was growing louder, but it did not require her to raise her voice yet. She only wanted to shout because she was terrified. "I am Estie Queen of Amika, daughter of King Smegin, made Queen when he surrendered his throne. I have come—"

"Good!" snapped the Keeper. She had a voice like an echo of thunder. Her features resembled slabs of slate fused together. The granite escarpment of her forehead sheltered the fury in her eyes. "I will kill you. I will kill every man who stands in my way. I will repay your father's evil by crushing every bone in his body until he is too broken to beg for death. Then I will exact the price of what the Nuuri have suffered from your despised land. I will demand blood and pain from every Amikan who did nothing while my people were tortured and made slaves by sorcery!"

She sounded like she meant to shatter Estie at that instant.

But she did not raise her club.

"No, Keeper," retorted Queen Estie, "you will not. Not yet. Not until you have heard me.

"I know what my father has done. I abhor it." She gathered strength as she spoke. "Every good man and woman in Amika abhors it. He deserves what you would do to him. But you cannot break him. I have already done it. He is powerless now, a crippled shell. And the men who served him are mine to use and punish. They will take the place of those Nuuri who were made slaves. Any of your people who still live will be returned to you when their wounds have been given our best care.

"I am the Queen of Amika. My word binds my people. The evil you have suffered is finished. While I live—"

Again, the Keeper interrupted her. "It is not enough," the woman snarled. "Are we children, to be pacified by empty promises when we have been wronged? You do not know us. For uncounted years, uncounted generations, we have lived in peace, dealing with your kind only when we must—and always fairly. Do you say the evil is ended? Of course, you do. You fear us. You will say whatever serves your purpose. But we will not be content until we have shed blood in recompense. We will not be content until we have shed a *river* of your blood to balance the scales."

"*No,*" repeated Queen Estie. "I am not done. You will not shed one drop of Amikan blood until you have heard me. You will not risk more Nuuri lives until you have *heard* me.

"Do you say you are not a child? Neither am I. I tell you that I am the Queen of Amika, and my word *binds*. If you seek Amikan blood in recompense, Nuuri blood will be shed as well. Lives on both sides will be lost when there is no need. But yours will be wasted. Amika will endure.

"It is true that you have always dealt fairly. Your honesty is proven. *Mine* is also. And you understand barter. Barter with me now. I have the power to command any restitution you require, if it is not *blood*."

The Keeper raised her face to the threatened sky, the encroaching storm. "And *I* say," she roared, "*it is not enough*! Your words are rain. They fall and wet the ground and are gone. We do not barter when Nuuri lives are lost. Our people have suffered more than slavery and death. They have been *tortured*! We have been ravaged by your father's lightning until there is no scream that can contain our agony! *We will have blood!*"

Estie clenched her fists as if she imagined that she could strike the Keeper. She had no answer for such rage. If her words were as heavy as the coming storm, they would not suffice. Lightning cracked, calling a shout of thunder from the clouds. The first drops of rain spattered her face as if the weather itself were mocking her.

Then the devotee of Spirit shouted, "If that is your word, Keeper, I challenge it! I challenge you!"

Nuuri men beat their chest-plates. Whirling, Queen Estie saw Lylin. The devotee had come halfway down the slope. There she stood, straight as a spear, and as fearless. She had pushed back the hood of the cloak, letting the Nuuri see who she was.

"*You*, little woman?" yelled the Keeper. "*You* challenge me?"

"That is your custom," retorted Lylin. "When there is conflict among the Nuuri, you do not war with each other." A step at a time, she descended toward Queen Estie and the Keeper. "Your lives are too precious to be spent in battle. The dispute is settled by the Keepers, woman to woman, until one prevails. Then the conflict is done."

The devotee reached Estie's side with early raindrops streaking her features. To Estie, she seemed more than eager: reflected streams of lightning made her look ecstatic.

"Queen Estie rules Amika, but I am her Keeper." The assassin sounded stronger than the wind, stronger than the massing downpour. "I will give you battle, woman to woman. And when I prevail, there will be no war. Instead, you will honor Queen Estie's offer of restitution."

Estie did not know how to read the Keeper's face. She thought that the huge woman was amazed. There was less fury in the Keeper's voice as she repeated, "You? *You* challenge me?" Brandishing her club, she snorted, "You are a child, little woman. I will kill you. Then I will kill your Queen, and her men hiding their fear in the trees, and as many Amikans as I choose until I am content!"

"You will not," retorted Lylin calmly. Wind hurled rain at her, but she ignored it. "However, I insist on fair dealing. It would be too easy for me to kill you." From each of her sleeves, she drew out a dagger. For a moment, she held them for all the Nuuri to see. Then she handed them to Estie. "Also," she continued, "I do not desire your death."

"I desire *yours*, woman!" shouted the Keeper.

"And you will have it," replied the devotee, "if you can earn it. I will allow you to strike three blows at me. To be fair, I will stand where I am while you strike. If even one of your blows hurts me, you will do what you wish. Kill me, kill Queen Estie, kill every Amikan you can find."

The Keeper tossed her club from hand to hand as if it were weightless. Her grin was sharp with relish. "I will."

"*But*," insisted Lylin. "If you cannot harm me, you will allow *me* to strike three blows. When I am done, I will call upon the other Keepers to determine who has prevailed.

"Do you call that fair dealing?"

"Oh, certainly." The woman's scorn was as heavy as her weapon. "When you are dead, I will allow you to strike me as often as you can."

"And if I am not dead?" Despite the stiff wind, the pelting scatter of raindrops, the devotee's voice revealed an authority that Estie had never heard her use before; an assurance of command. "Do you accept my terms, Hearth-Keeper?"

"Yes!" snapped the Nuuri. "Being dead, you will have no cause to complain when I honor *my* terms."

Lylin was laughing—positively *laughing*—as she turned to Queen Estie. "Then, Majesty," she said through her joy, "you should withdraw to a safe distance. I can stand my ground, but I have not asked the Keeper to do the same."

Stunned beyond words, Estie backed away. The assassin's daggers felt lifeless in her hands. After a moment, she dropped them. The storm was coming. Oh, it was *coming*. Rain stung her face, wet her hair. Every crash of thunder shook the air in her lungs. The wild dance and slash of lightning made her want to cower. The worst of it was still some distance away, but its leading edge was enough to stagger her.

Eight backward steps behind the devotee: ten: twelve. There Queen Estie determined to stand her own ground; to bear witness yet again.

That decision seemed to take the last of her resolve.

Held by the storm and her own shock, she felt no surprise at all when Prince Jaspid arrived at her side.

He was fully armed, but he had not touched his weapons. His rifle still hung from its strap over his shoulder. His saber rested in its scabbard against his thigh, his dagger in its sheath at his belt. In flashes of lightning, rain and sweat shone on his face.

Why had Commander Crayn permitted him to pass?

How could the Commander have stopped him?

Bending to Estie's ear, the Prince asked, as eager as Lylin, "Shall I intervene, Majesty? I have heard tales of your devotee. Your escort at the Fivebridge garrison had much to say. No doubt, she is skilled. But she is overmatched here. I live for this. I can do better."

His offer found a scrap of resistance in the Queen's foundering heart. "Do not!" she hissed at once. "I forbid it! You do not understand this, Highness." He could not: he did not know what had led her to this place. "It is woman to woman. If you intrude, you will not face a woman. A host of Nuuri men will oppose you. More than a hundred of them, Jaspid! They will batter you into a smear on the gravel."

The Prince scowled at her command. For a moment, he seemed to consider defying her. His hunger for overwhelming odds was well known. But then he relented. Perhaps he could imagine what his brother the King would say if he overruled her choices. Or perhaps he wanted to see what Lylin could do. Standing straight, he said like the rain, "Then I will protect you when your devotee fails. That, at least, you will not forbid."

Estie hardly heard him. Her attention had already fallen back into the storm and the rain; into Lylin's confrontation with the Keeper.

While Prince Jaspid joined his Queen-Consort, the devotee had taken a moment to mark out a square in the gravel with her foot: the spot where she had promised to stand. Then she faced the Keeper.

"Now!" she called like a cheer. Spreading her arms, she made herself available to be hit. "I am ready! Do what you can!"

She looked off-balance, leaning her head and her weight slightly to one side as if the wind had pushed her off her best stance.

The Keeper did not hesitate. Clearly, she had exhausted her tolerance for the smaller woman's audacity. Raising her club with both hands, she hammered it down at Lylin's head.

The force of the blow would have crushed anyone Estie had ever known; but it did not touch the devotee. With a small shift of her feet, a quick lean in the opposite direction, she made the massive bone miss her. The impact when it pounded the gravel sprayed stone shards in all directions. Estie saw sudden red appear on Lylin's ankles. But the cuts were small.

The Keeper needed only an instant to understand how she had been tricked. Despite her weapon's weight, she snatched it back with frightening speed. One-handed, she swung it like a scythe at Lylin's legs.

The assassin had promised to stand her ground. She had not promised to stand without protecting herself. Faster than the club, she lifted one leg in a wheeling arc, then chopped downward. Before the club reached her, she hacked her heel like the blade of an axe onto the Keeper's wrist.

Deflected the blow.

Again, the thick bone hit gravel instead of its target. This time, the force and surprise of Lylin's kick staggered the Keeper. The Nuuri champion stumbled aside.

If Queen Estie had taken that moment to glance at Prince Jaspid, she would have seen his eyes wide, his mouth hanging open. But she could not look away from the devotee. She had no time.

Howling with rage, the Keeper discarded her club and charged. Head down, arms wide, she meant to catch her tormenter in a killing hug, drive her to the ground, crush her.

With insulting ease, Lylin braced her hands on the Keeper's shoulders and somersaulted over her opponent's back, landing lightly while the Keeper plowed the gravel with her face and chest.

Under his breath, Prince Jaspid muttered a soldier's obscenities. He sounded poleaxed. The Queen ignored him.

"That was an attempt to rush me!" crowed the devotee. "It was not a blow. I will allow you one more attempt. Then I will expect you to receive three from me!"

Even the rain seemed to pause to hear her. The Nuuri men stood motionless, as still as gravestones. Their clubs dangled from their limp arms.

From their places among the mass of men, the other Keepers made guttural sounds that might have been laughter.

As Lylin's opponent climbed to her feet, the mighty woman passed from hot, impatient rage to a cold and calculating fury. She did not move quickly now. Instead, she watched while the devotee returned to the spot where she had promised to stand. Then the Keeper advanced, one deliberate step at a time, measuring the distance. When she was almost near enough to deliver a hit, she paused. Through her teeth, she snarled, "You have had your fun, little woman. Now it is time to die."

With frightening precision, she lunged. As fast as a striking viper, her fist lashed out.

Nevertheless the devotee was ready. Somehow, she gave the impression that she had time to move slowly as she took a step closer; reached out with one hand to guide the Keeper's fist; folded her other arm and drove her elbow squarely into the Keeper's punch.

The collision, fist and elbow, knocked Lylin back a pace. Despite the concussions of lightning and thunder, Estie heard bones break in the Nuuri's hand.

For a moment, the Keeper stared at her opponent. She peered at her fist. Then she began to curse like the storm, viciously, and with all her heart.

But she did not try to hit Lylin again.

Prince Jaspid was panting in amazement. "That woman," he gasped. "That woman." Those were the only words he had.

Queen Estie did not look away. She knew better.

The devotee braced her fists on her hips. "Now," she said, bright with anticipation. "*My* three blows."

For a short time, the Keeper did not respond. She tested the fingers of her damaged hand and found that they were useless. With a few deep breaths, she steadied herself. When she had mastered her anger, she returned to the spot where she had stood to shout at Queen Estie. There she faced the devotee.

"Very well, *little* woman," she rasped. "You have won half your challenge. But you have not won it all. I will not honor the Amikan Queen's desire for peace until you have won it all."

In a tone that seemed to glitter, Lylin demanded, "Will you stand?"

"Hah!" barked the Keeper. "I do not fear you. You cannot wound me. It was my own force that broke my hand, not yours. I will withstand your three blows. Then you will be killed, and all who are with you. Amika will learn what the Nuuri can do when they have been wronged."

With an air of languor—of hopelessness or confidence, Estie could not tell which—the devotee of Spirit approached the Keeper, the Nuuri queen. Reaching up with one hand, she patted the taller woman gently between the breasts. "You do not lack courage," said Lylin, "or toughness. And it is true that you deal fairly. I acknowledge it. You have won my respect.

"I do not desire to harm you. My blows will do no lasting hurt."

This time, the Keeper replied with a snort of scorn.

In wind and rain, thunder and lightning, the assassin stepped back to give herself a little space. With one hand, she pointed at her target, the hidden hollow where the Keeper's ribs met behind her chest-plate. Settling into her stance, she waited for some sign that her opponent was ready.

Briefly, the Nuuri's scowl suggested incomprehension. Then she answered with a stiff nod.

At once, Lylin struck.

One two three, faster than Estie could count, Lylin delivered her punches to her chosen target. The first snatched a small gasp between the Keeper's teeth. The second broke into her chest-plate, scattering splinters of bone. The third astonished her.

Clutching herself with both arms, she folded to her knees.

At the sight, one hundred fifty Nuuri men gave a terrible howl. But Queen Estie could not hear it. The full power of the storm had come, and its rush drowned out the world.

Moments later, she was ascending the slope, half carried by Prince Jaspid, and drenched to the skin. The wind and rain had an edged chill that reached into her everywhere. She was already shivering.

Lylin was with them. Between concussions of thunder, Estie heard the Prince pant to the devotee of Spirit, "*Teach* me. You must *teach* me."

"Foolish man," Lylin may have replied. Queen Estie was not sure. "I am more than you imagine. You do not know what you ask."

Then Commander Crayn came skidding downward with a bundle of rain-capes in his arms. Prince Jaspid took one and wrapped it around Estie before accepting another for himself. With a smile that looked faintly amused, the devotee also accepted a cape.

By the time they reached the comparative shelter of Solace Wood, channeled water began rushing into the basin. But there was no one left to wade through the new torrents. All of the Nuuri were gone.

Queen Estie had no idea how Prince Jaspid had contrived to arrive when he did. He was probably exhausted. She did not care. While she could still remember who she was and why she was here, she told him to take three of Crayn's men and follow the Nuuri. She wanted him to confirm her promise that she would offer restitution. In a few days, she would send emissaries to hear and accept the demands of the Nuuri.

The Commander did not object. Clearly, he knew Prince Jaspid. The Prince and his rifle would keep Crayn's guardsmen safe enough.

If King Bifalt's brother objected, Queen Estie did not hear it. When he and his companions had retrieved their horses, they rode around one side of the hollow and away. She did not see them again until the storm had spent the worst of its vehemence.

By that time, she was asleep, still shivering, under a makeshift canvas shelter beside a fire that Commander Crayn had contrived to light.

In the aftermath, she heard the tale of Prince Jaspid's ride from Belleger's Fist. When he left, she was five days ahead of him: he rode hard. Before he reached the place where she had been ambushed, he had been told about the dead in and around the narrows: Bellegerin men, apparently, but not soldiers, and no women among them. Thinking that she had been taken prisoner, perhaps as a hostage, he learned the truth from her escort when he arrived at the Fivebridge garrison. As soon as he procured the release of her riflemen from the garrison commander and sent them back to the King, he rode on.

Knowing that she meant to confront her father, the Prince saved time by heading straight for Solace Wood without passing through Maloresse.

There he fell silent. Queen Estie waited for a while. Then she prompted him.

"As you surely know, Majesty," he said with heavy reluctance, "I found King Smegin's retreat deserted. Barn, stables, servants' quarters, all empty. Briefly, I entered the manor-house. Then I came north." He avoided Estie's gaze by studying his hands as if they had disappointed him in some fashion. "Where else would you go? You had dealt with your father. Your next task would be to face the cost of his crimes."

His discomfort told Estie that he was withholding something. After all, how could he know she had dealt with her father? There could be a variety of reasons for King Smegin's absence. For the emptiness of his retreat.

"Tell me, Jaspid," she commanded softly. "Say what you do not want to say."

His mouth twisted into a snarl. Harsh as a curse, he answered, "The manor-house was not entirely empty. I found your father. He is dead. He hanged himself by the neck from one of the rafters."

Dead, thought Estie. Of course. Driven to kill himself by the loss of his power. In effect, his own daughter had destroyed him. After all, it was she, Estie, who had brought Magister Facile to his sanctuary.

Seen another way, the Queen of Amika had done nothing. Magister Facile had ended King Smegin, just as Lylin had ended the threat of war with the Nuuri. Estie's only achievement had been to arrange for other people to accomplish her goals for her.

Perhaps that was what queens did. Perhaps that was what ruling her realm meant. But she did not believe that her husband would have done the same.

For him, his given word meant something stronger. Something that cost him what he wanted most.

She was no match for him.

PART THREE

FOURTEEN

A COURTED MAN

The tavern called the Beleaguered Eagle sat among a collection of hovels on the eastern outskirts of the Open Hand. During the final years of the old wars, the region had been a reeking slum, a breeding ground for ruffians and thugs, whores and petty thieves, destitution and disease. The tavern had been there then, serving its thin ale and scummy wine to patrons who were too poor, too sick, or too bloody-minded to care what they drank. It retained its familiar place now. But since the creation of the alliance, King Bifalt's improvements to his city had gradually spread outward from the walls of the original Hand. Wherever they were needed, streets of packed gravel had gradually replaced muddy lanes and alleys; sewers had been dug outward to empty into drain-fields and fertilizer-wells beyond the boundaries of the slums; by increments, overcrowded hovels had been refurbished when they were not rebuilt entirely; and—a recent innovation—pipes had been laid to fill communal cisterns with clean water. The Beleaguered Eagle and at least three generations of disreputable proprietors, father to son to son, had seen significant changes.

Still, this far from the main roadways of the Open Hand and its comparatively few city guards, the outskirts were still known for poverty, sold flesh, brawls, and dirt; for stabbings and casual sanitation. And the tavern remained much as it had always been. The ale was a little stronger, the scummy wine had been replaced by more acid vintages, and the proprietor even kept a few bottles of distilled spirits behind the bar, an Amikan drink called—for lack of a better term—*grot*. But physically the Beleaguered Eagle resisted change. The floors were never swept. No one wiped down the tables or the bar, or washed the mugs and flagons. Most of the chairs had broken at one time or another, damaged in brawls or cracking under the weight of their occupants; but they were not replaced. Instead, they were patched with careless incompetence. Some of the tables leaned precipitously.

All things considered, the tavern served few self-respecting patrons. Nevertheless Prince Lome loved it. It suited his outraged vanity. He could feel superior to everyone around him without ever being expected to prove his worth. In his usual fog of drink, he was often happy here, where he never felt his brother the King's influence.

Since King Bifalt's last public council meeting, the Prince had been especially happy. When was that? Ten days ago? He had lost count. But he had played his small part in the fate of the realm, and his self-righteous brother—well, both of his brothers were self-righteous, but only one of them mattered—the King suspected nothing. Someday, the world would know that Prince Lome alone had understood what needed to be done, and had set it in motion. And while he waited for his day of recognition, he was being courted.

Despite his public rebuff, he was still being courted.

At the time, that rebuff had been especially bitter. It lingered in his memory: he probed it like an aching tooth. Both his brother and that cheap beauty the Queen-Consort had spoken against him. In front of witnesses. Between them, they had made him fear that he would no longer be considered worth courting.

But since then, he had found that he retained his value. The priest now sitting across the Beleaguered Eagle's best table from him continued to treat him as a man of consequence. As if nothing had gone wrong in the council meeting, the priest sought out Prince Lome, engaged him in long, desultory conversations. And the proof of the priest's courting was this: he paid for the Prince's drinks. Even when Prince Lome was in the mood for grot—when he felt a particular need for happiness—the priest paid.

The priest's name was Knout, and he wore the customary black robes of the Church of the Great God Rile. He had a round, innocent face, with the smooth cheeks of a babe, the bright blue eyes of a seducer, and a smile of the utmost sincerity. He smiled often, laughed often, and never sounded like anything other than what he appeared to be: a contented man who enjoyed ale and Prince Lome's company.

Being a priest, his conversation occasionally resembled preaching. He extolled the inner peace that came with ending the war within him through Truth and Faith. For the most part, however, he chatted about anything and everything: the price of grain, the state of relations between Belleger and Amika, the weather, the companionship of other priests, the joys of sharing his Truth and Faith, even the wonders of good ale, which he professed to believe was what the Beleaguered Eagle served. And he asked questions without any obvious purpose. How were the King and his Queen-Consort getting along? Why were they always arguing? Had Prince Bifalt's quest for the library been worth what it cost? How could farmers afford to sell wheat so cheaply? If Belleger and Amika were at peace, what were all the rifles for? And what was Elgart's story? How did he get that scar? Father Knout had never seen a man contrive to look so busy doing nothing.

Without any reluctance day after day, always in the evenings, Prince Lome answered the priest's questions from his own perspective. Why not? There was no harm in it. And most people deserved what the Prince said about them. King Bifalt and Queen-Consort Estie argued because she was Amikan, contrary by nature. Especially when she was whipping the mad horse of her desire for a road to the Last Repository. Of *course* young Bifalt's quest for the library had been worth it. He had needed two trips to do it, but he had brought sorcery back to Belleger. Amika's restoration was an unfortunate side effect—or a serious misjudgment on Bifalt's part. Only fools trusted Amikans, declared the Prince stoutly. Why else would Belleger need so many rifles? The King had made a mistake—or perhaps several, seduced by the cheap beauty he had married—but he was not a fool. He intended to be ready for Amikan treachery. As for Elgart, the man was a shameless weasel who had somehow tricked the King into taking him seriously.

In full spate, Prince Lome sometimes said more than he meant. His grievances were many and various. But he never forgot to be careful on certain points. After all, he was King Abbator's son: the youngest of them, yes, and the least regarded; but he had his father's blood in his veins. He was a drunk—he could confess that much to himself—but he was not dull-witted. During their long evenings together, Father Knout never missed his step, never made Prince Lome uncomfortable, never asked the wrong question, or asked any question in the wrong way. But despite the necessary haze of ale, wine, or grot, King Abbator's third son remained alert enough to distrust the priest.

He would have distrusted *anybody* who paid for his, Lome's, drinking cheerfully, without question. Nobody was *that* good-natured. But in addition, the Prince could not think of any innocent reason why a man with an innocent face would spend so much time sharing his, Lome's, table in the Beleaguered Eagle. He believed that he was worth the effort, despite his failures on behalf of the Archpriest; but he had not given anyone else a reason to think the same.

Well, no one except those Amikans—and he did not speak of them. If they did their part as well as he had done his, the world was going to change. Sooner rather than later.

Over the course of many long evenings and much drinking, Prince Lome had come to the conclusion that he knew exactly what Father Knout wanted. The priest was in pursuit of a secret, and he hoped the Prince would reveal it. Not directly, perhaps. But if he kept Prince Lome talking long enough, the truth might slip out. Unfortunately for him, Lome did not know the truth. He had been kept out of that secret. His vaunted brother the King had kept him out of most secrets.

Of course, he hated the fact that he was not trusted. But if he had known the secret, he might have revealed it eventually. And then he would have had to worry about the possibility that he had done something shameful. Something that would have grieved King Abbator. Where Father Knout was concerned, the Prince was better off not knowing. He had already done something that made him proud. He did not want to taint *that* memory.

On this particular evening, however, he was not given an opportunity to admire his own cleverness. Instead of saying anything that might be interpreted as prying, Father Knout was asking about the Queen-Consort. Again. Had she returned from Amika yet? No, not yet. But her departure was rather sudden, was it not? It was. But she was like that. Most of her departures were sudden. It was astonishing how often the King was able to drive her away.

"A troubled marriage," observed the priest. "They are at war in themselves, and so they war with each other."

Prince Lome drained his flagon, hoping to drown out the start of another sermon. But Father Knout did not pursue his favorite topic. Instead, he tilted his head toward the door, scanned the men teetering at the other tables, and announced—rather abruptly, thought the Prince—that he had stayed long enough. Scattering enough coins to pay for an entire bottle of grot, he smiled with his usual unblemished pleasure, bowed once, and headed for the door. In a moment, he was gone, leaving Lome to enjoy the Church's largesse alone.

The Prince absolutely did not trust that priest.

But he had his own reasons for supporting the Church—at least in the person of the Archpriest. And as a matter of pride, he did not refuse any gift of drink. Certainly not a gift of grot.

Sometimes, he wondered how Father Knout obtained so much coin. Sometimes, but not tonight. Tonight he was not in the mood to imagine the priest begging alms in the streets, or perhaps filling his purse as a purveyor of whores. Behind his chosen air of befuddlement, he felt a nagging anxiety. And it was getting worse. Gambling with his life, he had played his part in the fate of the realm. What was the outcome? He wanted to know. He *needed* to know.

He should have heard *some*thing by now. How could a secret like *that* have been kept from him?

On other nights, a full bottle of grot would have inspired eager anticipation. Tonight it was a necessary defense.

Like a man who had difficulty uncrossing his eyes, he regarded the room: the proprietor at the bar, the ruffians and wastrels at some of the other tables, the few souls spending their last coins in a futile attempt to escape their own despair. It was easy to feel superior to such people. Privately, he knew it was *too* easy. Outwardly, however, he showed only satisfaction as he poured grot into his mug and prepared to hit his heart with a gulp of liquid fire.

When the door opened, he thought later that it should have made a sound like a thunderclap. What followed was momentous enough. It changed his life. But in fact the door opened quietly. Nothing about the movement of the age-gnawed boards and their inadequate braces alerted the Prince to King Bifalt's arrival.

For an instant, Lome had genuine difficulty uncrossing his eyes. Then he saw his brother clearly.

Belleger's King entered with his habitual assurance, as grim as an accusation, as if he had every right to be there; as if the Beleaguered Eagle and everything in it did not already belong to his youngest brother by right of possession and comfort if not by actual ownership. For a moment, his gaze scanned the room. Then it fixed on Lome.

Two men followed the King, Jeck and Malder, veterans of the Amikan wars. They did not carry rifles—or even bows. In every other way, they were armed for a fight. Jeck was an artist with a saber. The bigger man, Malder, was a natural brawler. And they were certainly not alone. King Bifalt did not walk his city at night without four bodyguards. Obviously, the other two, Spliner and Boy, were on watch outside.

Deep in his guts, the Prince flinched. He could be confident that his brother would not lay hands on him. Jeck and Malder would not hesitate.

Without haste, King Bifalt crossed the room, his men at his back. When he reached Prince Lome's table, he spent a few heartbeats looking down at his besotted brother. Then he gestured to the proprietor, called for a second mug. He did not sit down in the priest's place opposite Lome until the mug arrived.

Prince Lome reminded himself that he wanted news. He wanted to know the outcome of his gamble. Maybe this was how tidings came to him. Maybe King Bifalt felt compelled to deliver the news in person.

Maybe everything in Belleger had changed while the Prince waited.

The King seated himself and poured a small amount of grot into his mug before he gazed at his brother again. His expression—his whole visage—had been formed and hardened to reveal nothing. But Prince Lome had become adept at reading faces through his inner haze. He saw the subtle lines of worry around King Bifalt's eyes, the slight tightening of pity at the corners of King Bifalt's mouth.

He did not see the consternation he desired.

Above all things, Prince Lome hated his brother's pity. Ignoring the way Jeck and Malder loomed behind the King's shoulders, Lome quenched his impulse to flinch with a mouthful of grot, then set down his mug like an announcement that he was ready to hear King Bifalt's latest reproach.

Without looking away, the King tasted his drink. Grimacing, he placed his mug like a challenge in front of Prince Lome's.

"So, Brother." King Bifalt sounded neither more nor less hoarse and harsh than usual. "This is your preferred sanctuary."

"It is, Brother." The Prince could not match the King's tone, but he could grimace as well as any man. "Although I prefer to be alone in it."

"Always?" asked the King. "You have no companions? No one drinks with you? No one shares your"—he paused over the word—"sadness?"

It was conceivable that Bifalt meant the question kindly.

Lome did not believe it.

"No one shares yours," he retorted with a smolder of grot in his mouth. "That is *your* preference. Why should I not feel the same? Perhaps it is a family trait. Jaspid would rather use his saber than exchange three words in an honest conversation."

As an attempt to deflect his brother, Lome's gambit failed. "On my way here," remarked Bifalt, "Boy saw a priest leaving. Does he speak with you, Brother? Perhaps you consider him a friend. You have been a steady advocate for his Church."

"Yes, Brother," sighed the Prince, "he speaks with me. He tries to convert me. He pretends he hopes I will join his congregation. But his real interest is ale. He *craves* it. He craves it so much that even this dunghole's brew pleases him."

"Indeed?" King Bifalt appeared to study Lome's reply. "If what you say is true," he continued, musing, "and his efforts to convert you are a pretense, why does he speak to you at all? What does he want from you, Brother?"

That question may not have been kindly meant. Malder's grin made his opinion plain enough.

Prince Lome took two more swallows of grot, summoning sarcasm. "What do all men want from me, *Brother*? Nothing. Nothing at all. I am merely a pretext. If he respected my wishes, he would leave me alone."

As would you, thought the Prince.

Or tell me what I want to know.

"These priests mystify me," confessed King Bifalt. "Perhaps one day you can explain them." Then, as if he were not changing the subject, he asked, "Do Amikans drink here?"

Lome snorted fumes. "How would *I* know? They do not wear signs."

The King seemed to take that retort seriously. "By their garments?" he suggested. "By their accents? By those waxed goatees and moustaches? Some are distinctive." After a pause, he added, "My lady Queen tells me that Amika's noble families favor goatees and moustaches, especially those families that have been stripped of their privileges."

Prince Lome heard malice in the background of King Bifalt's remark, and it hit him hard. As steadily as he could, he refilled his mug and drank deeply, thinking, Oh, hells! He *knows*. Some bastard has betrayed me!

But the effects of drink protected him. He did not expose his dismay. When he could breathe again, he said stiffly, "If Amikans drink here, they do not announce themselves. Why would they? No one here welcomes them."

"No. Of course not." The King's voice hardened slightly. His gaze did not leave Lome's face. "What would be the use? Your antipathy toward Amika is known. Naturally, it would discourage conversation."

He sipped from his mug again, twisted his mouth in disgust. "But here is a curious matter. At the conclusion of my last public council meeting, when you had repeated your appeal on behalf of the Archpriest

Makh, you came here. You were seen. Shortly afterward, three Amikans left this tavern. They left in haste. They, too, were seen. It is not difficult to imagine that you said something to chase them away."

Before Prince Lome could respond, King Bifalt added, "But it is their haste that makes their departure curious. Your tavern, Brother, is about as far as it can be from any of the roads into or out of the Open Hand. Why would Amikans who needed haste have come here at all? If they wanted only to refresh themselves, why did they not choose a more convenient alehouse?"

Given a moment to think, the Prince decided against bluster. Belleger's King was impervious to such tactics. Any man who married Estie of Amika had to be. When Bifalt paused, Prince Lome chose a slurred drawl.

"What do you imagine I could have said? Who *cares* what I say? Show me a man who claims he did not laugh when I insulted him, and I will show you a liar."

Staring hard, King Bifalt said slowly, "I hope, Brother, that you will tell me. It would ease my heart. What *did* you say?"

The Prince shrugged, spread his hands, then emptied his mug. "How can I remember?" he countered. "It was days ago. I have lost count. I suppose I may have said something. If they were Amikans, I may have irritated them. It is possible I questioned their loyalty. Were they devoted to their Queen, your refined Queen-Consort? Then why did they trouble a Bellegerin tavern? If they wanted ale, Amika has enough."

Lome admired his response. He thought it covered him nicely. Elevated by grot, he risked touching on the subject hidden behind his brother's questions.

Smiling as innocently as the buzz in his head allowed, he asked, "Has your Queen-Consort returned, Brother? Her reasons for leaving were imperative."

Just for an instant, King Bifalt dropped his gaze, and his shoulders sagged. Disappointment? Relief? Suppressed rage? Prince Lome could not tell. And when Bifalt straightened to face his brother again, he revealed nothing. Even the small signs that Lome watched for were controlled, concealing the King's heart.

"She will come." King Bifalt spoke as if the sound of his own voice bored him; as if even his ability to crush his youngest brother bored him. "She has many matters to settle in Maloresse. But she sent a messenger I can trust. He is the commander of her Amikan escort, a man named Crayn. He tells me that she has installed a new chancellor in Postern's place. And she has put an end to King Smegin's cruelty. A war with the Nuuri has been forestalled." He should have sounded proud of his wife, yet he betrayed no natural emotions. "When she comes, she will bring Magister Facile with her. But the Magister is old. They will return at their own pace."

Prince Lome filled his mug with grot, drank it down; repeated the process. Hells on earth! Estie was still alive! He had gambled—and he had lost. His life was forfeit. At his most self-righteous, King Bifalt was capable of having his own brother executed.

But the King was not done. "Also," he continued, as implacable as a waiting grave, "I have spoken with the captain of my lady Queen's Bellegerin escort. I know how she was ambushed, and how she survived. Her attackers were Amikan, but they were disguised as Bellegerins." He still sounded bored. "The ambush was treason in both realms, hers and mine."

Then he surged to his feet. With almost conversational calm, he announced, "Now, Brother, you will come with me."

The Prince stayed seated. That was as much defiance as he was able to muster. He could not meet King Bifalt's glare. Instead, he concentrated on grot. He wanted to finish the bottle before Jeck and Malder dragged him away.

Jeck's knuckles were white on the grip of his saber. Malder lifted his heavy fists until he was sure that the Prince saw them.

While he filled his mug for the last time, Lome drawled, "Are you going to torture me?" For no apparent reason, he was suddenly happy: as happy as he had ever been in his life. He had been exposed. He should have felt appalled or horrified. Fear should have loosened his bowels. But he was not afraid. The truth vindicated him. "Before you execute me?"

Do you see, Brother? Does the uneasiness of your alliance alarm you? You are not alarmed enough. Even here, in your own city, your own family, you are not safe.

"I will do worse than that," retorted the King. "I will ask my lady Queen to question you."

"No!" The Prince pretended dismay. "She terrifies me."

"She should," answered Bifalt. "She terrifies *me*."

He revealed nothing because he understood nothing.

Masking the vexation he must have felt, King Bifalt gestured Jeck and Malder toward Lome. "I will not put you in a cell." There was no hint of any concession in his tone; any comprehension. "You will have the freedom of your rooms. Belleger's Fist will be open to you. But you will not leave the keep until my lady Queen is ready for you. General Klamath commands my guards until Prince Jaspid returns. He will see that you do not escape."

Oh, well, thought Prince Lome as Jeck and Malder hauled him to his feet. The grot in his veins filled him with bright joy. True, he had gambled and lost. But his plight could be worse. The Queen-Consort was only Amikan, after all. Even sober, he had the wits to outplay her. And he still had a secret or two that might be useful as barter. There were truths his brother had not guessed. His gamble had failed, but he had reason to be proud of it nonetheless.

King Bifalt could have summoned his youngest brother whenever he wished, but Prince Lome had made the King of Belleger come to *him*.

FIFTEEN

DELIVERIES

When sub-Commander Waysel reached the Bay of Lights with his first wagon-train of cannon and his forty guardsmen, autumn had come to the coast of Belleger. Even in that season, the wind whipping up from the violent seas seemed eager for winter. To save time and leagues, he had crossed overland from the Fivebridge garrison instead of taking the road to the Open Hand and then following the beaten track to the bay. He arrived with oxen exhausted by their heavy burdens and men wearied by their slow plod across the rising landscape. From the day when Queen Estie had given the sub-Commander his orders, his task had cost him more than a fortnight.

Captain Flisk and Commander Forguile should have been there to meet him on the rim of the infamous bay. A messenger from King Bifalt had brought word that cannon were coming. The men working on the fortifications knew that Amika's Queen had begun the process of supplying them with guns.

But when sub-Commander Waysel approached, only his former superior in King Smegin's honor guard, Ennis Forguile, greeted him.

Alone, Commander Forguile supervised the unloading of the guns, shot, and powder, then organized the difficult chore of moving that tremendous weight of iron down the steep slope to the terraces where the cannon were needed. Without Flisk, he arranged food from the camp's kitchens for Waysel and his men, warmth in the dining halls, beds in the bunkhouses. His fellow officer and comrade had a different task.

Far below the rim of the cliffs, Heren Flisk was making himself frantic with worry.

Since he and Commander Forguile had listed their needs for Magister Lambent, only some of their requirements had been met. They had asked for two hundred men to speed the work and relieve the desperately exhausted laborers. So far, King Bifalt and Land-Captain Erepos had only been able to scrounge fifty. The bay's officers had asked for forty cannon. Queen Estie had given the necessary orders; but sub-Commander Waysel had not been able to find many wagons in Maloresse sturdy enough to bear the weight, and his first delivery consisted of only ten long guns.

Fortunately, other requests were better filled. The Land-Captain had provided an abundance of lumber and firewood as well as several carpenters, a number of big stoves, at least a league of ropes as heavy as hawsers, and a temporary surfeit of food and ale. The King's army had surrendered two stitchers and bonesetters, both willing enough, both inexperienced. And General Klamath had sent one man: Mattwil, the eldest son of his old friends Matt and Matta.

This last item was the cause of Captain Flisk's concern.

The General's instructions regarding Mattwil were explicit, and they were directed to Heren Flisk personally. The young man was a good stonemason, and stronger than most. But he had suffered a cruel hardship while working on the Queen-Consort's road, and the General wanted him treated with particular care. Specifically, Mattwil could not be asked to work with Amikans—and he could not be asked why. In addition, he was under Captain Flisk's sole command. And he would not be required to train, even casually, as a cannoneer.

To say that these orders were unusual was an understatement. Flisk explained them as best he could to Commander Forguile. Neither of them understood. But they both knew that any sign of preferential treatment would attract the resentment of the men, Bellegerin as well as Amikan, who strained until their sinews tore and their hearts threatened to burst.

To his credit, Mattwil worked hard, driven by a mute fury. And when his tasks involved stone, as most of them did, he accomplished more in less time than anyone else. His conduct gave the officers no cause for complaint. Even Commander Forguile did not object.

Still, General Klamath's restrictions were awkward. Worse, they were dangerous.

The Bellegerin and Amikan sides of the fortifications helped each other whenever help was needed. They had forgotten the distinctions between their homelands long ago. Work in the bay had become a stew of labor: every man there was cooked in the same pot. And they all knew they were running out of time. Magister Lambent had told them so. As a result, the common separations between Bellegerins and Amikans had collapsed.

However—and this was fortunate in Mattwil's case—there were always men on both sides who did not answer calls for help because they were engaged in tasks that could not be abandoned: setting heavy stones, for example, where the danger of mangled fingers or crushed limbs was extreme. Captain Flisk chose to believe that none of Forguile's countrymen noticed Mattwil's absence. He hoped devoutly that he was right.

And as far as he could see, Matt and Matta's son was safe. Everyone crawling and groaning over the terraces was too bone-weary to start a brawl with anyone, for any reason. But accidents were another matter. Men who did this kind of work under these conditions found accidents easy to arrange—and almost impossible to evade.

Well, there were always accidents. Too many of them. But none of the mishaps came near Mattwil. He caused none himself.

So far, he had not been harmed.

Or not until he vanished.

Captain Flisk remembered his last sight of the young man. With Commander Forguile and at least thirty other men, the two of them had been in one of the camp's crude-built dining halls when the King's messenger brought word that the first shipment of cannon was on its way, escorted by a large company of Amikan guardsmen. At once, there were a dozen different questions. How many cannon? What size? Did the shipment include shot and powder as well? In the clamor, everyone learned that the wagons carried ten long guns: not enough, but plenty for now. Their emplacements were ready. They could be used as soon as they were set on their new-made trucks and wheeled into position. And a large supply of twenty-pound balls and several casks of powder accompanied them.

Concentrating on the news, Captain Flisk forgot Mattwil for a while. When he remembered to look around, the young man was gone.

At first, and for the next few days, he assumed that Mattwil had simply gone back to work. The young man must have been sleeping in a different bunkhouse, eating in a different dining hall. It was just a coincidence that he did not cross Flisk's path. The Captain watched for Mattwil, but did not seek for him.

But days passed, and sub-Commander Waysel's wagon-train drew near, and Heren Flisk finally confessed to himself that he was worried. In fact, he was actively alarmed. Quite apart from General Klamath's orders, Flisk *liked* the young man. Yes, Mattwil hardly spoke. No, he did not make friends. But Flisk knew enough about the effects of old wounds to recognize them when he saw them. Mattwil had been hurt badly, and the pain had turned him inward. He worked efficiently and well, hour after hour after hour. When he was not working, he hardly seemed to be alive.

The old ache in Flisk's shoulder began to feel like shame. After a quiet word with Ennis Forguile, he abandoned his usual responsibilities and spent his time scouring the terraces—in fact, the whole width and depth of the bay—for some sign of Matt and Matta's boy.

On the day of sub-Commander Waysel's arrival, Heren Flisk was down on the strand, searching despite the lashing winds and stinging spray, the cold deluge of breakers, for a dead body.

He did not find one. Maddened by rocks and surge and pitiless winds, the bay inside its reef took everything it was given and gave nothing back.

By the time Captain Flisk forced himself to admit that his hunt was hopeless, the new cannon were being winched down the unforgiving slope that served as the bay's only access, and the carpenters were hard at work on the new trucks that Forguile and Flisk himself had designed to replace the comparatively flimsy wheeled frames provided by Amika.

Trudging upward like a man with a leaden weight in his mind, Heren Flisk rehearsed excuses for his own absence; practiced and then discarded them. Sub-Commander Waysel and his guardsmen were Amikan. No doubt, they knew about Flisk's role here, but they would naturally assume that Forguile was the senior officer. After all, he had once commanded King Smegin's honor guard. They would not miss Heren Flisk.

Instead of climbing all the way to the bay's rim, Captain Flisk stopped in the most convenient dining hall to make sure that the cooks were prepared to feed so many extra mouths.

That evening, when he and Commander Forguile were alone with the sub-Commander, they began an oblique campaign to convince Waysel that they needed some of his men. Kneading his shoulder, Flisk let his comrade do most of the talking.

"You have seen the work," Forguile told Waysel. "We have emplacements ready on three terraces and half of a fourth. If the war began tonight, we could make use of twenty-eight guns. We have only thirteen, with none to spare if one or another fails.

"The plans for this fortification call for forty guns. We still have twelve emplacements to build, with their stone housings for powder and their compartments for shot and chain. And we need at least twenty-seven cannon, long, medium, and siege guns, if we cannot get spares.

"No doubt, the war will not begin tonight. But we have been assured that it is coming. It will come soon. Tomorrow, we may see the first signs of the enemy, or the next day. And the men are beyond exhausted. We know what needs to be done. We fear we cannot do it in time."

At that point, the sub-Commander interrupted. With an air of complacency, he said, "Queen Estie has foreseen all this." He was a fleshy man, too soft to have the air of a veteran. But he was genial enough to be liked, firm enough to be obeyed. "My charge is to escort cannon. Now that I know the way, I will travel more easily. And new wagons are being made in Maloresse. My next train will be longer.

"But I have also been instructed to give you what aid I can. My company is too large. Some of the terrain in my path is hostile. The people are not. I do not need forty men. I will assign twenty to you. Use them where they are needed. If they balk, remind them that they are the Queen's guardsmen. Her displeasure is not to be taken lightly.

"When I return, I will bring more men."

Commander Forguile did his best to look pleased. Like Captain Flisk, he would have preferred to claim Waysel's whole company, leaving only the wagons, the teamsters and their oxen, and the sub-Commander himself to return to Maloresse.

But Flisk did not share Forguile's old loyalty to the Queen's honor guard. He did not hesitate to ask, "*How* many?"

"I cannot say." Waysel shrugged like a man who could not be expected to make promises. "That is in the new Chancellor's hands. As I am sure you know, Postern has lost his place. The Queen has appointed a chancellor of another kind altogether, a diligent man named Sikthorn. He understands your dilemma. No doubt, he will send as many as Queen Estie can afford to pay." The sub-Commander paused. "Always remembering that men are also needed for her road, and for King Bifalt's army."

The officers of the bay looked at each other for a moment. Postern's removal was good news: he had been a nagging obstacle. But Flisk and Forguile had not had *any* news from King Bifalt since Magister Lambent's last visit. Supplies and some men, yes: tidings, no, apart from word that cannon were on their way. At times, both Flisk and Forguile fretted over their ignorance of what might be happening elsewhere in Belleger and Amika.

More formally, Ennis Forguile expressed his gratitude to the sub-Commander. "We need all the help you can provide, sir. You have already done much. It comforts us to know you will do more."

After that, he spent a while questioning Waysel about events in Belleger and Amika. Unfortunately, the escort commander knew only what Queen Estie had told her honor guard in Maloresse. She was in haste because Amika faced an immediate threat: in the north, apparently. To meet that danger or enemy, she had split the honor guard into three companies. She and Commander Soulcess had taken one. Sub-Commander Hellick had been given another. But Waysel's only assignment was to deliver cannon. All he knew for certain was that she was in a hurry, and already worn-out.

Chewing his frustration, Commander Forguile asked, "How long ago was this, sir?"

Waysel gave one of his shrugs. "The others left a day ahead of me, so"—he consulted his memory—"eighteen days."

"And you do not know if the Queen succeeded." Forguile's glower made the statement sound like a threat. "You do not know if she still lives."

The sub-Commander smiled uncomfortably. "I prefer to believe that Commander Soulcess or Chancellor Sikthorn would have sent word if some calamity had befallen Queen Estie. I might have been recalled." Then he added, "I will know more when I come again."

With an effort that was probably more obvious to Flisk than to Waysel, Forguile mastered himself. "Of course," he replied. "Of course. We know our duty. We will do it. And now we have added reasons to be eager for your return."

After that, he and Flisk let sub-Commander Waysel go to his bed in one of the bunkhouses. For some time, the officers of the bay sat alone together; but neither of them had anything to say. Captain Flisk guessed that his comrade was worried about Queen Estie and events in his homeland. Flisk himself concentrated on the pain in his shoulder so that he would not think about how badly he had failed Mattwil—and General Klamath.

The next morning at dawn, Waysel left with his empty wagons and his remaining guardsmen. And while Captain Flisk and Commander Forguile were walking back down the road to inspect the placement of the new guns, Mattwil appeared.

In the shadow of the west-facing bay, the young man was barely visible. Flisk had not seen him arrive, or where he came from. He was simply there. Despite the gloom, however, or because of it, he seemed to have an air of fatality, the look of a man who had returned to die.

Instead of looking at the officers, he faced the seas as if he expected Flisk and Forguile to drag him downward and pitch him into the rabid waters.

After the first instant of surprise, Flisk grabbed Mattwil's arm to stop him. A step later, Forguile rounded on the two of them.

"Hells, Mattwil!" cried Flisk. "Where *were* you? We have lost too many men to this terrible work. I was *afraid* for you! You were *entrusted* to me!"

Mattwil did not meet Flisk's gaze. The young man's expression was indecipherable. But he stood unsteadily, wavered in the Captain's grasp. The erratic pummeling of wind and cold seemed to exhaust him; knock him off-balance. He said something, but a gust tore it from his mouth.

Between one heartbeat and the next, Captain Flisk understood that his charge had not eaten since his disappearance. "Mattwil!" he shouted. "Answer me!"

What in the name of every hell was Mattwil doing to himself?

The young man tried harder. "I could not bear it, Captain." His next sentence was weaker, lost in the wind. He forced himself to raise his voice. "I have seen too many Amikan soldiers."

"And *what*?" demanded Commander Forguile without compunction. He had consented to Flisk's absence from duty, not Mattwil's absence from everything. "You have seen too many Amikan soldiers, and now you have a morbid fear of them? Look around you. The men are coming to their tasks. They are coming to share *your* work. Can you say which of them were soldiers once? Can you say which of them were *Amikan* once? Whatever they were, they are not that now. Now they are only men beaten down by an impossible task. You abandoned them without leave or explanation.

"If we were soldiers, *any* of us, you would be accused of desertion."

The Commander's anger—or perhaps only his last word—found a spark of belligerence in Mattwil. His head snapped up. Shadows filled his eyes.

"I did not," he retorted, speaking distinctly despite the cutting wind, "*ask* for this duty. General Klamath is not a man of his word. He knows what I know about Amikan cruelty. He promised me work that would fit my skills without requiring me to suffer Amikan soldiers. If he were a man of his word, I would not be required to suffer *you*."

For a moment, Flisk thought that his friend would erupt. But instead the Commander tightened his grip on himself. "Think before you speak, *boy*," he answered, deliberately scornful. "Klamath is our *General*, not some backstreet thug. He knows more than you do about keeping his *word*.

"I will teach you. Return to the work for three days. Then come to me and identify the men you know to be Amikan. If you can do that—if you can *tell the difference*—Captain Flisk and I will find ways to spare your tender repugnance."

Wheeling away, Ennis Forguile let the slope carry him downward.

Mattwil might have followed, or might not. Captain Flisk still gripped his arm. Flisk stood as motionless as the wind allowed until the man turned his head.

When the Captain believed that he had Mattwil's attention, he said, "You will obey Commander Forguile. But first, Mattwil, you will eat and sleep. In your condition, you are a sure accident.

"After you have eaten and rested, you will speak with me again." Through his grasp on Mattwil's arm, he measured the young man's tension and weakness. "We will come to some arrangement that does not impose such a long absence when the next guns arrive." He waited until he felt the muscles start to loosen before adding, "Then, if you are in your right mind, you will tell me what you know of Amikan cruelty.

"I fought in our last battle with Amika. I saw Amikan Magisters kill their own wounded. I know that much of cruelty myself. I spent years distrusting Commander Forguile, until I learned to recognize my own foolishness. Now he is more than King Bifalt's ally. He is more than my comrade. He is the man I trust when I cannot trust myself."

For a moment, frowning as if he had no reason to rely on what he heard, Mattwil held Flisk's gaze. He seemed to probe Flisk's anxiety, Flisk's intentions. Then he nodded and looked away.

He did not speak again. His silence had the effect of a rejection. But he made no effort to shake off the Captain's hand until they reached the nearest dining hall.

Heren Flisk had to be content with that small reassurance.

Sub-Commander Waysel's return was as prompt as he had promised. At noon no more than thirty days after his departure, he arrived with his remaining guardsmen and fifteen wagons. This delivery included five long guns and ten medium; casks of gunpowder; crates of shot and chain. The defense of the bay now had two spare long guns in case one or another failed, and enough medium cannon to arm one full terrace and part of another.

In addition, Waysel brought people. Riding on the wagons with the medium guns were thirty Amikans.

They were all women. They looked like camp-followers.

Captain Flisk stared in confusion. Commander Forguile was more direct. Fuming, he demanded of the escort commander, "Is *this* what Queen Estie imagines we need?"

"Be at ease, sir." Waysel sounded more than complacent. He seemed pleased with himself. "The suggestion was mine, but the Queen approved. Some of these women are as strong as men. Test them and see. Others are better cooks than you have. I have eaten in your dining hall. I know what I say. Give them your kitchens. You can find better uses for your cooks.

"Three or four of these women, I confess, are little more than servants. You can find better uses for your serving-men as well. But three are seamstresses. I have brought enough oilcloth for rain-capes to shield a few dozen of your men from the weather and spray. And," he continued with an air of triumph, "five are apprentice wheelwrights. Their masters assure me they can make sturdier wheels than the ones that support your guns.

"Also," he concluded, "they have volunteered. During the old wars, women did the work of men. Why can they not do the same again?"

Ennis Forguile spent a moment or two with his mouth hanging

open. Then he shook himself like a man trying to accommodate a new view of the world. "Accept my apologies, sir. My weariness—" He dismissed excuses with a flip of one hand. "If I had given the matter enough consideration, I would have asked for women as well as men."

Sub-Commander Waysel beamed. Had he been standing in less wind and cold, he might have preened.

Satisfied, Commander Forguile went to the rim of the cliff and started shouting orders to organize the off-loading and placement of the new guns.

For his part, Captain Flisk approached the newcomers. The sight of thirty women crowding the sides of the wagons daunted him. They were all staring at him with mixed alarm, uncertainty, and defiance. Their scrutiny made him acutely aware of the ache in his shoulder. It seemed to lessen him. But he knew vulnerability when he saw it. Thirty women alone with so many men in such a place had good reason to be afraid. He did what he could for them.

"Ladies," he began, trying for a note of kindness, "I am Captain Heren Flisk. You are very welcome here. We need you.

"Let me say at once that Commander Forguile and I will tolerate no abuse toward you. Here only the work matters. We have set everything else aside," women, children, homes, comforts. "If you are hindered or insulted in any way, tell us. Do not be afraid to tell us." There were so *many* men in the bay, all starving for more sustenance than mere food could supply. "We will shield you."

Before he could say more, one of the women raised her voice. He expected some bolder woman to speak, one of those who most resembled a hardened camp-follower. But the voice came from a girl who could have passed for a child. She was more frail than any woman he had seen since the formation of the alliance, her eyes stared from a face that was too thin, and her voice shook.

"The officer was in a hurry," she said unsteadily. "He wanted to arrive in daylight. We have not eaten today."

Volunteered? Flisk had to swallow a snort. Volunteered, hells! If the other women had anything in common with the girl who spoke, they had all been volunteered by their poverty.

Including the apprentice wheelwrights? Perhaps not. They had the advantage of knowing why they were necessary.

"Well said," replied the Captain, "my lady." On the spur of the instant, he decided to call each of them *my lady*. He did not want to know their names. Courtesy aside, he did not want to think of them as women at all. "Come. I will guide you. You will learn that our kitchens work all day and much of the night. Soon some of you will help them. But not today. While you eat, beds will be prepared for you in one of the bunkhouses. I do not know how you have slept on your journey, but tonight you will have bedding and blankets against the cold.

"The cold, I fear, is constant. And it will get worse as the season turns."

He was starting to babble. Fortunately, the women forestalled him by leaving the wagons and gathering to follow him.

"Come," he said again. Gesturing, he led them to take their first look at the bay.

The sky was overcast. Most days were shrouded here, in autumn even more than in winter. But the uneasy seethe of clouds that dimmed the sun did nothing to obscure the savagery below the terraces, the ferocity that frothed and tore at the cliffs sealing the Bay of Lights on both sides of the fortifications. Goaded by the incessant winds, the seas piled and crashed over rocks that ripped them like fangs. Spume like hail battered at the strand. On gentle days, the spray of breakers collapsing like mountains struck near the lowest terrace, where the siege guns would be positioned eventually. On more violent days—days like this one—the distant men laboring on that ledge were drenched, their hands frozen, their faces and arms numb to the sting of flung seawater.

Nevertheless the frenzy of the waves was dwarfed by their assault on the reef that barricaded the bay. There the seas surged high and higher, carrying their fury inward until they broke and sank, exposing the jagged axe-heads and brutal truncheons, the spear-points and flensing-knives of the reef. In the evening, the spray of the sea's convulsion often rose so thickly that it diffused the sunset, making the west a smear of twisted light. Even now, in the early afternoon, the turmoil cast up by the reef looked as dense as fog.

Captain Flisk heard several women gasp at the sight. At least one of them cried out. Many were already shivering. But he ignored them. His attention had been snatched away by the sight of Mattwil slogging up the road.

Fortunately, Commander Forguile still stood at the crest of the slope, summoning haulers, rope, winches, and carpenters for the guns. Without glancing at the women, Flisk told them, "Forgive me, my ladies. I see I have an immediate duty. Come with me to Commander Forguile. He will care for you."

At once, he approached his comrade.

Behind him, one of the bolder women shouted an insult: the kind of insult that would have started a brawl in most Bellegerin taverns. But Flisk forgot it as soon as he heard it. The wind swept it out of his mind. Walking faster, he strode toward the top of the road. As he passed Ennis Forguile, he said only, "Those women have not eaten. They have hardly slept." Then he hurried down the slope to intercept Mattwil.

Thirty days ago, Captain Flisk had said that he would warn the young man of sub-Commander Waysel's next arrival. He had kept his promise. If Mattwil still felt compelled to hide from Amikan soldiers, Amikan cruelty, he would not need to conceal himself for more than a couple of nights. In response, Mattwil had nodded without any visible acceptance or gratitude. To the Captain, Mattwil's face had resembled an unmarked grave.

Later, Flisk learned that Mattwil had refused Commander Forguile's test. If he could see any difference between Bellegerin and Amikan workers, he declined to admit it. In fact, he declined to respond at all. But he was needed, so Forguile left him alone.

Yet now the young man was trudging upward? To confront the sub-Commander and his guardsmen? Heren Flisk could not let that happen. Not without some reassurance—

If Matt and Matta's son attacked any Amikan, he would be the one who suffered for it.

Captain Flisk stopped directly in front of Mattwil; forced Mattwil to stop as well or thrust him aside. But Flisk did not order the young man to retreat. He did not know what Mattwil wanted or needed. And he did not try to plead. He could not think of any appeal that would sway his charge.

Instead, he said like a challenge, "Amikan soldiers, Mattwil. Honor guardsmen."

Mattwil blinked as if he had not noticed Flisk standing in his way until that moment. He squared his shoulders, stood as straight as one of his stone walls. "Captain," he said like a man who had forgotten language, a man who did not remember words until he spoke them, "I must. I am shaming my parents. My mother would not permit me to hide from any man. My father would urge me to confront any man who knows what I know."

Flisk scrambled to understand. His shoulder throbbed like an echo of Mattwil's nameless wound. But he did not hesitate.

"Then the man you must speak with is sub-Commander Waysel. I will take you to him."

Mattwil nodded. He surprised his officer by saying, "Thank you." There was a tremor in his voice, but Heren Flisk could not identify it. It may have been fear or fury. Or both.

Flisk stood aside as if to let the young man pass. But when Mattwil started upward again, the Captain joined him; gripped Mattwil's arm to guide and control him as if he, Flisk, imagined that his own strength could match a stonemason's. Together, he and Mattwil ascended to the crest of the road, where Mattwil could see the wagon-train, the guns, and Waysel's company of guardsmen for the first time.

The wind beyond the rim of the bay was different. It kicked less than it did lower down; moaned in fewer voices. Off to one side, Commander Forguile was still talking to the gathered women, explaining why he could not accompany them to the dining hall yet, assuring them that they were safe. He glanced a question at Flisk as the Captain and Mattwil moved toward the guardsmen; but Flisk's expression advised Forguile not to interfere, and the Commander let them go by without a word.

Holding his breath, Flisk took Mattwil to the sub-Commander.

While Waysel waited for men from the bay to arrive and begin off-loading the cannon, he was talking to his teamsters about the care and feeding of their oxen. However, he broke off when he noticed Captain Flisk.

"Captain?" he asked pleasantly. "What can I do for you?"

More awkward than the Amikan, Flisk replied, "Sub-Commander Waysel, this is Mattwil. He needs to speak with you."

"Does he?" The man sounded mildly surprised. "Why?"

Now that he was facing an officer of the Queen's honor guard, Mattwil seemed to have forgotten why he had come; or perhaps the words he wanted eluded him. For a moment, he stood silent while a storm brewed on his mien. When he had decided what he wanted to say, his eyes flashed with inward lightning.

"I worked on your road."

Captain Flisk gritted his teeth; resisted an impulse to massage his shoulder; waited for Mattwil to say what he meant.

"Did you?" Waysel studied the young man more closely. "Why did you leave?" Perhaps attempting a small jest, he asked, "Did you think the work here would be easier?"

Like a challenge, Mattwil answered, "I deserted."

To his credit, the Amikan swallowed his immediate reaction. Flisk imagined him saying, Is this how King Bifalt punishes deserters? He sends them here? But Flisk's fears were groundless. The sub-Commander's response was more circumspect.

"You do not have the look of a lazy man or a coward. Why did you desert?"

With his hand on Mattwil's arm, Captain Flisk felt him trembling. Mattwil did not raise his voice, but his suppressed tone had the passion of a shout.

"I saw Nuuri slaves forced to work. They were whipped to it by your soldiers. I saw them tortured and killed. By your soldiers. I wanted to defend them, but I could not. Your soldiers were too many. They would have killed me as well.

"I deserted to tell Belleger what Amika did."

Mattwil's muscles were iron. He could have flung the Captain away at any time. Nevertheless Flisk tightened his grip. Everything he heard was new to him. General Klamath had not told him. He held on as much for his own sake as for Mattwil's. The young man's bald statement implied howls and weeping, helplessness, ravaged compassion. Flisk wanted to weep himself, but he needed to hear Waysel's reply.

At first, sub-Commander Waysel's eyes opened wide in shock. Then a grimace of ire twisted his features. "And now you want me to justify what was done? I cannot.

"It was a terrible crime." As he spoke, however, his manner softened. He may not have been a veteran, but he knew how to manage men. "It must have been terrible to witness.

"But listen to me," he urged Mattwil. "It is good that you did not speak to me when I was here before. I did not know how to answer you then. Now I can assure you that your outrage is misplaced."

Mattwil stood like stone. If he felt Flisk's fingers digging into his arm, he did not show it. Flisk hung on in the vain hope that he could stop Mattwil if the young man's self-control broke.

"Those soldiers were Amikan," declared the sub-Commander, "but they did not serve Amika. I mean they did not serve Queen Estie of Amika. They served her father, the former King, who gave her his throne long ago.

"He plotted some great evil. What it was, I do not know. Why he wanted it, I do not understand. But the slaves and soldiers you saw were *his* doing, not the Queen's. When she heard of it, she risked her life to stop him. She risked Amika itself to stop him.

"Now he is dead. The slaves have been returned to their people. Peace with the Nuuri has been restored. Queen Estie rules. She is not her father."

Waysel paused, watching Mattwil's face for some sign that the young man understood him, believed him; that Mattwil was satisfied. Then he added, "You will not find it difficult to confirm what I say. King Bifalt knows the truth. By now, all Belleger's Fist knows it."

Mattwil did not relent. "The soldiers?" he demanded. Flisk felt him trembling harder.

"Oh, the soldiers," snorted the sub-Commander. "I call them traitors. Amika has suffered generations of cruelty. We do not need more. I would have executed those men. But Queen Estie is wiser. They have been forced to take the place of the Nuuri. They work on her road. My comrade sub-Commander Hellick keeps watch on them. He and our guardsmen will ensure that they do not shirk or flee."

Finally, the genial side of the Amikan's nature overcame his vexation for his Queen's sake; his impulse to defend her against Mattwil's indirect accusation.

"It appears to me, Mattwil," he added with some of his former ease, "that your desertion was an act of considerable courage. It was well meant. And who knows? Someday, we may learn that your report inspired the Queen to go against her father."

Mattwil did not relax. He may have been incapable of leaving his wound alone. Nevertheless Captain Flisk relaxed on his behalf. A subtle change in the tension of Mattwil's arm told Flisk that the young man had weathered his crisis, at least temporarily.

After a long silence, Mattwil said, "My father would have done more, but I cannot match him. If I cannot live with my failure to resist evil when I saw it, I will do what I can to oppose an evil I cannot see."

The library's enemy—

Without another word to either officer, he turned away.

Captain Flisk let him go. What else could he do? He had never suffered anything as bitter as watching soldiers torture and kill helpless slaves, and he did not compare the brutality of fortifying the bay with what Mattwil had endured. But he knew that some wounds never healed. They only scabbed over and became habitual, saving their pangs for those times when they would be most difficult to bear. Sub-Commander Waysel had shown Mattwil more generosity than Flisk had expected. There was nothing more that anyone could do.

As it happened, however, Mattwil did not escape so easily. Before he started down into the bay, Commander Forguile stopped him. In his most detached manner, Forguile put Matt and Matta's son in charge of the Amikan women. "See them fed, Mattwil," instructed the Commander. "And arrange a place in one of the bunkhouses where they can sleep in decent privacy. They have had a hard journey."

Something in Mattwil's expression must have suggested a protest. "Yes," said Ennis Forguile impatiently, "I know you have other work. You are needed at the emplacements. But Captain Flisk and I are needed *here*. I will not ask these women to wait for some other escort. They have left their homes, as you have. They are here to help us. Give them the respect they deserve."

Mattwil's compliance had the effect of easing the ache in Heren Flisk's shoulder.

And sub-Commander Waysel's company of women did not take long to prove their worth. In a day or two, the food from the kitchens began to taste better. It seemed more nourishing. The former cooks could work elsewhere. And Waysel was right about his apprentice wheelwrights as well. The women made wheels that were stronger and more useful than the ones Captain Flisk and Commander Forguile had designed. Now the carpenters who had spent their days building gun-trucks had time for much-needed repairs and reinforcements for the bunkhouses, dining halls, and kitchens.

In addition, the sub-Commander had told the truth on other points. Some of his women were as strong as men. They did not have Mattwil's skills with stone; but they could chisel and shift rock as well as other workers, Bellegerin or Amikan. And the seamstresses making rain-capes were quick with their needles. Every man who received one had cause to be grateful.

But several of the women had a gift that Waysel had not recognized. They had better vision than anyone else in the bay: better even than Captain Flisk, who was known for keen sight. As soon as he and Commander Forguile realized how acute their eyes were, those women were assigned to take shifts in the lookout-post atop the cliff, where the gradual downward slope to the east and the endless expanse of the ocean in the west allowed them to keep watch in both directions.

Two women on duty together were the first to spot sails on the horizon of the sea.

SIXTEEN

TELLING EACH OTHER THE TRUTH

When his Queen-Consort left Belleger's Fist to confront her father, King Bifalt had believed that she would be safe. Magister Facile was going with her, and he had known the nature of the Magister's Decimate for years, since the day the librarian of the Last Repository had refused to release Hexin Marrow's *Seventh Decimate*. Bifalt had been confident that Amika's Queen would survive her meeting with King Smegin, if she could conceal the old woman's presence and power from her father.

In addition, Elgart had arranged for a devotee of Spirit named Lylin to accompany Queen Estie. Long ago, Bifalt had known Lylin's sister assassin, Amandis. Amandis had convinced him that the most holy devotees of Spirit were supremely capable. If he could not trust his wife to Lylin, he could not trust her to anyone.

Not even to Prince Jaspid. The now-former First Captain's prodigious gifts made it too easy for him to believe that every danger could be answered by direct combat, even threats like King Smegin's sorcery and the massing of the Nuuri. King Bifalt loved his brother, but he had preferred to leave his wife in Lylin's hands. He had only sent the Prince after the Queen-Consort's party at General Klamath's urging because her Bellegerin escort was late returning from the Fivebridge garrison.

During the first days of Estie's absence, King Bifalt's reliance on Magister Facile and the devotee of Spirit blocked the sword-thrust of his visceral fear for his wife. She was safer than she would have been under his own protection. And she had always been free to manage the problems of her realm herself. True, that freedom had been his choice before it was hers. But he had believed in her from the first. He trusted her now.

In any case, he had powerful reasons to avoid interfering in her sovereignty. To his way of thinking, using her as a pawn to forge his alliance with Amika had been a kind of crime. Since then, he promised himself and her that he would not misuse her again.

Certainly, he had no intention of intruding on her rule of Amika to relieve his personal longing.

But then the illusion that she was safe was banished by the return of her Bellegerin escort. They had taken far too long to come back from the borders of Amika, and their report made the blood burn like terror in his veins. Estie ambushed? In Belleger? By something like *eighteen* Amikans disguised as Bellegerins? And instead of sending his men back to him afterward, she had imprisoned them in the Fivebridge garrison?

His enemies had tried to kill her! Without Lylin and the courage of Estie's escort, King Smegin's heir and successor would be dead. The alliance would be shattered, and King Smegin would be free to reclaim the rule of Amika.

King Bifalt needed all of his self-control to keep his rage and dismay from striking at the wrong target: the first target he could find. Captain Rowt.

The young captain of Estie's escort believed he deserved blame. Clearly, he blamed himself. But he was wrong. King Bifalt could not fault the man or his command. They had risked their lives to save the Queen-Consort. The fact that they would have failed without Lylin's instructions and aid was a mere detail. It did not taint their valor or their fidelity. Swallowing rage, King Bifalt said what he could to ease Captain Rowt's shame.

Nevertheless he was brusque—or more brusque than usual. He needed to be alone. He did not want any Bellegerin to see that he felt like screaming.

They had tried to kill Estie!

That was King Smegin's doing. Chancellor Postern's, yes—but primarily King Smegin's. Bifalt had imagined that he had gauged the depth of King Smegin's depravity, King Smegin's obsession with sorcery. Now he knew that he had misjudged the man.

Still, they must have had help, Smegin and Postern. They could not have timed their ambush to catch Estie unless someone had told them when she would leave Belleger's Fist.

Fortunately, Bifalt could trust Elgart to find that traitor. His, the King's, immediate responsibility was to behave as if nothing had happened to disturb him. No matter what his wife suffered or did, his preparations for war had to go on. For days, grimly, he maintained an air of outward normalcy. But within himself, he struggled for balance on the rim of a precipice.

King Smegin had been enslaving Nuuri. He may have been doing so for seasons. What would he do when he learned that his ambush had failed? How far would he go to relieve Amika of its Queen; of its alliance with Belleger?

Commander Crayn's arrival both relieved and appalled King Bifalt. The Commander must have ridden straight to Belleger's Fist from his Queen's encounter with the Nuuri army. He brought news: that was relief. He was able to assure the King that Estie of Amika was safe. Prince Jaspid was with her now. The Prince would accompany her return to Belleger after she had made a number of arrangements for her people and the alliance in Maloresse. In addition, Crayn could tell King Bifalt that the process of delivering Amikan cannon to the Bay of Lights had begun. He could explain how his Queen had deployed her honor guard. And he could describe the outlines of what she and Magister Facile had done against King Smegin, and of how she and Lylin had faced the Nuuri.

Bifalt could not have put his relief into words to save his life.

Nevertheless he was left stunned by Crayn's report. He hardly spoke to the Commander, except to ask the most obvious questions. He felt stricken witless.

If he had ever believed in gods, even for a moment, he would have thanked them all for his wife's safety. And for her successes. And for the decisions she had made along the way: appointing a new chancellor; sending cannon; distributing her honor guard to better tasks; providing care for the abused Nuuri. King Bifalt's approval was absolute.

But the sheer *scale* of the risks she had taken—! She could have died in the ambush. King Smegin could have fried her with lightning before she entered his manor-house. The Keeper of the Nuuri could have killed her with a single blow.

King Bifalt was not a man who trembled. It was his nature to meet every challenge without hesitation; to choose his path and follow it. He did not ignore his mistakes, but he refused to let them undermine him. Nevertheless he trembled now. He could not conceal it.

He had always admired his wife. Desired her. Ached for her. Now he realized that he had underestimated his need for her.

Later—much later—he learned more about her time in Amika. When he questioned her, she dismissed her own accomplishments as if they were not worth mentioning. But she gave him a reassuring impression of prospects for peace with the Nuuri, of Chancellor Sikthorn's abilities and devotion, and of Amika's deliveries of cannon. And Prince Jaspid offered details. In particular, he overflowed with enthusiasm for the devotee of Spirit.

King Bifalt would have liked to speak with Lylin himself. Among other things, he wanted to know what had prompted her to risk her life for the Queen-Consort—or for the alliance. Had she given Estie her protection simply because Elgart had requested it, or did she have some deeper purpose? Was she obeying instructions from the Last Repository? If so, what did they entail? But Lylin had disappeared after she had seen Estie safely back to Maloresse. When Bifalt asked Elgart to locate the devotee for him, the scarred spy only shrugged and grinned as if he found the question of her whereabouts imponderable.

However, waiting for his Queen-Consort's return, King Bifalt knew only what Commander Crayn had told him. It was enough. If it relieved and horrified him, if it left him astonished with admiration and shaken with rage, it also tightened his impatience to see his wife until the desire felt like a physical wound.

He knew that she had stopped for the night at Beds, Food, Ale. She had sent a messenger ahead to announce her coming. The next day, when King Bifalt judged that she would be setting out for the Open Hand, he mounted his horse and went to meet her.

But he did not hurry. Burdened with Magister Facile, Queen Estie would travel slowly. Setting an easy pace himself, the King led Boy and Spliner from Belleger's Fist through the old city and its new sprawl out onto the stone road northward. There in the light and crispness of a bright morning on his way between pastures ripe for harvesting, he settled into his mount's gait and surrendered—uncharacteristically—to reveries.

King Smegin had tried to have Estie killed. She was responsible for this road; this smooth passage between the realms. Bifalt had memorized her face. He needed to see it again.

Drifting among his memories, he recalled that her road had caused a crisis between them. He could not say that he regretted the outcome of that confrontation. He was not a man who wasted time on regrets—or feared their consequences. Nevertheless the hurt of that particular conflict lingered. In its own way, it was worse than the night when he had told his new bride that he would never touch her.

In all their years of marriage, he had only visited her in her apartments twice. The first occasion had been on their wedding night, when he had announced his intention to leave immediately for the Last Repository so that sorcery could be restored to Belleger and Amika. The second had been some years later, prompted by her unexpected and surprisingly inflexible announcement that she intended to build a road between Belleger, Amika, and the library. At the time, they were alone in his private council chamber; unconstrained by witnesses. The ensuing argument found him at his most vehement, and her at her most sweetly unyielding.

He insisted that he wanted nothing more to do with the Repository's Magisters. Toying with him, they had forced him into preparing for a terrible war that had nothing to do with his realm or hers. The last thing Belleger and Amika needed was more manipulation by men who were too arrogant to bother telling the truth or keeping their promises.

Unfortunately, her decision was as reasonable as she made it sound. In fact, its very rationality infuriated him. First, she argued, the Last Repository was inherently precious. It had to be protected. The destruction of so much knowledge would be a crime against the world. Second, despite their arrogance and machinations, those Magisters possessed powers and insights that might save Amika and Belleger, if their help could arrive swiftly. It required a well-made road. And third, if worst came to worst, the survivors of both realms would be forced to flee to the only remaining refuge, the library. She wanted a road to speed their retreat. It might save hundreds or thousands of lives.

Fuming, he countered that Belleger and Amika together did not have enough men to restore the Open Hand, muster an army, form a western defense, *and* build a road, especially a road that would have to cross the bitter wasteland of the vast desert. Unruffled, she replied that no one knew when the war would come. Certainly, it was years away. It might be decades or more. The question was not one of having enough men. It hinged on having enough time.

She made him feel as thwarted as he had throughout his quest for the Last Repository. He caught himself wanting to hit her: an appalling impulse. Full of shame as well as ire, he stormed out of the council chamber.

But later that evening, when he had mastered himself, he realized that he had to talk to her. Not to continue the argument about her road. She was Amika's Queen: she could build whatever she wished in her own realm. No, he had to explain himself. He had to talk to her *about* himself.

Men like General Klamath and Elgart and even Prince Jaspid might have called him blind; but he could see what was in front of him. Over the years, she had given him signs enough to convince him that her consent to their marriage endured despite his distance, his clenched severity; his apparent disregard. Her refusal to match vehemence with vehemence on the subject of her road was just one demonstration among many. He could believe now that if he went to her on his knees, she would welcome him into her bed. She was willing to be whatever he needed her to be. More than willing.

But *he* was not. *That* was what he had to explain.

When he had dispatched a servant to forewarn her, he gave her an hour. Then he went to face her in her private domain.

The last time he had visited her there, on their wedding night, she had waited for him in her bedroom. On her bed. Practically naked. The sight had almost shattered his resolve.

This time, her maid ushered him into the smaller of her sitting rooms, a chamber for private conversations. It was lit only with candles, not with lamps. For some reason, she preferred candlelight. Perhaps she liked watching candles melt and shrink as they burned. Perhaps they had a symbolic meaning for her. But she or her servants had set out an abundance of them in single holders and plain candelabras. They seemed to banish every shadow. In addition, they emphasized the shabbiness of the old furnishings: the worn curtains, the three patched armchairs, the flimsy writing-desk and stool.

Unfortunately for him, the candles also lit her clearly. Her rooms were the best that the Fist could provide, but she was too beautiful to belong in them. She seemed to glow with a warmth that closed his throat. For the occasion, she had chosen a demure bed-gown that nevertheless made him want to pull it off her shoulders.

This time, he felt naked himself.

To greet him, she rose from her chair. "My lord King." Her tone was formal, but she did not extend him the formality of a curtsy. Instead, she resumed her seat; gestured at an armchair. "Will you sit?"

He needed a moment to find his voice. "My lady Queen." He would have been more comfortable riding into hell with his rifle and his men. "I prefer to stand."

Her delicate shrug said, Please yourself. These rooms were hers. He had sacrificed his claim on them long ago.

Chewing the inside of his cheek, he was silent until she asked, "Will you speak, my lord? Do you have more to say about my desire for a road?"

Her question had the effect of a sting. "No," he said at once. Too sharply. Hells, he had not come here to be sharp with her. "No," he repeated with more moderation. "The subject is not closed. No doubt, we will both find more to say. But you are Amika's Queen. You will do what you wish. You must. My loathing for the Magisters of the library is my concern, not yours. I distrust all Magisters, as you know. Nonetheless, we need them. If I cannot condone your purpose, I will ask the Land-Captain to argue on my behalf. We are allies, you and I. I have no power to command or deny you. I do not want that power."

Watching him, she nodded as if she had expected his response. Quietly, she said, "The fault is mine, my lord. I am familiar with your preference for discussing matters that affect both realms in public. It seems a wise policy. It shows that we can disagree without threatening our alliance.

"But I foresaw your objections. I hoped you would take it as a courtesy that I announced my intentions while we were alone."

Swallowing hard, he said, "I should have done so, my lady." He could not look away. She compelled his gaze as if she were the only sight in the world. "I am Bellegerin. We are known for our single-mindedness. It is a strength, but it can be a weakness as well." He knew to his cost that it could be a form of ignorance; a failure of imagination. "I am fixed to my path. I did not expect to be distracted from it."

She gave him a shallow smile. "Thank you, my lord." A shift of her shoulders opened the V of her bed-gown slightly. "Say what you have come to say. I am ready to hear it."

Oh, hells. Was she ready? He was not. His hard-learned habit of self-mastery hampered him. He could not expose himself, even to her—especially to her—without despising the necessity; without sounding angry at her when all of his vast wrath belonged elsewhere.

Trying to be honest, he began, "Forgive my vexation, my lady. It is not directed at you. You did not cause it. You cannot relieve it. But you should understand it, if you can. I have taken too long to explain myself."

In a small voice, almost whispering, as if he had made her afraid, she agreed, "You have taken a long time. You gave me a reason for refusing my bed. I did not understand it then. I do not now."

He clenched his fists. He wanted to hit something, anything. But not her. Not *her*.

"Then hear me."

In his hoarse voice, as raw as an exhausted scream, he said, "My lady, you have changed. In the years of our alliance, you have changed. I distrusted your first consent to our marriage. I had reason to distrust it. You were a girl commanded by a harsh father and used as a ploy by a dishonorable suitor. But now you are a woman. You make your own choices. You defend them clearly. When you are persuaded, you acquiesce. When you are not, you hold your ground. You rule your realm for the good of your people. And still, your consent endures. You have made it plain. It *endures*.

"That is a greater gift than I could have expected. It is greater than I deserve.

"Tell me if I am mistaken."

She was blinking as if the brightness of so many candles suddenly hurt her eyes. "You are not, my lord."

He tried to smile. "Do you see, my lady?" Her simple declaration twisted a blade in his chest. "Some truths can penetrate even *my* single-mindedness."

Then he flung himself back into the grip of his purpose.

"But out of respect for who you are and what you give, I must tell you that I have *not* changed. If I can, I must tell you why."

She did not move—and yet she seemed to lean toward him like a woman who yearned. "Then do so. I want to know."

For a moment, he contrived to look away. But everything in the room sent his gaze back to her. He studied her face so that he would not watch the way she breathed.

"The devotees of Spirit and Flesh," he said, forcing himself, "teach that only a man who loves his life can choose an honorable death. But I do not love my life. I am not living a life I can love. I aspire to honor, but I cannot choose to be honorable. The Magisters of the library have made it impossible. I aspire to well-being and safety for my people, and for yours, but I cannot devote myself to my proper task. Those Magisters have precluded it. My aspirations are empty. I am their servant, their tool, nothing more.

"If I had been allowed to choose freely, I might well have decided to seek an alliance with Amika. I might even have tried to defend the library's treasure of knowledge. But I was not permitted to choose. Instead, I was pushed and mocked and misled until my only path was the one those Magisters marked out for me. I cannot love what I do, or why I do it.

"In my life, I can find honor only in what I deny myself. It is the only choice left to me. Denial is all that allows me to remain who I am."

Her eyes glistened. "Truly, my lord?" The tightness at the corners of her mouth suggested an anguish like his. "I do not understand."

"You *do*," he insisted. "Remember how you felt when you first heard that you would be forced to wed me." He allowed himself to demand that much from her. "When we met, I came to you as a hated Bellegerin. Worse, I came to usurp your father's place in Amika. Not directly, no. I did not want the rule of Amika for myself. I do not want it now. But I did to him what the Magisters of the library did to me. I twisted his choices until his only path was mine. I twisted his choices until *your* only path was mine.

"Remember how you felt then. Remember how you resolved to suffer a loveless marriage for his sake, and for Amika's, not for your own. Remember your sense that you had been betrayed, and your determination to survive it by denying your natural desires, the life you wanted for yourself.

"You *do* understand me."

She seemed to flinch as he spoke; but he continued as if he were pitiless. "The difference between us is only this. Having used you once, I have refused to use you again. I have freed you to find a new path. And you have done so. You have *changed*, my lady—but it is a change of *your* choosing, a change that elevates you. A change that *confirms* you.

"I cannot match you. I have not been allowed to change. The compulsion that those Magisters have placed on me only increases. Every year, their war comes closer, and I am not ready. I lack the means to be ready. I am trapped where you were when your father bartered you to me. The only honorable choice left to me is to gain nothing for myself.

I must deny who I am and what I want so that I can serve my people, and yours, and you. Every other choice was made for me long ago, when I was hammered into the shape of a tool for the Last Repository."

Her multitude of candles found damp reflections in her eyes. Her lip trembled. Resting in her lap, her hands made small, aimless gestures: a twitch of a finger, the shift of a palm. He could see that he had hurt her. And he could guess at the depth of the wound. He was naked before her. She could repay her pain cut for cut, if that was her desire. But he did not turn away. This challenge, at least, he *had* chosen. He refused to shirk it.

Like a lost child, she asked, "Is that why you do not love me? Am I your denial? If that is your aspiration, it is empty. I have consented. I *do* consent. Your denial does not free me. It binds me to your misery. It serves no purpose, except to ensure that my path follows yours.

"I do not call that *honor*, my lord. I call it an excuse. You say what you do to conceal the truth."

Tears spilled from her eyes. Abruptly fierce, she wiped them away.

"The truth is that you do not love me because you cannot. You do not have it in you."

"No!" Her response wrung a cry from him. He needed every scrap of his self-command to soften it. Instead of wailing, he said again, "No, my lady. You underestimate yourself. Since you do not know it, I will tell you. It is impossible to look at you without wanting your love. You are more than beautiful. You are good-hearted, thoughtful, and brave. From the moment when I first saw you, I have desired nothing else, no one else.

"But I do not act on my desire because I know my flaw, my single-mindedness. Loving you, I will divide myself. I will become less than the man you know. It would dishonor you to give you less. Yet my people need all that I am, and more. If I give *them* less, I will dishonor myself. Worse, I will doom them.

"I cannot choose to divide myself. Belleger is not an excuse, my lady. The alliance is not an excuse. The library's war is not. They are my burdens. That they are in peril is not my doing, but I have accepted the responsibility for their defense. I am Bellegerin to the core, and

Belleger's need for me is limitless. While my realm is threatened with war, it must have all that I am. It demands more than I know how to give.

"I do not love you because I *will* not turn away from my people."

For the first time since he had entered her sitting room, she dropped her gaze. Her hands twisted each other in her lap. Watching their struggle, she commanded, "Then go. You have said enough."

"No," he insisted for the last time. "I will say one thing more.

"Have you considered the prospect of children, my lady? Have you considered the possibility of sons or daughters? Have you imagined loving them the way my father loved me—the way your father should have loved you—and then watching them burn in the conflagration of the library's war?

"You offer me your love. I ache for it. But my ache for it is selfish. The price is too high. It gives me nightmares."

So softly that he barely heard her, she breathed, "My mother loves me."

She did not weep to see him go. He did not weep to leave. But he could sense her pain through all of the doors between them. It resembled his.

Something inside him felt broken. Its shards filled his chest. She did not believe that he could love her.

Remembering that night, King Bifalt rode until he saw the Queen-Consort and her company ahead of him. Then he stopped, allowing his wife time to draw near at her own pace.

Magister Facile and Prince Jaspid were with her, as were Commander Crayn and her Amikan escort. But they halted when they saw him so that Queen Estie could approach him alone. Prompted by native courtesy, or by some command he did not hear, they gave her and her husband a degree of privacy to greet each other.

At once, King Bifalt told Splinter and Boy to withdraw. If his lady Queen wanted to speak without being overheard, so did he. His memories were too close to the surface. They left him raw.

As Estie came closer, the sight of her seemed to open a pit in his chest. Despite the midday sun and the sweat on his face and arms, he felt a chill in his bones. This was his first chance to gauge what her risks had done to her. Their effects made even the simplest words of welcome impossible. For a time, the challenge of speaking defeated him.

She was road-weary, yes. But her fatigue had a deeper source as well. She carried the weight of the challenges she had accepted, and of the ones still ahead of her. As a result, she looked thinner, although she had not lost weight. Rather, she had been refined or purified, reduced to her essence in the fires of her father's cruelty and the fierce anger of the Nuuri. She had been beautiful before. In Bifalt's eyes, she was more lovely now.

When he met her gaze, he saw that it was bright with tears.

He could count on two fingers the number of times he had seen her this close to weeping.

But the ease with which she blinked her eyes clear—the certainty—showed that she had changed in other ways as well. She was stronger, or harder— No, not harder. That word did not do her justice. Her smile was as sweet as he had ever seen it, and as sincere. She was not *hard*. But she had learned how to summon hardness when she needed it.

The prospect of what she might say now made her husband's guts shiver as if he had contracted a fever.

He deserved hardness from her. He had earned it. In the name of a severe standard that he called *honor*—the standard of denial—he had been relentlessly rigid toward her. But he knew, because she had told him so, that his rigidity did not protect her from him. *It binds me to your misery*. Its real purpose was to protect him from her, or from his desire for her.

As Belleger's King, he was glad to see that Amika's Queen had come back from her ordeals with so much strength, so much new clarity. As himself, he wanted to curse because she had surpassed him. She had become capable of more courage than he had.

Of course, he should have welcomed her. But he could not do it. Without speaking, he turned his mount to walk slowly at her side on the way to the Hand and the Fist. Magister Facile and Prince Jaspid followed in silence. Commander Crayn and his soldiers, like Spliner and Boy, kept a discreet distance.

The Open Hand sprawled ahead of the company, a smear across the horizon. King Bifalt had ridden some distance to meet his Queen-Consort, but not so far that he could not see his upthrust keep on its high ground watching over the city. He wanted to hurry toward it; to cut short his inadequacy in her presence. At the same time, he wanted to prolong his ride with her until he recovered his sense of himself.

After a while, disgust at his own weakness prodded him to speak. He had to say something. But when he opened his mouth, the only words that came to him were, "We know who betrayed your departure. It was Prince Lome. He has committed treason."

Tightening his grip on himself, he added, "When you are ready, perhaps you will consent to question him. He is my brother. I am inclined to judge him harshly. It may be that I will judge him too harshly."

He did not look at her. He hardly gave her a chance to respond. He had already revealed too much of himself. Searching for surer ground, he asked her why she had imprisoned his men when they reached the Fivebridge garrison.

Her question in reply—What would you have done if they had returned earlier?—silenced him again. She knew him too well. Certainly, she knew him well enough to recognize that any attack on her person—especially an attack in his own lands—would have driven him wild with rage. In effect, she had protected him from himself until she was beyond his reach.

In silence, he clung to the old pain that he called *honor*. What else could he do? Long ago, he had promised himself that he would give the dishonesty and manipulations of the library's Magisters the reward they deserved. He meant to humble their arrogance. Nevertheless he had done exactly what they wanted.

That was the essence of their singular cruelty. Hating them—hating what they had done to him—he served them nonetheless because any other choice would sacrifice his people.

Since he could not think of a way to address his wife that did not arise from pain and yearning, he walked his horse at her side, and gritted his teeth until his jaws ached, and said nothing.

Under other circumstances, he could have enjoyed these few hours away from his duties. The sun was warm on his face, and the clack of iron-shod hooves on smooth stone had a soothing rhythm. He was not Klamath: he did not share his General's love for fields and crops, herds and flocks, wildflowers and birds. But he liked open air and riding, the feel of the breeze, the flex of muscles under him, the muffled music of his mount's tack and the subtle creak of leather. At some other time—

At this time, he felt defenseless. He had been too afraid, too angry, and had remembered too much. His wife's return had too much power. The weight of his emotional shields seemed to drag him down.

But he did not realize how exposed he was until his wife said softly, too softly for anyone else to hear, "My lord, I must tell you something. It will not be easy for you to hear. It is hard for me to say. I must say it."

Her announcement was like a blade at his neck, a knife he had not seen coming. Instinctively, he tried to block and counter. Before he could recover his restraint, his awareness of what he did, he snapped, "Then say it." He still felt abraded by his own failings. "What is one more burden among so many?"

She did not raise her voice at his sudden rudeness, but he heard her tone harden. "It is this, my lord King. Magister Facile tells me I have a gift for sorcery."

Between one heartbeat and the next, his world stopped.

As if she were sliding a dagger into his heart, she added, "It slumbers now. It can be awakened. But she does not know what it will be when it is roused. She does not know who *I* will be. Nevertheless she is sure I possess a talent for power.

"She has no proof. There will be no proof until my theurgy shows itself. But I do not doubt her. A sleeping talent explains much about my father that I did not understand."

King Bifalt hardly heard her. *I have a gift for sorcery.* After she said those words, the rest became a buzzing in his ears, wasps of thought with numbing stings. He did not know that he had tugged his horse to a halt. He did not see Queen Estie waving her company back, keeping the Magister and the Prince and her Amikan escort at a distance; urging Boy and Spliner to stay away.

A gift for sorcery. His Queen-Consort. His *wife*.

For a time, he was not aware that he was alone with her. In his mind, he stood in the Last Repository, in the workroom of Magister Sirjane Marrow, struggling to retain his threatened integrity while the librarian prodded and sneered and explained and lied and broke promises until he, Prince Bifalt, made the fatal mistake that laid the foundation for his entire future; until he positively leapt at the chance to save his honor as well as Belleger's independence by mortal combat.

And then, in the Repository's vast refectory, he met his doom when he faced the library's champion. It was Elgart, his companion and friend, a man he could not fight. Elgart, who had been seduced or persuaded by the devotees of Flesh and Spirit to support Magister Marrow's demand for peace between Belleger and Amika. In that way, the librarian broke Prince Bifalt. Sick with shame and humiliation, Bifalt fell from one surrender to the next to the next until he reached a kind of ultimate abasement. And when his fall was complete, he had become a different man. The only piece of his former self that remained was a silent promise.

Someday, somehow, he was going to repay the arrogance of the Last Repository's Magisters.

Everything else that followed from that crisis was what Magister Marrow wanted. The librarian had designed it all.

A gift for *sorcery*.

And now Magister Facile had done something similar to the Queen-Consort. Bifalt could not begin to guess what the old sorceress hoped to accomplish. But he recognized the style of manipulation, the giving with one hand and taking with the other; the tacit dishonesty.

Oh, he did not think that Magister Facile had lied. Falsehood would have been too blatant. If she said Estie had a gift, Estie did. But the sorceress expected to get something in return. Something that was precious to her. And she did not care how much harm she did to anyone who had not been born with the blessing or curse of power.

To someone like the King himself, who abhorred theurgy.

He went that far. He did not go farther. He could not think. Like his world, he stopped on the brink of a precipice. A fall from that height would kill him. It would wipe out Belleger and Amika.

If Estie's talent awoke—

If she became like other Magisters, seduced by her own superiority—

If she turned away—

The shock was too great. He could not meet the challenge.

Lost in himself, he did not realize that Queen Estie was still speaking until she put her hand on his clenched fist.

"Bifalt," she breathed softly, urgently. "Husband. Hear me."

Had she ever called him by his name?

He turned his head; looked at her as if she had become venomous. For some reason, his mouth was full of blood.

"I know what I have done to you," she murmured, pleading. "I know what you fear. Only hear me."

After a moment, he managed to lean aside and spit blood; stain her road. Upright again, he asked as if he were weeping, "Do you expect me to trust you now?"

At once, her whole face hardened. "You have never trusted me. From the first, you have discounted my consent, my understanding, my support, my love. And yet I have never lied to you. I will not lie now.

"Magister Facile spoke to me on our way to Maloresse, before I faced my father. Until that moment, I spent my life believing that I had no gift. That I had inherited nothing except an abused realm and an abundance of enemies. Bifalt, *hear* me. If I had suspected the truth, I would have told you."

At last, her tone softened. "I would have told you."

Despite his turmoil, his sense of betrayal, his fury and grief, she reached him. To tell *him* that she had a gift—! At least for a moment, her bravery meant more to him than what she had taken away. She could so easily have kept silent; so easily have let him put his faith in a false image of her. But no. She wanted him to trust her for who she was, not for a mistaken belief. He was susceptible to the risk she had taken. It was like facing Elgart in mortal combat—

Harsh with strain, with weakness, he demanded, "Who else knows?"

For a moment, his question perplexed her. Then she understood. It would be a calamity if people heard that Amika's Queen—that Belleger's Queen-Consort—was an *unawakened* sorceress. The result would be a firestorm of shifting allegiances and animosities. Both realms would assume that he, King Bifalt, had known all along. That he was using her—

Distinctly, she answered, "Magister Facile. The devotee of Spirit. No one else."

The pitch of her voice reminded him that she did not lie. He had been her husband long enough to recognize her sincerity.

But then she said, "Ask Magister Facile. She will confirm what I say," and his world stopped again.

Ask Magister Facile? Talk to that—that—? Trust *any* representative of the Last Repository? No. He could not so much as turn to look at the old woman. The sight would be like stepping off a cliff. He would fall until he died.

But she would die first. She had no defense against common violence.

She was manipulating Estie. Through Estie, the sorceress was manipulating *him*. But he had no idea why. Unless she wanted to drive a wedge between Belleger's King and Amika's Queen? To turn them against each other?

That prospect was worse than infuriating. It was terrifying. Instinctively, he stepped back from it.

Instead of falling, he set his horse in motion with a nudge of his heels, a flick of the reins. At once, Queen Estie joined him. She did not take her eyes off his face, but he refused to glance at her. He fixed his gaze on the Open Hand and Belleger's Fist; on places where he understood what was required of him. To her, he said only, "Nothing has changed. We will do what we have done from the first."

He knew his path. He could not diverge from it. He *would* not.

But she had a talent for sorcery. She would become a Magister. For him, everything had changed.

SEVENTEEN

AN INTERROGATION

Prince Lome was kept waiting for a long time. Days stretched into fortnights, and still he was kept waiting.

He had been granted the freedom of Belleger's Fist, but he seldom left his rooms. Servants brought him food. To his surprise, they supplied him with as much wine and ale as he demanded: he had expected his brother the King to punish him with sobriety. On those occasions when he bothered to change his clothes, the servants took the soiled garments away and delivered clean ones. If he had been a man who enjoyed reading, he could have asked for texts from the King's collection of tomes and scrolls. And his rooms suited him well enough. The bed and chairs were comfortable. After a long summer, he did not need fires in his hearths despite the enduring chill of the Fist's stone. Whenever he wished, he could adjust the feel of the air by opening or closing windows. Passing his days in a haze of drink and his nights in blank slumber, he told himself that he could wait indefinitely for the day when King Bifalt sent the Queen-Consort to question him. He tried to believe that he was content.

Of course, he was not. More than anything else, he longed for the Beleaguered Eagle. Naturally, he missed the burn and lift of grot: a luxury the King and his abstemious advisers rejected. And he pined for the tavern's air of decrepitude—its decaying floors and walls, decaying tables and chairs, decaying patrons—where he could sit and feel superior without having to prove himself. But what he yearned for most was conversation. He wanted people he could talk to, people who would entertain him with their curiosity and despair, people whom he could dazzle or befuddle with his high-handed opinions.

Whenever he left his rooms, he was looking for someone, anyone, who would condescend to converse with him.

In his presence, unfortunately, the whole of Belleger's Fist had been struck dumb. Wherever he wandered, no one spoke. The servants and guardsmen, the counselors and their aides, the maids hurrying or loitering, the cooks and serving-men, the grooms and ostlers in the stables of the bailey, even the old friends and relations of King Abbator's family, Prince Lome's own relatives and acquaintances: none of them offered him a word. Except for the guards who kept watch on him and the servants who took care of him, they all walked away when they saw him, or passed him without answering his greeting or meeting his eyes.

King Bifalt had that kind of authority. With one command, he could erase his brother from the world of the Fist.

Eventually, the Prince was reduced to talking to himself. When the mood was on him, he walked around and around his rooms, declaiming at the walls. He cited his reasons for distrusting Amika and despising the alliance. He defended his own actions with elaborate eloquence, and shouted down objections that no one uttered. He confounded every claim that he had committed treason. He offered proofs both obvious and subtle of his brother's madness. And he found fault with every imaginable feature of the King's Queen-Consort, from her overrated beauty to her contrary and unreliable nature.

With the wiliness of habitual drink, Prince Lome did what he could to prepare himself for the crisis he had been promised.

As it happened, he had just finished his first flagon of ale one morning, and was contemplating his second, when a heavy fist pounded on the outer door of his rooms.

A heavy fist. Not a servant, then. For a moment, the Prince considered staying where he was—sprawled on his favorite couch—and shouting, "Enter!" with as much bluster as he could manage. Then he decided that he would prefer to face his fate on his feet. With an effort, he wedged himself off the couch, found his way to the door, and hauled it open.

His brother Jaspid stood outside, fist raised to belabor the door again.

Lome blinked in surprise. He had not seen King Abbator's middle son since, well, since King Bifalt's last public council meeting, whenever that was. Apparently, Jaspid had abandoned his duties as commander of the King's guardsmen. Otherwise Lome would have spotted him in the halls. He must have been kept busy by the challenge of serving as the army's First Captain under that jumped-up villager *General* Klamath.

But he did not look like a man who had been kept busy. In fact, he looked more than fresh: he looked like a man who had been buffed like his breastplate—face and arms, leggings and moccasins—until all of him shone. He had left his helm somewhere, but he wore his weapons, including his rifle, as if they were as natural to him as his limbs.

As soon as he saw Prince Lome, his features clenched in a scowl.

Wincing, Lome took an involuntary step backward. Almost at once, however, he rallied. After all, he was familiar with his older brother's scorn. The only difference now was that Jaspid did not try to hide it.

Prompted by an almost belligerent curiosity, Lome peered more closely at the First Captain.

Something in Jaspid's face had changed, something more than the general impression that he had just been burnished: something far in the background of his gaze, something that his displeased scowl could not mask. The Jaspid Lome had known since childhood had spent his life *coasting*: his natural skills and aptitudes had come so easily that they threatened to bore him. He had dreamed of fighting gloriously alone against impossible odds because no other contest stretched his limits. If he had inherited King Bifalt's personality to go with his own talents, he might have become a killer before he was twelve—and a tyrant by the time he was twenty-five. Fortunately for everyone around him, Prince Jaspid had a streak of fidelity in his nature that outweighed his desire to test himself. Lome considered it a form of romantic sweetness.

But *this* Jaspid, the one standing outside Prince Lome's door, had acquired something new, or it had been given to him, or he had been forced to accept it. Momentarily fascinated, Lome studied it until he knew what it was. Then he lifted his head and forced out a laugh that was supposed to sound delighted.

"Jaspid!" he crowed. "Brother! You have found a wife!"

That was the change in Jaspid. He had become *avid*, honed to a keenness that he had never felt while fighting. After all these years, he must have fallen in love.

In spite of his scowl, Prince Jaspid flinched as if Lome had accused him of an indecent act.

The younger Prince pursued his advantage. "Who is she? How did you meet her? Come in! Tell me. Tell me."

There must have been truth in it. The First Captain, veteran of a hundred fights and at least one hell, needed a moment to gather himself. Somehow, Lome had hit him hard. Harder than he would have thought possible.

But then Jaspid raised his open palm with such a force of rejection that he staggered Lome without touching him. "Brother!" said the First Captain like a slap. "You look disgraceful."

Still staggering inwardly, Lome looked down at himself.

Apparently, he had wasted a considerable quantity of wine on his doublet and blouse. The stains on his trousers looked more like ale. And now that he thought about it, he noticed that his hair hung in rank clumps clotted with sweat and body oils. He could not remember the last time he had washed his face, so his beard was probably filthy as well. He needed to hold a drink in front of his face to disguise his own odor.

He returned his blurred gaze to his brother. "Does it matter?"

"Hells!" snapped Prince Jaspid. "Queen Estie will be here in an hour. She wants to speak with you. Go. Bathe! Do you have clean garments? I will send for some.

"Go *now*."

Jaspid had not taken one step into the room.

Lome frowned to conceal his private satisfaction; his sense that his own judgments had been confirmed. Had he made himself so distasteful that his brother could not bear to come closer? Good. Very good. Perhaps the Queen-Consort would be actively repulsed.

Spreading his arms in a gesture of helplessness, the younger Prince said, "I am who and what I am, Brother. I see no reason to pretend otherwise. If our brother's harridan wishes to question me, she will find that I am as blameless as you, but less easily seduced."

Prince Jaspid was as devoted to Estie as his loyalty to King Bifalt allowed. He rasped, "She is more than our brother's wife, Lome. She is the Queen-Consort of Belleger, the Queen of Amika. Are you unable to respect who and what *she* is?"

Lome shrugged. "Let me judge her for myself. I will decide if she deserves my respect."

Grinding his teeth, Jaspid retorted, "If she decides to let you *live*, I will tell you tales. Until that time, do whatever pleases you."

With a sweep of his arm, the First Captain pulled the door shut and left.

Prince Lome felt that he had achieved an obscure victory. At the same time, he was overtaken by an unexpected weakness. He stumbled back to his couch, practically fell onto it. His hands shook as he reached for the nearest flask of wine. If she decides to let you *live*— It was still possible that he would be executed. Unable or unwilling to make the choice himself, King Bifalt had given his Queen-Consort the power to decide Lome's fate.

Well, he told himself. The stakes were higher than he had allowed himself to believe. He had been left alone for so long that he had become overconfident. But it did not matter. Did that woman have power over him? So what? *Everyone* had power over him. She was just one among many.

And he still had his secret. He drank deeply to prove it. No matter what his wretched brother and the Queen-Consort thought about him, he knew something they did not.

He could keep it to himself.

Or perhaps not. If he had enough to drink, he might hold on to what he knew. Unfortunately, he was aware of a fatal flaw in his nature. Behind his bluster—behind his walls of wine and ale—he was a frightened man. The kind of man who confessed. When he was scared, he babbled. People who sneered at him might learn the very thing he most wanted to conceal.

He told himself that he had to be *badly* scared before he betrayed himself. *Very* badly scared. But he did not believe it.

To save his life, he might give himself away while he was too scared to think.

He had consumed all of the wine in his rooms and had only ale left when a gentle hand tapped on his door.

He did not answer. Of *course* not. Was he expected to *welcome* the threat of execution?

But he had neglected to lock the door. After a polite pause, it opened, and the Queen-Consort of Belleger entered, Estie of Amika.

Before she closed the door behind her, Prince Lome glimpsed two guardsmen outside.

He might have found some small comfort in the fact that they stayed outside. His fate had not been decided yet. But the King's wife claimed his attention by simply approaching him. In her presence, he could not think about anything else.

"Highness," she said, "you have been abused." She spoke kindly. When she chose, she could make her voice as sweet as a well-played flute. "It saddens me to see you in such a state."

Lome stared at her. Despite her lengthy absence, she did not resemble a woman who had survived an ambush. Like Prince Jaspid, if in her own way, she was radiant. She wore a gown cut to entice, her hair reached in lush waves to her shoulders, and the skin of her face and arms glowed with clean health. Lome had known her for nineteen years, and she was still the loveliest woman he had ever seen.

Yet she had changed, as Jaspid had. But the alteration in her was of a different kind. If he had become avid, she had been forged. She had new iron in her. She hid it well: there were no obvious signs in her gaze, or her voice, or her manner. But her host had the discernment of a practiced drinker. He saw that she had been through fire. The woman facing him now had learned to make hard choices. She had become capable of demanding his life.

When Prince Lome did not speak, the Queen-Consort asked without rancor or embarrassment, "May I sit, Highness?"

He found himself nodding as if she already had the power to command whatever she wanted.

Unself-consciously graceful, she accepted a chair; arranged her gown like a woman who knew how to elicit admiration.

Despite his weakness, he noticed that she had taken the chair farthest from his couch. She was keeping her distance, perhaps because she held his life in her hands—or perhaps because she found his odor unpleasant.

Was she reluctant to decide his life or death? Did she consider him abused? Did she dislike his stink? All interesting possibilities. They had the effect of stiffening his spine. He sat up straight on his couch; folded his hands in his lap to conceal their trembling.

"You were away a long time," he ventured. Feeling compelled, he added, "My lady."

"Oh, yes, Highness," she admitted. "I had much to do. And every step made my journey longer."

To Lome, she seemed eager to explain her absence, as if she had come expressly for that purpose.

"You know that I left to confront my father. But you may not know that Magister Facile accompanied me. Sadly, she has grown old in her service here. I had to slow my pace for her sake.

"Also, I needed to spend a day in Maloresse. No doubt, you understand that I could not retain Postern as my chancellor. I was required to choose and advise his replacement. And I passed an evening with my mother, Queen Rubia. I needed her counsel."

The Prince gathered himself while she spoke. When she paused, he risked asking, "How so, my lady?"

The Queen-Consort sighed. Instead of answering his question, she replied, "And after *that*, Highness, I had to deal with the animosity of the Nuuri. Doing so added more days to my absence. And when I returned finally to my duties in Maloresse, I found that they required more attention. My actions had caused considerable consternation.

"This was not unexpected, Highness. I am sure you understand that choices which affect entire realms do not swing into motion instantly. I had hoped to return sooner, but I could not.

"My desire for peace with the Nuuri called for appropriate emissaries with appropriate gifts. And my chancellor was new to his post. We had much to discuss. For example, I had sent my honor guard elsewhere. He and I had to devise other means to secure Maloresse itself. I had to determine the best use of my remaining Magisters, those who do not already take part in King Bifalt's preparations. Also, there was my promise to provide cannon for the defense of the Bay of Lights. The guns were ready. They should have been delivered. But I did not have enough strong wagons to carry them. That was a further complication."

Lome wanted to stop her. He did not understand why she was telling him all this. She had survived the ambush. That was the only detail that mattered. But before he could find the words to interrupt her, she went on speaking, apparently struck by a different complication, a different memory.

"In addition, Highness, I owed some of my time to my mother. I did not expect her to grieve over her husband. He was a cruel man, meanspirited and capricious. As a girl, twice I saw him strike men dead for no better reason than because he was disappointed. I expected Queen Rubia's first and last response to her husband's end to be relief.

"But I was mistaken. She wept, Highness. After all that he had done—after he had dismissed and misused her for decades—she wept to lose him.

"What else could I do? I had to stay and comfort her."

The Prince was thinking, King Smegin? *Ended?* Somehow, the Queen-Consort had contrived to kill a powerful sorcerer? It was inconceivable. He needed to demand an explanation.

At that moment, nothing could have surprised him more than hearing himself ask, "How could she not grieve, my lady? He had given her you. Who would not treasure such a gift?"

Apparently, he still had his discernment—and his cunning.

His visitor—his judge—flashed him a look. He expected a moment of softening, of appreciation: he did not get it. Her glance was new iron, metal bright from the grindstone. It said that she knew his game and could play it better than he did.

Nevertheless her tone remained sweet, modulated for kindness. When she replied, "Thank you, Highness," she sounded sincere.

Prince Lome scrambled inwardly. He was desperate for a drink, but he did not trust his hands to reach for the nearest flagon and lift it without shaking. To control them, he clamped them between his knees.

Had she seen through him? Impossible. No one saw *him*. No one bothered to look past his veil of drink. Wine and ale, and especially grot, were better than any disguise.

He would have killed for a mug of grot—

Still, if she knew his game, he knew hers. He saw it now. She wanted to distract him from the seriousness of his peril. But she had a deeper purpose as well. She hoped to foster the illusion that she was capable of sympathy. That she could be convinced to grant mercy.

Understanding her steadied him. He recovered his poise. "So you were much delayed," he remarked. "How was your return to this old pile of stone? Did your husband greet you in his usual way?" With grim indifference? "Did you find him changed by your absence?"

A better man than King Bifalt would have feared for his wife. He would have welcomed her with relief, even with joy.

"He surprised me," admitted the Queen-Consort, unruffled by Lome's gambit. "He rode out to meet me, but his only apparent purpose was to ask a question. He wanted to know why I had made my Bellegerin escort prisoners in the Fivebridge garrison."

The Prince resisted an impulse to gape. He wanted to demand, What, *all* of them? Did that ambush accomplish nothing? Did it even take place? But he knew now that she had been accompanied by a Magister. He had no idea what Magister Facile's Decimate might be, but if Estie and her riflemen had reached Fivebridge unharmed, they must have been defended by strong sorcery.

Controlling himself, he asked, "Did you have some reason to distrust them?"

Her reply was prompt. "Certainly not. I know them well. They were freed as soon as Prince Jaspid spoke to the garrison commander." Then she said with more care, "To answer the King, I asked what he would have done if I had allowed his men to return to him immediately."

"And he said?" urged Prince Lome.

She shrugged delicately. "You know him, Highness. He said nothing. But he understood me. The imprisonment of his men did them no harm. Their report if they had returned to him at once might have provoked some rash act. I shudder to imagine it.

"Gods, Lome," she said as if she were addressing an old friend, "he might have invaded Amika to secure my safety."

Without pausing, she added in the same manner, "So I must ask you. Why did you conspire to have me killed?"

Prince Lome knew that tactic. In fact, he had been expecting it. Nevertheless it burned him like the jab of a glowing poker. Without thinking, he sprang to his feet, brandished his fists.

"I did not!"

Then he cursed himself for allowing her to breach his walls.

The Queen-Consort measured him with her gaze. "You are not slow-witted, Highness." She showed a little of her iron. "Some puzzles you are quick to grasp. And you are cunning. But you—" She hesitated. "I must say this frankly, Highness. You are also ignorant. You lack knowledge. You live in the world, but you are unaware of it. You cannot conspire effectively."

While she spoke, he wheeled away to pace around the couch and back, around and back. He could not meet her gaze: he could not so much as look at her.

"Knowledge is a mirage," he snapped, irate and frightened. "The priests say so. They are right." Trying to think, he trusted whatever came out of his mouth. "It confuses. Given time, it causes madness. Why do you think your husband is the way he is? He trusts knowledge. He fears it, but he also trusts it. If he cannot have it himself, he relies on those who do. He is—"

"Highness." She did not raise her voice, but her tone silenced him like a shout. "Do you know the devotees of Flesh and Spirit? Some call them 'most holy.' They are certainly *devotees*. Do you know that they are *here*, in the Open Hand? Are you acquainted with their abilities?"

Pacing, pacing, he muttered, "I have heard my brother speak of them. They belong to the library. They have nothing to do with Belleger and Amika. That is enough."

"It is *not*," asserted the Queen-Consort. "You do not know that I was accompanied by a devotee of Spirit. You do not know what women like her can *do*.

"The King has heard that you went directly to your favorite tavern after Postern's confession. Three Amikans were there. They left, hurrying, shortly after you arrived. There were witnesses."

"I insulted them," insisted the Prince.

She shook her head. "No, Highness. One of the witnesses described those men to Elgart. He has described them to me. I recognized two of them, a lesser son of an Amikan noble and one of my own Magisters. His name was Flense. His Decimate was fire. He participated in the assault on my life."

Lome froze with his back to his judge. If he could not look at her, he also could not let her see his face. A *Magister*—? One of *them*? Oh, hells!

He did not care. Why should he? But he did. Magisters were too well known. It was always possible that a man like that would be recognized.

What deranged fool sent a *Magister* to conspire with him?

Well, Chancellor Postern, of course. King Smegin indirectly. But the others should have known better. Any Amikan with the wits of a walnut should have known.

Nevertheless Prince Lome could not turn his back on one inescapable fact. The presence of a Magister should have guaranteed the success of the ambush.

What had gone wrong?

Too late, he realized that Estie was still speaking.

"—of Spirit killed him."

She did not sound hard now. She sounded sad—and strangely tolerant. "Oh, Lome, you poor, lost man. If you knew a fraction of what you think you know, you would have told your conspirators to flee as soon as they saw her. Against a devotee of Spirit, your ambush was doomed from the start. Every man who attacked me died. Now they have all been identified as Amikans disguised as Bellegerins."

The Prince had no response. His whole mind had become a blank gibber of fear. In a small voice, he commanded, "Get out."

Amika's Queen ignored him. "Since you do not confess, I must guess at your reasons. I imagine that your treachery was not aimed at *me*. You tried to arrange my death as a means to an end. And the end? What could it be, if not the end of the alliance?

"If I were killed in Belleger by men presumed to be Bellegerin, what would follow? King Bifalt would be helpless—and Amika would require a monarch. A monarch who was not allied to Belleger. A monarch who could never be seen as a servant of Belleger. A monarch like King Smegin, who had become more powerful than any ordinary Magister."

Barely aloud, Prince Lome demanded, "Get out. Leave me."

Again, she ignored him. "You struck at me, Lome, so that King Smegin could resume his throne. Then the alliance would end, and the old war would begin again, and Belleger and Amika would go back to slaughtering each other.

"And for what, Lome?" She seemed to restrain a cry of protest. "For *what*? Must I continue to guess? Did you hope that Prince Jaspid would die in battle? And King Bifalt? In his heart, he is a soldier. He could not refuse to fight for his realm. Did you imagine that *you* would become King in Belleger's Fist when your brothers were dead?" She said it with no hint of scorn. Her words were scornful enough. "Are you *that* petty?"

All he wanted to say was, Get out. Get out get out get out. But she had accused him of pettiness, *him*, the despised son who could have outshone both of his brothers if he had only been given the chance. It was more than he could bear.

If he became King, the world would finally make sense.

Whirling to face her, he braced his arms on the back of the couch so that he would not fall. "Think what you like of me," he sneered. "Despise me as much as you wish. You are married to a madman, but you refuse to see it. This alliance itself will destroy both Belleger and Amika.

"We prepare endlessly for a war that will never come. But there *must* be an end. There *will* be. And its name will be *resentment*. Nineteen years of struggle, strain, suffering, discord, and privation, all for nothing. The end will come when our people rise up against it.

"My brother will be overthrown. *You* will be overthrown. Without their own strong kings, Belleger and Amika will collapse into their many conflicts, one faction striving against another until both realms are overrun by bands of warlords without a thought in their heads except greed and survival.

"And all of this is inevitable because my brother was broken in the library. He is so rigid now because he did not heal, or did not heal straight. He has been driven beyond reason by people who have all the knowledge and sorcery they will ever need to defend themselves, people who find entertainment in their secure keep by destroying weaker realms. And you support him. You who are Amikan, and should know better."

He wanted to see chagrin on her face. Oh, he wanted that! Chagrin and recognition. Even despair. Her eyes were bright enough to betray a profound wound.

But their brightness was not any version of dismay. It was the gleam of a new blade. She had been whetted. She could show her edges whenever she chose to unsheathe herself.

Giving him nothing, she replied, "I cannot fault your eloquence, Highness. You speak well when you are pushed to it. But your entire defense rests on a single assumption, not a fact. You believe the library's enemy will never come. I believe he will. More than that, I have reason to believe he is already coming.

"No doubt, you will counter that my belief, like yours, rests on an assumption, not a fact. But because you have chosen ignorance, you do not know what I know, what the King your brother knows. We have spoken with Magister Facile.

"Using some theurgy beyond my comprehension, she communicates with the Last Repository. The Magisters there have told her that their enemy is closing on us. And if we were inclined to doubt her, your brother and I, we would believe because ships have been sighted approaching the Bay of Lights. *Ships*, Lome, when for generations no one in Belleger or Amika has ever seen such vessels.

"War is coming, Highness. It will trample Belleger and Amika underfoot."

Abruptly, the Queen-Consort rose from her chair. As if she had nothing more to say and had already dismissed Prince Lome from her mind, she went to the door. There, however, she faced him again for what might be the last time.

"Doubt me if you must, Highness." She had put her hardness away. He saw only pity in her eyes, heard only pity in her voice. "But have the honesty to doubt yourself as well. If you are wrong, your desires and conspiracies and secrets will hasten the ruin of our realms."

Watching her put her hand on the door-latch, Lome panicked. His discernment, his cleverness, his superiority, his defiance, all deserted him. She was going to open the door for the guardsmen outside. When they entered, they would take him to his death. This was his last chance—and yet he could not bring himself to confess. She had already proven his guilt.

Pleading, he asked, "What have you decided?"

Apparently, he had surprised her. She cocked an eyebrow. "Decided?"

"My life is in your hands." To save himself, he stifled his impulse to babble. "What will you do with it?"

"*I?*" The Queen-Consort frowned. "Nothing. You are too uninformed to act wisely, and too full of yourself to admit your guilt. I am done with you.

"If my husband is troubled by his responsibility for you, he may leave your fate to others. To Land-Captain Erepos, perhaps, or to General Klamath—or even to Elgart. I am done."

In desperation, Prince Lome tried to sway what she would say about him. "When that day comes," he urged, "when *someone* decides, tell them I know more than they think I do. I am not as ignorant as you suppose. I have a secret that is worth more than any confession."

She had abandoned sweetness. Her tone dripped skepticism.

"And your secret is?"

Fighting to keep himself alive, he clung to it. It was all he had. If he revealed it too soon, it would be wasted. There was nothing else he could do to keep his accusers from passing judgment.

He had to swallow terror and tears before he could say, "I will share it with King Bifalt when he is ready to believe me."

Just for an instant, he saw another question in the Queen-Consort's gaze. Almost at once, however, it was gone. Turning away, she opened the door and went out, closing it behind her.

Without ordering the guardsmen to enter.

Prince Lome endured his suspense for a few heartbeats, no more than half a dozen. Then he scrambled to the door and threw the bolt to lock it.

After that, he flung himself in a frenzy on the couch. He may have sobbed briefly. He was not sure—and did not care.

Hells and more hells. *All* of them. She was a terrible woman. Worse than he had allowed himself to imagine.

But she had set his death aside. For the time being, at least, he would be allowed to live.

Despite the way she had questioned him—and for the first time in his life—he felt grateful to the woman his brother had married.

EIGHTEEN

THE SPY AND THE ARCHPRIEST

The day of the Queen-Consort's return from Amika—in fact, while King Bifalt rode out to meet her—a messenger in a lather of haste reached Belleger's Fist from the Bay of Lights. Sails had been sighted on the distant rim of the ocean.

When he heard the news, the King would no doubt have snatched a fresh horse and rushed to the bay as soon as he and General Klamath could muster a response. But before he was ready to leave, a second message came from Captain Flisk and Commander Forguile. This rider brought a more detailed report, one that obviated the call for immediate action.

Like everyone else in living memory, the officers commanding the bay had never seen vessels that traveled the seas. They had heard words like *ships* and *sails*, but they could only imagine what the words meant. The second messenger described the ships, three of them, as "floating fortresses." They were obviously wind-driven: the great trees sprouting from the decks carried vast spreads of canvas to hold the air. The ships themselves were made of black wood. Their trees were black. They looked like dried blood shaped by sorcery. In contrast, the sails were so white that they seemed to ache with purity in direct sunlight.

The ships had approached the bay in a sawtooth fashion, angling to one side and then the other, but always sure of their destination. When they neared the biting reef that blocked the bay, however, they stood off.

Men made tiny by distance crowded the decks to study the reef. Then the ships turned and let the winds carry them away.

A portentous event beyond all question. Elgart would have preferred to be included in the haste and alarm of the bay's messages as they arrived. Being who he was, he wanted to know what was happening. But at the time, the self-styled Captain of Spies was absent from the Fist, consumed by his own concerns.

He had a sense that men who might betray either Belleger or Amika remained in the Open Hand, despite King Smegin's death. In addition, his distrust of the Church of the Great God Rile continued to nag at him. Father Skurn had mastered him. Worse, the priest had disturbed—had almost attacked—Magister Pillion. Elgart had a debt to repay there.

And King Bifalt did not send for him. Because the scarred veteran was always moving, and usually in places where he was not expected, two days passed before he heard about those ships.

Scouts, thought Elgart when the tidings reached him. The enemy was coming. That was certain now.

But the ships had seen the reef. That barrier might convince the enemy to begin his invasion somewhere else.

Then where? Elgart had studied Belleger's rudimentary maps. He could not think of another approach, unless the enemy tried the inlet of the Line's Cut, which would be stark folly, or came through the canyons of the Realm's Edge Mountains, which the General's scouts had been exploring for fortnights. In either case, there was nothing useful Elgart could do.

Instead of returning to Belleger's Fist, he continued on his personal quests.

But as soon as his web of eavesdroppers, informers, and spies brought him word that the Queen-Consort intended to question Prince Lome on the morrow, Elgart turned his apparently aimless rambling through the Open Hand toward King Bifalt.

When he saw his King late the next morning in the King's private council room, Elgart was taken aback. The change in Belleger's

King was remarkable to anyone who knew him well. Fortunately, Elgart's disfigured visage made it easy for him to conceal his reactions.

In the handful of days since Elgart had last seen him, Bifalt had aged ten years.

This was not the King's first sudden alteration. After his short time in the Last Repository, Prince Bifalt had looked a decade older than his twenty-three or twenty-four years. He had paid a high price for his submission to Magister Marrow. But during his reign as King, Bifalt had seemed strangely immune to age: untouched by the weight of his extravagant burdens, or preserved by it. He could have been mistaken for a man in his early thirties.

Now, abruptly, time had caught up with him. He looked every hour of his years. Oh, his mien was as severe as it had always been, his voice as hoarse. His attention when he concentrated had lost none of its force. But the lines of strain and weather around his eyes were more pronounced. The skin under them sagged. The furrows across his brow were deeper: they looked permanent. The creases at the corners of his mouth resembled galls. His shoulders slumped. And there were new streaks of grey in his cropped hair and short beard.

Elgart leapt to the conclusion that some crisis had weakened the clench of will by which King Bifalt had defied his age.

But what crisis?

Prince Lome's treachery? Elgart dismissed that explanation. Knowing that the Queen-Consort was safe, King Bifalt had faced his brother's crime with his familiar simmering ire. He had not relaxed his grip on himself.

The sight of sails on the horizon? The scouting ships? Elgart rejected that answer as well. King Bifalt had believed for decades that the enemy was coming. Mentally, emotionally, he was braced for it.

But what other possibilities were there? Queen Estie's return? How could *that* be a crisis? How could it have hit Bifalt hard enough to age him?

Unless she had told him something, explained something, revealed something that shook him to the core?

That notion shook Elgart himself. But he did not have time to pursue it. King Bifalt had already noticed that his Captain of Spies was staring. At Elgart's entrance, the King had risen to his feet. He stood expectantly behind his desk, watching Elgart with a puzzled lift of his eyebrows.

Elgart grinned and scowled on the opposing sides of his face. "Your pardon, Majesty." He was full of questions, but he knew better than to ask them. King Bifalt did not tolerate prying. "You know me. My mind wanders." He made a show of pulling himself together. "But I am here now.

"My informers"—in this case, Prince Jaspid—"assure me that the Queen-Consort is well. Has she questioned Prince Lome?"

For a moment, the King continued studying his old friend, his companion and antagonist in the library. He did indeed know Elgart. No doubt, he could imagine some of the issues that had distracted Elgart. Clearly, however, his own attention was elsewhere. Instead of probing his spy, he answered sourly, "She is with him now. If he does not frighten her by offering some wild proof of his innocence—perhaps by threatening to throw himself out a window—she will join us soon."

Then he said, "While we wait, tell me how you know Lylin."

That was comfortable ground for Elgart. "I do not, Majesty. The devotees of Spirit in the Open Hand keep to themselves for their own reasons. When I was told the Queen-Consort intended to confront King Smegin—and, presumably, the Nuuri—with only Magister Facile for protection, I asked a devotee of Flesh to tell a devotee of Spirit that the Queen-Consort might need her.

"I do not know how they contact each other, those devotees. If I did, I would boast of it. Ordinary spies I understand well enough. The devotees of Flesh and Spirit are a mystery."

King Bifalt nodded, apparently without much interest. "So you do not know where Lylin is now."

Elgart answered with a shrug. "I know only what Prince Jaspid told me. Oh, and Commander Crayn. Now *there* is a staunch man. He is devoted to his Queen. They agree that Lylin delivered the Queen-Consort back to Maloresse, then disappeared." Crayn in particular must have told King Bifalt the same thing fortnights ago. "If she is gone, she is gone. As I say, the devotees are mysteries."

The King said nothing. He was not listening—or not listening to Elgart. He was waiting for a different sound.

Fortunately, the two men did not have to wait long. Before King Bifalt lost patience, or Elgart surrendered to the pressure of impertinent questions, the servant outside the door opened it to announce the Queen-Consort.

As soon as she entered, and the door closed behind her, Elgart felt the tension between Belleger's King and Amika's Queen. It was like a cold breeze from the open windows.

It did not show in any outward sign, except perhaps in the way they did not quite meet each other's eyes. The King squared his shoulders. He stood like a soldier awaiting an inspection. But he often stiffened in her presence. And she wore her beauty and her alluring gown like shields: she betrayed nothing.

Nevertheless their discomfort chilled Elgart. He had studied with Amandis and Flamora long ago. And he had spent the better part of nineteen years training himself to feel the moods and emotions that people kept hidden. King Bifalt and his Queen-Consort had never been truly comfortable with each other; but Elgart knew at once that their tension was something new.

It was a hint. Like a good spy, Elgart grabbed it and held it close to his chest.

Both monarchs were too familiar with Elgart to behave formally in his presence. King Bifalt did not bow: Queen Estie did not curtsy. Instead, she only inclined her head. "My lord King." Nodding, he replied, "My lady Queen."

Then, too abruptly, he asked, "What have you learned?"

For a moment, she ignored him. With her perfect smile, she turned to the King's spy. "It is good to see you again, Elgart."

For his part, Elgart gave her his best bow. He saw at a glance that she, too, had changed. But in her, the change was strength, not weakness. "And you, Majesty," he replied, approximating a gallantry that was not natural to him. "Of course, I heard you are well. And successful. But I am glad to see it with my own eyes."

Her smile took on an inflection of humor, but her manner was serious. "The credit is yours, my friend. If you had not sent Lylin to accompany me—" She shrugged delicately. "You know the tale by now. I would not have kept my life without her."

Unable to stop himself, Elgart bowed again. "You are gracious, Majesty. But I cannot accept credit. I did not *send* Lylin. I only asked." He chuckled dismissively. "And I did so indirectly. The credit belongs to the most holy devotees."

"Then perhaps," returned the Queen-Consort, "you will let a devotee of Flesh know that I"—she glanced at her husband—"that King Bifalt and I would like to give Lylin our thanks in person. And Prince Jaspid wishes to speak with her. He would like that very much."

Elgart started to say, Of course, Majesty. But King Bifalt was too tense to suffer delays. He forestalled his Captain of Spies by asking, "You have spoken with Prince Lome, my lady? How does he justify himself?"

His tone said, Why should I not have my brother shot for trying to arrange your death?

She gave Elgart another moment of her smile before facing her husband again.

"He is lost in himself, my lord." She sounded sure in a way that was new to Elgart's experience of her. "You know that. Drink masks his pain, but only so that he will not look at it. No amount of drink will heal him."

"Did he confess?" demanded the King.

The Queen-Consort sighed. "He said many things, my lord. They were intended to justify him, but I took them as signs of guilt."

"Then should I—?" began King Bifalt.

She cut him off, which Elgart had never seen her do before. "You must accept that he conspired with Amikan traitors, my lord. I do. But there is more. He urged me to believe he has a secret. He knows"—she spread her hands—"something no one else has realized. *That* he is willing to confess. But he will not reveal his secret until we are ready to hear it."

For an instant, King Bifalt became a statue. Every natural movement stopped. He hardly seemed to breathe. Without blinking, he regarded his wife. But he was only surprised, not angry. Elgart knew the indications.

When the King replied, he sounded calm, in control of himself. "Thank you, my lady. That may prove useful.

"Were you able to form an impression of his secret? Does it appear to have value?"

Queen Estie allowed herself a delicate grimace. "I cannot say. I was done with him. I did not test his claim."

King Bifalt bit the inside of his cheek, considering possible responses. Without looking away from his wife, he asked Elgart, "And you? What do you know? Can you guess at my brother's secret?"

Elgart lifted one eyebrow, scowled with the other. He did not hesitate. "No, Majesty. I believe the Prince has come to the end of his dealings with Amikan traitors. I can only speculate that he has an understanding with the Great God's priests."

The spy thought he knew what that understanding was. He and King Bifalt had discussed it days ago. Lome wanted to help the Archpriest gain power over his brother. But if *that* was Lome's secret, he had an exaggerated opinion of its worth. The King had been forewarned.

Bifalt nodded. Still facing the Queen-Consort, he shook his shoulders to loosen them. "The question remains. What should be done with him?

"Will you advise me, my lady? If he were your subject, an Amikan conspiring with Bellegerins, how would you repay his treachery?"

That question brought out the change in her. Her eyes flashed, and the lines of her face seemed to harden. "I am outraged, my lord. His plot came close to killing me. He cost me Anina, my maid that I have known and trusted for many years. His death would please me.

"But I see no gain in punishing him. He is your brother. If you have him shot, you will set a harsh example for your people. You need their loyalty, not their fear. And no lesser penalty will match his crime.

"If he were my subject, my lord, I would set him free."

Then she added, "Of course, I would ask Elgart to watch him. I would like to know where he goes, what he does, who he encounters. If it can be done, I would like to know the import of every conversation he has. But I would give him his freedom. Let him declare himself by his actions, or his friendships, or his private discussions."

Clearly, her advice was not what King Bifalt had expected. While the King thought about it, Elgart took his opportunity to remark, "It can be done, my lady. I have men and women who are adept at such tasks." He was thinking especially of Flax, his personal guard, who had a keenly developed talent for remaining unnoticed while she eaves-dropped. "He will not know he is watched. Or heard."

King Bifalt gave a sharp nod of decision. "If Elgart says it can be done, my lady, it can be done. I will do what you suggest. He has shamed our father's memory. I want to drag his entrails through the streets. But your counsel is wiser.

"Accept my thanks."

"Of course, my lord." The severity was gone from the Amikan Queen's face. In its place, her smile resumed its perfection. "We dis-agree often, but I am grateful that you always consider what I say."

Still, she did not meet her husband's gaze.

As if her response were a trigger, Elgart felt the tightness between them increase. The King became a statue again. His attention was as fierce as rifle fire, but he did not seem to know where to aim it.

The Queen-Consort gave the impression that she was pursuing an advantage as she asked in her most melodious tones, "Have you spoken with Magister Facile yet, my lord?"

Elgart thought that he saw King Bifalt flinch. "No." Perhaps to conceal their clenching, the King gripped his hands behind his back. "I have summoned her. I have questions for her. I do not understand the delay." Then he said, "But I am told she will come this morning. Will you wait with me, my lady?"

Again, the tension in the room increased. The Queen-Consort gazed at Bifalt's chest rather than his face. "You do not wish to consult with her privately?"

The King made a low sound like a growl deep in his throat. "Not on this occasion."

While both monarchs ignored him, Elgart raised one of his own eyebrows, scowled with the other. He heard hints in their exchanges, undercurrents of meaning. Something had happened between King Bifalt and his Queen-Consort. It may have involved the old sorceress somehow. He could not imagine what it was. But he was beginning to believe that somehow Queen Estie—or Queen Estie and Magister Facile—had caused the King to show his years.

The Queen's challenges in Amika had made her stronger: that was obvious. But Elgart did not understand why or how her new courage and assurance had weakened her husband.

Secrets and more secrets. Prince Lome had at least one. Belleger's King and Amika's Queen had one or more. Despite his devotion to Bifalt and his respect for Estie, Elgart was eager to uncover them.

Before long, the door opened to admit another of King Bifalt's advisers. But this was not Magister Facile: it was General Klamath.

Elgart's companion on Prince Bifalt's search for the library looked worn. The strain of his duties had gouged lines like arguments on both sides of his mouth, contradictions of each other. Decisions scored his forehead. But this was not new. He had looked worn ever since his King had required him to assume the title and burdens of General. He was a tough fighter with a soft heart. He never forgot that eventually he would be expected to send men he liked and cared for to their deaths.

Without any real surprise, King Bifalt said in greeting, "General." Like Elgart himself, Klamath was always welcome in the King's presence. Bifalt kept his impatience to himself. "Do you have something to report?"

His tone asked, Has something happened? Has the enemy been sighted again?

Offering the King a cursory bow, General Klamath replied, "Majesty." To the Queen-Consort, he bowed more formally. "My lady Queen, I am glad to the heart that you have not been harmed." To Elgart, he added, "And you are here as well, old friend? This council is more portentous than I expected."

While Queen Estie smiled to acknowledge Klamath's greeting, and Elgart grinned his pleasure, the General answered King Bifalt. "My report is on your desk, Majesty. Perhaps you have not seen it yet? I have nothing to add. I am here because Magister Facile asked for my presence."

Oh, that was interesting. The sorceress wanted Klamath here?

The King lifted an eyebrow. He had seen the report, of course. But he did not say so. Instead, he muttered, "Did she? Then it is good that you have come." Complex emotions tugged at each other in his tone. "Can you spare the time to wait with us? We are all interested in what the Magister will say."

Klamath replied with a rueful smile. "My First Captain, Majesty, knows your army as well as I do. At times, I suspect he knows it better. I will not be missed. In any event, my time is always yours."

"Good." King Bifalt scowled his approval. "I have read your report. But the Queen-Consort has not seen it. Perhaps you will repeat it while we wait."

General Klamath frowned at the request. It was unusual: he did not ordinarily discuss the army's activities with Queen Estie. However, he answered promptly enough. "As you say, Majesty.

"I am now confident of what my trackers and riflemen have learned about the men who have been raiding across the Realm's Edge front. The southwest of Belleger," he added for the Queen-Consort's benefit. "Your suggestion was a good one, Majesty. The Amikan commanders have shown their worth. Their task required"—he grimaced sourly—"discretion.

"Those men commit atrocities, but they are not raiders."

Elgart saw concern in the Queen-Consort's gaze. Her mouth shaped the word, Not? but she did not say it aloud.

"As we suspected," continued Klamath, "they are scouts. They have spent seasons or more among the mountains, searching for ways into Belleger. If they have any other purpose, it is to test our response. That may be the reason for their savagery.

"There are many points of egress from the Realm's Edge, but among the peaks they join together in three main canyons. Wisely, my men did not follow the trails inward for more than two or three leagues. But they went far enough to conclude that those canyons extend deep into the south.

"They are not paths for mere raiders, Majesty. They are roads for armies."

Scouts, thought Elgart. And ships scouting the bay. Was that why the priests had come as well? To scout the realms?

King Bifalt's concentration seemed to heat the room. Grimly, he asked, "Can we block them?"

Now General Klamath sighed. "The commanders think not, Majesty. Cannon are our best weapons, but we could not use them. The terrain is against us. Our guns are difficult to move, and many of the mountainsides are sheer. We would have to rely on rifles and sorcery.

"Effective barricades in three canyons would require half our army and every Magister in Belleger. We might need my lady Queen's sorcerers as well. And I cannot assure you that our defense would hold. The positions necessary for us would be hard to reach and secure. A force powerful enough to threaten the Last Repository might slaughter its way through us."

"Then what—?" the Queen-Consort tried to ask. For an instant, words failed her. "What can we do?"

While her question waited for an answer, the servant at the door announced Magister Facile. Stamping her cane, the old woman hobbled into the room.

Clearly, she had recovered from the rigors of her journey with Amika's Queen, the stress of what she had endured. Hardy and stubborn, she had arranged her malleable features to convey anger. In her grey robe, she resembled an irate dove. However, Elgart had known her for a long time. He saw past her demeanor. Behind it lay a yearning that he had only glimpsed once or twice before. And he saw an entirely uncharacteristic defensiveness. She approached King Bifalt like a woman who had come to outface recriminations.

"Majesties," she said, addressing both monarchs without any particular respect. "And General Klamath. Elgart. Good."

"Magister Facile." When King Bifalt applied his full attention, he could be as discerning as Elgart. "You are angry. When I summoned you, did you imagine I meant to reprimand you? Is that why you have made me wait?"

Brusquely, she retorted, "The thought occurred to me."

To himself, Elgart chortled. He was right. There was definitely something here, something between the King, the Queen-Consort, and the old woman. Queen Estie's abruptly masked expression suggested that she knew what the Magister had in mind.

"I will." King Bifalt kept his anger under control, but he did not hide it. His tone made his wife wince. "I have much to say. I will demand answers. But I will not speak until we are alone."

"Speak now," returned the Magister without hesitation. "Speak later. Say whatever pleases you whenever you wish. I will tell you nothing."

"You *will*—" began the King hoarsely.

"I will *not*." The sorceress stamped her cane. "My choices are not yours to judge, King. I have done what I have done. And I have not forgotten that you despise sorcery. Revile me if you must. Send me away—if you believe you do not need my service. You will lose much and learn nothing. This burden does not belong to you."

Everything she said made the tension hotter. King Bifalt held his fists clenched at his sides. His sudden revulsion threatened to scorch Magister Facile. The Queen-Consort tried to intervene. "My lord," she murmured. "My lord." But she could not make herself heard through the force of his ire. Even the General tried to intervene. "Majesty, we must—" His voice faded away when he realized that King Bifalt was not listening.

Elgart held himself still, waiting for some word that he would be able to understand.

Abruptly, the King wheeled on Queen Estie. "Do you stand with me in this?" he demanded. "Am I alone?"

She had gone pale. Her lower lip trembled. But she met his gaze now; met it and held it. "In this, my lord," she answered softly. "Only in this. You know why I cannot stand with you."

For a moment, the way the King's hands shook and his lips bared his teeth made Elgart think that his restraint had snapped; that he was about to do or say something that neither the Queen of Amika nor the Magister of the Last Repository would forgive. But then he turned away from his wife. Unsteadily, he went to his desk. Supporting himself on it, he moved around the desk to his chair. With great care, he sat down.

"Then," he said, "I will bear it alone."

Without pausing, he added, "You did not come because I summoned you, Magister. You came because you have something to say in General Klamath's presence. Say it now."

Magister Facile studied him closely, appraising his self-command. By increments, she rearranged her expression. Lowering her head, she leaned more of her weight on her cane. When she answered, she no longer sounded defensive. She sounded grieved.

"I have tidings."

Sighing, the Queen-Consort allowed herself to relax a little. In contrast, General Klamath stood straighter. His chin came up as if he expected a call to battle. But King Bifalt only propped his elbows on his desk and lowered his head into the support of his hands. Almost calmly, he asked, "You have spoken with the Last Repository?"

The old woman nodded. "After a long absence, yes." Bitterness twisted her mouth. "Magister Avail has harried me, but I could not make myself heard. Much that was said is distressing, but it is a personal matter. Now I have news for you—and for General Klamath. It will interest Queen Estie as well."

"I do not mention Elgart. Everything interests *him*."

The King betrayed no reaction. "Tell us."

Magister Facile seemed to shrug. "The caravan is coming," she announced. "Set Ungabwey's wagons and men and mechanisms. They are on the Queen's road. They will reach the Open Hand in ten days, perhaps less."

General Klamath opened his mouth to request an explanation. The Queen-Consort spoke first.

"My road is complete?"

"Not entirely," answered the Magister. "Some leagues remain. But they are on your side of the Line. And Master Ungabwey has contributed a few skilled stonemasons to the task, men he can hardly spare. The last work will be done in a fortnight."

Elgart wanted to ask, But why? What brings that caravan *here*? For King Bifalt's sake, however, he restrained the impulse. Instead, he inquired, "How, Magister? Tell us how. That desert is vast. We have traveled it." He meant Prince Bifalt, Klamath, and himself. "With horses and a good map, it can be crossed without suffering. But wagons cannot follow those paths. They are too cunning, and too narrow. The sands clog them. And the chasm of the Line River deepens as it stretches eastward. Yet you say Set Ungabwey and his train are now in Amika.

"Tell us how."

Magister Facile made a rasping noise, a snarl of irritation. "I respect you, Elgart. I always have. But at times, you do not *think*.

"You have seen the size of that caravan. Do you imagine the Last Repository is its only destination? No. For a man of Master Ungabwey's wealth and hindrances, it would be an absurd trek. You know how he crosses the desert. You have seen his road. It is concealed among the dunes, but it is kept open. Did you suppose a chasm would stop him?"

At that, King Bifalt jerked up his head as if the old woman had slapped him. "There is a *bridge*? In *that* desert?"

His surprise seemed to please the Magister—or perhaps placate her. "It was made centuries ago, with footings of good stone. Strong wards sustain it." Then she turned to Queen Estie. "Your surveyors did not know of it. They would have needed seasons or years to accomplish what you asked of them. But Master Ungabwey's outriders came upon them before they lost hope. You will have your road."

This claim lit a smile on the Queen-Consort's face. But it was more than a smile of relief. Elgart saw vindication in it; even eagerness. And something else. An admixture of fear? A deeply personal dread?

Too many questions. Too many secrets. Fortunately, the spy had plenty of other things to think about while he waited for insight.

King Bifalt shook his head. He had heard enough about his wife's road. And he was beginning to recover his composure.

"Now," he said abruptly, "tell us why Set Ungabwey is coming." His tone took on an edge. "He will find no profit here. Yet he comes at a time of growing peril. What is his purpose?" Sitting straighter, he spoke to cut. "Did the Magisters of the library send him to put some new obstacle in our path?"

"Majesty!" Fuming, the sorceress hit the floor with her cane. "I know why you distrust Magisters, but there are times when your arrogance blinds you. He comes to *help*." In her ire, she struck the floor again at every phrase. "If he can do it, with the seasons passing, and time against him, he intends to seal the Realm's Edge against the enemy. He has already made the Wall impassable. He will strive to do the same in your mountains."

Staring, General Klamath asked, "He can *do* that?"

"I suspected him of sorcery," added the King. "Does he wield the Decimate of earthquake? Can he bring down mountainsides?"

Magister Facile shook her head. "He has no gift. His men are not sorcerers. He has mechanisms. You would call them catapults. But you cannot imagine their size and power. They are so heavy that only illirim can move them. No Decimate known to you can equal them. If the enemy does not prevent him, he can break cliffs and peaks to close the passes."

For a moment, silence held the room. The rest of the Magister's audience needed time to absorb what she said. Elgart did not. His mind ran in other directions. Now he understood why the sorceress wanted General Klamath to hear her. But it was not his place to say so.

"Nevertheless," muttered King Bifalt as if to himself, "he does not bring an army. He will need protection. The raiders may be unaware that they have been tracked. The caravan cannot hide itself from them."

At once, Klamath said, "If you command it, Majesty, I will send riflemen to watch over Master Ungabwey's efforts."

The King did not respond. He may have nodded.

The Queen-Consort watched her husband, apparently waiting for him to acknowledge the library's help. Then she answered Magister Facile for him.

"The Last Repository does us a great service. And you have done us a great service as well. No one else in Belleger or Amika can communicate with the library. It is arduous for you, but you do not shy from it. I hope you will accept my gratitude"—she glanced at the King again—"and King Bifalt's, when he remembers that you have earned his courtesy."

"Gratitude?" Bifalt shook off his lapse of attention. "Matters are not so simple. Set Ungabwey does not come to aid *us*. He serves the library. If the enemy is allowed to pass through the Realm's Edge, his horde can march straight to its target. It will not be slowed by our defenses. The library intends to hinder his advance by sacrificing Belleger and Amika."

That assertion shocked his wife. But it did not daunt the old woman. As harsh as a raven, she demanded, "Will you refuse Master Ungabwey, King? Will you abandon the Last Repository to its doom?"

He replied with a snort. "Hells, no! If we do not stand in the enemy's way when he arrives, he will come for us later. He cannot leave a living force behind him. He must destroy us, or he will be cut off from the other lands he has conquered.

"If Set Ungabwey wants *my* aid, I will give it. I will give whatever he asks. But I will not feign gratitude."

Elgart saw a gleam of approval in General Klamath's gaze. The Queen-Consort seemed to struggle with conflicting emotions. She may have hoped to hear Magister Facile contradict Bifalt's reasoning. But Elgart felt sure that the sorceress would not argue. What could she say? King Bifalt was right.

"Then, King"—Magister Facile only called him that when she was too angry for courtesy—"do what you can in the Bay of Lights. You have no other path."

Turning her back, she stormed as well as she could for the door. If she could croak like a raven, she was a raven with a damaged wing.

"Magister, wait," whispered Queen Estie. Throwing off her own dismay, she hurried after the old woman; caught her before she opened the door. "Please, Magister." Despite everything the Queen-Consort had heard, despite what she felt, she spoke gently. "You will not welcome my question, but I must ask it.

"Will you tell me what you heard from Magister Avail that has caused you so much distress?"

Elgart stared as the sorceress dropped her cane, covered her face with her hands. When she answered, she sounded like she might weep.

"Apprentice Travail has been ill. The shamans believe he was poisoned. They have brought him back from death, but they do not know how long he will live.

"I am lost—"

When her voice broke, she could not say more.

"Oh, Magister." Without hesitation, Amika's Queen put her arms around the old woman, held her close. "I am sorry. I am sorry."

Magister Facile accepted the embrace for a moment. Then she pulled away. Stooping, she retrieved her cane. Twice, she stamped it on the floor as if that jolt might restore her composure. When she left the room, she did not glance back at the men behind her, or the woman.

"What ails her?" King Bifalt sounded surprised. "Elgart, do you understand?"

The scarred spy stood stunned for a few heartbeats. Then he came back to himself. The night when Queen Estie had left for her encounter with her father, he had not overheard enough to be sure that he knew what Apprentice Travail meant to Magister Facile. But he was good at guessing. And he had other matters to discuss with the sorceress. He answered the question King Bifalt should have asked.

"There is treachery in the library."

If the Queen-Consort chose, she could say more. Sketching a bow, Elgart ran after Magister Facile.

S he had only gone a few steps. As soon as he reached her side, he clasped her arm to balance the support of her cane. At a glance, he saw the tears on her cheeks, the way her mouth clenched so that she would not sob aloud. Bowing his head to her ear, he said quietly, "Turn your mind to other matters, Magister. Perhaps you are lost. Or perhaps matters are not as dire as you suppose. You are still *needed*."

In a thick voice, she retorted, "Leave me, spy. You know nothing of grief."

He resisted an impulse to hide what he felt behind an air of amusement. "I am lost myself. That is grief enough for me.

"You expected King Bifalt to accuse you of some fault. What have you done that would anger him?"

She choked out a curse. "Spare me your curiosity. Ask the Queen, if you think she will tell you. I am not a cistern you can pump for answers."

To himself, he shrugged. He had already accomplished his first objective. He had made her too angry for weeping. Unrepentant, he persisted.

"Then explain the sorcery of the priests." He had his own ideas: he wanted to hear hers. "In the sanctuary of the Church, you said you sensed theurgy. You said it could 'end' you." She had also said, *I do not know what it is*, but he ignored that detail. "How could a sorcerer know you were present? How could his power threaten you?"

Using her cane hard, she tried to walk faster. He helped her along; but he did not let her go.

Trembling with exasperation, she retorted, "You are a fool, spy. You do not *think*. You are only *interested*. Your curiosity will drive you mad. It will see you dead.

"Those priests are not sorcerers. Ask as many Magisters as you wish. They will say the same. But the Great God's servants have sorcery at their command. They can wield a power they do not possess. How, I do not know. Why, I do not know. Where they get it, I do not know. What use they make of it, I cannot imagine. But it is *there*. And if I can sense it, it can sense me.

"I cannot defend myself against a power that is not *present*. Any *borrowed* theurgy can destroy me."

Her reply silenced him. She had struck a nerve, a point of weakness in his contradictory defenses. Without knowing it, she had told him that Father Skurn could have destroyed Magister Pillion. Elgart supported her a little farther along her way, then took his leave. As King Bifalt's Captain of Spies—as a man—he suddenly had a more urgent concern than any question she might or might not answer.

*Y*ou *are not the man you try to be*. Elgart's efforts to deny Father Skurn's assessment lost some of their effectiveness when Magister Facile reminded him of it. —*you are at war with yourself*.

Hells! thought the scarred spy. That priest had given him a hint; but he was too obtuse to see it. Or too cynical. Or he did not know enough about sorcery.

His friend Magister Pillion had tried to explain the influence of the priests. Father Skurn, at least, was not a sorcerer: not according to Pillion. Like Magister Facile, however, the unassuming little man believed that the priest *did* use sorcery, theurgy he drew from some other source. With sorcery, Skurn had tried to break Elgart's belief in himself. With sorcery, he had made Elgart unconscious. But he had treated Magister Pillion differently. The priest had used his borrowed power to ask for—no, to demand—Magister Pillion's *consent*.

Consent to *what*? Pillion felt that he had been urged to surrender his family; perhaps even his gift for theurgy. To become a servant of the Church. He had refused—he had been able to refuse—because he loved his wife and children.

If the Great God Rile's priests obtained or coerced Magister Facile's consent, what would be done with her? What use would be made of her surrender?

Were the priests sincere? Was their only desire to end the war inherent within everyone who heard them? Did they want nothing more than peace for Magister Pillion, for Elgart himself? For Belleger and Amika?

Or were they scouts for the Repository's enemy?

Without planning or premeditation, Elgart left Belleger's Fist and strode down the streets of the Open Hand, heading for the Church of the Great God. He needed better answers than his friend or Magister Facile had been able to give him.

What had Father Skurn said when Elgart had heard him read the scripture and give the sermon? *In* you, *there is war. In* each *of you, there is war.* Walking faster, Elgart retorted, Is *that* truth? It is *your* truth, certainly. But is it mine? You want me to believe it is. The devotees teach a different lesson.

After two visits to the Church, he was determined to question the Archpriest Makh.

When he had asked for the Archpriest days ago, he had been told that Makh was elsewhere, doing the Great God Rile's work outside the Hand. Elgart knew better. His network of watchers and eavesdroppers, informers and spies could not uncover every secret, but they could be relied on to track the movements of a personage like the Archpriest. Makh had not left the Hand. He had simply declined to be bothered by men like Elgart and Magister Pillion. Or perhaps—a happier thought—he had been reluctant to expose himself.

Not *this* time. Elgart knew something that even Facile did not: the sorcery of the priests could be shaped to affect different hearers in different ways. That was useful. And he was a veteran of the old wars, a soldier long before he became a spy. He knew how to shed blood, and was not ashamed to do it. He did not consider himself overconfident when he decided to speak with the head of the Great God's Church in Belleger.

Did the priests think that they could defend themselves by putting him to sleep again? He had weapons. This time, he would not hesitate to use them.

His discussion with King Bifalt, General Klamath, the Queen-Consort, and Magister Facile had taken longer than it seemed. He did not arrive at the crudely made Church until early in the afternoon.

No matter. One time was as good as another.

As always, he was being shadowed by his personal guards, Howel and Flax. With small gestures, he asked Howel to join him while Flax remained where she was. To Howel, he suggested one simple precaution, then sent the man on his way.

A moment later, King Bifalt's Captain of Spies entered the sanctuary, crossed among the pews to the dais, and began calling for attention. Because he was anxious and more than a little overwrought, he made a point of sounding especially cheerful.

The familiar lamps illuminated the back of the space. The dais and whatever lay behind it were filled with darkness. The pulpit suggested its shape among the shadows. He could barely discern the cross and its statue.

For a moment, no one responded. He considered repeating his call. But then a man manifested himself behind the pulpit. Clad entirely in black, with his black eyebrows and beard, he seemed to solidify like an incarnation of the dark.

Elgart recognized him before he spoke. When he said, "You have returned, my son," the sonorous depth of his voice confirmed his identity. "I am glad of it. You are always welcome in the Church of the Great God." He was Father Skurn.

"I have, Father." Elgart made his tone jovial. "And I am pleased by your welcome. I am in need."

"As are all men," replied the priest. "All who war with themselves are in need. But I surmise that your need is a particular one, my son. When we spoke before, I felt your exhaustion, the cost of your inward struggle. And this time, you have not brought a Magister to disguise your plight. You are not a common laborer.

"How can the Church of the Great God Rile serve you?"

Elgart had no qualms about lying. Blithely dishonest, he answered, "Your discernment does you credit, Father. If you can see that I am not common, you will understand that my need is not.

"I represent a force that is growing in the Open Hand. In fact, grows across Belleger. My comrades have chosen me to speak for them. I have been sent to seek insight from the Archpriest."

The light behind Elgart was too dim to reveal Father Skurn's expression, but the priest did not sound troubled—or even interested. "Then you have an awkward mission, my son. The Archpriest continues to do the Great God's work elsewhere. Will you allow me to assist you?"

Half of Elgart's face grinned. "With respect, Father, you are mistaken. Archpriest Makh is here. The men I represent are certain of it."

That assertion caused the priest to raise his black eyebrows. "Truly? How can they be certain?"

"Because he is nowhere else. If he is not here, he is not in Belleger. And if he is not in Belleger—really, I must insist that I say it with respect—he serves the Church poorly. He has lost an opportunity. My comrades and I can do many things to further the Great God's purposes. But first I must speak with the Archpriest. We believe that he alone has the authority to speak for the Great God Rile. We hope to reach an agreement with him. We must be sure of what we do.

"If you can, tell the Archpriest this. We have the ability to arrange an audience with King Bifalt."

In response, Father Skurn scowled like a man masking himself. Hiding surprise? Excitement? Suspicion? Elgart pondered the question, but it did not trouble him. He had found his path. Lies came easily when he could see his way forward.

"That is a grand claim, my son." The priest's tone hinted at bluster. "Do you want to be sure? How can I be sure of *you*?"

The spy failed to make both sides of his face smile at the same time. "Archpriest Makh will be sure when he hears me."

Then he adopted a more placating manner. "Come, Father. How can my wishes harm the Church, or the Great God, or you? I do not fault you for saying the Archpriest is elsewhere. His work is vital. You protect him from trivial interruptions. But my work is vital as well. My purpose is not trivial."

Careless of the risk, he added, "Prince Lome has done what he can on your behalf. It is not enough. I can do—" He caught himself. "The force I represent can do better."

"If that is true," insisted Father Skurn, "it must have more stature than the King's brother. What *is* it, my son? *Who* is it?"

"Father." Elgart sighed, admonishing the man. "How often have you reminded your congregation that Belleger and Amika are still at war with each other? How often have you preached that Belleger is at war with itself? Or that every Bellegerin is at war with himself? A number of us—a considerable number—chafe at King Bifalt's yoke. And some of us are known to him. Unlike Prince Lome, some of us are welcome in his private councils." Taking another risk, he chose a name he considered safe. "One is Crickin, the Captain of the Count." To Elgart's certain knowledge, the man was fifty leagues away, hard at work numbering villagers. "With his support, and that of others, we can promise the Archpriest a hearing."

The priest still scowled; but now Elgart believed that he could identify Father Skurn's expression. It was cupidity. His hunger for a meeting between Archpriest Makh and the King was too strong to conceal.

"Very well, my son," he conceded. "He *is* here, as you believe. I will take you to him."

In an instant, he seemed to dissolve into the obscurity of the dais. Between one heartbeat and the next, he was gone.

When a door hidden in the wall below the dais opened, and lamp-light from the corridor beyond it streamed inward, Elgart joined Father Skurn without hesitation.

In the chamber at the end of the corridor, there was light everywhere: half a dozen candles, as many lamps, two cressets set in the walls opposite each other. But there was no smell of smoke—or of burning wicks and lamp oil.

Elgart did not need more proof that the priests had access to sorcery. They may not have been theurgists themselves, but they could draw on strange powers for their own use.

He had spent enough time in the Last Repository to know that sorcery was not limited to the Decimates. In fact, he knew enough to realize that he had no idea what its limits were. If Magister Avail could speak in Prince Bifalt's mind across astonishing distances—if some theurgist far away could protect the Prince from a killing bolt of light-ning, or from the fatal blast of a grenade—*everything* seemed possible. Surely a "great god" could project his strength across oceans and conti-nents.

Of course, there had to be a trick to it. An implement of some kind. A *means*. But still—

Elgart was more fearful than he wanted to admit. He had no de-fense against sorcery except violence. He seemed to feel weary only because Father Skurn had suggested it.

Subtly, he confirmed that his hidden blade was in its sheath. As if he were adjusting his breeches, he checked his belt and its thin wire garrote.

The chamber was spacious by comparison with the room where the priest had talked with Elgart and Magister Pillion, but it was not large.

Its furnishings were practical rather than austere, made for use rather than self-denial: a bed against one wall, a desk on another, a small trestle table and several stools in the center. An inkpot and several quills were the only objects on the desk. There were no papers or books of any kind.

Sitting on a stool behind the table was an old man of medium height and considerable bulk. His flowing beard and long mane were as white as a devotee of Spirit's robe. He had the fleshy lips of a sybarite and the wide-set eyes of a goat. They gave him the look of a man who doted on unwilling girls. But his nose contradicted them. It resembled a wooden peg placed to anchor his desires so that they would not lead him astray. Seated, his posture and cassock hid the nature of his bulk. It could have indicated either strength or indulgence.

But the feature that held Elgart's attention was the man's hands. Large and heavy, with thick knuckles and strangling fingers, they looked like they belonged to a stonemason, someone as strong as the First Captain's son Mattwil: someone who spent all day every day chiseling, shifting, and setting blocks of granite; changing the world. A younger man with those hands might have been able to break the table simply by clenching his fists.

Glancing at the priest, the old man asked, "A seeker after truth, Father?" His voice had a curious liquid quality. It seemed to splash and swirl like a brook twisting over its rocks.

"No, Archpriest," replied Father Skurn, as resonant as an omen. "This man claims he can arrange an audience with King Bifalt."

"Indeed?" Archpriest Makh shifted his gaze to Elgart. "Then I must hear what he has to say. No doubt, he has questions. He will want to understand us before he explains himself."

A slight shift of one hand dismissed Skurn. "Thank you, Father."

The priest nodded. "Archpriest." At once, he turned and left. Elgart heard him walking back down the corridor for a few moments. Then the sound faded.

"So, my son," began Makh. "An audience with King Bifalt. That is a powerful inducement. What can I say or do to persuade you that only good will come of our meeting, King Bifalt's and mine?"

Uninvited, Elgart dropped onto a stool. His heart was beating too fast, and he did not trust his legs to keep him upright. The brightness in the room hurt his eyes. He was accustomed to dark streets and stealth, not this glare of revelation. It made him feel naked.

Emphasizing his awkwardness, he worked his stool closer to the table: close enough to rest his hands below the table's edge where Makh could not see them. Then he cleared his throat, hoping to clear his mind.

"Your purpose, Archpriest. What you do here. I think I grasp your Church's teachings. You seek peace in the world. To achieve it, you do what you can to show warring men and women that the way to peace is the way of Truth and Faith. Some of us—perhaps many of us—have tested what you say in our hearts, and we have found it good."

Archpriest Makh's smile looked benign; but to Elgart, it had a rapacious cast. Like the expression of the statue in the sanctuary, it resisted definition. How could any ungifted man trust his senses when he considered the Archpriest?

Groping for clarity, Elgart continued, "But I do not understand why you offer your teachings to *us*. We are a small land. Together, Belleger and Amika are small. More than that, we are a godless people. We know nothing of beings that transcend mortality. We have no conception of our place among them. Your teachings are more strange to us than a sun that rises at night or a plume of dust that drifts against the wind.

"Yet you have traveled a vast and troublesome distance to reach us. Why do you care what we believe or what we do? We do not know the world. We have no dealings with it. Whether we kill ourselves in war or join each other in peace, we will have no effect on your efforts in larger, more important realms."

Archpriest Makh folded his hands on his beard, rested them on his ample chest. "The answer is simple, my son," he said like a stretch of placid water. "We are here because the Great God Rile wills it. That is reason enough for us."

Elgart stifled a sudden impulse to yawn. Hells! he thought. It is happening again.

But now he knew what it was. Makh was probing him with theurgy.

And the Captain of Spies was not a weak man despite his lean frame and easy lies. Peril sharpened his attention. Without shifting his shoulders or his attention—without showing any movement that might betray him—he slipped his poniard from its sheath.

Amandis had taught him well. With one quick arc of his forearm, one flick of his wrist, he could throw his blade. He could hit his opponent in either eye, or in the throat.

"You confuse me, Archpriest," he admitted. "Do you mean to say that you are the Great God's instruments? You do what he commands? Forgive me if I seem disrespectful. How is your purpose consistent with the way of Truth and Faith? If you have found your own peace, how are you made to do another's bidding?"

Makh made a small gesture of impatience. It looked casual, but Elgart had the impression that it could have cracked boards.

"I misspoke, my son. The matter is so plain to us that we seldom consider how to express it. I will attempt a better answer.

"We are not servants or instruments. We were not commanded or sent. We follow the way of Truth and Faith. Doing so, we have been blessed in many ways. We are at peace ourselves. But we also see the value of sharing that peace. Because the truth of who and what we are draws its strength from our faith in the Great God Rile, we know his mind. That is, we know it as well as mortal men can. We choose to spend our lives as teachers in gratitude for what we have received, and to lessen the sorrow and misery of men and women who have not been blessed as we are."

"Then, Archpriest," asked Elgart more crisply, "Belleger was not chosen *for* you? *You* chose it?"

The Archpriest nodded. "And Amika, my son. And Amika."

"Now I am more confused. Why did *you* choose us?"

For no obvious reason, Makh glanced around him. He may have wanted to confirm that his candles, lamps, and cressets were all lit. Then he returned his attention to Elgart. With one hand, he rubbed absentmindedly at his chest.

"Because you are godless," he explained, "as you say. But it would be more insightful to say that you are *unaware* of gods. You do not know what drives you, what threatens you, what undermines you. Therefore you are vulnerable. Without Truth and Faith, you have no defense against Pride and Folly and their Lusts.

"Those gods are already among you."

Elgart had his next question ready. *How* could you choose us? How could you know of our existence? But he lost his chance to ask it. Another yawn swelled inside him, and the effort of swallowing it broke his concentration. He had to shield his eyes with his free hand while he tried to recover.

He meant to ask—

He could have gone to sleep where he sat. Who did these priests think they were? Did they consider *themselves* gods? What gave them the right to drain him of his most precious gift, his restless and inquiring mind?

What kind of theurgy could *do* this?

In the privacy of his divided mind, he readied his knife.

Howel and Flax knew where he was. They would know where to look for him when they grew impatient. They could call for help.

And of course, Makh would not kill him. None of the Archpriest's questions would be answered by a corpse.

Instead of fighting it, Elgart let himself yawn. Then he asked, "There are many gods?"

Makh shook his head. "Once there were." He sounded proud. He did not raise his voice, but he gave each sentence the weight of a plunge. "Now they are few. When the Great God's work is done, there will be only one."

While the Archpriest rubbed his chest, Elgart's impulse to sleep faded. In its place, a terrible weakness swept through him. Suddenly, his strength was gone. He needed to lie down. The sensation was so intense that he could hardly hold himself upright on his stool.

More sorcery. Hells!

Soon! he told himself. *Soon.* One more answer, one confession, and he would throw his poniard. If he could do it, if it could be done, he would hurl his blade into Makh's throat.

"You are here for the library," he panted. "You are here because Belleger is on your way to the Last Repository."

Archpriest Makh shrugged. "What of it?" One heavy hand clutched loosely at his chest. The movement resembled an old habit, nothing more. "Why would you object? The library is a feeding ground for degenerate gods, the corrupt get of Folly and Pride. Do you imagine that the men and women there worship knowledge? Perhaps they do. I would say, rather, that they *lust* for it. Their desire is born of Pride. It is a lust of the mind. And at their extremes, the lusts of the mind cannot be distinguished from the lusts of the flesh. You know this. You have felt it. You have lived it."

At some other time, in a different place, Elgart would have challenged that assertion. It was not fair to Amandis and Flamora. What they taught was so much more than lust. But he could not summon the strength to defend them. He could barely manage to go on breathing.

It was time. *Throw*, you fool! Kill him *now*.

The hilt of his poniard seemed to be slipping through his fingers. He had already lost his argument with Makh's sorcery.

How could the Archpriest know what he, Elgart, had felt or lived?

"We teach the way of Truth and Faith," continued the Great God's representative. "We serve peace. If our work diminishes lesser gods, where is the harm? How are you, or King Bifalt, or Belleger and Amika damaged by the truth that knowledge is a mirage? It is a snare and a seduction. You *know* this. If you do not see it in yourself, you have seen it in your King. His preparations for a useless war rule you all, to no good purpose."

Briefly, Makh's tone hinted at sinkholes and swift water. "Give me an audience with him. I will show him the difference between Truth and Pride, between Faith and Folly."

Obedient to the priest's command, Elgart promised, "I will. An audience. Yes." He meant, The enemy is coming. His ships were sighted. He meant, I know the truth about you. But he could not move his hand. Somewhere in the distance, he heard his blade clatter on the floor. Lies were his only hope. "I need two days. Three at most. Then King Bifalt will send for you."

Archpriest Makh studied him for a long moment. Still holding his chest with one hand, Makh reached out with the other and rested it on

Elgart's head. Elgart tried to block the contact, strike the man's hand away, retrieve his blade, but his whole body refused to obey him. He tried to scream, but he had no voice. Makh needed no force at all to bend him forward until he collapsed, half sprawling, on the table.

Leaning over him, the Archpriest asked like a chuckling stream, "Did you come to me thinking I did not know who you are? You are Elgart, a veteran of the old wars, Prince Bifalt's companion in the Last Repository, and now King Bifalt's spy. I do not doubt you can arrange the audience I crave. But I doubt your sincerity, my son. There is no truth in you. King Bifalt will not send for me. He will send riflemen instead.

"Be at ease, my son." He did not exert pressure to control Elgart. The weight of his hand was enough. "I will learn everything you do not say. The means will be painful for you. They will be excruciating. And they will be prolonged. A man such as you are—a man who lies with every breath, and whose very life is falsehood—does not unclose his secrets lightly.

"But I am adept at what I do in the Great God's name. In the end, you will satisfy me. Afterward, you will be made whole. When you are at peace with yourself, you will become an eager servant of the Great God Rile."

Elgart wasted his last moment of consciousness on a failed effort to pull away. Then the weight of Makh's hand on his head increased, and he dropped like a stone into a deep well.

NINETEEN

A CRISIS IN BELLEGER'S FIST

Behind his chosen face, his expression of controlled severity, King Bifalt felt like screaming. His familiar sense of incurable frustration had been pushed into the background: a kind of terror had taken its place. He resembled a man who had discovered suddenly, without any warning at all, that he stood on quicksand. Until Queen Estie's return from Amika, he had not realized how much he depended on her; how much of his ability to face his future, and Belleger's, relied on her place at his side.

Now he was afraid for her—and afraid *of* her. He did not know what she might become. She had a slumbering talent for sorcery. That was bad enough. His abhorrence of theurgy and theurgists was as much a part of him as his need for air. If she followed the path of the library's Magisters, the path of arrogance and scorn, he would never be able to trust her again. Worse, he might learn to despise her.

It was certainly true that he had lost his faith in Magister Facile, who had transformed Estie in his sight by speaking of her nameless gift. With one stroke, Facile had made his wife a woman Bifalt could not trust; a woman as potentially dangerous as a Decimate.

But now— Oh, hells! Now the harsh shock of Estie's confession had been pushed into the background by another loss, a more obvious act of treachery.

Elgart had disappeared.

Elgart, the divided man: clever, cunning spy and staunch friend. Elgart, who had both opposed and supported Prince Bifalt in the last crisis of his struggle against the library's Magisters. Elgart, who had done more than even his King could have expected to preserve Belleger's fragile peace with Amika.

Elgart was missing.

An absence of one day would have been unremarkable. He was always poking the stick of his curiosity into one beehive or another. His pursuits often delayed his contact with King Bifalt for a day. Perhaps even for two. An absence of two days would have been unusual, but not a cause for alarm.

Elgart's bodyguard Howel did not wait that long. Early on the day after Queen Estie had questioned Prince Lome, Howel presented himself at the gates of Belleger's Fist and demanded to speak with King Bifalt immediately.

He was met by Prince Jaspid, who commanded the King's guards in the Fist. The Prince had other matters on his mind; but he knew a crisis when it shouted in his face. He escorted the spy without delay.

At the time, King Bifalt was in his private council chamber with Wheal, the Royal Surveyor. They were engaged in an elaborate discussion of the Open Hand's defensive possibilities. Bifalt wanted barricades that could be wheeled or dropped into place quickly at crucial points along the city's streets. Assuming that the library's enemy attacked the Hand directly, he hoped to prepare obstructions that would serve two purposes. First, they would redirect the invaders toward the original walls of the city, where the fortifications might be strong enough to hold for a while. Second, the barriers would give defenseless people time to flee along prepared streets, leaving the city as the enemy entered.

Unfortunately, the Open Hand as a whole had not been planned with such eventualities in mind. It had not been planned at all: it had simply built itself during the worst years of the old wars. King Bifalt's desires posed a daunting challenge for the Royal Surveyor.

Standing over a large map of the city—Wheal's proudest accomplishment—he and King Bifalt were deep in their study of obvious problems and conceivable solutions when the servant at the door announced Prince Jaspid and Howel.

Howel hurried into the room ahead of the Prince. To King Bifalt's way of thinking, no Bellegerin was out of place in the Fist. Nevertheless Howel's arrival came as a shock. His intensity seemed to set the air on fire.

Like most of Elgart's people, he was nondescript at first glance, as ordinary as he could be and still have a name. In almost any tavern, he would have been entirely unremarkable. His bland features, colorless hair and beard, hooded eyes, and indifferent garb practically repelled notice. Oh, he had a strong frame—but so did half of Belleger's remaining laborers. His hands looked like they belonged on the handles of a plow or the haft of an axe. If he carried a weapon, King Bifalt could not spot it.

Still, Howel's extremity demanded attention. A dangerous passion congested his visage: his hands swung like bludgeons. When Prince Jaspid started to apologize for their intrusion, the spy's bodyguard cut him off.

"Elgart, Majesty!" His tone could have been a snarl of rage or a gasp of distress. "He is taken!"

Wheal froze over his map. Prince Jaspid cast a quick glance at his brother, a promise of instant action. Already glaring, King Bifalt turned toward Howel.

Softly, as if he were blind to the man's plight, the King commanded, "Say that again, Howel."

"And Flax!" retorted Howel. "My partner. Invisible, she was, when she wanted to be. As sweet between the sheets as she was with her knife. Killed!"

For a moment, King Bifalt's breath caught in his throat. He seemed to hear a distant rumble like the sound of his world breaking. He had prepared himself for a long list of catastrophes. He was not ready for this one.

Clearing his throat with a cough, he said more sharply, "Start again, Howel. Take small steps. Help me understand how each leads to the next.

"How do you know Elgart is taken?"

As silent as drifting dust, the Royal Surveyor began rolling up his precious map. He was squeamish about bloodshed at the best of times. Now he had the look of a man who wanted to be anywhere except where he was.

Howel clenched his fists in his hair, tried to pull it out in clumps. "Because," he yelled, "Flax was killed!"

But then he seemed to feel the force of the King's concentration. A shudder ran through him. He dropped his hands as if they were too heavy to lift. "As you say, Majesty."

His gaze avoided King Bifalt's. In a gruff voice, he muttered, "He wanted that Archpriest. To question. Makh. He was always suspicious. We went to the Church. 'The Great God Rile.'" He snorted his scorn. "Flax said no. *I* said no. We needed more men. Was he suspicious? Then the Church might be dangerous. But he did what he wanted, always. Me, he sent away with a message. Flax, he left to watch.

"He went in. He did not come out."

Unable to contain himself, Prince Jaspid demanded, "What, *never*? Not at all? How long ago did he enter?"

King Bifalt held Howel's attention with a small gesture. Both men ignored the Prince.

"This is what I want," said Bifalt. "Small steps."

"What message did Elgart send?"

"Those women." Howel sounded bitter. "The shameless ones. Devotees, he calls them. Find one, he told me. Tell her what he did. Tell her he went into the Church. To face Makh. He might need help. She would know what to do.

"*She* would know? Flax and I would not? He insulted us, her and me. But he is Elgart. I delivered his message. Searching for that kind of woman took hours. Evening came. But I did what he told me. Then I went back."

Absentmindedly, hardly aware of himself, the King explained to Prince Jaspid, "A devotee of Flesh. Elgart knows them better than I do."

His eyes and his thoughts were fixed on Howel.

"I saw a man kill Flax," rasped the bodyguard. "I can not understand why she did not cut his throat. Quick with her knife, she was. But she stood there. *Stood* there. Let him break her neck.

"I was too late. Too far away. I could not save her. It was sudden. I could not reach her fast enough. I could not *shout* fast enough. My Flax—"

For a moment, his voice broke. Straining, he forced the pieces back together.

"Then he ran. When I reached her, she was dead."

Bifalt could not contain his consternation. "A moment, Howel," he insisted. "Give me a moment.

"Was that man a *priest?*"

Howel shook his head. "It was dark. Those women are hard to find. And Flax stayed in shadows. I did not see him well. A laborer, I thought. Bellegerin.

"Now I know him."

So there was a traitor in the Hand. At least one. A traitor who could identify Elgart's bodyguards.

"You *know* him?" demanded King Bifalt: a croak of surprise. "Who *is* he? *How* do you know him?"

Howel faced his King with a glare as fierce as Bifalt's. "He came back for me. I knew he would. Why would he kill her and not me? When we were both outside the Church? Unless it was because Elgart went in?" The bodyguard spat fury. "Now he is dead."

While King Bifalt stared, Howel added, "I have seen him often enough. Entering the Church. Leaving it. For the services. I do not know his name. But he was Bellegerin. *That* I know."

"*Howel.*" For an instant, Bifalt's self-control broke. He almost screamed. "You *killed* him?"

"He killed Flax." The man's retort was granite. "He tried to kill me. We stood guard for Elgart."

"Fool!" cried the King. He fought to master himself. "You should—" By increments, he tightened his grip on his emotions. Howel had more to tell him. He needed to hear it. "You should have questioned him. Was he alone? Does he have allies? Is this part of a larger conspiracy? Who *told* him to kill Elgart's guards?"

Jaspid's features were taut with concern. He moved closer as if he meant to intervene. But he did not speak.

For a moment, Howel's rage matched Bifalt's. Then he looked down. Hoarse with bitterness, he asked, "Why? He serves the Church. Makh sent him. Because Elgart went in. I had no time to waste on questions. Worse might happen while my attention was turned away.

"I did not raise the alarm. I waited for other killers. I waited for Elgart. I waited"—he snarled a curse—"for that devotee to send help. He *trusted* her."

King Bifalt took deep breaths to calm his breathing. One finger at a time, he unclenched his fists. Howel did not deserve his outrage. He understood the man's impulse to repay blood with blood. He could not tell himself that he would have acted differently. And he could not fault Howel's reasoning.

Serves the Church. That made sense. Any man who wanted Flax and her partner dead for personal reasons could have attacked them anywhere at any time. And Elgart had told King Bifalt that the priests seemed to exert a sorcery of persuasion. That might explain Flax's failure to defend herself. It might explain the man who murdered her.

Grimly, Bifalt set his shock and ire aside. He had too many questions. At that moment, Howel or no one could answer them.

Why had the devotees failed Elgart? He had good reason to trust them.

At the edge of his concentration, the King noticed Wheal moving softly toward the door. Over the spy's shoulder, King Bifalt commanded, "Summon General Klamath. And the Queen-Consort." Giving the Royal Surveyor permission to leave. "Tell them I need them at once."

Clenching his restraint, he gave Wheal a moment to escape. Then he faced Howel again.

"You did what you could. I could not have done more. When you were done with Flax's killer, you waited. What then?"

Like acid, Howel replied, "I wanted to break in. Find Elgart. But I was one man. There are too many priests. And Elgart said wait. Wait for that woman. I waited.

"She did not come. For a long time, she did not. Then she did. Elgart is taken, she said. Alive, she said. You will not find him. Warn the King."

Abruptly, the man shrugged like a spasm. "She left. I came to you."

Prince Jaspid stood without moving. Nevertheless he conveyed the impression that he was trying to break the ropes of decorum or uncertainty that kept him still.

King Bifalt did not hesitate. "That woman," he ordered his brother curtly. "The devotee. *Any* devotee, Flesh or Spirit. Any of them may know where Elgart has been taken.

"*Find* a devotee, Brother. If you can, find the one who spoke to Howel. Bring her to me. Bring *any* of them, if you cannot find her. I want an answer."

At once, the Prince became a lit fuse. He paused only long enough to promise, "As you say, Majesty." Then he was gone, closing the door swiftly behind him.

For a while afterward, King Bifalt said nothing. Chewing the inside of his cheek, he held Howel with his glare. The two men were alone. But the King was always alone. Even with those few people he trusted, he did not reveal his heart. Yet he felt maimed, helpless, as if some innocent-seeming man had suddenly cut off one of his, King Bifalt's, hands. He did not know how to take hold of this crisis. He did not know how to bear it.

He tried to imagine a search for Elgart. He wanted a confrontation with the priests. He considered fire. But violence would not retrieve Elgart. He had nothing useful in his mind.

Still, he did not refuse the challenge. He had spent his life carrying burdens he had not chosen and did not understand. When he tasted blood in his mouth, he took his first step.

Howel represented the challenge. He was the only witness. And he was the only choice King Bifalt had.

"You have been badly hurt. I know that. But you must put it aside." He spoke harshly to compel Howel's attention. "I need you. Elgart is gone. Until we recover him, someone must take his place. I must know what happens in Belleger.

"That task is yours."

Howel's dismay was immediate. His features seemed to split open. "Majesty, no! I cannot. He had too many interests, too many. And too many men and women served him. Everywhere, they are. I hardly know half of them. I cannot *begin*—"

"You *can*," snapped the King. "There is no one better. You know what was done. You recognized Flax's killer. And you went everywhere with Elgart. You saw the people he met. You heard what they said. No one else in his service can take your place.

"It is a cruel burden to give you. I trust you to carry it. I do not expect you to become a second Elgart. But I have no one else. And you have cause to accept the task. If Flax's murder is not reason enough, think of Elgart's life. Think of Belleger's safety. Do what you must. Do it as well as you can. Your best efforts will content me."

Clearly, Howel's first impulse was to refuse. He crossed his arms on his chest, glowering like a workman unjustly reprimanded. His jaws chewed obscenities that were as familiar as breathing to King Bifalt. But then pain filled his eyes. In them, the King could almost see his memories of Flax. A moment later, his face flushed a darker, bloodier hue.

"As you say, Majesty," he rasped. "I know who to watch. I will assemble help. By sunset, I will know how to put my hands on every priest who is out in the city. I will send them to the Church."

King Bifalt allowed himself a small sigh, a slight slump. "Then accept my thanks, Howel. While you watch, I will decide my reply to this killer. And to the Church."

With a bow, he dismissed Elgart's bodyguard.

When Klamath came, the King might command a full assault on the Church of the Great God Rile. Certainly, he wanted to attack it. He wanted to lead the charge himself, with his rifle shouting in his hands. He could burn the building to ash. Elgart was more than his friend, more than his spy, more than his cleverest adviser. By turning Prince Bifalt away from his native rage during the crisis in the Last Repository, Elgart had done his part to make the alliance with Amika possible.

King Bifalt waited for General Klamath because he did not trust himself when he was this angry. But he also waited for Queen Estie.

She was Amikan. Despite the dismay that squirmed in his guts when he thought of her, he knew her mind was more complex than his. She could imagine possibilities that would never occur to him.

S he arrived while he was still pacing from wall to wall of his council chamber, batting his head against the conundrum of finding Elgart or tracking his captors without resorting to outright slaughter.

Clearly, his summons had been delivered with a sense of urgency. When had he ever said that he *needed* her? She had reason to think something dire had happened.

As soon as she entered, she dropped into a formal curtsy: another sign that she expected news of some calamity. In a low voice, but firmly, almost fearlessly, she greeted him. "My lord King. You asked for me?"

Grimacing, he suppressed a snarl. "Save your courtesies, my lady," he retorted. "I do not have time for them. I must act. I must act quickly. But I do not know what to do."

She rose with easy grace. In her eyes, he saw apprehension mixed with a desire to be of use. "Tell me, my lord." Her tone did not waver. "What has occurred?"

As calmly as he could, he complied.

His answer startled her: that was obvious. At first, she betrayed a hint of fright. But it was quickly replaced by the strength or resolve that she had brought back from her confrontation with her father and the Nuuri. Her first words took him by surprise. "Then it is well, my lord, that you did not risk meeting with the Archpriest." Her brief smile tugged at his heart. "What do you think of doing?"

Her manner slipped past his defenses. With more openness than he intended to show, he growled, "I want to burn that Church out of existence."

Again, she surprised him. "Why do you hesitate?"

Without thinking, he said, "I have too many reasons. Elgart may still be inside. Those priests may be blameless. Belleger does not need a King who answers every threat with bloodshed."

She nodded. "If Elgart still lives, an attack on the Church may ensure his death.

"Do you want my counsel, my lord?"

Howel had infected him. He felt like tearing his hair. "I do."

"Then you will have it." Opening her hands, she spread her arms as if she would have welcomed his embrace. Welcomed it, but did not expect it. "These are my first thoughts.

"The Church must be searched. General Klamath's men can do that for you. He will ensure that they remain mindful of Elgart's peril. If they proceed with courtesy and restraint, the priests will not oppose them. They can question every priest until they are sure they have heard the truth."

King Bifalt swallowed a curse. "Those priests have sorcery. They are not sorcerers themselves, but they call on power from some other source. Elgart has felt it. This was not his first encounter with what they can do. While they preach peace, they are able to sway or blind minds."

"Then send a sorcerer with them," replied the Queen. "Any Magister can sense the threat of theurgy. The General's men will be warned if the priests mislead them."

Bifalt nodded. He knew the right Magister for the task, Elgart's friend Pillion. If the situation inside the Church was bad enough, Pillion could bring down the whole building.

"But first, my lord—" began Estie. Then she hesitated.

He stared at her. He had no time for unexplained scruples. Howel had been told that Elgart was still alive. King Bifalt did not know how long that would remain true.

"'But first'?" he prompted.

The abrupt intensity of her gaze made him think of her father. King Smegin must have seen that expression when she faced him. It must have alarmed him despite his power and arrogance. If she could be calm, she could also go to unprecedented extremes.

An instant later, however, she softened. As if she had never doubted herself, she suggested, "But first, my lord, it might be wise to summon Prince Lome."

That suggestion seemed to catch him with his balance on the wrong foot. His mouth shaped his brother's name, but his voice failed him.

Without a tremor, she explained, "He has a secret, or thinks he does. He claims he will reveal it when you are ready to believe him. Perhaps he knows nothing. Perhaps he imagines that his offer is a form of cunning. Or perhaps you are ready now." She paused for a few heartbeats, then finished, "Elgart reported that the Prince spent some or much of his time in the Beleaguered Eagle conversing with a priest."

Oh, hells! She was right. The reminder jolted his thoughts, jarring them into a semblance of clarity. Hells and sorcery! Before he did anything else, he had to talk to Lome. His brother's secret—if Lome had one—might help him understand the nature of Elgart's peril. And Belleger's.

Forgetting restraint, he yelled for the servant outside his door. As soon as the man opened the door, King Bifalt ordered him to find Prince Lome. "Tell Prince Jaspid's men." Lome had the freedom of the Fist. Hells, he had the freedom of the Hand. Elgart should have assigned people to follow him, but the King did not know who they were. However, Jaspid's guardsmen would almost certainly have some idea where to look. "I need Prince Lome *now*."

As if he were fleeing, the servant hurried to obey.

To himself, the King went on cursing. The last thing he needed at this moment—the *last* thing—was to feel gratitude toward Amika's Queen. She was giving him good advice. She had a better mind than he did. But she also had a gift for sorcery. When it came to life in her, she would be a Magister. At that moment, she would cease to be his wife. She might even cease to be his ally. She would become a woman he did not know. She might decide that her first loyalty belonged to the Last Repository.

The cost of gratitude was too high.

By good fortune, Prince Lome was in his rooms, sleeping off the previous night's excesses. The Fist's guards hurried him into his clothes and hauled him before his brother the King without explanation or ceremony. Perhaps, like Queen Estie herself, they had never heard King Bifalt summon anyone with the word *need*.

Lome arrived blurred with sleep and gasping with alarm. As he usually did, he tried to put an uncaring face on his encounters with his brother. But the suddenness and indignity of King Bifalt's demand for his presence clearly frightened him.

"Well, Brother," he panted, breathing too hard to sneer. "Have you exhausted your compassion for lesser men? Have you decided to punish what you call my treason?"

Brief as it was, the wait before Lome appeared gave King Bifalt time to recover his composure, his command of his emotions. As well as he could, he matched Estie's air of calm.

"Thank you for coming, Lome. For you, nothing has changed. My lady Queen urged me to give you your freedom. I will not refuse her. You cannot expect me to forget what you have done. Nevertheless I have put it behind me.

"But *I* have changed. You spoke of a secret. I am ready to hear it now."

While the Prince struggled to master his breathing, a flush of relief reddened his cheeks: relief mingled with chagrin. He ignored the King's last statement. With as much gravity as he could manage, he bowed unsteadily to Queen Estie.

"My lady," he began. "I suppose I must be grateful." By increments, a familiar petulance crept into his tone. "But you give mixed gifts. You grant my life after you have thwarted its purpose.

"Your death would have been a sore loss. I feel that." He slapped at his heart with one hand. "Still, it would have foiled your husband's madness. It would have ended this alliance, these endless, useless preparations.

"No doubt, King Smegin would have honored my contribution with a quick death. To hide my share in his plots, he would have discarded me in an unmarked grave. But I would have died with one great accomplishment to my name. Future generations would have remembered me with more kindness.

"I have a life now, but it is empty."

King Bifalt listened with an expression of long-suffering patience. Only the patience was feigned. Lome spoke to Estie, but his self-justification was aimed at Bifalt. Inwardly, the King fumed with shame for his brother.

With only a feather's touch of irritation, he said, "You heard me, Lome. Time is short. We must act quickly. I am ready for your secret."

Still sluggish after a night of drinking, the Prince showed his brother a twisted smile. "'We,' Brother? A strange word to use. You do not mean you and me. You have never included me in your plans. You *say* you are ready. Are you confident of me now, after so many years? I will not waste what I know if you are not prepared to believe me."

King Bifalt let his voice sharpen. "And *I* will not waste my belief when I do not know what you will say. Do you hope to be remembered kindly? You have a chance now. You may not find another.

"Tell me what your secret concerns."

Lome hesitated. He peered at Bifalt, then turned a look of pleading on Estie while he fought a complex contest with himself: a battle between his resentment of his whole life, his desire to humble the King in some fashion, and his yearning for stature in the affairs of the realm. Abruptly, he walked away, went to one of the windows. Bracing his hands on the sill, he looked down at the battlements and the bailey as if he hoped to resolve his conflict by studying a view King Bifalt saw every day. The window was open: the King liked fresh air. If Prince Lome leaned out far enough, he could end his frustrations by falling.

Queen Estie glanced at her husband. Unexpectedly tense, she extended her hand like a warning toward the Prince.

King Bifalt shook his head. He could believe almost anything about his brother except that Lome would end his own life.

Keeping his back to the room—to Belleger's King and Amika's Queen—Prince Lome said sullenly, "It concerns the Church."

That declaration lit a flare in the King's chest. At once, he replied, "Then I am sure." He could not afford uncertainty. There was too much at stake. "I will value the truth."

"The truth?" snorted Prince Lome. He did not look away from the Fist's fortifications. "The priests want peace, Brother. *That* is the truth.

"For them, the road to true peace is faith in the Great God Rile. For that, you scorn them. But I tell you that their desire for peace is *sincere*. If you had agreed to meet with the Archpriest, he would have persuaded you. Above all things, the priests want peace for Belleger and Amika. Peace for the world. With every word and deed, they serve that desire."

After a moment, he added in a smaller, more tormented voice, "But they seek peace by more than one path."

As if to keep her husband silent, Queen Estie put her hand on his arm. Bifalt opened his mouth to prod his brother, then closed it again. He had no intention of telling Lome that he knew how Makh would "persuade" him. Chewing his cheek, he waited.

Like a sigh, Prince Lome explained, "They do not say what it is, but I hear it in them. Father Knout is more transparent than he supposes. He talks with me, and pays for what I drink, and gives me his sympathy, because he wants to know—because the Church wants to know—where you hide your stores of bullets."

The *bullets*? King Bifalt restrained a curse. A moment of panic clenched his heart. He was right to be suspicious of the Church. He had been right all along. Yet he was also appalled. He had not expected that kind of treachery.

He had made Elgart's spies responsible for guarding his secret storerooms. Now Elgart was gone. And Bifalt had already sent Howel away. He could not recall Elgart's bodyguard to give the man new orders.

"If they knew that," continued Prince Lome, "they could disarm you. *Then* we would have peace. Even if your imagined enemy chanced to appear, you could not oppose him. Your elaborate charade of preparation would evaporate like mist. There would be no more war."

With a glance at Estie, King Bifalt saw that she shared his alarm; that she understood the danger. But he had no time to ask for her advice now.

Hoarsely, he demanded of his brother, "What did you tell that priest?"

Slowly, Prince Lome turned from the window. A wracked grimace knotted his features. His eyes showed the pain of his wasted life. They flung it at Bifalt like an accusation.

"Nothing. What could I say? I do not *know* where the bullets are stored. I am not trusted enough to know."

The nakedness of Lome's distress convinced the King. Now he was sure that his brother had not betrayed him twice. Prince Lome had not used whatever cunning he possessed to learn the secret of those stores.

And his pain—

Until that moment, King Bifalt had never looked at his own disgust from his brother's side. He was accustomed to Lome's petulance and scorn, Lome's resentments. But he had never considered that he might deserve Lome's reproach.

With a gesture, he waved Queen Estie to the door. "Send another summons," he told her. "I *need* the General."

Clearly, she understood what was at stake. She complied without hesitation.

While she crossed the room, he approached his brother. When he put his hands on the younger man's shoulders, his own gentleness surprised him.

Quietly, he said, "You know why you are not trusted, Brother. But your path has not been an easy one. I have treated you badly. When I can, I will share my plans with you. When you speak, I will listen.

"If you wish it, you will remain with us until General Klamath comes. You will hear what we decide about the Church and the priests. You will give us your thoughts. Then you will take a place in my council."

In response, Prince Lome seemed to compress himself, gathering his strength. Then he screamed like a trapped beast in King Bifalt's face: a cry of such fury and anguish that it had no words.

While his howl held the chamber, he fled past Queen Estie and rushed away.

For a long moment, the King did not move. Time passed while he wondered why he had not knocked Lome to the floor. Would a blow from his fist have eased his brother's distress? Would Lome have called it a victory if he had broken through King Bifalt's self-possession? Would the Prince think that the King had finally treated him as an equal—as a *man*—instead of a wastrel child?

Trying to comfort Lome, had Bifalt succeeded only at pouring acid on his brother's wounds?

Then Queen Estie said, "You took a long step, my lord." Her voice trembled, but she did not hold back. "It was too long for him, or you took it too late. But you could not have done better. There was nothing better to be done."

King Bifalt stared at her as if a heavy punch had left him numb. But she held his gaze without flinching. More steadily, she added, "He chose his own path, my lord. He chose it long before you could have offered him another."

The King took a heavy breath; released it. It shuddered in and out of his lungs, but he repeated it until his muscles loosened and he could inhale freely. Trying to get the sound of Lome's cry out of his ears, he shook his head. He was never going to forget it. But he had more urgent concerns.

"As you say, my lady," he muttered finally. "He chose his own path."

"If General Klamath does not come soon, we will go to him."

He did not know how to interpret her smile, or the slight moisture in her eyes, or the way her hands twisted against each other as if they yearned to reach out. But for the first time since her return from Amika, he was glad of her company.

He was the King of Belleger, the *King*, but now there was nothing he could do for his people. He had to wait.

General Klamath was slow to arrive. King Bifalt's summons found him outside the city on the far edge of the training-fields, beyond the barracks, the hospital and kitchens, the huge stables with their many paddocks. He had a long way to come.

When he finally joined King Bifalt and Queen Estie, however, he did not waste time dealing with his own dismay at what he was told. He had spent long years as a soldier, and had learned how to set himself aside. But he had questions to ask, answers to understand.

"You want a raid of some kind on the Church, Majesty," he said after he heard what King Bifalt had to say. "A search for Elgart. Interrogations of the priests. What do you hope to gain? Elgart is my friend as well. I want to find him. Like you, I want to strike hard. But a devotee told Howel he is gone. She said we would not find him. And Howel is a good man. He would not mistake her words. Or imagine them.

"Do you trust the devotees, Majesty?"

"Yes," said the Queen before King Bifalt could reply.

Glowering, the King replied, "I have only met one devotee of Flesh, and that was long ago. But Elgart knows them well. He trusts them. And a devotee of Spirit did more than any Magister to aid me in the Last Repository. A devotee of Spirit brought Queen Estie back to us. If Elgart were here, I would say I trust them as much as he does."

"Then, Majesty," said Klamath like a man thinking aloud, "he is not in the Church. What do we gain by showing those priests we are aware of their treachery?" A moment later, he added, "Howel did not say the man who killed Flax was a priest."

With an edge in her voice, Estie countered, "We have seen killers disguised as Bellegerins before."

King Bifalt ignored her. "I want that Archpriest, General. I want Makh."

He meant, I want him in a cell. Where he will do no more harm.

He was thinking of his ammunition stores.

Klamath nodded. "I understand. If you approve, Majesty, I will take a small company and tell the priests I have been ordered to escort their Archpriest here. I will say you wish to consult with him about their conduct in the Open Hand. If they resist, I will insist." He grinned sourly. "A few rifles are often persuasive."

While he considered that suggestion, Bifalt struggled with a new rush of fury and frustration. More waiting. More helplessness. As if he were still searching for the library. He wanted to attack the Church. He wanted to do it *himself*. Prince Bifalt would not have hesitated. But he was Belleger's King now. He could not leave Belleger's Fist. Howel might come back. Prince Jaspid might. The King had to let other people do his fighting for him. And he had to trust their decisions.

Hoarse with ire, he commanded Klamath, "Take Magister Pillion with you." He was in no mood to rely on Magister Facile, even if her

Decimate could counter indirect theurgy. "He is Elgart's friend. He will protect you. One or more of those priests can wield a form of sorcery that clouds minds. Magister Pillion can warn you if he senses any threat."

"As you say, Majesty," replied General Klamath. He knew Pillion, of course. The army's duties included guarding Belleger's Magisters if the sorcerers were ever in danger.

Then he added, "At the same time, my First Captain will assemble our best marksmen. He will place them where they can watch over our hidden bullets while remaining hidden themselves."

"Tell them to be careful, General," put in Queen Estie quickly. "They must be sure of what they do. If they see threats where there are none, they will kill harmless men or women."

Klamath gave her a nod. "As you say, Majesty. You do not know First Captain Matt. His judgment is better than mine. He will ensure that his riflemen are cautious."

Hurrying now, King Bifalt said, "One thing more, General. Send riders to search the countryside around the Open Hand. I do not expect them to find Elgart's captors, but I will hope as long as I can."

Again, Klamath said, "As you say, Majesty."

After that, he did not wait to be dismissed. Time was against Elgart. The General left the council room like a man who would have preferred to run.

When General Klamath was gone, King Bifalt wanted to send Queen Estie away. At the same time, he felt strangely reluctant to let her go. Of course, he had to wait to hear from Howel. More than that, however, he was waiting for Prince Jaspid. The Prince would bring one of the devotees: Bifalt trusted his brother to use force if necessary. But when the King had one of those eerie women in front of him, he would have to question her, get the truth from her—and he did not know how. She would be a most holy devotee of Flesh. No devotee of Spirit would allow Jaspid to compel her. And the devotees of Flesh were a mystery to him.

When he forced himself to be honest, he confessed that he kept Estie with him because he wanted her help.

But still, he had to wait. To *wait*. Even in his search for the Last Repository, he had not been reduced to this extreme of passivity. He had been able to plod along—or to fight—or to argue. The Magisters of the library had not forced him to remain in one place, helpless, while his fate was decided elsewhere by people or forces he could not imagine.

Eventually, he found himself hoping that Queen Estie would say something.

Too tense to sit and stare at the wall—or at him—she walked around and around the chamber, passing the windows, moving along the wall behind the desk, circling beyond the seats in the middle of the room. At once fascinated and appalled by what she had become, or by what she would become when her talent was roused, he watched her whenever he could see her without turning his head. Her steps were too smooth to seem anxious, but her pacing betrayed her. The play of emotions on her face hinted at an argument with herself. She was alarmed, he could see that. Alarmed and sad. But she was also strong enough to act on what she decided, when she made up her mind.

Abruptly, she chose a chair in front of him. With a flourish of her skirts, she sat. While she adjusted their hems, she asked in her least challenging tone, "My lord, why did they do it? What do they want with Elgart?"

He stood the way he had been standing for hours, like a soldier on duty. He thought he knew the answer, but he did not say so. He wanted to see where her inner debate was headed.

"Why ask me? I am not a priest."

For a moment, she smiled at a quirky angle. "Are you not?" She seemed to be teasing him. "You underestimate yourself. You do not preach belief, but you inspire it. For every man or woman who considers the coming war a mirage, there are five hundred who trust you with their lives."

Then she shook her head to change her mood. "But I cannot ask you to see yourself as I do. Naturally, you do not know what their Great

God requires of his priests. Yet you can guess. Why do you imagine they took Elgart?"

King Bifalt snorted. "He provoked them. Deliberately, no doubt. That is what he does when other tactics fail."

"But *how*?" she protested. "What could he do to provoke men who preach peace? How could he make them see him as a threat?"

Then she caught herself. He saw a rush of dismay in her eyes, in the flush that tinged her cheeks. "Do you suppose they know who he *is*?"

"I do." The King scowled past her to mask his own distress. "Why else would they risk taking him? That single act has exposed them. Unless they are fools, they know that their time in Belleger is done. They *must* know who he is. They must believe they have accomplished their purpose here—or they can accomplish it through him."

Elgart was one of the few people who knew where the ammunition stores were hidden. Even the army's best marksmen could not protect those crates from fire arrows. Or from grenades.

"But *how*?" insisted Estie. "How could any priest know who he is? How could they know what he does to serve you?"

Like a growl, King Bifalt answered, "Lome may have mentioned him. He spoke with that Father Knout any number of times. They drank together. Lome may have consumed enough ale or wine or grot to loosen the tongue of an ox." He shrugged. "In any event, Elgart is easily recognized, once he has been described."

"Oh, gods," breathed Amika's Queen. She sounded shaken. "Oh, gods." A moment later, she asked, "Will he tell them?"

The King ground his teeth. "He will tell them or die." Then he remembered Elgart's time in the Last Repository, the time Elgart had spent studying with Amandis and Flamora. He remembered how often Elgart had surprised him. "Or he will trick them. Or they may not realize he is armed."

The knife in Elgart's sleeve would be easy to find. The garrote concealed around his waist might escape notice.

Bifalt's reply silenced her. The flush on her cheeks faded to pallor. Darkness seemed to fill her eyes. Her breathing quickened; slowed; quickened again.

Without warning, she rose to her feet. She did not look at him. "If you will not consult with Magister Facile, my lord, I will. And if she has nothing to offer, I will attend to the needs of my realm. Chancellor Sikthorn is diligent. Some of his messages must be answered."

King Bifalt forced himself into a brusque bow. She returned a brief curtsy, then left him.

He did not realize until after she was gone that the decision she had been wrestling with was not whether she should ask her questions. It was what she should do when he answered them.

After that, King Bifalt waited. He waited. His fury and frustration were an incoming tide, receding only to gather again and rise higher. Like Queen Estie earlier, he paced his council chamber as if he were measuring the confines of a prison. In a perfect world, he would have wrested what he wanted to know with his own hands from anyone who stood in his way. In *this* world, he felt that he was going mad.

Jaspid did not return.

Toward midafternoon, General Klamath came to report on his encounter with the Church and its priests.

"They did not protest, Majesty. They seemed bewildered." Klamath sounded bewildered himself. "They said their Archpriest was not there. They insisted he was not. Then they encouraged us to search. Majesty, they *helped* us search. With them, my men and I explored every room and closet in the Church. We tested every floor, every wall, every ceiling, looking for places to hide. We did not find Makh. We saw no sign that Elgart had been there.

"Again and again, the priests clutched at their chests. When I asked, they showed me that they all wore gold crosses on leather thongs under their cassocks. I did not have to insist, Majesty. They were eager to demonstrate that they were harmless.

"Magister Pillion assured me the priests were not sorcerers. There was no theurgy in the Church. The crosses might be instruments of power. He thought they were not. He touched one and felt nothing."

King Bifalt heard all this with a feral glower. Using both hands, he tried to rub his expression into its normal controlled severity. As soon as he stopped, his features twisted again.

When Klamath was done, Bifalt said like a man suppressing a wild laugh or a howl, "So, General. Makh has taken Elgart away. Or both Makh and Elgart have been taken. By someone with no fear of sorcery. Someone capable of overcoming two unwilling men and removing them from the Church in complete secrecy. Someone—" He faltered on the edge of a crisis that resembled hysteria. Then he pulled himself back. "Someone known to the devotees of Flesh.

"Someone those women do not oppose."

"But they wanted you to know," offered the General cautiously. "They may have meant to reassure you."

Elgart is taken. Alive. Warn the King.

"*Reassure* me?" barked King Bifalt like a cry. "A devotee of Flesh told Howel to *warn* me!"

You will not find him.

General Klamath had nothing to say. There was nothing to be said.

After a long silence, King Bifalt mastered himself. "I *must* question those women," he rasped. "If Prince Jaspid cannot find at least one, perhaps your men can. Send as many as you need." A wasted effort. The devotees could baffle discovery anywhere by the simple ploy of changing their garments. Nevertheless the King insisted. "Search the Open Hand." Then he added unnecessarily, "And *protect* our ammunition."

"As you say, Majesty." Hurrying, Klamath went back to his duties.

Alone again, King Bifalt felt like beating his head against a wall. He wanted to scream. He had the impression that the truth was worse than he could imagine. Worse than Elgart's abduction and the Archpriest's disappearance. Worse than Lome's betrayal: worse than priests hunting for hidden bullets and gunpowder. Worse than black ships scouting the bay. Worse than hearing that Estie might eventually become a Magister.

Jaspid should have returned hours ago.

King Bifalt went on waiting. For a while, he stood at one of the open windows and shouted curses at the uncaring sky. Later, he cursed only himself, and resumed pacing. With every step, he promised himself that he would become the man he should be after a hundred more: the Bifalt who stood to meet every challenge. But he might need a thousand. Or ten thousand. He was only the King of Belleger, trapped in his role. What else could he do, except wait? What else could he be, except helpless? Thinking otherwise was another wasted effort, like sending riflemen to search the Hand. Like his promise to humble the library's Magisters.

He continued waiting. Pacing. Cursing.

Eventually, the world outside his windows darkened. Night spread its cloak over the Open Hand, hiding its own secrets. And still hours passed before a guard burst into the room.

King Bifalt saw at a glance that the man had run all the way up from the bailey.

"Majesty!" the guard panted. "Prince Jaspid is found." He snatched a breath. "Beaten close to death." Another breath. "He is being carried. The army's hospital."

Jaspid—

A part of King Bifalt's mind went blank, as empty of thoughts and words as a wiped slate. Another part did what he had to do.

He was already leaving his chamber when he demanded, "My horse?"

"Ready, Majesty," gasped the guard clattering down the stairs behind him. "Waiting. And your men."

Your men meant Jeck and Malder, Spliner and Boy: his bodyguards. On a night like this, anything could happen. Beaten close to death. The King might need protection in his own realm.

He took the stairs two at a time, three; ran along the corridors, through the halls. From the doors of the keep, he crossed the bailey and sprang for his mount. With his escort around him, he pounded past the gates and away at a dread-filled gallop.

At many times in the past, he had enjoyed this ride through the Hand. He liked seeing the improvements in the lives and homes of his people. And he took pride in keeping a mental list of improvements that still needed to be made. He could have done the same now despite the darkness. Many of the homes were lit. The inns and alehouses, and a few of the merchantries, were open, shedding light into the streets. But he noticed nothing except the distance. The encampment of the army was too far away.

Beaten close— Jaspid should have been taken to the nearest hospital.

No. The army's resources were the best in Belleger. Its stitchers and bonesetters had the most experience.

It was still too far away. Only the blankness in part of King Bifalt's mind kept him sane.

He arrived in a rush that would have trampled anyone in his way. Fortunately, he was expected. When he threw himself from the saddle, he found two physicians and their aides waiting for him.

Clusters of riflemen were there as well, Bellegerin and Amikan. Prince Jaspid was loved by his own people. Even the most recalcitrant Amikans respected him. But First Captain Matt stood among them, keeping them well back. The King's bodyguards joined the soldiers.

"Majesty—" began one of the physicians, a woman.

King Bifalt pushed past her; strode into the hospital.

The building was a solid structure the size of a prosperous cattleman's barn. Heavy timbers supported the lofts. Rooms for scribes and storage, and quarters for the physicians and aides on duty, lined the walls; but the space between them was large enough to hold forty cots without crowding. On this night, only four of the cots were occupied. In three of them, men with bandages on their heads or splints on their arms were sitting up, watching the unexpected frenzy of activity. Prince Jaspid lay on the fourth.

Half a dozen lamps had been lit around him, covering him with light.

King Bifalt remembered now that Jaspid had not been wearing his helm or carrying his rifle when he brought in Howel early this morning; an eternity ago. The Prince must have neglected to take them in his haste to obey his brother. Why would he need them? In the Open Hand? In daylight? But his saber and dagger in their sheaths leaned beside his breastplate against a post near the head of his bed.

His breastplate had been battered useless, as if it had been pounded by cudgels.

The physicians or their aides had cut away his clothing so that they could assess his wounds. He lay naked in the light, covered by a sheet only from the waist down.

There were no red stains on the sheet. The rest of him was a bludgeoned mess, swollen and livid everywhere, seeping blood where he had been hit hard enough to tear the skin. King Bifalt had seen enough wounds to recognize some of Jaspid's.

"A broken arm, Majesty," said the woman. "The left." He probably knew her name. He did not try to remember it. "A dislocated elbow. The right. Broken ribs. Two breaks in the jaw. The eye may heal." It was hidden under a bruise the size of Bifalt's fist. "It may not. We will not know if it can still see until the swelling shrinks."

King Bifalt imagined a gang of thugs. At least ten men. Or twenty. Twenty was more likely.

"But the worst injuries," said the woman as if she were callous, "are inside. A rib or two have pierced the lung. The chest fills with blood. It suffocates him."

The King watched his brother's struggle to breathe. He could hardly breathe himself.

"We must cut into him. His other bones can wait. We know how to tend them. But those ribs— We must cut him open to find them. Remove them from the lung. Stanch the bleeding. Help him inhale.

"Another man might die. He is too stubborn to let go."

The pure fool had been beaten until he could not defend himself. Until he could only see out of one eye. Until he could barely draw breath. But he had refused to admit defeat. He had gone on fighting until all of his choices had been taken from him.

The blank part of King Bifalt's mind thought nothing, felt nothing. The other part of him did what he had to do.

Kneeling beside the cot, he touched his brother's cheek gently. "Jaspid," he murmured, "Brother," until Jaspid's good eye looked at him. Then he asked like a demand, "Who did this?"

Jaspid could not move his jaw. His lips were torn and bleeding. Somehow, he breathed like a sigh, "Lylin." A dying fall of air. "Refused us. Refused you."

Those words were claws. They shredded Bifalt's blankness. His heart felt like his brother's body, intolerably hurt.

"Jaspid," he protested. "Brother. What possessed you? She is a devotee of Spirit."

He had the terrible impression that Jaspid was trying to smile. "How else can I learn?"

Then the Prince gagged. His eye closed. Blood burst from his mouth. His whole body twisted, fighting for air.

When the physician thrust King Bifalt out of her way, he did not resist. There was nothing he knew how to do that might help her. He told himself his brother had lost consciousness. For all he knew, his brother was gone.

TWENTY

A DAY OF SQUALLS

When the physician had done what she could for Jaspid, King Bifalt sat with him for the rest of the night. After her efforts to relieve the pressure of blood cramping Jaspid's lungs, she had strapped much of his chest in tight bandages. The King feared that she had made a mistake. Those wrappings protected many of Jaspid's worst bruises and contusions, but they also constricted his breathing. Watching him strain for air was excruciating. Nevertheless Bifalt refused to leave. He was familiar with the sight of men in pain, men dying. If he went away, it would be too easy to imagine Jaspid gasping until he died.

Near dawn, however, the physician told King Bifalt to go. "He will outlive the day, Majesty." She sounded less callous now. She may have been exhausted. "You will see him breathing tonight. You may see him breathing more easily."

Urged by Malder and Jeck, who had ridden into hell with him long ago, Bifalt allowed himself to be taken back to Belleger's Fist.

But he did not sleep or rest. At sunset, he returned to the hospital over the objections of his bodyguards. Men like Land-Captain Erepos and General Klamath wisely kept silent.

When she saw King Bifalt, Jaspid's physician seemed to smile. "He will live, Majesty," she declared. "His healing prowess is a match for his skill in combat. If more of your soldiers had his hardiness, I would not be needed here."

Inside, Bifalt found his brother still unconscious, perhaps sleeping off the effects of some herbal potion. But Jaspid was able to inhale without struggling, and with only a faint rattle of blood in his lungs. Bifalt sat with him for an hour or two, hoping that he would awaken. Eventually, the King fell asleep on his stool.

When they roused him, he allowed his men to escort him back to the Fist. He did not resist when Spliner and Boy insisted on putting him to bed.

The third night, King Bifalt found the Prince awake. To some extent, Jaspid was alert. The swelling over his right eye had receded enough to reveal that the eye itself remained intact. Whether or not it could still see was another matter. The damaged ball was so black with blood that it looked blind.

"Brother," he whispered. He could not move his jaw. It had been splinted, then bound shut. But he had enough air now to make himself understood. "I must tell you."

Bifalt pulled a stool close to the head of the cot; seated himself. Stroking Jaspid's head with a feather's touch, he said hoarsely, "Tell me."

"Lylin," began the Prince. "She refused. She refused everything."

King Bifalt waited.

"She said"—longer sentences cost Jaspid an extra effort—"the devotees are gone. All of them. You will not find them. They will not return. Then she refused."

While Jaspid recovered his breathing, Bifalt prompted him: "Refused?"

Jaspid sighed a groan. "Refused to come with me. Refused to see you. Refused to explain. Refused to say Elgart's name." He panted for a moment. "Refused to be followed. We fought. I fought to make her see you. She fought to keep me from following." He paused for more air. "You see what happened."

She fought— But she had not used her daggers. If she had, he would be dead. And if he had drawn his own weapons, she would certainly have killed him.

"Brother." Now Jaspid sounded urgent. Despite his dislocated elbow, he managed to put his hand on Bifalt's knee. "Do not think ill of her. I forced her to hurt me. Every blow was a lesson. What I learned"—he gasped in pain or passion—"is worth a beating."

The pressure in the King's chest and throat threatened to choke him. "Promise me, Brother." He swallowed the anger that disguised his grief. "Promise you will not learn from her like this again."

"I will not." For a few heartbeats, Jaspid's whisper came easily. "I have learned not to fight her."

King Bifalt bowed his head so that his brother would not see how his face twisted.

For the next few days, the King visited Prince Jaspid every evening. During the rest of his waking hours, he slumped through his duties, giving them as much attention as he could while he waited for news.

As much as possible, he avoided Queen Estie by staying in his apartments. The thought of her was too much for him. He feared that seeing her would snap the last strands of his resolve. Nevertheless he forced himself to summon her once. The Queen of Amika had a right to know what he had learned from Prince Jaspid. She had put too much faith in Lylin.

To protect himself, he called her to meet with him in his public council room, along with most of his advisers, General Klamath, Land-Captain Erepos, Royal Surveyor Wheal, and Purse-Holder Grippe. Obviously, Jaspid could not attend. Crickin was far away. And the King excluded Magister Facile. He no longer trusted her.

In any case, Queen Estie would consult with the old sorceress afterward.

The meeting was brief. King Bifalt described Prince Jaspid's recovery. He repeated what Lylin had said to the Prince. He admitted that he did not know what had provoked the devotees of Flesh and Spirit to abandon or betray the Open Hand and—presumably—Belleger. Then he dismissed his council.

Even in so short a time, however, the Queen's demeanor was a sword-thrust he could not parry. She looked as radiant as ever, and more sure of herself. But she could not mask her quick shock when she first saw him. She hardly reacted to what he said. Instead, she seemed to study him as if he had become a man she no longer knew.

Defying her, he made an effort to lift his shoulders, hold up his head. But he could not sustain it. As soon as he returned to his apartments, he slumped again. In his condition, seeing her—and seeing her look at him that way—was a deeper wound than he knew how to treat.

He already had too many wounds.

The devotees were gone. Instead of saving Elgart—instead of rescuing him from the Archpriest—they had forsaken him altogether. They had turned their backs on him and the Open Hand and Belleger. King Bifalt did not expect to see them again.

If Makh knew who Elgart was, he also knew that Elgart could tell him where to find Belleger's stores of ammunition.

Any damage to those stores would be a crippling blow.

Since Elgart was lost to him, the King had to do what Elgart would have done to protect his realm. But that was not a challenge he could meet in person. He was too conspicuous. Every step he took outside the Fist declared his intentions. The nature of Elgart's work required King Bifalt to rely on other men, primarily Howel and General Klamath.

Once again, Bifalt's place in Belleger required him to wait.

Howel the King trusted to do what had been asked of him. The bodyguard's hunger to avenge Flax's death would goad him if King Bifalt's instructions did not; and Howel would never succeed if he did not first reestablish some or most of Elgart's network of informants and spies. The King would have wanted Flax's killer watched, not slain; but he accepted what Howel had done.

No one could take Elgart's place.

At first, the priests of the Great God were a more alarming concern. Prince Lome had suggested that they sought to destroy Belleger's supplies of bullets. The First Captain's marksmen might not be enough to protect those stores.

But while King Bifalt's attention had been focused on Prince Jaspid—then and afterward—General Klamath had continued his polite assault on the Church. Every day, he sent two of his most discerning men, both Amikan commanders, to question the priests in their home. *All* of them, sometimes separately, sometimes together, often for hours.

Klamath's reports reassured the King. Under the pressure of careful questioning, the priests had seemed more and more baffled, increasingly leaderless and lost. Men like Father Knout wilted. Even Father Skurn shrank into himself. If they were lying, they were the most skillful and consistent mummers the General's representatives had ever met. The priests still held services, but now they preached with less certainty, and their congregations dwindled.

"The Archpriest," concluded General Klamath, "took Elgart without sharing his intentions with his own people."

"Or," mused King Bifalt, "both men were taken."

But who could accomplish that feat? Without any witnesses? Without any commotion? Without leaving any hint of their passage through the Open Hand? Who, except the devotees of Spirit and Flesh?

After his own experiences in the Last Repository, and Queen Estie's in Amika, the King could hardly credit that the devotees would abduct both his most irreplaceable supporter and his worst immediate enemy. Certainly, he could not imagine *why* they would do such a thing.

After a moment, the General shrugged. "In either case, the priests can tell us nothing. I believe they can *do* nothing. We have been assured that they draw their sorcery from some other source. Their Archpriest must *be* their source. Why else are they so bewildered without him?"

King Bifalt had not considered that possibility. It fed new fuel to his dying alarm. If Makh were a sorcerer—and a sorcerer who could share his power with his priests—even women like the most holy devotees of Spirit and Flesh would be helpless against him.

For the sake of the devotees, if not for his own, Bifalt had to hope they were not involved. He had to believe that the Archpriest had taken Elgart. Presumably, to learn where Belleger's ammunition was stored.

As if he were choking, the King croaked, "Send more men. The marksmen protecting our bullets and gunpowder must also be protected."

If hidden archers contrived to loose fire arrows, no rifleman would be able to prevent some of those abandoned structures from becoming conflagrations in an instant.

Klamath smiled ruefully. "To my shame, Majesty, I did not consider that danger. But Matt did. We have men watching over our marksmen in all directions.

"He is an outstanding First Captain, Majesty. If you would listen to sense, you would make him General. I would happily serve as his First Captain."

King Bifalt knew that his old friend spoke only half in jest. But he was in no mood for it. Losing Elgart, suspicious of Magister Facile, and cut off from Queen Estie by her power in his heart, he needed to keep men like Klamath close.

He tried to smile; to acknowledge Klamath's value. Then he sent the General away.

During that time, Jaspid's healing was not the King's only source of relief. He also found comfort in the reports he received from Howel and Klamath's First Captain. Howel's tidings were brusque; often fragmentary. But he was working with Matt as well as with some of Elgart's people. The First Captain's information was more complete.

Aided by other spies and confidants, Howel learned the name of Flax's killer. That name led Howel to the man's wife and their small clutch of children. Abandoned without explanation, the woman talked freely and bitterly about her husband's passion for the Church—and about the five friends with whom he spent his nights instead of with his family as a man should. After she told Howel the names of those friends and where they lived, and the spy told Matt, the First Captain's men were able to take them with comparative ease.

The results when the killer's friends were questioned were both frustrating and reassuring. In effect, those men seemed as leaderless and confused as the priests of the Great God. They professed their devotion to the Church, but they could not explain why they had spent an uncounted number of nights together, wandering the streets of the Open Hand without any apparent—or conscious—purpose. No matter how hard they were pressed, they could not account for themselves.

Perhaps those men were somehow able to resist any form of questioning that stopped short of torture. Or perhaps they were as honestly baffled as they appeared. In either case, there were no attacks on Belleger's stores of bullets. The First Captain's snipers had nothing to do except watch.

King Bifalt spent a while grinding his teeth. Then he chose to believe that the Church's sorcery of "persuasion" had departed or disappeared with the Archpriest. It had lost its grip on the Great God's followers. After that, Bifalt was able to put the whole subject aside. In the few days remaining to him, he prepared himself and his advisers and the Open Hand for Set Ungabwey's arrival.

When Master Ungabwey's caravan reached the Open Hand, he could not enter the city. He had too many wagons, and some of them were too large. Three were the immense conveyances drawn by tusked and snorting illirim, wagons like platforms with their strange burdens tightly wrapped in canvas. They were too wide to navigate the Hand's twisting streets. They were certainly too tall to pass through the gates into the inner city's fortifications. Others, like the train's kitchen and refectory, or the warehouse on wheels that held both Master Ungabwey's supplies and his infirmary, were too long to round the corners.

In addition, there was no open space that could accommodate all of the vehicles: ten wagons like dormitories for the workmen, four that carried fresh oxen, three more laden with horses and fodder, three comfortable carriages for the mechanicians, stonemasons, and scouts who would not be needed until they reached the Realm's Edge front, a smaller one for Tchwee, the interpreter, and the caravan master's own elaborate domicile, where he lived with his daughters and—possibly—any advisers who happened to travel with him. The train could not have entered the Open Hand and made camp without demolishing buildings.

Accordingly, a site had been prepared just beyond the training-fields to the south and east of King Bifalt's city. The ground was cleared. Waste-pits and latrines were dug. Wagons loaded with barrels of water and ale, and with other provisions, were waiting. And First Captain

Matt spent part of every day working with the force of riflemen that would join the train to protect it. He had to arrange a system of signal relays those men could use to summon help. Master Ungabwey's efforts would be opposed. And if he succeeded at sealing one canyon, the next would be more fiercely defended. Eventually, he might require a small army to clear the way for the train's mechanicians and stonemasons, and its massive, irreplaceable catapults.

The messengers riding back and forth between the approaching caravan and Belleger's Fist brought King Bifalt only one surprise. Set Ungabwey needed more men. He had committed too many to the completion of Queen Estie's road. He did not have enough to open paths for his wagons through the canyons of the mountains.

That was a vexing challenge. The road, the fortification of the Bay of Lights, and the combined army of Belleger and Amika had already claimed every willing man, as well as a disturbing number of eager youths who were not yet men. But King Bifalt understood the necessity of the caravan's task. The library's survival depended on Master Ungabwey's success. Ultimately, so did Belleger's and Amika's. The King could not afford many of his own scruples. He put Land-Captain Erepos in charge of recruiting workers who could be persuaded, and of conscripting ones who could not. And when Erepos asked in the badgering tone he had formerly reserved for his arguments with Chancellor Postern, "If that is not enough, Majesty?" the King showed his teeth like a wolf.

"Then take the priests." The depths of King Bifalt's frustration and rage were in his voice. "All of them. Call on guards from the Fist if you need them. Assure those priests that their efforts will serve the cause of peace."

He found no comfort in the fact that none of the priests appeared to know where their Archpriest and Elgart had gone. Or why. When Makh had taken Elgart, he had declared the true loyalties of his Church.

Uncharacteristically, at least in his King's presence, the Land-Captain grimaced. "That is harsh, Majesty. It seems unlike you. There can be no doubt that the Archpriest serves our enemy. His priests surely do the same. But his absence has left them milling like lost sheep. Their sorcery—whatever it was—has forsaken them. To my mind, they are harmless enough.

"And there is another concern. The Church has won a number of followers. If they are true believers, and their priests are taken from them, they will speak against you. Will you take that risk, Majesty? When we know that the enemy is coming, and the alliance is still troubled by unrest?"

Bifalt studied Erepos. The man had served him ever since his father's Land-Captain had passed away. They were comfortable with each other. Erepos had never hesitated to say what he thought. Cursing to himself, the King relented.

"Then use your own judgment, Land-Captain. I say only that the Church should contribute to the realm's defense. If you are reluctant to claim conscripts, ask for volunteers. Speak during a service, where you will be heard by 'true believers.' Offer the priests a new congregation among the people of the caravan."

He wanted those men out of the Open Hand. He wanted them out of Belleger.

Erepos nodded his approval. "As you say, Majesty." He left looking relieved.

The King trusted him. The Land-Captain had proven his worth for many years. If Bifalt felt a need to distrust such men, he would have to start with himself.

On the day before the caravan's arrival, King Bifalt sent a messenger to inform Set Ungabwey that the caravan master's emissaries would be made welcome in Belleger's Fist. The King himself would not ride out to meet the wagon train. Why should he? he countered when General Klamath questioned him. He was *King* now, not a lost and despairing Prince. He was entitled to a show of respect.

Even after twenty years, however, the truth was that he did not want to spend another moment in Set Ungabwey's presence. Tchwee was bad enough: the caravan master was worse. King Bifalt despised the obese man's feigned kindness, his pretense of welcome. They were the masks

Master Ungabwey used to disguise his part in the machinations of the library's Magisters.

But the King also had a better reason for keeping his distance; for treating the caravan master with apparent disregard. He understood Set Ungabwey's real purpose. The man had not come so far from his normal trade routes to defend Belleger from enemies in the south. The Magisters of the Last Repository had sent him to ensure that their own enemy could not reach them without passing through King Bifalt's realm.

Those sorcerers did not care how many Bellegerin and Amikan lives they sacrificed. They cared only for the Repository's survival.

Bifalt could not object to the caravan's intentions. He had always assumed that the enemy would find a way to come through Belleger. If Master Ungabwey's mechanisms could close the passes through the mountains, Belleger's army would not be forced to wage war there. That was more help than Bifalt had expected to get. But he did not feel required to welcome it. Certainly, he did not intend to forgive the library's guardians.

In the meantime, he wanted to hear the truth from *someone* who spoke for the Last Repository.

On the day of Set Ungabwey's arrival, excitement filled the Open Hand. In the streets, shouts and clamor were everywhere. King Bifalt could hear them from his windows. The people of his city had never seen anything like Master Ungabwey's wagon-train. Some of them abandoned their tasks and ran out across the training-fields to watch the caravan make camp. Others yelled back and forth, asking what their neighbors, friends, and complete strangers had seen. Under different circumstances, the King might have declared a holiday for everyone. But when Belleger was in such peril, the thought of treating the train's mission like a cause for celebration sickened him.

The next morning, he summoned his advisers to his private council chamber to meet with Set Ungabwey's representatives. This time, he excluded only Magister Facile. He did not want to deal with her indignation toward him—or with her more personal wounds. But he could not think of a reason to refuse Amika's Queen. Instead, he braced himself to endure her presence.

Expecting his call, they all came promptly. Queen Estie and General Klamath entered with Land-Captain Erepos, followed by Royal Surveyor Wheal and Purse-Holder Grippe. Despite his injuries, Prince Jaspid could have accompanied them. He had recovered enough to walk around. In fact, his physician encouraged him to walk as much as possible. Being Jaspid, he could have walked all the way to the Fist from the army hospital. Or he could have come on a horse, although his arms were strapped to his chest, and his jaw remained bound. But the King had forbidden him to attend. Prince Jaspid's presence in his condition might prompt questions that Bifalt did not intend to answer.

As for the Captain of the Count, Crickin, he had more important duties. He was busy in the south, working his way along the Realm's Edge front in an effort to identify every Bellegerin who might still be in danger from raiders. King Bifalt wanted to know how many of his people would need to be evacuated, and where to find them, if the caravan's purpose failed.

The King's private council chamber was more than large enough to seat eight or ten people comfortably. If Tchwee brought more than three of Set Ungabwey's counselors with him, the space would begin to seem crowded; but the Land-Captain had made sure that there were enough chairs and stools. He had also lit several lamps. Even at midmorning with all the windows open, the atmosphere resembled twilight, dim and damp. Autumn was the season of rains in this region. A series of squalls was passing over the Hand, lashing Belleger's Fist and then scudding westward at irregular intervals. When they hit, a cold spray splashed from the windowsills, and faces faded in the gloom. The lamps were needed.

King Bifalt was glad for the rain because he wanted the caravan's spokespeople to have a discomforting journey from their camp. He might have kept the windows open in any case. He liked the cooler, damper air. But he also hoped that the squalls and spray would unsettle his visitors. *He* had certainly been unsettled when he had been introduced to Set Ungabwey in the caravan master's brightly lit and overheated conveyance twenty years ago. He wanted any slight advantage he might get from the displeasure and anxiety of Master Ungabwey's people.

Knowing Bifalt's preferences, Queen Estie wore a thick shawl over her shoulders. And Grippe had wrapped himself in a warm robe. The other men were accustomed to Belleger in all seasons and did not appear to feel the chill.

As they entered the room, the King's advisers chose seats. Bifalt himself remained on his feet, half sitting on the edge of his desk to keep everyone else in front of him.

They waited in silence. King Bifalt had already told them what they needed to hear, and had explained what he wanted them to do.

But when the servant at the outer door announced an arrival, it was Prince Lome who entered.

He looked only moderately drunk, only a little disheveled. Without meeting anyone's gaze, he gave King Bifalt an unsteady bow. But he did not offer a greeting. Nor did he seem to expect one. Instead, he walked across the room and propped himself in a corner away from the windows and the door.

Under his breath, King Bifalt cursed the impulse that had prompted him to offer Lome a place on his private council. However, he did not send Lome away. He had already shamed his brother enough. Over the course of his life, he had shamed the Prince too much.

Queen Estie smiled her approval. Erepos, who probably knew more about Lome's life than anyone else now that Elgart was gone, studied his hands and said nothing. No one ventured an objection.

During the distraction of Prince Lome's entrance, Set Ungabwey's emissary appeared to arrive unannounced. Tchwee walked into the chamber like an unwelcome herald.

He was alone.

He was almost exactly as King Bifalt remembered him: a tall man with gleaming black skin that looked oiled rather than wet; naked to the waist, and hairless on his chest and scalp; strong enough to wrestle an ox. His white teeth glistened like fangs when he grinned. He must have worn a rain-cape and hood on his way to the Fist: the long cloth that he wrapped around his waist and thighs was dry. Only his bare feet showed that he had walked through a league of mud.

He looked a little older than he had twenty years ago. His face showed a bit of extra crinkling at the corners of his eyes, deeper mirth lines around his mouth, but nothing more. Entering a room he had never seen before, encountering people he had never met, he seemed as sure of himself as ever; as confident of his safety, or of his wits and prowess. And yet—

With Set Ungabwey's caravan, he had looked like he belonged. The train was his home, his proper setting. Here he was strangely out of place: an intrusion from a world with which Belleger and Amika were entirely unfamiliar.

At once, the seated men jumped to their feet. Queen Estie remained in her chair, but she nodded like a formal bow. King Bifalt acknowledged the interpreter by standing up straight for a moment. The Royal Surveyor looked at the door, obviously longing to escape. From his corner, Prince Lome let out a sloppy giggle, then stopped himself when he realized that no one else saw the humor in the situation.

Tchwee ignored everyone except Bifalt. "Hail, King!" he began in his bone-shaking voice. "Master Ungabwey sends his best wishes, his hopes for a better future, and his regret that you declined his hospitality. I have come to speak on his behalf."

King Bifalt, who remembered that the caravan master seldom spoke for himself, snorted privately. With a gesture, he urged his counselors to reclaim their chairs. Then he glared at Set Ungabwey's emissary.

"My title," he said distinctly, "is 'Majesty.'"

If he could have disturbed Tchwee's composure with that opening, he might have relaxed a measure of his severity.

Apparently, he could not. "Is it?" asked the black man with a laugh. "If you require titles, mine include Lord of Languages, Peacemonger of Far Arrak, Holder of the Callish Medal of Service, and Adopted Scion of the Knights of Ardor. For convenience, I will forego the others."

Despite his mood, Bifalt forced himself to smile. "I take your point. I did not invite you here to debate honorifics. You may call me King. I will call you Interpreter."

Tchwee chuckled easily. "A wise choice, King. In your place, I would do the same." Then he looked around the room. "And these are your advisers. They would not impress Master Ungabwey. I see overindulgence"—he indicated Lome—"difficult choices"—Queen Estie—"men with too many burdens"—everyone else—"and not a Magister or devotee among them. If you will accept a suggestion, King, you will release them to their duties. You can hear what I will say without their aid."

Prince Lome giggled again. "But he needs them. The King of Belleger is not a subtle man. They may notice hints and omissions that elude him."

Reflexively, King Bifalt scowled. Nevertheless he was pleased. Whatever Lome's reasons might be, the Prince was playing a part his brother might have chosen for him.

"My brother, Prince Lome," said Belleger's ruler for Tchwee's benefit. Then he introduced his other counselors. The interpreter had done the same for him long ago. When he had named them all, he added, "I do have a Magister who advises me, but I distrust her counsel.

"Tell me, Interpreter," he continued before Tchwee could reply, "is Master Ungabwey content with the supplies and men we have provided? His purpose deserves our utmost. But Belleger is a poor land. His needs have not been met with largesse."

"He is content," replied the big man comfortably. "You have not offered him abundance, King, but you have given enough."

Without waiting for permission to speak, Grippe asked, "And will your master pay for our supplies?" A sour man by nature, he had become increasingly acidulous as the realm's preparations required more and more coin Belleger did not have. "King Bifalt does not exaggerate when he calls us poor."

Tchwee's amusement faded. He almost frowned. "Do you not call it payment enough that Master Ungabwey hazards his men and his caravan and his own life to shield you from your foes among the mountains?"

"But," persisted Grippe, doing what King Bifalt had asked of him, "everything we give to your master's efforts weakens us elsewhere. The enemy is coming. *Winter* is coming. We are threatened by treachery and spies." By *spies*, he meant the Great God's priests. "And Amika can offer us little. Queen Estie has already sacrificed her realm's wealth to aid us.

"What will you call it when our riflemen spend their lives so that your train can hope for success?"

King Bifalt's instructions were explicit: push that hard, no harder. The Purse-Holder did *not* add, What will you call it when Belleger and Amika are destroyed because they defend the library?

Studying the interpreter, Bifalt sensed his wrath. Tchwee seemed to grow taller. The muscles of his chest and arms tightened. For the first time, he gave the King reason to suspect that he was alarmed by the risks his master meant to take.

Good. Now Bifalt had an advantage.

But then Set Ungabwey's emissary calmed himself. Clearly, he had realized that Grippe's provocation was deliberate. His years with the caravan must have taught him to recognize that tactic, and to manage it.

With a forced smile, he replied like the rumble of a distant landslide, "The issue does not arise. There is no question of payment on either side. Master Ungabwey's dealings are with the Last Repository. If his costs are great, the Repository will reward him."

A brief stretch of clear sky above the Fist filled the room with unexpected light, etching faces out of the gloom. Amika's Queen sat limned with her hands clenched in her lap, frowning as if she shared the Royal Surveyor's desire to leave. War and defense were her husband's responsibility, not hers. She seemed to feel as out of place as Set Ungabwey's emissary.

Sitting straight and square in his chair, General Klamath concentrated with an intensity that made him glower. Despite his ready sympathies, he shared his King's single-mindedness.

Then another squall closed over the city, and the light was gone.

The King nodded. "But he has undertaken a similar task before, Interpreter?" Magister Facile had told him so.

Tchwee did not hesitate. "He has."

Still trying to provoke the man, Bifalt remarked, "Then surely he knows what his costs will be."

"No, King." The emissary sounded certain. "Every range of mountains is different. In the Realm's Edge, there is less snow and ice than in the Wall. However, there is opposition here. There was none in the Wall. Master Ungabwey must—"

King Bifalt interrupted him. "I did not finish my question. You say that Master Ungabwey's dealings are with the library's Magisters. We will suppose that he has already been paid for sealing the Wall. What is their agreement to reward similar efforts in the Realm's Edge? What further payment will your master expect? Will he claim a share of Belleger? Or of Belleger and Amika?"

Now Tchwee allowed himself anger. "I have said, King, that the issue does not arise. It does not concern you. The Last Repository has no interest in the possession of lands. And Master Ungabwey is a traveling merchant. He has no *use* for lands which he will then be required to defend."

Suppressing a snarl, King Bifalt retorted, "You mean to say that Master Ungabwey has been allied with the library for many years. Its safety is a personal concern for him. To preserve that alliance, no cost is too high.

"But he has no personal interest in Belleger. He will not help us as he would an ally. I want to know what reward your master has been offered for his work in our mountains."

Thunder rolled over Belleger's Fist. Lightning made the chamber lurid for an instant. Briefly, Tchwee looked away. The corners of his mouth tightened. There was outrage in his voice as he countered, "And I repeat. Master Ungabwey's dealings with the Magisters are his and theirs. They do not affect you."

King Bifalt swallowed a faint taste of success: a flavor he had never known while he was with the caravan. He had pierced the interpreter's pose of easy superiority. Grimly, he countered, "If you answer, I will know what your master expects to gain from Belleger."

He meant, I may be able to judge Set Ungabwey's honesty.

He could not trust the caravan master. More than that, he refused to trust the Repository's sorcerers.

But General Klamath spoke while Tchwee considered his response. "Majesty," he asked, "why do we care? Questions of payment have no substance when we are threatened with fire and slaughter. Master Ungabwey is here because he has come to terms with the Magisters of the library. Those terms do not require our assent. And we cannot refuse what we are offered.

"I comprehend the caravan's motives no better than you. But to my mind, there is only one question. Does Master Ungabwey intend to close the passes through the Realm's Edge, as we were assured, or does he have some other purpose? *That* his emissary must tell us."

A quick cloudburst drenched the windowsills. Grippe tightened his robe against the spray. Queen Estie's lips were pale with chill or alarm. She may have been shivering. But King Bifalt felt a thud of anticipation in his chest. He suppressed a feral grin. Day after day, Klamath proved his worth. He had changed the direction of the exchange, doing what he could to shift the ground under Tchwee's feet.

The King of Belleger looked at Tchwee. "Interpreter?"

The man who spoke *all known languages, and others as well* surprised everyone by bowing to Prince Lome. "Prince," rumbled the big man, "I see now that I misjudged you. Your King needs his advisers. I will not say that they hear what he does not. But his hearing is clouded by distrust. It lures him astray."

Then he returned his attention to King Bifalt.

"I, too, have been led astray, King. Why do we speak of payment? Master Ungabwey's purpose is indeed what you have been told. If it can be done, he will prevent your enemies from passing through the mountains. But he has another purpose as well. It will not threaten you."

Another crack of thunder. More lightning. King Bifalt ignored them.

"He hopes to save his daughters," explained Tchwee. "You have met them, King. They have served him for many years. Now they have taken refuge in the Last Repository. Master Ungabwey will do everything in his power to keep them safe. To that extent, he *is* your ally."

Abruptly, the Purse-Holder lifted his head. "Is that his payment from the library?" He sounded uncharacteristically hopeful. "Did the Magisters buy his support by giving refuge to his daughters? Or perhaps his daughters are held hostage to compel him?"

For an instant, Tchwee forgot circumspection. "Of *course* not!" he snapped. "Master Ungabwey is not such a man. He cannot be bought—or threatened."

He turned to Bifalt. "Rule your people, King. Master Ungabwey does not expect gratitude, but he relies on simple courtesy. He did not send me to receive insults. If his presence is unwelcome, he will withdraw. It will cost him nothing to abandon his purpose in the Realm's Edge."

Hells, Grippe! thought King Bifalt. Well done! The emissary was off-balance now. Bifalt was almost ready for him.

The Magister Marrow he knew was certainly capable of taking hostages to gain what he wanted.

"Let it drop," he told Grippe. "General Klamath is right. We have strayed from our own purpose."

Like Klamath, he changed the subject. "Satisfy me on one practical matter, Interpreter. If Master Ungabwey is content in other ways, is he also content with the force of riflemen we will send to protect him?"

The black man almost relaxed. "He is, King. Your soldiers look capable. They may suffice. And General Klamath has promised more if more are needed. That reassures Master Ungabwey. He has no complaint."

King Bifalt clasped his hands behind his back so that Tchwee would not see them clench. "Then I must ask a different question. Where are Master Ungabwey's other counselors? Why did they not accept my invitation?

"Do *they* have other purposes here?"

In response, Tchwee laughed outright. However, his laughter was not his usual comfortable bellow. It had an edge of vexation: it hinted at fury. "His other counselors, King? There have been many. Did you expect one or another in particular?"

Deliberately sharp, King Bifalt replied, "I speak of Alleman Dancer," although he had no curiosity about the leader of the Wide World Carnival. "I speak of the monk known as Third Father," who had treated Prince Bifalt with kindness and integrity, and had been willing to risk himself for Belleger's sake. "I speak of the courtesan and the assassin.

Did Master Ungabwey forbid them to accept my invitation? Does he fear what they will say? Or have they been given other tasks?"

He wanted to hear whatever Tchwee might tell him about Amandis and Flamora. Despite her other commitments, Amandis had helped him understand *why* Magister Marrow was manipulating him. And both she and Flamora had shaped Elgart into a man who could be the King's invaluable friend and spy. In the crisis of Elgart's abduction, they might side with King Bifalt.

The big man assumed an amused smile, but the tension in the muscles of his naked chest and shoulders contradicted it. "And you distrust them all, King?" he retorted. "Then I must pity you. But there can be no harm in answering.

"Alleman Dancer," he began, "is now an old man. His son leads the Wide World Carnival. Aided by some among the most holy devotees of Spirit, they have performed a great service by watching for signs of the enemy wherever they go. It is by their efforts that we know the enemy is near."

King Bifalt nodded. "Go on, Interpreter."

"The monk of the Cult of the Many," continued Tchwee, "was not with us when we left the Last Repository. However, he joined us while we delayed to assist the completion of Queen Estie's road." His tone was noncommittal. "Disturbed by troubles in Belleger and Amika, he begged passage to the Open Hand. Now he is abroad in the city. He did not speak of his intentions. I do not know his whereabouts."

At that, Queen Estie startled her husband. Sitting forward as if she had been stung, she demanded, "What did he say of those troubles?"

Tchwee cocked an eyebrow at her. "He said little, Queen," he answered like a shrug. "He seldom speaks. To Master Ungabwey, he said only that he suspected a confluence. Because he was unsure of it, he declined to explain.

"Accept my regrets, Queen. I do not—"

But she did not wait for his apology. Springing to her feet, she rushed a curtsy. "Forgive me, my lord King. I believe I can find this monk. When I do, I will bring him to you."

Her manner gripped King Bifalt's heart. Instinctively, he wanted to stop her. A *confluence*? What did *that* mean? But the whetted metal of her gaze defied him. And she knew how Third Father had served and saved him in the library: all of his advisers did. Feigning unconcern, he muttered, "Of course, my lady. Do what you must."

In a moment, she was gone, leaving the King and his men with the same question. A *confluence*?

Outside, the rain sank to a steady drizzle. Thunder muttered once more, but it was moving away. There was no lightning.

Prince Lome giggled again until Bifalt glared at him.

Swallowing a lump of apprehension that threatened to choke him, the King said as if he felt compelled to excuse Estie's departure, "She is a remarkable woman, Interpreter. *I* could not find Third Father. *She* will, although she has never seen him."

Without pausing for breath, he prompted Set Ungabwey's emissary. "You were saying?"

For a moment, Tchwee seemed to lose the thread of his reply. Then he wiped a look of puzzlement off his face. "We were speaking of Master Ungabwey's absent counselors, King.

"As for the most holy devotees of Flesh and Spirit, Amandis and Flamora, they also traveled with Master Ungabwey. But then they left the caravan. They did not give their reasons."

Thinking of Elgart, and of the disappearance of devotees from the Open Hand, King Bifalt fought his impulse to pounce. "*When* did they leave?"

Tchwee spread his strong hands. His manner suggested that he was in the mood to crush a few throats. "Ten days ago?" he offered. "Fifteen? I did not number them, King. Master Ungabwey's men come from many lands. They speak many languages. My duties as his interpreter fill my days."

By an act of will, King Bifalt did not pursue the subject. His confusion had too many pieces: he could not assemble them on such short notice. He only knew that Third Father's mention of a *confluence* was not an accident. Tchwee had not repeated the word by accident. It was not an accident that Amandis and Flamora had left the caravan, or that Elgart had been taken when he went to confront Archpriest Makh, or—

Queen Estie understood hints better than he did. If she had not left, he would have been tempted to question her in front of Set Ungabwey's emissary.

"Is there nothing more you can tell me, Interpreter?" he asked. "I relied on a chance to speak with the devotees. They have aided us, both here and in Amika. I hoped—"

More unsure of himself than he wanted to admit, he bit off his impulse to plead.

"You hoped?" echoed the interpreter. He seemed to mean, *You hoped?*

Abruptly, King Bifalt decided that he was ready. He had been given too many hints, and did not know which ones were trustworthy. But he was always unsure. And he had prepared himself for this: the moment when Tchwee had been made angry, and then had been encouraged to relax. It might not come again.

"I hoped for honesty. Tell me one thing more, Interpreter." Now he loosened his restraint; let out his own deep ire. "Why did your Master Ungabwey abandon me in the desert when I was only *Prince* Bifalt? He found me lost and dying. He promised me welcome. He seemed to offer me friendship. Then he left me at the mercy of the sun and the sands."

The emissary stared at him; *glared* at him. The big man bunched his fists. But before Tchwee could respond, King Bifalt continued harshly, "No. Tell me nothing. Let me guess.

"Magister Avail spoke in Set Ungabwey's mind. He said, 'Drug that Prince and leave him. We will not let him die. But he is arrogant. He must be humbled before he enters the Last Repository.' Then your master did what he was told. Like a servant. Like a *tool*. He did what he was told."

Confess the truth *now*, Interpreter, thought Bifalt. Admit that the library's Magisters have *always* intended to sacrifice Belleger and Amika.

But Tchwee did not. He betrayed an instant of shock. An instant of outrage. A fierce effort to control himself. For half a dozen heartbeats, he stood without moving.

Then he turned and walked away.

At the door, he snarled over his shoulder, "Farewell, King. We will not speak again."

With vehemence, he slammed out of the chamber.

Clouds opened and closed shutters of light as they drifted westward. King Bifalt saw his advisers' faces in waves of clarity. A different kind of shock held them for a moment. When it passed, General Klamath released an explosive sigh.

"That was dangerous, Majesty."

Grippe nodded. "The caravan may withdraw. You heard the interpreter, Majesty. He threatened to forsake us."

Wheal looked like he wanted to vomit.

The King settled his familiar severity on his features; in his voice. "I think not. Set Ungabwey's dealings are with the Magisters of the library, not with us. He will keep faith with them. Rudeness and accusations will not dissuade him."

After that, he had nothing more to say. Outside, the squall drifted westward. The rain ceased. But the sky remained overcast, swollen with threats. The lamps hardly seemed to pierce the gloom. They did not weaken it.

He wanted Amandis and Flamora. He could not think of anyone else from the library who might tell him the truth. Their sister-devotees had done much for Belleger and Amika. Devotees of Flesh had defused countless bursts of unrest in the Open Hand. More than once, Lylin had saved Queen Estie's life. If he could not talk to them, he could not count on anyone to relieve his ignorance.

His lack of knowledge might prove fatal. He had to live with it anyway.

When King Bifalt had dismissed his counselors, Prince Lome remained in his corner. For his own amusement, the Prince giggled until Bifalt turned to snarl a reproach. Then Lome held up his hands: a gesture of placation.

Glowering, the King controlled himself. "You have something further to say, Brother?"

Prince Lome rolled his eyes. "You are slow, *Brother*." His familiar slur was fading. "I have often said so.

"What is this 'confluence'? Your lady reacts to mention of her road. King Smegin made an attempt on her life. He sent slaves to the road. He tried to provoke war with the Nuuri. For wasted seasons of my wasted life, I have had conversations with Amikan traitors and devout priests. Your ridiculous friend Elgart disappeared when he went to the Church. Those women you esteem so highly are gone. The devotees you know have turned their backs on the caravan master. Both the monk you seek and Magister Facile serve the library."

He made a deliberate effort to face King Bifalt squarely. But the King's glare seemed to wither him. His gaze wandered away to the nearest window.

"Are you lost without Elgart, Brother?" The Prince was able to muster more sarcasm when he did not look at the King. "Have you been told too much? Do you need someone to think for you?

"*I* do not need spies to convince me that King Smegin must have been visited by priests before his crimes took shape. They came through Amika. They could have gone to his retreat. Who else could have inspired him to act after so many years in his sanctuary? How else did he make peace with his desires? They must have taught him to end the war within him. And I do not need informers to tell me that the monk has gone to consult with Magister Facile. They both serve the library. Your lady will find him with her."

To his surprise, Bifalt realized that he believed his brother. Everything Lome said made sense. More keenly, the King asked, "What else can you tell me?"

Prince Lome shrugged. If he could see anything more than the cloud-sealed sky from that window, his sight was better than his brother's; but he did not look away.

"Some of those courtesans or assassins have gone in search of El-gart. The rest have hidden themselves to avoid your questions." His tone dripped acid. "You trust them. I do not. If they do not want you to know their plans—you or that caravan's master—their intentions must be worse than the librarian's."

Inwardly, Bifalt winced. What, *worse*? The most holy devotees had plans that were *worse* than the librarian's? No. *That* he did not believe. He did not know those women as well as Elgart did. But Lome did not know them at all. And Elgart had trusted them. His trust had persuaded Prince Bifalt to accept his own utter humiliation in the Last Repository.

A devotee of Spirit had done far more than keep Queen Estie alive. Lylin had prevented a fatal war with the Nuuri.

"That is speculation, Lome." King Bifalt managed to sound almost neutral. "We cannot be sure of it. But your other observations are convincing.

"You are quick to judge others. Tell me something of yourself. You call the priests devout. You insist they are sincere. You say they search for my stores of bullets so they can prevent me from waging war. But now you tell me they urged King Smegin to his crimes.

"You are inconsistent."

Prince Lome started to giggle again; but at once the sound became a snort of disdain. "And you are *slow*. You do not listen closely. I did not *say* the priests persuaded King Smegin to commit his evils. How would I know? I inferred only that they taught him to make peace with himself.

"That is their lesson." Wrapping his arms around himself, he seemed to hunch over a private hurt. "It is the *whole* of their lesson. They urge us all to tell ourselves the truth about who and what we are. When we have done that, we will no longer be at war with ourselves. Then we will have no need for other wars.

"You cannot hold the Great God's priests responsible for what King Smegin chose to *do* after he found his own peace."

Tension thrummed in King Bifalt's mind, but he did not move. The rigidity of his mien masked his thoughts. He could not remember ever caring about his brother the way he did now. Suddenly, he wanted to understand Lome's pain. Until now, their father's eldest son and heir had not bothered—

"What do *you* believe, Lome?" asked Bifalt. "What truth have you told yourself?"

Again, Prince Lome started to giggle. Again, the sound of it changed. It became a sour laugh like a bark of revulsion.

"I want a drink."

For a long moment, Bifalt studied his brother. Then, carefully, he said, "That may be one truth. It is not the whole truth."

Lome whipped his head around. With an almost tangible snap, his gaze met his brother's. His eyes burned with the cold flame of distilled spirits when the liquid caught fire.

"It is enough."

In a stumbling rush, he flung himself past King Bifalt toward the door.

Bifalt let him go. He understood now that Lome's insistence on the sincerity of the priests was like his drinking. It was an excuse—or an escape. If he supported the Church, he only did so to convince himself that he had substance, that his choices and actions carried weight. He did not tell himself the truth because he was afraid of what he might hear.

To that extent, unexpectedly, King Bifalt found that he shared his brother's dilemma. The truth that he, Bifalt, refused to hear was that he had already failed his people. When the library's Magisters had chosen, they had done so because they knew he was not astute enough to evade their manipulations. Able to maneuver him however they wished, they had doomed both Belleger and him. They had doomed Belleger *through* him.

And they had done the same to Amika. Queen Estie's homeland was doomed because he had persuaded her to believe in him. When he failed, they would be lost.

Had he ever told his wife the truth about his use of her? The whole truth? He had not. He had never acknowledged it aloud because he could not bear to hear it. Instead, he had chosen a path like Lome's: the path of insisting that what he *could* bear to hear was enough.

K ing Bifalt waited a long time for Third Father, but the delay did not gall him. The monk needed to speak with Magister Facile. He needed to know whatever she could tell him. Otherwise he would not be able to advise the man he had supported and served in the Last Repository: the man for whom he had *stood surety*.

The cloud cover had thinned, letting more light in from the windows. One by one, Bifalt extinguished the lamps. He had a rifleman's preference for natural light.

Keeping busy, he immersed himself in reports; in endless lists of details and impediments from General Klamath, from Land-Captain Erepos, from the Royal Surveyor and the Purse-Holder. And eventually, the servant at the door announced a monk of the Cult of the Many.

Springing from his seat, King Bifalt crossed the room to greet the man who entered.

He was indeed the monk known as Third Father.

He had changed in twenty years. Clearly, he had not spent his time in the Last Repository, where sorcerous healing could have preserved him. Oh, his dun cassock belted with white rope was the same. He had shaved his pate into its familiar tonsure. And his demeanor was as unassuming as ever. Careless of his dignity, he kept his eyes downcast, modestly avoiding the challenge of a direct gaze. His unlined brow retained its former placidity.

But the fringes of his tonsure had grown sparse and white. Old sorrow had worn creases down his cheeks, and his skin was sere with age. He appeared shrunken in some way, diminished by lost weight or weakened posture. A subtle tremor marred his hands.

Nevertheless King Bifalt was glad to see him.

Standing in front of the monk, he felt an unaccustomed impulse to kneel. Instead, he offered his visitor a formal bow. "Third Father," he said gruffly. "I have never given up hope that we would meet again. The circumstances are grim. Soon they will get worse. But your coming is a gift nonetheless."

When Third Father bowed in return, the stiffness of his joints showed the years. As did his voice. It quavered slightly while he answered. "You are kind, King." Unlike Tchwee, he made the lack of Bifalt's honorific sound like an expression of respect. "Asking me to deliver Estervault's book on cannon to your father, you tested my devotion to its core. When you redirected the book to Amika, you relieved the distress I had caused for myself. You have earned my gratitude."

Instinctively, King Bifalt put his hand on the monk's arm, offering his support. "You are too self-effacing, Father. You stood surety for me. No other man in the library would have done as much. Yet I have done nothing for you, except to shift some of my burdens onto your shoulders.

"Come," he urged before the old man could contradict him. "Please sit with me. I have been on my feet too long." A polite fiction. "Will you accept water? Wine?" Holding the monk by the arm, he guided him to the nearest chair. "May I ask a servant to bring food and refreshment?"

With a thin sigh, Third Father sank into the chair. He did not lift his eyes. Again, he said, "You are kind, King. Water will suffice. I have no immediate needs. And you are too much in demand to provide for me."

Bifalt walked away to the pitcher of water his servants provided for him; filled a goblet. When he had put the drink in the monk's unsteady hands, he dragged another chair closer so that he could sit almost knee to knee with his visitor. Wincing at the caution with which Third Father lifted the goblet to his mouth, Bifalt said more harshly than he intended, "I am the King of Belleger. When I want time, I take it. You and I are in no hurry, Father."

A brief twist that might have been a smile touched the monk's lips. "No doubt," he murmured. "No doubt. It is the burden of kings to take only what they must and give all they can. But there is no 'must' between us, King. You are not my sovereign. I am not your subject. Do not let my presence interfere with what you give."

King Bifalt studied the old man for a moment. Third Father's journey—or his long session with Magister Facile—had drained him. In a wry way, hoping the monk would grasp his limited sense of humor,

Bifalt asked, "If you do not mean to interfere, Father, why did you come? Is your visit not interference in itself?"

With a flick of his eyes, the old man met King Bifalt's regard. Then he dropped his gaze. "I came to look at the King of Belleger." He seemed to study his drink as if he could read secrets on its surface. "Now I am content. I see that you have become the man I saw hidden inside you when you were Prince."

Long ago, he had claimed that his gift was to *see*.

Thinking of Lome, the King asked, "Which man is that, Father?"

He did not ask, The man who has not forgiven the Magisters of the library? The man who does not trust any sorcery or sorcerer?

Above all, he did not ask, The man who has used his wife and her realm to slow the destruction of his people?

The monk cocked his head as if he were listening to what Bifalt refused to say; to the words Bifalt would have repudiated if they had been thrown in his face. "The man Belleger needs," replied Third Father. "The man the Last Repository needs. The man who does not name himself among his responsibilities."

Then the old man surprised King Bifalt by stretching out one thin hand and resting it on Bifalt's knee. "That is the man I saw sleeping in the young Prince. That is the man I see awake in you now. Your alliance with Amika is an alliance with yourself. You have come to terms with your former war.

"But there is more. I see that you have suffered a mortal wound."

Startled, the King pulled back. A *mortal* wound? He spread his arms as if he were baring himself for an inspection. "See me as I am, Father. I am well. My only wounds are those Belleger has suffered."

He told himself he was being honest, but he knew he was not.

The monk shook his head. His hand stayed on Bifalt's knee. "It is a moral wound, King. To call it 'mortal' is only to say that it will kill you as surely as any physical harm. Long ago, Magister Marrow and his comrades committed a crime against your spirit. They dishonored you by means that allowed you to do only what they wished. Another man might have felt humiliation and rage. You felt unmade, doomed to dishonor in a war you did not choose and could not avoid.

"When you answered them, you surpassed them. You became more than they had imagined. Truly, King, you became more than I had hoped to see. You surpassed *yourself.* But the wound, the dishonor remains. It has not healed. It will not heal. It has made of you the man Belleger and the Last Repository need. And it will kill you. Your wound will not heal until you surpass yourself again."

What, *again?* thought King Bifalt. What does *that* mean? I can only be who I am. But he did not pursue those questions. In self-defense, he tried to change the subject, or shift its terms.

Harshly, he demanded, "What has Magister Facile told you?"

He meant, What has that old woman said about my childless marriage and my heartbroken wife's sleeping talent?

Third Father tightened his grip. Briefly, his voice lost its quaver. "We spoke of many things. Amika's Queen and I have done the same."

Unable to stop himself, Bifalt asked, "What did the Queen say?"

The monk shook his head. "Their words are not for you, King. Their hearts are their own." As if deliberately, he reminded Bifalt that he had once urged, *Say whatever gives you ease. It will be sacred to me. No other soul will know of it.*

Then he relaxed. Releasing the King, he leaned back in his chair; resumed his study of his goblet. "But Magister Facile also spoke of events in Belleger. She told me of the Queen's efforts to surpass herself. She described the crimes of Amika's former King. And she gave me tidings of the Church of the Great God Rile. She told me that your friend and spy, Elgart, has disappeared, taking Archpriest Makh with him, or taken by the Archpriest. In addition, it seems that the most holy devotees of Flesh and Spirit have made unforeseen choices.

"King, I am here because I suspected a confluence. In my travels, I have heard many people speak of the Church. I have sat in the sanctuary myself and heard the Great God's priests. The Cult of the Many does not judge, but we do discern. Clearly, they exert a strange theurgy. It makes them"—he paused to search for the right word—"persuasive. Still, I see no harm in their teachings.

"However, the timing of their arrival in Belleger alarmed me. It is a strange coincidence, King, that they came to your realm so soon after

Magister Marrow and his comrades learned that their enemy knows where the Last Repository is hidden. I find it difficult to imagine that the coming of the Church and the coming of the enemy are not connected in some way.

"That is one possible confluence. Another is the decision of the most holy devotees to forsake the Open Hand when Elgart and the Archpriest have vanished.

"King, it is difficult—it is impossible—to conclude that these events have no bearing on each other."

The monk paused to lift his goblet with both hands and drink. Then he sighed. "But now—" He smiled ruefully. "In an excess of self-esteem, I conceived that I was needed to give warning. Alas for my pride, I have learned that my concerns are already known." A brief grimace crossed his features. "Indeed, King, the Queen described my fears before I could express them.

"We were speaking of Belleger and Amika, as I did with Magister Facile. I am free to say that the Queen considers her father's crimes to be both a confluence in themselves and an aspect of a larger confluence. If she were not your wife and Amika's sovereign, she would be an asset in the Last Repository. Magister Marrow and the others would benefit from her counsel."

Estie? Consigned to the library? An appalling notion. She would be wasted on those Magisters, or they would corrupt her.

Shaking his head, King Bifalt tried to dismiss the idea. "As you say, Father," he growled. "Even I can see a confluence when it rises to overwhelm me.

"And there is more. Magister Facile may not have thought to mention that raiders from the Realm's Edge Mountains have ravaged farmsteads and hamlets across the south of Belleger. These raids began when the Church first appeared here."

"Then, King"—Third Father considered the floor, the King's boots, the open windows—"I have seen what I came to see. I have done what I came to do, although it has proved needless. Let us consider *your* dilemmas and desires.

"Once before, I inquired how I could best serve you." Again, he let

Bifalt see his rueful smile. "You offered me a challenging task. What would you ask of me now? If it lies within my strength, I will give it."

King Bifalt could have posed a number of questions. At a more relaxed moment, he might have asked the monk to tell him more about the Cult of the Many. He knew almost nothing. Or he might have urged Third Father to say as much about the devotees of Flesh and Spirit as his scruples allowed. But the monk's humble openness encouraged the King to be honest himself.

—she would be an asset in the Last Repository.

Honesty was dangerous.

I want a drink.

Belleger was threatened. Honesty might prove fatal. It might require more of Bifalt than he could bear.

Your wound will not heal until you surpass yourself again.

But he had nowhere else to turn. No one else *saw* him the way Third Father did.

Before he could summon the will to remain silent, he said hoarsely, "Give me your counsel, Father. What can I do about Queen Estie?"

The monk raised his eyebrows. Musing, he countered, "What is your dilemma?"

King Bifalt clenched his fists to restrain them. "You know me, Father. You know my loathing for sorcery and sorcerers." He had described his abhorrence to the monk in the library twenty years ago. "It sickens me that I must rely on Magisters.

"Now I know that the woman I married has a gift for sorcery. It is asleep in her, but it will awaken. When it does, she may become repulsive to me."

In the same tone, Third Father asked, "Why is this a dilemma, King?"

Bifalt wanted to shout, but he did not raise his voice. He said each word without emphasis.

"Because she is my wife. Because I love her. I can love her. I want to love her. And"—he swallowed a rush of pain—"she loves me. She has given me too many proofs. I cannot doubt her.

"I dishonored her, Father, when I made her my wife. I used her to seal my alliance with Amika. But I desired her as soon as I saw her. I desire her more now. I keep my distance because I dishonored her. She deserves better. But I have promised myself that when this war is done—if I live—if I have served my people honorably—I will claim my place as her husband.

"*Now*—" The force of his restraint made his voice tremble as if he were as old as the monk. "I cannot have a sorceress as my wife. I cannot be her husband."

Third Father made a low humming sound. He did not look up at King Bifalt. He seemed to find his reply in the grain of the floorboards, the shape of the worn rugs.

With ineffable gentleness, he said, "This touches you deeply, King. No man can fail to see your distress. No man can fail to grieve for you. But you make too much of it.

"You believe that your abhorrence of sorcery is who you *are*. You are mistaken. It is not inborn. I do not ask how you learned it. I do not fault your reasons for it. Nevertheless it is a choice, not a gift of birth.

"Choices can be made. It is your right to make them. But they can also be unmade. That also is your right. And you have shown me that you have the courage to unmake them. When you elected mortal combat in the Last Repository, you made a choice. You unmade that choice when you refused to fight.

"The day may come, King, when you will set aside your abhorrence. It may not. I do not see your future. I see only you. But I tell you this. On one point, the teachings of the Great God's Church are false. Choice is not a matter of truth and faith. It is a matter of truth and courage."

While Bifalt stared, cut to the heart and hardly able to breathe, the monk asked, "Can you tell yourself the truth, King? Do you have that much courage?"

King Bifalt did not jump up from his chair. He did not storm away, or yell at the monk, or dismiss him. But Third Father had laid him bare. Fresh blood pulsed from his wounds. He needed some way to stanch the bleeding; some way to distance himself from Third Father's insights.

"You urge me to surpass myself." He made no effort to soften his bitterness. "You do not mention the cost of unmaking my choices." His surrender in the library had cost him his whole life. "Have you ever surpassed *yourself*, Father?"

To Bifalt's surprise, Third Father's shoulders slumped. As they sagged, he seemed to age. The air of conviction that had brought him to Belleger's Fist and King Bifalt drained from him. With a hint of self-mockery, he admitted, "You gave me an opportunity when you trusted me with Sylan Estervault's book. Then you spared me the necessity of acting on my promise."

In an instant, the King's impulse to reproach his visitor vanished. The monk's confession defused his ire before he could defend himself. More than once in the library, this man had vexed and foiled him by asking questions and offering observations that cast him in a light he did not like. But Bifalt could not fault the monk for it. With two sentences, Third Father had demonstrated that he subjected himself to the same scrutiny.

The old man was more honest than King Bifalt. He had more courage.

Later, when the monk had left him, King Bifalt spent an hour alone, fuming as he paced from wall to wall. This was not the first time he had failed to meet the challenges Third Father presented. On one occasion, the monk had told him that he was at war with himself. And the man's offer to stand surety for him had tested him in ways that he had not been able to understand or answer. The present case was no different.

Can you tell yourself the truth, King? Do you have that much courage?

Like the Prince he had once been, Bifalt wanted to rage and bluster. But he had been pushed too far by Third Father. By Tchwee. By the loss of Elgart. Most of all by Queen Estie. He stood on the edge of an inner precipice. He seemed to have no defiance left in him.

Because he was alone, he told himself a portion of the truth.

Do you doubt my courage? So do I.

TWENTY-ONE

THE QUEEN'S CHOICE

The day after Tchwee's visit to Belleger's Fist—after Estie's long talk with Magister Facile and the monk known as Third Father—the Queen of Amika rode out in the first grey of dawn to watch Set Ungabwey's caravan depart. Taking Commander Crayn and her Amikan escort with her, she cantered past the boundaries of the Open Hand and across the army's training-fields to the crest of a ridge of hills. There she had a clear view of the train's many and strange wagons, conveyances, carriages, beasts, and people as they prepared to leave.

She did not need her own men here, in the armed heart of King Bifalt's domain. For that reason, her husband might take the presence of her escort as an affront. General Klamath might. After all, her guardsmen had only one duty. They were here to protect her. They did not answer to the King or the General. But she had her reasons for bringing Crayn and his company. She would explain herself when she had a chance.

Despite the early hour, she was not the first to reach the ridgecrest. A stone's throw away, King Bifalt on his horse was already there, accompanied by his bodyguards Malder and Jeck. He was in no more danger than the Queen-Consort. But he had learned the habit of taking precautions whenever he left Belleger's Fist. Amikan traitors had tried to kill her. A Bellegerin laborer had murdered one of Elgart's bodyguards. And the priests of the Great God Rile had tried to find King Bifalt's hidden stores of bullets. Now most of them had been commandeered to serve the caravan. But there was always a chance that other people might be plotting against her husband.

General Klamath and Land-Captain Erepos were with the King. As was Prince Jaspid. Although both of his arms were strapped to his chest, he was well enough now to sit his mount and manage it without using the reins. Anxious for him—and aching to talk to the only man who did not blame Lylin for his injuries—she had visited him in the hospital twice. There she had been relieved to learn that his damaged eye had not lost its sight.

For the moment, the three men were alone with Jeck and Malder. But they would not be alone for long. When Queen Estie looked behind her, she saw a throng of men and women, Bellegerin and Amikan, hurrying to catch sight of the long caravan before its horses, oxen, and illirim hauled it away. Like a river in flood, the city spilled a rush of its inhabitants. The train and every part of it were new sights in Belleger, as unfamiliar as the tusked beasts. Many people had left the Open Hand to witness the caravan's arrival. As many and more did not want to miss its departure.

Among the crowd, Third Father approached. His slower steps encouraged other people to stride past him; but Queen Estie suspected that he would arrive in plenty of time.

On one of the fields beyond the throng, First Captain Matt was mustering the horsemen who would guard the caravan: a hundred soldiers with rifles and bulging satchels of ammunition as well as bows, arrows, sabers, and daggers. In the dawn, their breastplates and helms had a dull grey hue. When the sun rose high enough to strike their armor, they would shine. The beleaguered eagles on their chests would look as vivid as shouts.

Down in the opposite direction from Estie's vantage, Master Ungabwey's men and women had already dismantled their encampment. And they had cleaned the site, burying their refuse and latrines; sweeping away the ashes of their fires. Leaving nothing to mark their passage except the cut of wheels and the imprint of hooves, they were preparing the conveyances that would carry them south. Men ran back and forth to secure the wagons, yelling in languages that Estie had never heard

before. Women hurried to toss the last bundles, kegs, and bales of supplies into wagons and carriages. Most of the wagoneers sat on their
benches, holding the traces ready. Oxen bawled at each other, or at what
was expected of them. Illirim snorted vapor in the lingering chill. A few
wagons had moved into line behind Set Ungabwey's carriage. And over
them all, Tchwee presided, stentorian and cheerful, as if he were speaking several different tongues at once.

But the last of the extra horses and oxen were still being prodded
into their vans. The caravan was not ready to begin its long plod toward
the Realm's Edge.

In any case, the First Captain's riflemen had not joined the train yet.
General Klamath's second-in-command was still giving their officers
his last orders. No doubt, he wanted to confirm that the officers understood where and how to set their signal-relays so that they could summon help if they needed it. Or when they did. Tchwee would not call
the train into motion until the soldiers Master Ungabwey had been
promised came to guard it.

Soon the leading edge of the throng reached the crest. There the
people hesitated, looking to King Bifalt for permission to obstruct his
view. With a brusque gesture, he sent them pouring downward for a
closer look at the conveyances and beasts. Hundreds of men, women,
and children from both realms followed.

When the first sunlight touched the ridge where Queen Estie sat her
horse, the contrast cast the caravan into deeper shadows. Before long, the
sun would reach the carriages and wagons as well; but it would not dispel
the gloom of their purpose. In the canyons and passes of the Realm's
Edge, the cliffs would cut off the sky's light more often than not. Master
Ungabwey's laborers and mechanicians, like their company of riflemen,
would not be able to rely on sunshine to reveal what awaited them.

Queen Estie shuddered to imagine the hazards the train would face:
the risk of being ambushed among unfamiliar mountains, attacked often; the danger of unexpected landslides; the brutal labor of clearing the
caravan's way until Master Ungabwey's strange siege engines were in
position to do their work.

While she distracted herself from her own intentions by imagining

other worries, the monk of the Cult of the Many finished his climb to
the crest. She half expected him to continue on his way to reclaim his
old place with the train, as Set Ungabwey's counselor. But he halted
where he was, in the middle distance between her and King Bifalt.
While stragglers from the city hurried past him, he stood alone with his
head bowed as if he were praying.

Perhaps he did not know where he was needed. Presumably, the
caravan master did not require his advice in the Realm's Edge. He had
said what he could to King Bifalt. And the previous day, while Magister
Facile had urged Queen Estie in one direction, and Estie's loyalties—to
Amika, to Belleger, to her husband—had called her in another, the
monk had prompted her decision by asking a question she could not
answer: How else will you know? At the time, he had seemed to mean,
How else will you know what your gift is, or whether you want it, or if
you can use it? But he may have meant, How else will you know who
you are? Or even, How else will you know your husband's heart?

Now Third Father kept his distance like a man with conflicting allegiances. If the Cult of the Many did not judge, it also refrained from
taking sides.

As the sun rose, a low breeze began to skirl along the ridge, nudging
the light's warmth westward. It was a cool, dry wind that smelled im-
plausibly of parched sand, as if it had come from the vast desert that
separated Belleger and Amika from the Last Repository and the Wall
Mountains. Of course, the faint scent was an illusion. The desert was
too far away. Still, the breeze made Queen Estie shiver. She pulled her
cloak more tightly around her shoulders, but she could not close out the
chill. The impression of baked, dead sand tasted like an omen. It seemed
to promise a coming wasteland: a time when the realm's life would be
plowed under and left to wither.

When the caravan left, it might not be seen again.

Come to me, Husband, she thought in silence. Come because you
chose me and do not regret it. Come because you want to hear and
understand what I will say.

But King Bifalt did not glance in her direction. As far as she could
tell at this distance, he had not noticed her arrival. He did not acknowl-

edge her now. With General Klamath and Land-Captain Erepos, he concentrated on the caravan as if his future and Belleger's depended on Set Ungabwey rather than on the Queen of Amika. Only Prince Jaspid gave her the courtesy of a direct look and a grin.

Behind her, the First Captain finally dispatched the train's escort. Wheeling away from Matt, the horsemen left the training-field at an easy canter. At first, their hooves thundered on the packed dirt of the field. But as they ascended the ridge-side, hardy grasses muted their coming, made the labor of hooves sound more distant. The riflemen and their mounts seemed to lose substance. Crossing the ridgecrest, they flashed into sunlight. Then they lost their brightness as if they were fading from Estie's world as they dropped into the gloom of dawn. When they reached Master Ungabwey's wagons and conveyances, they looked as elusive as shadows, as insignificant as mists.

At a slower pace, Matt rode upward to join the men gathered around King Bifalt. Like them—like Third Father—he gave no sign that he was aware of Queen Estie.

Their disregard was not an insult, she told herself. King Bifalt and his companions ignored her because they expected her to join them. That would have been her proper role, to approach her husband in his own realm. They assumed that she stayed away to avoid intruding on what they said to each other.

Few of them recognized the change in her. She had discussed it with Third Father. King Bifalt knew the truth. But Klamath, Erepos, and the First Captain had heard only the outlines of her recent experiences in Amika. Even Jaspid had been nothing more than a spectator, and then only at the end. She could not expect them to realize that she was now more truly Amika's Queen than she had been before.

And time was against her, just as it was against her husband and Belleger, and for the same reason. Estie needed to act before anything happened to forestall her intentions.

Gods, she sighed to herself. Aloud, she said softly, "Commander Crayn, please tell King Bifalt that I must speak with him. When he asks me to wait"—which he would certainly do under the circumstances—"tell him that I cannot."

The Commander brought his mount closer. "As you say, Majesty." However, he did not obey at once. His cropped beard disguised the lines of his expression, but the rising sun gave his sandstone eyes a troubled look. "Yet if I may, Majesty? Are you certain of what you do? We may be needed here."

More sternly than she intended, Queen Estie retorted, "I am not a girl, sir. Certainty is for children. I have outgrown it."

Then another thought struck her. "On your way, tell the monk that he must choose soon. His moment is passing."

Frowning, Crayn repeated, "As you say, Majesty." With a snap of his reins and a nudge of his heels, he sent his horse into motion toward the company around King Bifalt. When he was halfway there, he paused to address Third Father. Then he approached the King.

The breeze ruffled Estie's hair. It seemed to carry every sound away. As the horses, oxen, and illirim dragged their burdens into a row behind Master Ungabwey's carriage, and the riflemen took their positions around the train, the crowd from the city watched in a hush, as if they were witnessing an assemblage of ghosts. As if they knew they would never see the caravan and its escort again.

When Commander Crayn spoke, King Bifalt answered. With the wind in her ears, Estie could not hear them. But she saw anger in the way her husband sat his horse; in his quick, harsh gesture. Now all of his companions looked at her. No doubt, they disapproved. Nevertheless she trusted Crayn. He was Amikan, and hers. If King Bifalt wanted to send him away, the King would have to call on his bodyguards to intervene. General Klamath and Matt would not rebuff the Queen-Consort's personal guardsman. Land-Captain Erepos had no authority here.

The Commander insisted. King Bifalt barked a response that Queen Estie almost heard, a curse of some kind. With a vehement jerk of his reins, he turned his horse. Trailed closely by Crayn, he rode toward his wife.

His bodyguards started to follow. Prince Jaspid stopped them with a word. Estie had time for a small moment of satisfaction that the King was coming to her alone. Then she had to face her husband.

He had left his arms and armor in the Fist. Despite the chill, he had not brought a cloak: he liked the open air. His brown shirt, trousers, and boots could have been the same garments he had worn for their wedding. Queen Estie had never seen him pamper himself with expensive fabrics or other luxuries. Still, he was the man she had married. Even now, the heat in his gaze made her skin burn.

Nevertheless she was painfully aware that he was not the *same* man she had married. Instead of sitting upright, he slumped in his saddle. His shoulders were bowed. There were new lines around his mouth, under his eyes. And he had aged since she had told him that she had a gift for sorcery. Now his severity did not look like a mask for his familiar, embattled ire. It seemed to conceal a profound defeat.

But he could still be angry. Halting fiercely in front of her, he demanded, "*Now,* my lady? You need to speak to me *now?*"

As she had done so often in their many public arguments, Queen Estie replied with her sweetest smile. "And alone, my lord. We will not have another opportunity."

"So you mean to return to Amika," he retorted. "That is why you have brought your escort. What of it? You have done the same many times. Why is it urgent *now?*

"Do you not see that we have no hope in this war if Set Ungabwey fails?"

After nineteen years of marriage, the raw rasp of his voice still made the core of Estie's chest quiver. She forced her smile to the breaking point. "*Alone,* my lord," she insisted. "When you hear me, you will understand."

For a moment, she feared that his self-control might crack. Prince Lome had betrayed him; Elgart had been taken from him; his need for Master Ungabwey's aid undermined him. And he hated sorcery. He hated sorcerers. Despite his underlying dismay, his black scowl threatened a blow. Driven to extremity, he might be capable of striking his wife. Responding to his tension, his horse tried to shy away.

But he bit down on the inside of his cheek hard enough to draw blood. His face twisted into a red-lipped grimace. As hoarse as a man who had lost his voice—or himself—he relented.

"As you say, my lady."

Before King Bifalt could change his mind, or one of his men could call to him, Queen Estie told Crayn, "We will not be disturbed, Commander." An order, not an observation. Then she guided her mount off the ridgecrest. Deliberately, she trotted away from her soldiers and King Bifalt's companions and the sight of the caravan gathering itself.

Still chewing his cheek, the King followed her.

She did not stop until she was sure that they would not be overheard, even if he shouted at her. Briefly, she considered dismounting. But if he joined her, he might feel that he was at a disadvantage. And if he stayed in his saddle, he would tower over her. The disadvantage would be hers. Turning her horse, she moved to his side until they sat almost face to face.

"My lady," he demanded as if the words were an insult.

Her smile failed her. The ferocity of his concentration made it difficult for her to breathe. Despite her determination to believe in her own courage, she procrastinated.

"My lord King," she began, trying not to pant, "I have received a message from Chancellor Sikthorn. Ships have been sighted entering the Line's Cut"—the sheer rift where the Line River split the rising cliffs on its way to the sea. "Three ships like those that scouted the Bay of Lights."

"What of it?" he countered bitterly. "We studied the Cut together, you and I. It is easily defended. I am more interested in how you receive messages without my knowledge. Elgart could have told me, but he is gone."

"It *is* easily defended." Estie mastered her breathing as she spoke. "Before I left Maloresse, Commander Soulcess returned from the lands of the Nuuri. A bargain has been agreed. We now have peace there." King Bifalt had spent enough time in Amika to form his own opinion of Thren Soulcess. "I had no urgent use for him elsewhere, so I sent him and a dozen men to watch the Cut. As a precaution, they assembled a catapult on a suitable rim of the cliff. When the ships appeared, the Commander's men were ready. With three or four rocks and one hit, they persuaded the ships to turn back."

More firmly, she concluded, "My communications with my realm are not your concern, my lord."

The King dismissed that assertion. "This cannot be your reason for demanding to speak with me."

The passion in his eyes seared her. Queen Estie needed all of her willpower to hold his gaze.

Enough! she commanded herself. *Say* it. It must be said.

Her husband had never denied her freedom to make her own choices.

"No, my lord," she assented, "it is not. I merely wished to reassure you concerning the Nuuri and the Line's Cut." She meant, I had to remind myself that I was able to confront my father. "As you surmised, I intend to leave Belleger. My carriage has been made ready. We have our supplies. I will go when I am confident that you have heard me.

"But my journey will be a long one. I do not go to Amika."

There she faltered despite her resolve. She could imagine his reaction too easily.

"*Not*, my lady?" She had surprised him. The lines of his glower shifted into a frown. His attention, already fierce, became even sharper. He could have sliced her open with a glance. "Then where?"

As if she were as strong as she needed to be, she answered, "To the Last Repository."

Between one heartbeat and the next, he became stone. Only his chest moved, heaving for air. Unnoticed, blood gathered at one corner of his mouth. His silence had the vehemence of a howl.

He hated sorcerers. He could tolerate—even appreciate—those who served Belleger and Amika. He needed them. The lives of his people, and of hers, were more important to him than his personal revulsion. But he had never trusted any theurgist except Magister Facile. Now he did not trust even her.

As for the Magisters of the library—

Like her father, he did not forgive them. His reasons were better: his resentment was not.

If he had ever touched her as a woman, as his wife, she would have reached out to him. "Hear me a moment, my lord," she said quickly. "I could say that I have no place in your war. I am not a soldier. I know little of strategy, and nothing of tactics. I cannot aid you, except by standing at your side. That is the truth—but it is not *the* truth. If it were, I would not go.

"I will go because I have a gift for sorcery. Magister Facile sees it. She is sure it is there. But she does not know what it *is*. It may be trivial. It may be fatal. For that reason, she fears for me if it is awakened.

"In the Last Repository, there are students of sorcery who will be able to name my gift. They will tell me what I need to know to choose my future. Do I wish to become a Magister? Will I prefer to remain as I am? Either choice is impossible until I know what I can become.

"My lord husband," she pleaded. "Bifalt. You must understand. I have been your wife for nineteen years"—untouched, unloved. "During all that time, I have been waiting. I told myself that I was waiting for you. I waited for the day when you would choose to love me. But now I know the truth. I have been waiting for myself. I have been waiting to find out who I am."

Finally, King Bifalt's silence broke. As hoarse and raw as a rusty saw, he asked, "What is there to understand? Magister Facile says you have a gift. What of it? *I* have a gift. Its name is outrage. It enables me to stand my ground. It is not sorcery, but it is *born* in me. And it is wasted. No gift can save us. Will you learn to call down lightning like your father? You will *become* him, and still the enemy will trample us like insects."

Instantly affronted, she snapped, "Gods, Bifalt! You know me better than that."

"*Do* I?" His sarcasm was as brutal as a slap. "Do I know you at all? There is only one difference between sorcery and other gifts. It can be used without risk to the sorcerer. He can wreak intolerable harm without fear for himself. That safety makes him arrogant. Then his arrogance makes him cruel."

Angry herself, she replied, "You are mistaken, my lord. It may be that men and women who have spent their lives knowing that they are gifted are prone to arrogance. *I* have spent my life grieving that I am ungifted. I am not likely to forget my own littleness."

Certainly, she would not forget that he refused to love her.

"And what of Amika, *little* Queen?" he retorted. "What will become of your people when you are in the library? Beyond their reach? Amika has had too many cruel monarchs."

He stung her. She returned that pain with the most honest answer she had.

"I trust you to protect them until my return."

For a moment, he stared at her, blinking as if an accident of wind had stung his eyes with grit. His chest swelled, gathering a shout. With an effort of will, he quelled it. The strain of containing himself made his hands tremble on his reins. When he replied, he was only able to manage a raw whisper.

"I will never see you again."

He did not expect to survive the coming war.

The naked loss in his voice was more than she could bear. She refused it. For their entire marriage, he had rejected her as a woman. Did he claim the gift of standing his ground? She had the right to do the same.

Shivering as if her cloak did nothing to fend off the chill, she answered, "If that is your choice, my lord." There were many ways that he could contrive to reach the library ahead of its enemy. Oh, she knew he would not do so. She *knew*. If he had to, he would stand alone against the enemy's host. But whatever he did would still be a choice. "Mine is to leave."

That was too much for him. He jerked his head away. Tugging on his reins, he started to turn his mount.

Before he could go, she snatched at his reins; kept him where he was. Like a curse or a plea, she said, "I am not done, my lord. There is more."

The idea shocked him. *"More?"* he cried. "You ride away from our people, *our people*, and that is not *enough*?"

She kept her grip on his reins. "It is not. I will take Magister Facile with me."

For an instant, he gaped at her as if she had driven a dagger into his chest. Then his dismay became a storm. Like a crash of thunder, he shouted, *"You cannot!"*

The Queen of Amika winced; but she did not back down. As if she were impervious to regret or remorse, she added, "Also I will take the last of my cannon. I have supplied the Bay of Lights. There will be no more."

"Hells, woman!" He flung his rage into her face. "I do not care about your *cannon*. I *must have* Magister Facile!

"You cannot be blind to this! The seventh Decimate is our best weapon. It may be our only *useful* weapon. The library must have other Magisters who share her theurgy. They could have been sent to us, but they were not. We have only *her*. Her departure will cost hundreds of lives, thousands. She must not go!"

"Ask her yourself," retorted Estie. "Come with me now. Force her to refuse you in person." She took a deep breath to calm her tremors. "Or take pity on her.

"She is an old woman. She is weary and full of sorrow. When she came from the Last Repository to serve us, she left behind a man she loves. Since that day, nineteen years have passed, and she has aged, but he has not. That is cruel enough. But now she hears that there is treachery in the library. The man she loves and left has been poisoned.

"She wishes to see him before he dies, or she does.

"You can shout at her if you must, my lord. You can try to command her. You can throw all Belleger and Amika at her feet and beg for her service. She will not hear you."

While Estie spoke, a shutter seemed to close behind King Bifalt's eyes. His gaze flattened as if he had withdrawn into himself. Reflexively, he used the back of his hand to wipe the blood from his mouth. By increments, the cut lines of his face relaxed into their more familiar lines, their stern restraint.

Long ago, he had told her, *I do not love my life.* She remembered every word, every inflection. She seemed to remember every beat of his heart. *I am not living a life I can love.* The Magisters of the library had beaten him into the shape they desired. *Denial is all that allows me to remain who I am.*

Now she had reached him in the only way that he could be reached: by pushing him away. Refusing him herself had not been enough. Refusing the needs of his people was more powerful.

His gentleness surprised her as he removed her hand from his reins. "Then, my lady," he croaked like a man whose voice was gone, "we will do what we can with men and guns and lesser sorceries. When you discover your gift, remember that we need you. We have always needed you.

"And remember," he added, still gently, "we face true slaughter. Send your Magisters to me. *All* of them, my lady. If I am to save even one of our people, yours and mine, I must have all the sorcery I can command."

Without waiting for her answer, he turned and rode away.

As he left, he seemed to take her courage with him. A moment ago, she had been angry enough to say anything. Now she only wanted to say his name; to call him back. *Denial is all that allows me to remain who I am.* She was still no match for him. Even yet, she did not entirely believe in herself.

He had not said, *I need you.* Perhaps he could not. Or perhaps he refused to confess the truth. If he admitted that *he* needed her, he might consider it a betrayal; a broken promise. She did not know what commitments he had made to himself, apart from denial. But that was the promise he had given her.

Riding away, he kept it. He did not look back.

Was that all she had to do? Ride off as he did, and not look behind her?

She could have wept then. Instead, she summoned Commander Crayn and his men to her side. When they arrived, she let their momentum carry her among them down the slope and across the training-fields toward Belleger's Fist, where her carriage and servants and Magister Facile awaited her.

But she did look behind her.

When she saw Third Father following her at his own pace, she forgot her own turmoil for a moment. Clearly, he had elected to accompany her. That surprised her. She had expected him to make some other choice. Once long ago, he had stood surety for then-Prince Bifalt. And he had become Master Ungabwey's trusted counselor long before he had first met the Prince. She had imagined that the monk would stand by one of his older loyalties.

Now, however, she felt that she was beginning to understand him. He had nowhere else to go. Set Ungabwey did not need him. King Bifalt did not. Perhaps he thought the day might come when *she* would need him. If not—

Queen Estie shuddered. The day might come when the Last Repository fell. If that happened, how else would she expect a man like Third Father to meet his death, if not by standing surety for his oldest loyalty, the library itself?

When that notion struck her, another followed. She may have misunderstood her husband. *I will never see you again.* King Bifalt may have meant that she would die when the library did. That nothing he could do would save either the Last Repository or her. That only he would be left to gather the remnants of both realms and flee.

If he thought *that*, the idea must have appalled him. He believed that his own gifts were wasted; that they could not save Belleger and Amika. But she refused to accept his view of himself. In some ways, she had never accepted it. The man who had forged an almost inconceivable alliance between the realms had not come to the end of what he could accomplish. Not yet. He was capable of more.

If she did not fail him—

EPILOGUE

COMING

After a foreshortened autumn, winter was on the horizon in Belleger. In the Bay of Lights, it had already arrived. Too early, there were knots of ice among the stones of the strand and signs of frostbite on the men's fingers. At the top of the road, the wind's remorseless howl stuttered as the sharp rims of the cliffs shredded the brittle air. But it never ceased. Lower down, it shrilled in the ears of the workers until they felt like they were going deaf. Some of them were. Their eardrums were frozen.

Confused by wind and cold, and pummeled by exhaustion, men made mistakes. Accidents, a danger at all times, became more frequent. In rooms that could never be adequately heated, seamstresses pushed needles through their fingers and sewed their own flesh to the raincapes and heavy cloaks that the laborers outside needed. Unwieldy with their knives, cooks in the kitchens prepared meals laced with blood. And out among the fortifications, workers missed their footing, or dropped stone blocks onto their hands, or broke their necks when they fell. Others lost control of the cannon they were lowering down the steep road into the bay, leaving their skin on the raw ropes. One siege gun was bent out of use when it struck the bouldered shore. If it fired, it would rupture its barrel. It might kill the cannoneers. One medium cannon no longer looked trustworthy.

Through it all, every man and woman on the terraces lived for the times when they could retreat to the dining halls or kitchens or bunkhouses and cluster around the fierce heat of the stoves. The raptor winds forced cold through all the walls, but inside their own small circles the stoves gave warmth. No one complained at the jagged pain they endured while heat thawed the ice in their veins, brought the nerves of their skin back to life and anguish.

And out in the bay, between the arms of the indurate cliffs and the raw fangs of the barrier reef, massive seas rose and crashed, ripped to chaos by the flailing winds, and by the whetted fists and heads and blades of rock which jutted from the bay's floor, harrowing the surges of water. The heaviest swells flung spray onto the lowest terrace, and the next. The turmoil within the bay was impassable at all times, in every season. In this weather, the enclosed seas were a maelstrom as savage as any hell. When the spray struck, it hit like hail.

It was a cruel time for the men and the comparatively few women who strained and bled on the bay's fortifications. It was not less punishing for Captain Flisk and Commander Forguile. They worked beside their teams to secure sub-Commander Waysel's last delivery of cannon; but that was only one of their duties. They also had to organize their teams, train cannoneers, oversee the work to catch mistakes, and care for their people, doing what they could to ensure adequate meals and blankets and protective garb, and to ration what was expected of their few overwrought stitchers and bonesetters. The most common message they sent to Belleger's Fist was a plea for more men, more supplies, more physicians—and more wagons to carry home the dead.

It was already a cruel time, but it was going to get worse. True winter was coming. When ice began to clog the guns and make every exposed surface as slick as oil, even the road from the rim of the cliff down to the strand would become as treacherous as a precipice. The cold would be a killing force. Every day, frostbite would make more cripples.

Heren Flisk thought that he existed for the day when the last work would be done. Then he and Ennis Forguile could withdraw their whole command. They could have the bunkhouses, dining halls, and kitchens disassembled, to be rebuilt above the edge of the bay, where the winds were less brutal and there was no spray. The men and women could finally get warm, rest, and start to heal. After that, their only tasks would be to inspect and clean the guns every day, and to continue learning how to fire the cannon. Many of them could return to their homes.

Captain Flisk thought all that. But he was wrong.

After the black ships had been sighted—ships like fortresses under their stark white sails—Captain Flisk, Commander Forguile, and General Klamath had established a system of relays to carry warnings back and forth between the bay and Belleger's Fist as swiftly as possible. The distance was only half a day's ride on a sturdy horse; but it required a stable of mounts as well as cabins for riders near the stone hut of the lookout post. Every day in any weather, one horseman went from the bay to the Fist while another came in the opposite direction. Often, the riders who left the bay carried Flisk and Forguile's incessant appeals, or the most recent toll of the dead. Usually, the news from the Fist was sparse. King Bifalt did not trouble the officers of the bay with tidings they did not need. But the Captain and his comrade had been informed of Elgart's disappearance. They both knew the spy well: they felt the force of his loss. And more than a fortnight ago, messengers three days in a row had brought descriptions of the caravan's arrival and departure.

The caravan held little interest for Flisk: he had never seen Set Ungabwey's wagon train. It meant more to Forguile. But neither man paid much attention. The Realm's Edge and the incursion of raiders were not their problem. They still had work to do, and they had passed the boundaries of exhaustion long ago.

When the sails were spotted on the horizon for the second time, a rider sprang for his horse while one of the lookouts waved signal-flags to summon Captain Flisk and Commander Forguile. By the time the officers were able to finish what they were doing and make the long ascent from the lower terraces, the messenger was an hour on his way—and the lookouts could see that the ships were coming closer.

Heren Flisk and Ennis Forguile were too numb for urgency. Despite the excitement of the lookouts, both men spent a while huddled close to the stove in the hut before they forced themselves to look out at the sea.

There was nothing wrong with Commander Forguile's eyes, but Captain Flisk had always been known for keen sight. He saw the ships before his companion did: three vessels made of black wood, with tall black masts holding great sheets of white canvas. Even at this distance, Flisk could see that the ships were huge. The day was almost unnaturally clear, and the sun shining on the large sails lit them like omens.

He knew what they meant.

As soon as he was sure that the vessels were approaching, he stumbled outside; shouted for a messenger. The man who responded he sent after the first rider. "Tell the King," he panted, "these ships are not scouts. They have seen how the bay defends itself. They have seen us working to make it stronger. Now they will test their power."

Without waiting to watch the horseman leave, Captain Flisk returned to the hut and the Amikan Commander.

Forguile could see the ships more clearly now. "Do you suppose," he asked in a husky whisper, "they have cannon that can reach us? From outside the reef?"

The Bellegerin shook his head. "Guns like that would be enormous. How could a wooden vessel withstand the recoil?" Then he added, "What purpose would they serve? If they can reach us, they might destroy our emplacements"—years of brutal work. "But they still could not enter the bay. They would gain nothing."

Flisk did not fear sorcery here. Cannon that could strike at such a distance were scarcely imaginable. No sorcerer had so much range.

"Nevertheless," muttered Commander Forguile. "We must prepare for the worst."

"As you say," replied the Captain. "If those ships do not turn away, I will withdraw our people from the lower terraces. Our cannon I leave to you." The guns were Amikan, after all. "You will know when to fire."

After squinting at the ships for a moment, he added, "It seems the winds and currents force them to sail in wide sweeps. If they do not improve their pace, they can hardly near us before sunset."

Commander Forguile made a humming sound while he considered the situation. Finally, he said, "Long before then, you must bank or douse every fire. We cannot let those ships see our positions. We must make it difficult for them to aim when the light fades."

Bank or douse, thought Flisk. Hells! That would be a heavy blow to men and women who had worked themselves to the edges of delirium and beyond. But he understood his comrade. If they meant to prepare for the worst, the first necessity was to withdraw their people and make the emplacements look abandoned. In poor light, the fortifications might be indistinguishable from the native rock of the cliffs.

With luck, the enemy might imagine that rocks and wild swells and the reef were all that prevented a landing in the bay after dark.

At midafternoon, the ships were still more than a league outside the reef. Nevertheless Captain Flisk decided that the time had come to retrieve his people. With the westering sun lighting the cliffs, the enemy would be able to watch the men and women withdraw, apparently forsaking their duties; fleeing for their lives. Shivering, he began his trek down to the lowest terrace, the fifth, which still lacked its full complement of finished emplacements. That was where the main dining halls, kitchens, and bunkhouses stood. There were more accommodations higher up, primarily for the best cannoneers and their teams; but Flisk could pass through them and give his orders during his descent. His task now was to remove the men and women working on the fourth and fifth levels: three fourths of his people.

He knew from long experience that they could not see the ships. So close to the strand, even the reef was masked by the torn and towering waves, the vehement tumult of seas. But the workmen and women on the lower terraces would catch sight of the danger soon enough.

When the signal-flags summoned Captain Flisk back to the top of the road, he was searching for Mattwil. Again.

Of course, he remembered his orders: General Klamath had instructed him to keep the young man away from peril, away from even the prospect of combat. In addition, Flisk was expected to spare Mattwil contact with the Amikans; but with Mattwil's mute consent, Flisk had elected to ignore that restriction. At present, however, he had a better reason for wanting the son of Matt and Matta.

Despite what the young man had endured, or perhaps because of it, he had a steadying influence on the laborers around him. He worked hard, and his clenched concentration inspired effort from his fellows. In addition, he had an almost inhuman ability to make no mistakes. Nothing he did had to be redone. As a result, other workmen paid attention when he remarked on their misjudgments. But he also had a gift that Flisk needed more under the circumstances. Somehow, he had formed a bond with the youngest of the Amikan women, a girl as frail as a waif who nonetheless possessed the unlikely determination to speak up when the other women hesitated. She may have reminded him of his sister. Because of her, the rest of the women trusted Mattwil.

Captain Flisk ignored the signal-flags; continued his search.

Unfortunately, the young man was at the farthest end of the lowest terrace. But he was not hiding. With other men, Mattwil had completed one emplacement earlier. Now he was working alone, fitting blocks of stone to form the housing that would protect kegs of gunpowder for the siege cannon.

With the wind yammering in his ears, and his concentration as tight as a fist, Mattwil did not notice Captain Flisk until Flisk touched his arm. Then he stood upright, wiped cold spray from his eyes, and faced the Bellegerin officer.

"I need you." Flisk pitched his voice to carry through the clamor. "There are ships."

At first, Mattwil looked confounded, as if the Captain's words were nonsense. Almost at once, however, he jerked around to peer across the bay. "Ships?"

Of course, he could not see them.

"The reason for all this," retorted Heren Flisk. With a gesture, he indicated the whole expanse of the fortifications. "King Bifalt said an attack would come. Now it has. But I will not risk lives," not if he could avoid it. "We must withdraw."

Again, he said, "I need you."

Slowly, Mattwil turned back to the Captain. His face was already wet with spray. He had to blink hard to meet Flisk's gaze. "What do you need?"

"Gather the women," said Flisk at once. "Bank or douse every fire." As tersely as possible, he gave his reasons. "I will evacuate the men. Use the women. Work as quickly as you can. Then bring them to the lookout post.

"I *will not* risk lives."

The young man nodded. Without hesitation, he strode away, leading Flisk back toward the bunkhouses and the road.

Flisk did not try to keep up with him. He took a moment to sigh; rub his shoulder; marshal his thoughts. He had been called back to the rim of the cliff. He did not know why. But he was prepared to defy any order until he had located all of the remaining men and sent them to safety.

The women he trusted to Mattwil.

During Flisk's absence, Commander Forguile had ordered bonfires lit in the shelter of a low hill at the back of the lookout hut. When Flisk gained the top of the road, he found his men gathered around the fires, enduring the exquisite pain while life returned to their limbs, their chests, their faces. The women were still behind him. But they were on their way now, straggling up the steep track with the last of their strength. Mattwil followed them, helping the ones who fell, encouraging those who had to stop for breath.

With him was the girl he had befriended; or perhaps she had befriended him. She added her voice to his, goading the other women when his kindness did not suffice.

Near the hut, Captain Flisk also found King Bifalt.

The King had brought a substantial company, primarily riflemen and Magisters. While some of the soldiers walked their lathered horses—a detail that told Flisk they had ridden hard to come so soon—the rest crowded near the edge of the cliff, watching the bay; the ships. Among them, the Captain recognized Prince Jaspid and Magister Lambent. He would know more of them if he took the time to look: other Magisters; a number of the Prince's guardsmen from the Fist. They had all come to gauge the threat.

But King Bifalt kept his distance from the onlookers. Accompanied by his bodyguards and General Klamath, he was talking with Commander Forguile, a familiar companion and friend.

The King, Klamath, and Forguile turned to look at Flisk as the Bellegerin officer crossed the crest of the road.

Now Heren Flisk understood the signals he had ignored. They had summoned him to attend King Bifalt.

Despite his exhaustion, Flisk was able to be shocked at King Bifalt's appearance. When the King was only Prince Bifalt, his time in the library had added years to the lines on his cheeks and forehead, the severity of his mien. However, since the formation of the alliance, his marriage to the Queen-Consort, and his ascension to the throne, he had hardly seemed to age. But now—

Now his shoulders had acquired a stoop that Flisk had never seen before. There were faint brushstrokes of grey in his cropped beard and hair. The small muscles around his eyes seemed to flinch, and his gaze had a haunted cast, as if some essential source of strength had abandoned him. For the first time, King Bifalt showed his resemblance to his father, King Abbator.

Studying his King, Flisk felt an impulse to ask if anything had happened to the Queen-Consort. King Bifalt's expression made him think of grief; of bitter bereavement. With a deep bow, he masked his dismay—and his question.

As usual, King Bifalt did not complain when men he trusted kept him waiting. To that extent, at least, he remained unchanged. Answering Flisk's bow with a nod, he said hoarsely, "Well, Captain. Commander Forguile tells me you have been working too hard. I am sorry to see it. But those ships prove you have not wasted your efforts.

"Have you accounted for all of your people?"

At that moment, Mattwil herded his company of women out of the bay. Flisk glanced at them, did a quick tally, then replied, "We have, Majesty."

"And the cannon?"

The Captain referred the question to his comrade.

"They are not manned, Majesty," replied Forguile. "We do not know how those ships hope to hurt us. We can respond quickly enough when we see what they will do. Our cannoneers and their teams are ready. They have their orders. They can reach the long guns without delay if they are needed."

After a flicker of hesitation, the Amikan added, "We do not expect to need the lower cannon. They are three ships, Majesty, but they are only three. They cannot carry enough soldiers to force a landing. I would guess that they mean to attempt a test of some sort. Of themselves, perhaps. Or of us."

King Bifalt nodded again. "But first they must come closer. Their test may not begin until nightfall. There are wains coming behind us. The Land-Captain has dispatched food and blankets, canvas for shelters. If they make good speed, you may be able to feed your people before the test starts."

Rubbing his shoulder, Flisk groaned privately. An attack after dark? How would the cannoneers aim their guns at targets they could not see?

Like an echo of the Captain's concern, Magister Lambent protested loudly from the cliff's edge, "I cannot *see*!"

Someone near the sorcerer replied, "There is nothing to see. The ships are half a league from the reef. If they try to cross it, it will tear them apart. We will not need cannon to defeat them."

"But I want to *see* it," retorted the Magister. "I want to watch them go down." As if he did not realize—or care—that King Bifalt could hear him, he added, "I have always believed this fortification is a waste of men and time. A foolish waste."

"And when you are King, Magister," drawled Prince Jaspid distinctly, "your beliefs will be heeded. Until then, they are chaff. The wind blows them away, and they are gone."

Flisk felt a sudden desire to toss Magister Lambent off the precipice. But King Bifalt ignored the theurgist. With something like gentleness, he urged, "Warm yourself, Captain." He gestured at the lookout hut. "Rest while you can. When the ships begin to do"—he shrugged— "whatever they intend, I will ask you to descend partway and watch. I remember your keen sight. The men at the guns may need the help of an observer to improve their aim."

"You can take Magister Lambent with you," suggested Forguile with a glint in his eyes. "He needs a lesson in humility."

Heren Flisk accepted the King's command gratefully. He had done what he could. He had even stumbled on a role for Mattwil that the General would approve. And he had time. One look assured him that the ships were still distant. With a favorable wind, they could probably have neared the reef in under an hour. In the conflicted turmoil of these winds, the heave and smash of these swells, they would have to continue their sawtooth approach, veering repeatedly from one side to the other. Sunset, he thought dully. Sunset at the earliest.

Offering King Bifalt another bow, Captain Flisk went to the stone hut.

Inside, he slumped down to sit with his back against one wall, opened his rain-cape to get as much warmth from the stove as possible, and astonished himself by falling asleep.

When he woke, it was not the coming of the wains, or the wind-tattered calls of the laborers and servants, or the rush to distribute food and blankets that roused him. It was the sharp throbbing of his shoulder where it pressed on the cold stone wall.

Blinking at the fog of dreams, he imagined that he would simply change positions and go back to sleep. But then he realized that the dimness around him was not a residue of slumber. The hut was full of gloom. The lookout window cast ruddy light onto one wall above his head. Everything else was dusk. He was barely able to make out the shape of the woman taking her turn at the window.

Hells, he thought stupidly. I have slept too long. But of course, he had not. Ennis Forguile would have awakened him before he was needed.

Awkward with inadequate sleep, Captain Flisk shoved himself to his feet, clasped his rain-cape around him, and lurched outside.

In the west, the sun had begun its slow fall below the horizon. Light streaked the dozens, no, hundreds of people crowded along the rims of the cliff, but it was not bright enough to hold back the darkness. Flisk had to squint to identify individuals. King Bifalt and General Klamath stood back from the edge, keeping each other company; staying out of the way. Perhaps a third of the workmen and a number of the women remained around the fires, either too tired to care about ships or too frightened to watch what might happen. With Commander Forguile, everyone else stared out at the sea: guards from Belleger's Fist, riflemen from the army, servants sent by Land-Captain Erepos, the bay's men and women, and more Magisters than Flisk had expected. Even the King's bodyguards were there. No doubt, King Bifalt had sent them to satisfy their curiosity.

The only sound was the incessant flailing of the winds. Their cuts and slashes covered even the complex violence of the seas. The throng itself was silent, transfixed by the sight of the enemy.

Lit from behind by the half-blaze of the setting sun, the ships were little more than stark silhouettes against the lesser dark of the ocean. They showed no lights. No activity was visible on the decks. If orders were shouted, Flisk could not hear them. Nevertheless the general blur of the details made the outlines especially distinct.

The sails had been taken down, exposing spars like naked limbs. Without their spreads of canvas, the ships sat motionless, as still as if they had been nailed to some immovable stretch of rock below the surface. The heavy rise of the swells did not lift them: the swift rush and plunge as the waves went past did not affect them. Unnaturally stable, they looked fatal somehow, as if they were plague-ships, vessels packed with pestilence.

They were no more than a hundred paces off the reef.

If they meant to challenge that barrier, they did not show it. Heren Flisk could not imagine any power that would enable them to enter the bay. And if they managed that inconceivable trick, they would immediately shatter themselves on the rocks.

For a moment, the Captain considered joining the King, General Klamath, and Prince Jaspid. Then he shook his head. Massaging his shoulder, he went to stand with Commander Forguile, where he belonged.

The Commander had mustered his cannoneers and teams for the long guns. They were gathered around him, watching, waiting. As Flisk moved among them, Forguile met his gaze; gave him a wry grin. But he did not speak. There was nothing to be said.

Soon, the sun went down. The last of its shining clung to the horizon for a while, a long streak of red fading to the hue of blood. Then even that glow sank as if it had been swallowed by the ocean.

Following the sun, night swept over the bay. Flisk had no idea when the moon would rise, or what face it would present when it came. The stars were too far away to affect the darkness. Where the sky and the sea met in the west, the horizon seemed to vanish from the world.

At that moment, as if it had been waiting for its opportunity, the bay revealed its name.

The ships were invisible. The reef and the rocks could not be seen. But here and there on the breaking crests of the swells, small silver spangles appeared. They flickered and were gone—and came again. Soon they became streaks, ragged lines, tiny glowing clusters. Wherever the rocks and the reef forced the waves to break over themselves, the waters formed evanescent lips of argent foam. The silver appeared and faded in instants. Nevertheless the faint glimmering lines and streaks, the clusters and swirls of foam, seemed to map the bay.

While Captain Flisk watched, and every man around him held his breath, the virulent rapacity of the waters made the Bay of Lights beautiful.

Vaguely, almost mysteriously, the swift gleaming defined the black ships. Heavy swells and surges crashed against the sides of the vessels, limning them for heartbeats; but those pulses were enough to show where the ships sat amid the seas.

Everyone on the cliff could see it when one of the ships began to turn. Smoothly, steadily, as if its rigid moorings were a pivot, it shifted until its prow faced the reef.

The foaming and spray of silver defined the rocks, the reef, the ships, but did not cast its light higher. There could have been a dozen men on the deck of that ship, or a hundred, or none. With only the flickering loveliness across the waters to guide his gaze, Captain Flisk could not tell what was done on the vessel. Without its canvas, the ship looked abandoned; uninhabitable.

Nothing warned him when a bolt of lightning fell from the clear heavens and struck the reef directly in front of the ship.

Instinctively, he recoiled. People around him jumped back or cried out. Some of them screamed. He did not hear them. But he could see them. In the white glare of sudden theurgy, they looked like ghouls.

Accustomed to the Decimate of lightning in the hands of Amikan or Bellegerin sorcerers, Flisk expected a blast of force that would hit hard and hot enough to burn or melt stone and then exhaust itself almost at once. In his experience, no Magister could sustain such theurgy for more than one or two moments.

The bolt hitting the reef was impossibly fierce—and impossibly prolonged. It was so bright that he could not look at it directly, so bright that it lit the whole bay like a full moon; and still it did not waver or stop.

Instead, a second bolt called down by another sorcerer attacked the reef in the same spot as the first. Then a third shaft of lightning blazed as well. They made a distant frying sound that reached the top of the cliff despite the shrill yowling of the winds and the crashing of the nearer seas.

None of them faltered. Not one lost its fury.

Somehow, Commander Forguile made himself heard through the sizzle and flay of noise. "Go!" he shouted at his men. "So much light will blind even them! Go to your guns!"

Other men might have hesitated; but Forguile's authority ruled his cannoneers and their teams. In a rush, they hurried to the road; began to drop out of sight.

"Now!"

A moment passed before Flisk realized that his comrade was yelling at *him*.

"You have your orders! We may need an observer! Go while they cannot see you!"

When Commander Forguile thrust a set of signal-flags into Flisk's hands, the man who had failed to complete Prince Bifalt's quest long ago stumbled into a run.

Now that he was in motion, the Captain intended to keep going. The lightning made it easy for him to watch where he planted his feet. But before he could start downward, Prince Jaspid halted him with a roar: "Wait, Captain!"

Reeling on locked knees, Flisk turned to the Prince.

Jaspid had a splint on his left arm. A sling protected his right elbow. His movements were stiff. Nevertheless he approached quickly, dragging Magister Lambent behind him. Lambent's protests scaled into screams until Jaspid cut him off. "Be silent and watch!" demanded the King's brother. He seemed to shout without moving his jaws. "You are not a great sorcerer! See what *real* power can do!"

The theurgist gaped as if he were choking; but his fear of the Prince or the ships silenced him.

Behind him and Prince Jaspid came other Magisters, five of them. Like Lambent, one was Amikan. One was a woman. Captain Flisk did not know them all. But he did not wait for their names. As Jaspid released Magister Lambent, Flisk took him; pulled him staggering off the top of the road and down into the bay.

The third terrace, thought Flisk. The emplacements. He could shelter the Magisters there. He could join them. All he had to do was reach the nearest tier of medium guns, guard the theurgists following him, and watch—

Before he had taken ten steps, the intolerable light vanished as if some monstrous force had dropped a blanket over the bay. The lightning had ended. Heren Flisk was suddenly blind. Even the tenuous streamers and tendrils of light from the conflicting seas and rocks were lost from sight.

He had the presence of mind to croak, "Stop! Wait!"

Then he remembered to breathe.

"It will pass!" he called to his small company. "The blindness! Those sorcerers have exhausted themselves." Or they had stepped aside to make way for some other assault. "We will go on when we can see."

In absolute darkness like the bottom of a buried well, Captain Flisk stood where he was. The after-flashes behind his eyelids only made the dark worse. Magister Lambent clutched at him. Other Magisters bumped into them, then halted. His shoulder hurt as if only an hour had passed since it had been pierced by an Amikan arrow.

When he realized that Magister Lambent was sobbing, he was appalled.

Then he heard the sound of a slap. Abruptly, Lambent subsided. By feel, another Magister found his way to Flisk's side. In the Captain's ear, the sorcerer growled, "You would never guess that man is the most powerful theurgist here."

By his voice, Flisk recognized Magister Trench. His Decimate was wind.

"Perhaps, Magister," answered Flisk, "you can impose a little stillness around us."

"Hells!" retorted Trench. "I should have thought of that."

A moment later, the Captain found himself in a small zone of calm. He could still hear the bay's biting winds, but they seemed distant. They did not touch his face, or shriek in his ears, or try to knock him off his feet. Instead, he heard closer sounds: the panting of his companions, the curses, the muttered fear and awe.

"Magister Lambent." He compelled himself to speak softly. "Put your hands on my shoulders. Magister Trench, your hands on Lambent's. Each of you in a line, hold the shoulders in front of you. I will lead you down."

He heard a little shuffling, a quiet call of readiness. When Captain Flisk felt Magister Lambent's desperate grip on his damaged shoulder, his pain doubled; but he did not let himself flinch. Feeling his way, he drew the sorcerers downward.

One step at a time, he fought his own fear to win enough caution. A slip now could be fatal. Anyone behind him who fell would take others. Flisk could not hope to catch them, not in this darkness. He might tumble down the road himself.

Then he began to see again. As faint as flickers at the edges of his vision, the luminescence of the thrashing waters reappeared far below him. The road became a vague impression under his boots. After a moment, he was able to discern the crouched outlines of the first terrace, where Commander Forguile's men had taken their places at the long guns.

The Captain let the slope draw him and his string of Magisters downward a bit more quickly.

As they passed the second tier of emplacements, Flisk felt a strange shudder. Just for an instant, he thought that he had missed his footing; that he had forgotten to breathe; that his fear was too strong for him. Then the sensation came again, and he recognized it. It was not part of him. He felt it through his boots. The whole surface of the road had quivered like struck flesh.

In a rush, Captain Flisk went for the third terrace, dragging Magister Lambent behind him; leaving the other sorcerers to manage the descent for themselves. One of them did not watch his feet. He tripped, almost fell. But Magister Trench caught him. The others were more careful.

There was another shudder. It lasted longer. It made Flisk want to vomit. He had to swallow bile and nausea.

The effort of catching his companion had broken Trench's concentration. The full scourge of the winds returned.

Ignoring the shrill hurt of Lambent's grip on his shoulder, Flisk struggled through the renewed assault.

In moments, he gained the third terrace. With a rough heave, he shoved Lambent past him onto the level walkway between the wall of the higher tier and the parapet that shielded the medium cannon. The terrified Magister sprawled on his face, but Flisk did not care.

One by one, he guided the other Magisters onto the walkway.

Magister Trench hauled Lambent upright, then set about reasserting his control over the immediate air. The sorcerous quiet returned, pushing every other sound and wind into the background.

"That," declared one of the Magisters, the woman, when she could make herself heard, "was the Decimate of earthquake. They used lightning to weaken the reef. Now they are trying to force a gap with earthquakes."

Flisk nodded. He had only ridden into hell once, during the last battle between Belleger and Amika, but he remembered every horror theurgy could create.

The next shudder was stronger. It made the Captain and his companions stagger for balance, brace themselves on the parapet. Out in the bay, it transformed the swift glints of loveliness riding the waters into a wild dance, flinging arcs and spouts of silver in all directions.

The earthquake felt dangerously powerful where Flisk stood. It threatened ruin. But most of its energy was focused at its center: at the portion of the reef that had been hammered by the Decimate of lightning. He thought he saw part of the reef jump. Then he was sure of it. The sorcery unleashed by one or all of the ships shouldered even the mightiest seas aside as if a giant had risen from the floor of the bay.

The quakes that came next were less virulent. Flexing his knees, Flisk rode them while they passed. But now they struck more rapidly, each new shudder crowding closer to the one before. The effect on the reef became unmistakable. First, bits of it were tossed away like handfuls of pebbles. Then larger chunks erupted from the seas, crashed among the swells. Despite the winds outside Magister Trench's influence, Flisk heard a subterranean rumbling, a sound so deep, so profound, that he seemed to receive it in his chest rather than his ears.

The bass rumble stuttered and stopped.

It started again.

The sorceress who had recognized the Decimate of earthquake muttered a string of obscenities. Flisk found himself panting over and over again, "Hells. Hells. Hells."

As if he were fighting for his life, Magister Trench gasped, "I cannot sustain this quiet."

Then his stamina—or his lack of it—ceased to matter.

Suddenly, the deep rumbling became a roar, a scream; a howl like the shattering of the earth's bones. From the seas, forty or fifty paces of the reef *lifted*, thrust upward by more power than Flisk could imagine. That piece was only a minor portion of the whole reef, but it looked like a mountain as it rose. And as it rose, cracks ran through it. It began to break apart.

At once, the enemy sorcerers withdrew their Decimate. If the reef rose high enough, any piece of it might drive one or another of the black vessels to the bottom.

With a liquid crash that drowned out Magister Lambent's cries and Magister Trench's failing theurgy, the shattered part of the reef collapsed back into the depths.

It left a gap. Enormous swells thrashed through the breach as if they were desperate to hurl themselves against the strand.

Flisk had no idea how deep the gap might be, but it was plainly wide enough to admit one of the ships.

None of them moved, despite the new current ripping past them. The vessel with its prow pointed at the opening remained where it was. It seemed immovable.

Captain Flisk wiped his face, snatched gulps of air, and watched. He had studied the bay for years: he knew that a huge, raw rock with flensing edges stood directly in front of the gap. Closer in lay a stretch of uninterrupted water, but that rock barred the breach.

It jutted just beyond the reach of the long cannon.

His signal-flags hung, useless, in his hands. He knew what was coming. None of the cannoneers would need his guidance to correct their aim.

A heartbeat later, the Decimate of lightning returned. Sorcerers on all three ships directed their bright, hot power at the immediate obstacle.

The bolts struck. They endured.

Within moments, the rock burst into shards as if someone had ignited a warehouse of gunpowder at its base.

Through the dazzle of lightning, Captain Flisk saw the ship at the gap raise one small sail above its peak. Slowly, the black vessel began to glide closer.

Too late, Flisk remembered his signal-flags; forgot his aching shoulder. Frantically, he waved instructions to wait. At their best, the long guns could not send cannonballs so far.

But the first tier was already firing. One after another in the sequence their gunners had been taught, all eight cannon released their shots. Deafened by the winds, Flisk could not hear the guns booming. Like afterimages when the lightning ended, he saw cannonballs waste their force on open water.

Desperate now, he signaled again and again: *Wait.*

The men on the second terrace saw him, or Commander Forguile did. Those guns did not fire.

All of the cannoneers knew where that obstructing rock had been. They had time to remember the range and refine their aim.

And the darkness across the bay was easing. A partial moon had begun to rise. Covered by the shadow of the cliff, Flisk and the Magisters with him were barely discernible to each other. But the ships were visible. They resembled incarnations of malice in the night.

As stately as a monument over a grave, the first ship slid past the spot where the rock had stood. The rabid turmoil of winds and swells, cross-currents and tumbling waves did not touch it. Sorcerers on the vessel wielded theurgy stronger than anything Captain Flisk had witnessed. Even with the faint help of the moon, he only knew where the ship was by the smack and spray of silver against its sides.

Now, he signaled. For your lives! Fire *now!*

Shrill yowling filled his ears. He did not hear the cannon. But he watched two shots lose themselves in the warring seas.

The next balls hit.

So suddenly that the sight seemed to stop his heart, he saw the ship pitch forward, dig its prow into the waters, and go down. In the space of a gasp, the ship was gone. There was no sign that it had ever existed. The bay took everything: it gave nothing back.

"By the *stars!*" panted Magister Trench. "Heavens and earth! Did you *see*—?"

"What?" wailed Magister Lambent. "*What?* My eyes—! What is happening?"

Straining for air, Captain Flisk was slow to realize that a second ship had already broached the gap in the reef. It must have committed itself before the first vessel sank. It entered the bay, gliding as if it rode on rails.

But as it reached the clearer water past where the rock had been, its captain miscalculated; or the sorcerers ruling its movements faltered. The ship seemed to stagger. It appeared to lose headway. Then, heeling, it leaned away, swung broadside to the bay's fortifications.

Like a wild man, Flisk signaled, Now. *Now!*

If any of the guns had been reloaded—

The cannoneers and their teams knew their work. Commander Forguile had drilled them relentlessly. The first tier was ready.

Made soundless by the incessant howl, the long guns fired.

Apart from the quick gleaming of the waters, Flisk had only a sliver of moonlight to help him see. It was enough. He watched one ball strike, and another. They did damage; but they hit too high on the ship's side. The impact of the third was lower. The fourth and fifth found the waterline. The sixth and seventh seemed to skip over the waves to tear holes in the black wood. The eighth missed entirely.

Despite the seas gushing inward, the ship righted itself. It had been made to cross the oceans of the world in any weather. It could withstand—

Sooner than Flisk thought possible, the guns of the second terrace fired again. Their cannonballs struck true.

The abrupt destruction of the vessel's side was wonderful to watch. It was terrible. In an instant, the ship took on a greater weight of water than it could carry. With a strange slowness, as if its decline were deliberate, it fell over.

Just for a moment, Heren Flisk saw men on the vessel. As indistinct as scraps of shadow, some of them jumped from the decks. They were the first to die. Others were trying to launch longboats.

While they struggled to free the smaller craft, their ship was taken by the violence of the swells. It sank in a swirl of brief silver. Surrounded by spangles, the longest spars stood up from the waves as if they were reaching for air. Then they slipped out of sight.

Almost at once, the third vessel unfurled its sails and stood off from the reef. It had seen enough. The eerie ease with which it defied the winds and currents to float away gave it an appearance of disgust: the look of a foe who felt only scorn for the weapons of his enemy—or for the captain who had allowed the second ship to offer its whole side as a target.

There was no release from the bay's gales. If men and women up on the rim of the cliff were shouting, Captain Flisk could not hear them. He could hardly hear the astonishment and jubilation of his small company. Still, he was able to fill his lungs as if breathing had become easier.

Later, in the modest shelter of the hill behind the lookout post, all of the spectators—guards, riflemen, servants, messengers, laborers, women, cannoneers and their teams, Magisters, Commander Forguile and Captain Flisk—all gathered around a bonfire and waited for King Bifalt to address them.

He did not keep them long. "You have done well," he told them brusquely. "Do not doubt that. But now the enemy knows how we defend ourselves. And he knows he can force a landing despite our defenses. He has the strength to break open that reef. It will not fail him when he faces forty cannon instead of sixteen."

"Forty cannon," muttered Prince Jaspid, "our best Magisters, and a few hundred riflemen."

Standing beside the King, General Klamath suggested, "He may not attack us here. If Master Ungabwey fails to close the canyons of the Realm's Edge—"

"We know by signals," rasped King Bifalt, "that Set Ungabwey has reached the Realm's Edge front. It is too soon for other reports. But if he fails, we are lost. On open ground, we cannot defend every road through the mountains. And the enemy will surely kill our scouts. We will be forced to guess which pass or passes he will use. If we guess wrongly, we will give him a direct path to his goal.

"No." The King shook his head. "We must hope he comes against us here. We must be ready *here*. That is the only choice the Magisters of the library have given us. It is our only chance."

His King's certainty seemed to fill Captain Heren Flisk's mouth with blood and ashes. It made his shoulder throb. He would have preferred to savor one small triumph for a while. But he had felt the enemy's power: he knew the truth.

When it came, the real war would be worse than any hell he had ever faced. It would be worse than any destruction he had ever witnessed. Far worse.